Alexander Mackenzie

History of the Clan Mackenzie

Alexander Mackenzie

History of the Clan Mackenzie

ISBN/EAN: 9783743376861

Manufactured in Europe, USA, Canada, Australia, Japa

Cover: Foto ©Raphael Reischuk / pixelio.de

Manufactured and distributed by brebook publishing software (www.brebook.com)

Alexander Mackenzie

History of the Clan Mackenzie

HISTORY

OF THE

CLAN MACKENZIE;

WITH

GENEALOGIES OF THE PRINCIPAL FAMILIES.

BY

ALEXANDER MACKENZIE,

Editor of the "Celtic Magazine," "The Prophecies of the Brahan Seer," "Historical Tales and Legends of the Highlands," &c., &c.

LUCEO NON URO.

INVERNESS: A. & W. MACKENZIE.

MDCCCLXXIX.

INVERNESS: PRINTED AT THE ADVERTISER OFFICE.

To

SIR KENNETH S. MACKENZIE OF GAIRLOCH, BARONET;

AS A SLIGHT BUT GENUINE ACKNOWLEDGMENT

OF HIS

EXCELLENT QUALITIES

AS A REPRESENTATIVE HIGHLAND CHIEF,

AND

AS A GENEROUS AND BENEVOLENT LANDLORD,

THIS

HISTORY OF HIS CLAN

IS RESPECTFULLY

INSCRIBED BY

THE AUTHOR.

PREFACE.

WHILE submitting to the Subscribers the HISTORY AND GENEALOGIES OF THE MACKENZIES, I feel fully alive to its literary demerits, but I am, at the same time, sensible of having done some little service to my Clan and to the Literature of the Highlands ; and it is no small pleasure to find that this has been already acknowledged in the most tangible and gratifying form—evidenced by the large and high-class List of Subscribers printed herewith.

The amount of labour and research involved in the production of such a work is at once obvious.

For generous and effectual aid to increase the number of my patrons, and for valuable genealogical notes, I am specially indebted to Major THOMAS MACKENZIE of the 78th Highlanders (Ross-shire Buffs). For Mackenzie family MSS., and other valuable documents and information, I have to express my obligations to JAMES F. MACKENZIE, Esq. of Allangrange, Chief of the Clan ; to Sir KENNETH S. MACKENZIE of Gairloch, Baronet, my own immediate Chief; to Major JAMES D. MACKENZIE of Findon ; to Captain MACRA CHISHOLM, Glassburn ; and to Mr DUNCAN A. MACRAE, Monar. For the free use of an extensive and rare library, I have to express my gratitude to CHARLES FRASER-MACKINTOSH, Esq. of Drummond, M.P., F.S.A., Scot., and to his obliging Secretary, Mr ALEXANDER FRASER, our best known and most distinguished local Antiquarian ; as also to Bailie J. NOBLE, Bookseller, Inverness, who always granted me free access to the many curious and valuable historical and antiquarian books in his large stock.

The Genealogies of the various families will be found in the order in which they branched off from the main stem of Kintail and Seaforth.

A. M.

INVERNESS, *July 1879.*

CONTENTS.

Contents

LIST OF SUBSCRIBERS.

Aird, Rev. Gustavus, F.C. Manse, Creich
Aitken, Dr, District Asylum, Inverness
Allan, A. Stewart, Major-General, Richmond, Surrey
Allan, William, Esq., Scotland House, Sunderland
Anderson, Peter, Esq., Holly Mount, Wandsworth, Surrey
Athole, His Grace the Duke of
Bethune, Alex. Mackenzie, Esq., Upper Norwood, London
Black, George, Esq., banker, Inverness
Blair, Patrick, Esq., Sheriff-Substitute of Inverness-shire
Buccleuch, His Grace the Duke of—(quarto copy)
Buchan, Dr Patrick, Inverness—(quarto copy)
Burgess, Alex., Esq., banker, Gairloch
Burgess, Peter, Esq., factor for Glenmoriston
Burns, William, Esq., solicitor, Inverness
Campbell, Alex. D., Esq., Kirkintilloch
Campbell, G. J., Esq., solicitor, Inverness
Campbell, George Murray, Esq., Ceylon
Carruthers, ⚑ Walter, Esq., of the *Inverness Courier*—
 Carruthers, Walter, Esq. of the *Courier*
 Ferguson, John A., Esq., Mauritius
 Mackenzie, John Ord, Esq., George Street, Manchester
 Mackenzie, Mrs, Grove House, Bathwick Road, Bath
 Mackenzie, Rev. Wm., Galdra, Herbert River, Queens-
  land
 Young, John, Esq., 94 Cornwall Road, London
Cay, John, Esq., W.S., Edinburgh—(quarto copy)
Chisholm, Colin, Esq., Namur Cottage, Inverness
Chisholm, Dr Kenneth Mackenzie, Radcliffe, Manchester
Chisholm, The—(2 copies)
Cluny—(quarto copy)
Davidson, Duncan, Esq. of Tulloch
Davidson, D. H. C. R., Esq., yr. of Tulloch
Davidson, John, Esq., merchant, Inverness
Dawson, Messrs Wm., & Sons, booksellers, Cannon Street,
 London—(1 copy, 1 quarto copy)

Dickson, Thomas, Esq., Edinburgh
Dixon, John H., Esq., Inveran House, Poolewe
Dixon, Thomas, Register House, Edinburgh
Drummond, Mrs R., 1 Palace Gate, Kensington, London,
—(quarto copy)
Duncan, John M., Esq., Lockerbie—(3 copies)
Ferguson, Captain, Tullich, Lochcarron
Forsyth, Ebenezer, Esq., of the *Inverness Advertiser*
Forsyth, William B., Esq., Editor of the *Inverness Advertiser*
Fraser, Alexander, Esq., accountant, Inverness
Fraser, Alexander, Esq., banker, Inverness
Fraser-Mackintosh, Charles, Esq. of Drummond, M.P.—
(quarto copy)
Fraser, James, Esq., North Albion Street, Glasgow
Fraser, William, Esq., South Castle Street, Edinburgh—
. (quarto copy)
Fraser, Mrs, of Bunchrew—(quarto copy)
Fraser, Captain E., of Bunchrew, 60th Rifles—(quarto copy)
Fraser, William, Esq., Portman Square, London—(2 copies)
Gallie, Lachlan, Esq., George Street, Edinburgh
Gilchrist, Miss M., London
Gilfillan, The late Rev. George, Dundee
Gourlay, Mrs, The Gows, Dundee
Grant, Frances Mackenzie, Denmark House, Scarborough
Grant, General Sir Patrick, G.C.B., G.C.M.G., Colonel 78th
Highlanders (Ross-shire Buffs), Governor of Royal
Chelsea Hospital—(quarto copy)
Grant, P., Esq., banker, Fortrose—(quarto copy)
Green, William, Esq., bookseller, Edinburgh
Hanbury, C. A., Esq. of Strathgarve
Henderson, W. L., Esq., *Advertiser* Office, Inverness
Highlander Newspaper Company, Inverness—(5 copies)
Highlanders, The Officers of the 78th (Ross-shire Buffs)—
(quarto copy)
Hill, G. H., Esq., Ingram Street, Glasgow
Hollins, Mrs, Bodysgallen, Conway, Wales
Hornsby, James, Esq., Gairloch Hotel
Hornsby, Robert, Esq., Loch-Maree Hotel—(quarto copy)
Jeffrey, Allan R. Macdonald, Esq., London—(quarto copy)

Keith, Charles, Esq., bookseller, Inverness—(3 copies)
Kerr, Miss J. Mackenzie, Broughton Place, Edinburgh
Linn, James, Esq., Geological Survey of Scotland, Elgin
Lovat, The Right Hon. Lord—(quarto copy)
Low, Andrew B., Esq., Pitkerro House, near Dundee
Matheson, Alexander, Esq. of Ardross and Lochalsh, M.P.
Matheson, Kenneth, Esq., yr. of Ardross and Lochalsh
Mitchell, A. T., Esq., M.A., Pall Mall Club, London
Munro, Hector, Captain, younger of Fowlis
Macandrew, H. C., Esq., the Diriebught, Inverness
Macdonald, And., Esq., solicitor, Inverness—(quarto copy)
Macdonald, J. M., Esq., Harley Street, London—(quarto
    copy)
Macdonald, Kenneth, Esq., Garve
Macdonald, Kenneth, Esq., solicitor, Inverness—(quarto
    copy)
Macdonald, The Rev. Donald, D.D., Inverness
Macdonald, A. J., Esq., Suffolk Lane, Cannon Street, Lon-
    don—(2 copies)
Macgillivray, A., Esq., Bankend, Southwark, London
Macgillivray, Alex., Esq., Princes Street, Cavendish Square,
    London
Macgregor, Rev. Alexander, M.A., Inverness
Maciver, E., Esq., Scourie, factor, Lairg
Mackay, William, Esq., bookseller, Inverness
Mackay, D. J., Esq., solicitor, Inverness
Mackay, John, Esq., C.E., Rogart House, Swansea
Mackay, John, Esq. of Benreay, Fortrose
Mackay, William, Esq., solicitor, Inverness
Mackenzie, Alexander, Esq., china merchant, Inverness
Mackenzie, Alexander, Esq., Birnam Hotel, Birnam
Mackenzie, Alexander, Esq., merchant, Inverness
Mackenzie, Alexander, Esq., Muirton Street, Inverness
Mackenzie, Alex., Esq., Hotel Balmoral, Paris—(quarto
    copy)
Mackenzie, Alex. Kenneth, Esq., Boonara, Bondi, New
    South Wales
Mackenzie, Allan R., Esq., yr. of Kintail
Mackenzie, A., Esq., Office of Woods and Forests, Whitehall

Mackenzie, A., Esq., Quay Head, Bristol

Mackenzie, A. C., Esq., Maryburgh, Dingwall

Mackenzie, A. Kinaird, Esq., of Ravelrig, Midlothian

Mackenzie, Calvert, Esq., Forres

Mackenzie, Captain Colin, Pall Mall, London—(2 copies, 1 quarto do.)

Mackenzie, Captain Harry M., R.A., Eileanach, Inverness

Mackenzie, Captain Roderick, of Kincraig

Mackenzie, Captain Stewart, of Seaforth—(quarto copy)

Mackenzie, Colin, Esq., W.S., Edinburgh—(1 copy, 1 quarto do.)

Mackenzie, Colonel Hector, Fortrose

Mackenzie, Colonel, of Parkmount, Forres

Mackenzie, C. D., Esq., Grange Road, Middlesborough-on-Tees

Mackenzie, D., Esq., Inland Revenue, Shieldaig, Lochcarron

Mackenzie, Dr F. M., Inverness

Mackenzie, D. G., Esq., 2d Sind Horse, Abbotsford Park, Edinburgh

Mackenzie, D. H., Esq., Auckland, New Zealand—(6 copies, 3 quarto do.)

Mackenzie, Dr Morell, Harley Street, London—(2 copies)

Mackenzie, Evan J., Esq., solicitor, Inverness

Mackenzie, Finlay, Esq., Nicolson Square, Edinburgh

Mackenzie, Frank, Esq., Manilla, New South Wales

Mackenzie-Fraser, Colonel, of Castle Fraser—(quarto copy)

Mackenzie, George, Esq., Meadowside, Dundee

Mackenzie, Gordon, Esq., Madras Civil Service—(quarto copy)

Mackenzie, Hector, Esq., late of Gollanfield

Mackenzie, Henry, Esq., Oriental Bank, London

Mackenzie, Hugh, Esq., C.E., Elgin

Mackenzie, H. Munro, Esq., Distington, Whitehaven—(2 quarto copies)

Mackenzie, James, Esq., Athole Arms Hotel, Glasgow

Mackenzie, James, Esq., Lapeer, Michigan, U.S.A.

Mackenzie, James F., Esq. of Allangrange—(quarto copy)

Mackenzie, James H., Esq., bookseller, Inverness—(4 copies)

Mackenzie, John A., Esq., C.E., Inverness

Mackenzie, J. C., Esq., V.S., Rochester, New York
Mackenzie, J. Munro, Esq. of Mornish, Mull
Mackenzie, John, Esq., Auchenstewart, Wishaw
Mackenzie, John, Esq., Brodick, Arran
Mackenzie, John, Esq., Collector of Customs, Leith
Mackenzie, John, Esq., Mithankote, Mooltan, India
Mackenzie, John, Esq., Nevada Bank, San Francisco
Mackenzie, John, Esq. of Eileanach, M.D., Inverness
Mackenzie, John, Esq. of Glack, Aberdeenshire
Mackenzie, John Hope, Esq., Tarradale House—(1 copy,
    1 quarto do.)
Mackenzie, John J., Esq., Golspie
Mackenzie, John T., Esq., shipowner, Dunvegan, Skye
Mackenzie, John Whitefoord, Esq. of Lochwards, W.S.,
    Edinburgh—(quarto copy)
Mackenzie, Kenneth, Esq. of Hilton, Tyrl-Tyrl, Taralga,
    Sydney, Australia
Mackenzie, Lady, of Coul—(quarto copy)
Mackenzie, Landseer, Esq., Kensington Park Gardens,
    London
Mackenzie, Lieut.-Col., Royal Military Asylum, Chelsea
Mackenzie, Major Colin Lyon, of St Martins, Inverness—
    (quarto copy)
Mackenzie, Major James D., of Findon—(quarto copy)
Mackenzie, Major James K. D., 86th Regiment, Aldershot
Mackenzie, Major Roderick, of Flowerburn
Mackenzie, Major Thomas, 78th Highlanders (Ross-shire
    Buffs)—(quarto copy)
Mackenzie, Murdo C., Aberdeen, Sydney, N.S. Wales
Mackenzie, Murdo, Esq. of Dundonnell
Mackenzie, Murdo, Esq., Glasgow
Mackenzie, Miss, Lyne of Carron, Aberlour
Mackenzie, Miss M., Cheadle, Stoke-on-Trent
Mackenzie, Miss, Victoria Street, Aberdeen
Mackenzie, N. B., Esq.,banker, Fort-William—(quarto copy)
Mackenzie, Osgood H., of Inverewe
Mackenzie, Rev. Donald, C.C., Beauly　.
Mackenzie, Rev. James, Logan Terrace, South Shields
Mackenzie, Rev. Kenneth, Eddrachillis, Lairg

2

Mackenzie, Roderick, Esq., Mountpelier Road, Peckham, London—(2 copies)

Mackenzie, Roderick Fraser, paymaster-sergt., 84th Regt.

Mackenzie, Sir Evan, of Kilcoy, Baronet

Mackenzie, Sir Kenneth S., of Gairloch, Baronet—(3 copies, 1 quarto copy)

Mackenzie, The late Major-General A. M., of Gruinard, Queensborough Terrace, London—(quarto copy)

Mackenzie, Thomas, Esq. of Applecross, W.S., Edinburgh —(quarto copy)

Mackenzie, Thomas, Esq., Luskintyre, Harris

Mackenzie, Thomas, Esq. of Ord

Mackenzie, W., Esq., M.D., C.B., C.S.I., Honorary Physician to the Queen, London

Mackenzie, William, Esq., Achandunie, Alness

Mackenzie, William, Esq., Castlegate, Malton, Yorkshire

Mackenzie, William, Esq., *Free Press* Office, Inverness— (2 copies)

Mackenzie, William, Esq., merchant, Inverness

Mackenzie, William Ord, Esq. of Culbo, M.D., Deputy-Inspector-General of Army Hospitals—(quarto copy)

Mackinlay, D., Esq., Duchess Street, London—(quarto copy)

Mackinnon, Deputy Surgeon-General W. A., C.B., Aldershot

Mackintosh, Angus, Esq. of Holme

Mackintosh of Mackintosh—(quarto copy)

Macknight, The late James, Esq., W.S., Edinburgh

Maclauchlan, Rev. Thomas, LL.D., Edinburgh

Maclachlan & Stewart, Messrs, booksellers, Edinburgh

Macnab, James, Esq., Renfield Street, Glasgow

Macphee, John Cameron, Esq., surveyor, H.M. Customs, London

Macpherson, Rev. John, F. C. Manse, Lairg

Macrae, Alex. M. M., Esq., Glenoze, Skye—(6 copies)

Macrae, Donald, Esq., Denny Street, Inverness

Macrae, Duncan A., Esq., Monar

Macrae, Ewen, Esq. of Ardtulloch, Australia

Macrae, Ewen, Esq., Braintrath, Strome Ferry

Macrae, Finlay, Esq., Glasgow

Macrae, Kenneth, Esq., Achalorachan, Strathconon
Macraild, A. R., Esq., Church Street, Inverness
Masson, Rev. Donald, A.M., M.D., Edinburgh
Melven, James, Esq., bookseller, Inverness—(20 copies, 5 quarto do.)
Morrison-Duncan, Miss, of Naughton, Fife—(quarto copy)
Munro, David, Church Street, Inverness
Murray, Francis, Esq., Travancore, India
Noble, John, Esq., bookseller, Inverness—(80 copies, 20 quarto do.)
Pink, William D., Esq., bookseller, Leigh, Lancashire
Reid, Donald, Esq., solicitor, Inverness
Rhind, John, Esq., architect, Inverness
Robertson, George, Esq., bookseller, Warwick Square, London
Rose, Hugh, Esq., solicitor, Inverness
Ross, A., Esq., teacher, Alness
Ross, Alex., Esq., architect, Inverness—(quarto copy)
Ross, James, Esq., solicitor, Inverness
Ross, Jonathan, Esq., merchant, Inverness
Scobie, Captain, Mid-Fearn
Scott, Roderick G., Esq., solicitor, Inverness
Semple, Mrs, Moorside House, Neston, Cheshire
Shaw, Gilbert, Esq., Tongland, Kirkcudbright
Shaw, Alex. Mackintosh, Esq., Chipping Barnet, Herts
Simpson, Alex., Esq., Provost of Inverness—(quarto copy)
Sinton, Thomas, Esq., Nuide, Kingussie
Skues, Frederick M., Surgeon-Major, Army Medical Department, Sheerness
Skues, Miss, St Heliers, Jersey
Skues, William Mackenzie, M.D., Surgeon-Major, Army Medical Department, Jersey
Smith, J. Turnbull, Esq., C.A., Edinburgh
Soule, H. M., Esq., St John's Hill, Surrey
Stanley, Hon. Mrs, Wimpole Street, London—(quarto copy)
Steuart, James, Esq., Dalkeith House, Dalkeith
Stewart, Archibald, Esq., Auchallander, Tyndrum
Stewart, Duncan, Esq., Portlands, Sevenoaks, Kent
Stewart, Robert, Esq., bookseller, Forres

Stodart, R. R., Esq., Lyon Office, Edinburgh
Sutherland, George Miller, Esq., solicitor, Wick
Sutherland-Walker, Evan C., Esq. of Skibo
Symon, George, Esq., Salford
Tomlinson, George C. J., Esq., Torquay
Tweeddale, The Most Noble Julia, Marchioness of
Waddington, Major-General H. F., Eastbourne Terrace,
    London—(5 copies)
Walker, Mrs K. Robertson, of Gilgarran, Cumberland
Watson, James, Esq., bookseller, Elgin—(4 copies)
Wood, George, Esq., Baltic Chambers, Dundee

HISTORY OF THE MACKENZIES;

WITH

GENEALOGIES OF THE PRINCIPAL FAMILIES.

THE CLAN MACKENZIE, at one time one of-the most powerful in the Highlands, and still one of the most numerous and
influential, claims a very ancient descent. It has been long
maintained that the family is descended from an Irish nobleman named Colin or Cailean Fitzgerald. The authorities
who maintain this Irish origin of the Clan inform us, that
a certain Otho, who came to England with William the Con-
queror, and fought with him at the Battle of Hastings, was
created Castellan and Baron of Windsor, and that he was
the common progenitor of the Fitzgeralds, of the Windsors
and Earls of Plymouth. Most authorities concur in holding
that this Otho was succeeded by his son, surnamed Fitz-
Otho, who, we find, was Castellan of Windsor in 1078, and
married a daughter of Glady; of Ry Gwallan ap Comryn,
Prince of North Wales, by whom he had three sons, Gerald,
Robert, and William. Robert, who was afterwards Castellan
of Windsor, appears as a witness to a royal charter, granted
in favour of the Monks of Durham, in 1082, and had extensive possessions in several English counties.

Gerald or Gerard (for the two names are synonymous),
under the patronymic of Fitz-Walter, in 1112, married Nesta,
daughter of Rees ap Teudor Griffin, Prince of South Wales,
by whom he had three sons, (1) Maurice, (2) William, of
whom are said to be descended the Earls of Kerry, and (3)
David, Bishop of St David's, uncle to the celebrated Ger-
aldus Cambrensis, whom he afterwards appointed to the
Arch-Deanery of that See.

A

Maurice, the eldest son, succeeded his father, and was one of those who accompanied Richard Strongbow, Earl of Striguel, to Ireland, about 1170, where, after many distinguished and signal services in the subjection of that country, he was created Baron of Wicklow, and Naas Offelim of the territories of the Macleans, by Henry II., who, on his return to England, in 1172, left Maurice in the joint-Government. He had married Alicia, daughter of Amulphade Montgomery, brother of Robert, Earl of Shrewsbury, who bore him four sons, Gerald, William, Alexander, and Maurice.

Gerald Fitz-Maurice succeeded his father, and was created Lord Offally. By his wife Catherine, daughter of Hanno de Valois, Lord Chief-Justice of Ireland, he had a son, Maurice, who in due course succeeded his father. Maurice died on the 20th of May 1267, and left two sons, Thomas and Gerald.

Thomas Fitz-Maurice succeeded his father as Lord Offally, and was generally known as "Tomas Mor," or Great Thomas, in consequence of his distinguished valour and signal performances on the battlefield. This great warrior and powerful chief had a rupture with King Henry, and the neighbouring tribes finding that this was a great source of weakness to them, they, led by their chiefs, made harassing inroads on his territories. Thomas, however, continued to effect considerable division amongst them, and thus recovered much of his former power and influence, and cleared his territories of all his enemies. In 1262, however, these Irish mountain tribes concentrated their followers, and gained a victory over him in a pitched battle at Callan, where his son John, and grandson Maurice, with fifteen knights and a great number of followers of less note, were left dead on the field; but he was ultimately successful, and established for himself a high reputation, and secured the favour of the Sovereign.*

* The following is the *traditionary* account of the introduction of the race of Otho into Hibernian record, and how they became identified with the children of the Gael in Ireland, and afterwards with those of Scotland:—In 1167, according to this legend, Diarmad MacMhurchaidh, King of Leinster, committed a rape on Devorgil, the wife of Tighearnach, Roderick King of Bresinia, who entered into a league with Roderick O'Connor, the most powerful of the petty kings

The Kings of Desmond are admitted to have been of very ancient renown in Irish annals. During the conquest Diarmad of Desmond stood out boldly against the English, and, as a reward for his reduction, Henry gave the Kingdom of Cork, comprising originally that of Desmond, to the victor ; but that petty monarch having at length sub-. mitted to the English King, the seigniory of Desmond, was

of Ireland, to revenge the insult. This combination was too formidable for Diarmad, who was overwhelmed and totally defeated. He fled to England with the view of obtaining aid from King Henry II. Finding His Majesty was at the time at Antiquane, he proceeded thither and offered to hold his kingdom of that monarch if he would aid him to recover it from his victorious enemies. Henry readily entered into the project, and gave him a commission to recruit from among his English subjects such followers as he might consider expedient. On Diarmad's return to Bristol he met Richard Strongbow, Earl of Striguel, who willingly agreed to join him, on condition that Strongbow, in the event of success, wou'd marry Eva, Diarmad's daughter, and succeed him in his kingdom. The Irish king then proceeded to Wales, where he made arrangements with Maurice Fitz Gerald and his half-brother, Robert Fitz-Stephen, promising them, in the event of success, the town of Wrexford and the adjoining territories. The latter started immediately for Ireland, and arriving with a handful of followers, reduced Wrexford. Fitz Gerald soon after followed and joined his brother. Their combined forces, numbering ten knights, sixty horsemen, seventy men-at-arms, and four hundred and sixty archers, marched upon the city of Dublin, with such promptitude, that the garrison, then occupied by the Danes, surrendered after little or no resistance. Striguel arrived in 1170, and, according to agreement, married Eva, Diarmad's daughter, and was declared heir and successor to the kingdom of Leinster. The City of Dublin, which was unaccountably left under the charge of the Danish Governor Asculphus, revolted, and had to be again reduced. Asculphus escaped and fled to Orkney, and thus ended the reign of the Vikingr in that quarter. King Henry now became jealous of the success of Diarmad and his English confederates, and issued an order to all his English subjects serving under Strongbow to abandon him, at the same time commanding all adventurers from England not to join him further in the invasion. He was called Diarmad "Mor Onorach," or "Highly honourable," by his friends and allies, but by his own countrymen he was considered and looked upon as contemptible for having betrayed his country into the hands of the English. He died on the 4th of May 1171, when Striguel was proclaimed King of Leinster. On hearing this, Henry despatched Henry de Merisco to demand his surrender of authority and his instant return to England, at the same time, appointing Maurice Fitz Gerald governor *ad interim*. Striguel obeyed, and on his return to England he met Henry at Gloucester, and there made over all his rights to him. The King himself now embarked for Ireland, with four or five hundred knights, and four thousand men-at-arms. On his arrival with such an imposing and powerful following, all the petty kings found it most to their interest to do him homage, and retain possession of their respective kingdoms ; and it is on this visit he is said to have created Maurice Fitzgerald Baron of Wicklow and Naas Offelim.

remitted to him, to hold of the King of England, but failing heirs male, it ultimately fell to Thomas Carron, who had married his daughter. There was issue, only one daughter, of this union, who married Thomas Fitzgerald, and who had the seigniory of Desmond transferred to her in dowry. She bore him one son, John, who married first, Marjory, daughter of Sir Thomas Fitz-Antony, who bore him Maurice, ancestor of the Duke of Leinster; and secondly, he married Honora, daughter of Hugh O'Connor, by whom he had six sons—Cailean, the reputed progenitor of the Mackenzies; Galen (said to be the same as Gilleon, or Gillean, the ancestor of the Macleans of Mull), who fought at the Battle of Largs, and died in 1300; Gilbert, ancestor of the White Knights; John, ancestor of the Knights of Glynn; Maurice, ancestor of the Knights of Kerry; and Thomas, progenitor of the Fitzgeralds of Limerick.

It will be noticed, that although the name Gerald or Gerard descends through the ancestors of the family, beginning with Gerald Fitz-Walter, it does not appear to have become an established patronymic until a later period; but it has been maintained that the ancestors of the Clan Mackenzie were recognised *in limine* as "*e Familia Geraldorum.*"

During the reign of Alexander II., several of the North and West Highland Chiefs were very powerful, and so remote from the centre of Government that they could not be subdued to the King's authority. To bring them to subjection he determined to command an expedition in person against Angus of Argyll, but he died, on his way thither in 1249, leaving his son, Alexander III., only nine years of age, with the full weight and responsibilities of the Government of Scotland upon his shoulders. It is not, however, our present object to refer to Alexander's reign further than is necessary to introduce Cailean Fitzgerald, the reputed ancestor of the Clan Mackenzie to the reader, and to show the manner in which he is said to have obtained possession of Islandonain and the Lands of Kintail.

Driven from Ireland in 1262, Cailean is said to have taken refuge at the Court of the youthful Scottish King, by whom his rank and his established prowess were duly recognised. Alexander was at this time preparing for an expected attack from Haco, King of Norway ; and he, no doubt, in view of such a contingency, considered himself fortunate in being able to secure the friendship and active aid of such a renowned warrior as Cailean Fitzgerald. On the 2d of October 1262, Haco landed on the coast of Ayrshire, where he was at once met by a gallant force of fifteen hundred knights, splendidly mounted on horses—many of them of pure Spanish breed—wearing breastplates, while their riders were clad in complete armour, with a numerous army of foot well armed with spears, bows and arrows, and other weapons of war, according to the usage in their respective provinces, the whole led by the King in person. These splendid and well accoutred armies met at Largs; and then commenced that sanguinary and famous battle which was the first great blow to check the arrogance of the Norwegians and to open up a channel for the subsequent arrangements between Alexander and Magnus IV., and consequent introduction of an entirely new organisation into the Western Islands hitherto inhabited by a mixed race, composed of the natives and of the descendants of those who had gradually formed connections and intermarried with successive colonies of the Norse and Danes that settled in the Hebrides.*

Among the illustrious warriors who were most conspicuous for their gallantry and heroism at the Battle cf Largs was Cailean Fitzgerald, who, as we learn from the fragment of the Record of Icolmkill, arrived the previous year. This document says—" Callenus peregrinus Hybernus

---

* In this memorable engagement the Scots commenced the attack. The right wing, composed of the men of Argyle, of Lennox, of Athole, and Galloway, was commanded by Alexander, Lord High Steward, while Patrick Dunhar, Earl of March, commanded the left, composed of the men of the Lothians, Berwick, Stirling, and Fife. The King placed himself in the centre, at the head of the choice men of Ross, Perth, Angus, Mearns, Mar, Moray, Inverness, and Caithness, where he was confronted by Haco in person, who, for the purpose of meeting the Scottish King, took post in the Norwegian centre. The High Steward, by a dexterous movement, made the enemy's left give way, and he instantly, by another adroit manœuvre, wheeled back on the rear of Haco's centre,

nobilis ex e familia Geraldinorum qui proximo anno ab Hybernia pulsus apud Regum benigne acceptus hinc usque in curta permansit et in praefacto proelio strenue pugnavit." —(Colin, an Irish stranger and nobleman of the family of Geraldines, who, in the previous year, had been driven from Ireland, and had been well received by the King, remained up to this time at Court, and fought bravely in the aforesaid battle).

After the defeat of Haco, Alexander sent detachments to secure the Western Islands, and to check the Islanders, which, after his treaties with Magnus, served to reduce them to comparative subjection and a proper state of subordination. Among those sent in charge of the western garrisons was Cailean Fitzgerald, who, under the patronage of Walter Stewart, Earl of Menteith, was settled in the government of Islandonain, a strong castle in Kintail, built on an insulated rock at the extremity of Lochalsh and the junction of Loch Duich and Loch Long, the whole forming, it is said, by various authorities, the *Itus* of Ptolemy and Richard Cirencester. Cailean's jurisdiction extended over the adjoining districts of Lochalsh, Kintail, &c., and his vigilance is recognised by the already quoted document in the following terms :—" De· quo in proelio ad Largos, qui postea se fortiter contra Insulanos gessit et ibi inter eos in presidium relicto "—that is, " Of whom we have spoken at the battle of Largs, and who afterwards conducted himself with firmness against the Islanders, and was left a governor among them."

Sir George Mackenzie of Tarbat, afterwards first Earl of Cromarty, writing on this subject, says—Being left in Kintail, tradition records, that he married the daughter of Mac-

where he found the two warrior Kings desperately engaged. This induced Haco, after exhibiting all the prowess of a brave king and an able commander, to retreat from the field, followed by his left wing, leaving, as has been variously stated, sixteen to twenty-four thousand of his followers on the field, while the loss on the Scottish side is estimated at about five thousand. The men of Caithness and Sutherland were led by the Flemish Freskin. Those of Moray were probably led by one of their great chiefs, and we have every reason to believe, although without any distinct authority, that the men of Ross rallied round one of their native chiefs.

Mhathoin, heritor of the half of Kintail. This MacMhathoin is frequently identified with *Coinneach Gruamach* MacMhathoin, Cailean's predecessor, as governor of Eilean-Donnan Castle. The other half of Kintail belonged to O'Beolan, one of whose chiefs, Ferchair, was created Earl of Ross, and his lands were given by the King to Cailean Fitzgerald.

The reputed charter in favour of Colin runs thus:— "Alexander, Dei Gracia, Rex Scottorum, omnibus probis hominibus tocius terre sue clericis et laicis, salutem, Sciant presentes et futuri me pro fideli seruicio michi navato per Colinum Hybernum tam in bello quam in pace ideo dedisse, et hac presenti carta mea concessisse dicto Colino, et ejus successoribus, totas terras de Kintaile. Tenendas de nobis et successoribus nostris in liberam baroniam cum guardia. Reddendo servicium forinsecum et fidelitatem. Testibus Andrea episcopo. Moraviensi, Waltero Stewart. Henrico de Balioth camerario. Arnoldo de Campania. Thoma Hostiario, vice-comite de Innerness. Apud Kincardine, IX. die Jan.: Anno Regni Domini, Regis XVI."—"Alexander, by the grace of God, King of the Scots, to all honest men of his whole dominions, cleric and laic, greeting : Be it known to the present and future that I, for the faithful service rendered to me by Colin of Ireland in war as well as peace, therefore I have given, and by this my present charter, I concede to the said Colin and his successors, all the lands of Kintail to be held of us in free Barony with ward to render foreign service and fidelity. Witnesses (as above). At Kincardine, 9th day of January, in the year of the reign of the Lord the King, the 16th."

The Kincardine, at which the above charter is said to have been signed, is supposed to be that situated on the river Dee, for about this time an incident is reported to have taken place in the Forest of Mar, in consequence of which the Mackenzies adopted the stag's head as their coat of arms. Alexander was on a hunting expedition in the forest, when an infuriated stag, closely pursued by the hounds, made straight in the direction of His Majesty, and Cailean Fitzgerald, who accompanied the royal party,

gallantly interposed his own person between the exasperated animal and his sovereign, and shot it with an arrow in
the head. The King, in acknowledgment of his gratitude,
issued a diploma in favour of Cailean for his armorial bearings, which were to be, a stag's head puissant, bleeding at
the forehead where the arrow pierced him, to be borne on a
field azure, supported by two greyhounds. The crest to be
a dexter arm bearing a naked sword, surrounded with the
motto, "Fide Parta, Fide Aucta," which continued to be the
distinctive bearings of the Mackenzies of Seaforth until it was
considered expedient, as corroborating their claims on the
extensive possessions of the Macleods of the Lews, to substitute the crest of that ancient clan—viz., a mountain in
flames, surcharged with the words, "Luceo non uro," with
the ancient shield supported by two savages, naked, and
wreathed about the head with laurel, armed with clubs,
issuing fire, which are the bearings now used by the representatives of the ancient Mackenzies of Kintail.*

It would naturally, ere this, have occurred to the reader,
How, if this origin of the Clan Kenneth be correct, has the
original patronymic of Fitzgerald given place to that of
Mackenzie? The Earl of Cromarty says that Cailean had
a son by the daughter of Kenneth MacMhathoin, whom he
named *Coinneach*, or Kenneth, after his father-in-law, that
Cailean himself was killed in *Glaic Chailein* by MacMhathoin, who envied him, and was sore displeased at the
stranger's succession to his ancient heritage, that Cailean
was succeeded by his son Kenneth, and that all his descendants were, by the Highlanders, called MacChoinnich,
taking the patronymic from MacMhathoin rather than from
Cailean, whom they esteemed a stranger. No record exists
of the exact period of Cailean's death, but it is said that he
died about 1278, and was buried in Icolmkill.

* The incident of the hunting match and Colin Fitzgerald's gallant rescue of ·
the King was painted by West in one of those large pictures with which the old
Academician employed and gratified his latter years. He received £800 for the
noble painting, still to be seen in Brahan Castle, and in his later years was
willing to give the same sum for it to add to his own collection.

The preceding is the theory accepted hitherto by the Clan generally of their origin and that of their name. It has been adopted in all the Peerages and Baronetages, by all the principal men of the different branches of the Mackenzies, and almost without exception by every writer on their genealogy and history. The Laird of Applecross, in his "Genealogy of the Mackenzies preceding the year 1661, written in the year 1669," adopts it, and concludes a lengthy detail thus—"From the Battle of Largs, Walter Stewart was sent with forces to reduce the Isles, then associated with the Norwegians. To retain them in obedience, he built a fort in Kintail, which took its name from its intended use, and was called the Danting Isle, fitly situate to attack any who stirred in a great part of the Isles, and in it he placed Colin Fitzgerald with a garrison." The other half of Kintail at this time belonged to O'Beolan, whose chief, called Farquhar, was created Earl of Ross, and his lands in Kintail were given by the King to Colin Fitzgerald. "This tradition carries enough of probability to found historical credit, but I find no charter of these lands purporting any such grounds, for that the first Charter of Kintail is given by this King Alexander to this Colin, Anno 1266." He then quotes the charter in full as already given, describes how Colin saved the King in the Forest of Mar from the infuriated stag, and the granting of the stag's head as the armorial bearings on that occasion pretty much the same as already given from another old manuscript history of the Mackenzies in our possession. He also gives pretty much the same account of the murder of Colin, who had a son, Kenneth, by MacMhathoin's daughter; but the garrison in the castle, consisting mostly of Macraes and Maclennans, "did so valiantly defend their young master's right that, maugre his opponents, they retained his possessions to him. To Colin succeeded this Kenneth. . . . . . All the descendants of Kenneth were by the Highlanders called *MacChoinnich*, taking the patronymic from MacMhathoin rather than from Colin, whom they esteemed a stranger."

So much for the origin of the reputed Clan Mackenzie

from Colin Fitzgerald. We shall now dispose of it, and adduce reasons for adopting a native Gaelic descent.

Coinneach, or Kenneth, is really the first of the line of Mackenneth, and it seems ... a pity to controvert and reject the elaborate ... by which the origin of the Clan has hitherto been traced back through Ireland and Wales to a Norman and Florentine source—illustrious and flattering as this origin is to the successors of Kenneth, who, like most of the Highland Clans, since the begining of the seventeenth century, exhibit an unpatriotic preference for alien progenitors. Writing of the Clans who claim this foreign origin, Skene says :—" As the identity of the false aspect which the true tradition assumes in all these cases implies that the case was the same in all, we may assume that wherever these two circumstances are to be found combined, of a Clan claiming a foreign origin, and asserting a marriage with the heiress of a Highland family, whose estates they possessed and whose followers they led, they must invariably have been the oldest cadet of that family, who, by usurpation or otherwise, had become *de facto* chief of the Clan, and who covered their defect by right of blood by denying their descent from the Clan, and asserting that the founder had married the heiress of its chief." He then goes on to maintain that the general deduction from all our MS. genealogies is, that the Clans were divided into several great tribes descended from a common ancestor, while he draws a marked distinction between the different tribes which, by indications traceable in each, can be identified with the Earldoms or Maormorships into which the North of Scotland was anciently divided. By the aid of the old genealogies he divides the Clans into five different tribes as follows :—(1) The Descendants of Conn of the Hundred Battles, (2) Descendants of Ferchar Fata Mac Feradaig, (3) Descendants of Cormaig Mac Oirbertaig, (4) Descendants of Fergus Leith Dearg, and (5) Descendants of Krycul. Under the third heading he includes the *Old* Earls of Ross, the Mackenzies, the Mathesons, and several others.

There appears to be no doubt that the Earls of Ross were

descended from the ancient Maormors of that district ; and
the same authority informs us that the district of Ross is
very often mentioned in the Norse Sagas along with the
other districts which were governed by Maormors or Iarls;
that it was only on the downfall of those of Moray that the
Chiefs of Ross appear prominent in historical records, the
Maormors of Moray being in such close proximity, and
so great in power and influence that the less powerful
Maormor of Ross only held a subordinate position, and his
name was in consequence seldom or never associated with
any of the great events in Highland history. It was only
after the downfall of those local potentates that the chiefs
appear under the appellation of Comites or Earls. That
they were the descendants of the ancient Maormors there
can be little doubt, and the natural presumption is in
this instance strengthened by the fact that the oldest
authorities concur in asserting that the Gaelic name of the
Earls of Ross was O'Beolan, or the descendants of Beolan ;
"and we actually find," says Skene, "from the oldest Norse
Saga connected with Scotland that a powerful chief in the
North of Scotland, named Beolan, married the daughter of
Ganga Rolfe, or Rollo, the celebrated pirate, who became
afterwards the celebrated Earl of Normandy." From this
account it appears that the ancestor of the Earls of Ross
was Chief of Kintail in the beginning of the tenth century.
   The first known Earl of Ross is Malcolm, to whom a
precept was directed from Malcolm IV., desiring him to
protect and defend the Monks of Dunfermline in their
lawful privileges and possessions. This document is not
dated, but from the names of the witnesses it must have
been granted before 1162. The next Earl of Ross whom
we find recorded in history is Ferchard, or "Ferchair Mac
an t-Sagairt," son of the priest, who seems to have risen
rapidly to power on the ruins of the once powerful Earl of
Moray, Kenneth MacHeth, who was the last of his line.
   Skene is of opinion that this *Mac an t-Sagairt*, being
"the son of the priest," was not the son of the former Earl,
but was of a new line that came into possession on the

extinction of the older family. "Of what family this Earl
was, history does not say, but that omission may in some
degree be supplied by the assistance of the MS. of 1450."*
The surname of Ross has always been rendered in Gaelic
Clan Anrias, or *Clan Gilleanrias*, and the Rosses appear
under the form of these appellations in all the early Acts of
Parliament. There is also an unvarying tradition in the
Highlands that on the death of William, the last Earl of
Ross of this family, a certain Paul MacTire was for some
time chief of the Clan, and the tradition is corroborated by
the fact that there is a charter by the same William, Earl of
Ross, in favour of this very Paul MacTire, in which he

---

* To this ancient document, which is the oldest Gaelic genealogical account
on record, and which is given in the original, with a literal English translation,
in the Transactions of the Iona Club, Mr Skene adds the following note:—"From
the peculiar condition of society among the Highlanders the investigation of
family history becomes an important instrument in ascertaining and illustrating
the leading facts of their origin and history. The attention of the Club will,
consequently, be in a considerable degree directed to this object, and it is proposed to include in the Collectanea a series of genealogies of Highland Clans
which are still to be found in ancient MSS. In the present number the series
commences with the contents of the most ancient MS. now known to exist. It
was discovered accidentally in the Advocates Library last year, and consists of
eight parchment leaves, the last of which is covered with genealogies, written in
the old Irish character, but so very faded with time as to be read with difficulty,
and in many instances to be altogether illegible. Of the authenticity of the MS.
there can be no doubt, and a strict comparison of all the genealogies contained in
it has satisfied the editor of its general accuracy. The same careful examination
shows that it must have been written about the year 1450, and this conclusion,
with respect to its date, was afterwards corroborated by the discovering the date
1467 written upon one of the leaves. The author of the MS. appears to have
been a person of the name of Maclachlan, as the genealogy of the Clanlachlan is
given with much greater minuteness than any of the other Clans, and the various
intermarriages of that Clan alone are given. From this it seems probable that it
once formed a part of the well known Kilbride collection, which was long preserved by the family of MacLachlan of Kilbride. . . . . Of the very important effects which this MS. must produce upon the question of the origin of
the Highland Clans, it will be sufficient to state that it seems to establish these
three very remarkable facts—1st, The existence at a very early period of a
tradition in the Highlands of the common origin of all the Highland Clans; 2d,
The comparatively late invention of many of the traditionary origins of the
different Clans at present believed; and 3d, The mutual relationship of various
Clans which have hitherto been supposed to be altogether unconnected." In
another note, the editor informs us that he "has been enabled by means of a
chemical process to restore the writing which was so much decayed as to be in
many parts illegible," and has now been able to give the MS. in full.

styles him his cousin. There appears, however, among the numerous Clans contained in the MS. of 1450, one termed Clan Gilleanrias, which commences with Paul MacTire, so there can be little doubt of that Clan being the same as that of the Rosses, and in this MS. of 1450 they are traced upwards in a direct line to a certain "Gilleon na h' Airde," or Colin of the Aird, who lived in the tenth century, and who was, as we shall see in the sequel, also the remote progenitor of the Mackenzies. In this ancient Gaelic genealogy occurs the name of Gilleanrias, exactly contemporary with the generation preceding that of Ferchard, Earl of Ross.

The name GilleAnrias is the Gaelic for "servant of Andrew," or of St Andrew, and this would indicate that he was a priest. When we consider that the dates exactly correspond, and that the Earls of Ross were, as we have seen, an offshoot of the Clan Anrias—must indeed have descended from Anrias—and that among the Earls who besieged Malcolm IV. in Perth in the year 1160 is to be found the name of Gilleanrias, it appears beyond question that Ferchard Mac an t-Sagairt (Farquhar son of the priest) was the son of Gilleanrias, the founder of Clan Anrias, and that consequently he succeeded to the Earldom of Ross on the failure of the former family. Mr Charles Fraser-Mackintosh in "Antiquarian Notes," p. 216, says that "Ignorance of the (Gaelic) language deprives any writer, about Highland affairs of old, of the means of understanding what to others may be very obvious. Having occasion to refer lately to 'Dalrymple's Annals of Scotland'—esteemed a learned and correct work—we observed that anno 1215, 'M'Kentagar' attacked and defeated certain marauders, who had made an inroad into Moray; and in a foot-note that 'M'Kentagar is an unintelligible word.' Though barbarously spelt, there is no doubt the word means 'Son of the Priest,' and the person referred to is Farquhard, first Earl of Ross, of the line of Ross, who was known by this name. In the Chronicle of Melrose he is styled 'Comes Rossensis Machentagard.'" Ferchard Mac an t-Sagairt rendered great assistance to Alexander II. in his conquest of Argyle in 1222, leading

most of the western tribes to support the King, and as a
reward for his services he received from that monarch a
grant of North Argyle, a district known to be that which is
now called Wester Ross.   He is designed " Earl of Ross "
in a charter dated 1234.   In a manuscript in our possession,
and in which the writer supports the Irish origin of the
Clan, we find the following :—" It cannot be disputed that
the Earl of Ross was the lord paramount under Alexander
II., by whom Farquhard Mac an t-Sagairt was recognised
in the hereditary dignity of his predecessors, *and who, by
another tradition, was a real progenitor of the noble family of
Kintail."*

Sir Robert Gordon, in his " History of the Earldom
of Sutherland," p. 36, says :—" From the second son of
the Earl of Ross the lairds of Balnagowan are descended,
and had by inheritance the lands of Rariechies and Coul-
leigh, where you may observe that the Laird of Balnagown's surname should not be Ross, seeing there was never
any Earl of Ross of that surname ; but the Earls of Ross
were first of the surname of Beolan, then they were Leslies,
and last of all that Earldom fell by inheritance to the Lords
of the Isles, who resigned the same unto King James the
Third's hands, in the year of God 1477.   So I do think that
the lairds of Balnagown, perceiving the Earls of Ross
decayed, and that Earldom, fallen into the Lords of the
Isles' hands, they called themselves Rosses, thereby to
testify their descent from the Earls of Ross.   Besides, all
the Rosses in that province are unto this day called in the
Irish (Gaelic) language Clan-Leandreis, which race, by their
own tradition, is sprung from another stock." From the
same authority, p. 46, we find that the Earls of Ross were
O'Beolans as late as 1333, for Sir Robert Gordon informs
us, writing of the Battle of Hallidon Hill, that " in this field
was Hugh Beolan, Earl of Ross, slain."

It seems thus established that the O'Beolans were the
ancient and original Earls of Ross, and it is quite clear
from the MS. of 1450 that they continued to be represented
by the old Rosses of Balnagown down to the beginning of

the eighteenth century, when the last of that family finding
that the entail ended with himself, sold the estate to General
Ross, brother of Lord Ross of Hawkhead, and who was,
although of the same name, of quite a different origin. ·

It appears equally clear that the Rosses and the Mackenzies had a common origin, descended from the same
ancestor—"Gilleon na h' Airde," so called from having his
seat in the Aird, now the property of Lord Lovat. Some
maintain that the Macleans and Macraes are from the same
stock as the Mackenzies, and there appears to be little
doubt that these tribes had occupied lands and held strongholds in the district of the Aird.* The genealogy of the
Macraes is not preserved in the MS. of 1450, but reference
to the name will be found in the genealogy of the Macleans,
thus supporting the view of those who maintain that the
Mackenzies, the Macleans, and the Macraes are descended
from the same ancestor. It will also be seen by the following extract that Gilleoin, or Gilleain was the common
ancestor of the three.

These genealogies are from the MS. of 1450:—

ORIGINAL MANUSCRIPT.	SKENE'S TRANSLATION.
Genelach Clann Anrias.	*Genealogy of the Clan Andres.*
Pal ic Tire, ic Eogan, ic Muiredaigh, ic Poil, ic Gilleanrias, ic Martain, ic Poil, ic Cainig, ic Cranin, ic Eogan, ic Cainic, ic Cranin, Mc Gilleoin na hairde, ic Eirc, ic Loirn, ic Fearchar, Mc Cormac, ic Abertaig, ic Feradaig.	Paul son of Tire, son of Ewen, son of Murdoch, son of Paul, son of Gille-anrias, son of Martin, son of Paul, son of Kenneth, son of Crinan, son of Ewen, son of Kenneth, son of Crinan, son of Gilleoin of the Aird, son of Erc, son of Lorn, son of Ferchar, son of Cormac, son of Oirbeirtaigh, son of Feradach.
Do Genelach Clann Gilleain.	*Genealogy of the Macleans.*
Lachlan ic Eon, ic . . . . . mc Maelsig, mc Gilleain, mc Icrait, ic Suan, ic Neill, ic Domlig, i'Ablesanid Sanobi, mc Ruingr, mc Sean Dubgall Airlir, mc Fearchair Abr. mc Feardach, ic . . . . . mc Neachtain, mc Colman, mc Buadan, &c.	Lachlan son of John, son of . . . . .* son of Maelsig, son of Gilleain, son of Icrath, son of Suan, son of Neill, son of Domlig, son of Ruingr, son of Old Dougall, son of Ferchard, son of Fera- dach, son of . . . . son of Neach- tan, son of Colman, son of Buadan,&c.

* They, "as vassals of the Bysets, inhabited the Clunes, Achryvaich, Obri-
achan, Kilfinnand, and Urquhart."—*Wardlaw Manuscript.*

Genelach Clann Cainig.	*The Genealogy of the Clan Kenneth.*
Muiread ic Cainig, mc Eoin, ic Cainig, ic Aengusn, ic Cristin, ic Agam, mc Gillaeon Oig, ic Gilleon na hairil.	Murdoch son of Kenneth, son of John, son of Kenneth, son of Angus, son of Christiau, son of Adam, son of Gilleoin Og, son of Gilleoin of the Aird.

To devote so much space to the origin of the Clan Andreas, or Ross, in a history of the Clan Kenneth, or Mackenzie, may be thought out of place ; but on considera- tion, the necessity of this will be admitted, for in tracing the genealogy of this Clan from the Earls of Ross, and from " Gilleon na h' Airde," this Gilleon being—as will be seen by the above extract from the MS. of 1450—also the ances- tor of the Mackenzies, we are at the same time establishing the Gaelic descent and origin of the Clan Kenneth.

If it be admitted that the MS. of 1450 is authentic— and this has not been seriously disputed by any respectable authority, while we have the high authority of Skene and others in support of its authenticity and general accuracy— it now appears doubtful, notwithstanding all the labour and learned attempts made in the past to foist a successful Irish adventurer upon this great Clan as their ancestor, whether, although hitherto accepted without much question, this Irish origin can be ultimately maintained and finally ac- cepted by the impartial student of history, or by the Clan themselves.

It is true that we have the reputed charter of the lands of Kintail, said to have been granted by King Alexander III. to Colin Fitzgerald, and extensively quoted by all the writers on the question of the origin of the Mackenzies, to controvert and dispose of. This, from the great strides made in recent years in independent historical research, and the results obtained, is much easier than will at first sight appear. Mr Skene unhesitatingly asserts that no trace of any traditions assigning a foreign origin to any of the Highland Clans can be found in any writings prior to the seventeenth century, and it is superfluous to state that, had any existed, no one was more likely to discover them than this laborious

Celtic scholar and eminent antiquarian. The first notice we find of such a charter is by George, first Earl of Cromarty, in his MS. History of the Clan Mackenzie, written in the seventeenth century. All the later genealogists seem to have taken its authenticity for granted, and quoted it accordingly. Dr George Mackenzie accepted and believed in its genuineness, as did also the Laird of Applecross, who wrote the MS. history of the Mackenzies already quoted, in 1669, for he not only copies the charter from Earl George, but quotes pages of his MS. *verbatim et literatim*. Skene gives it as his decided opinion that the charter is a forgery, and perfectly worthless as evidence in favour of the Fitzgerald origin of the Clan, and he is supported in this view by other high authority. The editor of the "Origines Parochiales Scotiæ," pp. 392-3, vol ii., says :—" The lands of Kintail are said to have been granted by King Alexander III. to Colin, an Irishman of the family of Fitzgerald, for service done at the Battle of Largs. *The charter is not extant*, and its genuineness has been doubted." In a footnote he gives the text of the charter in exactly the same terms as already given in these pages from another source, and which, he says, is from a copy of the seventeenth century, "*in the handwriting of the Earl of Cromarty.*" "If the charter be genuine," he continues, "it is not of Alexander III., or connected with the Battle of Largs (1263). Two of the witnesses, Andrew, Bishop of Moray, and Henry de Baliol, chamberlain, *would correspond with the sixteenth year of Alexander II.* The writers of the history of the Mackenzies assert also charters of David II. (1360) and of Robert II. (1380) to 'Murdo filius Kennethi de Kintail,' but without furnishing any description or means of testing their authenticity. No such charters are recorded."

Alexander II. began to reign in 1214, so that the charter, according to this excellent authority, must have been signed and witnessed in 1230—thirty-three years before the Battle of Largs was fought, and thirty-six years earlier than the actual date of the charter itself. This, in the opinion of all reasonable men, will settle finally the question of the

B

genuineness of a charter, which has been the main, indeed
the only, support of any weight ever adduced in favour of
the Irish origin of the Clan Mackenzie. We shall, however,
quote the same authority still further, and show pretty conclusively, not only that at that early period no Fitzgerald,
nor even a Mackenzie, was the actual proprietor of, although
no doubt even then the latter was a very powerful chief in
Kintail. " In 1292 the Sheriffdom of Skey, erected by King
John Baliol, included the lands of the Earl of Ros in North
Argail, a district which comprehended Kintail and several
other large parishes in Ross.* Between 1306 and 1329,
King Robert Bruce confirmed to the Earl of Ross all his
lands, including North Argyll (Borealis Ergadia).† In
1342, William Earl of Ross, the son and heir of the deceased
Hugh Earl of Ross, granted to Reginald, the son of Roderic
(Ranald Rorisoune, or *MacRuairidh*) of the Isles, the ten
davachs (or ten pennylands) of Kintail in North Argyle.‡
The grant was afterwards confirmed by King David II.§
About the year 1346 Ranald was succeeded by his sister
Amie, the wife of John of Isla.|| Between the years 1362
and 1372 William Earl of Ross, the son and heir of the
deceased Hugh Earl of Ross, exchanged with his brother
Hugh of Rosse, lord of Fylorth, and his heirs, his lands of
all Ergile, *with the Castle of Elandonan*, for Hugh's lands in
Buchan.¶ In 1463 the lands of Kintail were held by Alexander Mackenzie."**

We are thus irresistibly driven to the conclusion that, if
this charter be genuine, it must have been written when the
witnesses whose names are upon it were in existence—about
thirty years before Colin Fitzgerald crossed the Irish Channel,
and, probably, several years before he was born. There is
no doubt that the Mackenzies were in Kintail before 1463,
although this appears to be the first authentic record of

* Acta. Parl. Scot., vol. i., p. 91.
† Rob. Index, p. 16, No. 7; Register Moraviense, p. 342.
‡ Rob. Index, p. 48, No. 1; p. 99: p. 100; No. 1.
§ Ibid. || Gregory, p. 27.
¶ Balnagown Charters.   ** Gregory, p. 83

them in the district; but we are quite satisfied that they were there only as an important branch of the native and Gaelic Earls of Ross, closely related to them, and rapidly increasing in numbers, power, and influence. Even Dr George Mackenzie, who strongly maintains the Fitzgerald origin of the Clan, informs us that the Earl of Ross, in 1296, " sent a messenger to the Kintail men to send their young chieftain to him *as being his nearest kinsman by his marriage with his aunt.*" Before, however, proceeding with the general history of the Clan, we shall, in further support of the view here adopted, and, we venture to assert, now pretty well established, place Skene's conclusions before the reader.

In his " Highlands of Scotland" (pp. 223-5) he says:— "The Mackenzies have long boasted of their descent from the great Norman family of Fitzgerald in Ireland, and in support of this origin they produce a fragment of the records of Icolmkill, and a charter by Alexander III. to Colin Fitzgerald, the supposed progenitor of the family, of the lands of Kintail. At first sight these documents might appear conclusive, but, independently of the somewhat suspicious circumstance, that while these papers have been most freely and generally quoted, no one has ever yet seen the originals, the fragment of the Icolmkill record merely says that among the actors in the Battle of Largs, fought in 1262, was 'Peregrinus et Hibernus nobilis ex familia geraldinorum qui proximo anno ab Hibernia pulsus apud regem benigne acceptus hinc usque in curta permansit et in praefacto proelio strenue pugnavit,' giving not a hint of his having settled in the Highlands, or of his having become the progenitor of any Scottish family whatever; while as to the supposed charter of Alexander III., it is equally inconclusive, as it merely grants the lands of Kintail to 'Colino Hiberno,' the word 'Hibernus' having at the time come into general use as denoting the Highlanders, in the same manner as the word 'Erse' is now frequently used to express their language: but inconclusive as it is, this charter cannot be admitted at all, as it bears the most palpable marks of having been a forgery of a later time, and one by no means happy in its execution.

"How such a tradition of the origin of the Mackenzies ever could have arisen it is difficult to say ; but the fact of their native origin and Gaelic descent is completely set at rest by the Manuscript of 1450, which has already so often been the means of detecting the falsehood of the foreign origins of other Clans.   In that MS., the antiquity of which is perhaps as great, and its authenticity certainly much greater than the fragments of the Icolmkill records, the Mackenzies are brought from a certain Gilleon Og, or Colin the younger, a son of ' Gilleon na h' Airde,' the ancestor of the Rosses."

Another able and unbiassed modern writer is of the same opinion, and says :—"This chivalrous and romantic origin of the Clan Mackenzie, though vouched for by certain charters and local histories, is now believed to be fabulous. It seems to have been first advanced in the seventeenth century, when there was an absurd desire and ambition in Scotland to fabricate or magnify all ancient and lordly pedigrees.   Sir George Mackenzie, the Lord Advocate, and Sir George Mackenzie of Tarbat, the first Earl of Cromarty, were ready to swear to the descent of the Scots nation from Gathelus, son of Cecrops, King of Athens, and Scota his wife, daughter of Pharoah, King of Egypt ; and, of course, they were no less eager to claim a lofty and illustrious line-age for their own clan.   But authentic history is silent as to the two wandering Irish knights, and the reported charters (the elder one being palpably erroneous) can nowhere be found.   For two centuries after the reigns of the Alexanders the district of Kintail formed part of the lordship of the Isles, and was held by the Earls of Ross.   The Mackenzies, however, can be early traced to their wild mountainous and picturesque country—*Ceann-da-Shail*—the Head of the Two Seas."*

The descendants of Gilleon na h' Airde have already been fully identified as the ancestors of the old Earls of Ross, and it therefore follows that the Mackenzies, whose

---

* The late Robert Carruthers, LL.D., of the *Inverness Courier*, in an original unpublished MS. sketch of the Mackenzies, which he kindly presented to us, and which is now in our possession.

descent from the same ancestor is also, we submit, incontestably established, must always have formed an integral part of the ancient and powerful native Gaëlic tribe of Ross. All historical records show that, until the forfeiture of the Lords of the Isles, the Mackenzies held their lands from the Earls of Ross, and invariably followed their banner in the field.

The first Chief of Clan Kenneth who is known with any degree of certainty in history is Murdoch, son of Kenneth of Kintail, the "Murdo filius Kennethi de Kintail" already referred to as having obtained a charter from David II. as early as the year 1362, and that he lived about this time is confirmed by the MS. of 1450, for the last two generations named in it are found to be "Muiread ic Cainig," or Murdoch the son of Kenneth, after which it proceeds, as we have already seen—"Kenneth son of John, son of Kenneth, son of *Angus*, &c." ; whereas the genealogy given in all our Peerages and by all our family historians would read— "Murdoch, son of Kenneth, son of *Kenneth*, son of Kenneth, son of *Colin*." The only difference will be found in those names printed in *italics*.

In Skene's genealogy, from the MS. of 1450, we find *Angus* representing *Colin* Fitzgerald in the other ; and *John*, a very common name among the Mackenzies, standing for *Kenneth* in the family genealogy. It would certainly appear somewhat uncommon that we should have three Kenneths in the family in immediate succession ; and the probabilities are in favour of the Gaelic genealogy, which gives a John between two of the Kenneths; and as for Colin we think he has been already pretty satisfactorily disposed of as having had no connection whatever with the family.

When mere tradition was the only authority to be depended upon, one Kenneth, more or less, made no serious difference to those who, from time to time, recited the traditional family genealogy, so, on the whole, and considering all the *pros* and *cons*, we prefer the written authority, which gives a Kenneth and a John alternately, to the mere traditional record, which is so lavish with that from which the family name is derived as to supply us with three in immediate succession.

The craze for a foreign origin, which all the best authorities admit to have been almost universal among the Highland genealogists during the seventeenth century—which was indeed the creation of that period,—and with which the Earl of Cromarty, the Laird of Applecross, and Dr George Mackenzie have been so strongly saturated, would not affect, in any material degree, their records of the general history of the Clan, beyond what was necessary to make it fit in with the Irish origin which they themselves first brought into being, and stoutly maintained all along. We shall, therefore, in the following history of Clan Kenneth, in addition to the information and views derived from and founded upon modern historical research, draw pretty freely on the large and complete collection of private MSS. in our possession.

The History and Genealogies of the Chiefs of Kintail and Seaforth will be proceeded with in their order, beginning with the first *Kenneth*, he being the one from whom the Clan name is derived; after which the various offshoots, beginning with the oldest cadet, will be treated, in the same manner, in order of seniority.

It may be well to explain, at the outset, how the Clan name came to be pronounced and written as we now have it. Mackenzie was originally *MacChoinnich*, and the second chief of the family was designated, according to the manuscript of 1450, *Eoin*, or *Ian MacChoinnich—John*, son of Kenneth. The Gaelic patronymic was, in that form, unpronounceable to a non-Gaelic speaker, and the nearest that he could get to it would be *MacCoinni*, or MacKenny. In those days the letter " Z " possessed no sound or value different from the letter " Y." Indeed, in our own day we find it in many names simply doing duty in place of that accommodating letter, for we still find it quiescent in such names as Menzies, MacFadzean, and others—pronounced exactly, at any rate by Scotsmen, as if the names were written with the letter " Y." The two, being of the

same value, came to be used indiscriminately in the word
Kenny or Kenzie; and the letter "Z" having, in later times,
acquired a different and independent value, we now pro-
nounce the name as if it were written Mackenzie.

In the preceding pages, which are necessarily of an
introductory character, it has been shown from authentic
records that Kintail was in the possession of the Earls of
Ross in and before 1296; that King Robert Bruce confirmed
him in those lands in 1306-29; that in 1342 Earl William
granted the ten pennylands or davachs of Kintail to another
—Reginald of the Isles; that this grant was confirmed by
the King; and that in 1362-72 Kintail was, "with the Castle
of Eileandonan," exchanged by the Earl with his brother
Hugh for lands in Buchan. How could these lands be possessed by the Mackenzies and the Earls of Ross at one and
the same time? is a question which the upholders of the
Irish origin are bound to answer. The Mackenzies could
not have possessed a single acre of it, there being only ten
davachs or pennylands in Kintail altogether. It cannot be
assumed that the Earl of Ross had taken illegal possession,
for in the Acts of Parliament in 1296 Kintail is mentioned
as " the lands of the Earl of Ros," and these possessions are
later on confirmed to him by the King.

These facts, which are founded on authentic records (see
page 18), must be disposed of before we can accept the
reputed charter to Colin Fitzgerald, even were it possible
any longer, after it has been shown that it must have been
written at least thirty-three years before the Battle of Largs
was fought, and thirty-six before the date of the charter
itself, to attach any importance to it. William Fraser, in
his " Earls of Cromartie," recently published, admits that
the charter is not of Alexander the Third, and says—" In
the middle of the seventeenth century, when Lord Cromartie
wrote his history, the means of ascertaining, by the names
of witnesses and otherways, the true granter of a charter
and the date were not so accessible as at present. The
mistake of attributing the Kintail charter to King Alexander
the Third, instead of King Alexander the Second, cannot

be regarded as a very serious error in the circumstances."
When the upholders of the Fitzgerald origin are obliged to
make such admissions and apologies as these, their case
must be considered as practically given up ; for, once admit,
as is here done, that the charter is of Alexander the Second
(1230), even if genuine, it cannot possibly have any reference
to Colin Fitzgerald, who, according to his supporters, only
came over from Ireland about 1261 ; and it is simply absurd
to maintain that a charter granted in 1230 can be a reward
for valour displayed at a battle fought in 1263 ; and Mr
Fraser, having given up that point, was in consistency bound
to give up Colin Fitzgerald. Mr Fraser further informs us
that the charters of 1360 and 1380 are not now known to
exist. "But the terms of them as quoted in the early
histories of the family are consistent with either theory of
the origin of the Mackenzies, whether descended from Colin
Fitzgerald or Colin of the Aird."

Another very significant fact to which no attention has
been hitherto directed by any writer is that from 1263 down
to 1568—a period of three centuries—not a trace of the
name Colin is to be found in any of the family genealogies.
Cailean Cam, who became chief in the latter year, is the
first of the name. He was, on the mother's side, descended
from the houses of Athole and Argyll ; and being a second
son, he was, no doubt, according to the prevailing custom,
named after some of her numerous relatives of that name.
Is it at all probable, if Colin Fitzgerald had really been
the progenitor of the family, that his name would have
been totally ignored for 300 years in the face of the invari-
able practice among the other Highland families to honour
the names of their ancestors by continuing them in the
family names ? Keeping all this in view, we have no hesi-
tation in commencing the general History of the Clan Mackenzie with the first of the name.

I. COINNEACH.

KENNETH, according to our view and the MS. of 1450,
was the eldest son of Angus, a scion, and near relative

of the O'Beolans, the ancient Earls of Ross, who before
and during the thirteenth and fourteenth centuries were
the superior lords of Kintail.* Kenneth was in all probability a nephew of Earl William. From all accounts it
appears that Kenneth, whose followers were already powerful, succeeded his father in the government of Islandonain
Castle, garrisoned by his own immediate relatives, the
Macraes and the Maclennans. The Earl of Ross of the
day (William, third Earl) found his subaltern and relative
was getting too powerful for his comfort and satisfaction
as supreme lord of the district. About this time the Earl
laid claim to the superiority of the Western Isles, which he
and his father Fearchair had been recently chiefly instrumental in wresting from the Norwegians ; and he naturally
considered it safer to have the stronghold of Islandonain in
his own possession than in that of a dependant who was
rapidly rising in influence among the surrounding tribes ;
who had given unmistakable indications already of a disposition not to be treated contemptuously even by such a
powerful superior ; and who might, backed by a powerful
and loyal garrison, at any moment assert his rights as hereditary governor of the Castle, and, from self-interest and
other considerations, act contrary to those of his superior.
He might even go over to the other side, on condition that the
prospects of his own house and those of his more immediate

* At this time "Macbheolan had Glensheal and the south side of Lochduich
and to the Firth of Kyle Rhea, which divides the Isle of Skye from the Continent ; MacIver had Glenlichd, the Croe of Kintail, and the north side of Lochduich, and one Charles, called Tearlach, had Glenelchaig and . . . . whose
posterity were called Clan Tearlaich, of whom several to this day remain in Kintail and the Letter of Lochalsh. . . . . Kenneth MacMhathon also had the
garrison of Ellandonnan as Constable. Neither were heritors of these lands;
but movable at the King's pleasure ; otherwise it might be thought that the
King had wronged them in disposing their heritage to another, while there was
nothing to he laid to their charge, and it is possible they would have disputed
their rights. As for MacMhathon he had no heritage in Kintail, nor in Lochalsh,
which last he held of the Earl of Ross, not as heritor ; but he and many of his
name possessed it for duty and service, as a number of the MacMhathons had
some places and lands in the Braes of Sutherland in those days, and the successors of both are numerous to this day in the Lochalsh and the Braes of Sutherland. . . . . The MacRas and the MacCalamains did not for many years
after come into Kintail.—*Ardintoul MS.*

kindred would be advanced. The Earl, in these circumstances, demanded possession of the young governor of the
fortress,* which demand was peremptorily refused; and,
finding that Kenneth was determined to hold the stronghold at all hazards, the Earl sent a strong detachment to
take the castle by storm, and, if possible, to carry away the
governor. Kenneth, however, was so very popular among
the surrounding tribes that he was promptly reinforced by
the Macivers, and the brave Macaulays of Lochbroom,
and by their aid he was able, in spite of a desperate and
gallant onset by the followers of the Earl, to maintain his
position, and drive back the enemy with great slaughter.
The hitherto generally successful Earl felt so exasperated
by this defeat that he at once decided upon returning to the
attack with a largely increased force, threatening the young
governor with vengeance and extirpation. Before he was
in a position, however, to carry out his threatened retaliation,
he found himself in the clutches of another—a more powerful—enemy. The king of terrors had now taken him in
hand, and having been conquered, he succumbed and died
about 1274. His son Hugh, the fourth Earl, was diverted
from carrying out the intentions of his father against the
gallant defender of Islandonain, in consequence of the distracted state of the nation, brought about by the recent death,
in 1286, of Alexander III. This state of affairs proved
advantageous to Kenneth, for, in the general chaos which
followed, he was able to strengthen his position among the
local tribes, and, through a combination of native prudence,
popularity, and power, heightened by the *eclat* of his having
defeated the powerful Earl of Ross, he was able to keep
order in his own district, while his influence was felt over

---

* Dr George Mackenzie, in his MS. History of the Clan says that "at the
same time [1267] William, Earl of Ross, laying a claim of superiority over the
Western Isles, ... thought this a fit opportunity to seize the Castle of
Eileandonnan. . . . . He sent a messenger to the Kintail men to send their
young chieftain to him as being his nearest kinsman by *his marriage with his
aunt*; and the Doctor goes on to inform us that Kenneth, "joined by the Macivers, Macaulays, Macbollans, and Clan Tarlichs, the ancient inhabitants of Kintaile, all descended from Norwegian families, refused to deliver him up—in short,
the Earl attacked them and was beaten."

most of the adjoining isles. He was married to Morba, daughter of Macdougall of Lorn,* and niece, on her mother's side, to Cumming, Earl of Badenoch ; he died about 1304, and was succeeded by his son,

II. IAN MACCHOINNICH.†

JOHN, son of Kenneth, regarding whom we find little in history ; it has been, however, pretty well established that he, almost alone among the Western Chiefs, befriended Robert Bruce during his wanderings in the Western Isles, after his defeat by and escape from Macdougall of Lorn, who tenaciously adhered to the cause of Baliol. Bruce would certainly not be safe anywhere else in the Western Isles until after the defeat of the Lord of the Isles in Buchan by his brother Edward in 1308, the discomfiture of Lorn, and the imprisonment of the Earl of Argyll in 1309. After Bruce left the Island of Rachrin, in the north of Ireland, he was for a time lost sight of—many supposing that he had perished in his wanderings from the hardships he had to endure in his various contrivances to escape the vigilant look-out and rigid search of his enemies. The traditions of Kintail have it that he was concealed and protected by the Chief of Clan Kenneth in the stronghold of Islandonain until he again found a favourable opportunity to take the field against the enemies of his country ; and this tradition, which we record as a proud incident in the history of the Clan, is supported by the family historians. The Earl of Cromarty says:—"Kenneth (John?) did owne ye other partie, and was one of those who sheltered the Bruce in his retreat, and assisted him in his

---

* Earl of Cromartie and other Mackenzie MSS. "According to the vulgar tradition he married Maciver's daughter, partly that he might the more peaceably and pleasant take possession of that part of Kintail which Maciver formerly possessed, but Maciver gave him easy access and possession of his own will. . . . The King banished Maciver to Ireland for favouring the Danes."—*Letterfearn MS.*

† We have perused genealogies in which this chief is not included. His successor, Coinneach na Sroine is made to succeed the first Kenneth, and to occupy the period of the two reigns ; but most of the family genealogies follow the Earl of Cromartie, and present us with three Kenneths in immediate succession. In view of such differences among the authorities, we prefer the genealogy of the MS. of 1450.

recovery." The Laird of Applecross, writing in 1669, says:
—" He married Morba, daughter of Macdougall of Lorn,*
yet albeit Macdougall sided with the Baliol against the
Bruce. Kenneth (John?) did own the other party, and was
one of those who sheltered the Bruce, and assisted in his
recovery. I shall not say he was the only one, but this
stands for that assertion, that all who were considerable in
the hills and isles were enemies to the Bruce, and so cannot
be presumed to be his friends. The Earl of Ross (William,
the third Earl) did, most unhandsomely and inhumanely,
apprehend his lady at Tain, and delivered her to the English, anno 1305. Donald of the Isles, or Rotholl, or rather
Ronald, with all the Hebrides, armed against the Bruce, and
were beat by Edward Bruce in Buchan, anno 1308. Alexander, Earl of Argyll, partied (sided with) the Baliol; his
country, therefore, was waisted by Bruce, anno 1304, and
himself taken prisoner by him, 1309. Macdougall of Lorn
fought against the Bruce, and took him prisoner, from whom
he notably escaped, so that there is none in the district left
so considerable as this Chief (Mackenzie), who had an immediate dependence on the Royal family, and had this
strong fort (Islandonain), which was never commanded by
the Bruce's enemies, either English or Scots; and that his
shelter and assistance was from a remote place and friend is
evident from all our stories. But all their neighbours, being
stated on a different side from the Mackenzies, engendered
a feud betwixt him and them, especially with the Earl of
Ross and Donald of the Isles, which were ended but with
the end of the Earl of Ross, and lowering of the Lord of the
Isles." The Laird of Applecross quotes the above extract
—as he indeed does largely throughout his work—*verbatim*
from his noble kinsman, the Earl of Cromarty, whose manuscript, he informs us, he had seen and perused.

We can fairly assume, from subsequent events in the
history of these powerful families, as well as from the united
testimony of all the genealogists of the Mackenzies, that

* This is an error ; she was *his mother*.

their Chief did really befriend Robert Bruce against the
wishes and united power of his own immediate superior,
the Earl of Ross, and the other great families of the Western
Isles and Argyll ; and here we discover the true grounds of
the local rancour which afterwards existed between them,
and which only terminated in the collapse of the Earls of
Ross and the Lords of the Isles, upon the ruins of which,
as a reward for proved loyalty to the reigning monarch, and
as the result of the characteristic prudence of the race of
MacKenneth, the House of Kintail gradually rose in power,
subsequently absorbed the ancient inheritance of all the
original possessors of the district, and ultimately extended
their influence more widely over the whole province of
Wester Ross. The genealogists further inform us that this
Chief of Kintail waited on the King during his visit to Inverness in 1312.* This may now be accepted as a certainty,
as well as that he fought with him at the head of his followers at the Battle of Inverury, where Bruce defeated
Mowbray and the Comyn, in 1308. After this important
engagement, Fenton informs us, " all the nobles, barons,
towns, cities, garrisons, and castles north of the Grampians submitted to Robert the Bruce," when, undoubtedly,
and with good reason, the second Chief of Clan Kenneth
was fully confirmed in the favour of his sovereign, and in
the government of the stronghold of Islandonain. The
Lord of the Isles had meanwhile, after his capture at Inveraray, died in confinement in Dundonald Castle, and his
brother and successor, Angus Og, declared in favour of
Bruce. Argyll and Lorn left, or were driven out of the
country, and took up their residence in England. With
Angus Og of the Isles now on the side of Bruce, and the
counties of Argyll and Lorn at his mercy in the absence of
their respective Chiefs, it was an easy matter for the King,

* The MSS. Histories of the Mackenzies give the date of Robert Bruce's visit
to Inverness as 1307, but from a copy of the " Annual of Norway," at the negotiation and arrangement of which " the eminent Prince, Lord Robert, by the
like grace, noble King of Scots (attended) *personally* on the other part," it will
be seen that the date of the visit was 1312.—*See "Invernessiana,"* by Charles
Fraser-Mackintosh, F.S.A.S., M.P., *pp.* 36-40.

during the varied fortunes of his gigantic struggle, defending
and wresting Scotland from the grasp of the English, to
draw largely upon the resources of the Western Highlands
and Islands, now unmolested, particularly after the surprise
at Perth in the winter of 1312, and the reduction of all the
strongholds in Scotland—except Stirling, Berwick, and
Dunbar—during the ensuing summer. The decisive blow
was, however, yet to be struck, by which the independence
and liberties of Scotland were to be for ever established and
·confirmed, and the time drawing nigh when every nerve
would have to be strained for a final effort to clear it, once
for all, of the hated followers of the tyrannical and grasping
Edwards, roll them back before an impetuous wave of
Scottish pluck and valour, and for ever put an end to England's claim to lord it over a free-born people whom it was
impossible to crush or cow by such a tyrant. Nor will we
affect a morbid indifference to the fact that on the 24th of
June 1314, Bruce's heroic band of thirty thousand warriors
—who, on the glorious field of Bannockburn, as regards
Scotland, crushed for ever the great power of England, and
secured to Scotland, in all future ages, her independence,
her laws, and her religion—contained ten thousand Western
Highlanders and men of the Isles, under Angus Og of the
Isles, Mackenzie of Kintail (who led five hundred of his
followers), and other Chieftains of the mainland, of all of
whom Major specially relates, that "they made an incredible
slaughter of their enemies, slaying heaps of them around
wherever they went, and running upon them with their
broadswords and daggers like wild bears without any regard
to their own lives." Alluding to the same force, Barbour
writes :—

> Angus of the Isles and Bute alsne,
> And of the plain lands he had mae
> Of armed men a noble route,
> His battle stalwart was and stout.

General Stewart of Garth, in a footnote to his "Sketches of
the Highlanders," informs us that the eighteen Highland
Chiefs who fought at this glorious battle were—Mackay,

Mackintosh, Macpherson, Cameron, Sinclair, Campbell, Menzies, Maclean, Sutherland, Robertson, Grant, Fraser, Macfarlane, Ross, Macgregor, Munro, Mackenzie, and Macquarrie ; and that "Cumming, Macdougall of Lorn, Macnab, and a few others were unfortunately in opposition to Bruce, and suffered accordingly."

In due time the Western Chiefs returned home, where, on their arrival, many of them found local feuds still glimmering—encouraged in the absence of the natural protectors of their people—amidst the surrounding blaze. John appears to have lived peaceably at home during the remainder of his days. He was married to Margaret, daughter of David de Strathbogie, Earl of Athole ; died in 1328, and was succeeded by his son,

III. COINNEACH NA SROINE,

OR KENNETH OF THE NOSE, so called from the great protuberance of that organ. Little or nothing is known of this Baron. It appears, however, that he soon found himself in trouble, and quite unable to cope successfully with the difficulties by which he was surrounded, from the attempts made by the Earls of Ross to re-establish their power in Kintail. According to Wyntoun, the rhyming Prior of Lochleven, we find, in 1331, Randolph, Earl of Moray, nephew of Robert the Bruce, and then Warden of Scotland, dispatching his crowner to Islandonain to prepare the Castle for his reception, and to arrest "mysdoaris," fifty of whom that officer had put to death, and, according to the cruel and barbarous practices of the time, exposed their heads, for the edification of the surrounding lieges, high upon the Castle walls. Randolph shortly afterwards arrived, and, the same author informs us, was "right blithe" to see the goodly show of heads "that flowered so weel that wall"—a ghastly warning to all treacherous and plundering clansmen. This state of matters clearly demonstrates a sad lack of power and influence on the part of Kenneth to govern his people, and keep the district secure from lawlessness and "mysdoaris."

It is evident that at this time the Earl of Ross regained a considerable hold in the district, over which he had throughout claimed the rights of superiority; for, on the 4th of July 1342, we find William, fifth Earl, granting a charter in favour of Reginald, son of Roderick of the Isles, of the ten davachs of Kintail. The charter was granted at the Castle of Urquhart, was witnessed by the Bishops of Moray and Ross, and many other influential dignitaries, cleric and laic; and was confirmed by King David in the year 1344.* It would have been already seen that in 1350, the same Earl William dated a charter *at Islandonain*. This fact clearly proves that the line of Mac-Kenneth was getting very frail, and almost at the point of snapping during the reign of Coinneach na Sroine.

Some of the followers of the Earl of Ross at this time made a raid into Kenlochewe, and carried away a great spoil and heirschip from that district. Mackenzie pursued them, recovered a great part of the spoil and killed a large number of the raiders. The Earl of Ross was greatly incensed at this, and determined to use all means for his apprehension. In this he was ultimately successful, and for this and previous quarrels he had him executed at Inverness, and at the same time he granted the lands of Kenlochewe, hitherto possessed by Mackenzie, to Leod Mac-Gillandries.

The Laird of Applecross informs us that Kenneth "married Finguala, daughter to Macleod of Lewis. Before his marriage he had three bastard sons—viz., Hector Birrach, who married Helen Loban or Logan, of Drumnamargne; but forced from his rights by the oppressions of the Earl of Ross, superior of Drumnamargne, he turned outlaw, and died at Edderachilish, in Sutherlandshire, leaving a son called Hendrie, of whom are descended the Sleight Hend-riech *(Sliochd Ionraic)* there. The second bastard was called Tewald Deirgallach. From him descended John Mackenzie, Commissary-Depute of Ross, afterwards in

* "Invernessiana," p. 56.

Cromarty, and Mr Rory Mackenzie, minister of Croy, with several others. The third bastard was called Alexander, of whom are descended many of the Commons of Brae Ross. . .'. . He had by Macleod's daughter Murdoch Dow, and by another wife Murdoch Riach." The Earl of Cromarty gives substantially the same account, and concludes that, " murdered thus, his estate was possessed by the oppressor's followers; but Island Donain keeped still out, maintaining themselves on the spoyle of the enemie, all being trod under by insolince and oppression, right had no place. This was during David Bruce's imprisonment in England." He was succeeded by his son,

IV. MURCHADH DUBH NA H'UAGH,

OR, BLACK MURDOCH OF THE CAVE. Duncan Macaulay of Lochbroom, a friend of Mackenzie, commanded in Islandonain Castle during Kenneth's absence, and when he was murdered at Inverness. Becoming apprehensive about the safety of " Murchadh Dubh," then very young, he sent him to his grandfather, Macleod of the Lews, while he sent his own son, also named Murdo, to Macdougall of Lorn, to save them from the grasping clutches of the Earl of Ross. The Earl, however, managed to seize young Macaulay, and put him to death, out of revenge for his father's gallant defence of Islandonain, during the absence of Mackenzie, against the Earl's repeated attacks to reduce it. The actual murderer of young Macaulay was a desperate character, Leod Macgilleandreis, a vassal of the Earl of Ross, who was chiefly instrumental in the apprehension of Mackenzie, incessantly harrassed the gallant defender of Castle Donain, and, in one of his incursions, discovered the whereabouts of Macaulay's son, cruelly murdered him, and for a time became master of Lochbroom and Kintail. As a reward for his conduct the Earl of Ross gave him Kenlochewe, which he found a convenient centre of operations ; but the brave garrison of the fortress, under Macaulay, continued to make desperate reprisals, and held out, in spite of all the attempts made to reduce it, until the restoration of King David, by

C

which time Murdo Dubh had grown up a powerful and
intrepid youth, fast approaching manhood :—He was called
Murdo of the Cave because, being perhaps not well tutored,
he preferred sporting and hunting in the hills and forests to
going to the Ward School, where the ward children, or the
heirs of those who held their lands and wards of the King,
were wont or bound to go, and he resorted to the dens and
caves about Torridon and Kenlochewe, hoping to get a hit
at Leod Macgilleandreis, who was instrumental, under the
Earl of Ross, to apprehend and cut off his father. In the
meantime Macgilleandreis hearing of Murdo's resorting to
these bounds, that he was kindly entertained by some of
the inhabitants, and fearing that he would withdraw the
services and affections of the people from himself, and con-
nive some mischief against him for his ill-usage of his father,
he left no means untried to apprehend him, so that Mackenzie was obliged to start privately to Lochbroom, from
whence, with only one companion, he went to his uncle,
Macleod of Lews, by whom, after he had revealed himself
to him alone, he was well received, and both of them resolved to conceal his name until a fit opportunity offered to
make known his identity.   He, however, met with a certain
man named Gille Riabhach, a natural son of Maclean of
Duart, who came to Stornoway with twelve men about the
same time as himself, and he, in the strictest confidence, told
Gille Riabhach that he was Mackenzie of Kintail, which
secret the latter kept strictly inviolate.   Macleod entertained his nephew, keeping it an absolute secret from others
who he was, that his enemies might think that he was dead,
and so feel the greater security, till such time as they
would deem it wise that he should act for himself, and
make an attempt to rescue his possessions from Macgilleandreis, who now felt quite secure, thinking that Mackenzie
had perished, having for so long heard nothing concerning
him.   When a suitable time arrived his uncle gave Murdo
one of his great galleys, with as many men as he desired, to
accompany him, the Gille Riabhach and his twelve followers,
all of whom determined to seek their fortune with young

Kintail. They embarked at Stornoway, and securing a favourable wind they soon arrived at Sanachan in Kishorn, where they landed, marched straight towards Kenlochewe, and arrived at a thick wood near the place where Macgilleandreis had his residence. Mackenzie commanded his followers to lie down and watch, while he and his companion, Gille Riabhach, went about in search of intelligence. He soon found a woman cutting·rushes, she at the same time lamenting his own supposed death, and Leod Macgilleandreis' succession to the lands of Kenlochewe in consequence. He at once recognised her as the woman's sister who nursed or fostered him, drew near, spoke to her, sounded her, and discovering her unmistakeable affection towards him, he felt that he could with perfect safety make himself known to her. She was overjoyed to find that it was really he, whose absence and loss she had so intensely and so long lamented. He then requested her to go and procure him information of Leod's situation and occupation that night. This she did with great propriety and discretion. Having satisfied herself, she returned at the appointed time, and assured him that Macgilleandreis felt himself perfectly secure, and quite unprepared for an attack, and had just appointed to meet the adjacent people next morning at a place called Ath-nan-Ceann (the Ford of the Heads), preparatory to a hunting match, instructing those who might arrive before him to wait his arrival. Mackenzie considered this an excellent opportunity to punish Leod. He in good time went to the ford accompanied by his followers. Those invited by Leod soon after arrived, and, seeing Mackenzie before them, thought he was Macgilleandreis and some of his men, but soon discovered their mistake. Mackenzie killed all those he did not recognise as soon as they appeared. The natives of the place, who were personally known to him, he pardoned and dismissed. Leod soon arrived, and seeing such a gathering awaiting him, naturally thought they were his own friends, and hastened towards them, but upon approaching them he found himself "in the fool's hose." Mackenzie and his band fell upon them with their

swords, and after a slight resistance Macgilleandreis and his
party fled, but they were soon overtaken at a place called
to this day "Featha Leoid," or Leod's Ditch or Bog, where
they were all slain, except his son Paul, who was taken
prisoner and kept in captivity for some time, but was afterwards released upon plighting his faith that he would never
again trouble Mackenzie or resent against him his father's
death. Murdoch Mackenzie being · thus re-possessed of
Kenlochewe, "gave Leod Macgilleandreis' widow to Gillereach to wife for his good services and fidelity, whose posterity
live at Kenlochewe and thereabout, and to this day some of
them live there."*

Paul repaired to the confines of Sutherland and Caithness, prevailed upon Murdo Riabhach, the Chief of Kintail's brother, to join him, and, according to one authority,
became "a common depredator," while according to
another, he became what was perhaps not inconsistent in
those days with the character of a common thief—a person
of considerable state and property. They often spoiled
Caithness. Ultimately Murdo Riabhach and Paul's only
son were killed by Budge of Fortingall. Paul was so mortified at the death of his promising young depredator son,
that he gave up building the fortress of Duncrcich. which
he was at that time erecting to strengthen still more his
position in the country. He gave his lands of Strathoykel,
Strathcarron, and Westray, with his daughter and heiress
in marriage, to Ross of Balnagown, on which condition he
obtained pardon from the Earl of Ross, their respective
Chief.†

* Ardintoul MS.

† Murdo Riabhach's descendants are still known in Sutherland as Clann
Mhuirich, and from them can he traced Daniel Mackenzie, who arrived at the
rank of colonel in the service of the Stratholder. He had a son, Barnard, who
was a major in Seaforth's regiment, and was killed at the battle of Auldearn.
He left a son, also named Barnard, who became a distinguished Greek and Latin
scholar, and who taught those languages for four years at Fortrose. He was
afterwards ordained as a clergyman by the Bishop of Ross, and presented to the
Episcopal Church of Cromarty, where, after a variety of fortunes, he died, and
was buried in the Cathedral Church of Fortrose. His eldest son, Alexander,
studied medicine under Boerhave, and afterwards practised his profession at

Young Kintail, after disposing of Macgilleandreis, returned to his own country, where he was received with open arms by the whole population of the district. He then married the only daughter of his gallant friend and defender, Macaulay—whose only son, as already stated, had been killed by Macgilleandreis—and through her Mackenzie succeeded to the lands of Lochbroom and Coigeach, granted to Macaulay's predecessor by Alexander II. Mackenzie now engaged himself principally in preserving and improving his possessions until the return of David II. from England in 1357-8, when he laid before his Majesty a complaint against the Earl of Ross for the murder of his father, and claimed redress; but the only satisfaction he could obtain was a confirmation of his rights previously granted by the King to "Murdo filius Kennethi de Kintaile, &c.," dated "Edinburg 1362, et Regni Domini Regis VI., Testibus Waltero senescollo et allis."* Of Murdo Dubh's reign, the Laird of Applecross, says:—"During this turbulent age, securities and writs, as well as laws, were little regarded; each man's protection lay in his own strength." Kintail regularly attended the first Parliament of Robert II., until it was decreed by that monarch and his Privy Council that the services of the "lesser Barons" would not be required in future Parliaments or General Councils. He then returned home, and spent most of his time in hunting and wild sports, to which he was devotedly attached, living peaceably and undisturbed during the remainder of his days.

This Baron of Kintail took no share in the late rebellion under the Lord of the Isles, who, backed by most of the other West Highland Chiefs, attempted to throw off his independence and have himself proclaimed King of the Isles. The feeble and effeminate Government of David II., and the evil results consequent thereon throughout the country, en-

Fortrose. He married Ann, daughter of Alexander Mackenzie of Belmaduthy, purchased the lands of Kinnock, and had a son, Barnard, and two daughters—Catherine and Ann.
    * MS. Histories of the Mackenzies.

couraged him in this desperate enterprise ; but, as Tytler informs us, King David on this occasion, " with an unwonted energy of character, commanded the attendance of the Stewart, with the prelates and barons of the realm, and surrounded by this formidable body of vassals and retainers, proceeded against the rebels in person." This expedition proved completely successful, and John of the Isles, with a numerous train of the wild Chieftains who joined him in the rebellion, met the King at Inverness, and submitted to his authority. He there engaged, in the most solemn manner, for himself and for his vassals, that they should yield themselves faithful and obedient subjects to David their liege· lord, and not only give due and prompt obedience to the ministers of the King in suit and service, as well as in the payment of taxes and public burdens, but that they would coerce and put down all others, and compel all who dared to rise against the King's authority to make due submission, or pursue them from their respective territories. For the fulfilment of these obligations, the Lord of the Isles not only gave his most solemn oath before the King and his nobles, on condition of forfeiting his whole possessions in case of failure, but offered his father-in-law, the High Stewart, in security; and delivered his son Donald, his grandson Angus, and his natural son, also named Donald, as hostages for the strict performance of the articles of the treaty, which was duly signed and attested, and dated the 15th November 1369.* Fordun says that in order to crush the Highlanders, and the more easily, as the King thought, to secure obedience to the laws, he used artifice by dividing the chiefs, and promising high rewards to those who would capture or kill their brother chiefs ; and, the writer continues, " this diabolical plan, by implanting the seeds of dis-union amongst the chiefs, succeeded, and they gradually destroyed one another."

This was the turbulent and insecure state of affairs throughout the Kingdom when the Chief of Mackenzie was

* For a full copy of this instrument, see " Invernessiana," pp. 69-70.

peaceably and quietly enjoying himself in his Highland home. He died in 1375.* By his wife Isabel, only daughter of Macaulay of Lochbroom, he had a son and successor,

V. MURCHADH NA DROCHAID,

OR, MURDOCH OF THE BRIDGE, so called from the circum-stance, as the Laird of Applecross relates, that "his mother, being with child of him, had been saved after a fearful fall from the Bridge of Scotall (Scatwell) into the water of Conon." The writer of the Ardintoul MS. says that he was called "Murchadh na Drochaid," by reason of some bad treatment his lady met with at the Bridge of Scatwell, which happened on this occasion. He having lived for many years with his lady and getting no children, and so fearing that the direct line of his family might fail in his person, was a little concerned and troubled thereat, which being under-stood by some sycophants and flatterers that was about him, and would fain carry his favour, they thought that they could ingratiate themselves more to him by putting his lady out of the way, whereby he might marry another; and they waited an opportunity to put their design in execu-tion (some say not without his connivence), and so on a certain evening, or late at night, as she was going to Achilty, where her laird lived, these wicked flatterers did presump-tuously and barbarously cast her over the bridge of Scatwell, and then, their consciences accusing them for that horrid

* Murdo became a great favourite latterly with all those with whom he came in contact. "He fell in company with the Earl of Sutherland, who became his very good friend afterwards, as that he still resorted his court. In end (being comely of personage an ane active young man) the Earl's lady (who was King Robert the Bruce's young daughter) fell in conceit of him, and both forgetting the Earl's kindness, by her persuasion, he got her with child who she caused name Dougall," and the Earl suspecting nothing amiss "caused bred him at Schoolls with the rest of his children ; but Dougall being as ill-given as gotten, he still injured the rest, and when the Earle would challenge or offer to beat him, the Ladie still said, 'Dear heart, let him alone, it is bard to tell Dougall's father, which the good Earle always took in good part. In end, he comeing to years of descretion, she told her husband that Mackenzie was his father, but shortly thereafter, by way of merriment, told the King how his lady cheated him. The King, finding him to be his own cousine and of parts of learning, with all to pleasure the Earle and his lady, he made Dougall prior of Beauly."—*Ancient MS.*

act, they made off with themselves. But the wonderful providence of God carried the innocent lady (who was then with
child), notwithstanding of the impetuousness of the river,
safe to shore, and enabled her in the night time to travel the
length of Achilty, where her husband did impatiently wait
her coming, that being the night she promised to be home,
and entertaining her very kindly, being greatly offended at
the maltreatment she met with. The child she had then in
the womb was afterwards called Alexander, and some say
was off-named Inrick, because by a miracle of Providence
he escaped the danger and afterwards became heir to his
father and inherited his estate. Others say he was called so
because of his uprightness."

The author of the "Ancient" MS. brings the diabolical
act nearer home to Mackenzie himself, and says:—"They
lived a considerable tyme together childless, but men in these
dayes (of whom be reasone) preferred succession and manhood to wedlock. He caused throw her under silence of night
over the Bridge of Scatwell. But by providence by the
course of the river she was cast ashore and escaped, went
back immediately to his house, then at Achiltree, and went
to his bedside in a fond condition. But commiserating her
caice, and repenting of the deed, took her to bed and finds
a child lopping in her womb, so afterwards they lived together contentedly all their days."

During, at least, the early years of his government,
Murdo appears to have lived quietly, following the example set him by his father, keeping the laws himself, and
compelling those under his jurisdiction to do the same.
Nor was such dutiful and loyal conduct allowed long to go
unrewarded. At Edinburgh, 1380, a charter is granted in
his favour attested by "Willielmo de Douglas, Achibaldo
de Galloway, et Joanne Cancellario Scotiæ."* He was one
of the sixteen Highland Chiefs who accompanied the Scots,
under James, second Earl of Douglas, to England, and defeated Sir Henry Percy, the renowned Hotspur, at the famous

---

* MS. Histories of the Family.

battle of Otterburn. This engagement raged furiously for several hours. Douglas, who wielded a battle-axe with both hands, cut his way into the thickest of the enemy, where, getting separated from his men, he was overcome and mortally wounded. The English were, however, ultimately defeated all along the line. Hotspur and his brother, Sir Ralph Percy, were taken prisoners; and scarcely a single man of note among the English escaped death or captivity. Froissart informs us:—"Of all the battles that have been described in this history, great and small, this was the best fought and most severe." It is related that in a personal encounter, a few days before the battle, Hotspur lost his pennon, and Douglas boasted in his hearing that he would place it on the tower of his castle of Dalkeith. "That," said Percy, stung to the quick, "shalt thou never do; you shall not even bear it out of Northumberland." "Well," replied Douglas, "your pennon shall this night be placed before my tent; come and win it if you can." The battle of Otterburn three days after was Hotspur's reply to this bold challenge.

This was a turbulent period among the Highlanders. Then occurred the feuds between the Lochaber and Badenoch tribes which culminated for a time at the famous conflict before King Robert III., in 1396, on the North Inch of Perth; the ferocious and savage cruelties, robberies, and murders of the "Wolf of Badenoch," and of his son Alexander Stewart, afterwards Earl of Mar. In a desperate encounter between the latter and Sir Walter Ogilvy, Sheriff of Angus, an incident occurred which is preserved by Winton, illustrating, in a ghastly manner, the fierceness of Mar's followers. Sir David Lindsay had run one of them, a powerful and "brawny" man, through the body with a spear, and brought him to the ground; but although in the agonies of death, he writhed and pulled himself up, and, with the spear sticking in his body, struck Lindsay a desperate blow with his sword, which cut through his stirrup, his boot, and into his bone; he then instantly expired. There were also the feuds and fights in Sutherlandshire between Mackay of Farr, his son Donald, and the Earl of Sutherland, in which many lives were sacrificed and great depredations committed on both sides, and which ultimately resulted in the death of Mackay and his son, by the Earl's own hands in the Castle of Dingwall. Then followed the fierce conflict between Mackay, aided by Alexander Murray of Cubin, and Malcolm Macleod of Lewis, at Tuiteam Tarbhach, on the marches between Ross and Sutherland. Great valour was displayed by both sides on this occasion. Sir Robert Gordon describes the conflict as "long, furious, cruel, and doubtful, rather desperate and resolute." Macleod was crushed, himself and all his men slaughtered—only one man escaping to carry back the sorrowful news, who was so severely wounded that he had scarcely told the sad tale when he expired.

These feuds were followed by the formidable invasion by Donald, Lord of the Isles, which threatened to overturn the Government, and bring about the dismemberment of the Kingdom of Scotland, and which culminated in the memorable battle of Harlaw, the history of which is already well known to the reader.*

For more than a hundred years, it is said, the battle of Harlaw continued to be fought over and over again by schoolboys in their play.

It fixed itself in the music and poetry of Scotland. A march, called the "Battle of Harlaw," continued to be a popular air down to the time of Drummond of Hawthornden; and a spirited ballad, on the same event, is still repeated in our own age, describing the meeting of the armies, and the deaths of the chiefs, in no ignoble strain.†

* For a good account of it see the *Celtic Magazine*, vol. iii., pp. 122-4; and the "History of the Highland Clans."

† We have also that famous poem, "The War Song, by Lachlan Mor Mac-Mhuirich, to Donald of the Isles, King of the Isles, and Earl of Ross, on the day of the Field of Harlaw," composed to excite the enthusiasm of the Highlanders at that famous battle. There are, in alphabetical order, lines beginning with every letter in the Gaelic alphabet, excepting the letter H—the poem altogether consisting of three hundred and thirty-eight lines, each letter being exhausted in its order, some of them having forty alliteratives, and the whole forming a chain of epithets so copious, but so pointed and incisive, as to excite astonishment and admiration. This poem will be found, most appropriately the first in Stewart's collection, published in 1804, and now very rare. It should be studied by those who maintain that the Gaelic language is of limited compass.

Mar and the few brave companions in arms who survived the battle passed the night on the field. When morning dawned they found that the Lord of the Isles had retreated during the night by Inverury and the hill of Banochy. To pursue him was impossible, and he was therefore allowed to retire without molestation, and to recruit his exhausted strength.

As soon as the news of the disaster at Harlaw reached the ears of the Duke of Albany, then Regent of Scotland, he set about collecting an army, with which, in autumn, he marched in person to the north with a determination to bring the Lord of the Isles to obedience. Having taken possession of the Castle of Dingwall, he appointed a governor, and from thence proceeded to recover the whole of Ross. Donald retreated before him, and took up his winter quarters in the Western Islands. Hostilities were renewed next summer, but the contest was not long or doubtful, notwithstanding some little advantages obtained by the Lord of the Isles. He was compelled to give up his claim to the Earldom of Ross, to become a vassal of the Scottish crown, and to deliver hostages to secure his future good behaviour.

Murdo Mackenzie must have felt secure in his stronghold of Islandonain, and must have been a man of great prudence, sagacity, and force of character, when, in spite of all the solicitations of his superior—the Lord of the Isles—to support him in these unlawful and rebellious proceedings against his King, and threats in case of refusal, he resolutely refused to join him in his desperate and treasonable adventures, at the same time informing him that, even were his claims just in themselves, they would not justify him in rising against the existing Government; and, independently of that consideration, he boldly told his lordship that he felt no great incentive to aid in the cause of the representative of the murderer of his own grandfather. Mackenzie was one of those prudent and loyal chiefs who remained at home in the Highlands, looking after his own affairs, the comfort of his followers, and laying a solid foundation for the future prosperity of his house. " This was so characteristic of them

that they," as one authority informs us, "always esteemed
the authority of the magistrate as an inviolable obligation."

The Macraes were on the best terms of friendship with
the Mackenzies—were, indeed, from the aid that they
always afforded them, known as "Mackenzie's shirt of mail."
They originally came from Clunes, on the territory of the
Frasers of Lovat, under the following circumstances :—
"One of the brothers went to Braeross and lived at Brahan,
where there is a piece of land called Knock Vic Ra, and the
spring well which affords water to the castle is called Tober
Vic Ra. . . . . Other two of MacRa's sons, elder than
the above, went off from Clunes several ways ; one is said
to have gone to Argyleshire and another to Kintail. In the
meantime their father remained at Clunes all his days, and
had four Lord Frasers of Lovat fostered in his house. He
that went to Argyle, according to our tradition, married the
heiress of Craignish, and on that account took the surname
of Campbell. The other brother who went to Kintail, earnestly invited and encouraged by Mackenzie, who then had
no kindred of his own blood, *the first six Barons, or Lords of
Kintail, having but one lawful son to succeed the father*, hoping
that the MacRas, by reason of their relation, as being originally descended from the same race . . . . would prove
more faithful than others, wherein he was not disappointed,
for the MacRas of Kintail served him and his successors very
faithfully in every quarrel that they had with neighbouring
clans, and by their industry, blood, and courage, have been
instrumental in raising that family."*

The statement here made respecting the succession of
the Mackenzies is certainly remarkable and curious, but it
is borne out by every genealogy of the house of Kintail
we have ever seen. There is no trace of any other legitimate offspring during the first six generations beyond
the immediately succeeding chief.

Murdoch married Finguala, daughter of Malcolm Macleod of Harris, by his wife Martha, daughter of Donald,

---

* Genealogical Account of the MacRas, by John MacRa, minister of Dingwall, who died in 1704.

Earl of Mar, and nephew of King Robert the Bruce. By this marriage the royal blood of the Bruce was introduced into the family of Kintail, as also that of the ancient Kings of Man. Norman, third in descent from Olaus, King of Man, married Finguala MacCrotan, the daughter of an Irish Chief. She bore to him Malcolm Macleod of Harris, whose daughter had now become the wife of Murdo Mackenzie, and the mother of Alastair Ionraic, who carried on the succession of the ancient line of Kintail. Murdo died at Achilty about 1416, leaving issue, an only son and successor,

VI. ALASTAIR IONRAIC,

OR, ALEXANDER THE UPRIGHT, said to be so called "for his righteousness." He was among the western barons summoned in 1427 to meet King James I. at Inverness, who, immediately on his return from his long captivity in England, in 1424, determined to put down the rebellion and oppression then, and for some time previously, so rampant in the Highlands. In a Parliament held at Perth on the 30th September 1426, James exhibited a foresight and appreciation of the conduct of the lairds in those days, and passed laws, which might with good effect, and with equal propriety, be applied to the state of matters in our own. In that Parliament an Act was passed which, among other things, ordained that, north of the Grampians, the fruit of those lands should be expended in the country where those lands lie. The Act is as follows* :—" It is ordanit be the King ande the Parliament that everilk lorde hafande landis bezonde the mownthe (the Grampians) in the quhilk landis in auld tymes there was castellis, fortalyces, and maner-plaicis, big, reparell, and reforme their castellis and maneris, and duell in thame, be thameself or be ane of thare frendis for the gracious gournall of thar landis, be gude polising and to expende ye fruyt of thar landis in the countree where thar landis lyis."

James was determined to bring the Highlanders to sub-

---

* Invernessiana, p. 102.

mission, and Fordun relates a characteristic anecdote in which the King pointedly declared this determination. When these excesses were first reported to him by one of his nobles, on entering the kingdom, he thus expressed himself:—" Let God but grant me life, and there shall not be a spot in my dominions where the key shall not keep the castle, and the furze bush the cow, though I myself should lead the life of a dog to accomplish it"; and it was in this frame of mind that he determined to visit Inverness in 1427 or 1428,* to establish good government in the Highlands, then in such a deplorable state of insubordination that neither life nor property was secure. The principal chiefs, on his order or invitation, met him there, from what motives it is impossible to determine—whether hoping for a reconciliation by a ready compliance with the royal will, or from a dread of suffering, in case of refusal, the fate of the southern barons, who had already fallen victims to His Majesty's severity. The order was, however, obeyed, and they all repaired to meet him at the Castle of Inverness. As they entered the hall where Parliament was sitting, they were, one by one, by order of the King, arrested, ironed, and imprisoned in different apartments, and debarred from having any communication the one with the other, or with their followers. Fordun informs us that James exhibited marks of great joy as these turbulent and haughty spirits, caught in the toils which he had prepared for them, came within the clutches of his regal power, and that he " caused to be arrested Alexander of the Isles, and his mother, Countess of Ross, daughter and heiress of Sir Walter Lesley, as well as the more notable men of the north, each of whom he wisely invited singly to the Castle, and caused to be put in strict confinement apart. There he also arrested Angus Duff (Angus Dubh Mackay) with his four sons, the leader of 4000 men from Strathnarven (Strathnaver). Kenneth More, with his son-in-law, leader of two thousand

---

* Fordun gives the date as 1427, the MS. History of the Mackintoshes as 1428.

men ;* John Ross, William Lesley, Angus de Moravie, and
Macmaken, leaders of two thousand men ; and also other
lawless caterans and great captains in proportion, to the
number of about fifty. Alexander Makgorrie (MacGodfrey)
of Garmoran, and John Macarthur (of the family of Campbell), a great chief among his own clan, and the leader of
a thousand and more, were convicted, and, being adjudged
to death, were beheaded. Then James Cambel was hanged,
being accused and convicted of the slaughter of John of the
Isles. The rest were sent here and there to the different
castles of the noblemen throughout the kingdom, and were
afterwards condemned to different kinds of death, and some
were set at liberty." Among the latter was Alexander of
Kintail. The King sent him, then quite a youth, to the
High School at Perth, then the principal and most celebrated
literary seminary in the kingdom, while the city was frequently the seat of the Court. During young Kintail's
absence, it appears that his three bastard uncles were ravag-
ing the district of Kenlochewe, for we find that, insulting
and troubling "Mackenzie's tenants in Kenlochewe and
Kintail, Macaulay, who was then Constable in Islandonain,
not thinking it proper to leave his post, proposed Finlay
Dubh Mac Gillechriost as the fittest person to be sent to
Saint Johnston, now Perth, and by general consent he accordingly went to inform his young master, who was then
there with the rest of the King's ward children at school, of
his Lordship's tenants being imposed on as above, which,
with Finlay's remonstrance on the subject, prevailed on
Alexander, his young master, to come home, and being
backed with all the assistance Finlay could command, soon
brought his three bastard uncles to condign punishment."†
The Ardintoul MS. History of the Mackenzies says, Finlay "prevailed on him to go home without letting the master

* All writers on the Clan Mackenzie have hitherto claimed this Kenneth
More as their Chief, and argued from the above that the Chief of Mackenzie had
a following of two thousand fighting men in 1427. It will be seen that Alexander
was Chief at this time, but Kenneth More may have been intended for MacKenneth More, or the Great Mackenzie. He could have no following of *his own name.*
† Genealogical Account of the Macras.

of the school know of it. Trysting with him at a certain place
and set hour they set off, and, lest any should surprise them,
they declined the common road and went to Macdougal of
Lorn, he being acquainted with him at St Johnston. Macdougall entertained him kindly, and kept him with him for
several days. He at that time made his acquaintance with
Macdougal's daughter, whom afterwards he married, and
from thence came to his own Kintail, and having his authority and right backed with the power of the people, he calls
his bastard uncles before him, and removes their quarters
from Kenlochewe, and gave them possessions in Glenelchaig
in Kintail, prescribing measures and rule for them how to
behave, assuring them, though he pardoned them at that
time, they should forfeit favours and be severely punished if
they transgressed for the future ; but after this, going to the
County of Ross to their old dwelling at Kenlochewe, they
turned to practice their old tricks and broke loose, so that
he was forced to correct their insolency and make them
shorter by the heads, and thus the people were quit of their
trouble."

The young Lord of the Isles was at the same time sent
to Edinburgh, from which he soon afterwards, at the instigation of the old Countess, escaped to the North, raised his
vassals, and, joined by the outlaws and vagabonds in the
country, numbering about ten thousand, he, with this
formidable body, laid waste the country, plundered and
devastated the crown lands, against which his vengeance was
specially directed, razed the royal burgh of Inverness to
the ground, pillaged and burned the houses, and perpetrated
all sorts of cruelties, after which he besieged the Castle,
unsuccessfully however, and then retired precipitately towards Lochaber, where he was met by the King's forces
commanded by His Majesty in person. Alexander prepared for battle, but he had the mortification to notice the
desertion of those of Clan Chattan and Clan Cameron who
had previously joined him, and to see them going over to
the Royal standard. The King immediately attacked him,
and completely routed his whole army, while he himself

sought safety in flight. He was vigorously pursued, and finding escape or concealment equally impossible, and being reduced to the utmost distress, hunted from place to place by his vigilant pursuers, the haughty chief, who had hitherto considered himself on a level with kings, resolved to throw himself entirely on the mercy of His Majesty, and finding his way to Edinburgh in the most secret manner, and on the occasion, in 1429, of a solemn festival at Holyrood, on Easter Sunday, he suddenly appeared, in his shirt and drawers, before the King and Queen surrounded by all the nobles of the Court, while engaged in their devotions before the High Altar, and implored, on his knees, with a naked sword held in his hand by the point, the forgiveness of his sovereign. With bonnet in hand, his legs and arms quite bare, his body covered only with a plaid, in token of absolute submission he offered his sword to the King. His appearance, with the solicitations of the affected Queen and all the nobles, made such an impression on His Majesty that he completely submitted to the promptings of his heart, against the wiser and more prudent dictates of his better judgment. He accepted the sword offered him, and spared the life of his captive, but immediately committed him to Tantallon Castle, under the charge of William Douglas, Earl of Angus. The spirit of his followers, however, could not brook this mortal offence, and the whole strength of the Clan was mustered under Donald Balloch, a cousin of the Lord of the Isles. They were led to Lochaber, where they met the King's forces, under the Earls of Mar and Caithness, killed the latter, gained a complete victory over the Royal forces, and returned to the Isles in triumph, with a great quantity of spoil. James again came north in person as far as Dunstaffnage ; Donald Balloch fled to Ireland; and, after several encounters with the Highlanders, the King received the submission of most of the chiefs who were engaged in the rebellion; others were apprehended and executed, to the number of about three hundred, after which he released the Earl from Tantallon Castle, and granted him a free pardon for all his rebellious

D

acts, confirmed him in all his titles and possessions, and
conferred upon him the Lordship of Lochaber, which
had previously, on its forfeiture, been granted to the Earl of
Mar.

After the first escape of the Lord of the Isles from
Edinburgh, he again, in 1429, raised the standard of rebellion. He burnt the town of Inverness while the Baron of
- Kintail was "attending to his duties at Court," from whence
he was recalled by his followers, who, armed for the King,
and who, led by their young Chief on his return home,
materially aided in the overthrow of Alexander of the Isles,
at the same time securing peace and good government in
his own extensive domains, and among most of the surrounding tribes. We also find him actively supporting the King,
and fighting with the Royal army during the turbulent rule
of John, successor to Alexander, Lord of the Isles, who
afterwards, in 1447, died at peace with the ruling powers.
James I. died in 1460, and was succeeded by James II. When,
, in 1462, the Earl of Douglas, the Lord of the Isles, and
Donald Balloch entered into a treaty with the King of England for the proposed subjugation of Scotland, on condition that, in the event of success, the whole of Scotland
north of the Firth of Forth should be divided between
them, Alexander Mackenzie stood firm in the interest of·
the·ruling monarch, the result being that nothing came
of this rebellious compact. We soon after find him rewarded by a Royal charter in his favour, dated 7th January
1463, confirming him in his lands of Kintail, with a further
grant of the "5 merk lands of Killin, the lands of Garve,
and the 2 merk lands of Coryvulzie, with the three merk ·
lands of Kinlochluichart, and 2 merk lands of Achana-
clerich, the 2 merk lands of Garbat, the 2 merk lands of
Delintan, the 4 merk lands of Tarvie, all lying within the
shire and Earldom of Ross, to be holden of the said John
and his successors, Earls of Ross."

Alexander continued to use his great influence at Court,
and with John, Lord of the Isles, to bring about a reconciliation with the King during the unnatural rebellion of

Angus Og against his father. The King, however, proved inexorable, and refused to treat with the Earl, on any other condition than the absolute and unconditional surrender of the Earldom of Ross to the Crown, of whom, however, he would be permitted to hold his other possessions in future. These conditions he refused, again flew to arms, and, in 1476, invaded Moray, but finding he could offer no effectual resistance to the powerful forces sent against him by the King, he, by the seasonable grants of the lands of Knapdale and Kintyre, secured the influence of Argyll in his favour, and with the additional influence of Kintail, procured remission of his past offences on the conditions already stated ; and, resigning for ever, in 1476, the Earldom of Ross to the Crown, he "was infeft of new" in the Lordship of the Isles and in the other possessions which he had not been called upon to renounce. The Earldom was irrevocably annexed to the Crown, in the same year, in the 9th Parliament of James III., where the title and honours still remain, held by the Prince of Wales. The great services of the Baron of Kintail to the reigning family during these negotiations, and generally throughout his long rule at Islandonain, were recognised by a charter from the Crown, dated Edinburgh, November 1476, of the lands renounced by the Earl of Ross, viz., Strathconan, Strathbran, and Strathgarve ; and after this the Barons of Kintail continued to hold their lands independently of any superior but the Crown.

During the disputes between the Earl of Ross and Mackenzie, no one was more zealous in the cause of the Island Chief than Allan of Moydart, who made several raids into Kintail, ravaged the country, and carried away large numbers of cattle. After the forfeiture of the Earldom of Ross, Allan's younger brother, supported by a faction of the tenantry, rebelled against his elder brother, and possessed himself for a time of the Moydart estate. John of the Isles, unwilling to appear so soon in these broils, or, perhaps, favouring the pretensions of the younger brother, refused to give any assistance to Allan, who, however, hit upon a

device as bold as it ultimately proved successful. He
started for Kinellan, "being ane ile in ane loch," where
Alexander resided at the time, and presented himself
personally before his old enemy, who was naturally much
surprised to receive a visit from such a quarter, and
from one to whom he had never been reconciled. Allan
coolly related how he had been oppressed by his own
brother and his nearest friends, and how he had been refused aid from those from whom he had a right to expect
it. In these circumstances he thought it best to apply to
his greatest enemy, who perhaps might in return gain as
faithful a friend as he had previously been his "diligent
adversary." Alexander, on hearing the story and moved
by the manner in which Allan had been oppressed by his
immediate relatives, promised to support him, went in
person with a sufficient force to repossess him, and finally
accomplished his purpose. The opposing party at once represented to the King that Alexander Mackenzie invaded their
territory as a "disturber of the peace, and ane oppressor,"
whereupon he was cited before His Majesty at Edinburgh,
"but here was occasion given to Allan to requite Alexander's
generosity, for Alexander having raised armies to assist
him, without commission, he found in it a transgression of
the law, though just upon the matter; so to prevent Alexander's prejudice, he presently went to Holyrood House,
where the King was, and being of a bold temper, did truly
relate how his and Alexander's affairs stood, showing withal that he, as being the occasion of it, was ready to suffer
what law would exact rather than to expose so generous a
friend to any hazard. King James was so taken with their
reciprocal heroisms, that he not only forgave, but allowed
Alexander, and of new confirmed Allan in the lands of
Moydart."*

A desperate skirmish, which took place some time
before this, at Bealach na Broige, "betwixt the heights of
Fearann Donuil and Lochbraon," was brought about by

* The Earl of Cromartie's MS. History of the Mackenzies.

some of Kintail's vassals, instigated by Donald Garbh Maciver attempting to seize the Earl of Ross, but the plot
having been discovered, Maciver was seized by the Lord of
the Isles' followers, and imprisoned in Dingwall. He was
soon released, however, by his undaunted countrymen from
Kenlochewe, consisting of Macivers, Maclennans, Macaulays, and Macleays, who, by way of reprisal, pursued
and seized the Earl's son at Balnagown, and carried
him along with them. His father, Earl John, at once
apprised the Lord Lovat, who was then His Majesty's
Lieutenant in the North, of the illegal seizure of his son,
and he at once despatched northward two hundred men,
who, joined by Ross's vassals, the Monroes of Fowlis, and
the Dingwalls of Kildun, pursued and overtook the western
tribes at Bealach na Broige, where they were resting themselves. A desperate and bloody conflict ensued, aggravated
and exasperated by a keen and bitter recollection of ancient
feuds and animosities. The Kenlochewe men seem to have
been almost extirpated. The race of Dingwall were actually
extinguished, one hundred and forty of their men having
been slain, and the family of Fowlis lost eleven members
of their house alone, with many of the leading men of their
clan.[*]

The following version of this skirmish and the cause
which led to it is worth recording :—Euphemia Leslie,
Countess Dowager of Ross, lived at Dingwall. She would
gladly have married Alexander of Kintail, he being a proper
handsome young man, and she signified no less to himself.
He refused the offer, perhaps, because he plighted his faith
to Macdougal's daughter, but though he had not done so,
he had all the reason imaginable to reject the Countess's
offer, for, besides, that she was not able to add to his estate,
being but a life-rentrix. She was a turbulent woman, and
therefore, in the year 1426, the King committed her to ⌐

---

[*] "Among the rest ther wer slain eleven Monroes of the House of Foulls,
that wer to succeed one after another ; so that the succession of Foulls fell unto
a chyld then lying in his cradle."—*Sir Robert Gordon's History of the Earldom
of Sutherland, p. 36.*

prison in St Colin's Isle, because she had instigated her
son, Alexander, Earl of Ross, to rebellion. She invited
Kintail to her Court in Dingwall to make a last effort, but
finding him obstinate she converted her love to hatred and
revenge, and made him prisoner, and either by torturing or
bribing his page, she procured the golden ring which was the
token between Mackenzie and Macaulay, the governor of
Islandonain, who had strict orders not to quit the castle or
suffer any one to enter it until he sent him that token. The
Countess sent a gentleman to Islandonain with the ring,
who, by her instructions, informed Macaulay that his master
was, or shortly would be, married to the Countess of Ross,
desiring the Governor to repair to his master, and to leave
the stronghold with him. Macaulay seeing and receiving
the ring believed the story, and gave up the castle, but in a
few days he discovered his mistake, and that his chief was
a prisoner instead of being a bridegroom. He went straight
to Dingwall, and finding an opportunity to communicate
with Mackenzie, the prisoner made allegorical remarks by
which Macaulay understood that nothing would secure his
release but the apprehension of Ross of Balnagown, who
was grand uncle, or grand uncle's son to the Countess.
Macaulay returned to Kintail, made up a company of the
" prettiest fellows " he could find of Mackenzie's family, and
went back with them to Easter Ross, and in the morning
apprehended Balnagown in a little arbour near the house,
in a little wood to which he usually resorted for an airing,
and, mounting him on horseback, carried him westward
among the hills. Balnagown's friends were soon in pursuit,
but fearing capture, Macaulay sent Balnagown away under
guard, resolving to fight and detain the pursuers at Bealach
nam Brog, as already described, until Balnagown was safely
out of their reach. After his success here Macaulay went
to Kintail, and at Glenluing, five miles from Islandonain, he
overtook thirty men, sent by the Countess, with meal and
other provisions for the garrison, and the spot, where they
seized them, is to this day called Innis nam Balg. Macaulay secured them, and placed his men in their upper

garments and plaids, who took the burdens of the sacks of meal on their backs, and went straight with them to the garrison, whose impoverished condition induced the Governor to admit them without any inquiry, not doubting they were not his own friends. Once inside they threw down their burdens, drew forth their weapons from under their plaids, seized the new Governor and all his men, and kept them in captivity until Mackenzie was afterwards exchanged for the Governor and Balnagown.*

There has been a considerable difference of opinion as to the date of this encounter, but it is now finally set at rest by the discovery of a positive date in the Fowlis papers, where it is said that "George, the fourth Laird, and his son, begotten on Balnagown's daughter, were killed at the conflict of Beallach na Brog, in the year 1452, and Dingwall of Kildun, with several of their friends and followers, in taking back the Earl of Ross's second son from Clan Iver, Clan Tarlich or Maclennans, and Clan Leod."†

Angus Og, after many bloody conflicts with his father, finally overthrew him at the battle of the Bloody Bay,‡ at Ardnamurchan, obtained possession of all the extensive territories of his clan, and was recognised as its legitimate head. He now determined to punish Mackenzie for having taken his father's part at Court, and otherwise, during the rebellion, and swore that he would recover from him the great possessions which originally belonged to his predecessors, the Lords of the Isles, but now secured by Royal charter to the Baron of Kintail. With this view he decided to attack him, and marched for Inverness, where he expected to meet the now aged Mackenzie returning from his attendance at Court. He, however, missed his object, and instead of killing Mackenzie, he was himself assassinated

---

* Ardintoul MS. History of the Mackenzies.

† The Earl of Cromarty gives a different version, and says that the battle or skirmish took place in the year immediately after the Battle of Harlaw. In this he is manifestly incorrect. The Highlanders to defend themselves from the arrows of their enemies, with their belts tied their shoes on their breasts, hence the name " Bealach nam Brog," or the Pass of the Shoes.

‡ Tobermory.

by an Irish harper. This violent, but well-merited, close to his diabolical career, is recorded in the "Red Book" of Clan-ranald as follows :—"Donald, the son of Angus that was killed at Inverness by his own harper, son of John of the Isles, son of Alexander, son of Donald, son of John, son of Angus Og." This occurred about 1485.

Alexander was the first who lived at Kinellan, while he had Brahan as a "maines," or farm, both of which his successors held from the King for a yearly rent until Kenneth feued Brahan and his son, Colin, feued Kinellan. The Earl of Sutherland had been on friendly terms with Mackenzie, and appointed him as his deputy in the management of the Earldom of Ross. On one occasion, the Earl of Sutherland being in the south at Court, the Strathnaver men and the men of the Braes of Caithness took the opportunity to invade Sutherland. Their intention soon spread abroad, and reached the ears of the Chief of Kintail, who at once, with a party of six hundred men, passed into Sutherland, and the Earl's followers joining him, he defeated the invaders, killed many of them, forced the remainder to sue for peace, and compelled them to give substantial security for their peaceful conduct in future.

Mackenzie was now a very old man. His prudence and sagacity well repaid the judicious patronage of the first King James, confirmed and extended by his successors on the throne, and, as has been well said of him by his biographer, secured to him "the love and respect of three Princes in whose reign he flourished, and as his prudent management in the affairs of the Earldom of Ross, showed him to be a man of good natural parts, so it very much contributed to the advancement of the interest of his family by the acquisition of the lands he thereby made ; nor was he less commendable for the quiet and peace he kept among his Highlanders, putting the laws punctually in execution against all delinquents." Such a character as this, justly called Alastair Ionraic, or the Just, was certainly well fitted to govern, and deserved to flourish, in the age in which he lived. Various important events occurred in his latter

years, but as Kenneth, his son and successor, was the actual
leader of the Clan for many years before his father's death,
and especially at the celebrated Battle of Park, we shall
record them under the next heading.

There is a considerable difference among the genealogists and family historians respecting Alexander's wives.
Both Edmonston in his "Baronagium Genealogicum," and
Douglas in his "Peerage" say that Alexander's first wife
was Agnes, sixth daughter of Colin, first Earl of Argyll.
This, we think, can be shown to be absolutely impossible
without a violation of the laws of nature. Colin succeeded
as a minor in 1453, his uncle, Sir Colin Campbell of Glen-
urchy, having been appointed his tutor. Colin of Argyll
was created Earl in 1457, probably on his coming of age.
He married Isabel Stewart of Lorn, and had two sons, and,
according to Crawford, five daughters. If he had a daughter
Agnes she must have been his eighth child. Assuming that
Argyll married when he became of age, about 1457, Agnes,
as his eighth surviving child, could not, in all probability,
have been born before 1470. Her reputed husband, Alexander of Kintail, was then close upon 70 years of age, having died in 1488, bordering upon 90, just at a time when his
reputed wife would barely have arrived at a marriageable
age, and when her reputed son, Kenneth a Bhlair, pretty
well advanced in years, had fought the famous Battle of
Park. John of Killin, her reputed grandson, was born about
1480, when at most she could only have been 10 to 15 years
of age, and, in 1513, at the age of 33, he fought at Flodden,
where Archibald, second Earl of Argyll, this lady's brother,
at least ten years older than Agnes, was slain. How could
these things be? Further comment is unnecessary.

The same difficulty has arisen, from what appears to
be a very simple cause, about his second marriage. The
authors of all the family MS. histories are unanimous in
stating that Alexander's first wife was Anna, daughter of
Macdougall of Lorn, or Dunollich. Though the direct line
of the house of Lorn ended in two heiresses who, in 1388,
carried away the property to their husbands, the Macdou-

galls of Dunollich became the male representatives of the
ancient and illustrious house of Lorn ; and this fully accounts
for the difference and confusion about the families of Lorn
and Dunollich in some of the family histories.

Regarding Alexander's second marriage the same authorities, who affirm that Agnes of Argyll was his first wife,
assert that Anna Macdougall, above-mentioned, was his
second.   There is ample testimony that she was his first,
though some confusion has again arisen in this case from
a similarity of names and patronymics.   Some of the
family MSS. say that Alexander's second wife was Margaret,
daughter of " M'Couil," " M'Chouile," or " Macdougal " of
Morir, or Morar, while several others, among them the
Allangrange "Ancient" MS., say that she was "Mac-
Ranald's daughter."   The Ardintoul MS. has it that she
was " Muidort's daughter."   One of the Gairloch MSS. in
our possession says that she was ' Margarite, the daughter
of Macdonald of Morar, of the Clan Ranald Race, from
the Stock of Donald Lord of the Æbudæ Islands," while in
another, also in our possession, she is described as " Margaret Macdonald, daughter of Macdonald of Morar."   There
is here an apparent contradiction, but it can be shown, we
think, with perfect accuracy, that the lady so variously described was one and the same person.   Gregory, in his
" Highlands and Isles of Scotland," p. 158, clearly shows
that "Macdougal" was the patronymic of one of the Families
of Clan Ranald of Moydart and Morar.   Speaking of
Dougal MacRanald, son and successor to Ranald Bàn
Ranaldson of Moydart, he says, " Allan, the eldest son of
Dougal, and the undoubted male heir of Clan Ranald, acquired the estate of Morar, which he transmitted to his
descendants.   He and his successors were always styled,
in Gaelic, MacDhughail Mhorair, i.e., MacDougal of Morar,
from their ancestor, Dougal MacRanald."   At p. 65 he informs us that "the Clan Ranald of Garmoran comprehended
the families of Moydart, Morar, Knoydart, and Glengarry ; "
and they were descended from Ranald, younger son of
John of the Isles, by his marriage with the heiress of the

MacRorys, or MacRuairies of Garmoran, whose ancestry, from Somerled of the Isles, is as illustrious as that of any family in Britain. A district north of Arisaig is still known among the Western Islanders as " Mor-thir Mhie Dhughail," or the mainland possession of the son of Dougal. The MS. histories of the Mackenzies having been all written after the patronymic of "MacDhughail" was acquired by the Macdonalds of Moydart and Morar, they naturally enough called Alexander of Kintail's second wife, a daughter of Macdougal of Morar, of Muidort, and of Clan Ranald, indiscriminately, for they were all one and the same person. It has also been suggested that the "M'Couil" and " M'Chouile " of the family historians were their equivalents for " MacDhomh'uill" (mh silent), the Gaelic for Macdonald. This is likely enough.

Alexander died, in 1488, about ninety years of age, at Kinellan, and was buried in Beauly Priory. He was twice married, first, as we have seen, to Anna, daughter of John Macdougall of Dunolly, who fostered him in his minority, and secondly, to Margaret, daughter of Macdonald of Morar, of the family of Clanranald. He is also said to have had a natural son, who was superior of, and repaired, the Priory of Beauly, about 1478, where he is buried.* He is said by others to have been his brother. By his first wife, Anna of Dunolly, Alexander had two sons, Kenneth, who succeeded him, and Duncan, from whom are descended the families of Hilton and Loggie. By the second marriage he had one son, Hector, known among the Highlanders as Heetor Roy, or *Eachainn Ruadh*, from whom descended the family of Gairloch, and of whom more hereafter. He also had a daughter by the second marriage, who married Allan Macleod of Gairloch. Alexander was succeeded by his eldest son by the first marriage,

VII. COINNEACH A BHLAIR,

Or, KENNETH OF THE BATTLE, who was served heir to his father, at Dingwall, on the second of September 1488. He

* Anderson's Historical Account of the Family of Fraser, p. 66, and MS. History of the Mackenzies.

secured the cognomen "of the battle" from the distinguished
part he took in the Battle of Park, fought during his father's
lifetime, in the neighbourhood of Kinellan. His father
was far advanced in years before Kenneth married, and
the latter arriving at the age of twenty, Alexander
thought it prudent, with the view of establishing peace with
John of Isla, to match Kenneth, his heir and successor, with
Isla's daughter, Margaret, and extinguish their ancient feuds
for ever in that alliance. The Island chief willingly consented, and the marriage was not long afterwards solemnised.
Some time after, Isla's nephew and apparent heir, Alexander
of Lochalsh, came to Ross, and feeling more secure in
consequence of this matrimonial alliance between the family
of Mackenzie and his own, took possession of Balcony House
and the adjacent lands, where, at the following Christmas,
he provided a great feast for his old dependants, inviting to
it most of the more powerful chiefs and barons north of the
Spey, and, among others, his cousin's lord, Kenneth Mackenzie. The House of Balcony * was at the time very much
out of repair, so that he could not conveniently lodge all his
distinguished guests within it. He had to arrange some of
them in the outhouses as best he could. Kenneth did not
arrive until Christmas eve, accompanied by a train of able-
bodied men numbering forty, according to the custom of
the times, but without his lady, which gave great umbrage
to Macdonald. One of the Macleans of Duart had the
chief charge of the arrangements in the house. Some days
previously he had a disagreement with Kenneth at some
games, and on his arrival, Maclean, who had the disposal
of the guests, told the heir of Kintail that, taking advantage
of his connection with the family, they had taken the
liberty of providing him with lodgings in the kiln. Kenneth, who was very powerful, considered himself thus insulted, more especially as he imagined the slight proceeded
from Maclean's ill-will against him, and he instantly struck

* Ardintoul MS. places this feast at Balnagown House. "In 1455, Beatrice,
Countess of Ross, submitted to King James II., who then granted her the Barony
of Balknie."—*Orig. Par. Scot.*, vol. ii., p. 480.

Maclean a blow on the ear, which threw him to the ground. The servants in the house viewed this as a direct insult against their Chief, Macdonald, and at once took to arms. Kenneth, though sufficiently bold, soon perceived that he had no chance to fight successfully, or even to beat a retreat, and, noticing several boats lying on the shore, which had been provided for the transport of the guests, he took as many of them as he required, sank the rest, and passed with his followers to the opposite shore, where he remained during the night. He took up his quarters in the house of a tenant "who haid no syrnam but a patronimick ;" and Kenneth, boiling with passion, was sorely affronted at the personal insult offered him, and at being from his own house on Christmas, staying with a stranger, and off his own property. He, in these circumstances, requested his host to adopt the name of Mackenzie, promising him protection in future, that he might thus be able to say he slept under the roof of one of his own name. His host at once consented, and his posterity were ever after known as Mackenzies. Next morning (Christmas day) Kenneth went to the hill above Chanonry, and sent word to the Bishop, who was at the time enjoying his Christmas with others of his clergy, that he desired to speak to him. The Bishop, knowing his man's temper, and the turbulent state of the times, thought it prudent to meet the young chieftain, though he considered it very strange to receive such a message, on such a day from such a quarter, and wondered what could be the object of his visitor. He soon found that Mackenzie simply wanted a feu of a small piece of land on which was situated the house in which he lodged the previous night, and stated his reason to be, "lest Macdonald should brag that he had forced him on Christmas eve to lodge at another man's discretion and not on his own heritage." The Bishop, willing to oblige him, probably afraid to do otherwise, and perceiving him in such a rage, at once sent for his clerk, and there and then granted him a charter of the township of Cullicudden, whereupon Kenneth returned to the place, and remained in it all day, lording over it as his own property.

The place was kept by him and his successors until Colin acquired more of the Bishop's lands in the neighbourhood, and afterwards exchanged the whole with the Sheriff of Cromarty for lands in Strathpeffer.

Next day Kenneth started for Kinellan, where the old Chief, Alexander, resided, and related what had taken place. His father was much grieved, for he well knew that the smallest difference between the families would revive their old grievances, and, although there was less danger since Macdonald's interest in Ross was smaller than in the past, yet he knew the Clan to be a powerful one still, more so than his own, in their number of able-bodied warriors ; but these considerations, strongly impressed upon the son by the experienced and aged father, only added fuel to the fire in Kenneth's bosom, which was already fiercely burning to revenge the insult offered him by Macdonald's servants. His natural impetuosity could ill brook any such insult, and he considered himself wronged so much that he felt it his duty personally to retaliate and revenge it. While this was the state of his mind, matters were suddenly brought to a crisis by the arrival, on the fourth day, of a messenger from Macdonald with a summons requesting Alexander and Kenneth to remove from Kinellan, with all their family, within twenty-four hours, allowing only that the young Lady Margaret, his own cousin, might remain until she had more leisure to remove, and threatening war to the knife in case of non-compliance. Kenneth's rage can easily be imagined, and without consulting his father or waiting for his counsel, he requested the messenger to tell Macdonald that his father would remain where he was in spite of him and all his power. For himself he was to receive no rules for his staying or going, but he would be sure enough to hear of him wherever he was ; and as for his (Macdonald's) cousin, Lady Margaret, since he had no desire to keep further peace with his family, he would no longer keep his relative. Such was the defiant message sent to young Macdonald, and immediately after receipt thereof Kenneth despatched Lady Margaret in the most ignominious manner

·to Balnagown. The lady was blind of an eye, and to insult her cousin to the highest pitch he sent her mounted on a one-eyed horse, accompanied by a one-eyed servant, followed by a one-eyed dog. She was in a delicate state of health, and this inhumanity grieved her so much that she never after wholly recovered. Her son, the only issue of the marriage, was named Kenneth, and to distinguish him from his father, was called Coinneach Og, or Kenneth the younger.

It appears that Kenneth had no great affection for the Lady Margaret, for a few days after he sent her away he went to Lord Lovat's country, accompanied by two hundred of his followers, and besieged his house. Lovat was naturally much surprised at such conduct, and demanded an explanation, when he was coolly told by Kenneth that he came to demand his daughter Anne, or Agnes, in marriage, now that he had no wife, having, as he told him, disposed of the other in the manner already described. Without further deliberation, he demanded a favourable answer to his suit, on which condition he promised to be on strict terms of friendship with her family ; but if his demand was refused, he would swear mortal enmity against Lovat and his house ; and as evidence of his intention in this respect, he pointed out to his Lordship that he already had a party of his men outside gathering together the men, women, and goods that were nearest in the vicinity, all of whom should " be made one fyne to evidence his resolution." Lovat had no particularly friendly feelings towards Macdonald of the Isles, and was not at all indisposed to procure Mackenzie's friendship on the terms proposed, and considering the exigencies and danger of his retainers, and knowing full well the bold and determined character of the man he had to deal with, he consented to the proposed alliance, provided the young lady herself was favourable. She fortunately proved submissive. Lord Lovat delivered her up to her suitor, who immediately returned home with her; and ever after they lived together as husband and wife.*

---

* History of the family of Fraser, Ardintoul MS., and Earl of Cromartie's MS. History of the Mackenzies.

Macdonald was naturally very much exasperated by
Kenneth's defiant answer to himself, and the repeated
insults heaped upon his relative, and, through her, upon all
her family. He thereupon dispatched his great steward,
Maclean, to collect his followers in the Isles, as also to
advise and request the aid of his nearest relations on the
mainland—the Macdonalds of Moidart, and Clan Ian of
Ardnamurchan. In a short time they mustered a force
between them of about fifteen hundred men—some say
three thousand—and arranged with Macdonald to meet him
at Contin. They assumed that Alexander Mackenzie, now
so aged, would not have gone to Kintail, but would stay in
Ross, judging that the Macdonalds, so recently come under
obligations to their King to keep the peace, would not venture to collect their forces and invade the low country. But
Kenneth, foreseeing the danger from the rebellious temper
of Macdonald, went to Kintail at the commencement of
Macdonald's preparations, and placed a strong garrison, with
sufficient provisions, in Islandonain Castle ; and the cattle
and other goods in the district he ordered to be driven and
taken to the most remote hills and secret places. He took
all the remaining able-bodied men along with him, and on
his way back to Kinellan he was joined by his dependants
in Strathconan, Strathgarve, and other glens in the Braes
of Ross, all fully determined to defend Kenneth and his
aged father at the cost of their lives, small as their united
forces were in comparison with that against which they
would soon have to contend.

Macdonald had meanwhile collected his friends, and at
the head of a large body of Western Highlanders, advanced
through Lochaber into Badenoch, where he was joined by
the Clan Chattan ; marched to Inverness, where they were
joined by the young Laird of Kilravock and some of Lovat's
people ; reduced the Castle (then a Royal fortress), placed a
garrison in it, and proceeded to the north-east, and plundered
the lands of Sir Alexander Urquhart, Sheriff of Cromarty.
They next marched westward to the district of Strathconan,
ravaged the lands of the Mackenzies as they proceeded, and

put the inhabitants and more immediate retainers of the family to the sword—resolutely determined to punish Mackenzie for his ill-treatment of Lady Margaret, and recover possession of that part of the Earldom of Ross so long possessed by the Earls of that name, but now the property of Mackenzie by Royal Charter from the King. Macdonald wasted Strathconan, and arrived at Contin on Sunday morning, where he found the people in great terror and confusion ; and, the able-bodied men having already joined Mackenzie, the aged, the women, and the children took refuge in the church, thinking themselves secure within its precincts from an enemy professing Christianity. They soon, to their horror, found themselves mistaken. Macdonald, having little or no scruples on the score of religion, ordered the doors to be closed and guarded, and then set fire to the building. The priest, helpless and aged men, women, and children, were all burnt to ashes.

This sacrilegious and cruel act has often been confused with the horrible burning of the Church of Cille-Chriost by the Macdonalds of Glengarry, at a later date, and of which hereafter. Some of those who were fortunate enough not to have been in the church immediately started for Kinellan, and informed Mackenzie of the hideous and cruel conduct of the advancing enemy. Alexander, sorely grieved in his old age at the cruel destruction of his people, expressed his gratitude that the enemy, whom he had hitherto considered too numerous to contend with successfully, had now engaged God against them, by their impious and execrable conduct. Contin was not far from Kinellan, and Macdonald, thinking that Mackenzie would not remain at the latter place with such a comparatively small force, ordered Gillespick to draw up his followers to the large moor known as "Blar na Pàirc," that he might review them, and send out a detachment to pursue the enemy. Kenneth Mackenzie, who commanded, posted his men in a strong position—on ground where he thought he could defend himself against a superior force, and conveniently situated to attack the enemy if a favourable opportunity occurred.

E

His followers only amounted to six hundred, while his opponent had at least nearly three times that number; but he had the advantage in another respect, inasmuch as he had sufficient provisions for a much longer period than Macdonald could possibly procure for his larger force, the country people having driven their cattle and all provender that might be of service to the enemy out of his reach. About mid-day the Islesmen were drawn up on the moor, about a quarter of a mile distant from the position occupied by the Mackenzies, their forces only separated from each other by a peat moss, full of deep pits and deceitful bogs. Kenneth, fearing a siege, shortly before this prevailed upon his aged father to retire to the Raven's Rock, above Strathpeffer, to which place, strong and easily defended, he resolved to follow him in case he was compelled to retreat before the numerically superior host of his enemy. This the venerable Alexander did, recommending his son to the assistance and protection of a Higher Power, at the same time assuring him of success, notwithstanding the superior forces of his adversary. By the nature of the ground, Kenneth perceived that Macdonald could not bring all his forces to the attack at once. He courageously determined to maintain his ground, and adopted a stratagem which he correctly calculated would mislead his opponent, and place him at a serious disadvantage. He acquainted his brother Duncan with his resolution and plans, and sent him off, before the struggle commenced, with a body of archers to be placed in ambush, while he determined to cross the peat bog himself and attack Macdonald in front with the main body, intending to retreat as soon as his adversary returned the attack, and thus entice the Islesmen to pursue him. He informed Duncan of his intention to retreat, and commanded him to be in readiness with the close body of archers under his command to fall down and charge the enemy whenever they got fairly into the moss, and entangled among its pits and bogs. Having made all these preliminary arrangements, he boldly marched to meet the foe, leading his resolute band in the direction of the intervening moss. Macdonald seeing him, in derision, called upon Gillespick to see "Mackenzie's impudent madness, daring thus to face him at such disadvantage." Gillespick being a more experienced general than the youthful but bold Alexander said "that such extraordinary boldness should be met by more extraordinary wariness in us, lest we fall into unexpected inconvenience." Macdonald, in a furious rage, replied to this wise counsel, "Go you also and join with them, and it will not need our care nor move the least fear in my followers ; both of you will not be a breakfast to me and mine." Meanwhile, Mackenzie advanced a little beyond the moss, avoiding, from his intimate knowledge of it, all the dangerous pits and bogs, when Maclean of Lochbuy, who led the van of the enemy's army, advanced and charged him with great fury. Mackenzie, according to his pre-arranged plan, at once retreated, but so masterly that in so doing he inflicted "as much damage upon the enemy as he received." The Islesmen soon got entangled in the moss, and Duncan observing this, rushed forth from his ambush and furiously attacked them in flank and rear, slaughtering most of those who entered the bog. He then turned round upon the main body, who were taken unprepared. Kenneth seeing this, charged with his main body, who were all well instructed in their Chief's design, and before the enemy were able to form in order of battle, he fell on their right flank with such impetuosity, and did such execution amongst them, that they were compelled to fall back in confusion before the splendid onset of the small force which they had so recently sneered at and despised. Gillespick, stung at Alexander's taunt before the engagement commenced, to prove to him that "though he was wary in council, he was not fearful in action," sought out Mackenzie, that he might engage him in single combat, and followed by some of his bravest followers, he, with signal valour, did great execution among his opponents as he was approaching Kenneth, who was in the hottest of the fight ; and who, seeing Gillespick coming in his direction, advanced to meet him, killing, wounding, or scattering any of the

enemy that came between them. He made a signal to
Gillespick to advance and meet him in single combat ; but
finding him hesitating, Kenneth, who far exceeded him in
strength, while he equalled him in courage, would " brook
no tideous debate, but pressed on with fearful eagerness, he
at one blow cut off Gillespick's arm and past very far into
his body, so that he fell down dead."

Just at this moment Kenneth noticed his standard-
bearer, in his immediate neighbourhood, without his colours,
and fighting desperately to his own hand.   He turned
round upon him and angrily asked what had become
of his colours, when he was coolly answered, " I left Macdonald's standard-bearer, quite unashamed of himself, and
without the slightest concern for those of his own Chief,
carefully guarding mine."   Kenneth naturally demanded an
explanation of such an extraordinary state of matters, when
Donald coolly informed him that they (the standard-bearers)
happened to meet in the conflict, when he was fortunate
enough to slay his opponent ; that he had thrust the staff
of his own standard through the other's body ; and as there
appeared to be some good work to be done among the
enemy, he had left his other attendants to guard the standard, and devoted himself to do what little he could to aid his
master, and protect him from his adversaries.   Maclean of
Lochbuy (Lachlainn Mac Thearlaich) was killed by Duncan
Mor na Tuaighe, Mackenzie's " great scallag," or plough-
man.*   What remained of the Macdonalds were completely

* The following account is given of the manner in which Duncan overcame
his powerful opponent, and some other of his curious adventures :—A raw, ungainly, but powerful-looking youth from Kintail was seen looking about as
they were starting to meet the enemy, in an apparently stupid manner, as if
looking for something.   He ultimately fell in with an old, big, rusty battle-axe,
set off after the others, and arrived at the scene of strife as the combatants were
closing with each other.   Duncan (for such was his name) from his stupid and
ungainly appearance was taken little notice of, and was going about in an
aimless, vacant, half-idiotic manner.   Hector Roy noticing him, asked him why
he was not taking part in the fight and supporting his Chief and clan ? Duncan
replied, ' Mar a faigh mi miabh duine, cha dean mi gniomh duine ' (Unless I get
a man's esteem, I shall not perform a man's work).   This was in reference to his
not having been provided with a proper weapon.   Hector answered him, ' Deansa
gniomh duine 's gheibh thu miabh duine ' (Perform a man's work and you will

routed and put to flight, but most of them were killed,
"quarter being no ordinar complement in thos dayes."
The night before the battle young Brodie of Brodie, accompanied by the accustomed train of retainers, was on a
visit at Kinellan, and as he was preparing to leave the next
morning he noticed Mackenzie's men in arms, whereupon
he asked if the enemy were known to be so near that for a
certainty they would fight before night. Being informed
that they were close at hand, he determined to wait and
take a part in the battle, in spite of Kenneth's persuasion
that he should not, saying "that he was an ill fellow and

receive a man's share). Duncan at once rushed into the strife, exclaiming,
'Buille mhor bho chul mo laimhe, 's ceum leatha, am fear nach teich romham,
teicheam roimhe' (A heavy stroke from the back of my hand (arm) and a step to
(enforce) it. He who does not get out of my way, let me get out of his). Duncan
soon killed a man, and drawing the body aside he coolly sat upon it. Hector
Roy, noticing this extraordinary proceeding as he was passing by in the heat of
the contest, accosted Duncan, and asked him why he was not still engaged with
his comrades. Duncan answered, 'Mar a faigh mi ach miahh aon duine cha
dean mi ach gniomh aon duine' (If I only get one man's due I shall only do one
man's work. I have killed my man). Hector told him to perform two men's
work and that he would get two men's reward. Duncan returned again to the
field of carnage, killed another, pulled his body away, placed it on the top of the
first, and sat upon the two. The same question was again asked, and the same
answer given, 'I have killed two men, and earned two men's wages.' Hector
answered, 'Do your best and we shall not be reckoning with you.' Duncan instantly replied, 'Am fear nach biodh ag cuuntadh rium cha hhithinn a cunntadh
ris' (He that would not reckon with me I would not reckon with him), and
rushed into the thickest of the battle, where he mowed down the enemy with
his rusty battle-axe like grass, so much so that Lachlan MacThearlaich, a most
redouhtable warrior, placed himself in Duncan's way to check him in his murderous career. The heroes met in mortal strife, but MacThearlaich being a very
powerful man, clad in mail, and well versed in arms, Duncan could make no impression upon him, but being lighter and more active than his heavily mailed
opponent, he managed to defend himself, watching his opportunity, and retreating backwards until he arrived at a ditch, where his opponent, thinking he had
him fixed, made a desperate stroke at him, which Duncan parried, and at the
same time jumped backwards across the ditch. MacThearlaich, to catch his
enemy, made a furious plunge with his weapon, hut it instead got fixed in the
opposite hank of the ditch, and in withdrawing it he bent his head forward,
when the helmet, rising, exposed the back of his neck, upon which Duncan's
battle-axe descended with the velocity of lightning, and such terrific force as to
sever MacThearlaich's head from his body. This, it is said, was the turning-
point in the struggle, for the Macdonalds, seeing the brave leader of their van
falling, at once retreated and gave all up for lost. The hero was ever afterwards
known as 'Donnchadh Mor na Tuaighe,' or Big Duncan of the axe; and many a
story is told in Kintail and Gairloch of the many other prodigies of valour which

worse neighbour that would leave his friend at such a time."
He took a distinguished part in the battle, and behaved "to
the advantage of his friend and notable loss of his enemy,"
and the Earl of Cromartie informs us that immediately
after the battle he went on his journey. But his conduct
produced a friendship between the Mackenzies and the
family of Brodie, which continued between their posterity,
"and ever yet remains betwixt them, being more sacredly
observed than the ties of affinity and consanguinity amongst
most others," and a bond of manrent was entered into between the families.   Some authorities assert that young

he performed in the after contests of the Mackenzies and the Macraes against
their common enemies. "Such of Macdonald's men as escaped the battle together,
and as they were going homewards began to spulzie Strathconnan, which Mackenzie hearing, followed them with a party, overtakes them at Inverchorran,
kills shoals of them, and the rest fled diverse ways. That night, when he sat at
supper, he missed his man Duncan More, *alias* MacCay (?Macrae), and said to
the company—'I am more vexed for want of my skallag more this night than
any satisfaction I had of this day.' One of the company says, '.I thought (as the
people fled) I perceived him following four or five men that ran up the burn.'
He had not well spoken the word when Duncan More came in with four heads
bound on a woody, and threw them before his master, 'Tell me now,' says he,
'if I have not deserved my supper,' for which (as is reported of him) he could
not want a stomach. This minds me of a cheat he once played to an Irishman,
being a traveller, withal a strong, lusty fellow, well-proportioned, but of an extraordinary stomach. He resorted into gentlemen's houses, and (was) very oft
in Mackenzie's.   Having come on a time to the same Mackenzie's house in
Islandonain two or three years after this battle (of Park), he was cared for as usual,
and when the Laird went to dinner, he was set aside, at a side-table to himself,
and a double proportion allowed him, which this Duncan More envying, went on
a day and sat side for side with him, drew his skyn or short dagger and eats
with him. 'How now,' says the Irishman, 'how comes it that you fall in eating
in any manner of way.' 'I cannot tell,' says Duncan, 'but I do think I have as
good will to eat as you can have.' 'Well,' says the other, 'we shall try that when
we have done.' So when the Laird had done of his dinner, the Irishman went
where he was and said, 'Noble sir, I have travelled now almost among all the
clans in Scotland, and was resorting their houses, as I have been several times
here, where I cannot say but I was sufficiently cared for, but I never met with
such an affront as I have this day.' The Laird asked what he meant. So he
tells him what injury Duncan had done him in eating a share of his proportion.
'Well,' says the Laird, 'I hope M'IlleChruimb,' for so the Irishman was called,
'you will take no notice of him that did that ; for he is but a fool that plays the
fool now and then.' 'I cannot tell,' says he, 'but he is no idiot at eating, nor will
I let my affront pass so ; for I must have a turn or two of wrestling with him for it
in your presence.' Whereupon a stander-by asks Duncan if he would wrestle
with him. 'I will,' says he, 'for I think I was fit sides with him in eating and
might be so with this.' They yocks, and Duncan threw him thrice on his back.

Brodic was slain, but of this no early writer makes any · mention ; and neither in Sir Robert Gordon's Earldom of Sutherland, in the Earl of Cromartie's and other MS. Histories of the Mackenzies, nor in Brown's History of the Highland Clans, is there any mention made of his having been killed, though all refer to the distinguished part he took in the battle. He was, however, seriously wounded. Next morning, Kenneth, fearing that those few who escaped might rally among the hills, and commit cruelties and robberies on those of his people who might lie in their way, marched to Strathconan, where he found, as he expected, that about three hundred of the enemy had rallied and were destroying everything which they may have passed over in their eastward march ; as soon, however, as they noticed him in pursuit they instantly took to their heels,

The Irishman was so angry he wist not what to say. He invites him to put the stone, and at the second cast he worried him four feet, but could never reach him. Then he was like to burst himself. Finding this, he invites him to lop so that he outlopped him as far a length. The Irishman then said, ' I have travelled as far as any of my equals, both in Scotland, England, and Ireland, and tried many hands, but I never met with my equal till this day, but comrade,' says he, ' let us now go and swim a little in the Laird's presence.' ' With all my heart,' says Duncan, ' for I never sought better ' (with this Duncan could swim not at all), but down to the shore they go to the next rock, and being full sea, was at least three fathoms deep, but before the Irishman had off half of his clothes Duncan was stark naked, lops over the rocks and ducks to the bottom and up again. Looking about him he calls to a boy that stood by, and said, ' Lad, go where the Lady is, and bid her send me a hutter and four cheese.' The Irishman, hearing this, asks ' What purpose.' ' To what purpose,' says he, ' yous the least we will need this night and to-morrow wherever we be.' ' Do you intend a journey,' says the Irishman. ' Aye, that I do,' answered the other, ' and am in hopes to cross the Kyle ere night.' Now, this Kyle was 20 leagues off with a very ill stream, as the Irishman very well knew, so that he said, with a very great oath, he would not go with him that length, but if he liked to sport the Laird with several sorts of swimming, he would give a trial. ' Sport here, sport there, wherever I go you must go.' With this the cheese and butter comes, and Duncan desires the Irishman to make ready, but all his persuasions (not against his will) would not prevail with Mac a Chruimh, whereupon all the company gave over with laughter, knowing the other could swim none at all, but the fellow thought they jeered him. The Laird made Duncan forbear him ; but Duncan swore a great oath he would make him swim or he left the town, otherwise he would want of his will. So it came to pass ; for the Irishman got away that same night, was seen on the morrow in Lochalsh, but none (were) found that ferried him over. But never after resorted (after this affront) Mackenzie's house."—*Ancient MS. History of the Mackenzies.*

but they were all killed or taken prisoners. Kenneth now
returned to Kinellan, conveying Alexander, whom he had
taken prisoner, in triumph. His aged father, Alastair Ionraic, had now returned from the Raven's Rock, and warmly
embraced his valiant son—congratulated him upon his
splendid victory over such a numerically superior force ;
but, knowingly, and with some complaining emphasis, told
his son that "he feared they made two days' work of one,"
since, by sparing Macdonald, whom he had also taken prisoner, and his apparent heir, Alexander of Lochalsh, they
preserved the lives of those who might yet give them trouble. But Kenneth, though a lion in the field, could not,
from any such prudential consideration, be induced to commit such a cowardly and inhuman act as was here inferred.
He, however, had no great faith in his more immediate followers if an opportunity occurred to them, and he sent Macdonald, under strong guard, to Lord Lovat, to be kept by
him in safety until he should advise him how to dispose of
him. He kept Alexander of Lochalsh with himself, but
contrary to all the expectations of their friends, he, on the
intercession of old Macdonald, released them both within
six months, having first bound them by oath and honour
never to molest him nor his, and never again to claim any
right to the Earldom of Ross, which Alexander of the Isles
had formerly so fully resigned to the King.[*]

Many of the Macdonalds and their followers who escaped
from the field of battle perished in the River Conon. Flying from the close pursuit of the victorious Mackenzies, they
took the river, which in some parts was very deep, wherever
they came up to it, and were drowned. Rushing to cross
at Moy, they met an old woman—still smarting under the
insults and spoliations inflicted on her and on her neighbours by the Macdonalds on their way north—and asked
her, "Where was the best ford on the river?" "Oh !
Ghaolaich, is aon ath an abhuinn ; ged tha i dubh cha'n eil
i domhain" (Oh ! dear, answered she, it is all one ford to-

<hr />

[*] This account of the Battle of Park is given mainly on the authority of the
Earl of Cromartie's MS. History of the Clan.

gether ; though it looks black it is not at all deep). In their pitiful plight, and on the strength of this misleading information, they rushed into the water in hundreds, and were immediately carried away by the stream, many of them clutching at the shrubs and bushes which overhung the banks of the river, and crying pitifully for assistance. This amazon and her lady friends had meanwhile procured their sickles, and now exerted themselves in cutting away the bushes on which the wretched Macdonalds hung with a death grasp, the old woman exclaiming, in each case, as she applied her sickle, " As you have taken so much already which did not belong to you, my friend, you can take that into the bargain." This instrument of the old lady's revenge has been for many generations, and still is, by very old people in the district, called " Cailleach na Maigh," or the old wife of Moy. The victors then proceeded to ravage the lands of Ardmeanach and those belonging to William Munro of Foulis—the former because the young Baron of Kilravock, whose father was governor of that district, had assisted the other party; the latter probably because Munro, who joined neither party, was suspected secretly of favouring Lochalsh. So many excesses were committed at this time by the Mackenzies that the Earl of Huntly, Lieutenant of the North, was compelled, notwithstanding their services in repelling the invasion of the Macdonalds, to act against them as oppressors of the lieges.*

A blacksmith, known as Glaishean Gow or " Gobha," one of Lovat's people, in whose father's house Agnes Fraser, Mackenzie's wife, was fostered, hearing of the advance of the Macdonalds to the Mackenzie territory, started with a few followers in the direction of Conan, but arrived too late to take part in the battle. They were, however, in time to meet those few who managed to ford or swim the river, and killed every one of them, so that they found an opportunity " to do more service than if they had been at it."

This insurrection cost the Macdonalds the Lordship of

* Gregory, p. 57. Kilravock Writs, p. 170, and Acts of Council.

the Isles, as others had previously cost them the Earldom
of Ross. In a Parliament held in Edinburgh in 1493, the
possessions of the Lord of the Isles were declared to be
forfeited to the Crown. In the following January the aged
Earl appeared before King James IV., and made a voluntary surrender of everything, after which he remained for
several years in the King's household as a Court pensioner.
By Act of the Lords of Council in 1492, Alexander Urquhart, Sheriff of Cromarty, obtained restitution for himself
and his tenants for the depredations committed by Macdonald and his followers.*

The Earl of Cromartie, says of this Baron, "Kenneth raised
great fears in his neighbours by his temper and power, by
which he had overturned so great anc interest as that of
Macdonald, yet it appearit that he did not proceid to such
attemptts but on just resentments and rationall grounds;
for dureing his lyfe he not only protected the country by
his power, but he caryed so that non was esteemed a better
neighbour to his freinds nor a juster maister to his de-
penders. In that one thing of his caryadge to his first wife
he is justly reprowable; in all things else he merits justly
to be numbered amongst the best of our Scots patriots.
. . . . The fight at Blairnapark put Mackenzie in great
respect through all the North. The Earl of Huntly, George ,
who was the second Earle, did contract a friendship with
him, and when he was imployed by King James 3d to
assist him againest the conspirators in the South, Kenneth
came with 500 men to him in Summer 1488; but erre they
came the lengthe of Perth, Mackenzie had nottice of his
father Alexander's death, whereupon Húntly caused him
retire to ordor his affaires, least his old enimies might tack
advantage on such a change, and Huntly judgeing that
they wer rather too numberous than weak for the conspirators, by which occasion he (Kenneth) was absent from that

---

* According to the Kilravock papers, p. 162, the spoil amounted to " 600 cows
and oxen, each worth 13s 4d ; 80 horses, each worth 26s 8d ; 1000 sheep, each
worth 2s ; 200 swine, each worth 3s ; with plenishing to the value?of £300 ; and
also 500 bolls of victual and £300 of the mails of the Sheriff's lands."

vnfortunat battl wher King James 3d wes kild, yet evir
after this, Earl George, and his son Alexander, the 3d Earl
of Huntly, keipt a great kyndness to Kenneth and his successors. From the yeir 1489 the kingdom vnder King
James 4d wes at great peace, and therby Mackenzie toock
opportunity to setle his privat affaires, which for many yeirs
befor, yea, severall ages, had bein almost still disturbed by
the Earls of Ross and Lords of the Illes, and so he lived in
pcaee and good correspondences with his neighbours till the
yeir 1491, for in the moneth of February that yeir he died
and wes buried at Bewlie. All his predecessors wer buried
at Icolmkill [except his father], as wer most of the considerable chieffs in the Highlands. But this Kenneth, after his
marriage, keipt frequent devotiones with the Convent of
Bewlie, and at his owin desyre wes buried ther, in the ille
on the north syd of the alter, which wes built by himselfe
in his lyftyme or he died ; after that he done pennance for
his irregular maricing of Lovit's daughter. He procured
recommendationes from Thomas Hay (his lady's uncle),
Bishop of Ross, to Pope Alexander the 6, from whom he
procured a legittmatione of all the cheildrein of the mari-
adge, daited apud St Petri, papatus nostri primo, anno
Cristiano 1491."*

Bishop Hay strongly impressed upon Mackenzie the
propriety of getting his marriage with Agnes of Lovat
legitimized, and to send for a Commission to the Pope for
that purpose. Donald Dubh MacGhregar, priest of Kirkhill, was despatched to the Pope with that object, and
procured the legitimation of the marriage. " This priest
was a native of Kintail, descended from a clan there called
Clan Chreggir, who, being a hopefull boy in his younger days,
was educat in Maekenzie's house, and afterwards at Beullie
he the forementioned Dugall Mackenzie, pryor yrof. In
end he was made priest of Kirkhill. His successors to this
day are called Frasers. Of this priest is descended Mr

---

* This is corroborated by Anderson's Account of the Family of Fraser, where
we are told that "Application was made to the Pope to sanction the second marriage, which he did, anno 1491."

William Fraser and Mr Donald Fraser."*   " They were both
made knights to the boot of Pope Clement the VIII., but
when my knights came home, they neglected the decree of
Pope Innocent III. against the marriage and consentrinate
of all the clergy : or otherwise they got a dispensation from
the then Pope Clement VIII. for both of them married—
Sir Dugall was made priest of Kintail and married nien
(daughter) Dunchy Chaim in Glenmorriston.   Sir Andrew
likewise married, whose son was called Donald Du Mac
Intagard, and was priest of Kirkhill and chapter of Ross.
His tack of the vicarage of Kilmorack to John Chisholm of
Comar stands to this day.   The present Mr William Fraser,
minister of Kilmorack, is the fifth minister in lineal and uninterrupted succession."†

Sir Kenneth of Kintail, knighted by James IV. " for being highly instrumental in reducing his fierce countrymen
to the blessings of a civilized life," was twice married ; first,
as we have seen, to Lady Margaret, daughter of John of
Isla, by whom he had one son, Kenneth Og, who succeeded
him ; and secondly, to Agnes or Anne Fraser, daughter of
Hugh, third Lord Lovat, by whom he had four sons—John,
who succeeded Kenneth Og as Baron of Kintail ; Alexander,
the first of the family of Davochmaluag ; Roderick, who
was killed at Flodden, and was the progenitor of the families
of Achilty, Fairburn, Ardross, &c. ; and Mr Kenneth, better
known as " the Priest of Avoch," from whom descended the
families of Suddie, Ord, Corryvulzie, Highfield, Inverlaul,
Little Findon, and others of lesser note.   By the second
marriage he had two daughters—Agnes, who married
Roderick Macleod of the Lewis, who afterwards sent her
away charging her with infidelity ; and Catharine, who
married Hector Munro of Fowlis.   .

Of Roderick, who was an exceedingly powerful man, the
following is told :—He was a man of great strength and
stature, and in a quarrel which took place between him and
Dingwall of Kildun, he killed the latter, and " that night

abode with his wife." Complaint was made to King James the Fifth, who commanded the Baron of Kintail to give Roric up to justice. His brother, knowing he could not do so openly and by force without trouble and considerable danger, went to Kintail professedly to settle his affairs there, and when he was about returning home he requested Roric to meet him at Glassletter, that he might privately consult and discourse with him as to his present state. Rorie duly met him on the appointed day with fifty men of his "coalds," the Macleays, besides ordinary servants and some Kintail men. While the two brothers went to discourse, they passed between the Kintail men and the Macleays, who sat at a good distance from one another. When Mackenzie, came near the Kintail men, he clapped Roric on the shoulder, which was the sign between them, and Roric was immediately seized. Gillecriost MacFhionnla instantly ran to the Macleays, who had taken to their arms to relieve their Coald Roric Mor, and desired them in a friendly manner to compose themselves, and not be rash, since Rorie was seized not by his enemies, but was in the hands of his own brother, and of those who had as great a kindness for him, and interest in him, as they had themselves ; and further he desired them to consider what would be the consequences, for if the least drop of blood was shed, Roric would be immediately put to death, and so all their pains would be lost. He thus prevailed upon them to keep quiet. In the meantime Rorie struggled with the Kintail men, and would not be taken or go along with them, until John More, afterwards agnamed Ian Mor Nan Cas, brother to Gillecriost MacFhionnla, took Rorie by the feet and cast him down. They then bound him and carried him on their shoulders, until he consented to go along with them willingly, and without further objection. They took him to Islandonain, whence shortly after he was sent south to the King, where he had to take his trial. He, however, denied the whole affair, and in the absence of positive proof, the judges declined to convict him ; but the King, quite persuaded of his guilt, ordered him to be sent a prisoner to the Bass·

Rock, with strict injunctions to have him kept in chains. This order was obeyed, and Rorie's hands and legs were much pained and cut with the irons. The governor had unpleasant feuds with one of his neighbours, which occasioned several encounters and skirmishes between their servants, who came in repeatedly with wounds and bruises. Rorie noticing this to occur frequently, said to one of them, "Would to God that the laird would take me with him, and I should then be worth my meat to him and serve for better use than I do with these chains." This was communicated to the governor, who sent for Rorie and asked him if he would fight well for him. "If I do not that," said he, "let me hang in these chains." He then took his solemn oath that he would not run away, and the governor ordered the servants to set about curing Rorie's wounds with ointments. He soon found himself in good condition to fight, and an opportunity was not long delayed. The governor met his adversary accompanied by his prisoner, who fought to admiration, exhibiting great courage and enormous strength. He soon routed the enemy, and the governor became so enamoured of him that he was never after out of his company whenever he could secretly have him unknown to the Court. About this time an Italian came to Edinburgh, who challenged the whole nation to a wrestling match for a large sum of money. One or two grappled with him, but he disposed of them so easily that no one else could be found to engage him. The King was much annoyed at this, and expressed himself strongly in favour of any one who would defeat the Italian, promising to give him a suitable reward. The governor of the Rock having heard of this, thought it an excellent opportunity for his prisoner to secure his liberty, and at the same time redeem the credit of the nation, and he informed the King that a prisoner committed to the Bass by his Majesty if released of his irons would, in his opinion, match the Italian. The King immediately answered, " His liberty, with reward, shall he have if he do so." The governor, so as not to expose his own intimate relations with, and treatment of, the prisoner, warily asked that time

should be allowed to cure him of his wounds, lest his own
crime and Rorie's previous liberty should become known.
When sufficient time had elapsed for this purpose a day was
appointed, and the governor brought Rorie to Holyrood
House to meet the King, who enquired if he " would undertake to east the Italian for his liberty?"   " Yes, sir,"
answered Rorie, "it will be a hard task· that I will not
undertake for that ; but, sir, it may be, it will not be so easy
to perform as to undertake, yet I shall give him a fair trial."
" Well," said the King, "how many days will you have to
fit yourself?"   " Not an hour," replied Rorie.   His Majesty
was so pleased with his resolution that he immediately sent.
to the Italian to ask if he would aecept the challenge at
once.   He who had won so many victories so easily already
did not hesitate to grapple with Rorie, having no fear as to
the result.   Five lists were prepared.   The Italian was first
on the ground, and seeing Rorie approaching him, dressed
in his rude habit, without any of the usual dress and
accoutrements, laughed loudly.   But no sooner was he in
the Highlander's grasp than the Italian was on his knee.
The King cried with joy ; the Italian alleged foul play, and
made other and frivolous excuses, but His Majesty was so
glad of the apparent advantage in his favour that he was
unwilling to expose Rorie to a second hazard.   This did
not suit the Highlander at all, and he called out, " No, no,
sir ; let me try him again, for now I think I know his
strength."   His Majesty hearing this, consented, and in the
second encounter Rorie laid firm hold of the foreigner,
pulled him towards him with all his might, breaking his
back, and disjointing the back-bone.   The poor fellow fell
to the ground groaning with pain, and died two days after.
The King, delighted with Rorie's prowess, requested him to
remain at Court, but this he refused, excusing himself on
the ground that his long imprisonment quite unfitted him
for Court life, but if it pleased his Majesty he would send
him his son, who was better fitted to serve him.   He was
provided with money and suitable clothing by Royal command.   The King requested him to hasten his son to Court,

which he accordingly did. This son was named Murdoch,
and His Majesty became so fond of him that he always retained him about his person, and granted him, as an earnest
of greater things to follow, the lands of Fairburn, Moy, and
others adjoining, also the Ferry of Scuideal ; but Murdoch
being unfortunately absent from the Court when the King
died, he missed much more which his Majesty had designed
for him.*

The following anecdote told of him and Kenneth, the
fourth son, is also worth recording :—He was Chaunter of
Ross, and perpetual Curate of Coeirbents, which vicarage he
afterwards resigned into the hands of Pope Paulus in favour
of the Priory of Beauly. Though a priest and in holy orders
he would not abstain from marriage, for which cause the
Bishop decided to have him deposed. On the appointed day
for his trial he had his brother Roric at Chanonry, where the
trial was to take place, with a number of his followers. Kenneth presented himself before the Bishop in his long gown, but
under it he had a two-edged sword, and drawing near his
Lordship, who sat in his presiding chair, whispered in his
ear, " It is best that you should let me alone, for my brother
Rorie is in the churchyard with many ill men, and if you
take off my orders he will take off your head, and I myself
will not be your best friend," and then coolly exposed his
penknife, as he called his great sword, " which sight, with
Roric's proximity, and being a person whose character was
well enough known by his Lordship, he was so terrified that
he incontinently absolved and vindicated the good Chaunter,
who ever after enjoyed his office (and his wife) unchal-
lenged."

There has been a considerable difference of opinion
among the family genealogists as to the date of Sir Kenneth's death, but there is now no doubt that he died in 1491,
having only ruled as actual Chief of the Clan for the short
space of three years. This is clearly proved from his tomb
in the Priory of Beauly, where there is a full length re-

* Ardintoul MS. History of the Mackenzies, and MS. History by the Earl of
Cromartie.

cumbent effigy of him, in full armour, with arms folded across his chest as if in prayer, and on the arch over it is the following inscription :—" Hic Jacet, Kanyans, m. kynch d'us de Kyntayl, q. obiit vii. die Februarii, a. di. m.cccc.lxxxxi." Mr William Fraser, in his history of the " Earls of Cromartie," gives, in his genealogy of the Mackenzies of Kintail, the date of his death as "*circa* 1506," and disposes of his successor Kenneth Og altogether. This is incomprehensible to readers of the work ; for in the book itself, in various places, it is indubitably established that Mr Fraser's genealogy is incorrect in this, as well as in other important particulars.*

The following extract from the published " Acts of the Lords of Council," p. 327, under date " 17th June 1494," places the question absolutely beyond dispute. " The King's Highness and Lords of Council decree and deliver that David Ross of Balnagown shall restore and deliver again to Annas Fresale, the spouse of THE LATE Kenneth Mackenzie of Kintail, seven score of cows, price of the piece (each), 20s; 30 horses, price of the piece, 2 merks ; 200 sheep and goats, price of the piece, 2s ; and 14 cows, price of the piece, 20s ; spuilzied and taken by the said David and his Complices from the said Annas out of the lands of Kynlyn (? Killin or Kinellan), as was sufficiently proved before the Lords ; and ordain that letters be written to distrain the said David, his lands, and goods therefor, and he was present at his action by this pro- curators." It is almost needless to point out that the man who, by this undoubted authority, was THE LATE Kenneth Mackenzie of Kintail in 1494 could not have died about, or "*circa* 1506," as Mr Fraser asserts in his " Earls of Cromartie." He died in 1491, and was succeeded by his only son by his first wife, Margaret of Isla,

VIII. COINNEACH OG,

OR KENNETH THE YOUNGER, who was also known as Sir Kenneth. When, in 1488, King James the IV. succeeded to the throne, he determined to attach to his interest the

---

* Mr Fraser appears to have adopted Douglas in his genealogies, who, as already shown, cannot bo depended upon in many instances.

F

principal chiefs in the Highlands. "To overawe and subdue
the petty princes who affected independence, to carry into
their territories, hitherto too exclusively governed by their
own capricious or tyrannical institutions, the same system of
a severe, but regular and rapid administration of civil and
criminal justice, which had been established in his Lowland
dominions, was the laudable object of the King; and for
this purpose he succeeded, with that energy and activity
which remarkably distinguished him, in opening up an in-
tercourse with many of the leading men in the northern
counties. With the Captain of the Clan Chattan, Duncan
Mackintosh; with Ewen, the son of Alan, Captain of the
Clan Cameron; with Campbell of Glenurghay; the Mac-
gillcouns of Duart and Lochbuy; Mackane of Ardnamurchan; the Lairds of Mackenzie and Grant; and the Earl of
Huntley, a baron of the most extensive power in these
northern districts—he appears to have been in habits of
constant and regular communication—rewarding them by
presents, in the shape either of money or of grants of land,
and securing their services in reducing to obedience such
of their fellow chieftains as proved contumacious, or actually
rose in rebellion."*

To carry out this plan he determined to take pledges
for their good behaviour from some of the most powerful
clans, and, at the same time, educate the younger lairds
into a more civilised manner of governing their people.
Amongst others he took a special interest in Kenneth
Og, and Farquhar Mackintosh, the young lairds of
Mackenzie and Mackintosh, who were cousins, their
mothers being sisters, daughters·of John, last Lord of
the Isles. They were both powerful, the leaders of
great clans, and young men of great spirit and reckless
habits. They were accordingly apprehended in 1495,†

---

* Tytler, vol. iv., pp. 367-368.

† "The King having made a progress to the North, was advised to secure
these two gentlemen as hostages for securing the peace of the Highlands, and
accordingly they were apprehended at Inverness and sent prisoners to Edinburgh
in the year 1495, where they remained two years."—*Dr George Mackenzie's MS.
History.*

and sent to Edinburgh, where they were kept in custody in the Castle, until a favourable opportunity occurring, in 1497, they escaped over the ramparts by the aid of ropes secretly conveyed to them by some of their friends. This was the more easily managed, as they had liberty granted them to roam over the whole bounds of the Castle within the outer walls; and the young Chieftains, getting tired of restraint, and ashamed to be idle while they considered themselves fit actors for the stage of their Highland domains, resolved to attempt an escape by dropping over the walls, when Kenneth injured his leg, so as to incapacitate him from rapid progress; but Mackintosh manfully resolved to risk capture himself rather than leave his fellow-fugitive behind in such circumstances. The result of this accident, however, was that after three days' journey they were only able to reach the Torwood, where, suspecting no danger, they put up for the night in a private house.

The Laird of Buchanan, who was at the time an outlaw for some murder he had committed, happened to be in the neighbourhood, and, meeting the Highlanders, entertained them with a show of kindness; by which means he induced them to divulge their names and quality. A proclamation had recently been issued promising remission to any outlaw who would bring in another similarly circumstanced, and Buchanan resolved to procure his own freedom at the expense of his fellow-fugitives; for he knew well that such they were, previously knowing them as His Majesty's pledges from their respective Clans. In the most deceitful manner, he watched until they had retired to rest, when he surrounded the house with a band of his followers, and charged them to surrender. This they declined; and Mackenzie, being of a violent temper, and possessed of more courage than prudence, rushed out with a drawn sword " refusing delivery and endeavouring to escape," whereupon he was shot with an arrow by one of Buchanan's men. His head was severed from his body, and forwarded to the King in Edinburgh; while young Mackintosh, who made no

further resistance, was secured and sent a prisoner to the
King. Buchanan's outlawry was remitted, and Mackintosh
was confined in Dunbar, where he remained until after the
death of James the Fourth at the battle of Flodden Field.*
Buchanan's base conduct was universally execrated, while
the fate of young Mackenzie was lamented throughout the
whole Highlands, having been accused of no other crime
than the natural forwardness of youth, and having escaped
from his confinement in Edinburgh Castle.

It is admitted on all hands that Kenneth Og was killed,
as above, in 1497, and he must, therefore—his father having
died in 1491—have ruled as one of the Barons of Kintail,
though there is no record of his having been formally served
heir. He was not married, but left two bastard sons—one
by the daughter of the Baron of Moniack, known as Rorie
Beag ; and the other by the daughter of a gentleman in Cromar, of whom are descended the Sliochd Thomais in Cromar
and Glenshiel, Bracmar, the principal families of which are
those of Dalmore and Renoway.† He was succeeded by
his eldest brother by his father's second marriage with Agnes
or Anne, daughter of Hugh, third Lord Lovat,

IX. JOHN OF KILLIN,

Known by that designation from his having generally
resided at that place. He was, as we have seen, the first
son of Kenneth, seventh Baron of Kintail, by his second
wife Agnes, or Anne of Lovat, and being never regularly
married, the great body of the Clan did not consider John
the legitimate heir. Hector Roy Mackenzie, his uncle, progenitor of the House of Gairloch, a man of great prudence

---

* Gregory, p. 93 ; and MS. History by the Earl of Cromartie.

† "In his going to Inverness, as I have said, to meet the King, he was the
night before his coming there in the Baron of Muniag's house, whose daughter
he got with child, who was called Rory Begg. Of this Rory descended the
parson of Slate ; and on the same journey going along with the King to Edinburgh he got a son with a gentleman's daughter, and called him Thomas Mackenzy, of whom descended the Mackenzies—in Braemar called Slyghk Homash
Vic Choinnich. That is to say Thomas Mackenzie's Succession. If he had
lived he would be heir to Mackenzie and Macdonald (Earl of Ross)."—*Ancient
MS.*

and eourage, was by Kenneth a Bhlair appointed tutor to Kenneth Og, then under age, though Dunean, an elder brother, by Alexander's first wife, had, aecording to custom, a prior claim to that honourable and important trust. Dunean is, however, deseribed as one who was "of better hands than head"—more brave than prudent. Hector, took charge, and on the death of Kenneth Og found himself in possession of valuable and extensive estates. He had already secured great popularity among the Clan, which he had before now often led to victory against the eom- mon enemy. He objeeted to John's succession on the ground that he was the illegitimate son of Lovat's daugh- ter, with whom his father, Kenneth, at first did "so irregu- larly and unlawfully cohabit," and John's youth encour- aging him, it is said,[*] Hector proposed an arrangement to Duncan, whom he considered the only legitimate obstacle to his own succession, by which he would transfer his rights as elder brother in Hector's favour, in return for which he would receive a considerable portion of the estates for himself and his successors. Duncan declined to enter into the proposed arrangement, on the ground that the Pope, in 1491, the year in which John's father died, had legiti- mised Kenneth a Bhlair's marriage with Agnes of Lovat, and thereby restored the children of that union to the rights of succession. Finding Duncan unfavourable to his project, Hector declared John illegitimate, and held possession of the estates for himself; and the whole Clan, with whom he was a great favourite, submitted to his rule.[†] It can hardly be supposed that Lord Lovat would be a disinterested speetator of these proceedings, and in the interest of his sister's children he proeured a precept of *clare constat* from James Stewart, Duke of Ross,[‡] and Arehbishop of St

---

* MS. History by the Earl of Cromartie.

† Though we have given this account on the authority of the MS. histories of the family, it is now generally believed that Duncan was dead at this period, and that his son Allan, who would have succeeded, failing John of Killin's legitimacy, was a minor when his father died.

‡ After the forfeiture of the ancient Earls of Ross, the district furnished new titles under the old names, to members of the Royal family. James

nephew

Andrews, in favour of his grandson, John, as heir to the estates. The document is "daited the last of Apryle 1500 and seasin thereon 16 Mey 1500 be Sir John Barchaw and William Monro of Foulls, as Baillie to the Duk."* This precept included the Barony of Kintail, as well as the lands held by Mackenzie of the Earldom of Ross, for, the charter chest being in the possession of Hector Roy, Lovat was not aware that Kintail was at this time held direct from the Crown ; but notwithstanding all these precautions and legal instruments, Hector kept possession and treated the entire estates as his own.

Sir William Munro of Fowlis, the Duke's Lieutenant for the forfeited Earldom of Ross, was dissatisfied with Hector's conduct, and resolved to punish him. Munro was in the habit of doing things with a high hand, and on this occasion, during Hector's absence from home, he, accompanied by his Sheriff, Alexander Vass, went to Kinellan, where Hector usually resided, held a court at the place, and as a mulct or fine took away the couples of one of Hector's barns as a token of his power. When

Stewart, second son of King James the Third, was created in 1487 Duke of Ross, Marquis of Ormond, Earl of Ardmanach, and Lord of Brechin and Navar. The Duke did not long hold the territorial Dukedom of Ross. On the 13th of May 1503, having obtained the rich Abbey of Dunfermline, he resigned the Dukedom of Ross into the hands of the King. The Duke reserved for his life the hill of Dingwall beside that town, for the style of Duke, the hill of Ormond (above Avoch) for the style of Marquis, the Reidcastle of Ardmanach for the style of Earl, and the Castle of Brechin, with the gardens, &c., for the name of Brechin and Navar. The Duke of Ross died in 1504. It was said of him by Ariosto, as translated by Hoole --

"The title of the Duke of Ross he bears,
No chief like him in dauntless mind compares."

The next creation of the title of the Duke of Ross was in favour of Alexander Stewart, the posthumous son of King James the Fourth. The Duke was born on the 30th April 1514, and died on the 18th December 1515. In the reign of Mary Queen of Scots, John, Earl of Sutherland, acquired from Mary, the Queen Dowager, a certain right in the Earldom of Ross, which might ultimately have joined in one family both Sutherland and Ross. Lord Darnley, on the prospect of his marriage with Queen Mary, was created Earl of Ross, a title by which he is little known, as it was only given to him a short time before he obtained the higher titles of Duke of Albany and King of Scotland.—*Fraser's Earls of Cromartie.*

* MS. History by the Earl of Cromartie.

Hector discovered what had taken place in his absence,
he became furious, and sent a message to Fowlis telling him that if he were a man of courage and a "good
fellow" he would come and take away the couples of the
other barn when their owner was at home. Munro, greatly
offended at this message, determined to accept the bold
challenge conveyed in it, and promptly collected his followers, with the Dingwalls, and the Maccullochs, who were
then his dependants, to the number of nine hundred, and
with this force started for Kinellan, where he arrived much
sooner than Hector, who hurriedly collected all the men he
could in the neighbourhood, anticipated. He had no time
to advise his Kintail men nor those at a distance from Kinellan, and was consequently unable to collect more than
one hundred and forty men. With this small force he
wisely deemed it imprudent to venture on a regular battle,
but decided upon a stratagem which, if it proved successful, as
he anticipated, would give him an advantage that would
more than counterbalance the enemy's superiority of numbers. Having supplied his small but resolute band with
provisions for twenty-four hours, he led them secretly, during
the night, to the top of Knock-farrel, a place so situated
that Munro must needs pass near its north or south side in
his march to and from Kinellan. Early next morning
Fowlis marched past, quite ignorant of Hector's position,
and expecting him to have remained at Kinellan to implement the purport of his message. He was allowed to pass
unmolested, and, supposing Hector had fled, he proceeded
to demolish the barn, ordered its couples to be carried away,
broke all the utensils about the place, and drove away all
the cattle, as trophies of his visit. In the evening he returned, as Hector conjectured, carrying his plunder in front
of his party, accompanied by a strong guard, while he placed
the rest of his picked men in the rear, fearing that Hector
might pursue him, little imagining that he was between him
and his destination. On his way to Kinellan, Munro
marched through Strathpeffer, round the north side of
Knock-farrel, but for some cause or other he returned by

the south side where the highway touched the shoulder of
the hill where Heetor's men were posted. Munro had no
fear of attaek from that quarter, and his men, feeling
themselves quite safe, marehed loosely and out of order.
Heetor diseovering his opportunity, allowed them to pass
until the rear was within musket shot of him. He then
ordered his men to eharge, which they did with such furious
impetuosity, that most of the enemy were cut to pieees
before they were properly aware from whenee they were
attacked, or could make any effectual attempt to resist the
dashing onset of Heetor's followers. The groans of the
dying in the gloaming, the uncertainty as well as the unex-
peetedness of the attaek, frightened them so much that they
fled in eonfusion, in spite of every attempt on the part of
Fowlis, who was in front in charge of the spoil and its
guard, to stop them. Those flying in disorder from the
rear soon confused those in front, and the result was a eom-
plete rout. Hector's men followed, killing every one they
met ; for it was ordered that no quarter should be given to
sueh a number, who might again turn round, attaek and
defeat the vietors. In this retreat almost all the men of
the Clan Dingwall and Maccullochs eapable of bearing
arms were killed, and so many of the Munros that for a
long time after " there eould not be ane seeure friendship
made up twixt them and the Mackenzies, till by frequent
allyance and mutuall beneffets at last thes animosities are
setled ; and in ordor to a reconciliation, Hector, sone to
this William of Foulls, wes maried to John Maekenzie's
sister."

At this eonflict, besides that it was notable for its neat
eontrivanee, the inequality of forees engaged, and the number
of the slain, there are two minor ineidents worth not-
ing. One is that the pursuit was so hot, that they not
only fled in a erowd, but there were so many of them killed
at a plaee on the edge of the hill where a descent fell
from each shoulder of it to a well ; and most of Hector's
men being armed with axes and two-edged swords, they
had eut off so many heads in that small space, that, tum-

bling down the slope to the well, nineteen heads were counted in it ; and to this day the well is called "Tobar nan Ceann," or the Fountain of the Heads. The other incident is that one, nicknamed "Suarachan," otherwise better known as "Donnchadh Mor na Tuaighe," or Big Duncan of the Axe, previously referred to, pursued one of the enemy into the Church of Dingwall, to which he had fled for shelter. As he was entering in at the door, Suarachan caught him by the arm, when the man exclaimed, "My sanctuary saves me!" "Aye," returned Suarachan, "but what a man puts in the sanctuary against his will he can take it out again;" and so, pushing him back from the door, he killed him with one stroke of his broadsword.*

Sir William Munro returned that night to Fowlis, where happened to be, passing the evening, a harper of the name of MacRa, who, observing Sir William very pensive and dispirited, advised him to be more cheerful and submit patiently to the fortunes of war, since his defeat was not his own fault, nor from want of personal courage and bravery, but arose from the timorousness of his followers, who were unacquainted with such severe service. This led Sir William to take more particular notice of the harper than he had hitherto done, and he asked him his name. On hearing it, Munro replied, "You surely must have been fortunate, as your name imports, and I am sure that you have been more so than I have been this day ; but it's fit to take your advice, MacRath." This was a play on the minstrel's name—Mac-Rath literally meaning "Son of Fortune"—and the harper being, like most of his kind, smart and sagacious, made the following impromptu answer :—

> Eachainn le sheachd fichead fear,
> Agus thusa le d' ochd ciad,
> Se Mac Rath a mharbh na daoine
> Air hathaois Cnoc faireal.

Which may be rendered in English as follows :—

---

* MS. History by the Earl of Cromartie.

Although MacRath doth "fortunate" import,
It's he deserves that name whose brave effort
Eight hundred men did put to flight
With his seven score at Knockfarrel.*

In 1499, George, Earl of Huntly, the King's Lieutenant,
granted a warrant to Duncan Mackintosh of Mackintosh,
John Grant of Freuchie, and other leaders, with three thousand men, to pass against the Clan Mackenzie, "the King's
rebels," for the slaughter of Harold of Chisholm, dwelling
in Strathglass, "and for divers other heirschips, slaughters,
spuilzies, committed on the King's poor lieges and tenants
in the Lordship of Ardmeanoch,"† but Hector Roy and his
followers gave a good account of them, and soon defeated
and dispersed them. He seems to have held undisturbed
possession until the year 1507, when John and his brother
Roderick were on a visit in the Aird, at the house of
their uncle, Lord Lovat, when a fire broke out at the
castle. According to the Earl of Cromartie, when the
house took fire, no one was found bold enough to approach
the burning pile but John, who rushed boldly through
the flames and carried away the Lovat charter chest, "a
weight even then thought too much for the strongest man,
and that cheist, yett extant, is a load sufficient for two. His
uncle, bothe oblciged by the actione, and glad to sie such
strength and boldnes in the young man, desyred (him) to
do as much for himself as he haid done for him, and to discover his (own) charter cheist from his uncle, and that he
should have all the concurrance which he (Lovat) could
give to that effect." Anderson's "History of the Family
of Fraser" ascribes this bold act to Roderick, for which
he was "considered amply recompensed by the gift
of a bonnet and a pair of shoes." It matters little which is
the correct version, but probably Lovat's valuable charter
chest was saved by one or other of them, and it is by
no means improbable that his Lordship's suggestion that
they should procure their own charter chest and his offer to
aid them in doing so were made on this occasion.

* Ardintoul MS.   † Kilravock Papers, p. 170.

John, who had proved himself extremely prudent, even in his youth, was satisfied that his uncle Hector, a man of proved valour and wisdom, in possession of the estates, and highly popular with the clan, could not be expelled without great difficulty and extreme danger to himself. Any such attempt would produce feuds and slaughter among his people, with the certain result of making himself personally unpopular with the clan, and his uncle more popular than ever. John therefore decided, upon what turned out a more prudent course; resolving to strike only at Hector's person, judging that, if his uncle failed, his claims and the personal respect of his followers would fall with him. To carry out his resolution, he concocted a scheme which proved completely successful. He had an interview with Hector, who then resided at Wester Fairburn, and pleaded that since he had taken his estates from him, and left him in such reduced circumstances, it was not in accordance with his feelings and his ambition for fame to remain any longer in his native country, where he had neither position nor opportunities to distinguish himself. He therefore begged that his uncle should give him a galley or birlinn, and as many of the ablest and most determined youths in the country as should voluntarily follow him in his adventures for fame and fortune in a foreign land. With these he would pass to Ireland, then engaged in war, and " there purchase a glorious death or a more plentiful fortune than he was likely to get at home." The idea pleased Hector exceedingly, who not only gave him his own birlinn or galley, then lying at Torridon, but furnished him with all the necessary provisions for the voyage, at the same time assuring him that, if he prosecuted his intentions, he should annually transmit him a sufficient portion to keep up his position, until his own personal prowess and fortune should place him above any such necessity; whereas, if he had otherwise resolved or attempted to molest him in what he called his rights, he would bring sudden and certain ruin upon himself. Thirty brave and resolute young men joined the supposed adventurer, after he had informed them that

he would have none except those who would do so of their
own free will, from their affection for him, and determination to support him in any emergency; for he well judged
that only such were suitable companions in the desperate
aims which he had laid out for himself to accomplish.
These he dispatched with the galley to Torridon, one of
the most secluded glens on the West Coast, and distant
from any populated place; while he himself remained with
his uncle, professedly to arrange the necessary details of
his journey, and the transmission of his portion, but really
to notice "his method and manner of converse." John soon
took farewell of Hector, and departed with every appearance of simplicity. His uncle sent a retinue to convoy him
with becoming respect, but principally to assure himself of
his nephew's departure, and to guard against surprise or
design on John's part. Accompanied by these, he soon
arrived at Torridon, where he found his thirty fellow adventurers and the galley awaiting him. They at once set
sail, and with a fair wind made for the Isles, in the direction
of, and as if intending to make for, Ireland. The retinue
sent by Hector Roy now returned home, and informed
their master that they saw John and his companions started
before a fair wind, with sails set, in the direction of Ireland,
when Hector exclaimed, referring to Anne of Lovat, "We
may now sleep without fear of Anne's children."

John, sailing down Loch Torridon, and judging that
Hector's men had returned home, made for a sheltered and
isolated creek; landed in a wood; and dispersed his men
with instructions to go by the most private and unfrequented
paths in the direction of Allt Corrienarnich, in the Braes of
Torridon, where he would meet them. This done, they
followed Hector's men, being quite close behind them by
the time they reached Fairburn. John halted at some little
distance from Hector's house until about midnight, when,
calling his men together, he feelingly addressed them thus:—
"Now, my good friends, I perceive that you are indeed
affectionate to me, and resolute men, who have freely for-
saken your country and relations to share in my not very

promising fortune ; but my design in seeking only such as would voluntarily go along with me was that I might be certain of your affection and resolution, and since you are they whom I ought only to rely upon in my present circum-stances and danger, I shall now tell you that I was never so faint-hearted as to quit my inheritance without attempting what is possible for any man in my capacity. In order to this I feigned this design for Ireland for three reasons : first, to put my uncle in security, whom I have found ever hitherto very circumspect and well guarded ; next, to find out a select, faithful number to whom I might trust ; and thirdly, that in case I fail, and that my uncle shall prevail over my endeavours, that I might have this boat and these provisions as a safe retreat, both for myself and you, whom I should be loath to expose to so great a danger without some probability in the attempt, and some security in the disappointment. I am resolved this night to fall on my uncle ; for he being gone, there is none of his children who dare hope to repone themselves to his place. The country-men who now, for fear, depend on him and disown me, will, no doubt, on the same motives, promoved with my just title, own me against all other injurious pretenders. One thing I must require of you, and it is that albeit those on whom we are to fall are all related both to you and to me, yet since on their destruction depends the preservation of our lives, and the restitution of my estate, you must all promise not to give quarter to my uncle or to any of his company."

To this horrid resolution they all agreed, disregarding the natural ties of blood and other obligations, and, marching as quietly as possible, they arrived at Hector's house, sur-rounded, and set fire to it—guarding it all round so that not a soul could escape. The house was soon in flames, and the inmates, Hector and his household, were crying out for mercy. Their pitiful cries made an impression on those outside, for many of them had relatives within, and in spite of their previous resolution to give no quarter, some of them called out to their nearest friends to come out and surrender, on assurance of their lives being spared. John,

seeing so many of his followers moved to this merciful conduct, and being unable to resist them, exclaimed, " My uncle
is as near in blood to me as any in the house are to you,
and therefore I will be as kind to him as you are to them.'
He then called upon Hector to surrender and come forth from
the burning pile, assuring him of his life. This he did; but
Donald Dubh MacGillechriost mhic Gillereach, a Kenlochewe man, made for the door with his two-edged sword drawn,
whereupon Hector seeing him he called out to John that
he would rather be burned where he was than face Donald
Dubh. John called the latter away, and Hector rushed out
into his nephew's arms and embraced him. That very same
night John and Hector, without "Dysman," saving God and
such commons as were then present, agreed and condescended that Hector should have the estate till John were
twenty-one years of age, and that John should live on his
own purchases till then. Hector was to set the whole estate
immediately, as tutor to John, which upon the morrow he
went about. " I cannot forget what passed betwixt him and
the foresaid Donald at the set of Kenlochewe, who was one
of the first that sought land from him, which when he
sought, Hector says to him : ' I wonder, Donald, how you
can ask land this day, that was so forward to kill me the
last day.' Donald answered that ' if he had such a leader
this day as he had that night he should show him no better
quarters, for Kenneth's death (meaning Kenneth Aack) struck
nearer my heart than any prejudice you can do me in denying
me land this day.' Hector said, ' Well, Donald, I doubt ye
not if you had such coildghys (coldhaltas=fosterage) to me
as you had to that man but you would act the like for me.
Therefore, you shall have your choice of all the land in the
country.' Hector having set the whole estate as tutor, all
things seemed fair, only that Allan and his faction in Kintail,
who previously urged John to possess himself of Islandonain
Castle, were not satisfied with the arrangement, as John
was still kept out of the stronghold, ' which Hector would
not grant, not being condescended on (and as he alleidged)
lest John should faill on his part ; but the factions—the

commons—within that country could not be satisfied herewith, being, as it was said, moved hereto by ane accident
that fell out a year or two before.'"* This "accident" is
described further on, and refers to Hector's reputed attempt
to get Allan out of the way at Inversheal. .

Donald Dubh was Kenneth Og's foster-brother, and
imagining that Hector was accessory in an underhand
manner to Kenneth's captivity in Edinburgh Castle, and
consequently to his death in the Torwood, he conceived an
inveterate hatred for Hector, and determined to kill him
in revenge the first opportunity that presented itself.
Hector, knowing that his resolution proceeded from fidelity
and affection to his foster-brother and master, not only forgave him, but ultimately took an opportunity to reward
him ; and, as we have seen, afterwards gave him his choice
of all Kenlochewe.

John immediately sent word of what had taken place to
his uncle of Lovat, and next day marched for Kintail, where
all the people there, as well as in the other parts of his
property, recognised him as their chief. The Castle of
Islandonain was delivered up to him, with the charter
chest and other evidence of his extensive possessions.

It has been maintained by the family of Gairloch that
there is no truth in the charge against their ancestor, Hector
Roy, which we have given above mainly on the authority of the
Earl of Cromartie. The writer of the Ardintoul MS. of the
Mackenzies,† however, corroborates him, and says that John
"was but young when his father died ; and Hector, his younger
uncle (Duncan, Hector's eldest brother, who should be tutor
being dead, and Allan, Duncan's son, not being able to oppose or grapple with Hector), meddled with the estate. It
is reported that Hector wished Allan out of the way, whom
he thought only to stand in his way from being laird, since
he was resolved not to own my Lord Lovat's daughter's
children, being all bastards and· gotten in adultery. The

* Ancient MS.
† Dr George Mackenzie gives substantially the same account,

reason why they entertained such thoughts of him was partly
this: Hector going to Islandonain (where he placed Malcolm
MacEancharrich constable) called such of the country
people to him as he judged fit, under pretence of setting
and settling the country, but asked not for, nor yet called
his nephew Allan, who lived at Inversheal, within a few
miles of Islandonain, but went away. Allan, suspecting this
to have proceeded from unkindness, sends to one of his
familiar friends to know the result of the meeting, or if
there was any spoken concerning him. The man, perhaps,
not being willing to be an ill instrument 'twixt so near relations, sends Allan the following Irish lines :—

> Inversheala na struth bras,
> Tar as, 's fear foill ga d' fheitheamh,
> Nineag, ga caol a cas,
> Tha leannan aice gun fhios,
> A tighinn ga'm fhaire a shios,
> Tha i, gun fhios, fo mo chrios
> Tha 'n sàr lann ghuilbneach ghlas,—
> Bheirinn urchair dha le fios.

Allan put his own construction on them, and thought a
friend warned him to have a care of himself, there being
some designs on him from a near relation ; and so that very
night, in the beginning thereof, he removed himself and
family and anything he valued within the house to an hill
above the town, where he might see and hear anything that
might befall the house ; and that same night about cock
crow he saw his house and biggings in flames, and found
them consumed to ashes on the morrow. The perpetrators
could not be found ; yet it was generally thought to be
Hector his uncle's contrivance."

The writer describes the legitimation of Agnes Fraser's
children by the Pope, and continues, " Hector, notwithstanding of the legitimation, refused to quit the possession of the
estate," and he then gives the same account of John's feigned
expedition to Ireland, and the burning of Hector's house at
Wester Fairburn, substantially as given above from another
source, but adding—" That very night they both entered
upon terms of agreement without acquainting or sending for

any, or to advise a reconciliation betwixt them. The sum of their agreement was, that Hector, as a man able to rule and govern, should have (allowing John an aliment) the estate for five or six years, till John should be major, and that thereafter Hector should render it to John as the right and lawful undoubted heir, and that Hector should ever afterwards acknowledge and honour him as his chief, and so they parted, all being well pleased.* But Allan and the most of the Kintail men were dissatisfied that John did not get Islandonan, his principal house, in his own possession, and so desired John to come to them and possess the castle by fair or foul means wherein they promised to assist him. John goes to Kintail, desires him to render the place to him, which he refused, for which cause John ordered bring all his cattle to those he employed to besiege the castle till Malcolm (the governor) would be starved out of it. Yet this did not prevail with the governor, till he got Hector's consent, who, being acquainted, came to Lochalsh and met with his nephew, and after concerting the matter, Hector sends word to Malcolm to render the place to John. But Malcolm would not till he would be paid of his goods that were destroyed. But Hector sending to him the second time, after considerable negotiation for several days, telling him he was a fool, that he might remember how himself was used, and that that might be a means to take his life also. Whereupon Malcolm renders the house, but John was so much offended at him that he would not continue him governor, but gave the charge to Gillechriost Mac Fhionnla Mhic Rath, making him Constable of the Isle. So after that there was little or no debate twixt John and Hector during the rest of the six years he was Tutor."†

The various MSS. Histories of the family are to some extent borne out by Gregory,‡ who informs us

---

* John and Hector did condescend that Hector should have the estate till John were one and twentie years, and that John should live on his own purchase till then.—*Letterfcarn MS.*

† Ardintoul and Ancient MSS. of the Mackenzies,

‡ Highlands and Isles of Scotland, p. 111.

that "Hector Roy Mackenzie, progenitor of the House
of Gairloch, had, since the death of Kenneth Oig Mackenzie
of Kintail, in 1497, and during the minority of John, the
brother and heir of Kenneth, exercised the command of
that clan, nominally as guardian to the young chief. Under
his rule the Clan Mackenzie became involved in feuds with
the Munroes and other clans, and Hector Roy himself became obnoxious to Government as a disturber of the public
peace. His intentions towards the young Lord of Kintaill
were considered very dubious; and the apprehensions of
the latter having been roused, Hector was compelled by
law to yield up the estate and the command of the tribe to
the proper heir." Gregory gives the "Acts of the Lords of
Council, xxii., fo. 142," as that upon which, among other
authorities, he founds. We are enabled to place the following extract from these before the reader; and except that
the spelling is so far modernised as to make it intelligible
to the ordinary reader, it is as follows :—"7th April 1511.—
Anent the summons made at the instance of John Mackenzie of Kintail against Hector Roy Mackenzie for the
wrongous intromitting, uptaking, and withholding from him
of the mails 'fermez,' profits, and duties of all and whole
the lands of Kintail, with the pertinents lying in the Sherrif-
dom of Inverness, for the space of seven years together,
beginning in the year of God 1501, and also for the space
of two years, last bye-past, and for the masterful withholding from the said John Mackenzie of his house and Castle
of Eleandonain, and to bring with him his evidence if (he)
any has of the constabulary and keeping thereof, and to
hear the same deemed of none avail, and diverse other
points like as at more length is contained in the said summons, the said John Mackenzie being personally present,
and the said Hector Roy being lawfully summoned to this
action, oft-times called and not compearing, the said John's
rights, &c. The Lords of Council decree and deliver, that
the said Hector has forfeited the keeping and constabulary
of the said Castle of Eleandonain, together with the fees
granted therefor, and decern all evidents, if he any has

made to him thereupon, of none avail, force, nor effect, and the said John Mackenzie to have free ingress and entry to the said Castle, because he required the said Hector for deliverance thereof and to thole him to enter thereunto, howbeit the said Hector refused and would not give him entry to the said Castle, bot gif his servants would have delivered their happinnis from them to his men er their entries, like as one actentit instrument taken thereupon shown and produced before the said Lords purported and bore, and therefore ordains our sovereign Lords' letters (to) be directed to devode and rid the said Castle and to keep the said John in possession thereof as effeirs and continues the remanent points contained in the said summons in form, as they are now, unto the 20th day of July next to come, with continuation of days, and ordains that letters be written in form of commission to the Sheriff of Inverness and his deputies to summon witnesses and take probations thereupon, and to summon the party to hear them sworn and thereafter send their depositions closed to the Lords again, the said day, under the said Sheriff's or his Deputy's seal, that thereafter justice may be ministered thereuntill."

Whatever truth there may be in the accounts given by the family historians, Hector Roy was undoubtedly at this period possessed of considerable estates of his own ; for, we find a "protocol," by John Vass, "Burges of Dygvayll, and Shireff in this pairt," by which he makes known that, by the command of his sovereign lord, letters and process was directed to him as Sheriff, granting him, to give Hector Mackenzie heritable state and possession "of all and syndri the landis off Gerloch, with thar pertinens, after the forme and tenor off our soucrane lordis chartyr maide to the for-saide Hector," lying between the waters called Inverew and Torridon. The letter is dated "At Alydyll (? Talladale) the xth of the moneth off December the yher off Gode ane thousande four hundreth nynte and four yheris."

It is quite clear that Hector did not long continue under a cloud ; for in 1508 the King directed a man-date to the Chamberlain of Ross, requesting him to

enter Hector Roy Mackenzie in the "males and pro-
ffitis of our landis of Braane and Moy, with ariage,
cariage and vther pertinence tharcof . . . . for his
gude and thankfull service done and to be done to us .
. . and this on na wise ye leif vndone, as ye will incur
our indignatioun and displesour. This our letrez . . .
efter the forme of our said vther letres past obefor, given
vnder our signet at Edinburgh the fift day of Marche and
of Regne the twenty yere.—(Signed) James R." In 1513
he received a charter under the great seal of the lands of
Gairloch formerly granted him, with Glasletter and Coru-
guellen, with their pertinents.* Hector Roy's conduct towards John has been unfavourably criticised, but if we keep
in mind that no regular marriage ever took place between
Kenneth a Bhlair and John's mother, Agnes of Lovat ; that
their union was not recognised by the Church until
1491, the same year in which Kenneth died; we can
quite understand why Hector should conscientiously do
what he probably considered his duty—oppose John of
Killin in the interest of those whom he considered the
legitimate successors of Kenneth a Bhlair and his unfortunate son, Kenneth Og, to whom only, so far as we can discover, Hector Roy was appointed Tutor, for when his
brother, Kenneth a Bhlair, died, there was every appearance
that Hector's ward, Kenneth Og, would succeed when he
came of age. The succession of John of Killin was at most
only a remote possibility when his father died, and no
Tutor to him would be appointed. Meanwhile further consideration of this question must be left until we come to
treat of the history of the House of Gairloch.

In terms of an Act passed in 1496, anent the education of young gentlemen of note, John, when young, was sent
by Hector Roy to Edinburgh to complete his education at
Court. He thus, in early life, acquired a knowledge of legal

* The original charter ; the " protocol " from John Vass; the mandate to the
Chamberlain of Ross ; and various other documents, for copies of which we are
indebted to Sir Kenneth S. Mackenzie, Baronet, are in the Gairloch Charter
Chest.

principles and practice of great service and value to him in after life, not only in the management of his own affairs, but in aiding his friends and countrymen in their peculiar difficulties by his counsel and guidance, and thus he secured such universal esteem and confidence as seldom fell to the lot of a Highland Chief in that rude and unruly age. The standard of education necessary at Court in those days must have been very different from that required in ours, for we find that, with all his opportunities, John of Killin could not write his name. To a bond in favour of the Earl of Huntly he subscribes, "Jhone M'Kenze of Kyntaill, with my hand on the pen led by Master William Gordone, Notar."

Referring to the power of the House of Kintail at this period, and to the rapid advance made by the family under Alexander and his successor, we quote the following from a modern MS. history of the family*:—" We must observe here the rapid advance which the family of Kintail made on every side. The turbulent Macdonalds, crushed by the affair of Park, Munro, sustained by his own Clan, and the neighbouring vassals of Ross humbled at their own door, when a century had not yet passed since the name of Mackenzie had become familiar to their ears; and it is gratifying to trace all this to the wise policy of the first James and his successors. The judicious education of Alastair Ionraic, and consequent cultivation of those habits which, by identifying the people with the monarch through the laws, render a nation securely great, is equally discernible in John of Killin and his posterity. The successors of the Earls of Ross were turbulent and tenacious of their rights, but they were irreclaimable. The youthful Lord of the Isles, at the instigation of his haughty mother, deserted the Court of James I., while young Kintail remained, sedulously improving himself at school in Perth, till he was called to display his gratitude to his Royal master in counteracting the evil arising from the opposite conduct of Macdonald. Thus, by one happy circumstance, the attention of the King

* By the late Captain John Matheson of Bennetsfield.

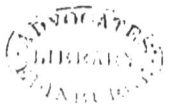

was called to a chieftain, who gave such early promise of
steady attachment, and his future favour was secured. The
family of Kintail was respectably recognised in the Calendar
of the Scottish Court, while that of the once proud Macdonalds frowned in disappointment and barbarous independence amidst their native wilds, while their territories, extending beyond the bounds of good government and protection, presented, gradually, such defenceless gaps as became inviting, and easily penetrable by the intelligence of ·
Mackenzie, and Alastair Ionraic acquired a great portion
of his estates by this legitimate advantage, afterwards
secured by the intractable arrogance of Macdonald of
Lochalsh and the valour and military capacity of Coinneach
a Bhlair."

In 1513 John of Killin is found among those Highland
Chiefs summoned to rendezvous with the Royal army at
Barron Moor preparatory to the fatal advance of James IV.
into England, when the Mackenzies, forming with the Macleans, joined that miserably-arranged and ill-fated expedition which terminated so fatally to Scotland on the disastrous
field of Flodden, where the killed included the King, with
the flower of his nobility, gentry, and even clergy. There
was scarcely a Scottish family of distinction that did not lose
at least one, and some of them lost all the male members
who were capable of bearing arms. The body of the King was
found, much disfigured with wounds, in the thickest of the
slain.   Abercromby, on the authority of Crawford, includes,
in a list of those killed at Flodden, "Kenneth Mackenzie of
Kintail, ancestor to the noble family of Seaforth." This
is an undoubted error ; for it will be seen that John, not
Kenneth, was chief at the time of Flodden.   It was he
who joined the Royal army, accompanied by his brave and
gallant uncle, Hector Roy of Gairloch ; and it is established
beyond dispute that though almost all their followers fell,
both John and Hector returned home. They, however, narrowly escaped the charge of Sir Edward Stanley in rear of
the Highlanders during their disorderly pursuit of Sir
Edward Howard, who had given way to the furious and

gallant onset of the mountaineers. The Chief, John of Killin, was made prisoner, but he afterwards escaped in a very remarkable manner. When his captors were carrying him and others of his followers to the south, they were overtaken by a violent storm which obliged them to seek shelter in a retired house occupied by the widow of a shipmaster. After taking up their quarters, and, as they thought, providing for the safe custody of the prisoners, the woman noticed that their captives were Highlanders ; and, in reference to the boisterous weather raging outside, she, as if unconsciously, exclaimed, " The Lord help those who are to-night travelling on Leathad Leacachan." The prisoners were naturally astonished to hear this allusion, in such a place, to a mountain so familiar to them in the North Highlands, and they soon obtained an opportunity, which she appeared most anxious to afford them, of questioning her regarding her acquaintance with so distant a place; when she told them that during a sea voyage she took with her husband, she had been taken so ill aboard ship, that it was found necessary to send her ashore on the north-west coast of Scotland, where, travelling with only a maid and a single guide, they were caught in a severe storm, and she was suddenly taken in labour. In this distressing and trying predicament a Highlander passing by took compassion upon her, and seeing her case so desperate, with no resources at hand, he, with remarkable presence of mind, killed one of his horses, ripped open his belly, and taking out the bowels, placed her and the newly-born infant in their place, as the only effectual shelter from the storm. By this means he secured sufficient time to procure female assistance, and ultimately saved herself and her child.

But the most remarkable part of the story remains to be told. The same person to whom she owed her preservation was at that moment one of the captives under her roof. He was one of Kintail's followers on the fatal field of Flodden. She, informed of his presence and of the plight he was in, managed to procure a private interview with him, when he amply proved to her, by more detailed reference

to the incidents of their meeting on Leathad Leacachan,
that he was the same man—"Uisdean Mor Mac 'Ille Phad-
raig"—and in gratitude, she, at the serious risk of her own
personal safety, successfully planned the escape of Hugh's
master and his whole party. The story is given on uninterrupted tradition in the country of the Mackenzies; and
a full and independent version of the hero's humane proceedings on Leathad Leacachan will be found in the
Celtic Magazine, vol. ii., pp. 468-9, to which the Gaelic
reader is referred.

"Tradition has preserved a curious anecdote," says
Gregory, p. 112, "connected with the Mackenzies, whose
young chief, John of Kintail, was taken prisoner at Flodden.
It will be recollected that Kenneth Oig Mackenzie of Kintail, while on his way to the Highlands, after making his
escape from Edinburgh Castle, was killed in the Torwood
by the laird of Buchanan. The foster-brother of Kenneth
Oig was a man of the district of Kenlochew, named Donald
Dubh MacGillecrist vic Gillercoch, who with the rest of the
clan were at Flodden with his chief. In the retreat of the
Scottish army this Donald Dubh heard some one near him
exclaiming, 'Alas, Laird! thou hast fallen.' On enquiry,
he was told it was the Laird of Buchanan who had sunk
from his wounds or exhaustion. The faithful Highlander,
eager to revenge the death of his chief and foster-brother,
drew his sword, and, saying, 'If he has not fallen he shall
fall,' made straight to Buchanan, whom he killed on the
spot."

As to the safe return of John of Kintail and Hector Roy
to their Highland home, after this calamitous event, there is
now no question whatever; for we find John was, among
others, afterwards appointed, by Act of Council, a lieutenant or guardian of Wester Ross,[*] to protect it from Sir
Donald Macdonald of Lochalsh, when he proclaimed himself
Lord of the Isles. In 1515, Mackenzie, without legal warrant, seized the royal castle of Dingwall, but professed

* Gregory, p. 115. Acts of Lords of Council, xxvi., fo. 25.

his readiness to give it to any one appointed by the Regent, John, Duke of Albany.* In 1532 we find him included in a commission by James V. for suppressing a disorderly tribe of Mackintoshes. He secured the esteem of this monarch so much that he appointed him a Privy Councillor.

To put the question of John's return beyond question, and to show how the family rose so rapidly in influence and power during his rule, we shall quote the following from the "Origines Parochiales Scotiæ," from which it will also be seen that Kenneth, his heir, received considerable grants for himself during his father's lifetime :—"In 1509 King James IV. granted to John Makkenze of Keantalle (the brother of Kenneth Oig) the 40 marklands of Keantalle —namely, the davach of Cumissaig, the davach of Letterfearn, the davach of Gleanselle, the davach of Glenlik, the davach of Letterchall, the two davachs of Croo, and three davachs between the water of Keppach and the water of Lwying, with the castle and fortalice of Eleandonnan, in the earldom of Ross and sheriffdom of Innernis, with other lands in Ross, which John had resigned, and which the King then erected into the barony of Eleandonnan.† In 1530 King James V. granted to James Grant of Freuchy and Johne Mckinze of Kintale liberty to go to any part of the realm on their lawful business.‡ In 1532, 1538, and 1540, the same John M'Kenich of Kintaill appears in record.§ In 1542, King James V. granted to John Mckenzie of Kintaill the waste lands of Monar, lying between the water of Glencak on the north, the top or summit of Landovir on the south, the torrent of Towmuk and Inchclochill on the east, and the water of Bernis running into the water of Long on the west ; and also the waste lands of lie Ned lying between Loch Boyne on the north, Loch Tresk on the south, lie Ballach on the west, and Dawclach on the

* Acts of Lords of Council, xxvii., fo. 60.

† Reg. Mag. Sig., lib. xv., No. 89. Gregory, p. 83.

‡ Reg. Sec. Sig., vol. viii., fol. 140.

§ Reg. Sec. Sig., vol. ix., fol. 3 ; vol. xii., fol. 21 ; vol. xiv., fol. 32.

cast, in the carldom of Ross and sheriffdom of Inncres—
lands which were never in the King's rental, and never
yielded any revenue—for the yearly payment of £4 to the
King as Earl of Ross.* In 1543 Queen Mary granted to
Kenneth Mackenzie of Kintaill, and Isabel Stewart, his
wife, the lands of Auchnaccyric, Lakachanc, Strome-nc-
mowklach, Kilkinternc, the two Rateganis, Torlousicht,
Auchnashellicht, Auchnagart, Auchewranc, lie Knokfreith,
Aucharskclanc, and Malcgane, in the lordship of Kintaill;
and other lands in Ross, extending in all to 36 marks,
which he had resigned.† In 1551 the same Queen granted
to John M'Kenze of Kintaill, and Kenzeoch M'Kenze, his
son and apparent heir, a remission for the violent taking of
John Hectour M'Kenzesone of Garlouch, Doull Hectoursone, and John Towach Hectoursone, and for keeping them
in prison 'vsurpand thairthrou our Soucrane Ladyis autorite.'‡ In 1554 there appear in record John Mackenzie of
Kintaile and his son and heir-apparant, Kenneth Mackenzie
of Brahan—apparently the same persons that appear in
1551.§

Donald Gorm Mor Macdonald of Sleat laid waste the
country of Macleod of Dunvegan, an ally of Mackenzie,
after which he passed over in 1539 to the mainland and
pillaged the lands of Kenlochewe, where he killed Miles or
Maolmuire, son of Finlay Dubh MacGillechriost MacRath
at the time governor of Islandonain Castle. Finlay was
a very "pretty man," and the writer of the Genealogy of
the Macras informs us that "the remains of a monument
erected for him, in the place where he was killed, is still
(1704) to be seen." Kintail was naturally much exasperated at this unprovoked raid upon his territory, as also
for Macdonald's attack upon his friend and ally, Macleod of
Dunvegan; and to punish Donald Gorm, he dispatched
his son, Kenneth, with a force to Skye, who made ample

* Reg. Mag. Sig., lib. xxviii., No. 417.
† Reg. Mag. Sig., lib. xxviii., No. 524.   Reg. Sec. Sig., vol. xvii., fol. 56.
‡ Reg. Sec. Sig., vol. xxiv., fol. 75.
§ Reg. Mag. Sig., lib. xxxii., No. 211.

reprisals in Macdonald's country, killing many of his followers, and at the same time exhibiting great intrepidity and
sagacity. Donald Gorm almost immediately made an
incursion into Mackenzie's territories of Kintail, where he
killed Sir (Rev.) Dougald Mackenzie, "one of the Pope's
knights"; whereupon Kenneth, younger of Kintail, paid a
second visit to the Island, wasted the country; and on his
return, Macdonald learning that Islandonain was garrisoned
by a very weak force, under the new governor, John Dubh
Matheson of Fernaig,—who had married Sir Dugald Mackenzie's widow—he made another raid upon it, with fifty
birlinns or large boats full of his followers, with the intention of surprising the small garrison, and taking the castle
by storm. The gallant defenders consisted at the time
of only the governor, his watchman, and Duncan Mac-
Gilléchriost MacFhionnladh MhicRath, a nephew of Maolmuire killed in the last incursion of the Island Chief. The
advance of the boats was, however, noticed in time by the
sentinel or watchman, who at once gave the alarm to the
country people, but they arrived too late to prevent the
enemy from landing. Duncan MacGillechriost was on the
mainland at the time; but, flying back with all speed, he
arrived at the postern of the stronghold in time to kill
several of the Islesmen in the act of landing; and, entering the castle, he found no one there but the governor
and watchman; almost immediately, Donald Gorm Mor
furiously attacked the gate, but without success, the brave
trio having strongly secured it by a second barrier of
iron within a few steps of the outer defences. Unable to
procure access, the Islesmen were driven to the expedient
of shooting their arrows through the embrazures, and in
this way they succeeded in killing the governor.

Duncan now found himself, except the watchman, sole
defender of the castle; and worse still, he found his ammunition reduced to a single barbed arrow, which he
wisely determined to husband until an opportunity occurred
by which he could make good use of it. Macdonald at this
stage ordered his boats round to the point of the Airds, and

was personally reconnoitring with the view of discovering the weakest part of the wall wherein to effect a breach. Duncan considered this a favourable opportunity, and aiming his arrow at Donald Gorm, it struck him and penetrated his foot through the master vein. Macdonald, not having perceived that the arrow was a barbed one, instantly wrenched it out, and in so doing separated the main artery. Notwithstanding that every available means were used, it was found impossible to stop the bleeding, and his men conveyed him out of the range of the fort to a spot—a sand bank—on which he died, called to this day, " Larach Tigh Mhic Dhomhnuill," or the site of Macdonald's house, where the haughty Lord of Sleat ended his career.* The Islesmen burnt all they could find ashore in Kintail, which is confirmed by the following :—" In 1539 Donald Gorm of Sleat and his allies, after laying waste Trouterness in Sky and Kenlochew in Ross, attempted to take the Castle of Eileandonan, but Donald being killed by an arrow shot from the wall, the attempt failed."† In 1541 King James V. granted a remission to Donald's accomplices—namely, Archibald Ilis, *alias* Archibald the Clerk, Alexander McConnell Gallich, John Dow Donaldsoun, and twenty-six others whose names will be found in the " Origines Parochiales," p. 394, vol. ii., for their treasonable fire-raising and burning of the " Castle of Allanedonnand" and of the boats there, for the "Herschip" of Kenlochew and Trouteness, &c.

Duncan MacGillechriost now naturally thought that he had some claim to succeed as governor of the castle, but being considered "a man more bold and rash than

* Genealogy of the MacRas and the Ardintoul MS. "This Donald Gorme was son to Donald Gruamach, son to Donald Gealach, son to Hugh, natural son to Alexander, Earl of Ross, for which the elegy made on his death calls him grand-child and great-grandchild to Rhi-Fingal (King Fingal)—

> A Dhonnchaidh Mhic Gillechriost Mhic Fhionnla,
> 'S mor am houd a thuit led' aon laimh,
> Ogha 's iar-ogha Mhic Righ Fhinghaill,
> 'Thuiteam le bramag an aon mhic."

—*Letterfearn MS.*

† Gregory, pp. 145-146. Border Minstrelsy. Anderson, p. 283. Reg. Sec. Sig., vol. xv., fol. 46.

prudent and politick," Mackenzie decided to pass him over. Duncan then put in a claim for his brother Farquhar, but it was thought best, to avoid local quarrels and bitterness between the respective claimants, to pass them all over and appoint another, John MacMhurchaidh Dhuibh, priest of Kintail, to the constableship of Islandonain. Duncan was so much offended at this treatment in return for such excellent service that he, in disgust, left Kintail and went to the country of Lord Lovat, who received him kindly, and gave him the lands of Crochel and others in Strath-glass, where he lived for several years, until Lovat's death. Mackenzie, however, often visited him, and finally prevailed upon him to return to Kintail, and Duncan, who always re-tained a lingering affection for his native country, ultimately became reconciled to Mackenzie, who gave him the quarter-land of Little Inverinate and Dorisduan, where he lived the remainder of his days, and which his descendants continued to possess for generations after his death.

For this service against the Macdonalds, King James V. gave Mackenzie Kinchulidrum, Achilty, and Comery in feu, with Meikle Scatwell, under the great seal, in 1528. The lands of Laggan Achidrom, being four merks, the three merks of Killianan, and the four merk lands of Invergarry, being in the King's hand, were disposed by him to John Mackenzie, after the King's minority and revocation, in 1540, under the great seal, with a precept under the great seal and sasine thereupon by Sir John Robertson in January 1541. But before this, in 1521, he acquired the lands of Fodderty and mill thereof from Mr John Cadell, which King James V. confirmed to John Mackenzie at Linlithgow in September, in 1522. In 1541 he feued Brahan from the King to himself and his heirs male, which failing, to his eldest daughter. In 1542 he obtained the waste lands and forest of Neid and Monar from King James V., for which sasine is granted in the same year by Sir John Robertson. In January 1547 he acquired a wadset of the half of Culte-leod (Castle Leod) and Drynie from Denoon of David-ston. In September of the same year, old as he was, he

went in defence of his Sovereign, young Queen Mary, to
the unfortunate Battle of Pinkie, where he was taken prisoner; and the Laird of Kilravock meeting with him advised
him that they should own themselves among the commons,
Mackenzie passing off as a bowman, while Kilravock would
pass himself off as a miller, which plan succeeded so well as
to secure Kilravock his release; but the Earl of Huntly,
who was also a prisoner, having been conveyed by the Duke
of Somerset to view the prisoners, espying his old friend
Mackenzie among the common prisoners, and ignorant of
the plot, called him by his name, desiring that he might
shake hands with him, which civility two English officers
noticed to Mackenzie's disadvantage; for thenceforward he
was placed and guarded along with the other prisoners of
quality, but afterwards released for a considerable sum, to
which all his people contributed without burdening his own
estate with it,* so, returning home he set himself to arrange
his private affairs, and in the year 1556 he acquired the
heritage of Cultelcod and Drynie from Denoon, which was
confirmed to him by Queen Mary under the great seal, at
Inverness, 13th July of the same year. He had previously,
in 1544, acquired the other half of Cultelcod and Drynie
from Magnus Mowat, and Patrick Mowat of Bugholly.
In 1543 John Mackenzie acquired Kildins, part of Lochbroom, to himself, and Elizabeth Grant, his wife, holding
blench for a penny, and confirmed in the same year by
Queen Mary.†

In 1540 Mackenzie with his followers joined King James
at Loch Duich, while on his way with a large fleet to secure
good government in the Western Highlands and Isles,
upon which occasion many of the suspected and refractory
leaders were carried south and placed in confinement. His
Majesty died soon after, in 1542. Queen Mary succeeded,
and, being a minor, the country generally, but particularly
the northern parts, was thrown into a state of anarchy
and confusion.

---

* " He was ransomed by cows that was raised through all his lands."—
Letterfearn MS.

† MS. History by the Earl of Cromartie.

In 1544 the Earl of Huntly, holding a commission as Lieutenant of the North from the Queen Regent, Mary of Guise, commanded Kenneth Mackenzie, younger of Kintail (his father, from his advanced age, being unable to take the field), to raise his vassals and lead an expedition against the Clan Ranald of Moidart, who, at that time, held lands from Mackenzie on the West Coast; but Kenneth, who, in these circumstances, thought it would be much against his personal interests to attack Donald Glas of Moidart, refused to comply with Huntly's orders. To punish him for his contumacy, the Earl ordered his whole army, consisting of three thousand men, to proceed against both Moidart and Mackenzie with fire and sword, but he had not sufficiently calculated on the constitution of his force, which was composed chiefly of Grants, Rosses, Mackintoshes, and Chisholms; and Kenneth's mother being a daughter of John, then laird of Grant, and three of his daughters having married respectively Ross of Balnagown, Mackintosh of Mackintosh, and the Chisholm of Comar, Huntly found his followers as little disposed to molest Mackenzie as he had been to attack Donald Glas of Moidart. In addition to the friendly feelings of the other chiefs in favour of young Kintail, fostered by these family alliances, Huntly was not at all popular with his own followers, or with the Highlanders generally. He had incurred such odium for having some time before executed the Laird of Mackintosh, contrary to his solemn pledge, that it required little excuse on the part of the exasperated kindred tribes to counteract his plans, and on the slightest pretext to refuse to follow him. He was therefore obliged to retire from the West without effecting any substantial service; was ultimately disgraced; committed to Edinburgh Castle; compelled to renounce the Earldom of Moray and all his other possessions in the north; and sentenced to banishment in France for five years.

On the 13th December 1545, at Dingwall, the Earl of Sutherland entered into a bond of manrent with John Mackenzie of Kintail for mutual defence against all enemies,

reserving only their allegiance to their youthful Queen,
Mary Stuart.* Two years later the Earl of Arran sent the
fiery cross over the nation calling upon all between the ages
of sixteen and sixty to meet him at Musselburgh for the
protection of their infant Queen. Mackenzie of Kintail, at
the age of between sixty and seventy, when he might fairly
have considered himself exempt from further military service, duly appeared with all the followers he could muster,
prudently leaving his only son, Kenneth, at home ; and
when remonstrated with for joining in such a perilous
journey at his time of life, especially as he was far past the
stipulated age for active service, the old chief bravely and
patriotically remarked that one of his age could not possibly
die more decorously than in the defence of his country. In
the same year (1547) he fought bravely, as we have already
seen, at the head of his clan, with all the enthusiasm and
gallantry of his younger days, at the battle of Pinkie, where
he was wounded in the head and taken prisoner, but was
soon afterwards released, through the influence of the Earl of
Huntly, who had meanwhile again got into favour, received
a full pardon, and was appointed Chancellor.

The Earl of Huntly on one occasion paid a visit to
Ross, intending, if he were kindly received by the great
chiefs, to feu a part of the earldom of Ross, still in the
King's hands, and to live in the district for some period of
the year. Mackenzie, although friendly disposed towards
the Earl, had no desire to have him residing in his immediate neighbourhood, and he arranged a plan which had the
effect of deciding Huntly to give up any idea of remaining
or feuing any lands in Ross. The Earl, having obtained a
commission from the Regent to hold courts in the county,
came to the castle of Dingwall, where he invited the principal chiefs to meet him. John of Killin, though very advanced in years, was the first who arrived, and he was very
kindly received by Huntly. Mackenzie in return made a
pretence of heartily welcoming and congratulating his lord-

ship on his coming to Ross, and trusted that he would be the means of protecting himself and his friends from the violence of his son, Kenneth, who, taking advantage of his frailty and advanced years, was behaving most unjustly to him. He, indeed, expressed a hope that the Earl would punish Kenneth for his illegal and unnatural rebellion against his father. While they were thus speaking, a message came in that a large number of armed men, three or four hundred strong, with banners flying and pipes playing, were just in sight on the hill above Dingwall. The Earl became alarmed, not knowing whom they might be or what their object was, when Mackenzie informed him that it could be no other than his son Kenneth and his rebellious followers coming to punish him for paying his lordship this visit without his son's consent; and he advised the Earl to leave at once, as he was not strong enough to resist the enemy, and to take him (the old chief) along with him to protect him from Kenneth's violence, which would now, in consequence of this visit be directed against him more than ever. The Earl and his retinue at once made off to Easter Ross, when Kenneth ordered his men to pursue them. He overtook them as they were crossing the bridge of Dingwall and killed several of them; but having attained his object of frightening Huntly out of Ross, he ordered his men to desist. This skirmish is known as the "affair of Dingwall Bridge."*

In 1556 Y Mackay of Farr, progenitor of the Lords of Reay, refused to appear before the Queen Regent at Inverness, to answer serious charges made against him for depredations committed in Sutherlandshire; and she issued a commission to John, fifth Earl of Sutherland, to lay Mackay's country waste. Mackay, satisfied that he could not successfully oppose the Earl's forces in the field, pillaged and plundered another district of Sutherland. The Earl conveyed intelligence of how matters stood to John of Kintail, who, in terms of the bond of manrent previously

* Ardintoul MS.

H

entered into between them in 1545, instantly despatched his
son Kenneth with an able body of the clan to arrest Mackay's progress, which duty Mackenzie performed most effectually. Meeting Mackay at Brora, a severe contest ensued,
which terminated in the defeat of Mackay, with the loss of
Angus MacIain Mhoir, one of his chief commanders, and
many of his clan.   Kenneth Mackenzie was thereupon,
conjointly with his father, John, appointed by the Earl of
Sutherland, then the Queen's Lieutenant north of the Spey,
and Chamberlain of the Earldom of Ross,* his deputies in
the management of this vast property, at the same time
placing them in possession of Ardmeanoch, or Redcastle,
which remained ever since, until within a recent period,
in the possession of the family, becoming the property of
Kenneth's third son, Ruairidh Mor, first of the house of
· Redcastle, and progenitor of the family of Kincraig and
others.

After this, Kintail seems to have lived in peace during
the remainder of his long life and died at his house at
Inverchonan, in 1561, about eighty years of age. He was
buried in the family aisle at Beauly. That he was a man
of proved valour is fully established by the distinguished
part he took in the battles of Flodden and Pinkie ; and the
Earl of Cromarty informs us that, " in his time he purchased
much of the Brae-lands of Ross, and secured both what he
acquired and what his predecessors had, by well ordered
and legal security, so that it is doubtful whether his predecessors' courage or his prudence contributed most to the
rising of the family." In illustration of the latter qualtiy, we
shall quote the following curious story :—John Mackenzie
of Kintail "was a very great courtier and counsellor of
Queen Maries. Much of the lands of Brae Ross were
acquired by him, which minds me how he entertained the
Queen's Chamberlain who she sent North to learn the state
and condition of the gentry of Ross, minding to feu her
interest of that Earldome. Sir John, hearing of their com-

* Sir Robert Gordon, p. 134.

ing to his house of Killin, he caused his servants put
on a great fyre of ffresh arn wood newly cutt, which when
they came in (sitting on great jeasts of wood which he
caused sett there a purpose) made such a reek that they were
almost blinded, and were it not the night was so ill they
would rather goe than byde it. They had not long sitten
when his servants came in with a great bull, which presen-
ently they brained on the floor, and or they well could look
about, this fellow with his dirk, and that fellow with his,
were cutting collops of him. Then comes in another sturdie
lusty fellow with a great calderon in his hand, and ane axe
in the other, and with its shaft stroak each of these that
were cutting the collops, and then made Taylzies of it and
put all in the kettle, sett it on the same fire before them all
and helped the fire with more green wood. When all was
ready as he had ordered, a long, large table was covered and
the beef sett on in great scaills of dishes instead of pleats.
They had scarcely sitten to supper when they let loose six
or sevin great hounds to supp the broth, but before they
made ane end of it, they made such a tulzie as made them
all start at the table. The supper being ended, and longing
for their bedds (but much more for day), there comes in 5
or 6 lustie women with windlings of strae (and white plaids)
which they spread on each side of the house, whereon the
gentlemen were forced to lye in the cloaths, thinking they
had come to purgatory before hand ; but they had no
sooner seen day light, without stayeing dinner they made to
the gett, down to Ross where they were most noblie entertained be Ffowlis, Belnagowin, Miltoun, and severall other
gentlemen. But when they were come south the Queen
asked who were the ablest men they saw there. They
answered all they did see lived like princes, except Her
Majesty's great courtier and counsellor, Mackenzie. So
tells her all their usage in his house, and that he slept with
his doggs and sat with his hounds, wherat the Queen leugh
mirrily (whatever her thoughts was of M'Kenzie) and said,
'It were a pitty of his poverty ffor he is the best and hon-
estest man among them all.' The Queen thereafter having

called all the gentry of Ross to hold their lands of the Crown in feu, Mackenzie gote (by her favour and his pretended poverty) the easiest feu, and for his 1000 merks more than any of the rest had for three."*

He had a natural son named Dugall, who lived in Applecross, and married a niece of Macleod of Harris, by whom he had a son and one daughter. The son, also named Dugall, was a schoolmaster in Chanonry, and died without issue. The daughter was married to Duncan Mackenzie, Reraig, and after his death to Mackintosh of Strone. Dugall, the elder, was killed by the Mathesons at Kishorn. John of Killin had also a natural daughter who married Macleod of Raasay.

He married Elizabeth, daughter of John, tenth Laird of Grant, and by her had an only son and successor,

X. COINNEACH NA CUIRC,

OR KENNETH OF THE WHITTLE, so called from his skill in carving on wood and general dexterity with that primitive instrument, the Highland "Sgian Dubh." He succeeded his father in 1561. In the following year he was among the chiefs who, at the head of their followers, met Queen Mary at Inverness, and helped her to get possession of the Castle after Alexander Gordon, the governor, refused her access. In the same year we find an Act of Privy Council, dated the 21st of May, which bears that he had delivered up Mary Macleod, the heiress of Harris and Dun-vegan, of whom he had previously by accident obtained the custody, into the hands of Queen Mary, with whom she afterwards remained for several years as a maid of honour. The Act is as follows:—" The same day, in presence of the Queen's Majesty and Lords of Secret Council, compeared Kenneth Mackenzie of Kintail, who, being commanded by letters and also by writings direct from the Queen's Grace, to exhibit, produce, and present before her Highness Mary Macleod, daughter and heir of the umquwhile William

*Ancient MS,

Macleod of Harris, conform to the letters and charges direct thereupon: And declared that James Macdonald had an action depending the Lords of Session against him for deliverance of the said Mary to him, and that therefore he could not gudlie (well) deliver her. Notwithstanding the which the Queen's Majesty ordained the said Kenneth to deliver the said Mary to her Highness and granted that he should incur 'no scaith thairthrou' at the hands of the said James or any others, notwithstanding any title or action they had against him therefor; and the said Kenneth knowing his dutiful obedience to the Queen's Majesty, and that the Queen had ordained him to deliver the said Mary to her Highness in manner foresaid which he in no wise could disobey—and therefore delivered the said Mary to the Queen's Majesty conform to her ordinance foresaid."* Prior to this Mackenzie refused to give her up to her lawful guardian, James Macdonald of Dunyveg and the Glens. In 1563 we find him on the jury, with James, Earl of Moray, and others, at Inverness, by whom John Campbell of Cawdor was served heir to the Barony of Strathnairn.† This Chief of Kintail was advanced in years before he came into posses- sion, and took, as we have seen, an active and distinguished part in all the affairs of his clan during the life of his long- lived father. He seems after his return from Inverness, on the occasion of meeting Queen Mary there, to have retired very much into private life, for we find him, on Mary's escape from Lochleven Castle, sending his son Colin, who was then quite a youth and attending his studies at Aber- deen, at the head of his vassals and followers, to join the Earl of Huntly, by whom Colin was sent, according to the Laird of Applecross, "as one whose prudence he con- fided, to advise the Queen's retreat to Stirling, where she might stay in security till all her friends were convocate, but by an unhappy council she refused this advice and fought at Langside, where Colin was present, and when by

* Transactions of the Iona Club, p. 143-4.
† Invernessiana, p. 220.

the Regent's* insolence, after that victory, all the loyal
subjects were forced to take remissions for their duty, as if
·it were a crime. Amongst the rest Mackenzie takes one,
the only one that ever any of his family had ; and this is
rather a mark of his fidelity than evidence of failure, and
an honour, not a task of his posterity." It would have been
already seen that a second remission had been received, for
the imprisonment and murder of John Glassich, son and
successor to Hector Roy Mackenzie of Gairloch, in Islandonain Castle. Dr George Mackenzie informs us that
Kenneth apprehended him and sent him prisoner to the
Castle, where he was poisoned by the constable's lady,†
whereupon " ane certain female, foster-sister of his, composed a Gaelic rhyme to commemorate him." The Earl
of Cromarty gives us the reason for his imprisonment and
murder—that it was rumoured that John Glassich intended to
prosecute his father's claim to the Kintail estates, and Kenneth hearing of this sent for him to Brahan. John suspecting nothing came, accompanied only by his ordinary ser- ·
vants. Kenneth questioned him regarding the suspicious
rumours abroad, and not being quite satisfied with the
answers received, he caused John Glassich to be at once
apprehended. One of John's servants, named John Gearr,
seeing his master thus apprehended, struck at Kenneth of
Kintail a fearful blow with a two-handed sword, but fortunately Kenneth, who was standing close to the table,
nimbly moved aside, and the blow missed him, else he

* Earl of Moray appointed to the office after Mary's defeat.
† This lady was Nighean Iamhair, and was spouse to John MacMhurchaidh
Duibh, the priest of Kintail, who was then chosen Constable of Islandonain for
the following reason :—A great debate arose between the Maclennans and the
Macraes about this important and honourable post, and the laird finding
them irreconcilable, lest they should kill one another, and he being a stranger in
the country himself, Mackenzie, on the advice of the Laird of Fairburn, elected the
priest constable of the castle. This did not suit the Maclennans, and, as soon as
Mackenzie left the country, they, one Sabbath morning, as the priest was coming
home from church, " sends a man in ambush in his road who shot him with an
arrow in the buttocks, so that he fell. The ambusher thinking him killed, and
perceiving others coming after the priest that road, made his escape, and he (the
priest) was carried to his boat alive. *Of this priest are all the Murchisons in these
countries descended,"—Ancient MS.*

would have been cloven to pieces. The sword made a deep cut in the table, "so that you could hide your hand edgeways in it," and the mark remained in the table until Colin, Earl of Seaforth, "caused cut that piece off the table, saying that he loved no such remembrance of the quarrels of his relations." Kenneth was a man of good endowments; "he carried so prudently that he had the good-liking of his prince and peace from his neighbours." He had a peculiar genius for mechanics, and was seldom found without his core— " Sgian Dubh," or some other such tool in his hand, with which he produced excellent specimens of hand-carving on wood.

He married early, during his father's lifetime, Lady Elizabeth Stewart, daughter of John, Earl of Athol, by his lady, Mary Campbell, daughter of the Earl of Argyll, by whom he had three sons—first, Murdoch, who, being fostered in the house of Bayne of Tulloch, that gentleman, on his being sent home, presented him with a goodly stock of milk cows, with the grazing of Strathvaich in the Forest of Strathrannich, but he died before attaining his majority; second, Colin, who succeeded him; third, Roderick, to whom he gave the lands of Redcastle. Of many daughters, the eldest was married, first, to Macdonald of Glengarry, and, secondly, to Chisholm of Comar; the second to Ross of Balnagown; the third to Lachlan Mackintosh of Mackintosh;* the fourth to Walter Urquhart of Cromarty; the fifth to Robert Munro of Fowlis; and the sixth to Innes of Inverbreaky. By these inter-marriages he left his house singularly powerful in family alliances, and, as we have seen, in 1554 he derived no small benefit from them himself. He

* The following anecdote is related of this match :—Lachlan Mackintosh being only an infant when his father, William Mackintosh of that ilk, was murdered in 1550, was carried for safety by some of his humble retainers to the county of Ross. This came to the knowledge of Colin, younger of Kintail, who took possession of the young heir of Mackintosh, and carried him to Islandonain Castle. The old chief retained him, and treated him with great care until the years of pupilarity had expired, and then married him to his daughter Agnes, by no means an unsuitable match for either, apart from the time and manner in which it was consummated.

died, during his son's absence fighting for Queen Mary, at
Killin, on the 6th of June 1568, was buried at Beauly, and
succeeded by his second and eldest surviving son,

XI. CAILEAN CAM,

OR ONE-EYED COLIN, who soon became a special
favourite at Court, particularly with the young King himself; so much so, according to the Earl of Cromartie, that
"there was none in the North for whom he hade a greater
esteem than for this Colin. He made him one of his Privie
Councillors, and oft tymes invited him to be nobilitate
(ennobled); but Colin always declined it, aiming rather to
have his familie remarkable for power, as it were, above
their qualitie than for titles that equalled their power.
"In 1570 King James VI. granted to Coline Makcainze, the
son and apparent heir of the deceased Canzeoch of Kintaill,
permission to be served heir in his minority to all the lands
and rents in the Sheriffdom of Innerness, in which his
father died last vest and seised.   In 1572 the same King
confirmed a grant made by Colin Makcanze of Kintaill to
Barbara Graunt, his affianced spouse, in fulfilment of a
contract between him and John Grant of Freuchie, dated
25th April 1571, of his lands of Climbo, Keppach, and
Ballichon, Mekle Innerennet, Derisduan Beg, Little Innerennet, Derisduan Moir, Auchadrein, Kirktoun, Ardtulloch,
Rovoch, Quhissil, Tullych, Derewall and Nuik, Inchchro,
Morowoch, Glenlik, Innersell and Nuik, Achazarge, Kin-
lochbeancharan, and Innerchonray, in the Earldom of Ross,
and Sheriffdom of Inverness.   In 1574 the same Colin was
served heir to his father Kenneth M'Keinzie in the davach
of Letterfernane, the davach of Glenshall, and other lands
in the barony of Ellendonane of the old extent of five
marks."*

In 1570 a quarrel broke out between the Mackenzies
and the Munros.   Leslie, the celebrated Bishop of Ross,
who had been secretary to Queen Mary, dreading the effect

* Origines Parochiales Scotiæ, p. 393, vol, ii,

of public feeling against prelacy in the North, and against himself personally, made over to his cousin Leslie, the Laird of Balquhair, his rights and titles to the Chanonry of Ross, together with the castle lands, to divest them of the character of church property, and so save them to his family; but notwithstanding this grant, the Regent Murray gave the custody of the castle to Andrew Munro of Milntown, a rigid presbyterian, and in high favour with Murray, whó promised Leslie some of the lands of the barony of Fintry in Buchan as an equivalent; but the Regent died before this arrangement was carried out—before Munro obtained titles to the castle and castle lands as he expected. Yet he ultimately obtained permission from the Earl of Lennox, during his regency, and afterwards from the Earl of Mar, his successor in that office, to get possession of the castle.

The Mackenzies were by no means pleased to see the Munros occupying the stronghold; and, desirous to obtain possession of the castle themselves, they purchased Leslie's right, by virtue of which they demanded delivery of the fortress. This was at once refused by the Munros. Kintail raised his vassals, and, joined by a detachment of the Mackintoshes,* garrisoned the steeple of the Cathedral Church, and laid siege to Irvine's Tower and the Palace. The Munros held out three years, but one day the garrison getting short of provisions, they attempted a sortie to the Ness of Fortrose, where there was a salmon stell, the contents of

---

* In the year 1573, Lachlan More, Laird of Mackintosh, favouring Kintail, his brother-in-law, required all the people of Strathnairn to join him against the Munros. Colin, Lord of Lorn, had at the time the administration of that lordship as the jointure lands of his wife, the Countess Dowager of Murray, and he wrote to Hugh Rose of Kilravock :—" My Baillie off Strathnarne, for as much as it is reported to me that Mackintosh has charged all my tenants west of the water of Nairn to pass forward with him to Ross to enter into this troublous action with Mackenzie against the Laird of Fowlis, and because I will not that any of mine enter presently this matter whose service appertains to me, . . . wherefore I will desire you to make my will known to my tenants at Strathnarne within your Bailliary, that none of them take upon hand to rise at this present with Mackintosh to pass to Ross, or at any time hereafter without my special command and goodwill obtained under such pains," &c., &c. (Dated) Darnoway, 28th of June 1573.—*Kilravock Writs*, p. 263.

which they attempted to secure. They were commanded by John Munro, grandson of George, fourth laird of Fowlis, who was killed at the Battle of " Bealach na Broige." · They were immediately discovered, and quickly followed by the Mackenzies, under Iain Dubh Mac Ruairidh Mhic Alastair, who fell upon the starving Munros, and, after a desperate struggle, killed twenty-six of their number, among whom was their commander, while the victors only sustained a loss of two men killed and three or four wounded. The defenders of the castle immediately capitulated, and it was taken possession of by the Mackenzies. It was afterwards confirmed to the Baron of Kintail by King James VI.*

The disturbed state of the country was such, in 1573, that the Earl of Sutherland petitioned to be served heir to his estates, at Aberdeen, as he could not get a jury to sit at Inverness, and " in consequence of the barons, such as Colin Mackenzie of Kintail, Hugh Lord Lovat, Lachlan Mackintosh of Dunachton, and Robert Monro of Fowlis, being at deadly feud among themselves."†

In 1580 a desperate feud broke out between the Mackenzies and Macdonalds of Glengarry. The Chief of Glengarry inherited part of Lochalsh, Lochcarron, and Lochbroom, from his grandmother, Margaret, one of the sisters and co-heiresses of Sir Donald Macdonald of Lochalsh. Kenneth, during his father's life, had acquired the other part by purchase from Dingwall of Kildun, son of the other co-heiress of Sir Donald, on the 24th November 1554, and Queen Mary confirmed the grant by royal charter. Many causes leading to dispute and quarrel can easily be conceived with such men in close proximity. Glengarry and his followers " sorned " on Mackenzie's tenants, not only in those districts in the immediate vicinity of his own property, but also, during their raids from Glengarry, on the outskirts of Kintail, and thus Mackenzie's dependants were continually harrassed by Glengarry's cruelty and ill-usage. His

---

* Sir Robert Gordon, p. 154, and MS. Histories of the Family.
† Antiquarian Notes, p. 79.

own tenants in Lochalsh and Lochcarron fared little better, particularly the Mathesons in the former, and the Clann. Ian Uidhir in the latter, originally the possessors of Glengarry's lands in the district. These tribes, finding themselves in such miserable slavery, though they regularly paid their rents and other dues, and seeing how kindly Mackenzie used the neighbouring tenants, envied their more comfortable state and "abhorred Glengarry's rascality, who would lie in their houses (yea, force their women and daughters) so long as there was any good to be given, which made them keep better amity and correspondence with Mackenzie and his tenants than with their own master and his followers. This may partly teach how superiors ought always to govern and oversee their tenantry . and followers, especially in the Highlands, who are ordinarily made up of several clans, and will not readily underlie such slavery as the Incountry Commons will do."

The first serious outbreak between the Glengarry Macdonalds and the Mackenzies originated thus : One Duncan Mac Ian Uidhir Mhic Dhonnachaidh, known as "a very honest gentleman," who, in his early days, lived under Glengarry, and was a very good deerstalker and an excellent shot, often resorted to the forest of Glasletter, then the property of the Mackenzies of Gairloch, where he killed many of the deer. Some time afterwards, Duncan was, in consequence of certain troubles in his own country, obliged to leave it, and he, with all his family and goods, took up his quarters in Glen Affrick, close to the forest. Soon after, he went, accompanied by a friend, to the nearest hill, and commenced his favourite pursuit of deerstalking. Mackenzie's forester perceiving him, and knowing him as an old poacher, cautiously walked up to him, came upon him unawares, and demanded that he should at once surrender himself and his arms. Duncan, finding that Gairloch's forester was accompanied by only one gillie, "thought it an irrecoverable affront that he and his man should so yield, and refused to do so on any terms, whereupon the forester being ill-set, and remembering former abuses in their passages," he and his

companion instantly killed the poachers, and buried them
in the hill. Fionnla Dubh Mac Dhomh'uill Mhoir, and
Donald Mac Ian Leith, a native of Gairloch, were
suspected of the crime, but it was never proved against
them, though they were both repeatedly put on their trial
by the Barons of Kintail and Gairloch.

About two years after the deed was committed, Duncan's
bones were discovered by one of his friends who continued most diligently to search for him. The Macdonalds
always suspected foul play, and this being now placed beyond question by the discovery of the victims, a party of
them started, determined to revenge the death of their
clansmen ; and, arriving at Inchlochell, in Glenstrathfarrar,
then the property of Rory Mor of Redcastle, they found
Duncan Mac Ian Mhic Dhomh'uill Mhoir, a brother of the
suspected Finlay Dubh, without any fear of approaching
danger, busily engaged ploughing his patch of land, whom
they at once attacked and killed. The celebrated Rory
Mor, hearing of the murder of his tenant, at once
despatched a messenger to Glengarry to demand redress
and the punishment of the assassins, but Glengarry refused.
Rory determined to have satisfaction, and resolved, against
the counsel of his friends, to have retribution for this
and previous injuries as best he could. Having thus determined, he immediately sent for his trusted friend, Dugall
Mackenzie of Applecross, to consult with as to the best
mode of procedure to ensure success.

Macdonald at the time lived in the Castle of Strome,
Lochcarron, and, after consultation, the two Mackenzies
resolved to use every means in their power to capture him,
or some of his nearest relatives. For this purpose Dugall
suggested a plan by which he would, he thought, induce the
unsuspecting Glengarry to meet him on a certain day at
Kishorn. Rory Mor, to avoid any suspicion, would start at
once for Lochbroom, under cloak of attending to his interests there ; and if Glengarry agreed to meet Dugall at
Kishorn,he would immediately send notice of the day to Rory.
No sooner had Dugall arrived at home than he despatched

a messenger to Glengarry to inform him that he had matters
of great importance to communicate to him, and that he
wished, for that purpose, to meet him on any day which he
might deem suitable.

Day and place were soon arranged, and Dugall at
once sent a messenger, as arranged, with full particulars of
the proposed meeting to Rory Mor, who instantly gathered his friends, the Clann Allan, and marched along with
them to Lochcarron. On his arrival, he had a meeting with
Donald Mac Ian Mhic Ian Uidhir, and Angus Mac Eachainn, both of the Clann Ian Uidhir, and closely allied to
Glengarry by blood and marriage, and living on his lands.
"Yet notwithstanding this alliance, they, fearing his, and
his rascality's further oppression, were content to join Rory
in the plot." The appointed day having arrived, Glengarry
and his lady (a daughter of the Captain of Clan Ranald, he
having previously sent away his lawful wife, a daughter of
the laird of Grant) came by sea to Kishorn. He and Dugall
Mackenzie having conferred together for a considerable time
discussing matters of importance to each other as neighbours, Glengarry took his leave, but while being convoyed
to his boat, Dugall suggested the impropriety of his going
home by sea in such a clumsy boat, when he had only a
distance of two miles to walk, and if he did not suspect
his own inability to make the lady comfortable for the
night, he would be glad to provide for her and see her home
safely next morning. Macdonald declined the proffered
hospitality to his lady ; sent her home by the boat accompanied by four of his followers, and told Dugall that he would
not endanger the boat by overloading, but that he and the
remainder of his gentlemen and followers would go home
on foot.

Rory Mor had meanwhile placed his men in ambush in
a place called Glaic nan Gillean. Glengarry and his train,
on their way to Strome Castle, came upon them without the
slightest suspicion, when they were suddenly surrounded
by Rory's followers, and called upon to surrender. Seeing
this, one of the Macdonalds shot an arrow at Rory, which

fixed in the fringe of his plaid, when his followers, thinking their leader had been mortally wounded, furiously attacked the Macdonalds; but Rory commanded his friends, under pain of death, to save Glengarry's life, who, seeing he had no chance of escape, and hearing Rory's orders to his men, threw away his sword, and ran into Rory's arms, begging that his life might be spared. This was at once granted to him, but not a single one of his men escaped from the infuriated followers of Rory Mor, who started the same night, taking Glengarry along with him, to Lochbroom.

Even this did not satisfy the cruel disposition of Donald Mac Ian Mhic Ian Uidhir and Angus Mac Eachainn, who had an old grudge against their chief, Glengarry, his father having some time previously evicted their father from a davoch of land, Attadale, Lochcarron, to which they claimed a right. They, under silence of night, gathered all the Clann Ian Uidhir, and proceeded to Arinaskaig and Dalmartin, where lived at the time three uncles of Glengarry—Gorrie, Rory, and Ronald—whom they, with all their retainers, killed on the spot. "This murder was un-doubtedly unknown to Rory or any of the Mackenzies, though alleged otherwise; for as soon as his nephew, Colin of Kintail, and his friends heard of this accident, they were much concerned, and would have him (Rory) set Glengarry at liberty; but all their persuasions would not do till he was secured of him by writ and oath, that he and his would never pursue this accident either legally or unlegally, and which, as was said, he never intended to do, till seventeen years thereafter, when, in 1597, the children of these three uncles of Glengarry arrived at manhood," determined, as will be seen hereafter, to revenge their father's death.[*]

Gregory, however, says (p. 219) that after his liberation, Glengarry complained to the Privy Council, who, investi-gating the matter; caused the Castle of Strome, which Mac-donald yielded to Mackenzie as one of the conditions of his release, to be placed under the temporary custody of the

---

[*] Ancient and Ardintoul MSS.

Earl of Argyll; and Mackenzie of Kintail was detained at
Edinburgh in what was called open ward to answer such
charges as might be brought against him. This is confirmed by the Records of the Privy Council.* In 1586 King
James VI. granted a remission to "Colin M'Kainzie of Kintaill, and Rodorie M'Kainzie of Auchterfailie" (Redcastle
and Arpafeelie), "his brother, for being art and part in the
cruel murder of Rodoric M'Allester in Stroll ; Gorie M'Allester, his brother, in Stromcraig ; Ronnald M'Gorie, the son
of the latter; John Roy M'Allane v' Allester, in Pitncàn ;
John Dow M'Allane v' Allester, in Kirktoun of Lochcarroun;
Alexander M'Allanroy, servitor of the deceased Rodoric ;
Sir John Monro in Lochbrume; John Monro, his son ;
John Monro Huchcoun, and the rest of their accomplices,
under silence of night, upon the lands of Ardmanichtyke,
Dalmartene, Kirktoun of Lochcarroun, Blahat, and other
parts within the baronies of Lochcarroun, Lochbrume, Ros,
and Kessane, in the Sheriffdom of Innerness," and for all
other past crimes.†

During Colin's reign Huntly obtained a commission of
fire and sword against Mackintosh of Mackintosh (who was
married, as we have seen, to a sister of Colin Mackenzie of
Kintail), and reduced him to such a condition that he had
to remove with all his family and friends for better security
to the Island of Moy. Huntly, determined to crush him, came
to Inverness and prepared a large fleet of boats, with which
to besiege the island. These preparations having been completed, and the boats being ready to be drawn across the hills
to Moy, Mackenzie heard of Huntly's intentions, and despatched a messenger—John Mackenzie of Kinnock—to
Inverness, desiring his Lordship to be as favourable as
possible to his sister, Mrs Mackintosh of Mackintosh, and to
treat her as a gentlewoman ought to be treated when he
came to Moy, and that he (Colin) would consider it a great
act of personal courtesy to himself. The messenger de-

* See those of 10th August and 2d December 1582 ; and 11th January and
8th March 1582 3.
† Origines Parochiales Scotiæ and Retours.

livered his message, to which Huntly replied, that if it were
his good fortune, as he doubted not it would be, to apprehend her husband and her, she would " be the worst used
lady in the North ; that she was an ill-instrument against
his cause, and therefore he would cut her tail above her
houghs." "Well, then," answered Kinnock, "he (Mackenzie)
bade me tell your Lordship if that were your answer, that
perhaps he or his would be there to have a better care of
her." " I do not value his being there more than herself,"
Huntly replied, "and tell him so much from me." The
messenger departed, when some of Huntly's principal officers
who heard the conversation found fault with his Lordship
for sending Mackenzie such an uncivil answer, as he might
have cause to regret it if Mackenzie took it amiss. Kinnock having returned to Brahan, informed his master of
what had occurred, and delivered Huntly's defiant message.
Colin, who was in delicate health, sent for his brother,
Rory Mor of Redcastle, who next day crossed the ferry of
Ardersier with a force of four hundred warriors ; marched
straight through the hills for the Island of Moy ; and just
as Huntly, on his way from Inverness, was coming in sight,
on the west of Moy, Rory and his followers were marching
along the face of the hill on the east side of the island, when
his Lordship, perceiving such a force, asked his officers who
they could be. One of them, who was present during the
interview with Mackenzie's messenger on the previous day,
answered, "Yonder is the effect of your answer to Mackenzie." " I wonder," replied Huntly, "how he could have
so many men ready almost in an instant." The officer replied, " Their leader is so active and fortunate that his men
will flock to him from all parts on a moment's notice when
he has any ado. And before you gain Mackintosh or his
lady you will lose more than he is worth, since now, as
it seems, her friends take part in the quarrel;" whereupon,
and on further consideration, the Earl retired with his
forces to Inverness, "so that it seemed fitter to Huntly to
agree their differs friendly than prosecute the laws further
against Mackintosh."

About this time commenced the great troubles in the
Lews which ultimately ended in that extensive principality
coming into the possession of the House of Kintail, and
although the most important events connected with, and
leading up to that great result will principally fall to be
treated under the next head, the quarrel having originated
during Colin Cam's life, it may be more convenient to explain its cause under the present.

Roderick Macleod of the Lews married, first, Barbara
Stewart, daughter of Lord Methven, by whom he had one
son, Torquil Oighre, or the Heir. This youth, arriving at
manhood, gave proofs of a fierce and warlike disposition,
but in sailing from Lews to Skye on one of his raids, he,
with two hundred men, perished in a great storm. Upon
the death of Torquil's mother, Roderick married, secondly,
Janet, daughter of John of Killin, by whom he had a son,
Torquil Cononach, so called from his having been brought
up with his mother's relations in Strathconon. Roderick,
by all accounts, was not so purely virtuous in his domestic
character as one might wish, for we find him having no less
than five bastard sons, named respectively, Tormod Uigeach,
Murdoch, Neil, Donald, and Rory Og, all of whom arrived
at maturity. In these circumstances it can hardly be supposed that his lady's domestic happiness would have been
of the most complete and felicitous description. It has
been alleged, by this paragon of virtue, that she had proved
unfaithful to him, and that she had criminal intimacy with
the Brieve *(Breitheamh)*, or consistorial judge of the Island.
On the other hand, it has been maintained that the Brieve,
in his capacity of judge, had been somewhat severe on the
Island chief for his reckless and immoral habits, and for his
bad treatment of his lady ; and that the unprincipled villain,
as he throughout his whole career proved himself to be,
boldly, and in revenge, turned round and accused the judge
of adultery with his wife. Be that as it may, the unfortunate
woman, attempting to escape from his cruel and harsh treatment, while passing in a large birlinn, or boat, from the
Lews to Coigeach, on the opposite side of the coast, was

I

pursued and run down by some of her husband's followers, when she, with all on board, perished. Roderick now disinherited her son, Torquil Cononach, grandson of John of Killin, maintaining that Torquil was not his legitimate son and heir, but the fruit of his wife's unfaithfulness,* Macleod married a third time, a daughter of Maclean of Dowart, by whom he had two sons—Torquil Dubh, whom he declared his heir and successor, and Tormod, known as Tormod Og. Torquil Cononach, now designated "of Coigeach," married a daughter of Glengarry, who bore him two sons—John and Neil—and five daughters; and, raising as many men as would accompany him, he, with the assistance of two of his natural brothers—Tormod and Murdoch—started for the Lews to vindicate his right as his father's legitimate heir and successor. He defeated his father, and confined him in the Castle of Stornoway for four years, when he was finally obliged to acknowledge Torquil Cononach as his lawful son and successor. The bastards now quarrelled among themselves. Donald killed Tormod Uigeach. Murdoch, in resentment, seized Donald and carried him to Coigeach; but he afterwards escaped and complained to old Rory, who was highly offended at Murdoch for seizing, and with Torquil Cononach for detaining Donald. Roderick ordered Murdoch to be captured, and confined in his own old quarters in the Castle of Stornoway. Torquil Cononach again returned to the Lews,

---

* Most of the MS. Histories of the family which we have perused state that Rory Macleod's wife was a *daughter* of Kenneth a Bhlair, but it is scarcely possible that the daughter of a chief who died in 1491 could have been the wife of one who lived in the early years of the seventeenth century. She must have been Kenneth's *granddaughter*, as above described, a daughter of John of Killin. This view is corroborated by a decree arbitral in 1554, in which Torquil Cononach is called the *oy* (*ogha*, or grandson) of John Mackenzie.—*Acts and Decreets of Session*, *X., folio* 201. The Roderick Macleod who married, probably for his second wife, Agnes, daughter of Kenneth a Bhlair, must have been Roderick Macleod, seventh of the Lews, who died some time after his father early in the sixteenth century. According to the "Ancient" MS. already quoted, Rory married—first, Barbara Stewart, and "after her death he married the Lady Reah (McKayes Robert), who was Mackenzie's daughter. She was mother to Torquil Cononigh. . . . This Lady Reah was afterwards ravished from this Rory by a kinsman of his own, called John MacGillechallum,' brother of Alexander, then Laird of Rasaay,

reduced the castle, liberated Murdoch, again confined his
father, and killed many of his followers, at the same time
carrying off all the writs and charters, and depositing them
for safety with his relative, Mackenzie of Kintail. He had
meanwhile left his son John (who had been in the service
of Huntly, and whom he now called home) in charge of the
castle, and in possession of the Lews. He imprudently
banished his natural uncles, Donald and Rory Og out of
the island. Rory Og soon after returned with a considerable number of followers; attacked his nephew, Torquil
Cononach's son John, in Stornoway, killed him, and released his own father, old Roderick, who was allowed after
this to possess the island in peace during the remainder of
his life. "Thus was the Siol Torquil weakened, by private
dissensions, and exposed to fall a prey, as it did soon afterwards, to the growing power of the Mackenzies."

In 1594 Alexander Bayne, younger of Tulloch, granted
a charter of the lands of Rhindoun in favour of Colin Mackenzie of Kintail and his heirs male, proceeding on a contract of sale betwixt them, dated 10th of March 1574. On
the 10th of July in the same year there is "a contract
of alienation" of these lands by the same Colin Mackenzie
of Kintail in favour of Roderick Mackenzie of Ardefillie
(Redcastle), his brother-german, and his heirs male. A
charter implementing this contract is dated the 20th of
October following, by which the lands "are to be holden
blench and for relieving Kintail of the feu-duty and services
payable to his superiors." These lands are, in 1625, resigned by Murdoch Mackenzie of Redcastle into the hands
of Colin, second Earl of Seaforth, the immediate lawful
superior thereof, for new infeftments to be granted to
Roderick Mackenzie, his second lawful son.*

Colin, in addition to his acquisition in Lochalsh and
Lochcarron, "feued the Lordship of Ardmeanach, and the
Barony of Delnys, Brae Ross, with the exception of Western
Achnacherich, Wester Drynie, and Tarradale, which Bayne

* Writs and Evidents of Lands of Rhindoun. Antiquarian Notes, pp. 172 73.

of Tulloch had feued before, but found it his interest to
hold of him as immediate superior, which, with the former
possessions of the lands of Chanonry, greatly enhanced his
influence. Albeit his predecessors were active both in war
and peace, and precedent in acquiring their estate ; yet this
man acquired more than all that went before him, and made
such a solid progress in it, that what he had acquired was
with the goodwill of his sovereign, and clear unquestionable
purchase." He protected his cousin, Torquil Macleod of the
Lews, when he was oppressed by his unnatural relations
and natural brothers, and from this he acquired a right to
the lands of Assynt.*

He married Barbara, daughter of John Grant of Grant,
by Lady Marjory Stewart, daughter of John, third Earl of
Athol, by whom he had five sons—first, Kenneth, who
succeeded, and was afterwards created Lord Mackenzie of
Kintail ; second, Sir Roderick Mackenzie of Coigeach, progenitor of the families of Cromarty or Tarbat, Scatwell, Tarvie, Ballone, and others ; third, Alexander, first of Kilcoy ;
fourth, Colin of Kinnock and Pitlundie ; and fifth, Murdoch of
Kernsary, whose only lawful son was killed at the battle of
Auldearn. Colin also had a natural son, Alexander, by Margaret, daughter of Roderick Mackenzie, second of Davochmaluag, who became the founder of the family of Applecross
and Coul.   His eldest daughter married Simon, eighth Lord
Lovat ; the second married Eachainn Og, or Hector Maclean of Duart ; while a third married Macdonald of Sleat.
"This Colin lived beloved by princes and people, and died,
regretted by all, on the 14th of June 1594, at Redcastle,
and was buried at Bewlie." He was succeeded by his eldest
son,

XII. KENNETH,

First Lord Mackenzie of Kintail, who began his
rule among those domestic quarrels and dissensions in the

---

* Earl of Cromartie and other MS. Histories of the Family.

Lews to which we have already introduced the reader,* and which may, not inappropriately, be designated the strife of the bastards. Upon the death of Roderick Macleod, Torquil Dubh succeeded him, excluding Torquil Cononach from the succession on the plea of his being a bastard. The latter, however, held Coigeach and his other possessions on the mainland, with a full recognition by the Government of his rights to the lands of his forefathers in the Lews. His two sons having been killed, and his eldest daughter, Margaret, having married Roderick Mackenzie of Coigeach, progenitor of the Cromarty family, and better known as the Tutor of Kintail, Torquil Cononach threw himself into the hands of Kintail for aid against the bastards. By Roderick's marriage with Torquil Cononach's eldest daughter, he became heir of line to the ancient family of Macleod, an honour which still remains in his descendants, the Cromarty family. Torquil Dubh secured considerable support by a marriage with a sister of Macleod of Harris, and, thus strengthened, made a descent on Coigeach and Lochbroom, desolating the whole district, aiming at permanent occupation. Kintail, following the example of his predecessors—always prudent, and careful to keep within the laws of the realm—in 1596 laid the following complaint before James VI.:—

" Please your Majesty,—Torquil Dow of the Lews, not contenting himself with the avowit misknowledging of your

---

* The country generally was in such a lawless condition in this year, 1594, that an Act of Parliament was passed by which it was ordained " that in order that there may be a perfect distinction, by names and surnames, betwixt those that are, and desire to be, esteemed honest and true men, and those that are, and are not ashamed to be, esteemed thieves, sorners, and resetters of them in their wicked and odious crimes and deeds ; that therefore a roll and catalogue be made of all persons, and the *surnames* therein mentioned, suspected of slaughter, &c." It was also enacted "that such interposed persons as take upon themselves to sell the goods of thieves, and disobedient persons and clans, *that dare not come to public markets in the Lowlands themselves,* whereby the execution of the Acts made against sorners, clans, and thieves, is greatly impeded," should be punished in the manner therein contained. Another Act provided " that the inbringer of every robber and thief, after he is outlawed, and denounced fugitive, shall have two hundred pounds, Scots, for every robber and thief so inbrought,"—*Antiquarian Notes.*

Hieness authority wherebe he has violat the promises and
compromit made before your Majesty, now lately the 25th
day of December last, has ta'n upon him being accompanied
w 7 or 800 men, not only of his own by ylands neist adjacent, to prosecute with fire and sword by all kind of gud
order, the hail bounds of the Strath Coigach pertaining to
M'Leod his eldest brother, likewise my Strath of Lochbroom, quhilks Straths, to your Majesty's great dishonour,
but any fear of God ourselves, hurt and skaith that he hath
wasted w˜fire and sword, in such barbarous and cruel
manner, that neither man, wife, bairn, horse, cattle, corns,
nor bigging has been spared, but all barbarously slain, burnt,
and destroyit, quhilk barbarity and cruelty, seeing he was
not able to perform it, but by the assistance and furderance
of his neighbouring Ylesmen, therefore beseeches your
Majesty by advice of Council to find some sure remeid
wherebe sick cruel tyrannie may be resisted in the begining.
Otherway nothing to be expectit for but dailly increasing of
his malicious forces to our utter ruin, quha possesses your
Majesty's obedience, the consideration quharof and inconveniences quhilk may thereon ensue. I remit to your
Highness guid consideration of whom taking my leif with
maist humble commendations of service, I commit your
Majesty to the holy protection of God eternal.

"At the Canonry of Ross, the 3d day, Jany. 1596.
"Your Majesty's most humble and obt. subject,
"(Signed)   KENNETH MACKENZIE of Kintail."

Kintail now obtained a commission of fire and sword against
Torquil Dubh, as also the forfeiture of the Lews, on which
Torquil Cononach made over his rights to Mackenzie, on
the plea that he was the next male heir, but reserving the
lands of Coigeach to his own son-in-law.   The Mackenzies
did all they could to obtain possession for Torquil Cononach,
the legitimate heir, but mainly through his own want of activity and indolent disposition, they failed with their united
efforts to secure for him undisturbed possession.   They succeeded, however, in destroying the family of Macleod of the

Lews, and most of the Siol-Torquil, and ultimately became complete masters of the island. The Brieve by strategem captured Torquil Dubh and some of his friends, and, delivering them up to Torquil Cononach, they were, by his orders, beheaded in July 1597.*

In 1598 some gentlemen in Fife, known afterwards as the "Fife Adventurers," obtained a grant of the Island of Lews with the professed object of civilising the inhabitants. The object here is not to detail their proceedings or to describe the squabbles and constant disorders, murders, and robberies which took place while they held possession of the Island. The speculation proved ruinous to the adventurers, who in the end lost their estates, and were obliged to leave the islanders to their fate.

Mackenzie had for some time kept Tormod Macleod, the lawful brother of Torquil Dubh, a prisoner, but now released him, correctly premising that on his appearance in the Lews all the islanders would rise in his favour. In the meantime, Murdoch Dubh was taken by the Fife adventurers to St Andrews, and there put to death; but at his execution he revealed, in his confessions, the designs of Mackenzie, who was in consequence apprehended and com-

---

* "It fell out that the Breve (that is to say, the judge) in the Lewis, who was Chief of the Clan Illevoric (Morrison), being sailing from the Isle of Lewis to Ronny in a great galley, met with a Dutch ship loaded with wine, which he took; and advising with his friends, who were all with him there, what he would do with the ship lest Torquil Du shou'd take her from him, they resolved to return to Stornoway and call for Torquil Du to receive the wine, and if he came to the ship, to sail away with him where Torquil Conanach was, and then they might be sure of the ship and the wine to be their own, and besides, he would grant them tacks in the best parts in the Lewis; which accordingly they did, and called for Torquil to come and receive the wine. Torquil Du noways mistrusting them that were formerly so obedient, entered the ship with seven others in company, where he was welcomed, and he commended them as good fellows that brought him such a prize. They invited him to the quay to take his pleasure of the feast of their wine. He goes, but instead of wine they brought cords to tie him, telling him he had better render himself and his wrongously possessed estate to his eldest brother; that they resolved to put him in his mercy, which he was forced to yield to. So they presently sail for Coigeach, and delivered him to his brother, who he had no sooner got but he made him short by the head in the month of July 1597. Immediately he was beheaded there arose a great earthquake, which astonished the actors and all the inhabitants about them as a sign of God's judgment."—*Ancient MS.*

mitted to Edinburgh Castle, from which, however, he contrived to escape without trial, through his influence with the Lord Chancellor. After various battles and skirmishes had been fought between the brothers, the adventurers returned in strong force to the Island, armed with a commission of fire and sword, and all the Government power at their back against Tormod. The quarrel between the parties continued with varied success and failure on both sides; the adventurers again relinquished their settlement, and returned to Fife to bewail their losses, having solemnly promised never again to return to the Island or molest Mackenzie.

Kintail now, in virtue of Torquil Cononach's resignation in his favour, obtained a gift, under the great seal, of the Lews for himself through the influence of the Lord Chancellor. This he had, however, ultimately to resign into the hands of the King, and His Majesty, in 1608, vested these rights in the persons of Lord Balmerino, Sir George Hay, and Sir James Spence of Wormistoun, who undertook the colonisation of the island. For this purpose they made great preparations, and, assisted by the neighbouring tribes, invaded the Lews for the double purpose of planting a colony in it and of subduing and apprehending Neil Maelcod, who now alone defended the island. Mackenzie dispatched his . brother, Roderick, and Alexander Mackenzie of Coul, with a party of followers numbering 400, ostensibly to aid the colonists now acting under the King's commission, to whom he promised active friendship. At the same time he despatched a vessel from Ross loaded with provisions, but privately sent word to Neil Macleod to intercept her on the way, so that the settlers, being disappointed of their supply of the provisions in which they trusted for maintenance, should be obliged to abandon the island for want of the necessaries of life. Matters turned out just as Kintail anticipated : Sir George Hay and Spence (Lord Balmerino having meanwhile been convicted of high treason, and forfeited his rights) abandoned the Lews, leaving a party behind them to hold the fort, and intending to send

a fresh supply of men and provisions back to the island on
their arrival in Fife. But Neil Macleod and his followers
took and burnt the fort, apprehended the garrison, and
sent them safely to their homes " on giving their oath that
they would never come on that pretence again, which they
never did." Finding this, the Fife adventurers gave up
all hope of establishing themselves in the island, and sold
their acquired rights therein, as also their share of the
forfeited districts of Troternish and Waternish in Skye, to
Kenneth Mackenzie of Kintail, who at the same time obtained a grant from the King of Balmerino's forfeited share
of the Lews, thus finally acquiring what he had so long
and so anxiously desired. In addition to a fixed sum of
money, Mackenzie granted the adventurers " a lease of the
woods of Letterewe, where there was an iron mine, which
they wrought by English miners, casting guns and other
implements till their fuel was exhausted and their lease expired." The King confirmed this agreement, and " to encourage Kintail and his brother Roderick in their work of
civilizing the people of the Lews," he elevated the former
to the peerage as Lord Mackenzie of Kintail, at the same
time, on the 19th of November 1609, conferring the honour
of knighthood on his brother, Roderick Mackenzie of Coig-
cach.

In 1610 his Lordship returned to the Lews with 700
men, and finally brought the whole island to submission,
with the exception of Neil Macleod and a few of his followers, who retired to the rock of Berissay, and took possession of it. At this time religion appears to have been at
a very low ebb—almost extinct among the inhabitants; and,
to revive Christianity among them, his Lordship selected
and took along with him the Rev. Farquhar Macrae, a
native of Kintail and minister of Gairloch,* who had been
recommended to the latter charge by the Bishop of Ross.

* He brought with him Mr Farquhar Macrae who was then a young man and
minister of Gairloch and appointed by the Bishop of Ross (Lesley) to stay with
Sir George Hay and the Englishmen that were with him in Letterewe, being a
peaceful and eloquent preacher.—*Ardintoul MS.*

Mr Macrae found quite enough to do on his arrival in the
island, but he appears to have been very successful among
the uncivilised natives ; for he reports having gained many
over to Christianity; baptised a large number in the fortieth
year of their age ; and, to legitimise their children, married
many others to those women with whom they had been
for years cohabiting.   Leaving the rev. gentleman in the
prosecution of his mission, his Lordship returned home,
having established good order in the island, and promising
to return again the following year, to the great satisfaction
of the natives.

We must now follow him to the mainland, where, in 1597,
another fierce feud had broken out between the Mackenzies
and the Munros.[*]   John MacGillechallum, a brother of
the Laird of Raasay, annoyed the people of Torridon,
which place then belonged to the Baynes of Tulloch.   He
alleged that Tulloch, in whose house he was fostered, had
promised him these lands as a gift of fosterage ; but Tulloch, whether he had made a previous promise to John
MacGillechallum or not, left the lands of Torridon to his
own second son, Alexander Mor MacDhonnchaidh Mhic
Alastair, *alias* Bayne.   He afterwards obtained a decree·
against young MacGillechallum for interfering with his
lands and molesting the people, and, on a Candlemas market, with a large following of armed men, composed of most
of the Baynes, and a considerable number of Munros,
he came to the market stance, at that time held at Logie.
John MacGillechallum, quite ignorant of Tulloch "getting
the laws against him," and in no fear of his life or liberty,
came to the market as usual, and, while standing buying
some article at a chapman's stall, Alastair Mor and his followers came up behind him unperceived, and, without any
warning, struck him on the head with a two-edged sword
—instantly killing him.   A gentleman of the Clann Mhurchaidh Riabhaich Mackenzies, Ian Mac Mhurchaidh Mhic

---

[*] Sir Robert Gordon's Earldom of Sutherland, p. 236, and MS. Histories of
the Family.

Uilleam, a very active and powerful man, was at the time
standing beside him, and asked who dared to have spilt
Mackenzie blood in that dastardly manner. He had no
sooner said the words than he was run through the body
with one of the swords of the enemy ; and thus, without an
opportunity of drawing their weapons, fell two of the best
swordsmen in the North of Scotland. The alarm and the
news of their death immediately spread through the market.
" Tulloch Ard," the war cry of the Mackenzies, was instantly
raised ; whereupon the Baynes and the Munros took to
their heels—the Munros eastward to the Ferry of Fowlis,
and the Baynes northward to the hills, both followed by a
band of the infuriated Mackenzies, who slaughtered every
one they overtook. Iain Dubh Mac Choinnich Mhic
Mhurchaidh of the Clann Mhurchaidh Riabhaich, and Iain
Gallda Mac Fhionnla Dhuibh, two gentlemen of the Mackenzies, the latter of whom was a Kintail man, were on
their way from Chanonry to the market, when they met
in with a batch of the Munros flying in confusion, and,
learning the cause to be the murder of their friends at
Logie market, they instantly pursued the fugitives, killing
no less than thirteen of them between Logie and the wood
of Millechaich. All the townships in the neighbourhood of
the market joined the Mackenzies in the pursuit, and Alastair Mor Bayne of Tulloch only saved himself, after all his
men were killed, by taking shelter and hiding for a time in
a kiln-logie. Two of his followers, who managed to escape
from the market people, met with some Lewsmen on their
way to the fair, who, noticing the Baynes flying half naked,
immediately stopped them, and insisted upon their giving a
proper account of themselves. This proving unsatisfactory
they came to high words, and from words to blows, when
the Lewsmen attacked and killed them at Acha-n-cilich,
near Contin. The Baynes and the Munros had good
cause to regret the cowardly conduct of their leaders on
this occasion at Logie market, for they lost no less than
the fifty able-bodied men in return for the two gentlemen of
Clan Mackenzie whom they had so basely murdered at the

fair. One lady of the Clan Munro lost her three brothers, on whom she composed a lament, of which the following is all we could obtain :—

> 'S olc a' fhuair mi tus an Earraich,
> 'S na feill Bride 'chaidh thairis,
> Chaill mi mo thriuir bhraithrean geala,
> Taobh ri taobh a' sileadh fala.
> 'Se n dithis a rinn mo sharach',
> Fear beag dubh a chlaidheamh laidir,
> 'S mac Fhionnla Dhuibh á Cinntaile
> Deadh mhearlach nan adh 's nan aigeach.

When night came on, Alastair Mor Bayne escaped from the kiln, and went to his uncle Lovat, who at once despatched James Fraser of Phopachy south, with all speed to prevent information from the other side reaching the King before he had an opportunity of relating his version of the quarrel. His Majesty was at the time at Falkland, and a messenger from Mackenzie reached him, before Alastair Mor, pursuing for the slaughter of Mackenzie's kinsman. He got the ear of his Majesty and would have been successful had not John Dubh Mac Choinnich Mhic Mhurchaidh meanwhile taken the law into his own hands by burning, in revenge, all Bayne's cornyards and barns at Lemlair, thus giving Bayne an opportunity of presenting another and counter claim ; but the matter was ultimately arranged by the King and Council obliging Kintail and Tulloch mutually to subscribe a contract of agreement and peaceful behaviour towards each other in all time coming.

In the same year, Alexander MacGorrie and Ranald MacRory, sons of Glengarry's uncles murdered in Lochcarron in 1580, having arrived at maturity, and being brave and intrepid fellows, determined to revenge upon Mackenzie the death of their parents. With this object they went to Applecross, where lived one of the murderers, John Og, son of Angus MacEachainn, surrounded his house, and set fire to it, burning to death himself and his whole family. Kintail sought redress from Glengarry, who, while he did not absolutely refuse, did not grant it, or punish the wrongdoers; and encouraged by Glengarry's eldest son, Angus, who had now attained his majority, the cousins, taking advantage of Mackenzie's absence, who had gone on a visit to France, continued their depredations and insolence wherever they found opportunity. Besides, they made a complaint against him to the Privy Council, whereupon he was charged at the pier of Leith to appear before the Council on an appointed day under pain of forfeiture. In this emergency, Mr John Mackenzie, minister of Dingwall, went privately to France in search of his chief, whom he found and brought back in the most secret manner to Edinburgh, fortunately in time to present himself next day before the Council, in terms of the summons at Glengarry's instance; and, after consulting his legal adviser and other friends, he appeared quite unexpectedly before their Lordships.

Meantime, while the gentlemen were on their way from France, Alexander MacGorrie and Alexander MacRory killed in his bed Donald Mackenneth Mhic Alastair, a gentleman of the family of Davochmaluag, who lived at Kishorn. The shirt, covered with his blood, had been sent to Edinburgh to await Mackenzie's arrival, who, the same day presented it before the Privy Council, as evidence of the foul crime committed by his accusers. Glengarry was quite unable to prove anything material against Kintail or his followers; but, on the contrary, the Rev. John Mackenzie of Dingwall charged Glengarry with being instrumental in the murder of John Og and his family at Applecross, as also in that of Donald Mackenzie of Darochmaluag, and undertook not only to prove this, but also that he was a sorner, an oppressor of his own and of his neighbours' tenants, an idolater, who had a man in Lochbroom making images, in testimony of which he carried south the image of St Coan, which Glengarry worshipped, called in Edinburgh Glengarry's God, and which was, by public order, burnt at the Town Cross; that Glengarry was a man who lived in constant adultery with the Captain of Clan Ranald's daughter, after he had put away the laird of Grant's daughter, his lawful wife; whereupon Glengarry was summoned there and then to appear next day before the Council, and to lodge defences to this unexpected charge. He naturally became alarmed, and fearing the worst, fled from the city during the night, "took to his heels," and gave up further legal proceedings against Mackenzie. Being afterwards repeatedly summoned, and failing to put in an appearance, most of the charges were found proven against him; and, in 1602,* he was declared an outlaw and a rebel; a commission of fire and sword was granted to Mackenzie against Glengarry and all his followers, with a decree of ransom for the loss of those who were burnt and plundered by him, and for Kintail's charges and expenses, making altogether a very large sum. But while these legal matters were being arranged, Angus Macdonald, younger of Glengarry, who was of a restless, daring disposition, went with some of his followers under silence of night to Kintail, burnt the township of Cro, killed and burnt several men, women, and children, and carried away a large spoil of cattle.

Mackenzie, hearing of this sudden raid, became much concerned about the loss of his Kintail tenants, and decided to requite the quarrel by at once executing his commission against the Macdonalds of Glengarry, and immediately set out in pursuit, leaving a sufficient number of men at home to secure the safety of his property. He took with him a force of seventeen hundred men, at the same time taking three hundred cows from his farm of Strathbran to maintain his followers. Ross of Balnagowan sent a party of a hundred and eighty men, under command of Alexander Ross of Invercharron, to aid his neighbour of Kintail, while John Gordon of Embo commanded a hundred and twenty men sent to his aid by the Earl of Sutherland, in virtue of the long standing bond of manrent between the two families; but, according to our authority, Sir John "retired at Monar, growing faint-hearted

* Record of Privy Council, 9th September 1602; Sir Robert Gordon's Earldom of Sutherland, p. 248; Letterfearn, Ardintoul, and other MS. Histories of the Mackenzies.

before he saw the enemie." Andrew Munro of Novar also accompanied Kintail on this, as on several previous expeditions. The Macdonalds, hearing of Mackenzie's approach, drove all their cattle to Morar, where they gathered in strong force to guard them. Kintail, learning this, marched straight where they were ; harried and wasted all the country through which he had to pass ; defeated and routed the Macdonalds, and drove into Kintail the largest booty ever heard of in the Highlands of Scotland, "both of cows, horses, small bestial, duin-uasals, and plenishing, which he most generously distributed amongst his soldiers, and especially amongst such strangers as were with him, so that John Gordon of Embo was at his repentance for his return." Mackenzie had only two men killed in this expedition, though a few of the Kintail men, whom he caused to be carried home on litters, were wounded.

Several instances are recorded of the prowess and intrepidity of Alexander of Coul on this occasion. He was, excepting John MacMhurchaidh Mhic Ghillechriost, the fastest runner in the Mackenzie country. On his way to Kintail, leading his men and driving the creach before them, he met three or four hundred Camerons, who sent his Chief a message demanding "a bounty of the booty" for passing through their territory. This Mackenzie was about to grant, and ordered thirty cows and a few of the younger animals to be given, saying that it "was fit that hungry dogs should get a collop ;" whereupon Alexander of Coul and his brave band of one hundred and twenty followers started aside, and swore with a great oath that if the Camerons dared to take away a single head, they would, before night, pay dearly for them, and have to fight for their collop ; for he and his men, he said, had already nearly lost their lives driving them through a wild and narrow pass where eighteen of the enemy fell to their swords before they were able to get the cattle through ; but he would now let them pass in obedience to his Chief's commands. The messengers, hearing the ominous threat, notwithstanding Kenneth's personal persuasion, declined on any

account to take the cattle, and marched away "empty as
they came."

Before starting from home on this expedition, Kintail
drove every one of Glengarry's followers out of their hold-
ings in Lochalsh and Lochcarron, except a few of the
"Mathewsons and the Clann Ian Uidhir," and any others
who promised to submit to him and to prove their sincerity
by "imbrowing their hands in the enemy's blood." The
Castle of Strome, however, still continued in possession of
the Macdonalds.

Mackenzie, after his return home, had not well dissolved
his camp when Alexander MacGorrie and Ranald MacRory
made an incursion to the district of Kenlochewe, and there
meeting some women and children who had fled from Lochcarron with their cattle, he attacked them unexpectedly,
killed many of the defenceless women, all the male children,
killed and took away many of the cattle, and "houghed"
all they were not able to carry along with them.

In the following autumn, Alexander MacGorrie made a
voyage to Applecross in a great galley, contrary to the advice of all his friends, who looked upon that place as a
sanctuary which all Highlanders had hitherto respected, it
being the property of the Church. Notwithstanding that
many took refuge in it in the past, he was the first man who
ever pursued a fugitive to the place, "but," says our authority, "it fared no better with him or he rested, but he being
informed that some Kintail men, whom he thought no sin to
kill anywhere," had taken refuge there with their cattle, he
determined to kill them, but on his arrival he found only
two poor fellows, tending their cows. These he murdered,
slaughtered all the cows, and took away as many of them
as his boat would carry.

A few days after this Glengarry combined with the
Clann Alain of Moydart (whose chief was at the time
captain of Clan Ranald's men), the Clann Ian Uidhir, and
several others of the Macdonalds, who gathered together
amongst them thirty-seven birlinns with the intention of
sailing to Lochbroom, and on their return to burn and harry

the whole of the Mackenzie territories on the west coast.
Coming to an arm of the sea on the east side of Kyleakin,
called Loch na Beist, opposite Lochalsh, they sent Alexander MacGorrie forward with eighty men in a large galley
to examine the coast in advance of the main body. They
first landed in Applecross, in the same spot where Mac-
Gorrie had previously killed the two Kintail men. Kintail
was at the time on a visit to Mackenzie of Gairloch, at his
house on Island Rory in Loch-Maree, and hearing of Glengarry's approach and the object of his visit, he ordered all
his coasts to be placed in readiness, and sent Alexander
Mackenzie of Achilty with sixteen men and eight oarsmen,
in an eight oared galley belonging to John Tolmach Macleod, son of Rory Mhic Allan Macleod, who still possessed
a small portion of Gairloch, to watch the enemy and examine the coast as far as Kylerhea. John Tolmach himself
accompanied them, in charge of the galley. On their way
south they landed by the merest chance at Applecross, on
the north side of the point where MacGorrie landed, where
they noticed a woman gathering shellfish on the shore, and
who no sooner saw them than she came and informed them
that a great galley had landed in the morning on the other
side of the promontory. They at once suspected it to be
an advanced scout of the enemy, and, ordering their boat·
round the point, in charge of the oarsmen, they took the
shortest cut across the neck of land, and, when half way
over, they met one of Madonald's sentries lying sound
asleep on the ground. He was soon sent to his long rest ;
and the Mackenzies blowing up a set of bagpipes found
lying beside him, rushed towards the Macdonalds, who, suddenly surprised and alarmed by the sound of the bagpipes,
and thinking a strong force was falling down upon them,
fled to their boat, except MacGorrie, who, when he left it,
swore a great oath that he would never return with his back
to the enemy ; but finding it impossible single-handed to
resist them, he retired a little, closely followed by the Mackenzies, who furiously attacked him. He was now forced
to draw aside to a rock, against which he placed his back,

K

and fought right manfully, defending himself with extraordinary intrepidity, receiving the enemy's arrows in his targe. He was ultimately wounded by an arrow which struck him under the belt, yet no one dared to approach him ; but John Dubh MacChoinnich Mhic Mhurchaidh noticing his amazing agility, seeing his party had arrived with the boat, and fearing they would loose Glengarry's galley unless they at once pursued it, went round to the back of the rock against which the brave Macdonald stood, carrying a great boulder, which he dropped straight on to MacGorrie's head, instantly killing him. Thus died the most skilful and best chieftain—had he possessed equal wisdom and discretion— then alive among the Macdonalds of Glengarry.

The Mackenzies immediatly took to their boat, pursuing Macdonald's galley to Loch na Beist, where, noticing the enemy's whole fleet coming out against them, John Tolmach recommended them to put out to sea ; but finding the fleet gaining upon them, they decided to land in Applecross, where they were nearly overtaken by the enemy. They were obliged to leave their boat and run for their lives, hotly pursued by the Macdonalds; and were it not that one of Mackenzie's men—John Mac Rory Mhic Mhurchaidh Matthewson—was so well acquainted with the ground, and led them to a ford on the river between two rocks, which the Macdonalds missed, and the night coming on, they would have been unable to escape with their lives. The Macdonalds retraced their steps to their boats, and on the way discovered the body of Alexander MacGorrie, whose death " put their boasting to mourning," and conceiving his fate ominous of additional misfortunes, they, carrying him along with them, prudently returned home, and disbanded all their followers. In the flight of the Mackenzies Alexander of Achilty, being so stout that he fainted on the way, was nearly captured. John MacChoinnich, who noticed him falling, threw some water on him, and, drawing his sword, swore that he would kill him on the spot if he did not get up at once rather than that the enemy should have the honour to kill or capture him. They soon arrived at Gairloch's house in Loch-Maree, and gave a full account of their expedition, whereupon Kintail immediately decided upon taking active measures against the Macdonalds. In the meantime he was assured that they had returned to their own country. He soon returned home, and found that the people of Kintail and Glengarry, tiring of those incessant slaughters and mutual injuries, agreed, in his absence, in the month of May, to cease hostilities until the following Lammas. Of this agreement Kintail knew nothing ; and young Glengarry, who was of an exceedingly bold and restless disposition, against the earnest solicitations of his father, who became a party to this agreement between his people and those of Kintail, started with a strong force to Glenshiel and Letterfearn, while Allan Macdonald of Lundy with another party went to Glenelchaig, harried those places, took away a large number of cattle, killed some of the aged men, several women, and all the male children. They found none of the principal and able-bodied men, who had withdrawn some distance that they might, with greater advantage, gather together in a body and defend themselves, except Duncan Mac-Ian Mhic Ghillechallum in Killichirtorn, whom the enemy apprehended, and would have killed, had not one of the Macdonalds, formerly his friend and acquaintance, prevailed upon young Glengarry to save his life, and send him to the Castle of Strome, where he still had a garrison, rather than kill him.

The successful result of this expedition encouraged Angus so much that he began to think fortune had at last turned in his favour, and he set out and called personally upon all the chiefs and leaders of the various branches of the Macdonalds throughout the west, soliciting their assistance against the Mackenzies, which they all agreed to give in the following spring.

This soon came to Mackenzie's knowledge, who was at the time residing in Islandonain Castle ; and fearing the consequences of such a powerful combination against him, he went privately to Mull by sea to consult his brother-in-law, Maclean of Duart, to whom he told that he had a com-

mission of fire and sword against "the rebels of Glengarry
and such as would rise in arms to assist them, and being informed that the Macdonalds near him (Maclean) had combined to join them, and to put him to further trouble, that,
therefore, he would not only, as a good subject but as his
fast friend, divert these whenever they should rise in arms
against him."* Maclean undertook to prevent the assistance
of the Clan Ranald of Isla, Glencoe, and Ardnamurchan, by,
if necessary, invading their territories, and thus compelling
them to protect their own interests at home. It appears
that old Glengarry was still anxious to arrange a permanent
peace with Mackenzie ; but young Angus, restless and turbulent as ever, would not hear of any peaceful settlement,
and determined to start at once upon an expedition, from
which his father told him at the time he had little hopes of
his ever returning alive—a presentiment or shrewd forecast
which turned out only too true.

Angus, taking advantage of Mackenzie's absence in
Mull, gathered, in the latter end of November, as secretly
as he could, all the boats and great galleys within his
reach, and, with this large fleet, loaded with his followers,
passed through the Kyles under silence of night ; and, coming to Lochcarron, he sent his marauders ashore in the
twilight. The inhabitants perceiving them, escaped to the
hills, but the Macdonalds cruelly slaughtered the aged men
who could not escape, and many of the women and children ;
seized all the cattle, and drove them to the Island of Slum-
bay, where their boats lay, which they filled with the car-
cases. Before, however, they had fully loaded, the alarm
having gone through the districts of Lochalsh and Kintail
some of the natives of those districts were seen coming
in the direction of Lochcarron. The Macdonalds deemed
it prudent to remain no longer, and set out to sea pursued
by a shower of arrows by way of a farewell, which, however,
had but very little effect upon them, as they were already
out of range.

* Ardintoul MS.

. The Kintail men, by the shortest route, now returned to
Islandonain, sending twelve of the swiftest of their number
across country to Inverinate, where lay, newly built, a
twelve-oared galley which had never been to sea belonging
to Gillecriost MacDonnchaidh, one of Inverinate's tenants.
These heroes made such rapid progress that they were back
at the castle with the boat before many of their companions
had arrived from Lochcarron. During the night they set to
work, superintended and encouraged by Lady Mackenzie in
person, to make arrangements to go and meet the enemy.
The best men were quickly picked out. The Lady supplied
them with all the materials and necessaries within her reach,
handed them the lead and powder with her own hands,
and gave them two small pieces of brass ordnance. She
ordered Duncan MacGhillechriost, a powerful handsome
fellow, to take command of the galley in his father's absence,
and in eloquent terms charged them all with the honour of
her house and her own protection in her husband's absence.
This was hardly necessary, for the Kintail men had not yet
forgotten the breach of faith which had been committed by
Macdonald regarding the recent agreement to cease hostilities for a stated time, and other recent sores. Her ladyship
wishing them God-speed, they started on their way rejoicing,
and in the best of spirits. She mounted the castle walls,
and stood there encouraging them until, by the darkness of
the night, she could no longer see them.

On their way towards Kylerhea they met a boat from
Lochalsh sent out to inform them of the enemy's arrival at
Kyleakin. Learning this, they cautiously kept their course
close to the south side of the loch. It was a calm moonlight
night, with occasional slight showers of snow. The tide had
already began to flow, and, judging that the Macdonalds
would wait the next turning of the tide to enable them to
get through Kylerhea, the Kintail men, longing for their
prey, resolved to advance and meet the enemy. They had
not proceeded far, rowing very gently, after placing seaweed
in the rowlocks so as not to make a noise, when they noticed
a boat rowing at the hardest and coming in their direction ;

but from its small size they thought it must have been sent
by the Macdonalds in advance to test the passage of Kylerhea. They therefore allowed it to pass unmolested, and
proceeded northward, looking for Macdonald's own galley.
When they neared the Cailleach, a low rock midway between
both Kyles, it was seen in the distance covered with snow.
The night also favoured them, the sea, calm, appearing
black and mournful to the enemy. Here they met his first
galley, and drawing up near it, they soon discovered it to be
no other than Macdonald's own great galley, some distance
ahead of the rest of the fleet. Macdonald, as soon as he
noticed them, called out " Who is there?" twice in succession,
but received no answer, and finding the Kintail men drawing nearer he called out the third time, when, in reply, he
received a full broadside from Mackenzie's cannon, which
disabled his galley and threw her on the Cailleach Rock.
The men on board Macdonald's galley thought they had
been driven on shore, and flocked to the fore part of the
boat, striving to escape, thus capsizing and filling the galley.
Discovering their position, and seeing a long stretch of sea
lying between them and the mainland, they became quite
confused, and were completely at the mercy of their enemies,
who sent some of their men ashore to despatch any of the
poor wretches who might swim ashore, while others remained in their boat killing and drowning the Macdonalds.
Such of them as managed to reach the shore were killed or
drowned by those of the Kintail men who went ashore, not
a soul out of the sixty men on board the galley having
managed to escape, except Angus Macdonald himself, still
breathing, though he had been wounded twice in the head
and once in the body. He was yet alive when they took
him aboard their galley, but he died before the morning.
Hearing the uproar, several of the Lochalsh people went
out with all speed in two small boats, under the command
of Dugall MacMhurchaidh Matthewson, to take part in the
fray ; but by the time they arrived few of Macdonald's followers were alive. Thus ended the career of Angus, younger
of Glengarry, a chief to whom his followers looked up, and

whom they justly regarded as a bold and intrepid leader, though deficient in prudence and strategy.

The remainder of Macdonald's fleet, to the number o twenty-one, following behind his own galley, having heard the uproar, returned to Kyleakin in such terror and confusion that each thought his nearest neighbour was pursuing him. Landing in Strathardale, they left their boats " and their ill-cooked beef to these hungry gentlemen," and before they slept they arrived in Sleat, from whence they were sent across to the mainland in the small boats of the laird.

The great concern and anxiety of her ladyship of Islandonain can be easily conceived, for all that she had yet learnt was the simple fact that an engagement of some kind had taken place, and this she only knew from having heard the sound of cannon during the night. Early in the morning she noticed her protectors returning with their birlinn, accompanied by another great galley. This brightened her hopes, and going down to the shore to meet them, she heartily saluted them, and asked if all had gone well with them. " Yea, Madam," answered their leader, Duncan MacGillechriost, " we have brought you a new guest, without the loss of a single man, whom we hope is welcome to your ladyship." She looked into the galley, and at once recognising the body of Angus of Glengarry, she ordered it to be carried ashore and properly attended to. The men proposed that he should be buried in the tomb of his predecessors, " Cnoc nan Aingeal," in Lochalsh; but this she objected to, observing that, if he could, her husband would never allow a Macdonald, dead or alive, any further possession in that locality, at the same time ordering young Glengarry to be buried with her own children, and such other children of the predecessors of the Mackenzies of Kintail as were buried in Kilduich, saying that she considered it no disparagement for him to be buried with such cousins; and if it were her own fate to die in Kintail, she would desire to be buried amongst them. The proposal was agreed to, and everything having been got ready suitable for the funeral of a gentleman of his rank—such as the place could afford in the circumstances—he was buried next day in Kilduich, in the same tomb as Mackenzie's own children. This is not the most generally received account regarding Angus Macdonald's burial ; but we are glad, for the credit of our common humanity, to find the following conclusive testimony in an imperfect but exeellently written MS. of the seventeeth century, otherwise remarkably correct and trustworthy :—" Some person, out of what reason I cannot tell, will needs affirm he was buried in the church door, as men go out and in, which to my certain knowledge is a malicious lie, for with my very eyes I have seen his head raised out of the same grave and returned again, wherein there was two small cuts, noways deep."*

The author of the Ardintoul MS. informs us that Mac-Lean had actually invaded Ardnamurchan, and carried fire and sword into that and the adjoining territory of the Macdonalds, whereupon the Earl of Argyll, who claimed the Macdonalds of those districts as his vassals and dependants, obtained criminal letters against MacLean, who, finding this, sent for his brother-in-law Mackenzie of Kintail, at whose request he had invaded the country of the Macdonalds. Both started for Inveraray. The Earl seemed most determined to punish MacLean, but Mackenzie informed him that "he should rather be blamed for it than MacLean, and the King and Council than either of them, for he having obtained, upon good grounds, a commission of fire and sword against Glengarry and such as would assist him, and against these men's rebellion and wicked courses, which frequently his lordship seemed to own, that he did charge, as he did severall others of the king's loyal subjects, MacLean to assist him." So that, if MacLean was to be punished for acting as his friend and as a loyal subject, he hoped to obtain a hearing before the King and Council under whose orders he acted. After considerable discussion, they parted good friends, Argyll having agreed not to molest MacLean any further. Mackenzie and Mac-

* Ancient MS.

Lean returned to Duart, where his lordship was warmly received and sumptuously entertained by MacLean's immediate friends and kinsmen for the services which he had just rendered to their chief. While thus engaged, a messenger arrived at the castle from Mackenzie's lady and the Kintail men.

After the funeral of young Glengarry, she became concerned about her husband's safe return, and was at the same time most anxious that he would be advised of the state of matters at home. She therefore despatched Robert Mac Dhomh'uill Uidhir to arrange the safest plan for bringing her lord safely home, as the Macdonalds were still prowling among the creeks and bays further south. Robert, after the interchange of unimportant preliminaries, informed his master of all that had taken place during his absence. MacLean, amazed to hear of such gallant conduct by the Kintail men in the absence of their chief, asked Mackenzie if any of his own kinsmen were amongst them, and being informed there were not, MacLean replied, " It was a great and audacious deed to be done by fellows." " Truly, MacLean," returned Mackenzie, " they were not fellows that were there, but prime gentlemen, and such fellows as would act the enterprise better than myself and kinsmen." " You have very great reason to make the more of them," said Maclean; " he is a happy superior who has such a following." Both chiefs then went outside to consult as to the best and safest means for Mackenzie's homeward journey. MacLean offered him all his chief and best men to accompany him by land, but this he declined, saying that he would not put his friend to such inconvenience, and would return home in his own boat just as he came ; but he was ultimately persuaded to take MacLean's great galley, his own being only a small one. He sailed in his friend's great birlinn, under the command of the Captain of Cairnburgh, accompanied by several other gentlemen of the MacLeans.

In the meantime, the Macdonalds, aware that Mackenzie had not yet returned from Mull, "convened all the boats and galleys they could, to a certain island which lay in his course, and which he could not avoid passing. So, coming within sight of the island, having a good prospect of a number of boats, after they had ebbed in a certain harbour, and men also, making ready to set out to sea. This occasioned the captain to use a stratagem, and steer directly to the harbour, and still as they came forward he caused lower the sail, which the other party perceiving made them forbear putting out their boats, persuading themselves that it was a galley they expected from Ardnamurchan, but they had no sooner come ' forgainst the harbour but the captain caused hoist sail, set oars and steers aside, immediately bangs up a bag-piper and gives them shots. The rest, finding the cheat and their own mistake, made such a hurly-burly setting out their boats, with their haste they broke some of them, and some of themselves were bruised and had broken shins also for their prey, and such as went out whole, perceiving the galley so far off, thought it was folly to pursue her any further, they all returned wiser than they came from home."

" This is, notwithstanding other men's reports, the true and real narration of Glengarrie Younger his progress, of the Kintail men their meeting him in Kyle Rhea, of my lord's coming from Mull, and of the whole success, which I have heard *verbatim* not only from one but from several that were present at their actings."*

. Mackenzie arrived at Islandonain late at night, where he found his lady still entertaining her brave Kintail men after their return from Glengarry's funeral. While not a little concerned about the death of his troublesome relative, he heartily congratulated his gallant retainers on the excellent manner in which they had protected his interests during his absence. Certain that the Macdonalds would never rest satisfied until they had wiped out and revenged the death

---

* Ancient MS. The authors of the Letterfearn and Ardintoul MSS., give substantially the same account, and say that among those who accompanied Mackenzie to Mull, was " Rory Beg Mackenzie, son to Rory More of Achigluni-chan, Fairburn and Achilty's predecessor, and who afterwards died parson of Contine, from whom my author had the full account of Mackenzie's voyage to Mull."

of their leader, Mackenzie determined to drive them out of
the district altogether. The castle of Strome, still in possession of Glengarry, was the greatest obstacle in carrying out
this resolution, for it was a good and convenient asylum for
the Macdonalds when pursued by Mackenzie and his followers; but he ultimately succeeded in wresting it from
them.

We give the following account of how it was taken from
the Ancient MS., slightly modernising the spelling:—" In
the spring of the following year, Lord Kintail gathered together considerable forces and besieged the castle of Strome
in Lochcarron, which at first held out very manfully, and
would not surrender, though several terms were offered,
which he (Mackenzie) finding, not willing to lose his men,
resolved to raise the siege for a time; but the defenders
were so unfortunate as to have their powder damaged by
the women they had within. Having sent them out by
silence of night to draw in water, out of a well that lay just
at the entrance of the castle, the silly women were in such
fear, and the room they brought the water into being so
dark for want of light, when they came in they poured the
water into a vat, missing the right one, wherein the few
barrels of powder they had lay. And in the morning, when
the men came for more powder, having exhausted the supply
of the previous day, they found the barrels of powder floating
in the vat; so they began to rail and abuse the poor women,
which the fore-mentioned Duncan Mac Ian Mhic Gilliechal-
lum, still a prisoner in the castle, hearing, as he was at liberty
through the house, having promised and made solemn oath
that he would never come out of the door until he was ransomed or otherwise relieved." This he was obliged to do to
save his life. But having discovered the accident which befel
the powder, he accompanied his keepers to the ramparts of
the castle, when he noticed his countrymen packing up their
baggage as if intending to raise the siege. Duncan instantly
threw his plaid over the head of the man that stood next to
him, and jumped over the wall on to a large dung heap that
stood immediately below. He was a little stunned, but in-

stantly recovered himself, flew with the fleetness of a deer
to Mackenzie's camp, and informed his chief of the state of
matters within the stronghold.   Kintail renewed the siege
and brought his scaling ladders nearer the castle.   The
defenders seeing this, and knowing that their mishap and
consequent plight had been disclosed by Duncan to the
enemy, they offered to yield up the castle on condition that
their lives would be spared, and that they be allowed to carry
away their baggage.   This was readily granted them, and
" my lord caused presently blow up the house with powder,
which remains there in heaps to this day.   He lost only but
two Kenlochewe men at the siege.   Andrew Munro of
Teannouher (Novar) was wounded, with two or three others,
and so dissolved the camp."*   Another writer says :—" The
rooms are to be seen yet.   It stood on a high rock, which
extended in the midst of a little bay of the sea westward,
which made a harbour or safe port for great boats or vessels
of no great burden, on either side of the castle.   It was a
very convenient place for Alexander Mac Gillespick to
dwell in when he had both the countries of Lochalsh and
Lochcarron, standing on the very march between both."

A considerable portion of the walls is still (1879) standing, but no trace of the apartments.   The sea must have
receded many feet since it was in its glory ; for now it
barely touches the base of the rock on which the ruin stands.
We have repeatedly examined it, and with mixed feelings
ruminated upon its past history, and what its ruined walls,
could they only speak, might bear witness to.

In the following year (1603) the chief, Donald Gruamach,
having died, and the heir being still under age, the Macdonalds, under Donald's cousin, Allan Dubh MacRanuil of
Lundy, made an incursion into the country of Mackenzie,
in Brae Ross, plundered the lands of Cillechriost, and fero-
ciously set fire to the church during divine service, when full
of men, women, and children, while Glengarry's piper
marched round the building cruelly mocking the heartrend-

* Ardintoul MS.

ing wails of the burning women and children, playing the well-known pibroch, which has been known ever since by the name of " Cilliechriost," as the family tune of the Macdonalds of Glengarry. " Some of the Macdonalds chiefly concerned in this inhuman outrage were afterwards killed by the Mackenzies ; but it is somewhat startling to reflect that this terrible instance of private vengeance should have occurred in the commencement of the seventeenth century, without, so far as we can trace, any public notice being taken of such an enormity. In the end the disputes between the chiefs of Glengarry and Kintail were amicably settled by an arrangement which gave the Ross-shire lands, so long the subject of dispute, entirely to Mackenzie ; and the hard terms to which Glengarry was obliged to submit in the private quarrel, seemed to have formed the only punishment inflicted on this clan for the cold-blooded atrocity displayed in the memorable raid on Kilchrist."*

The following account of this atrocious and inhuman act is extracted from a recent publication :—" Macranuil of Lundi, captain of the clan, whose personal prowess was only equalled by his intense ferocity, made many incursions into the Mackenzie country, sweeping away their cattle and otherwise doing them serious injury ; but these were but preludes to that sanguinary act on which his soul gloated, and by which he hoped effectually to avenge the loss of influence and property of which his clan was deprived by the Mackenzies, and more particularly to wash out the records of the death of his chief and clansman at Kyleakin. In order to form his plans more effectually, he wandered for some time as a mendicant among the Mackenzies, in order the more successfully to fix on the best means and place for his revenge. A solitary life offered up to expiate the manes of his relatives was not sufficient in his estimation, but the life's blood of such a number of his bitterest foemen, and an act at which the country should stand aghast was absolutely necessary.

* Gregory, pp. 302 3.

" Returning home, he gathered together a number of the
most desperate of his clan, and by a forced march across
the hills arrived at the Church of Cilliechriost on a Sunday
forenoon, when it was filled by a crowd of worshippers of
the Clan Mackenzie. Without a moment's delay, without
a single pang of remorse, and while the song of praise ascended to heaven from fathers, mothers, and children, he
surrounded the church with his band, and with lighted
torches set fire to the roof. The building was thatched, and
while a gentle breeze from the east fanned the fire, the song
of praise mingled with the crackling of the flames, until the
imprisoned congregation, becoming conscious of their situation, rushed to the doors and windows, where they were
met by a double row of bristling swords. Now, indeed,
arose the wild wail of despair, the shrieks of women, the
infuriated cries of men, and the helpless screaming of children ; these mingled with the roaring of the flames appalled
even the Macdonells, but not so Allan Dubh. ' Thrust
them back into the flames,' cried he, ' for he that suffers
aught to escape alive from Cilliechriost shall be branded
as a traitor to his clan ;' and they were thrust back or mer-
cilessly hewn down within the narrow porch, until the dead
bodies, piled upon each other, opposed an insurmountable
barrier to the living. Anxious for the preservation of their
young children, the scorching mothers threw them from the
windows in the vain hope that the feelings of parents
awakened in the breasts of the Macdonells would induce
them to spare them, but not so. At the command of Allan
of Lundi they were received on the points of the broadswords of men in whose breasts mercy had no place. It
was a wild and fearful sight, only witnessed by a wild and
fearful race. During the tragedy they listened with delight
to the piper of the band, who, marching round the burning
pile, played, to drown the screams of the victims, an extem-
pore pibroch, which has ever since been distinguished as the
war tune of Glengarry, under the title of ' Cilliechriost.'
The flaming roof fell upon the burning victims ; soon the
screams ceased to be heard, a column of smoke and flame

leaped into the air, the pibroch ceased, the last smothering groan of existence ascended into the still sky of that Sabbath morning, whispering as it died away that the agonies of the congregation were over.

" East, west, north and south looked Allan Dubh Macranuil. Not a living soul met his eye. The fire he kindled had destroyed, like the spirit of desolation. Not a sound met his ear, and his own tiger soul sunk within him in dismay. The parish of Cilliechriost seemed swept of every living thing. The fearful silence that prevailed, in a quarter lately so thickly peopled, struck his followers with dread : for they had given in one hour the inhabitants of a whole parish one terrible grave. The desert which they had created filled them with dismay, heightened into terror by the howls of the masterless sheep dogs, and they turned to fly. Worn out with the suddenness of their long march from Glengarry, and with their late fiendish exertions, on their return they sat down to rest on the green face of Glenconvinth, which route they took in order to reach Lundi through the centre of Glenmorriston by Urquhart. Before they fled from Cilliechriost, Allan divided his party into two, one passing by Inverness and the other as already mentioned.

" The Macdonells, however, were not allowed to escape, for the terrible deed had roused the Mackenzies as effectually as if the fiery cross had been sent through their territories. A youthful leader, a cadet of the family of Seaforth, in an incredibly short time, found himself surrounded by a determined band of Mackenzies eager for the fray; these were also divided into two bodies, one commanded by Murdoch Mackenzie of Redcastle proceeded by Inverness, to follow the pursuit along the southern side of Loch-Ness. Another, headed by Alexander Mackenzie of Coul, struck across the country from Beauly, to follow the party of the Macdonells who fled along the northern side of Loch-Ness under their leader Allan Dubh Macranuil.

" The party that fled by Inverness were surprised by Redcastle in a public house at Torbreck, three miles to the west of the town, where they stopped to refresh themselves. The house was set on fire, and they all—thirty-seven in number—suffered the death which, in the earlier part of the day, they had so wantonly inflicted.

"The Mackenzies, under Coul, after a few hours hard running, came up with the Macdonells as they sought a brief repose on the hills towards the burn of Aultsigh. There the Macdonells maintained an unequal conflict ; but as guilt only brings faint hearts to its unfortunate votaries, they turned and again fled precipitately to the burn. Many, however, missed the ford, and the channel being rough and rocky several fell under the swords of the victorious Mackenzies. The remainder, with all the speed they could make, held on for miles, lighted by a splendid and cloudless moon, and when the rays of the morning burst upon them, Allan Dubh Macranuil and his party were seen ascending the southern ridge of Glen-Urquhart, with the Mackenzies close in their rear. Allan, casting an eye behind him, and observing the superior numbers and determination of his pursuers, called upon his band to disperse, in order to confuse his pursuers, and so divert the chase from himself. This being done, he again set forward at the height of his speed, and after a long run, drew breath to reconnoitre, when, to his dismay, he found that the avenging Mackenzies were still on his track in one unbroken mass. Again he divided his men and bent his flight towards the shore of Loch-Ness, but still he saw the foe bearing down upon him with redoubled vigour. Becoming fearfully alive to his position, he cried to his few remaining companions again to disperse, until they left him, one by one, and he was alone. Allan, who, as a mark of superiority and as Captain of the Glengarry Macdonells, always wore a red jacket, was thus easily distinguished from the rest of his clansmen, and the Mackenzies, being anxious for his capture, easily singled him out as the object of their joint and undivided pursuit. Perceiving the sword of vengeance ready to descend on his head, he took a resolution as desperate in its conception as it was unequalled in its accomplishment. Taking a short course towards the fearful ravine of Aultsigh, he divested himself of his plaid and buckler, and turning to the leader of the Mackenzies, who had nearly come up to him, beckoned him to follow, then, with a few yards of a run, he sprung over the yawning chasm, never before contemplated without a shudder. The agitation of his mind at the moment completely overshadowed the danger of the attempt, and being of an athletic frame, he succeeded in clearing the desperate leap. The young and reckless Mackenzie, full of ardour and determined at all hazards to capture the murderer, followed ; but, being a stranger to the real width of the chasm, perhaps of less nerve than his adversary, and certainly not stimulated with the same feelings, he only touched the opposite brink with his toes, and slipping downwards, he clung by a slender shoot of hazel which grew over the tremendous abyss. Allan Dubh, looking round on his pursuer and observing the agitation of the hazel bush, immediately guessed the cause, and returning with the ferocity of a demon who had succeeded in getting his victim into his fangs, hoarsely whispered, ' I have given much to your race this day, I shall give them this also ; surely now the debt is paid ;' then cutting the hazel twig with his sword, the intrepid youth was dashed from crag to crag until he reached the stream below, a bloody and mis-shapen mass.*

" Macranuil again commenced his flight, but one of the Mackenzies, who by this time had come up, sent a musket shot after him, by which he was wounded, and obliged to slacken his pace. None of his pursuers, however, on coming up to Aultsigh, dared dream of taking a leap which had been so fatal to their youthful leader, and were there-

---

* It is historically incorrect to say that Alexander Mackenzie of Coul leaped and perished on this occasion as described. It is possible one of his more daring followers may have done so, or it may more probably have been introduced to adorn the tale. The burning of Cillechriost took place in 1603, and it is beyond question that Alexander of Coul lived long after that date. He had a sasine of the lands of Kildun in 1607, and one of the lands of Pittonachty, or Rosebaugh, and others, as late as 1619—16 years after the burning of Cillechriost. He died a very old man in 1650,

L

fore under the necessity of taking a circuitous route to gain
the other side. This circumstance enabled Macranuil to
increase the distance between him and his pursuers, but the
loss of blood, occasioned by his wound, so weakened him
that very soon he found his determined enemies were fast
gaining on him. Like an infuriated wolf he hesitated
whether to await the undivided attack of the Mackenzies or
plunge into Loch-Ness and attempt to swim across its
waters. The shouts of his approaching enemies soon decided him, and he sprung into its deep and dark wave.
Refreshed by its invigorating coolness he soon swam beyond the reach of their muskets ; but in his weak and
wounded state it is more than probable he would have sunk
ere he had crossed the breadth had not the firing and the
shouts of his enemies proved the means of saving his life.
Fraser of Foyers seeing a numerous band of armed men
standing on the opposite bank of Loch-Ness, and observing
a single swimmer struggling in the water, ordered his boat
to be launched, and pulling hard to the individual, discovered him to be his friend Allan Dubh, with whose family
Fraser was on terms of friendship. Macranuil, thus rescued,
remained at the house of Foyers until he was cured of his
wound. The influence and the Clan of the Macdonells
subsequently declined, while that of the Mackenzies surely
and steadily increased.

"The heavy ridge between the vale of Urquhart and
Aultsigh, where Allan Dubh Macranuil so often divided
his men, is to this day called Monadh-an-leumanaich, or
'the Moor of the Leaper.'"*

Eventually Mackenzie succeeded in obtaining a crown
charter to the disputed districts of Lochalsh, Lochcarron,
and others, dated 1607 ; and the Macdonalds having now
lost the three ablest of their leaders, Donald's successor, his
second son, Alexander, thought it prudent to seek peace
with Mackenzie. This was, after some negotiation, agreed
to, and a day appointed for a final settlement.

* " Historical Tales and Legends of the Highlands," compiled by the Author
of this work, and published by A. & W. Mackenzie, Inverness,

In the meantime, Kintail sent for twenty-four of his ablest men in Kintail and Lochalsh, and took them, along with the best of his own kinsmen, to Baile Chaisteil, where his uncle Grant of Grant resided, with the view to purchase from him a heavy and long-standing claim he held against Glengarry for depredations committed on Grant's neighbouring territories in Glenmoriston and Glen-Urquhart. The uncle was unwilling to sell, but ultimately, on the persuasion of mutual friends, he offered to take thirty thousand merks for his claim. Mackenzie's kinsmen and other friends from the West were meanwhile lodged in a great kiln in the neighbourhood, amusing themselves with some of Grant's men who went to the kiln to keep them company. Kintail sent a messenger to the kiln to consult his people as to whether he would give such a large amount for Grant's "comprising" against Glengarry. The messenger was patiently listened to until he had finished, when he was told to go back and tell Grant and Mackenzie, that had they not entertained great hopes that the uncle would "give that paper as a gift to his nephew after all his trouble," he would not have been allowed to cross the Ferry of Ardersier ; for they would like to know where he could find such a large sum, unless he intended to harry them and his other friends, who had already suffered sufficiently in the wars with Glengarry ; and, so saying, they took to their arms, and desired the messenger to tell Mackenzie that it was their wish that he should leave the paper where it was. And if he desired to have it, they would sooner venture their own persons and those of their friends at home to secure it by force, than to give a sum which it would probably be more difficult to procure than to dispossess Glengarry altogether by their doughty arms. They then left the kiln, and sent one of their own number for their master, who, arriving, was strongly abused for entertaining such an extravagant proposal, and requested to leave the place at once. This he consented to, and went to inform Grant that his friends would not hear of his giving such a large sum, and that he preferred to dispense with the claim against Glengarry al-

together than lose the goodwill and friendship of his retainers, who had so often endangered their lives and fortunes
in his quarrels. Meanwhile, one of the Grants who had been
in the kiln communicated to his master the nature of the
conversation which had passed there when the price asked
by Grant was mentioned to the followers of Mackenzie,
which made such an impression upon Grant and his advisers,
that he prevailed upon Mackenzie, who was about starting
for home, to remain in the castle for another night. To
this he consented, and before morning he obtained the
"paper" for ten thousand merks—a third of the sum originally asked for it.

"Such familiar relationship of the chief with his people,"
our authority says, "may now-a-days be thought fabulous ;
but whoever considers the unity, correspondence, and amity
that was so well kept and entertained betwixt superiors
and their followers and vassals in former ages, besides as it
is now-a-days, he need not think it so ; and I may truly say
that there was no clan in the Highlands of Scotland that
would compete with the Mackenzies, their vassals and followers, as to that ; and it is sure their superiors in former
times would not grant their daughters in marriage without
their consent. Nor durst the meanest of them, on the other
hand, give theirs to any stranger without the superior's
consent ; and I heard in Earl Colin's time of a Kintail man
that gave his daughter in marriage to a gentleman in a
neighbouring country without the Earl's consent, who never
after had kindness for the giver, and, I may say, is yet the
blackest marriage for that country, and others also, that
ever was among their commons. But it may be objected
that now-a-days their commons' advice or consent in any
matter of consequence is not so requisite, whereas there are
many substantial friends to advise with ; but its an old
Scots phrase, ' A king's advice may fall from a fool's head.'
I confess that is true where friends are real friends, but we
ordinarily find, and partly know by experience, that, where
friends or kinsmen become great and rich in interest, they
readily become emulous, and will ordinarily advise for

themselves if in the least it may hinder them from becoming a chief or head of a family, and forget their former headship, which was one of the greatest faults, as also the ruin of Monro of Miltown, whereas a common man will never eye to become a chief so long as he is in that state, and therefore will advise his chief or superior the more freely."

The day appointed for the meeting of Mackenzie and Glengarry to arrange terms arrived. The former had meanwhile brought up several decrees and claims against Glengarry at the instance of neighbouring proprietors, for "cost, skaith and damage," which altogether amounted to a greater sum than the whole of Macdonald's lands were worth. They, however, settled their disputes by an arrangement which secured absolutely to Mackenzie all Glengarry's lands in Ross, and the superiority of all his other lands, but the latter Glengarry was to hold, paying Mackenzie a small feu as superior. In consideration of these humiliating concessions by Glengarry. Mackenzie agreed to pay twenty thousand merks Scots, and thus ended for ever the ancient and long-continued quarrels between the powerful families of Glengarry and Kintail.*

Kenneth, first Lord of Kintail, to quote the Earl of Cromarty, " was truly of an heroic temper, but of a spirit too

---

* "Thus ended the most of Glengarries' troubles tho' there was severall other bloody skirmishes betwixt ym—such as the taking of the Stank house in Knoidart, where there was severalls burnt and killed by that stratagem ; as also young Glengarries' burning and harrying of Croe in Kintail, where there was but few men killed, yet severall women and children were both burned and killed. I cannot forget ane pretty fellow that was killed there, who went himself and three or four women to ane outsett in the Croe, where there was a barn (as being more remote), where they sleept yt night. But in the morning the breaking of the dore was their wakening, whereupon the man, (called Patrick McConocby Chyle) started and finding them about the barn, bad them leave of and he would open it. So, getting his bow and arrow, he opens the door, killed 4 of them there, (before) they took nottice of him, which made them all hold off. In end they fires the barn and surrounds it, which he finding still started out, and as he did he still killed one of them, till he had killed 11. The barn in end almost consumed and his arrows spent, he took him to his heels, but was killed by them and two of the women, the third having stayed in the reek of the barn, and a rough hide about her."—*Ancient MS.*

great for his estates, perhaps for his country, yet bounded
by his station, so as he (his father) resolved to seek employment for him abroad; but no sooner had he gone to France,
but Glengarry most outrageously, without any cause, and
against all equity and law, convocates multitudes of people
and invades his estates, sacking, burning, and destroying
all. Kenneth's friends sent John Mackenzie of Tollie to
inform him of these wrongs, whereupon be made a speedy
return to an affair so urgent, and so suitable to his genius,
for as he never offered wrong so he never suffered any.
His heat did not overwhelm his wit, for he took a legal
procedure, obtained a commission of fire and sword against
Glengarry and his complices, which he prosecuted so bravely
as in a short time by himself and his brother he soon forced
them to retreat from his lands, and following them to their
own hills, he soon dissipated and destroyed them, that
young Glengarry and many others of their boldest and
most outrageous were killed, and the rest forced to shelter
themselves amongst the other Macdonalds in the islands
and remote Highlands, leaving all their estates to Kenneth's
disposal. This refers to the atrocious affair of Cilliechriost
narrated elsewhere, and the consequent depression of the
house of Glengarry after this period (1603). This tribe of
the Clan Ranald seem to have been too barbarous for even
those lawless times, while by a strange contumacy in latter
times, a representative of that ancient family pertinaciously
continued to proclaim its infamy and downfall by the adherence to the wild strain of bagpipe music (their family
pibroch called Cillechriost), at once indicative of its shame
and submission. Kenneth's character and policies were of
a higher order, and in the result he was everywhere the
gainer by them." He was supported by Murdoch, second
of the family of Redcastle; and by his own brothers—
Sir Roderick Mackenzie of Coigeach, Alexander of Coul,
and Alexander of Kilcoy, all persons of more than common
intelligence and intrepidity.

   Lord Kenneth married, first, Ann, daughter of George
Ross of Balnagown, and by her had issue—first, Colin

Ruadh, his successor, afterwards created first Earl of Seaforth; second, John of Lochslinn, who married Isobel, eldest
daughter of Alexander Mackenzie, fifth of Gairloch, and
died without lawful male issue; and, third, Kenneth, who
died unmarried. By this marriage he had also two daughters, Barbara, who married Donald, Lord Reay; and Janet,
who married Sir Donald Macdonald of Sleat, Baronet.
Kenneth married, secondly, Isobel, daughter of Sir Gilbert
Ogilvie of Powrie, by whom he had—first, George, who
afterwards succeeded Earl Colin as second Earl of Seaforth;
Thomas Mackenzie of Pluscardine, whose male line has
been proved extinct; and Simon Mackenzie of Lochslinn.
Simon was twice married and left a numerous offspring,
who shall afterwards be more particularly referred to, his
descendants having carried on the male line of the ancient
family of Kintail. Kenneth had also, by the second marriage,
a daughter, Sibella. She married, first, John Macleod of
Harris; secondly, Alexander Fraser, Tutor of Lovat; and
thirdly, Patrick Grant, Tutor of Grant. His lordship appears also to have had another son, Alexander, who died
young.

He died in 1611, in the forty-second year of his age;
buried "with great triumph" at Chanonry,* and was succeeded by his second and eldest surviving son,

XIII. COLIN RUADH, OR RED,

SECOND LORD MACKENZIE OF KINTAIL, afterwards
created first Earl of Seaforth, a minor only fourteen years
of age when he succeeded his father. The estates were
heavily burdened in consequence of the long-continued
wars with Glengarry and other demands upon Lord Kenneth, who, in these circumstances, acted prudently by appointing his brother, Sir Roderick Mackenzie of Coigeach
—in whose judgment he placed the utmost confidence—

* "As is proved by an old MS. record kept by the Kirk Session of Inverness,
wherein is this entry :—'Upon the penult day of February 1611 My Lord Mackenzie died in the Chanonrie of Ross and was buried 28th April anno foresaid in
the Chanonrie Kirk with great triumph.'"—*Allangrange Service.*

Tutor to his son and successor, Lord Colin. Knowing the
state of affairs—financial and various other difficulties
staring him in the face, while the family were still much
involved with the affairs of the Lews and other broils on
the mainland—Sir Roderick hesitated to accept the great
responsibilities of the position, but, in the words of the
Laird of Applecross, "all others refusing to take the charge
he set resolutely to the work. The first thing he did was
to assault the rebels in the Lews, which he did so suddenly,
after his brother's death, and so unexpectedly to them, that
what the Fife adventurers had spent many years and much
treasure in without success, he, in a few months, accomplished ; for having by his youngest brother Alexander,
chased Neill, the chief commander of all the rest, from the
Isle, pursued him to Glasgow, where, apprehending him, he
delivered him to the Council, who executed him immediately. He returned to the Lews, banished those whose
deportment he most doubted, and settled the rest as
peaceable tenants to his nephew ; which success he had,
with the more facility, because he had the only title of succession to it by his wife, and they looked on him as their
just master. From thence he invaded Glengarry, who was
again re-collecting his forces ; but at his coming they dissipate and fled. He pursued Glengarry to Blairy in Moray,
where he took him ; but willing to have his nephew's estate
settled with conventional right rather than legal, he took
low-countrymen as sureties for Glengarry's peaceable deportment, and then contracted with him for the reversion
of the former wadsets, which Colin of Kintail had acquired
of him, and for a ratification and new disposition of all his
lands, formerly sold to Colin, and paid him thirty thousand
merks in money for this, and gave him a title to Laggan-
achindrom, which, till then, he possessed by force, so that
Glengarry did ever acknowledge it as a favour to be overcome by such enemies, who over disobligements did deal
both justly and generously. Roric employed himself therefore in settling his pupil's estate, which he did to that advantage, that ere his minority passed, he freed his estate,

leaving him master of an opulent fortune and of great superiorities, for he aequired the superiority of Troternish with the heritable stewarty of the Isle of Skye, to his pupil' the superiority of Raasay and some other Isles. At this time, Maeleod, partly by law and partly by foree, had possessed himself of Sleat and Troternish, a great part of Macdonald's estate. Rory, now knighted by King James, owned Maedonald's eause, as an injured neighbour, and by the same method that Maeleod possessed himself of Sleat and Troternish, he recovered both from him, marrying the heir thereof, Sir Donald Macdonald, to his neiee, sister to Lord Colin, and caused him to take the lands of Troternish, holden of his pupil. Shortly after that he took the management of Maelean's estate, and recovered it from the Earl of Argyll, who had fixed a number of debts and pretences on it, so by his means all the Isles were eomposed, and accorded in their debates and settled in their estates whence a full peace amongst them, Maeneill of Barra excepted, who had been an hereditary outlaw. Him, by eommission, Sir Rorie reduced, took him in his fort of Kisemull, and earried him prisoner to Edinburgh, where he proeured his remission. The King gifted his estate to Sir Rorie, who restored it to Macneill for a sum not exeeeding his expenses, and holding it of himself in feu. This Sir Rory, as he was beneficial to all his relations, establishing them in free and secure fortunes, he purchased eonsiderable lands to himself in Ross and Moray, besides the patrimony left him by his father, the lands of Coigeach and others, which, in lieu of the Lews, were given him by his brother. His death was regretted as a public calamity, which was in September 1626, in the 48th year of his age. To Sir Rory sueeeeded Sir John Mackenzie ef Tarbat ; and to him Sir George Maekenzie, of whom to write might be more honour to him than of safety to the writer as matters now stand."

Sir Roderiek was a most determined man, and extremely fertile in such schemes as enabled him to gain any object he had in view. One of these, eonnected with Mackenzie's final possession of the Lews, in its most abhorrent details

of conception and execution, almost equalled the Raid of
Cillicchriost, though the actual result was different; and for
that no credit can be given to the Tutor of Kintail. Neil
Macleod, accompanied by his nephews, Malcolm, William,
and Roderick, the three sons of Roderick Og; the four sons
of Torquil Blair; and thirty of their more determined and
desperate followers, retired, when Kintail obtained possession of the whole of the Lews, to the impregnable rock of
Berrisay, at the back of the island, to which Neil, as a precautionary measure, had been, for years previously, sending
food and other necessaries as a provision for possible future
necessity. They held out on this rock for three years, and
were a source of great annoyance to the Tutor and his followers. On a little rock opposite Berrissay, Neil, by a
well-directed shot killed one of the Tutor's followers
named Donald MacDhonnchaidh Mhic Ian Ghlais, and
wounded another called Tearlach MacDhomh'uill Roy
Mhic Fhionnlaidh Ghlais. This exasperated their leader
so much, that all other means having failed to oust Neil
from his impregnable position, the Tutor conceived the
inhuman scheme of gathering together all the wives and
children of those who were on Berrissay, and all those
in the island who were in any way related to them by
blood or marriage affinity, and, having placed them on a
rock in the sea during low water, so near Berrissay that
Neil and his companions could see and hear them, Sir
Roderick and his men avowed that they would leave those
innocent creatures—helpless women and children—on the
rock to be overwhelmed and drowned on the return of the
flood tide, if Neil and his companions did not instantly
surrender the stronghold of Berrissay. Macleod knew, no
doubt by stern experience, that even to the extent of carrying out such an atrocious deed, the promise of the Tutor
once given was as good as his bond. It is due to the greater
humanity of Macleod that the terrible position of his helpless
countrywomen and relations appalled him so much that he
decided immediately to yield up the rock on condition that
he and his followers were allowed to leave the Lews with

their lives. It is impossible to doubt that were it not for Macleod's more humane conduct the villanous and ferocious act would have been committed by Sir Roderick and the Clan Mackenzie; and we have to thank the humanity of their enemies for saving the clan from the commission of a crime which would have secured to its perpetrators the deserved execration of posterity.

After Neil had left the rock he went privately, during the night, to his relative, Macleod of Harris. The Tutor learning this caused Macleod to be charged, under pain of treason and forfeiture, to deliver him up to the Council. Discovering the danger of his position, he prevailed upon Neil and his son to accompany him to Edinburgh, and to seek forgiveness from the king; and under pretence of this he delivered them both up on arriving in the city, where Neil, in April 1613, was at once executed, and his son banished out of the kingdom. Such conduct on the part of Macleod of Harris can hardly be excused, but it was, perhaps, a fair return for a piece of treachery which Neil had been guilty of some little time . previously. He met, when on Berrissay, with the captain of a pirate, with whom he entered into a mutual bond by which they were to help one another, both being outlaws. The captain agreed to defend the rock from the seaward while Neil made his incursions on shore ; they promised faithfully to live and die together, and it was arranged, to make the agreement more secure, that the captain should marry Neil's aunt, a daughter of Torquil Blair. The day fixed for the marriage having arrived, and Neil and his adherents having discovered that the captain possessed several articles of value aboard his ship, he, when the captain was naturally most completely off his guard, treacherously seized the ship, and sent the captain and his crew prisoners to Edinburgh, thinking that by so doing he would secure pardon for himself in addition to all that was in the ship. By order of the Council they were all hanged at Leith. Much of the silver and gold taken from the ship Neil carried to Harris, where probably it helped to tempt

Macleod, as it had previously tempted himself, to break faith with Neil.

In 1614, while the Tutor was busily engaged in the Island of Lews, dissensions broke out between different branches of the Camerons, instigated by the rival claims of the Marquis of Huntly and the Earl of Argyll. The latter had won over the aid of Allan MacDhomhnuill Duibh, Chief of the Clan, while Huntly had secured the support of Erracht, Kinlochiel, and Glen Nevis, and, by force, placed them in possession of all the lands belonging to the Chief's adherents who supported Argyll. Allan, however, managed to deal out severe retribution to his enemies, who were commanded by Lord Enzie, the eldest son of the Marquis, and, as is quaintly said, "teaching ane lesson to the rest of kin that are alqui in what form they shall carry themselves to their chief hereafter." Huntly obtained a commission from the King to suppress these violent proceedings, in virtue of which he called out all his Majesty's loyal vassals to join him. Kintail and the Tutor demurred, and submitted the difficulties and trials they experienced in reducing the Lews to good and peaceable government, and they were exempted from joining Huntly's forces by a special commission from the king. Closely connected as it is with the final settlement of the island in the possession of the House of Kintail, we shall place it before the reader :—

" James Rex,—James, by the grace of God, King of Great Britain, France, and Ireland, defender of the faith, to all and sundry our lieges, and subjects whom it effeirs to whose knowledge this our letters shall come greeting. For as much as we have taken great pains and travails, and bestoun great charge and expense for reducing the Isles of our kingdom to our obedience :   And the same Isles being now settled in a reasonable way of quietness, and the chieftains thereof having come in and rendered their obedience to us ; there rests none of the Isles rebellious, but only the Lews, which being inhabitated by a number of godless and lawless people, trained up from their youth in all kinds of ungodliness :   They can hardly be reclaimed from their impurities and barbarities, and induced to embrace a quiet and peaceable form of living; so that we have been constrained from time to time to employ our cousin, the Lord Kintail, who rests with God, and since his decease the Tutor of Kintail his brother, and other friends of that House in our service against the rebels of the Lews, with ample commission and authority to suppress their insolence and to reduce that island to our obedience, which service has been prosecuted and followed these divers years by the power, friendship, and proper services of the House of Kintail, without any kind of trouble and charge or expense to us, or any support or relief from their neighbours; and in the prosecution of that service, they have had such good and happy success, as divers of the rebels have been apprehended and executed by justice: But seeing our said service is not yet fully accomplished, nor the Isle of the Lews settled in a solid and perfect obedience, we have of late renewed our former commission to our cousin Colin, now Lord of Kintail, and to his Tutor and some other friends of his house, and they are to employ the hale power and service in the execution of the said commission, whilk being a service emporting highly our honour, and being so necessary and expedient for the peace and quiet of the whole islands, and for the good of our subjects, haunting the trade of fishing in the Isles, the same ought not to be interrupted upon any other intervening occasion, and our Commissioners and their friends ought not to be distracted therefrae for giving of their concurrence in our services: Therefore, we, with advice of the Lords of our Privy Council, have given and granted our licence to our said cousin Colin, Lord of Kintail, and to his friends, men, tenants, and servants to remain and bide at home frae all osts, reeds, wars, assemblings, and gadderings to be made by George, Marquis of Huntly, the Earl of Enzie, his son, or any other our Lieutenants, Justices, or Commissioners, by sea or land, either for the pursuit of Allan Cameron of Lochiel and his rebellious complices, or for any other cause or occasion whatsoever, during or within the time of our commission foresaid granted against the

Lews, without pain or danger to be incurred by our said cousin the Lord of Kintail and his friends in their persons, lands or goods ; notwithstanding whatsoever our proclamation made or to be made in the contrair whatever, and all pains contained in, we dispense be their pretts, discharging hereby our Justices, Justice Clerk, and all our Judges and Ministers of law, of all calling, accusing, or any way proceeding against them for the cause aforesaid, and of their officers in that part.

"Given under our signet at Edinburgh, the 14th day of September 1614, and of our reign the 12th, and 48 years. Read, passed, and allowed in Council. All ; Concr. Hamilton, Glasgow, Lothian, Binning.

"(Signed)   " PRIMEROSE."

Having procured this commission, the Mackenzies were able to devote their undivided attention to the Lews and their other affairs at home ; and from this period that island principality remained in the undisturbed possession of the family of Kintail and Seaforth, until, at a later period, through the misfortunes and extravagance of the "last of the Seaforths," it was sold to its late owner, Sir James Matheson of the Lews. The inhabitants ever after adhered most loyally to the illustrious house to whom they owed such peace and prosperity as was never before experienced in the history of the island.

The commission proved otherwise of incalculable benefit to Kintail ; for it not only enabled him to pacify and establish good order in the Lews with greater ease, but provided his Lordship at the same time with undisturbed security in his extensive possessions on the mainland at a time when the most violent disorders prevailed over every other district of the West Highlands and Islands.

Sir Robert Gordon writing about this time, but referring to the year 1477, says* :—" From the ruines of the familie of Clandonald, and some of the neighbouring Hylanders, and also by their own vertue, the surname of the Clankenzie,

---

* Earldom of Sutherland, p. 77.

from small beginnings, began to floorish in these bounds ; and by the freindship and favor of the house of Southerland, chieflie of Earle John, fyfth of that name, Earle of Souther-land (whose chamberlaines they wer, in receaveing the rents of the carledome of Rosse to his use) ther estate afterward came to great height, yea above divers of ther more auncient nighbors. The cheiff and head of the familie at this day is Colin Mackenzie, Lord of Kyntale, now created Earle of Seaforth." If the family was so powerful in 1477, what must we consider its position under Lord Colin. The Earl of Cromarty informs us that " This Colin was a noble person of virtuous indowments, beloved of all good men, especially his Prince. He acquired and settled the right of the superiority of Moidart and Arisaig, the Captain of Clan-donald's lands, which his father, Lord Kenneth, formerly claimed right to but lived not to accomplish it. Thus, all the Highlands and Islands from Ardnamurchan to Strath-naver were either the Mackenzie's property, or under his vassalage, some few excepted, and all about him were tied to his familie by verie strict bonds of friendship or vassalage, which, as it did beget respect from many it begot envie in others, especially his equals."

It is difficult to discover any real aid which the Mackenzies ever received from the Earls of Sutherland of the kind stated by Sir Robert Gordon. We have carefully gone over the work from which the above quotation is made, and were unable to discover a single instance prior to 1477, where the Sutherlands were of any service whatever to the family of Mackenzie ; and the gratuitous assumption is only another instance of that quality of " partiality to his own family," so characteristic of Sir Robert, and for which even the publishers of his work deemed it necessary to apologise in the Advertisement prefaced to his History of the Earl-dom of Sutherland. They " regret the hostile feelings which he expresses concerning others who were equally entitled to complain of aggression on the part of those whom he de-fends," but " strict fidelity to the letter of the manuscript " would not allow them to omit " the instances in which this disposition appears." After Mackenzie's signal victory over the Macdonalds at Blar na Pairc, and Hector Roy's prowess at Drumchait, the Earl of Sutherland began to think the family of Mackenzie, rapidly growing in power and influence, might be of some service in the prosecution of his own plans and in extending his power, and he accordingly entered into the bond of manrent already noticed. It has been seen that for a long time after the advantages of this arrangement were entirely on the side of the Sutherlands, as at the battle of Brora and other places already referred to. The appointment of Kintail as Deputy-Chamberlain of the Earldom of Ross was due to, and in acknowledgment of, these signal and repeated services, and the obligations and advantages of the office were found to be reciprocal. The first and only instance in which we find the Earl's connection with Mackenzie likely to have been of service in the field, is on the occasion when, in 1605, he sent "six score," men to support him against Glengarry, and they, we have seen, fled before they saw the enemy. So much for the favour and friendship of the House of Sutherland and its results before and after 1477.

Lord Colin during his rule became involved in legal questions with the Earl of Argyll about the superiority of Moidart and Arisaig, and thus spent most of the great fortune accumulated for him by the Tutor; but he was ultimately successful against Argyll. He was frequently at the Court of James VI., with whom he was a great favourite. In 1623 he was raised to the peerage by the title of Earl of Seaforth, and Viscount Fortrose. From his influence at Court he was able to be of great service to his followers and friends; nor did he neglect the opportunity, while he exerted himself powerfully and steadily against those who became his enemies from jealousy of his good fortune and high position.

His Lordship imposed high entries and rents upon his Kintail and West Coast tenants, which they and their successors considered a most "grievous imposition." In Lord Kenneth's time and in that of his predecessors, the

people had their lands at very low rents. After the wars
with Glengarry the inhabitants of the West Coast properties devoted themselves more steadily to the improvement
of their stock and lands, and accumulated considerable
means. The Tutor, discovering this, took advantage of their
prosperity and imposed a heavy entry or grassum on their
tacks payable every five years. "I shall give you one
instance thereof. The tack of land called Muchd in Letterfearn, as I was told by Farquhar Mac Ian Oig, who paid
the first entry out of it to the Tutor, paid of yearly duty before but 40 merks Scots, a cow and some meal, which cow
and meal was usually converted to 20 merks; but the Tutor
imposed 1000 merks of entry upon it for a five years tack.
This made the rent very little for four years of the tack, but
very great and considerable for the first year. The same
method proportionately was taken with the rest of the lands,
and continued so during the Tutor's and Colin's time, but
Earl George, being involved in great troubles, contracted
so much debt that he could not pay his annual rents yearly
and support his own state, but was forced to delay his
annual rents to the year of their entry, and he divided the
entry upon the five years with the people's consent and
approbation, so that the said land of Muchd fell to pay
280 merks yearly and no entry."

"Colin lived most of his time at Chanonry in great state
and very magnificently. He annually imported his wines
from the Continent, and kept a store for his wines, beers,
and other liquors, from which he replenished his fleet on
his voyages round the West Coast and the Lews, when he
made a circular voyage every year or at least every two
years round his own estates. I have heard John Beggrie,
who then served Earl Colin, give an account of his voyages
after the bere seed was sown at Allan (where his father and
grandfather had a great mains, which was called Mackenzie's
girnel or granary), took a journey to the Highlands, taking
with him not only his domestic servants but several young
gentlemen of his kin, and stayed several days at Killin,
whither he called all his people of Strathconan, Strathbran,

M

Strathgarve, and Brae Ross, and did keep Courts upon them and saw all things rectified. From thence he went to Inverewe, where all his Lochbroom tenants and others waited upon him, and got all their complaints heard and rectified. It is scarcely credible what allowance was made for his table of Scotch and French wines during these trips amongst his people. From Inverewe he sailed to the Lews, with what might be called a small navy, having as many boats, if not more loaded with liquors, especially wines and English beer, as he had under men. He remained in the Lews for several days, until he settled all the controversies arising among the people in his absence, and setting his land. From thence he went to Sleat in the Isle of Skye, to Sir Donald Macdonald, who was married to his sister Janet, and from that he was invited to Harris, to Macleod's house, who was married to his sister Sybilla. While he tarried in these places the lairds, the gentlemen of the Isles, and the inhabitants came to pay their respects to him, including Maclean, Clan Ranald, Raasay, Mackinnon, and other great chiefs. They then convoyed him to Islandonain. I have heard my grandfather, Mr Farquhar MacRa (then Constable of the Castle), say that the Earl never came to his house with less than 300, and sometimes 500 men. The Constable was bound to furnish them victuals for the first two meals, till my Lord's officers were acquainted to bring in his own customs. There they consumed the remains of the wine and other liquors. When all these lairds and gentlemen took their leave of him, he called the principal men of Kintail, Lochalsh, and Lochcarron together, who accompanied him to his forest of Monar, where they had a great and most solemn hunting day, and from Monar he would return to Chanonry about the latter end of July."[*]

He built the Castle of Brahan, which he thought of building where the old castle of Dingwall stood, or on the hill to the west of Dingwall, either of which would have been very fine and suitable situations; but the Tutor of

---

* Ardintoul MS. History of the Mackenzies.

Kintail, who had in view to build a castle, where he afterwards built Castle Leod, induced the Lord High Chancellor,
Seaforth's father-in-law, to prevail upon him to build his
castle upon his own ancient inheritance, which he did, and
which was one of the most stately houses then in Scotland.
He also built the greater part of the Castle of Chanonry,
and "as he was diligent in secular affairs, so he and his
lady were very pious and religious." They went yearly to
take the Sacraments from Mr Thomas Campbell, the young
minister of Carmichael, a good and religious man, and staid
eight days with him ; nor did their religion consist in form
and outward show, but they proved its reality by their good
works. He had usually more than one chaplain in his house.
He provided the kirks of the Lews without being constrained
to do so, and the five kirks in Kintail, Lochalsh, Lochcarron,
Lochbroom, and Gairloch, of all of which he was patron,
with valuable books from London, the works of the latest
and best authors, "whereof many are yet extant." He also
laid the foundation for a kirk in Strathconan and Strathbran,
of which the walls are "yet to be seen in Main in Strathconan, the walls being built above the height of a man
above the foundation, and he had a mind to endow it had
he lived longer." He mortified 4000 merks for the Grammar
School of Chanonry, and had several works of piety in his
view to perform if his death had not prevented it. The last
time he went to Court some malicious person, envying his
greatness and favour at Court, laboured to give the King a
bad impression of him, as if he were not thoroughly loyal ;
but the King himself was the first who told him what was
said about him, which did not a little surprise and trouble
the Earl, but it made no impression on the King, who was
conscious and sufficiently convinced of his loyalty and
fidelity. After his return from Court his only son, Lord
Alexander, died of smallpox at Chanonry, on the 3d of
June 1629, to the great grief of all who knew him, especially
his father and mother. His demise hastened her death at
Edinburgh, on the 20th February 1631. She was buried
with her father at Fife on the 4th of March ; after which the

Earl contracted a lingering sickness, which, for some time
before his death, confined him to his chamber, during which
period "he behaved most Christianly, putting his house in
order, giving donations to his servants, &c." He died at
Chanonry on the 15th of April 1633, in the 36th year of his
age, and was buried there with his father on the 18th of
May following, much lamented and regretted by all who
knew him. The King sent a gentleman all the way to
Chanonry to testify his respect and concern for him, and to
attend his funeral, which took place, on the date already
stated, with great pomp and solemnity. "Before his death
he called his successor, George of Kildene, to his bedside,
and charged him with the protection of his family; but
above all to be kind to his men and followers, for that he
valued himself, while he lived, upon their account more than
upon his great estate and fortune."* On his last visit to
London the King complimented him on being the best
archer in Britain.

Colin, first Earl of Seaforth, Viscount Fortrose, and
second Lord Mackenzie of Kintail, married, first, Lady
Margaret Seton, daughter of Alexander, Earl of Dunfermline, Lord High Chancellor of Scotland, by whom he had a
numerous family, all of whom died young, except two
daughters, the elder of whom, Anna, married Alexander,
second Lord Lindsay, who was, in 1651, by Charles II.,.
created Earl of Balcarres, by whom Lady Anna had two
sons, Charles and Colin. Charles succeeded his father, and
died unmarried. Colin then became third Earl, and married
Jane, daughter of David, Earl of Northesk, by whom he had
issue an only daughter, who married Alexander Erskine,
third Earl of Kellie. Secondly, this Earl of Balcarres
married Jane, daughter of William, second Earl of Rox-
burgh, by whom he had an only daughter, who married
John Fleming, sixth Earl of Wigton. This Earl Balcarres
married a third time, Margaret, daughter of James Campbell, Earl of Loudon, by whom he had two sons, Alexander

* Ardintoul, Letterfearn, and other Family MS. Histories.

and James. Alexander succeeded his father, but died without issue, and was succeeded by James, fifth Earl of Balcarres, from whom the present line descends uninterruptedly,
carrying along with it in right of the said Anna, daughter
of Colin, first Earl of Seaforth, first Countess of Balcarres,
the lineal representation of the ancient House of Kintail.
Anna married, secondly, Archibald, ninth Earl of Argyll
beheaded in 1685, and died in 1706. The second, Jean,
married John, Master of Berriedale, to whom she had issue,
a son, George, sixth of Caithness, who died without issue in
1676. She afterwards married Lord Duffus, with issue, and
died in 1648.

Colin, first Earl of Seaforth, died, as already stated, at
Fortrose in 1633, and was buried in the Cathedral Church
there, in a spot chosen by himself. His son, Lord Alexander, having died before his father, on the 3d of June
1629, and having no other male issue, he was succeeded by
his brother,

XIV. GEORGE, SECOND EARL OF SEAFORTH,

THIRD LORD MACKENZIE OF KINTAIL, elder son of
Kenneth, first Lord, by his second marriage. He was
the *first* George of Kildun, and was in 1633 "served
heir male to his brother Colin, Earl of Seaforth, Lord Mackenzie of Kintail, in the lands and barony of Ellandonan,
including the barony of Lochalshe, in which was included
the barony or the lands and towns of Lochcarron, namely,
the towns and lands of Auchnaschelloch, Coullin, Edderan-
charron, Attadill, Ruychichan, Brecklach, Achachoull, Del-
martyne, with fishings in salt water and fresh, Dalcharlarie,
Arrinachteg, Achintie, Slumba, Doune, Stromcarronach,
in the Earldom of Ross, of the old extent of £13 6s 8d, and
also the towns of Kisserin, and lands of Strome, with fishings
in salt and fresh water, and the towns and lands of Torridan,
with the pertinents of the Castle of Strome; Lochalshe,
Lochcarron, and Kisserin, including the davach of Achvanie,
the davach of Achnatrait, the davach of Stromcastell, Ard-
nagald, Ardneskan, and Blaad, and the half davach of San-

nachan, Rassoll, Meikle Strome, and Rerag, in the Earldom
of Ross, together of the old extent of £8 13s 4d."* He
was served heir male of his father Kenneth, Lord Mackenzie
of Kintail, in the lands and barony of Pluscardine, on the
14th January 1620; and had charters of Balmungie and
Avoch, 18th July 1635; of Raasay, 18th February 1637;
and of Lochalsh, 4th July 1642.

His high position in the North, and his intimate friendship at this period with the powerful House of Sutherland, is
proved by the fact that he and Sir John Mackenzie of Tarbat, on the 2d November 1633, stood godfathers to George
Gordon, second son of John, Earl of Sutherland; and there can
be little doubt that to the influence of the latter we must mainly
attribute Seaforth's vacillating conduct during the earlier
years of the great civil wars which continued the curse of
Scotland for so many years after. In 1635 the Privy Council
with the view to put down the irregularities then prevalent in
the Highlands, demanded securities from the chiefs of clans,
heads of families, and governors of counties, in conformity
with a general bond, previously agreed to, that they should
be responsible for their clans and surnames, their men-tenants,
and servants. The first called upon to give this security
was the Earl of Huntly; then followed the Earls of Sutherland and Seaforth, and afterwards Lord Lorne and all the
chiefs in the Western and Northern parts of the Kingdom.

In the following year the hitherto suppressed embers of
religious differences broke out into a general blaze all over the
country. Then began those contentions about ecclesiastical
questions, church discipline and liturgies, at all times fraught
with the seeds of discontent, and danger to the common
weal, and which in this case ultimately led to such sad and
momentous consequences as only religious feuds can produce. Charles I. was playing the despot with his subjects,
not only in Scotland, but in England. He was governing
without a parliament, defying and attempting to crush the
desires and aspirations of a people born to govern themselves

* Origines Parochiales Scotiae, p. 401.

and to be free. His infatuated attempt to introduce the
Liturgy of the Church of England into the Calvinistic and
Presbyterian pulpits of Scotland was as insane as it was
unavailing. "In no part of Europe had the Calvinistic
doctrine and discipline taken such a hold on the public
mind as in Scotland. The Church of Rome was regarded
by the great body of the people with a hatred that might
justly be called ferocious, and the Church of England, which
seemed to be coming every day more and more like the
Church of Rome, was scarcely an object of less aversion.
. . . . To this step, taken in the mere wantonness of
tyranny and in criminal ignorance, or more criminal con-
tempt of public feeling, our country owes her freedom. The
first performance of the Liturgy produced a riot. The riot
soon broke out into a revolution, and the whole of Scotland
was soon in arms."* His English subjects were at the same
time almost in a state of open rebellion for their liberties.
In these circumstances he tried to put down the rising in
Scotland by the sword, but his military means and his military skill were unequal to the task. He failed to impose
the English Liturgy on his Scottish subjects, but his attempt
in this direction proved the deliverance of his English subjects from high-handed tyranny. It is only natural that in
such circumstances Seaforth, though personally attached to
the King, should be found on the side of the Covenant, and
that he should have joined the Assembly, the clergy, and
the nobles in their well-known Protest, and in favour of the
renewal of the Confession of Faith, previously accepted and
confirmed by James VI. in 1580, 1581, and in 1590; at the
same time that they entered into a covenant or bond of
mutual defence among themselves against all opposition from
whatever source. The principal among the Northern nobles
who entered into this engagement were the Earls of Seaforth
and Sutherland, Lord Lovat, the Rosses, Munroes, the Lairds
of Grant, Mackintosh of Mackintosh, Innes, the Sheriff of
Moray, Kilravock, the Laird of Altyre, and the Tutor of

* Macaulay's History of England,

Duffus. These, under command of the Earl of Seaforth, appointed General of the Covenanters north of the Spey, marched to Morayshire, where they met the Royalists on the northern banks of the river ready to oppose their advance.* An arrangement was here agreed to between Thomas Mackenzie of Pluscardine, Seaforth's brother, on behalf of the Covenanters, and a representative from the Gordons on the other side, that the latter should recross to the south side of the Spey, and that the Highlanders should return home. About the same time Seaforth received a despatch from Montrose, then at Aberdeen, also fighting for the Covenant, intimating the pacification entered into on the 20th of June, between the King and his subjects at Berwick, requesting Seaforth to disband his army. This order was obeyed. Shortly after, however, Montrose dissociated himself from the Covenanters, took up the King's cause, and raised the royal standard. The Earl of Seaforth soon after became suspected of lukewarmness in the cause of the Covenant. In 1640 the King arrived at York on his way to reduce the Covenanting Scots, when they resolved to invade England, and, as a precautionary measure, imprison or expel all suspected Royalists from the army. Among the latter we find the Earl of Seaforth, Lord Reay, and several others, who were taken before the Assembly, kept in ward at Edinburgh for two months; and, on the King's arrival in Scotland, in 1641, the Earl of Traquair, who had been summoned before Parliament as an opponent to the Lords of the Covenant, persuaded the Earls of Montrose, Wigton, Athole, Hume, and Seaforth (who had meanwhile escaped), with several others, to join in a bond against the Covenanters.

* On May 14, 1639, 4000 men met at Elgin under the command of the Earl of Seaforth, and the gentlemen following, viz. :—The Master of Lovat, the Master of Ray, George, brother to the Earl of Sutherland, Sir James Sinclare of Murkle, Laird of Grant, Young Kilravock, Sherriff of Murray, Laird of Innes, Tutor of Duffus, Hugh Rose of Achnacloich, John Munro of Lemlare, &c. They encamped at Speyside, to keep the Gordons and their friends from entering Murray ; and they remained encamped till the pacification, which was signed June 18, was proclaimed, and intimated to them about June 22.—*Shaw's MS. History of Kilravock*.

Soon after we find Montrose leaving Elgin with the main body of his army, and marching towards the Bog of Gight, accompanied by the Earl of Seaforth, Sir Robert Gordon, the Lairds of Grant, Pluscardine, and several other gentlemen who came in to him at Elgin to support the King. After this, however, fearing depredations would be committed on his followers by the garrison of two regiments stationed at Inverness, and the other Covenanters of that district, he permitted Seaforth, the Laird of Grant, and other Moray gentlemen, to return home to defend their estates, but before allowing them to depart he made them swear a solemn oath of allegiance to the King, and promise that they should never again take up arms against his Majesty or any of his loyal subjects, and to rejoin him with all their forces as soon as they could do so. Seaforth, however, with an unaccountable want of decision, disregarded his oath, again joined the ranks of the Covenanters, and excused himself in a letter to the Committee of Estates, saying that he joined the Royalists through fear of Montrose, at the same time avowing that he would abide by "the good cause to his death."

Seaforth is soon in the field, now against Montrose, for Wishart informs us that "the Earl of Seaforth, a very powerful man in those parts (and one of whom he entertained a better opinion) with the garrison of Inverness, which were old soldiers, and the whole strength of Moray, Ross, Sutherland, and Caithness, and the sept of the Frasers, were ready to meet him with a desperate army of 5000 horse and foot." Montrose at this time had only 1500—the Macdonalds of Glengarry and the Highlanders of Athole having previously gone home, against the earnest solicitude of Montrose that they should complete the campaign, according to their usual custom, to deposit the booty obtained in their repeated victories under the great chief, but on the plea of repairing their houses and other property which had been so much injured by their enemies in their absence. The great commander, however, although he knew many of the garrison to be old soldiers, decided to attack their pre-

ponderating numbers, correctly calculating that a great
many of the others were only newly raised "from among
husbandmen, cowherds, pedees, tavern-boys, and kitchen-
boys," and would be altogether raw and unserviceable.
Fortunately for Seaforth and his forces, it turned out otherwise. The gallant Marquis, on his way to Inverness, was
informed of Argyll's descent on Lochaber, and, instantly
changing his route, he fell down upon him at Inverlochy so
unexpectedly, that when Argyll, by an ignominious flight
in one of his boats, made himself secure, he had the well-
merited reward of personal cowardice and pusillanimity of
witnessing fifteen hundred of his devoted adherents cut
down, among whom were a great number of the leading
gentlemen of the clan,* who deserved to fight under a better
and less cowardly commander. The power of the Camp-
bells was thus broken, and so, probably, would that of Seaforth had Montrose attacked him first.

After this brilliant victory at Inverlochy, on the 2d
February 1645, Montrose returned to Moray, by Badenoch,
where, on his march to Elgin, he was met by Thomas
Mackenzie of Pluscardine and others, sent by Seaforth and
the Covenanters as commissioners to treat with him. They
received an indignant answer, the Marquis declining any
negotiation, but at the same time offering to accept the
services of such as would join and obey him as the King's
Lieutenant-General. The Earl of Seaforth was then sent
by the Committee of Ross and Sutherland, in person, and
meeting the Marquis between Elgin and Forres, was for
several days detained prisoner. He was afterwards released,
but on what terms all the authorities plead ignorance. It
appears that when the Royalists marched south, the Laird
of Lawers, who was then Governor of the Castle of Inverness, cited all those who had communications with Montrose
in Moray, and compelled them to give bonds for their ap-

* Among those who fell were Campbell of Auchinbreck, Campbell of Lochnell, his eldest son, and his brother Colin ; Macdougall of Rara, and his eldest
son, Major Menzies, brother to the Chief of Achattens Parhreck, and the Provost
of the Church of Kilmuir.—*History of the Highlands, p.* 199.

pearance, to answer for their conduct, before the Parliament, if required to do so. Among those we find Thomas Mackenzie of Pluscardine, and, after the affair at Fettercairn, and the retreat of Montrose from Dundee, we find the Earls of Seaforth and Sutherland, with the whole of the Clan Fraser, and most of the men of Caithness and Moray, assembled at Inverness, where General Hurry, who had been retreating before Montrose, joined them with a force of Gordons—1000 foot and 200 horse—the whole amounting to about 3500 foot and 400 horse, which included Sutherlands, Mackenzies, Frasers, Roses, and Brodies, while Montrose's followers consisted of Gordons, Macdonalds, Macphersons, Mackintoshes, and Irish, to the number of about 3000 foot and 300 horse.* Montrose halted at the village of Auldearn. General Hurry finding such a large army waiting for him at Inverness, decided to retrace his steps with this force the next morning, and give battle to the Marquis.

The author of the Ardintoul MS. informs us how the Earl of Seaforth came to take part in the battle of Auldearn, and gives the following account of the cause and of the engagement:—General Hurry sent for Seaforth to Inverness, and during a long conference informed him that although he served the States himself he favoured the King's cause, and advised Seaforth to dismiss his men and make a pretence that he had only sent for them to give them new leases of their lands, and in case it was necessary to make an appearance to fight Montrose, he could bring, when commanded to do so, two or three companies from Chanonry and Ardmeanach, which he would accept. It was, however, late before they parted, and Lady Seaforth, who was waiting for her lord at Kessock, prepared a sumptuous supper for Seaforth and his friends. He and his friends kept up the festivities so long and so well that he "forgot or delayed to advertise his men to dismiss till to-morrow," and going to bed very late, before he could stir in the morning all the lairds and gentlemen of Moray came to him, most earnestly

* Shaw's MS. History.

entreating his lordship by all the laws of friendship and good neighbourhood, and for the kindness they had for him while he lived among them, and which they manifested to his brother yet living amongst them, that his lordship would not see them ruined and destroyed by Montrose and the Irish, when he might easily prevent the same without the least loss to himself and his men, assuring his lordship that if he should join Hurry with what forces he had then under his command, Montrose would make off with his Irish and not fight them. Seaforth, believing the gentle-men, and thinking, as they said, that Montrose with so small a number would not venture to fight, the rest being twice the number, and many of them trained soldiers. Hurry acquainted him that he was to march immediately against Montrose, and being of an easy and compassionate nature, he yielded to their request, and sent immediately in all haste for his Highlandmen, crossed the ferry of Kessock, and marched straight with the rest of the forces to Auldearn, where Montrose had his camp; but the Moray men found themselves mistaken in thinking that he (Montrose) would make off, for he was not only resolved but glad of the op-portunity to fight them before Baillie, whom he knew was on his march north with considerable forces, could join Hurry, and so drawing up his men with great advantage of ground, he placed Alexander Macdonald, with the Irish, on the right wing beneath the village of Auldearn, and Lord Gordon with the horse on the left. On the south side of Auldearn, he himself biding in town, and making a show of a main battle with a few men, which Hurry understanding, and making it his business that Montrose should carry the victory, and that Seaforth would come off without great loss, set his men, who were more than double the number of their adversaries, to Montrose's advantage, for he placed Sutherland, Lovat's men, and some others, with the horse under Drummond's command, on the right wing opposite to my Lord Gordon, and Loudon and Laurie's Regiments, with some others, on the left wing, opposite to Alexander Macdonald and the Irish, and placed Seaforth's men for the most in the midst opposite Montrose, where he knew they could not get hurt till the wings were engaged. Seaforth's men were commanded to retire, and make off before they had occasion or command to fight ; but the men hovering, and not understanding the mystery, were commanded again to make off and follow Drummond with the horse, who gave only one charge to the enemy and then fled, which they did by leaving both the wings and some of their own men to the brunt of the enemy, because their own men stood at a distance from them, the right wing being sore put to by my Lord Gordon, and seeing Drummond with the horse and their neighbours fly, they began to follow, while Suther-land and Lovat suffered great loss, while on the left wing, Loudon's Regiment and Lawrie with his Regiment were both totally cut off betwixt the Irish and the Gordons, who came to assist them after Sutherland's and Lovat's men were defeated. Seaforth's men got no hurt in the pursuit, nor did they lose many men in the fight, the most consider-able being John Mackenzie of Kernsary, cousin-german to the Earl, and Donald Bain, brother to Tulloch and Cham-berlain to Seaforth in the Lews, both being heavy and cor-pulent men not fit to fly, and being partly deceived by Seaforth's principal ensign or standard-bearer in the field, who stood to it with some others of the Lochbroom and Lewis men, till they were killed, and likewise Captain Bernard Mackenzie, with the rest of his company, which consisted of Chanonry men and some others thereabouts, being somewhat of a distance from the rest of Seaforth's men, were killed upon the spot. There were only four Kintail men who might make their escape with the rest if they had looked rightly to themselves, namely, the Banner man of Kintail, called Rory Mac Ian Dhomh'uill Bhàin, *alias* Mac-lennan, who, out of foolhardiness and indignation, to see that banner, which had wont to be victorious, fly in his hands, fastens the staff of it in the ground, and stands to it with his two-handed sword drawn, and would not accept of quarter, though tendered to him by my Lord Gordon in person, nor would he suffer any to approach him to take him alive, as the gentlemen beholders wished, so that they were forced to shoot him. The other three were Donald, the bannerman's brother, Malcolm Macrae, and Duncan Mac Ian Oig. Seaforth and his men, with Colonel Hurry and the rest, came back that night to Inverness, all the men laying the blame of the loss of the day upon Drummond, who commanded the horse, and fled away with them, for which, by a Council of War, he was sentenced to die ; but Hurry assuring him that he would get him absolved, though at the very time of execution he made him keep silence, but when Drummond was like to speak, he caused him to be shot suddenly, fearing, as was thought, that he would reveal that what was acted was by Hurry's own directions. This account of the Battle of Auldearn I had from an honourable gentleman and experienced soldier, as we were riding by Auldearn, who was present from first to last at this action, and who asked Hurry, Who set the battle with such advantage to Montrose and to the inevitable loss and overthrow of his own side? to whom Hurry, being confident of the gentleman, said, "I know what I am doing, we shall have by-and-bye excellent sport between the Irish and the States Regiments, and I shall carry off Seaforth's men without loss ;" and that Hurry was more for Montrose than for the States that day is very probable, because, shortly thereafter, when he found opportunity, he quitted the States service, and is reckoned as first of Montrose's friends, who, in August next year, embarked with Montrose to get off the nation, and returned with him again in his second expedition to Scotland, and was taken prisoner at Craigchonachan, and sent south and publicly executed with Montrose as guilty of the same fault.

Montrose gained another engagement at Alford on the 2d of July, after which he was joined by a powerful levy of West Highlanders under Colla Ciotach Macdonald, Clan Ranald, and Glengarry, the Macnabs and Macgregors, headed by their respective chieftains, and the Stewarts of Appin. In addition to these some of the Farquharsons of Bracmar and small parties of smaller septs from Badenoch

rallied round the standard of Montrose. Thus, as a contemporary writer says, "he went like a current speat (spate)
through this kingdom." Seeing all this—the great suc-
cesses of Montrose and so many of the Highlanders joining
—Seaforth, who had never been a very hearty Covenanter,
began to waver. The Estates of Scotland sent a commission to the Earl of Sutherland appointing him as their
Lieutenant north of the Spey, but he refused to accept it.
It was then offered to Seaforth, who likewise declined it,
but instead "contrived and framed ane band, under the
name of ane humble remonstrance, which he perswaded
manie and threatned others to subscryve. This remonstrance gave so great a distast to both the Church and
State, that the Earl of Seaforth was therefore excommuni-
cate by the General Assemblie; and all such as did not
disclaime the said remonstrance within some days thereafter, were, by the Committee of Estates, declared inimies
to the publick. Hereupon the Earl of Seaforth joyned
publickly with Montros in Aprill one thousand six hundreth
fortey-six, at the seidge of Inverness, though before that
time he had only joyned in private councells with him."*

At Inverness, through the conduct of the Marquis of
Huntly and the treachery of his son, Lord Lewis Gordon,
Montrose was taken by surprise by General Middleton, but
he promptly crossed the river Ness in the face of a regiment
of cavalry, under the command of Major Bromley, who
crossed the river by a ford above the town, while another
detachment crossed lower down towards the sea with a view
to cut off his retreat. These he managed with his brave
followers to beat back with a trifling loss on either side,
after which he retreated unmolested to Kinmylies, a short
distance west of Achnagairn, and the following morning he
marched round by Beauly and halted at a place called
Fairley, where slight marks of field works are still to be
seen; and now, for the first time, he found himself in the
country of the Mackenzies, accompanied by Seaforth in

* Gordon's Earldom of Sutherland, p. 529

person. Montrose, finding himself in a level country with
an army mainly composed of raw levies newly raised by
Seaforth among his people, and who were taught by their
chief's vacillating conduct and example to have but little
interest or enthusiasm in either cause, thought it imprudent
to give battle to Middleton, who pursued him with a di-
sciplined force, and a considerable following of cavalry, ready
to engage with every favourable advantage in such a level
country. He therefore rapidly moved up through the valley
of Strathglass, crossed to Loch-Ness, and passed through
Strathcrrick towards the river Spey. Meanwhile Middleton
advanced to Fortrose and laid siege to the castle, which was
at the time under charge of Lady Seaforth. She surrendered after a siege of four days ; and taking away a considerable quantity of stores and ammunition, sent by Queen
Henrietta for the use of Montrose on his arrival there, the
General gave Lady Seaforth, whom he treated with the
greatest civility and respect, possession of the stronghold.

The Committee on Public Affairs, which, throughout the
great contest, acted in opposition to the Royal authority,
and had sederunts at Aberdeen and Dundee, as well as at
Edinburgh, gratified their malignity, after Montrose gave
up the contest in 1646, by fining the loyalists in enormous
sums of money, and decerning them to " lend " to the committee such sums—in many cases exorbitant—as they
thought proper. Sir Robert Farquhar, at one time a Bailie
of Aberdeen, was treasurer, and in the sederunt in that city,
the Committee threw a comprehensive net over the Clan
Mackenzie ; for sixteen of the name were decerned to
lend the handsome sum of £28,666 13s 4d Scots ; but
we are not sorry to find from the other side of the balance-
sheet that the Mackenzies declined to lend a penny ; and
Sir Robert credits himself as treasurer thus :—" Item of the
loan moneys above set down there is yet resting unpaid,
and wherefore no payment can be gotten, as follows—viz.
—Be the name of Mackenzie, sixteen persons, the sum
of £28,666 13s 4d Scots." These are the respective
names and sums decerned :—Mr Thomas Mackenzie of

Pluscardine, £2000; Mr Alexander Mackenzie of Kilcoy, £2000; Roderick Mackenzie of Redcastle, £2000; Alexander Mackenzie of Coul, £6000; Kenneth Mackenzie of Gairloch, £3333 6s 8d; Hector Mackenzie of Scotsburn, £2000; Roderick Mackenzie of Davochmaluag, £1333 6s 8d; John Mackenzie of. Dawach-Cairne, £1333 6s 8d; William Mackenzie of Multavie, £1000; Kenneth Mackenzie of Scatwell, £2000; Mr Thomas Mackenzie of Inverlael, £1333 6s 8d; Colin Mackenzie of Mullochie, £666 13s 4d; Donald Mackenzie of Logie, £666 13s 4d; Kenneth Mackenzie of Assint, £1000; Colin Mackenzie of Kincraig, £1000; Alexander Mackenzie of Suddie, £1000. Among the other sums decerned is one of £6666 13s 4d against "William Robertson in Kindeace, and his son Gilbert Robertson," and in Inverness and Ross the loan amounted to the respectable sum of £44,783 6s 8d, of which the treasurer was allowed to retain £15,000 in his own hands. The sum, with large amounts of disbursements by the committee, show that they were more fortunate with others than with the Clan Mackenzie.[*]

The Earl of Seaforth taking advantage of being on opposite sides to the Earl of Sutherland, now asserted some old claims against Donald Macleod or Donald Ban Mór, 7th Baron of Assynt, a follower of the house of Sutherland, and who afterwards became notorious as the captor of the great Montrose himself. Mackenzie laid siege to his castle, but a peace was soon arranged without any serious damage having been done to either party. In 1648 Seaforth again raised a body of 4000 men in the Western Islands and in Ross-shire, whom he led south, to aid the King's cause, but after joining in a few skirmishes under Lanark, they returned home to "cut their corn which was now ready for their sickles." During the whole of this period Seaforth's fidelity to the Royal cause was not without considerable suspicion, and when Charles I. threw himself into the hands of the Scots at Newark, and ordered Montrose to disband

---

[*] Antiquarian Notes, pp. 307-308 309.

his forces, Earl George, always trying to be on the winning side, came in to General Middleton, and made terms with the Committee of Estates ; but the Church, by whom he had previously been excommunicated, continued implacable, and would only be satisfied by a public penance in sackcloth within the High Church of Edinburgh. The proud Earl gave in, underwent this ignominious and degrading ceremonial, and his sentence of excommunication was removed. Notwithstanding this public humiliation, in 1649, after the death of the ill-fated and despotic Charles I., Seaforth went over to Holland, joined Charles II., by whom he was made Principal Secretary of State for Scotland, the duties of which, however, he never had the opportunity of exercising. Charles was proclaimed King of Scotland in Edinburgh, on the 5th of February 1649, and it was decided by the King and his friends in exile, that Montrose should make a second attempt to recover Scotland ; for the King, on the advice of his friends, declined the humiliating terms offered him by the Scottish faction, and, in connection with the plans of Montrose, a rising took place in the North, under Thomas Mackenzie of Pluscardine, brother to the Earl of Seaforth, Sir Thomas Urquhart of Cromarty, Colonel John Munro of Lumlair, and Colonel Hugh Fraser. On the 22d February they entered the town of Inverness, expelled the troops from the garrison, and afterwards demolished the walls and fortifications. On the 26th of February a Council of War was held. Present—Thomas Mackenzie of Pluscardine, Preses, Sir Thomas Urquhart of Cromarty, H. Fraser of Belladrum, Jo. Cuthbert of Castlehill, R. Mackenzie, fifth of Davochmaluak ; Kenneth Mackenzie of Gairloch, R. Mackenzie of Redcastle, John Munro of Lumlair, Simon Fraser of Craighouse, and Alex. Mackenzie of Suddie. This Committee passed certain enactments, by which they took the customs and excise of the six northern counties entirely into their own hands. The Provost of Inverness was made accountable " for all the money which, under the name of excise, has been taken up in any of the foresaid shires since his intromissions with the office of

excise taking." Another "item" is that Duncan Forbes be
pleased to advance money "upon the security which the
Committee will grant to him," to be repaid out of the readiest of the "maintaince and excise." Cromarty House was
ordered to be put in a position of defence, for which it was
"requisite that some faill be cast and led," and all Sir James
Fraser's tenants within the parishes of Cromarty and Cullicudden, together with those of the laird of Findrassie, within
the parish of Rosemarkie, were ordered "to afford from six
hours in the morning to six hours at night, one horse out of
every oxengait daily for the space of four days, to lead the
same faill to the House of Cromarty." By the tenth enact-
ment the Committee find it expedient for their safety that
the works and forts of Inverness be demolished and levelled
to the ground, and they ordained that each person appointed
to this work should complete his proportion thereof before
the 4th day of March following "under pain of being
quartered upon, and until the said task be performed."
They further enacted that a garrison be placed in Culloden
House, "which the Committee is not desirous of for any
intention of harm towards the disturbance of the owner,
but merely because of the security of the garrison of Calder,
which, if not kept in good order, is like to infest all the
well-affected of the country circumjacent."* General Leslie
being sent against them, they retired to the mountains of Ross.
Leslie advanced to Fortrose and placed a garrison in the castle.
He managed to make terms with all the other leaders except
Mackenzie, who would not listen to any accommodation,
and who, immediately on Leslie's return south, descended
from his mountain fastnesses, attacked and took the Castle
of Chanonry. Mackenzie was then joined by his nephew,
Lord Reay, at the head of three hundred men, which increased his force to eight or nine hundred. Now joined by
General Middleton and Lord Ogilvie, he advanced into
Badenoch, with the view of raising the people in that and
the neighbouring districts, where they were joined by the

* For a copy of these Minutes see "Antiquarian Notes," pp. 157-8.

Marquis of Huntly, formerly Lord Lewis Gordon, and at once attacked and took the Castle of Ruthven. After this they were pressed closely by Leslie, and fell down from Badenoch to Balvenny Castle, whence they sent General Middleton and Mackenzie to treat with Leslie, but before they reached their destination, Carr, Halket, and Strachan, who had been in the North, made a rapid march from Fortrose, and on the 8th of May surprised Lord Reay with his nine hundred followers at Balvenny, but not without considerable loss on both sides. Eighty Royalists fell in the defence of the castle. Carr at once dismissed the Highlanders to their homes on giving their oath never again to take up arms against the Parliament, but he detained Lord Reay and some of his kinsmen, and Mackenzie of Pluscardine, with a few of the leaders of that name, and sent them prisoners to Edinburgh. Having there given security to keep the peace in future, Lord Reay, Ogilvy, Huntly, and Middleton were forgiven, and allowed to return home, Roderick Mackenzie of Redcastle and Mackenzie of Pluscardine, being the only two kept in prison. Carr now returned to Ross-shire and laid siege to Redcastle, the only place in the North which still held out for the Royal cause. The captain in charge recklessly exposed himself on the ramparts, and was pulled down by a well-directed shot from the enemy. The castle was set on fire by the exasperated soldiers. Leslie then placed a garrison in Brahan Castle and in the stronghold of Chanonry, and returned south. The garrison was expelled, some of whom were hanged, the walls were demolished, and the fortifications razed to the ground. Thus ended an insurrection which probably would have had a very different result had it been delayed until the arrival of the great Montrose. The same year General Leslie himself came to Fortrose with nine troops of horse, and forwarded detachments to Cromarty and Eilean-Donan Castle, "Seaforth's strongest hold."

We shall quote again from the account by a contemporary writer:—Immediately after the battle of Aldern Seaforth met and communed with Montrose, the result of which was that Seaforth should join Montrose for the King against the Parliament and States, whom they now discovered not to be for the King as they professed ; but in the meantime that Seaforth should not appear, till he had called upon and prevailed with his neighbours about him, namely, My Lord Reay, Balnagowan, Lovat, Sir James Macdonald of Sleat, Macleod of Dunvegan, and others, to join him and follow him as their leader. Accordingly, Seaforth having called them together, pointed out to them the condition the King was in, and how it was their interest to rise and join together immediately for the King's service and relief. All of them consented and approved of the motion, only some of them desired that the Parliament who professed to be for the King as well as they, and desired to be rid of Montrose and his bloody Irish, should first be made acquainted with their resolution. Seaforth, being unwilling to lose any of them, condescended, and drew up a declaration, which was known as Seaforth's remonstrance, as separate from Montrose, whereof a double was sent them ; but the Parliament was so far from being pleased therewith that they threatened to proclaim Seaforth and all who should join him as rebels. Now, after the battle of Alford and Kilsyth, wherein Montrose was victorious, and all in the south professing to submit to him as the King's Lieutenant, he was, by the treachery of Traquhair and others of the Covenanters, surprised and defeated at Philiphaugh. In the beginning of the next year, 1646, he came north to recruit his army. Seaforth raised his men and advertised his foresaid neighbours to come, but none came except Sir James Macdonald, who, with Seaforth, joined Montrose at Inverness, which they besieged, but Middleton, who then served in the Scots armies in England, being sent with nearly 1000 horse and 800 foot, coming suddenly the length of Inverness, stopped Montrose's progress. Montrose was forced to raise the siege and quit the campaign, and retired with Seaforth and Sir James Macdonald to the hills of Strathglass, to await the arrival of the rest of their confederates, Lord Reay, Glengarry, Maclean, and several others, who, with such as were ready to join him south, were likely to make a formidable army for the King; but, in the meantime, the King having come to the Scots army, the first thing they extorted from him was to send a herald to Montrose, commanding him to disband his forces, and to pass over to France till his Majesty's further pleasure. The herald came to him in the last of May 1646, while he was at Strathglass waiting the rest of the King's faithful friends who were to join him. For this Montrose was vexed, not only for the King's condition, but for those of his faithful subjects who declared themselves for him ; and before he would disband he wrote several times to the King, but received no answer, except some articles from the Parliament and Covenanters, which, after much reluctance, he was forced to accept, by which he was to depart the Kingdom against the first of September following, and the Covenanters were obliged to provide a ship for his transportation, but finding that they neglected to do so, meeting with a Murray ship in the harbour of Montrose, he went aboard of her with several of his friends, namely, Sir John Hurrie, who served the States the year before, John Drummond, Henry Brechin, George Wishart, and several others, leaving Seaforth and the rest of his friends to the mercy of these implacable enemies ; for the States and Parliament threatened to forfeit him for acting contrary to their orders, and the Kirk excommunicated him for joining with the excommunicated traitor, as they called him, James Graham; for now the Kirk began to rule with a high hand, becoming more guilty than the bishops, of that of which they charged him with as great a fault for meddling with civil and secular affairs ; for they not only looked upon them to form the army and to purge it of such as whom, in their idiom, they called Malignants, but really such as were loyal to the King ; and also would have no Acts of Parliament to pass without their consent and approbation. Their proselytes in the laity were also heavy upon and uneasy to such as they found or conceived to have found with a tincture of Malignancy, whereof many instances might be given.

But now to return to Seaforth. After he was excommunicated by the Kirk he was obliged to go to Edinburgh,
where he was made prisoner and detained two years; till in
the end he was, with much ado, released from the sentence
of excommunication, and the process of forfeiture against
him discharged ; for that time he returned home in the end
of the year 1648, but King Charles I. being before that time
murdered, and King Charles II. being in France, finding
that he would not be for any time on fair terms with the
States and Kirk, he proposed to remove his family to the
Island of Lews, and dwell there remote from public affairs,
and to allocate his rents on the mainland to pay his most
pressing debts, in order to which, having sent his lady in
December to Lochcarron, where boats were attending to
transport himself and children to the Lews by way of Lochbroom, wherein his affairs called him, he, without acquainting his kinsmen and friends, went aboard a ship which he
had provided for that purpose, and sailed to France, where
the King was, who received him most graciously and made
him one of his secretaries. This did incense the States
against him, so that they placed a garrison in his principal
house at Brahan, under the command of Captain Scott, who
(afterwards) broke his neck from a fall from his horse in the
Craigwood of Chanonry, as also another garrison in the
Castle of Islandonan, under the command of one William
Johnston, which remained to the great hurt and oppression
of the people till, in the year 1650, some of the Kintail
men, not bearing the insolence of the garrison soldiers, dis-
corded with them, and in harvest that year killed John
Campbell, a leading person among them, with others, from
having wounded several at little Inverinate, without one
drop of blood drawn out of the Kintail men, who were only
10 in number, while the soldiers numbered 30.

After this the garrison was very uneasy and greatly
afraid of the Kintail men, who threatened them so, that
shortly thereafter they removed to Ross, being commanded
then by one James Chambers ; but Argyll, to keep up the
face of a garrison there, sent ten men under the command

of John Muir, who lived there civilly without molesting the people, the States were so incensed against the Kintail men for this brush and their usage of the garrison, that they resolved to send a strong party next spring to destroy Kintail and the inhabitants thereof. But King Charles II., after the defeat of Dunbar, being at Stirling recruiting his army against Cromwell, to which Seaforth's men were called, it proved an act of oblivion and indemnity to them, so that the Kintail men were never challenged of their usage of the garrison soldiers. Though the Earl of Seaforth was out of the kingdom, he gave orders to his brother Pliscardy to raise men for the King's service whenever he saw the King's affairs required it; and so, in the year 1649, Pliscardy did raise Seaforth's men, and my Lord Reay joining him with his men, marched through Inverness, went through Moray, and crossed the Spey, being resolved to join the Gordons, Atholes, and several others who were ready to rise, and appeared for the King. Lesley, who was sent from the Parliament to stop their progress, called Pliscardy to treat with him, while Seaforth's and my Lord Reay's men encamped at Balveny, promising a cessation of hostilities. For some days Colonel Carr and Strachan, with a strong body of horse, surprised them in their camp, when they lay secured, and taking my Lord Reay, Rory Mackenzie of Redcastle, Rory Mackenzie of Fairburn, John Mackenzie of Ord, and others, prisoners, threatening to kill them unless the men surrendered and disbanded; and the under officers fearing they would kill them whom they had taken prisoners, did their utmost to hinder the Highlanders from fighting, cutting their bowstrings, &c., so they were forced to disband and dissipate. Pliscardy, in the meantime, being absent from them, and fearing to fall into their hands, turned back to Spey with Kenneth of Coul, William Mackenzie of Multavie, and Captain Alexander Bain, and swam the river, being then high by reason of the rainy weather, and so escaped from their implacable enemies. My Lord Reay, Redcastle, and others were sent to Edinburgh as prisoners, as it were to make a triumph, where a solemn day of thanks-

giving was kept for that glorious victory. My Lord Reay
and the rest were set at liberty, but Redcastle was still kept
prisoner, because when he came from home he garrisoned
his house of Redcastle, giving strict commands to those he
placed in his house not to render or give it until they had
seen an order under his hand, whereupon Colonel Kerr and
Strachan coming to Ross, after the defeat of Balveny, summoned the garrison to come forth, but all in vain ; for they
obstinately defended the house against the besiegers until,
on a certain day, a cousin of Kerr's, advancing in the ruff of
his pride, with his cocked carbine in his hand, to the very
gates of the castle, bantering and threatening those within to
give up the castle under all highest pain and danger, he was
shot from within and killed outright.   This did so grieve
and incense Colonel Kerr, that he began fairly to capitulate
with them within, and made use of Redcastle's own friends
to mediate and persuade them, till in the end, upon promise
and assurance of fair terms, and an indemnity of what
passed, they came out, and then Kerr and his party kept
not touches with them, but apprehending several of them,
and finding who it was that killed his cousin, caused him to
be killed, and thereafter, contrary to the promise and articles
of capitulation, rifled the house, taking away what he found
useful, and then burnt the house and all that was within it.
In the meantime Redcastle was kept prisoner at Edinburgh,
none of his friends being in a condition to plead for him, till
Ross of Bridly, his uncle by his mother, went south, and
being in great favour with Argyll, obtained Redcastle's
-liberation npon payment of 7000 merks fine.*

While these proceedings were taking place in the Highlands, Seaforth was in Holland at the exiled Court of Charles
II., and when Montrose arrived there Seaforth strongly supported him in urging on the King the bold and desperate
policy of throwing himself on the loyalty of his Scottish
subjects, as also in strongly protesting against the accept-
ance by the King and his friends of the arrogant and

* Ardintoul MS.

humiliating demand made by the commissioners sent over to treat with him by the Scottish faction. It is difficult to say whether Seaforth's zeal for his royal master or the safety of his own person influenced him most during the remainder of his life, but whatever the cause may have been, he adhered steadily to the exiled monarch to the end of a life which, in whatever light we may view it, cannot be commended as a good example to others. Such vacillating and time-serving conduct ended in the only manner it deserved. We might have admired him for taking a consistent part on either side, but with Earl George self and self-interest appear to have been the only governing principles throughout the whole of this trying period of his country's history. The Earl of Cromarty thought differently, and says that "this George, being a nobleman of excellent qualifications, shared the fortune of his Prince, King Charles I., for whom he suffered all the calamities in his estate that envious or malicious enemies could inflict. He was made secretary to King Charles II. in Holland, but died in that banishment before he sawe ane end of his King and his countrie's calamities, or of his own injuries." We have seen that his conduct was not so very steadfast in support of Charles I., and it may now be safely asserted that his calamities were due more to his own indecision and accommodating conduct than to any other cause.

While these great national questions were being fought out between the rival parties, some comparatively unimportant squabbles occasionally occurred at home. One may be mentioned which took place between the Mackenzies and the Roses of Kilravock, who, being cousins, were generally good friends. An unlucky difference, however, arose between the Roses and Mackenzies of Kilcoy, respecting the privilege of casting peats in the "Month of Mulbuy," which Kilravock claimed in right of his lands of Coulmore, and which privilege his kinsman Kilcoy maintained had hitherto been only tolerated. A discussion took place, at first sufficiently courteous, though firm and warlike. Kilcoy addresses—" To the rycht honorabil my loving brother, the

Laird of Kilrawok there," and concludes, " I shall be als loith to offend you deservedly by my neglek as my borne brother, and I so shal remaine still your affectionat brother to command in quhat is just and lawful to my utermost power. (Signed) A. Mackenzie of Culcowie : the 16th of June 1640." On the 12th of July the same year, a notary attests that while twelve tenants of the "twa Culmores were peacefully leading peats with carts and sleds from the Month of Mulbuy, Mr Alexander McKenzie of Culcowie cam ryding upon ane quhyt hors, accompanied with certain of his domestic servands, and causit his said servands to tim the said pettis and turris furth of the said carttis." Kilravock appears to have written to Seaforth to get the matter adjusted, who replied saying that " I spoke Culcovij, who stands to his richt, and thinks that the letter your father directed to his predecessour to be ane sufficient attollerance which he has aduysed with the best advocates in Edinburgh. . . . Do not think that I shall in any measour authorise any wrong to your tenants; for none shall moir really approve himselfe unto you then your affectionate good freind (signed), Seafort, Chan: 16th July 1641."

Each party apparently "stood to his right," and used every means of annoyance which the law placed in his power, with all diligenge. A warrant of Lawburrows was obtained at the instance of Kilravock, setting forth that Kilcoy " having conceived ane deidlie haitred, evill-will, and malice causles, &c., daylie and continuallie molestis, trublis, &c., in the peaceable possession of their lands." The following certificate, under the hand of the Clerk of Register, announced similar proceedings on the other side. It was too good a quarrel to be speedily settled, and it is more than likely that it lasted until the sale of Kilravock's lands of Coulmores to Colin Mackenzie of Redcastle in 1678.

" Apud Edinburgh, vltimo Novembris 1642. The whilk day sovertie and lawborrowis is fundin by Hucheon Ros of Kilraak and Hew Ros, younger thereof, that Maister Alexander McKenyee of Culcowie, his wyff, bairnis, men tennentis, and servandis sal be harmles and skaithles in their

bodeis, landis, herctages, takis, stcidingis, rowmes, possessions, &c., aiher of the saidis persones, vnder the pane of
ane thowsand merkis money. This I testifie to be of virtie
be ther presentis subscryvit with my hand.

(Signed) " Jo. SKENE."

Earl George married, early in life, Barbara, daughter
of Arthur, Lord Forbes, by whom he had issue, four sons
and three daughters—first, Kenneth, his successor ; second,
George of Kildun ; third, Colin, father of Captain Robert
Mackenzie and Dr George Mackenzie—author of " Lives
of Eminent Scotsmen," and a MS. " History of the Fitzgeralds and Mackenzies"—of either of whom there is no existing representative ; fourth, Roderick, whose only son, Alexander, had issue one daughter, Anne, who died without
issue. Roderick's son, Kenneth, also died without issue. The
Earl's eldest daughter, Jean, married, first, John, Earl of Mar,
and secondly, Lord Fraser ; the second, Margaret, married
Sir William Sinclair of Mey ; and the third, Barbara, married
Sir John Urquhart of Cromarty. Earl George had also a
natural son, John, first of the family of Gruinard.

When the tidings of the disastrous defeat of Worcester
were made known to his Lordship, he sank into a pro-.
found melancholy, and, in 1651, died at Schiedam, in Holland, in the forty-third year of his age. He was succeeded
by his eldest son,

XV. KENNETH MÒR, THIRD EARL OF SEAFORTH.

He was born at Brahan Castle in 1635, and when he
arrived at five or six years of age, his father placed him
under the care of the Rev. Farquhar MacRa, minister of
Kintail, and constable of Islandonain Castle, who had a
seminary in his house attended by the sons of the neighbouring gentlemen who kept young Seaforth company.*

---

* The author of the Ardintoul MS. says on this subject :—" This might be
thought a preposterous and wrong way to educate a nobleman, but they who would
consider where the most of his interests lay, and how he was among his people,
followers, and dependants, on which the family was still valued, perhaps will

He followed the example of his father in his latter days, became entirely identified with the fate of Charles II., and devoted himself unremittingly to the services of that monarch during his exile. Earl Kenneth was, from his great stature, known among the Highlanders as "Coinneach Mòr." On the King's arrival at Garmouth, in June 1650, his reception throughout all Scotland was of a most cheering character, but the Highlanders, who always favoured the Stuarts, were particularly joyous on the return of their exiled king. After the defeat of the Scottish army at Dunbar by Oliver Cromwell—a defeat entirely brought about by the interference of the Committee of Estates and Kirk with the duties of those in charge of the forces, and whose plans, were they allowed to carry them out, would have saved our country from the first great defeat Scotland ever received at the hands of an enemy—the King determined to come north

---

not think so, for by this the young lord had several advantages; first, by the wholesome, though not delicate or too palatable diet he prescribed to him, and used him with, he began to have a wholesome complexion, so nimble and strong, that he was able to endure stress and fatigue, labour and travel, which proved very useful to him in his after life; secondly, he did not only learn the language but became thoroughly acquainted with, and learned the genius of, his several tribes or clans of his Highlanders, so that afterwards he was reputed to be the fittest chief or chieftain of all superiors in the Highlands and Isles of Scotland; and thirdly, the early impressions of being among them, and acquaint with the bounds, made him delight and take pleasure to be often among them and to know their circumstances, which indeed was his interests and part of their happiness, so that it was better to give him that first step of education than that which would make him a stranger at home, both as to his people, estate, and condition; but when he was taken from Mr Farquhar to a public school, he gave great evidence of his abilities and inclination for learning, and being sent in the year 1651 to the King's College at Aberdeen, under the discipline of Mr Patrick Sandylands, before he was well settled or made any progress in his studies King Charles II., after his army had been defeated at Dunbar the year before, being then at Stirling recruiting and making up his army, with which he was resolved to march into England, the young laird was called home in his father's absence, who was left in Holland (as already described), to raise his men for the King's service, and so went straight to Kintail with the particular persons of his name, viz., the the Lairds of Pluscardy and Lochsline, his uncles; young Tarbat, Rory of Davochmaluak, Kenneth of Coul, Hector of Fairburn, and several others, but the Kintail men, when called upon, made a demur and declined to rise with him, because he was but a child, and that his father, their master, was in life, without whom they would not move, since the King, if he had use for him and for his followers, might easily bring him home."

and throw himself on the patriotism and loyalty of his
Highland subjects. He was, however, captured and taken
back to Perth, and afterwards to Edinburgh, by the Committee of Estates, on whom his attempted escape to the
Highlands "produced a salutary effect;" and they commenced to treat him with some respect, even going the length
of admitting him to their deliberations. A considerable
number of the Highlanders were already in arms to support
the King; but the Committee, having Charles in their power,
induced him to write to the Highland chiefs commanding
them to lay down their arms. This they refused, and to
enforce the King's orders a regiment, under Sir John Brown,
was despatched to the North, but it was surprised and defeated on the night of the 21st October by Sir David Ogilvy
of Airley. On learning this intelligence, General Leslie
hastened north with a force of 3000 cavalry. General
Middleton, who supported the King's friends in the North,
and who was then at Forfar, hearing of Leslie's advance,
sent him a letter enclosing a copy of "a bond and oath of
engagement, which had been entered into by Huntly, Athole,
the Earl of Seaforth, and other leading Highland chiefs, by
which they had pledged themselves on oath, to join firmly
and faithfully together, and 'neither for fear, threatening,
allurement, nor advantage, to relinquish the cause of religion,
of the king, and of the kingdom, nor to lay down their arms
without a general consent; and as the best undertakings
did not escape censure and malice, they promised and swore,
for the satisfaction of all reasonable persons, that they would
maintain the true religion, as then established in Scotland,
the National Covenant and the Solemn League and Covenant, and defend the person of the King, his prerogative,
greatness, and authority, and the privileges of parliament,
and the freedom of the subject.'" Middleton pointed out
that the only object of himself and friends was to unite
Scotsmen in defence of their common rights, and that, as
would be seen from this bond, the grounds on which they
entered into association were exactly the same as those professed by Leslie himself. Considering all this, and seeing

that the independence of Scotland was at stake, all Scotsmen should join for the preservation of their common liberties. Middleton proposed to join Leslie, to place himself under his command, and expressed a hope that he would not shed the blood of his own countrymen nor force them to shed the blood of their brethren in self-defence. These communications ended in a treaty between Leslie and the leading Royalists on the 4th November, at Strathbogie, by which Middleton and his followers received an indemnity, and laid down their arms.*

In 1651, after the disastrous battle of Worcester, at which Charles was completely defeated by Cromwell—where we find Thomas Mackenzie of Pluscardine as one of the Colonels of foot for Inverness and Ross, and Alexander Càm Mackenzie, fourth son of Alexander, fifth of Gairloch —Charles fled to the Continent, and, after many severe hardships and narrow escapes, he ultimately found refuge in France, where, and in Flanders, he continued to reside, often in great distress and want, until the Restoration, in May 1660, when he returned to England "indolent, selfish, - unfeeling, faithless, ungrateful, and insensible to shame or reproach." The Earl of Cromarty says that subsequent to the treaty agreed to between Middleton and Leslie at Strathbogie, "Seaforth joined the King at Stirling. After the fatal battle of Worcester he continued a close prisoner till the Restoration of Charles." He was excepted from Oliver Cromwell's Act of Grace and Pardon in 1654, and his estates were forfeited without any provision being allowed out of it for his lady or family, He supported the cause of the King as long as there was an opportunity of fighting for it in the field, and when forced to submit to the opposing powers of Cromwell and the Commonwealth, he was committed to prison, where, with "much firmness of mind and nobility of soul," he endured a tedious captivity for many years, until Charles II. was recalled, when his old and faithful friend Seaforth was released, and became a

---

* Balfour, vol. iv., p. 129.   Highland Clans, p. 285.

favourite at his licentious and profligate Court. During the
remainder of his life little or nothing of importance is known
regarding him, except that he lived in the favour and
merited smiles of his sovereign, in undisputed possession
and enjoyment of the extensive estates and honours of his
ancestors, which, through his faithful adherence to the
House of Stuart, had been nearly overwhelmed and lost
during the exile of the second Charles and his own captivity.
Referring to the state of matters at the time, the Laird of
Applecross, a contemporary writer, says that the "rebels,
possessing the authority, oppressed all the loyal subjects,
and him with the first ; his estate was overburthened to its
destruction, but nothing could deter him so as to bring him
to forsake his King or his duty. Whenever any was in the
field for him, he was one, seconding that falling cause with
all his power, and when he was not in the field against the
enemy, he was in the prison by him until the restoration of
the King."

Seaforth, restored to liberty, received, on the 23d of
April 1662, a Commission of the Sheriffship of Ross
afterwards renewed to him and his eldest son, Kenneth,
jointly, on 31st July 1675 ; and when he had set matters
right at Brahan, he again visited Paris, leaving his
Countess, Isobel Mackenzie, daughter of Sir John Mackenzie of Tarbat, and sister to the first Earl of Cromarty, in
charge of his domestic affairs in the North. During his
absence occurred that incident, already so well-known to the
reader, which, it is said, ended in the Brahan Seer uttering
the famous and remarkable prediction regarding the fate of
the family of Seaforth, which has been so literally and
so curiously fulfilled.

His Lordship's heir and successor, Kenneth, Lord Kintail, was "undoubted Patron of the Paraich Kirk and Paro-
chin of Inverness," for, in consideration of Robert Robertson, Burgess of Inverness, paying a certain sum for the teind
sheaves and parsonage teinds of all and sundrie these 50
acres and a-half of land of the territerie and burgage lands
of the burgh of Inverness, "therefore will ye us, the said

Kenneth, Lord Kintail, with consent foresaid, as having right in manner above-written—and as the said Kenneth, Earl of Seaforth, as taking the full burden in and upon us for the said Kenneth, Lord Kintail, our son, to the effect after-rehearsed, to have sold, annailzed, and disponed, &c., &c., and we, the said Kenneth, Lord Kintail, as principale, and the said Kenneth, Earl of Seaforth, our father, as cautioneer, &c., &c."*

Kenneth was married early in life to Isobel, daughter of Sir John Mackenzie of Tarbat, father of the first Earl of Cromarty, by whom he had issue, first, Kenneth Og, who succeeded; second, John Mackenzie of Assynt, who had a son, Alexander, by Sibella, daughter of Alexander Mackenzie, third of Applecross, by whom he had one son, Kenneth, who married his cousin, Frances, daughter of Colonel Alexander Mackenzie of Conansbay, and, in 1723, died without issue; and third, Colonel Alexander Mackenzie, also designed of Assynt and Conansbay, and of whom the line of the last Lord Seaforth, Francis ↲ Humberston Mackenzie; another son, Hugh, died young. Of four daughters, Margaret married James, second Lord Duffus, with issue; Ann died unmarried; Isabel, first married Roderick Macleod of Macleod, without issue; and secondly, Sir Duncan Campbell of Lochnell; Mary married Alexander Macdonell of Glengarry. This Earl died in December 1678, and was succeeded by his eldest son,

XVI. KENNETH OG, FOURTH EARL OF SEAFORTH.

By the Highlanders, he was called *Coinneach Og*, to distinguish him from his father. At an early age he discovered the benefits of the faithful adherence of his father to the fortunes of Charles II. In 1678 we find his name among the chiefs who, by a proclamation issued on the 10th October, were called upon to give the bond and caution for

---

* Disposition recorded in the Commissary Court Books of Inverness, dated at Fortrose, 17th June 1698.

the security of the peace and quiet of the Highlands, which the leaders of the clans were to give, not only for themselves but for all the members of their Clan. Notwithstanding all the laws and orders hitherto passed, the inhabitants and broken men in the Highlands were "inured and accustomed to liberty and licentiousness" during the late troubles, and "still presumed to sorn, steal, oppress, and commit other violences and disorders." The great chiefs were commanded to appear in Edinburgh on the last Tuesday of February 1679, and yearly thereafter on the second Thursday of July, to give security, and to receive instructions as to the peace of the Highlands. To prevent any excuse for non-attendance, they were declared free from caption for debt or otherwise while journeying to and from Edinburgh, and other means were to be taken which should be thought necessary or expedient until the Highlands were finally quieted, and "all these wicked, broken, and disorderly men utterly rooted out and extirpated." A second proclamation was issued, in which the lesser barons—heads of the several branches of clans—whose names were given, were to go to Inverlochy by the 20th of November following, as they are, by reason of their mean condition, not able to come in to Edinburgh and find caution, and there to give in bonds and caution for themselves, their men, tenants, servants, and indwellers upon their lands, and all of their name descended of their family, to the Earl of Caithness, Sir James Campbell of Lawers, James Menzies of Culdares, or any two of them. These lists are interesting, showing, as they do, those who were considered the greater and lesser chiefs at the time. We find four Mackenzies in the former but none in the latter.*

Kenneth was, on the 1st March 1681, served heir male to his great-grandfather, Lord Mackenzie of Kintail, in his lands in the Lordship of Ardmeanach and Earldom of Ross; was made a member of the Privy Council by James II. on his accession to the throne in 1685, and chosen a Companion

* For full lists, see Antiquarian Notes, pp. 184 and 187.

of the most noble Order of the Thistle, on the revival of that ancient order in 1687. The year after the Revolution, which finally and for ever lost the British throne to the House of Stuart, Seaforth accompanied his royal master to France, but when that unfortunate Prince returned to Ireland in the following year to make a final effort for the recovery of his kingdom, he was accompanied by Earl Kenneth. Here he took part in the siege of Londonderry and other engagements, and as an expression of gratitude, he was created Marquis of Seaforth, under which dignity he repeatedly appears in different legal documents. This well-meant and deserved honour came too late in the falling fortunes and declining powers of the ex-sovereign, and does little more than mark the sinking monarch's testimonial and confirmation of the steady adherence of the chiefs of Clan Kenneth to the unfortunate cause of the Stuarts.

Dundee in his letter to "the Laird of Macleod," dated "Moy, June 23, 1689,"* in which he details his prospects, and gives a list of those who are to join him, says, "My Lord Seaforth will be in a few dayes from Ireland to raise his men for the King's service ;" but the fatal shot which closed the career of that brilliant star and champion of the Stuart dynasty at Killiecrankie, arrested the progress of the family of Seaforth in the fair track to all the honours which a grateful dynasty could bestow ; nor was this powerful family singular in this respect—seeing its flattering prospects withered at, perhaps, a fortunate moment for the prosperity of the British Empire. Jealousies have now passed away on that subject, and it is not our business here to discuss or confound the principles of contending loyalties. To

---

* About this time Viscount Tarbat boasted to General Mackay of his great influence with his countrymen, especially the Clan Mackenzie, and assured him "that though Seaforth should come to his own country and among his friends, he (Tarbat) would overturn in eight days more than the Earl could advance in six weeks; yet he proved as backward as Seaforth or any other of the Clan. And though Redcastle, Coul, and others of the name of Mackenzie came, they fell not on final methods, but protested a great deal of affection for the cause,"— *Mackay's Memoirs, pp.* 25 *and* 237.

check the proceedings of the Clan Mackenzie, Mackay
placed a garrison of a hundred Mackays in Brahan Castle,
the principal seat of the Earl of Seaforth, and an equal
number of Rosses in Castle Leod, the mansion of Viscount
Tarbat, both places of strength, and advantageously situated
for watching the movements of the Jacobite Mackenzies.*

Earl Kenneth seems to have left Ireland immediately
after the Battle of the Boyne, and to have returned to the
Highlands. The greater part of the North was at the time
hostile to the Government, and General Mackay was obliged
to march north, with all haste, before a general rising could
take place under Buchan, who now commanded the Highlanders that stood out for King James. Mackay was within
four hours' march of Inverness before Buchan knew of his
approach, who was then at that place "waiting for the Earl
of Seaforth's and the other Highlanders whom he expected
to join him in attacking the town." Hearing of the proximity of the enemy, he at once retreated, crossed the River
Ness, and retired along the north side of the Beauly Firth,
eastward through the Black Isle. In this emergency, Seaforth, fearing the consequences to himself personally of the
part he had acted throughout, sent two of his friends to
Mackay with offers of submission and of whatever securities
might be required for his good behaviour in future, informing him that although he was forced to appear on the side
of King James, he never entertained any design of molesting
the Government forces or of joining Buchan in his attack
on Inverness. Mackay replied that he could accept no other
security than the surrender of his Lordship's person, and
conjured him to comply, as he valued his own safety and the
preservation of his family and people, assuring him that in
the case of surrender he should be detained in civil custody
in Inverness, and treated with the respect due to his rank,
until the will of the Government should be made known.
Next day his mother, the Countess Dowager of Seaforth, and
Sir Alexander Mackenzie of Coul, went and pleaded with

---

* Life of General Mackay, by John Mackay of Rockfield, pp. 36-37.

Mackay for a mitigation of the terms proposed, but finding the General inflexible, they informed him that Seaforth would accede to any conditions agreed upon between them. It was then stipulated that he should deliver himself up and be kept prisoner in Inverness, until the Privy Council decided as to his ultimate disposal. With the view of concealing the voluntary submission of the Earl from his own clan and his other Jacobite friends, it was agreed that he should allow himself to be seized at one of his seats by a party of horse under Major Mackay, as if he were taken by surprise. He, however, disappointed the party sent out to take him, in excuse of which, his mother and he, in letters to Mackay, pleaded the delicate state of his health, which, it was urged, would suffer from imprisonment ; and really few can blame him for unwillingness to place himself absolutely at the disposal of such a body as the Privy Council of Scotland then was—many of whom would not hesitate to sacrifice him, if by so doing they saw a chance of obtaining a share of his extensive estates.

General Mackay became so irritated at the deception practised upon him that he resolved to treat the Earl's vassals " with all the rigour of military execution," and sent him a message that if he did not surrender forthwith according to promise, he should at once carry out his instructions from the Privy Council, enter his country with fire and sword, and seize all property belonging to himself or to his vassals as lawful prize; and, lest Seaforth should suspect that he had no intention of executing his terrible threat, he immediately ordered three Dutch regiments from Aberdeen to Inverness, and decided on leading a competent body of horse and foot in person from the garrison at Inverness, to take possession of Brahan Castle. He, at the same time, wrote instructing the Earl of Sutherland, Lord Reay, and the Laird of Balnagown, to send 1000 of their men, under Major Wishart, an experienced officer acquainted with the country, to take up their quarters in the more remote districts of the Seaforth estates, should that extreme step become necessary. Having, however, a friendly disposition

towards the followers of Seaforth, on account of their being
"all Protestants and none of the most dangerous enemies,"
and being more anxious to get hold of the Earl's person
than to ruin his friends, he caused information of his intentions to be sent to Seaforth's camp by some of his own
party, as if from a feeling of friendship for him ; the result
being that, contrary to Mackay's expectations, Seaforth
surrendered—thus relieving him from a disagreeable duty,*
—and he was committed a prisoner to the Castle of Inverness.

Writing to the Privy Council about the state of the disaffected chiefs at the time, Mackay says—"I believe it shall
fare so with the Earl of Seaforth, that is, that he shall haply
submit when his country is ruined and spoyled, which is the
character of a true Scotsman, *wyse behinde the hand.*"†
By warrant, dated 7th October 1690, the Privy Council
directed Mackay "to transport the person of Kenneth, Earl
of Seaforth, with safety from Inverness to Edinburgh, in
such way and manner as he should think fit." This done,
on the 6th November following he was confined within the
Castle of Edinburgh, but, little more than a year afterwards,
liberated on the 7th January 1692, having found caution to
appear when called upon, and on condition that he would
not go ten miles beyond Edinburgh. He appears not to
have kept long within these conditions, for shortly afterwards he is again in prison ; almost immediately makes his
escape ; is again apprehended on the 7th of May, the same
year, at Pencaitland; and again kept confined in the Castle
of Inverness, from which he is ultimately and finally liberated
on giving satisfactory security for his peaceable behaviour.‡

---

* Though the General " was not immediately connected with the Seaforth
family himself, some of his near relatives were, both by the ties of kindred and
of ancient friendship. For these, and other reasons, it may be conceived what
joy and thankfulness to Providence he felt for the result of this affair, which at
once relieved him from a distressing dilemma, and promised to put a speedy
period to his labours in Scotland."—*Mackay's Life of General Mackay.*

† Letters to the Privy Council, dated 1st September 1690.

‡ History of the Highland Clans, Records of the Privy Council, and Mackay's
Memoirs. The following is the order for his release :—" William R., Right

During the remaining years of his life, Seaforth appears to have lived mainly in France. His necessary absence from his own country during the protraction of political irritation and, indeed, the exhausted state of his paternal revenues, would have rendered his residence abroad highly expedient, and we find accordingly discharges for feu-duties granted, by others, viz.:—"I, Maister Alexander Mackenzie, lawful brother - to the Marquis of Seaforth, grants me to have received from John Mathesone, all and hail the somme of seaven hundred and twentie merks Scots money, and that in complete payment of his duties and of the lands of both the Fernacks and Achnakerich, payable Martimass ninety (1690), dated 22d November 1694;" and another by "Isabel, Countess Dowager of Seaforth, in 1696, tested by 'Rorie Mackenzie, servitor to the Marquis of Seaforth.'" There is another original discharge by "me, Isabel, Countess Dowager of Seaforth, Lady Superior of the grounds, lands, and oyes under-written," to Kenneth Mackenzie of Achterdonell, dated at Fortrose, 15th November 1697. Signed, "Isobell Seaforth."* All this time it may be presumed that Earl Kenneth was in retirement, and took no personal part in the management of his estates for the remainder of his life.

His clansmen, however, seem to have been determined to protect his interest as much as lay in their power. A certain Sir John Dempster of Pitliver had advanced a large sum of money to Seaforth and his mother, the Countess Dowager, and obtained a decreet of Parliament to have the money refunded to him. The cash was not forthcoming, and

trusty and right-well-beloved Councillors, &c., we greet you well. Whereas we are informed that Kenneth, Earl of Seaforth, did surrender himself prisoner to the commander of our garrison at Inverness, and has thrown himself on our Royal mercy ; it is our will and pleasure, and we hereby authorise and require you to set the said Earl of Seaforth at liberty, upon his finding bail and security to live peaceably under our Government and to compear before you when called. And that you order our Advocate not to insist in the process of treason waged against him, until our further pleasure be known therein. For doing whereof this shall be your warrant, so we bid you heartily farewell. Given at our Court at Kensington, the first day of March 1696-7, and of our reign the eighth year. By his Majesty's command.   (Signed)   "TULLIBARDINE."

* Allangrange Service, on which occasion the originals were produced.

Sir John obtained letters of horning and arrestment against
the Earl and his mother, and employed several officers to
execute them, but they returned the letters unexecuted, not
finding *notum accessum* in the Earl's country, and they refused altogether to undertake the due execution of them,
unless they were assisted by some of the King's forces in
the district.   Sir John petitioned for this, and humbly
craved their Lordships to allow him "a competent assistance of his Majesty's forces at Fort-William, Inverness, or
where they are lying adjacent to the places where the said
diligence is to be put in execution to support and protect
the messengers" in the due execution of the legal diligence
against the Earl and his mother, "by horning, poinding,
arrestment, or otherways," and to recommend to the Governor at Fort-William or the commander of the forces at
Inverness, to grant a suitable force for the purpose.   The
Lords of the Privy Council, having considered the petition,
recommended Sir Thomas Livingstone, commander-in-chief
of his Majesty's forces, to order some of these officers already
mentioned to furnish the petition "with competent parties
of his Majesty's forces" to support and protect the messengers in the due execution of the "legal diligence upon the
said decreet of Parliament."*   We have not learned the
result, but it is not likely to have proved very profitable to
Sir John Dempster.

Kenneth married Lady Frances Herbert, second daughter of William, Marquis of Powis (an English nobleman), by
Lady Elizabeth Somerset, daughter of Edward, Marquis of
Worcester, by whom he had issue, one son, William, his
successor, and a daughter, Mary, who married John Careyl,
with issue. He died in 1701, at Paris, and was succeeded
by his only son,

XVII. WILLIAM, FIFTH EARL OF SEAFORTH,

Known among the Highlanders as "William Dubh."
He succeeded at a most important era in the history of

---

* For this document see "Antiquarian Notes," pp. 118-119.

Scotland, just when the country was divided on the great question of Union with England, which, in spite of the fears of most of the Highland chiefs and nobles of Scotland, turned out in the end so beneficial to both. He would, no doubt, during his residence with his exiled parents in France, have imbibed strong Jacobite feelings. But little information of his proceedings during the first few years of his rule is obtainable. He seems to have continued abroad, for on the 23d of May 1709 an order appears addressed to the forester at Letterewe signed by his mother, the Dowager "Frances Seaforth." On the 22d of June 1713 she addresses a letter to Colin Mackenzie of Kineraig, in which she says—"I find my son William is fully inclined to do justice to all. Within fifteen days he will be at Brahan."*

At this time a great majority of the southern nobles were ready to break out into open rebellion, while the Highland chiefs were almost to a man prepared for a rising in favour of the Stuarts. This soon became apparent to the Government. Bodies of armed Highlanders were seen moving about in several districts in the North. A party appeared in the neighbourhood of Inverness which was, however, soon dispersed by the garrison. The Government became alarmed, and the lords justices sent a large number of half-pay officers, chiefly from the Scottish regiments, to officer the militia, under command of Major-General Whitham, commander-in-chief at the time in Scotland. These proceedings alarmed the Jacobites, most of whom returned to their homes. The Duke of Gordon was confined in Edinburgh Castle, and the Marquis of Huntly and Lord Drummond in their respective residences. The latter fled to the Highlands and offered bail for his good behaviour. Captain Campbell of Glendaruel, who had obtained a commission from the late Administration to raise an independent company of Highlanders, was apprehended at Inverlochy and sent prisoner to Edinburgh. Sir Donald Macdonald of Sleat was also seized and committed to the same place, and

* Original produced at Allangrange Service in 1829.

a proclamation was issued offering a reward of £100,000 sterling for the apprehension of the Chevalier should he land or attempt to land in Great Britain. King George, on his arrival, threw himself entirely into the arms of the Whigs, who alone shared his favours. A spirit of the most violent discontent was excited throughout the whole kingdom, and the populace, led on by the Jacobite leaders, raised tumults in different parts of the King's dominions. The Chevalier, taking advantage of this excitement, issued his manifesto to the chief nobility, especially to the Dukes of Shrewsbury, Marlborough, and Argyll, who handed them to the Secretaries of State.

The King dissolved Parliament in the month of January 1715, and issued an extraordinary proclamation calling together a new Parliament. The Whigs were successful both in England and Scotland, but particularly so in the latter, where a majority of the peers, and forty out of the forty-five members then returned to the Commons, were in favour of the King's Government. The principal struggle was in the county of Inverness, between Mackenzie of Prestonhall, strongly supported by Glengarry and the other Jacobite chiefs, and Forbes of Culloden, brother of the celebrated President, who carried the election through the influence of Brigadier-General Grant and the friends of Lord Lovat.

The Earl of Mar, who had rendered himself extremely unpopular among the Jacobite chiefs,·afterwards rewarded some of his former favourites by advocating the repeal of the Union. He was again made Secretary of State for Scotland in 1713, but was unceremoniously dismissed from office by George I., and vowed revenge. He afterwards found his way north to Fife, and subsequently to the Braes of Mar. On the 19th of August 1715, he despatched letters to the principal Jacobites, among whom was Lord Seaforth, inviting them to attend a grand hunting match at Braemar on the 27th of the same month. This was a ruse meant to cover his intention to raise the standard of rebellion, and that the Jacobites were let into the secret is evident from

the fact that as early as the 6th of August those in Edinburgh and the neighbourhood were aware of his intentions
to come to Scotland. Under pretence of attending this
grand match, a considerable number of noblemen and
gentlemen arrived at Aboyne about the appointed time,
among whom were the Marquis of Huntly, eldest son of the
Duke of Gordon ; the Marquis of Tullibardine, eldest son of
the Duke of Athole; the Earls of Nithsdale, Marischal,
Traquair, Errol, Southesk, Carnwarth, Seaforth, Linlithgow,
and others; the Viscounts Kilsyth, Kenmure, Kingston,
and Stormont; Lords Rollo, Duffus, Drummond, Strath-
allan, Ogilvie, and Nairne ; and about twenty-six gentlemen
of influence in the Highlands, among whom were Generals
Hamilton and Gordon, Glengarry, Campbell of Glendaruel,
and the lairds of Auchterhouse and Auldbar.* Mar made
a stirring address, expressing regret for his past conduct in
favouring the Union, and, now that his eyes were opened,
promising to do all in his power to retrieve the past and
make his countrymen again a free people. He produced a
commission from James appointing him Lieutenant-General
and Commander of all the Jacobite forces in Scotland,
informed the meeting that he was supplied with money, and
that an arrangement had been made by which he would be
enabled to pay regularly any forces that might be raised, so
that no gentleman who should join his standard with his
followers would be put to any expense, and the country
would be entirely relieved of the expenses of conducting the
war ; after which the meeting unanimously resolved to take
up arms to establish the Chevalier on the Scottish throne.
They then took the oath of fidelity to the Earl as representative of James VIII. and to each other, and separated,
each going home promising to raise his vassals and be in
readiness to join Mar whenever they were summoned to do
so. They had scarcely arrived at their respective destina-
tions when they were called upon to meet the Earl at
Aboyne on the 3d of September following, where, with only

* History of the Highland Clans ; Rae, p. 189 ; Annals of King George, pp. 15-16.

sixty followers, Mar proclaimed the Chevalier at Castletown
in Braemar, after which he proceeded to Kirkmichael, where,
on the 6th of September, he raised his standard in presence
of a force of 2000 men, mostly consisting of horse. · When
in course of erection, the ball on the top of the pole fell off.
This, which was regarded by the Highlanders as a bad omen,
cast a gloom over the proceedings of the day.

Meanwhile Colonel Sir Hector Munro, who had served
as Captain of the Earl of Orkney's Regiment with reputation
in the wars of Queen Anne, raised his followers, who, with
a body of Rosses, amounted to about 600 men. With these
in November 1715, he encamped at Alness, and on the 6th
of October following he was joined by the Earl of Sutherland, accompanied by his son, Lord Strathnaver, and by
Lord Reay, with an additional force of 600, in the interest
of the Whig Government, and to cover their own districts
and check the movements of the Western clans in effecting
a junction with the Earl of Mar, whom Earl William and
Sir Donald Macdonald had publicly espoused, as already
stated, at the pretended hunting match in Braemar. · This
meeting at Alness had the effect of keeping Seaforth in the
North. If the Earl and his mother's clans had advanced a
month earlier the Duke of Argyll could not have dared to
make head against Mar's united forces, who might have
pushed an army across the Forth sufficient to have paralyzed
any exertion that might have been made to have preserved
a shadow of the existing Government in Scotland. It may
be said that if Dundee had lived to have held the commission of Mar, such a junction would not have been necessary
to effect, which amounts to no more than that the life of
Dundee would have been tantamount to a restoration of the
Stewarts. Mar was not trained in the camp, nor did he
possess the military genius of a Dundee. Had Montrose a
moiety of his force things would have been otherwise. Mar,
trusting to Seaforth's reinforcement, was inactive, and Seaforth was for a time kept in by the collocation of Sutherland's levies, till he was also joined by 700 Macdonalds and
detachments from other names, amounting, with his own

' followers, to 3000 men, with which he instantly attacked the
Earl of Sutherland, who fled with his mixed army precipit-
ately to Bonar-Bridge, where they dispersed. A party of
Grants on their way to join them, on being informed of
Sutherland's retreat, thought it prudent to retrace their
steps. Seaforth, thus relieved, levied considerable fines on
Munro's territories, which were fully retaliated in his absence
with the Jacobite army, to join which he now set out ; and
Sir John Mackenzie of Coul, whom he had ordered to occupy
Inverness, was, after a gallant resistance, forced by Lord
Lovat, at the head of a mixed body of Frasers and Grants,
to retreat with his garrison to Ross-shire. "Whether he
followed his chief to Perth does not appear ; but on Seaforth's arrival that Mar seems for the first time to have
resolved on the passage of the Firth—a movement which
led to the Battle of Sheriffmuir—is evident and conclusive
as to the different features given to the whole campaign by
the Whig camp at Alness, however creditable to the noble
Earl and his mother's confederates. But it is not our present province to enter on a military review of the conduct
of either army preceding this consequential conflict, or to
decide to which party the victory, claimed by both parties,
properly belonged ; suffice it to say that above 3000 of Seaforth's men formed a considerable part of the second line,
and seem from the general account on that subject to have
done their duty."* A great many of Seaforth's followers
were slain, among whom were four gentlemen who appear
to have signally distinguished themselves. These were
John Mackenzie of Hilton, who commanded a company of
the Mackenzies, John Mackenzie of Applecross, John Mac-
Ra of Conchra, and John Murchison of Achtertyre. Their
prowess on the field has been commemorated by one of
their followers, John MacRae, who escaped and returned
home, in an excellent Gaelic poem, known as "Latha Blàr
an t-Siorra," or the "Day of Sheriffmuir." The fate of these
renowned warriors was keenly regretted by their Highland

* Bennetsfield MS.

countrymen, and they are still remembered and distinguished among them as " Ceithear Ianan na h-Alba," or the " Four Johns of Scotland."

During the previous troubles Islandonain Castle got into the hands of the King's troops, but some time before Sheriffmuir it was again secured by the following stratagem :—A neighbouring tenant applied to the Governor for some of the garrison to cut his corn, as he feared from the appearance of the sky and the croaking of ravens that a heavy storm was impending, and that nothing but a sudden separation of his crop from the ground could save his family from starvation. The Governor readily yielded to his solicitations, and sent the garrison of Government soldiers then in the castle to his aid, who, on their return, discovered the ruse too late; for the Kintail men were by this time reaping the spoils, and had possession of the castle. "The oldest inhabitant of the parish remembers to have seen the Kintail men under arms, dancing on the leaden roof, just as they were setting out for the Battle of Sheriffmuir, where this resolute band was cut to pieces."[*]

Inverness continued meanwhile in possession of the Mackenzies, under command of the Governor, Sir John Mackenzie of Coul, and George Mackenzie of Gruinard. Macdonald of Keppoch was on the march to support Sir John at Inverness, and Lord Lovat, learning this, gathered his men together, and on the 7th of November decided to throw himself across the river Ness and place his forces directly between Keppoch and the Governor. Sir John, on discovering the movement of Lovat, resolved to make a sally out of the garrison and place the enemy between him and the advancing Keppoch, where he could attack him with advantage, but Keppoch became alarmed and returned home through Glen-Urquhart, whereupon Lord Lovat marched straight upon Inverness, and took up a position about a mile to the west of the town. The authorities were summoned to send out the garrison and the Governor, or

* Old Statistical Account of Kintail, 1792.

the town would be burnt and the inhabitants put to the sword. Preparations were made for the attack, but Sir John Mackenzie, considering any further defence hopeless, on the 10th of November collected together all the boats he could find, and at high water safely effected his escape from the town, when Lovat marched in without opposition. His Lordship advised the Earl of Sutherland of his possession of Inverness,.and on the 15th November the latter, leaving Colonel Robert Munro of Fowlis as Governor of Inverness, went with his followers, accompanied by Lord Lovat with some of his men, to Brahan Castle, and compelled the responsible men of the Clan Mackenzie who were not in the South with the Earl of Seaforth, to come under an obligation for their peaceable behaviour, and to return the arms previously taken from the Munros by Lord Seaforth at Alness; to release the prisoners in their possession, and promise not to assist Lord Seaforth directly or indirectly in his efforts against the Government; that they would grant to the Earl of Sutherland any sum of money he might require from them upon due notice for the use of the Government; and, finally, that Brahan Castle, the principal·residence of the Earl of Seaforth, should be turned into a garrison for his Majesty King George.

Seaforth returned from Sheriffmuir, and again collected his men near Brahan, but the Earl of Sutherland, with a large number of his own men, Lord Reay's, the Munros, Rosses, Culloden's men, and the Frasers, marched to meet him and encamped at Beauly, within a few miles of Seaforth's camp, and prepared to give him battle, "which, when· my Lord Seaforth saw, he thought it convenient to capitulate, own the King's authority, disperse his men, and propose the mediation of these Government friends for his pardon. Upon his submission the King was graciously pleased to send down orders that upon.giving up his arms and coming into Inverness, he might expect his pardon; yet upon the Pretender's Anvil?.at Perth and my Lord Huntly's suggestions to him that now was the time for them to appear for their King and country, and that what honour

they lost at Dunblane might yet be regained; but while he
thus insinuated to my Lord Seaforth, he privately found
that my Lord Seaforth had by being an early suitor for the
King's pardon, by promising to lay down his arms, and
owning the King's authority, claimed in a great measure to
an assurance of his life and fortune, which he thought proper for himself to purchase at the rate of disappointing
Seaforth, with hopes of standing by the good old cause, till
Seaforth, with that vain hopes, lost the King's favour that
was promised him; which Huntly embraced by taking the
very first opportunity of deserting the Pretender's cause,
and surrendering himself upon terms made with him of
safety to his life and fortune.   This sounded so sweet to
him that he sleeped so secure as never to dream of any
preservation for a great many good gentlemen that made
choice to stand by him and serve under him than many
other worthy nobles who would die or banish rather than
not show their personal bravery, and all other friendly
offices to their adherents."*

In February 1716, hopeless of attaining his object, the
unfortunate son of James II. left Scotland, the land of his
forefathers, never to visit it again, and Earl William followed him to the common resort of the exiled Jacobites of
the time.   On the 7th of the following May an act of
attainder was passed against the Earl and other chiefs of
the Jacobite party.   Their estates were forfeited, though
practically in many cases, and especially in that of the Earl ·
of Seaforth, it was found extremely difficult to carry the
forfeiture into effect.   The Master of Sinclair is responsible
for the base and unfounded allegation that the Earl of Seaforth, the Marquis of Huntly, and other Jacobites, were in
treaty with the Government to deliver up the Chevalier to
the Duke of Argyll, that they might procure better terms
for themselves than they could otherwise expect.   "This
odious charge, which is not corroborated by any other
writer, must be looked upon as highly improbable."† If

---

* Lord Lovat's Account of the Taking of Inverness.   Patten's Rebellion.
† Fullarton's Highland Clans, p. 471.

any proof of the untruthfulness of this charge is necessary it will be found in the fact that Earl William returned afterwards to the Island of Lews, and re-embodied his vassals there under an experienced officer, Campbell of Ormundel, who had served with distinction in the Russian army, and it was not until a large Government force was sent over against him, which he found it impossible success-fully to oppose, that he recrossed to the mainland and escaped to France.

Among the "gentlemen prisoners" taken to the Castle of Stirling on the day after the Battle of Sheriffmuir we find the following in a list published in "Patten's Rebellion"— Kenneth Mackenzie, nephew to Sir Alexander Mackenzie of Coul; John Maclean, adjutant to Colonel Mackenzie's Regiment; Colin Mackenzie of Kildin, captain of Fairburn's Regiment; Hugh MacRa, Donald MacRa, and Chris-topher Macrae.

The war declared against Spain in December 1718 again revived the hopes of the Jacobites, who, in accordance with a stipulation between the British Government and the Duke of Orleans, then Regent of France, had previously, with the Chevalier and the Duke of Ormond at their head, been ordered out of France. They repaired to Madrid, where they held conferences with Cardinal Alberoni, and concerted an invasion of Great Britain. On the 10th of March 1719 a fleet, consisting of ten men-of-war and twenty-one trans-ports, having on board five thousand men, a large quantity of ammunition, and thirty thousand muskets, sailed from Cadiz under the command of the Duke of Ormond, with instructions to join the rest of the expedition at Corunna, and to make a descent at once upon England, Scotland, and Ireland. The sorry fate of this expedition is well known. Only two frigates reached their destination, the rest having been dispersed and disabled off Cape Finisterre by a violent storm which lasted about twelve days. The two ships which survived the storm and reached Scotland had on board the Earl of Seaforth and Earl Marischal, the Marquis of Tullibardine, some field officers, three hundred

P

Spaniards, and arms and ammunition for two thousand men. They entered Lochalsh about the middle of May; effected a landing in Kintail and were there joined by a body of Seaforth's vassals, and a party of Macgregors under command of the famous Rob Roy; but the other Jacobite chiefs, remembering their previous disappointments and misfortunes, stood aloof until the whole of Ormond's forces should arrive. General Wightman, who was stationed at Inverness, hearing of their arrival, marched to meet them with 2000 Dutch troops and a detachment of the garrison at Inverness. Seaforth's forces and their allies took possession of the pass of Glenshiel, but on the approach of the Government forces they retired to the pass of Strachell, which they decided to defend at all hazards. They were here engaged by General Wightman, who, after a smart skirmish of about three hours' duration, and after inflicting some loss upon the Highlanders, drove them from one eminence to another till night came on, when the Highlanders, their chief having been seriously wounded, and giving up all hopes of a successful resistance, retired during the night to the mountains, carrying Seaforth along with them ; and the Spaniards, next morning, surrendered themselves prisoners of war.* Seaforth, Marischal, and Tullibardine, with the other principal officers, managed to effect their escape to the Western Isles, from which they afterwards found their way to the continent. Rob Roy was placed in ambush with the view of attacking the Royal troops in the rear, and it is recorded that, having more zeal than prudence, he attacked the rear of the enemy's column before they had become engaged in front ; his small party was routed, and the intention of placing the King's troops between two fires was thus defeated.† General Wightman

---

* The Spaniards kept their powder magazine and balls behind the manse, but after the Battle of Glenshiel they set fire to it lest it should fall into the hands of the King's troops. These balls are still gathered up by sportsmen, and are found in great abundance upon the glebe.—*Old Statistical Account of Kintail.*

† *New Statistical Account of Glenshiel*, by the Rev. John Macrae, who gives a minute description of the scenes of the battle, and informs us that in constructing the parliamentary road which runs through the Glen a few years ago, several

sent a detachment to Islandonain Castle, which he ordered to be blown up and demolished.

Wightman advanced from the Highland Capital by Loch-Ness, and a modern writer pertinently asks "Why he was allowed to pass by such a route without opposition? It is alleged that Marischal and Tullibardine had interrupted the movements of the invaders by ill-timed altercations about command, but we are provoked to observe that some extraordinary interposition seems evident to frustrate every scheme towards forwarding the cause of the ill-fated house of Stuart. Had the Chevalier St George arrived earlier, as he might have done; had William Earl of Seaforth joined the Earl of Mar some time before, as he ought to have done; and strengthened as Mar would then have been, had he boldly advanced on Stirling, as it appears he would have done, Argyll's force would have been annihilated, and James VIII. proclaimed at the Cross of Edinburgh. Well did the brave Highlanders indignantly demand, ' What did you call us to arms for ? Was it to run away ? · What did our own King come for ? Was it to see us butchered by hangmen ?' There was a fatuity that accompanied all their undertakings which neutralised intrepidity, devotedness, and bravery; which the annals of no other people can exhibit, and paltry jealousies which stultified exertions, which, independently of political results, astonished Europe at large."*

An Act of Parliament for disarming the Highlanders was passed in 1716, but in some cases to very little purpose; for some of the most disaffected clans were better armed than ever, though by the Act the collectors of taxes were allowed to pay for the arms given in none were delivered except those which were broken, old, and unfit for use, and these were valued at prices far above what they were really worth. Not only so, but a lively trade in old arms was

---

bullets and pieces of musket barrels were found ; and the green mounds which cover the graves of the slain, and the ruins of a rude breast-work, which the Highlanders constructed on the crest of the hill to cover their position, still mark the scene of the conflict.

* Bennetsfield MS.

carried on with Holland and other continental countries,
and these arms were sold to the commissioners as Highland
weapons, at exorbitant prices. General Wade also found
in the possession of the Highlanders a large quantity of
arms which they obtained from the Spaniards who took
part in the Battle of Glenshiel, and he computed that those
Highlanders opposed to the Government possessed at this
time no less than five or six thousand arms of various kinds.

Wade arrived in Inverness on the 10th of August 1725,
and in virtue of another Act passed in the same year, he
was empowered to proceed to the Highlands and to summon the clans to deliver up their arms, and carry several
other recommendations of his own into effect. On his
arrival he immediately proceeded to business, went to
Brahan Castle, and called on the Mackenzies to deliver up
their weapons. He took those presented to him on the
word of Murchison, factor on the estate ; and by the representation of Tarbat, Sir Kenneth Mackenzie of Cromarty,
and Sir Colin Mackenzie of Coul, at the head of a large
deputation of the clan, he compromised his more rigid
instructions and accepted a selection of worn-out and
worthless arms, and at the same time promised that if the
clan exhibited a willing disposition to comply with the
orders of the Government he would use his influence in the
following Parliament to procure a remission for their chief
and his followers; and we find, to quote our last-named
authority, that "through his means, and the action of other
minions of Court (Tarbat was then in power), Seaforth
received a simple pardon by letters patent in 1726, for himself and clan, whose submission was recognised in the sham
form of delivering their arms, a matter of the less consequence as few of that generation were to have an opportunity
of wielding them again in the same cause."

General Wade made a report to the Government, from
which an extract follows :—" The Laird of the Mackenzies,
and other chiefs of the clans and tribes, tenants to the late
Earl of Seaforth, came to me in a body, to the number of
about fifty, and assured me that both they and their followers

were ready to pay a dutiful obedience to your Majesty's
commands, by a peaceable surrender of their arms; and if
your Majesty would be graciously pleased to procure them
an indemnity for the rents that had been misplaced for the
time past, they would for the future become faithful subjects
to your Majesty, and pay them to your Majesty's receiver
for the use of the public. I assured them of your Majesty's
gracious intentions towards them, and that they might rely
on your Majesty's bounty and clemency, provided they
would merit it by their future good conduct and peaceable
behaviour; that I had your Majesty's commands to send
the first summons to the country they inhabited; which
would soon give them an opportunity of showing the
sincerity of their promises, and of having the merit to set
the example to the rest of the Highlands, who in their
turns were to be summoned to deliver up their arms, pursuant to the Disarming Act; that they might choose the
place they themselves thought most convenient to surrender
their arms; and that I would answer, that neither their
persons nor their property should be molested by your
Majesty's troops. They desired they might be permitted
to deliver up their arms at the Castle of Brahan, the
principal seat of their late superior, who, they said, had promoted and encouraged them to this their submission; but
begged that none of the Highland companies might be present; for, as they had always been reputed the bravest, as
well as the most numerous of the northern clans, they
thought it more consistent with their honour to resign their
arms to your Majesty's veteran troops; to which I readily
consented.

"Summonses were accordingly sent to the several clans
and tribes, the inhabitants of 18 parishes, who were vassals
or tenants of the late Earl of Seaforth, to bring or send in
all their arms and warlike weapons to the Castle of Brahan,
on or before the 28th of August.

"On the 25th of August I went to the Castle of Brahan
with a detachment of 200 of the regular troops, and was
met there by the chiefs of the several clans and tribes, who

assured me they had used their utmost diligence in collecting all the arms they were possessed of, which should be
brought thither on the Saturday following, pursuant to the
summons they had received ; and telling me they were
apprehensive of insults or depredations from the neighbouring clans of the Camerons and others, who still continued
in possession of their arms.   Parties of the Highland companies were ordered to guard the passes leading to their
country ; which parties continued there for their protection,
till the clans in that neighbourhood were summoned, and
had surrendered their arms.

"On the day appointed the several clans and tribes
assembled in the adjacent villages, and marched in good
order through the great avenue that leads to the Castle ;
and one after the other laid down their arms in the court-
yard in great quiet and decency, amounting to 784 of the
several species mentioned in the Act of Parliament.

"The solemnity with which this was performed had undoubtedly a great influence over the rest of the Highland
clans ; and disposed them to pay that obedience to your
Majesty's commands, by a peaceable surrender of their
arms, which they had never done to any of your royal predecessors, or in compliance with any law either before or
since the Union."

The following account of Donald Murchison's proceedings and that of Seaforth's vassals during his exile in France
is taken from a most interesting and valuable work,* and
it will bring out in a prominent light the state of the Highlands and the futility of the power of the Government at
that period in the North.   With regard to several of the
forfeited estates which lay in inaccessible situations in the
Highlands, the commissioners had up to this been entirely
baffled, never having been able even to get them surveyed.
This was the case in a special manner as regards the immense
territory of the Earl of Seaforth, extending from Brahan
Castle near Dingwall in the East across to Kintail, and

* Chambers's Domestic Annals of Scotland.

including the large island of Lewis. The districts of Lochalsh and Kintail, on the west coast, the scene of the Spanish
invasion of 1719, were peculiarly difficult of access, there
being no approach from the south, east, or north, except by
narrow and difficult paths, while the western access was only
assailable by a naval force. To all appearance this tract of
ground, the seat of many comparatively opulent "tacksmen"
and cattle farmers, was as much beyond the control of the
six commissioners assembled at their office in Edinburgh,
as if it had been amongst the mountains of Tibet or upon
the shores of Madagascar.

For several years after the insurrection, the rents of this
district were collected, without the slightest difficulty, for
the benefit of the exiled Earl, and regularly transmitted to
him. At one time a considerable sum was sent to him in
Spain. The chief agent in the business was Donald Murchison, descendant of a line of faithful adherents of the "high
chief of Kintail." Some of the later generations of the
family had been intrusted with the keeping of Islandonain
Castle, a stronghold dear to the modern artist as a picturesque ruin,but formerly of serious importance as commanding
a central point from which radiate Loch Alsh and Loch
Duich, in the midst of the best part of the Mackenzie
country. Donald was a man worthy of a more prominent
place in his country's annals than he has yet attained ; he
acted under a sense of right which, though unfortunately
defiant of Acts of Parliament, was still a very pure sense of
right; and in the remarkable actions which he performed,
he looked solely to the good of those towards whom he had
a feeling of duty. A more disinterested hero—and he was
one—never lived.

When Lord Seaforth brought his clan to fight for King
James in 1715, Donald Murchison and a senior brother,
John, accompanied him as field officers of the regiment—
Donald as lieutenant-colonel, and John as major. The late
Sir Roderick I. Murchison, the distinguished geologist,
great-grandson of John, possessed a large ivory and silver
" mill," which once contained the commission sent from

France to Donald, as colonel, bearing the inscription:—
"James Rex: forward and spare not." John fell at Sheriffmuir, in the prime of life; Donald returning with the remains
of the clan, was entrusted by the banished Earl with the
management of estates no longer legally his, but still virtu-
ally so. And for this task Donald was in various respects
well qualified, for, strange to say, the son of the castellan of
Islandonain—the Sheriffmuir Colonel—had been "bred a
writer" in Edinburgh, and was as expert at the business of
a factor or estate-agent as in wielding the claymore.*

In bold and avowed insubordination to the Govern-
men of George the First, Mackenzie's tenants continued for
ten years to pay their rents to Donald Murchison, setting
at nought all fear of ever being compelled to repeat the
payment to the commissioners.

In 1720 these gentlemen made a movement for asserting
their claims upon the property. In William Ross of Easterfearn and Robert Ross, a bailie of Tain, they found two
men bold enough to undertake the duty of stewardship in
their behalf over the Seaforth property, and also the estates
of Grant of Glenmoriston, and Chisholm of Strathglass.
Little, however, was done that year beyond sending
out notices to the tenants, and preparing for strenuous
measures to be entered upon next year. The stir they
made only produced excitement, not dismay. Some of
the duine-uasals from about Lochcarron, coming down with
their cattle to the south-country fairs, were heard to declare
that the two factors would never get anything but leaden
coin from the Seaforth tenantry. Donald went over the
whole country showing a letter he had got from the Earl,
encouraging the people to stand out; at the same time telling them that the old Countess was about to come north'
with a factory for the estate, when she would allow as paid
any rents which they might now hand to him. The very
first use to be made of this money was, indeed, to bring

---

* For a short time before the insurrection, he had acted as factor to Sir John
Preston of Preston Hall, in Mid-Lothian, now also a forfeited estate, but of
minor value.

both the old and the young Countesses home immediately
to Brahan Castle, where they were to live as they used to do.
Part of the funds thus acquired, he used in keeping on foot
a party of about sixty armed Highlanders, whom, in virtue
of his commission as colonel, he proposed to employ in re-
resisting any troops of George the First which might be
sent to Kintail. Nor did he wait to be attacked, but in
June 1720, hearing of a party of excisemen passing near
Dingwall with a large quantity of *aqua vitæ*, he fell upon
them and rescued their prize. The collector of the district
reported this transaction to the Board of Excise, but no
notice was taken of it.

In February 1721, the two factors sent officers of their
own into the western districts, to assure the tenants of good
usage, if they would make a peaceable submission ; but the
men were seized, robbed of their papers, money, and arms,
and quietly remanded over the Frith of Attadale, though
only after giving solemn assurance that they would never
attempt to renew their mission. Resenting this procedure,
the two factors caused a constable to take a military party
from Bernera Barracks into Lochalsh, and, if possible, capture those who had been guilty. They made a stealthy
night-march, and took two men ; but the alarm was given,
the two men escaped, and began to fire down upon their
captors from a hillside ; then they set fire to the bothy as a
signal, and such a coronach went over all Kintail and Lochalsh as made the soldiers glad to beat a quick retreat.

After some further proceedings, all of them ineffectual,
the two factors were enabled, on the 13th day of September,
to set forth from Inverness with a party of thirty soldiers
and some armed servants of their own, with the design of
enforcing submission to their legal claims. Let it be remembered there were then no roads in the Highlands, nothing but a few horse-tracks along the principal lines in the
country, where not the slightest effort had ever been made
to smooth away the natural difficulties of the ground. In
two days the factors had got to Invermoriston ; but here
they were stopped for three days, waiting for their heavy

luggage, which was storm-stayed in Castle Urquhart, and
there nearly taken in a night attack by a partisan warrior
bearing the name of Evan Roy Macgillivray. The tenantry
of Glenmoriston at first fled with their bestial; but afterwards a number of them came in and made at least the
appearance of submission. The party then moved on towards Strathglass, while Evan Roy respectfully followed, to
pick up any man or piece of baggage that might be left behind. At Erchless Castle, and at Invercannich, seats of the
Chisholm, they held courts, and received the submission of
a number of the tenants, whom, however, they subsequently
found to be "very deceitful."

There were now forty or fifty miles of the wildest Highland country before them, where they had reason to believe
they should meet groups of murderous Camerons and Glengarry Macdonalds, and also encounter the redoubtable Donald Murchison, with his guard of Mackenzies, unless their
military force should be of an amount to render all such
opposition hopeless. An appointment having been made
that they should receive an addition of fifty soldiers from
Bernera, with whom to pass through the most difficult part
of their journey, it seemed likely that they would appear
too strong for resistance; and, indeed, intelligence was already coming to them, that "the people of Kintail, being a
judicious opulent people, would not expose themselves to
the punishments of law," and that the Camerons were absolutely determined to give no further provocation to the
Government. Thus assured, they set out in cheerful mood
along the valley of Strathglass, and, soon after passing a
place called Knockfin, were reinforced by Lieutenant Brymer
with the expected fifty men from Bernera. There must
now have been about a hundred well armed men in the invasive body. They spent the next day (Sunday) together
in rest, to gather strength for the ensuing day's march of
about thirty arduous miles, by which they hoped to reach
Kintail.

At four in the morning of Monday, the 2d of October,
the party set forward, the Bernera men first, and the factors

in the rear. They were as yet far from the height of the country, and from its more difficult passes ; but they soon found that all the flattering tales of non-resistance were groundless, and that the Kintail men had come a good way out from their country in order to defend it. The truth was, that Donald Murchison had assembled not only his stated band of Mackenzies, but a levy of the Lewis men under Seaforth's cousin, Mackenzie of Kildun ; also an auxiliary corps of Camerons, Glengarry and Glenmoriston men, and some of those very Strathglass men who had been making appearances of submission. Altogether, he had, if the factors were rightly informed, three hundred and fifty men, with long Spanish firelocks, under his command, and all posted in the way most likely to give them an advantage over the invading force.

The rear-guard, with the factors, had scarcely gone a mile when they received a platoon of seven shots from a rising ground near them to the right, which, however, had only the effect of piercing a soldier's hat. The Bernera company, as we are informed, left the party at eight o'clock, as they were passing Lochanachlee, and from this time is heard of no more ; how it made its way out of the country does not appear. The remainder still advancing, Easterfearn, as he rode a little before his men, had eight shots levelled at him from a rude breast-work near by, and was wounded in two places, but was able to appear as if he had not been touched. Then calling out some Highlanders in his service, he desired them to go before the soldiers and do their best, according to their own mode of warfare to clear the ground of such lurking parties, so that the troops might advance in safety. They performed this service pretty effectually, skirmishing as they went on, and the main body advanced safely about six miles. They were here arrived at a place called Ath-na-Mullach (Ford of the Mull People), where the waters, descending from the Cralich and the lofty mountains of Kintail, issue eastwards through a narrow gorge into Loch Affric. It was a place remarkably well adapted for the purposes of a resisting party. A

rocky boss, called Tor-a-Bheathaich, then densely covered
with birch, closes up the glen as with a gate. The black
mountain stream, "spear-deep," sweeps round it. A narrow
path wound up the rock, admitting of passengers in single
file. Here lay Donald with the best of his people, while in-
ferior adherents were ready to make demonstrations at a little
distance. As the invasive party approached, they received a
platoon from a wood on the left, but nevertheless went on.
When, however, they were all engaged in toiling up the
pass, forty men concealed in the heather close by fired with
deadly effect, inflicting a mortal wound on Walter Ross,
Easterfearn's son, while Bailie Ross's son was also hurt by
a bullet which swept across his breast. The Bailie called
to his son to retire, and the order was obeyed ; but the two
wounded youths and Bailie Ross's servant were taken
prisoners, and carried up the hill, where they were quickly
divested of clothes, arms, money, and papers. Young
Easterfearn died next morning. The troops faced the
ambuscade manfully, and are said to have given their fire
thrice, and to have beat the Highlanders from the bushes
near them ; but, observing at this juncture several parties
of the enemy on the neighbouring heights, and being informed of a party of sixty in their rear, Easterfearn deemed
it best to temporise.

He sent forward a messenger to ask who they were that
opposed the King's troops, and what they wanted. The
answer was that, in the first place, they required to have
Ross of Easterfearn delivered up to them. This was pointedly
refused ; but it was at length arranged that Easterfearn
should go forward and converse with the leader of the opposing party. The meeting took place at Beul-ath-na-Mul-
lach (The Mouth of the Mull Men's Ford), and Easterfearn
found himself confronted with Donald Murchison. It ended
with Easterfearn giving up his papers, and covenanting,
under a penalty of five hundred pounds, not to officiate in
his factory any more ; after which he gladly departed homewards with his associates, under favour of a guard of
Donald's men, to conduct them safely past the sixty men

lurking in the rear. It was alleged afterwards that the commander was much blamed by his own people for letting the factors off with their lives and baggage, particularly by the Camerons, who had been five days at their post with hardly anything to eat; and Murchison only pacified them by sending them a good supply of meat and drink. He had in reality given a very effective check to the two gentlemen-factors, to one of whom he imparted in conversation that any scheme of a Government stewartship in Kintail was hopeless, for he and sixteen others had sworn that, if any person calling himself a factor came there, they would take his life, whether at kirk or at market, and deem it a meritorious action, though they should be cut to pieces for it the next minute.

A bloody grave for young Easterfearn in Beauly Cathedral concluded this abortive attempt to take the Seaforth estates within the scope of a law sanctioned by statesmen, but against which the natural feelings of nearly a whole people revolted.

A second attempt was now made to obtain possession of the forfeited Seaforth estates for the Government. It was calculated that what the two factors, and their attendants, with a small military force, had failed to accomplish in the preceding October, when they were beat back with a fatal loss at Ath-na-Mullach, might now be effected by means of a good military party alone, if they should make their approach through a less critical passage. A hundred and sixty of Colonel Kirk's regiment left Inverness under Captain M'Neil, who had at one time been Commander of the Highland Watch. They proceeded by Dingwall, Strathgarve, and Loch Carron, a route to the north of that adopted by the factors, and an easier, though a longer way. Donald Murchison, nothing daunted, got together his followers, and advanced to the top of Màm Attadale, by a high pass from Loch Carron to the head of Loch Long, separating Lochalsh from Kintail. Here a gallant relative, named Kenneth Murchison, and a few others, volunteered to go forward and plant themselves in ambush in the defiles of the Coille Bhàn (White Wood), while the bulk of the party should remain where they were. It would appear that this ambush party consisted of thirteen men, all peculiarly well armed.

On approaching this dangerous place, the captain went forward with a sergeant and eighteen men to clear the wood, while the main body came on slowly in the rear. At a place called Altanbadubh, in the Coille Bhàn, he encountered Kenneth and his associates, whose fire wounded himself severely, killed one of his grenadiers, and wounded several others of the party. He persisted in advancing, and attacking the handful of natives with sufficient resolution they slowly withdrew, as unable to resist; but the captain now obtained intelligence that a large body of Mackenzies was posted in the mountain pass of Attadale. It seemed as if there was a design to draw him into a fatal ambuscade. His own wounded condition probably warned him that a better opportunity might occur afterwards. He turned his forces about, and made the best of his way back to Inverness. Kenneth Murchison quickly rejoined Colonel Donald on Màm Attadale, with the cheering intelligence that one salvo of thirteen guns had repelled the hundred and sixty red-coats. After this we hear of no renewed attempt to comprise the Seaforth property.

Strange as it may seem, Donald Murchison, two years after this, a second time resisting the Government troops, came down to Edinburgh with eight hundred pounds of the Earl's rents, that he might get the money sent abroad for his lordship's use. He remained a fortnight in the city unmolested. He would on this occasion appear in the garb of a Lowland gentleman; he would mingle with old acquaintances, "doers" and writers; and appear at the Cross amongst the crowd of gentlemen who assembled there every day at noon. Scores would know all about his doings at Ath-na-Mullach and the Coille Bhàn; but thousands might have known, without the chance of one of them, betraying him to the Government.

General Wade, in his report to the King in 1725, states

that the Seaforth tenants, formerly reputed the richest of any in the Highlands, are now become poor, by neglecting their business, and applying themselves to the use of arms. "The rents," he says, "continue to be collected by one Donald Murchison, a servant of the late Earl's, who annally remits or carries the same to his master in France. The tenants, when in a condition, are said to have sent him free gifts in proportion to their several circumstances, but are now a year and a-half in arrear of rent. The receipts he gives to the tenants are as deputy-factor to the Commissioners of the Forfeited Estates, which pretended power he extorted from the factor (appointed by the said Commissioners to collect those rents for the use of the public), whom he attacked with above four hundred armed men, as he was going to enter upon the said estate, having with him a party of thirty of your Majesty's troops. The last year this Murchison marched in a public manner to Edinburgh, to remit eight hundred pounds to France for his master's use, and remained fourteen days there unmolested. I cannot omit observing to your Majesty that this national tenderness the subjects of North Britain have one for the other, is a great encouragement for rebels and attainted persons to return home from their banishment."

Donald was again in Edinburgh about the end of August 1725. On the 2d of September, George Lockhart of Carnwath, writing from Edinburgh to the Chevalier St George, states, amongst other matters of information regarding his party in Scotland, that Daniel Murchison (as he calls him) " is come to Edinburgh, on his way to France"— doubtless charged with a sum of rents for Seaforth. " He's been in quest of me, and I of him," says Lockhart, "these two days, and missed each other; but in a day or two he's to be at my country house, where I'll get time to talk fully with him. In the meantime, I know from one that saw him, that he has taken up and secured all the arms of value in Seaforth's estate, which he thought better than to trust them to the care and prudence of the several owners; and the other chieftains, I hear, have done the same."

The Commissioners on the Forfeited Estates concluded their final report in 1725, by stating that they had not sold the estate of William, Earl of Seaforth, "not having been able to obtain possession, and consequently to give the same to a purchaser."*

The end of Donald's career can scarcely now be passed over in a slighting manner. The story is most painful. The Seaforth of that day—very unlike some of his successors—proved unworthy of the devotion which this heroic man had shown to him. When his lordship took possession of the estates which Donald had in a manner preserved for him, he discountenanced and neglected him. Murchison's noble spirit pined away under this treatment, and he died in the very prime of his days of a broken heart. He lies in a remote little church-yard in the parish of Urray, where his worthy relative, the late Sir Roderick I. Murchison, raised a suitable monument over his grave.†

---

* In a Whig poem on the Highland Roads, written in 1737, Donald is characteristically spoken of as a sort of cateran, while, in reality, as every generous person can now well understand, he was a high-minded gentleman. The verses, nevertheless, as well as the appended note, are curious :—

> Keppoch, Rob Roy, and Daniel Murchison,
> Cadets or servants to some chief of clan,
> From theft and robberies scarce did ever cease,
> Yet 'scaped the halter each, and died in peace.
> This last his exiled master's rents collected,
> Nor unto king or law would be subjected.
> Though veteran troops upon the confines lay,
> Sufficient to make lord and tribe a prey,
> Yet passes strong through which no roads were cut,
> Safe-guarded Seaforth's clan, each in his hut.
> Thus in strongholds the rogue securely lay,
> Neither could they by force be driven away,
> Till his attainted lord and chief of late
> By ways and means repurchased his estate.

"Donald Murchison, a kinsman and servant to the Earl of Seaforth, bred a writer, a man of small stature, but full of spirit and resolution, fought at Dunblane against the Government, anno 1715, but continued thereafter to collect Seaforth's rents for his lord's use, and had some bickerings with the King's forces on that account, till, about five years ago, the Government was so tender as to allow Seaforth to re-purchase his estate, when the said Murchison had a principal hand in striking the hargain for his master. How he fell under Seaforth's displeasure, and died thereafter, is not to the purpose here to mention."

† The traditional account of Donald Murchison, communicated to Chambers by F. Macdonald, Druidaig, states that the heroic commissioner had been promised a handsome reward for his services ; but Seaforth proved ungrateful. "He

The death of George I., in 1726, suggested to the Chevalier a favourable opportunity to attempt a second rising,
and of again stirring up his adherents in Scotland, whither
he was actually on his way, until strongly remonstrated
with on the folly and hopelessness of such an undertaking.
It was pointed out to him that it could only end in the ruin
of his family pretensions, and in that of many of his friends
who might be tempted to enter on the rash scheme more
through personal attachment to himself than from any
reasonable prospect they could see of success.   He
therefore retraced his steps to Boulogne ; and, the Earl of
Seaforth, having been pardoned in the same year,* felt
at liberty once more to return to his native land,
where, according to Captain Matheson, he spent the remainder of his life in retirement, and "with few objects to
occupy him or to interest us beyond the due regard of his
personal friends and the uninterrupted loyalty of his old
vassals." He must, however, have been in tightened circumstances, for, on the 27th of June 1728, he writes a letter to the
Lord Advocate, in which he refers to a request he made to
Sir Robert Walpole, who advised him to put his claim in writing that it might be submitted to the King. This was
done, but "the King would neither allow anything of the
kind or give orders to be granted what his royal father had
granted before. On hearing this, I could not forbear
making appear how ill I was used. The Government in

was offered only a small farm called Bun-Da-Loch, which pays at this day to Mr
Matheson, the proprietor, no more than £60 a year ; or another place opposite to
Inverinate House, of about the same value. It is no wonder he refused these
paltry offers. He shortly afterwards left this country, and died in the prime
of life near Conon. On his death-bed, Seaforth went to see him, and asked how
he was. He said, 'Just as you will be in a short time,' and then turned his ·
back. They never met again."

* By letters dated 12th July 1726, King George I. was pleased to discharge
him from imprisonment or the execution of his person on his attainder, and King
George II. made him a grant of the arrears of feu duties due to the Crown out of
his forfeited estate.   An Act of Parliament was passed iu 1733, to enable William
Mackenzie, late Earl of Seaforth, to sue or maintain any action or suit notwithstanding his attainder, and to remove any disability in him, by reason of his said
attainder, to take or inherit any real or personal estate that may or shall hereafter descend to him.—*Wood's Douglas' Peerage.*

Q

possession of the estate, and I in the interim allowed to
starve, though they were conscious of my complying with
whatever I promised to see put in execution." He makes
a strong appeal to his friend to contribute to an arrangement that would tend to the mutual satisfaction of all concerned, "for the way I am now in is most disagreeable, consequently, if not rectified, will choose rather to seek my
bread elsewhere than continue longer in so unworthy a
situation.*

Notwithstanding the personal remission granted in his
favour for the part he had taken in the Rising of 1715, the
-title of Earl of Seaforth, under which alone he was proscribed, passed under attainder, while the older and original
dignity of Kintail, which only became subordinate by a
future elevation, remained unnoticed, and, consequently, un-
vitiated in the male descent of Kenneth, first Lord Mackenzie of Kintail, granted by patent on the 19th November
1609, and it has accordingly been claimed.†

Earl William, in early life, married Mary, only daughter and heiress of Nicholas Kennet of Coxhow, Northumberland, and by her had issue, three sons—Kenneth, who
succeeded him; Ronald, died unmarried; and Nicholas,
drowned at Douay, without issue. He had one daughter,
Frances, who married the Honourable John Gordon of Kenmure whose father was beheaded in 1715. He died in 1740 in
the Island of Lews, was buried there in the Chapel of Ui,
and succeeded by his eldest son,

* Culloden Papers, pp. 103-4.

† This Act (of Attainder) omits all mention of the subordinate though older
title of "Lord Kintail," which he and all the collateral branches descended of
George, the second Earl, had taken up and assumed in all their deeds and transactions, though there was no occasion to use it in Parliament as they appeared
there as *Earls of Seaforth.* It is questionable therefore if the Act of Attainder
of *William, Earl of Seaforth*, by that designation only could affect the *barony of
Kintail ;* and as the designation to the patentee of it, "Suisque heredibus maxu-
lis," seems to render the grant an *entailed fee* agreeable to the 7th of Queen
Anne, c. 21, and the protecting clause of 26th Henry VIII., c. 13, the claimant,
George Falconer Mackenzie, is entitled to the benefit of such remainder, and in
fact such remainder was given effect to by the succession of Earl George, to his
brother Colin's titles as his heir male collateral.—*Allangrange Service.*

XVIII. KENNETH, LORD FORTROSE,

Which courtesy title he bore as the subordinate title of his father; and under this designation we find him named as a freeholder of Ross in 1741. In the same year he was returned Member of Parliament for the Burgh of Inverness; for the County of Ross in 1747, and again in 1754. In 1741, the year after Earl William's death, the Crown sold the Seaforth estates, including the lands of Kintail, and the barony of Islandonain, and others, for the sum of £25,909 8s 3½d, under burden of an annuity of £1000 to Frances, Countess Dowager of Seaforth. The purchase was for the benefit of Kenneth, Lord Fortrose, our present subject.* He does not appear to have passed much of his time at home, but in the last-named year he seems, from a warrant issued by his authority, to have been in the North. It is signed by "Colin Mackenzie, Baillie," and addressed to Roderick Mackenzie, officer of Locks, commanding him to summon and warn Donald Mackenzie, tacksman of Lainbest, and others, to compear before "Kenneth, Lord Fortrose, heritable proprietor of the Estate of Seaforth, at Braan Castle, or before his Lordship's Baron Baillies, or other judges appointed by him there, upon the 10th day of October next, to come to answer several unwarrantable and illegal things to be laid to their charge:" Dated at "Stornoway, 29th September 1741." There appears to be no doubt that in early life Lord Fortrose had, during the exile of his father, Earl William, communications with the representative of the Stewart family. It is a common tradition in Kintail to this day that Kenneth and Sir Alexander Macdonald of Sleat, were school companions of Prince Charles in France, and were among those who first imbued his mind with the idea of attempting to regain possession of his Kingdom of Scotland, promising him that they would use their influence with the other northern chiefs to rise in his favour, although, when the time for action came, neither

* Fraser's Earls of Cromartie.

of themselves arose. The position in which Lord Kenneth found himself placed by the Jacobite proclivities of his ancestors, and especially those of his father, appears to have made a deep impression upon his mind, and to have induced him to be more cautious in supporting a cause which appeared certain to land him in final and utter ruin. Though he personally held aloof, several of the clan joined the Prince, mostly under George, third Earl of Cromarty, and a few others under John Mackenzie, III. of Torridon. Several young and powerful Macraes, who strongly sympathised with Prince Charles, though unaccompanied by any of their natural leaders, left Kintail never again to return to·it; and, it is said, that several others were bound with ropes by their friends, to keep them at home. The influence of President Forbes weighed strongly with Lord Fortrose in deciding him to take the side of the Government, and, in return for his loyalty, the honours of the house of Seaforth were, in part, afterwards restored.

In 1744 an incident occurred in Inverness in which his Lordship played a conspicuous part, and which exemplifies the impetuous character of the Highland Chiefs of the day. A Court of the Freeholders of the county was held there at Michaelmas to elect a collector of the land tax, at which were present, among·others, Lord President Forbes, the Laird .of Macleod, Lord Fortrose, Lord Lovat, and many other leading members of the Clan Fraser. A warm debate upon some burning business arose between their Lordships of Lovat and Fortrose, when the Chief of the Frasers gave the Chief of the Mackenzies the lie direct, and the latter replied by striking Lovat a smart blow in the face. Mutual friends at once intervened between the distinguished antagonists. The Fraser blood was up, however, and Fraser of Foyers, who was also present, interfered in the interest of the Chief of his Clan, but, it is said, more in that capacity than from any personal esteem in which he held him. In his chief's person he felt that the whole Clan was insulted as if it had actually been a personal blow to every one of the name. He at

once sprung down from the gallery and presented a loaded
and cocked pistol at Lord Fortrose, to whom it would undoubtedly have proved fatal had not a gentleman present,
with great presence of mind, thrown his plaid over the
muzzle, and thus arrested its deadly contents.   In another
instant swords and dirks were drawn on either side ; but
the Lord President and Macleod laid hold of Fortrose and
hurried him out of the Court.   Yet he no sooner gained the
outside than one of the Frasers levelled him to the ground
with a blow from a heavy bludgeon, notwithstanding the
efforts of his protectors to support him.   The matter was ·
afterwards, with great difficulty, arranged by mutual friends,
between the great clans and their respective chiefs, otherwise
the social jealousies and other personal irritations which
then prevailed throughout the whole Highlands, fanned by
this incident, would certainly have produced a lasting and
bloody feud between the Frasers and the Mackenzies.

Shortly after the President had arrived at Culloden from
the south he wrote a letter to Lord Fortrose, under date
of 11th October 1745, in which he informed his correspond-
ent that the Earl of Loudon came the day before to Cromarty, and brought some "credit" with him, which "will
enable us to put the independent companies together for
the service of the Government and for our mutual protection." He desired his Lordship to give immediate orders
to pick those which are first to form one of the companies,
that they might receive commissions and arms.   Mackenzie
of Fairburn was to command.   There was, he said, a report
that Barrisdale had gone to Assynt to raise the men of that
country, to be joined to those of Coigeach who were said
to have orders to be in readiness to join him, and with instructions to march through Mackenzie's territories to try
how many of his Lordship's vassals could be persuaded, by
fair means or foul, to join the standard of the Prince.   " I
hope this is not true ; if it is, it is of the greatest consequence to prevent it.   I wish Fairburn were at home ; your
Lordship will let me know when he arrives, as the Lord
Cromartie has refused the company I intended for his son.

Your Lordship will deliberate to whom you would have it given."*

Exasperated by the exertions made by President Forbes to obstruct the designs of the disaffected, a plan was formed to seize him by some of the Frasers, a party of whom, amounting to about 200, attacked Culloden House during the night of the 15th of October, but the President being on guard they were repulsed.†

On the 13th of October Lord Fortrose writes that he surmised some young fellows of his name attempted to raise men for the Prince; that he sent expresses to the suspected parts, with orders to the tenants not to stir under, pain of death without his leave, though their respective masters should be imprudent enough to desire them to do so. The messengers returned with the people's blessings for his protection, and with assurances that they would do nothing without his orders, "so that henceforward your Lordship need not be concerned about any idle report from benorth Kessock."

Lord Fortrose in a letter dated "Brahan Castle, 19th October 1745," refers to the attempt on the President's house, which surprised him extremely, and "is as dirty an action as I ever heard of," and he did not think any gentleman would be capable of doing such a thing. "As I understand your cattle are taken away, I beg you will order your steward to write to Colin, or anybody else here, for provisions, as I can be supplied from the Highlands. I am preparing to act upon the defensive, and I suppose will soon be provoked to act on the offensive. I have sent for a strong party to protect my house and overawe the country. None of my Kintail men will be down till Tuesday, but as the river is high, and I have parties at all the boats, nothing can be attempted. Besides, I shall have reinforcements every day. I have ordered my servants to get, at Inverness, twelve or twenty pounds of powder, with a proportionable quantity of shot. If that cannot be bought at Inverness, I

* Culloden Papers, pp. 421-2.   † Ibidem, p. 246.

must beg you will write a line to Governor Grant to give
my servant the powder, as I can do without the shot. . .
. . Barrisdale has come down from Assynt, and was col-
lared by one of the Maclauchlans there for offering to force
the people to rise, and he has met with no success there. I
had a message from the Mackenzies in Argyllshire to know
what they should do. Thirty are gone from Lochiel ; the
rest, being about sixty, are at home. I advised them to
stay at home and mind their own business."

On the 28th of the same month he writes to inform the
President that Cromarty, his son, Macculloch of Glastullich,
and Ardloch's brother, came to Brahan Castle on the previous Friday ; that it was the most unexpected visit he had
received for some time, that he did not like to turn them
out, that Cromarty was pensive and dull ; but that if he
knew what he knew at the date of writing he would have
made them prisoners, for Lord Macleod had since gone to
Lochbroom and Assynt to raise men. He enclosed to the
President the names of the officers belonging to the two
Mackenzie companies, and said that he offered the commission to Coul and Redcastle, but that both refused. It was
from Coul's house that Lord Macleod started for the north,
and that vexed him. On the same date the President ac-
knowledges receipt of this letter, and says that the officers
in the two companies should be filled up according to Mackenzie's recommendations, " without any further consideration than that you judge it right," and he desires to see Sir
Alexander of Fairburn for an hour next day to carry a proposal to his Lordship for future operations. " I think," he
writes, " it would be right to assemble still more men about
Brahan than you now have ; the expense shall be made
good ; and it will tend to make Caberfey respectable, and
to discourage folly among your neighbours." In a letter of
6th November the President writes, " I supposed that your
Lordship was to have marched Hilton's company into town
(Inverness) on Monday or Tuesday ; but I dare say there
is a good reason why it has not been done."

On the 8th November Mackenzie informs the President

that the Earl of Cromarty crossed the river at Contin, with
about a hundred men, on his way to Beauly, "owing to the
neglect of my spies, as there's rogues of all professions."
Lord Macleod, Cromarty's son, came · from Assynt and
Lochbroom the same day, and followed his father to the
rendezvous, but after traversing the whole of that country
he did not get a single man. "Not a man started from
Ross-shire, except William, Kilcoy's brother, with seven
men, and a tenant of Redcastle with a few more; and if
Lentran and Terradon did go off last night, they did not
carry between them a score of men. I took a ride yesterday to the westward with two hundred men, but find the
bounds so rugged that it's impossible to keep a single man
from going by if he has a mind. However, I threatened to
burn their cornyards if any body was from home this day,
and I turned one house into the river for not finding its
master at home. It's hard the Government gives nobody
in the north power to keep people in order. I don't choose
to send a company to Inverness until I hear what they are
determined to do at Lord Lovat's." The Earl of Loudon
writes to Marshal Wade, Commander-in-Chief in the North,
under date of 16th November, that 150 or 160 Mackenzies,
seduced by the Earl of Cromarty, marched in the beginning
of that week up the north side of Loch-Ness, expecting to
be followed by 500 or 600 Frasers, under command of the
Master of Lovat, but the Mackenzies had not on that date
passed the mountains. On the 16th December Lord Fortrose writes asking for £400 expended during two months
on his men going to and coming from the Highlands, for
which he would not trouble him only that he had a very
" melancholy appearance" of getting his Martinmas rent, as
the people would be glad of any excuse for non-payment,
and the last severe winter, and their having to leave home,
would afford them a very good one. He was told, in reply,
that his letter was submitted to Lord Loudon, that both
agreed that his Lordship's expenses must have been greater
than what he claimed, "but as cash is very low with us at
present, all we can possibly do is to let your Lordship have

the pay of the two companies from the date of the letter signifying that they were ordered to remain at Brahan for the service of the Government. The further expense, which we are both satisfied it must have cost your Lordship, shall be made good as soon as any money, to be applied to contingencies, which we expect, shall come to hand, and if it should not come so soon as we wish, the account shall be made up and solicited, in the same manner with what we lay out of our own purses, which is no inconsiderable sums."

This correspondence will show the confidence which existed between the Government and Lord Fortrose.

On the 9th of December the two companies were marched into Inverness. Next day; accompanied by a detachment from Fort-Augustus, they proceeded to Castle Downie to bring Lord Lovat to account. The crafty old chief agreed to come to Inverness and to deliver up his arms on the 14th of the month, but instead of doing so he effected his escape.

After the battle of Prestonpans, on the recommendation of the Earl of Stair, the Government forwarded twenty blank commissions to President Forbes, to raise as many companies, of 100 men each, among the Highlanders. Eighteen of them were sent to the Earls of Sutherland and Cromarty, Lords Fortrose and Reay, the Lairds of Grant and Macleod, and Sir Alexander Macdonald of Sleat, with instructions to raise companies in their respective districts. The Earl of Cromarty, while pretending to comply with the instructions of the President, offered the command of one of the companies to a neighbouring gentleman, whom he well knew to be a strong Jacobite, and at the same time made some plausible excuse for his son's refusal of one of the commissions.

When Lord John Drummond landed with a body of Irish and Scotch troops, in the service of the French, to support Prince Charles, he wrote Lord Fortrose announcing his arrival, and earnestly requesting him at once to declare for the Stewart cause, as the only means by which he could "now expect to retrieve his character." All the means at Drummond's disposal proved futile, and the Mackenzies were kept out of the unfortunate affair of the Forty-five. The commissions were finally entrusted to those on whom the President and his advisers thought prudent to depend as supporters of the King's Government.*

That Prince Charles fully appreciated the importance of having the Clan Mackenzie, led by their natural chief, for or against him, will be seen from the following extract from Lord Macleod's "Narrative of the Rebellion."† "We set out from Dunblain on the 12th of January, and arrived the same evening at Glasgow. I immediately went to pay my respects to the Prince, and found that he was already set down to supper. Dr Cameron told Lord George Murray, who sat by the Prince, who I was, on which the Lord Murray introduced me to the Prince, whose hand I had the honour to kiss, after which the Prince ordered me to take my place at the table. After supper I followed the Prince to his apartment to give him an account of his affairs in the North, and of what had passed in these parts during the time of his expedition to England. I found that nothing

* The following is a list of the officers of eighteen of the Independent Companies, being all that was raised, with the dates of their commissions on the completion of their companies, and of their arrival in Inverness:—

CLANS.	CAPTAINS.	LIEUTENANTS.	ENSIGNS.	DATES.
Monros.....	George Monro.....	Adam Gordon.....	Hugh Monro......	1745. Oct. 23
Sutherlands	Alexander Gun....	John Gordon......	Ken. Sutherland..	,, ,, 25
Grants	Patrick Grant	William Grant	James Grant......	,, Nov. 3
Mackays....	George Mackay....	John Mackay......	James Mackay	,, ,, 4
Sutherlands	Peter Sutherland..	William Mackay ..	John Mackay......	,, ,, 8
Macleods ..	John Macleod.....	Alex. Macleod	John Maccaskill...	,, ,, 15
Do.	Norman Macleod of Waterstein	Donald Macleod...	John Macleod	,, ,, 15
Do.	Norman Macleod of Bernora	John Campbell....	John Macleod	,, ,, 15
Do.	Donald Macdonald	William Macleod..	Donald Macleod ..	,, ,, 15
Inverness ..	Wm. Mackintosh..	Kenneth Mathison	William Baillie....	,, ,, 18
Macleods of Assynt	Hugh Macleod....	George Monro.....	Roderick Macleod.	,, ,, 28
Mackenzies of Kintail	Alex. Mackenzie ..	John Mathison....	Simon Murchison..	,, Dec. 20
Do.	Colin Mackenzie of Hilton	Alex. Campbell....	John Macrae......	,, ,, 20
Macdonalds of Skye	James Macdonald.	Allan Macdonald..	James Macdonald.	,, ,, 31
Do.	John Macdonald..	Allan Macdonald..	Donald Macdonald	1746. Jan. 6
Mackays....	Hugh Mackay.....	John Mackay......	Angus Mackay....	,, ,, 6
Rosses......	William Ross......	Charles Ross......	David Ross........	,, ,, 8
Mackenzies of Lewis	Colin Mackenzie ..	Donald Macaulay..	Ken. Mackenzie...	,, Feb. 2

—*Culloden Papers.*

† Printed in full in Fraser's Earls of Cromartie.

surprised the Prince so much as to hear that the Earl of
Seaforth had declared against him, for he heard without
emotion the names of the other people who had joined the
Earl of Loudon at Inverness ; but when I told him that
Seaforth had likewise sent two hundred men to Inverness
for the service of the Government, and that he had likewise
hindered many gentlemen of his Clan from joining my
father (Earl of Cromarty) for the service of the Stewarts,
he turned to the French Minister and said to him, with
some warmth, *Hé! mon Dieu! et Seaforth est aussi contre
moi!*"

In this connection we may mention a hero of the name
of Mackenzie who had done good service to the Prince in
his wanderings through the Highlands after the battle of
Culloden.   Such a tribute is due to the gallant Roderick
Mackenzie, whose intrepidity and presence of mind in the
last agonies of death, saved his Prince from pursuit at the
time, and who was consequently the means of his ultimate
escape in safety to France.   He had hitherto been pursued with the most persevering assiduity, but Roderick's
ruse proved so successful that further search was at the
time considered unnecessary.   Mackenzie was a young man,
of very respectable family, who joined the Prince at Edinburgh, and served as one of his life-guards.   Being about
the same age as his Royal Highness, and, like him, tall,
somewhat slender, and with features in some degree re-
sembling his, he might, by ordinary observers not accustomed to see the two together, have passed for the Prince.
As Roderick could not venture with safety to return to
Edinburgh, where lived his two maiden sisters, after the
battle of Culloden, he fled to the Highlands, and lurked
among the hills of Glenmoriston, where, about the middle
of July, he was surprised by a party of Government soldiers.
Mackenzie endeavoured to escape, but, being overtaken, he
turned round on his pursuers, and, drawing his sword,
bravely defended himself.   He was ultimately shot by one
of the red-coats, and as he fell, mortally wounded, he exclaimed, "You have killed your Prince! You have killed

your Prince!" after which he immediately expired. The
soldiers, overjoyed at their supposed good fortune, cut off
his head, and hurried off to Fort-Augustus with their prize.
The Duke of Cumberland, fully convinced that he had now
obtained the head of his Royal relative, packed it up carefully, ordered a post-chaise, and at once went off to London,
carrying the head along with him. After his arrival there
the deception was discovered, but meanwhile it proved of
essential benefit to Prince Charles in his ultimately successful efforts to escape.*

Soon after the battle of Culloden a fleet appeared off
the coast of Lochbroom, under the command of Captain
Fergusson. It dropped anchor at Loch-Ceannard, when a
large party went ashore and proceeded up the Strath to the
residence of Mr Mackenzie of Langwell, connected by marriage with the Earl of Cromarty. Langwell having sided
with the Stewart Prince, fled out of the way of the hated
Fergusson ; but his lady was obliged to remain to attend to
the children, who were at the time confined with smallpox.
The house was ransacked. A large chest containing the
family and other valuable papers, including a wadset of
Langwell and Inchvennie from her relative, George, Earl of
Cromarty, was burnt before her eyes ; and about fifty head
of fine Highland cattle were mangled by their swords and
driven to the ships of the spoilers. Nor did this satisfy them.
They continued to commit similar depredations, without
discriminating between friend or foe, during the eight days
which they remained in the neighbourhood.†

It is well known that Lord Fortrose had strong Jacobite
feelings, though his own prudence and the influence of President Forbes secured his support to the Government. This
is the opinion of the writer already quoted, who concludes
his sketch of his Lordship thus:—Though many respectable
individuals of the Clan Mackenzie had warmly espoused
the cause of Charles, Lord Fortrose seems at no time to

* Highland Clans. Chambers's Rebellion. Stewart's Sketches.
† New Statistical Account of Lochbroom, by the late Dr Ross, minister of
the Parish.

have proclaimed openly for him, whatever hopes he might
have countenanced, when in personal communication with
the expatriated sovereign, as indeed there is cause to infer
something of the kind from a letter which, towards the end
of November 1745, was addressed by Lord John Drummond to Kenneth, pressing him instantly to join the Prince,
then successfully penetrating the West of England, and
qualifying the invitation by observing that it was the only
mode for his Lordship to retrieve his character. Yet so
little did Fortrose or his immediate followers affect the
cause, that when Lord Lovat blockaded Fort-Augustus,
two companies of Mackenzies, which had been stationed at
Brahan, were withdrawn, and posted by Lord Loudon, the
commander-in-chief of the Government forces, at Castle
Downie, the stronghold of Fraser, and, with the exception
of these, the Royal party received no other support from
the family of Seaforth, though many gentlemen of the Clan
served in the King's army. Yet it appears that a still greater
number, with others whose ancestors identified themselves
with the fortunes of the House of Kintail, were inclined to
espouse the more venturous steps of the last of the Stewarts.
George, the last Earl of Cromarty, being then paramount in
power, and, probably so, in influence, even to the Chief himself, having been, for certain reasons, liable to suspicions as
to their disinterested nature, declared for Charles, and under
his standard his own levy, with all the Jacobite adherents of
the Clan ranged themselves, and were mainly instrumental
in neutralizing Lord Loudon's and the Laird of Macleod's
forces in the subsequent operations of 1746, driving them,
with the Lord President Forbes, to take shelter in the Isle
of Skye.*

Kenneth, Lord Fortrose, married on the 11th September
1741, Lady Mary Stewart, eldest daughter of Alexander,
sixth Earl of Galloway, and by her had issue, one son and
six daughters. She died in London on the 18th of April
1751, and was buried at Kensington, where a monument

* Bennetsfield MS.

was raised to her memory. The eldest daughter, Margaret, married on the 4th June 1785, William Webb; Mary, Henry Howard of Effingham; Agnes, J. Douglas; Catherine, 1st March 1773, Thomas Griffin Tarpley; Frances, General Joseph Wald; and Euphemia, 2d of April 1771, William Stewart of Castle Stewart, M.P. for the County of Wigton.

His Lordship died in London, on the 19th of October 1761 ; was buried in Westminster Abbey, and succeeded by his only son,

XIX. KENNETH MACKENZIE,   ·

Afterwards created Earl of Seaforth, Viscount Fortrose, and Baron Ardelve, in the Peerage of Ireland. From his small stature, he was commonly known among the High-landers as the " Little Lord." Born in Edinburgh on the 15th of January 1744, he at an early age entered the army. As a return for his father's loyalty to the House of Hanover in 1745, and his own steady support of the reign-ing family, George III. raised him to the peerage by the title of Baron Ardelve in 1744, Viscount Fortrose in 1766, in the Kingdom of Ireland, and in 1771 he was created Earl of Seaforth in the peerage of the same kingdom. To evince his gratitude for this mag-nanimous act, he, in 1778, offered to raise a regiment for general service. The offer was accepted by his Majesty, and a fine body of 1130 men were in a very short time raised by his Lordship, principally on his own estates in the north, and by gentlemen of his own name. Of these, five hundred were raised among his immediate vassals, and about four hundred from the estates of the Mackenzies of Scatwell, Kilcoy, Redcastle, and Applecross. The officers from the south to whom he gave commissions in the regi-ment brought about two hundred men, of whom forty-three were English and Irish. The Macraes of Kintail, always such faithful followers and able supporters of the House of Seaforth, were so numerous in the new regiment that it was known more by the name of the Macraes than by that of Seaforth's own kinsmen, and so much was this the case that

the well-known mutiny which took place in Edinburgh, on
the arrival of the regiment there, is still called " the affair of
the Macraes."* The regiment was embodied at Elgin in
May 1778, and there inspected by General Skene, when it
was found so effective that not a single man was rejected.
Seaforth, on the 29th of December 1777 appointed Colonel,
was now promoted to the rank of Lieutenant-Colonel-Commandant, and the regiment was called the 78th (now the
72d), or Ross-shire Regiment of Highlanders.

The grievances complained of at Leith being removed,
the regiment embarked at that port, accompanied by their
Colonel, and the intention of sending them to India then
having been abandoned, one half of the regiment was sent
to Guernsey and the other half to Jersey. Towards the end
of April 1781 the two divisions assembled at Portsmouth,
whence they embarked for India on the 12th of June following, being then 973 strong, rank and file. Though in
excellent health, the men suffered so much from scurvy, in
consequence of the change of food, that before their arrival
at Madras, on the 2d of April 1782, 247 of them died, and
out of those who landed alive only 369 were in a fit state
for service. Their Chief and Colonel died in August 1781,
before they arrived at St Helena, to the great grief and
dismay of his faithful followers, who looked up to him as

---

* The Seaforth Highlanders were marched to Leith, where they were quartered for a short interval, though long enough to produce complaints about the
infringement of their engagements, and some pay and bounty which they said
were due them. Their disaffection was greatly increased by the activity of
emissaries from Edinburgh, like those just mentioned as having gone down from
London to Portsmouth. The regiment refused to embark, and marching out of
Leith, with pipes playing and two plaids fixed on poles instead of colours, took a
position on Arthur's Seat, of which they kept possession for several days, during
which time the inhabitants of Edinburgh amply supplied them with provisions
and ammunition. After much negotiation, a proper understanding respecting
the causes of their complaint was brought about, and they marched down the hill
in the same manner in which they had gone up, with pipes playing ; and, "with
the Earls of Seaforth and Dunmore, and General Skene, at their head. They
entered Leith, and went on board the transports with the greatest readiness and
cheerfulness." In this case, as in that of the Athole Highlanders, none of the
men were brought to trial, or even put into confinement, for these acts of open
resistance.—*Stewart's Sketches—Appendix p. lxxxiv.*

their principal source of encouragement and support. His loss was naturally associated in their minds with recollections of home, with melancholy remembrances of their absent kindred, and with forebodings of their own future destiny; and so strong was this feeling impressed upon them that it materially contributed to that prostration of mind which made them the more readily become the victims of disease. They well knew that it was on their account alone that he had determined to forego the comforts of a splendid fortune and high rank to encounter the privations and inconveniences of a long voyage, and the dangers and other fatigues of military service in a tropical climate.[*]

His Lordship, on the 7th of October 1765, married Lady Caroline Stanhope, eldest daughter of William, second Earl of Harrington, and by her—who died in London from consumption, from which she suffered for nearly two years, on the 9th of February 1767, at the early age of twenty,[†] and was buried at Kensington—he had issue, an only daughter, Lady Caroline, born in London on the 7th of July 1766, who formed a union with Count Melfort, a nobleman of the Kingdom of France, originally of Scottish extraction, and died without issue in 1847.

Thus the line of George, second Earl of Seaforth, who died in 1633, became extinct; and the reader must accompany us back to Kenneth Mòr, the third Earl, to pick up the chain of legitimate succession. It has been already shown that the lineal descent of the original line of Kintail was directed from heirs male in the person of Anna, Countess of Balcarres, daughter of Colin, first Earl.

Kenneth Mòr, the third Earl, had three sons—(1) Kenneth Og, his heir and successor, whose line terminated in Lady Caroline, as above ; (2) John of Assynt, whose only son Kenneth died without issue ; (3) Hugh, who died young ; and (4) Colonel Alexander, afterwards designated of Assynt and Conansbay, who married Elizabeth, daughter of John Pater-

---

son, Bishop of Ross, and sister of John Paterson, Archbishop
of Glasgow. Colonel Alexander had an only son and six
daughters. The daughters were (1) Isabella, married Basil
Hamilton of Baldoon, became mother of Dunbar, fourth -·
Earl of Selkirk, and died in 1725 ; (2) Frances, married her
cousin, Kenneth Mackenzie of Assynt, without issue ; (3)
Jane, married Dr Mackenzie, a cadet of the family of Coul,
and died at New Tarbat, 18th September 1776 ; (4) Mary,
married Captain Dougal Stewart of Blairhall, a Lord of
Session and Justiciary, and brother of the first Earl of
Bute, with issue ; (5) Elizabeth, died unmarried at Kirkcud-
bright, on the 12th of March 1796, aged 81 ; and (6) Maria,
who married Nicholas Price of Saintfield, County Down,
Ireland, and had issue. She was maid of honour to Queen
Caroline, and died in 1732. Colonel Alexander's only son
was

Major William Mackenzie, who died 12th March 1770.
He married Mary, daughter and co-heiress of Matthew
Humberston, Lincoln, by whom he had issue, two sons—(1)
Thomas Frederick Mackenzie, who assumed the name of
Humberston on succeeding to his mother's property, and
who was Colonel of the 100th Regiment of foot ; and (2)
Francis Humberston Mackenzie. He had also four daugh-
ters—(1) Frances Cerjat, who married Sir Vicary Gibbs, ·
M.P., his Majesty's Attorney-General, with issue ; (2) Maria
Rebecca, married Alexander Mackenzie of Breda, younger
son of John Mackenzie of Applecross, with issue ; and (3)
Helen, who married Major-General Alexander Mackenzie-
Fraser of Inverallachy, fourth son of Colin Mackenzie of
Kilcoy, Colonel of the 78th Regiment, and M.P. for the
County of Ross, with issue.

Major William died 12th of March 1770, at Stafford,
Lincolnshire. His wife died on the 19th of February 1813,
at Hartley, Herts.

Colonel Thomas F. Mackenzie-Humberston, it will be
seen, thus became male heir to his cousin, Earl Kenneth, who
died, without male issue, in 1781, and who, finding his property heavily encumbered with debts from which he could

R

not extricate himself, conveyed the estates to his cousin and
heir male, Colonel Thomas, in the year 1779, on payment
to him of £100,000. Earl Kenneth died, as already stated,
in 1781, and was succeeded by his cousin,

XX. COLONEL THOMAS FREDERICK MACKENZIE-HUMBERSTON,

In all his extensive estates, and in the command of the
78th Ross-shire Highland Regiment, but not in the titles
and dignities, which terminated with his predecessor. When,
the 78th was raised, in 1778, Thomas T. F. Mackenzie-Humberston was a captain in the 1st Regiment of Dragoon
Guards, but notwithstanding this he accepted a captaincy
in Seaforth's regiment of Ross-shire Highlanders. He was
afterwards quartered with the latter regiment in Jersey, and
took a prominent share in repelling the attack made on that
island by the French. On the 2d September 1780 he was
appointed from the 78th Lieutenant-Colonel-Commandant
of the 100th Foot. In 1781 he embarked with this regiment to the East Indies, and was at Port Preya when the
outward bound East Indian fleet under Commodore Johnston was attacked by the French. He happened at the
time to be ashore, but such was his ardour to share in the
action that he swam to one of the ships engaged with the
enemy. As soon as he arrived in India he obtained a separate command on the Malabar Coast, but in its exercise he
met with every discouragement from the Council of Bombay. This gave him a greater opportunity of distinguishing
himself, for, under all the disadvantages of having money,
stores, and reinforcements withheld from him, he undertook,
with 1000 Europeans and 2500 Sepoys to wage an offensive
war against Calicut. He was conscious of great resources
in his own mind, and harmony, confidence, and attachment
on the part of his officers and men. He drove the enemy
out of the country, defeated them in three different engagements, took the city of Calicut, and every other place of
strength in the kingdom. He concluded a treaty with the
King of Travancore, who was reinforced with a body of

1200 men. Tippoo now proceeded against him with 30,000 men, more than one-third of whom were cavalry; Colonel Mackenzie-Humberston repelled their attack, and by a rapid march regained the Fort of Panami, which the enemy attempted to carry, but he defeated them with great loss. He served under General Mathews against Hyder Ali in 1782; but during the operations of that campaign, Mathews gave such proofs of misconduct, incapacity, and injustice, that Colonels Macleod and Humberston carried their complaints to the Council of Bombay, where they arrived on the 26th of February 1783. The Council ordered General Mathews to be superseded, appointed Colonel Macleod to succeed him in command of the army, and desired Colonel Humberston to join him. They both sailed from Bombay on the 5th of April 1783, in the *Ranger* sloop of war; but, notwithstanding that peace had been concluded with the Mahrattas, that vessel was attacked on the 8th of that month by the Mahratta fleet, and after a desperate resistance of four hours, was taken possession of. All the officers on board were either killed or wounded, among them the young and gallant Colonel Mackenzie-Humberston, who was shot through the body with a four pound ball, and died of the wound at Geriah, on the 30th April 1783, in the 28th year of his age. He had thus only been Chief of the Clan for the short space of two years, and, dying unmarried, he was succeeded by his only brother,*

XXI. FRANCIS HUMBERSTON MACKENZIE,

Afterwards raised to the peerage by the title of Lord Seaforth, Baron Mackenzie of Kintail. This nobleman, in many respects a most able and remarkable man, was born in 1754, in full possession of his faculties; but a severe attack of scarlet fever, from which he suffered when about twelve years of age, deprived him of hearing and almost of speech. As he advanced in years he again almost entirely

---

* Douglas' Peerage. He had a natural son, Captain Humberston Mackenzie, of the 78th, killed at the storming of Ahmadnugger, on the 8th of August 1803.

recovered the faculty of speech, but during the latter two years of his life, grieving over the loss of his four promising sons, all of whom predeceased him, he became unable, or rather never made any attempt to articulate. He was in his youth intended by his parents to follow the naval profession, but his physical misfortunes made such a career impossible.

Little or nothing is known of the history of his early life. In 1784, and again in 1790, he was elected M.P. for the County of Ross. In 1787, in the thirty-third year of his age, he offered to raise a regiment on his own estates for the King's service, to be commanded by himself. In the same year the 74th, 75th, 76th, and 77th Regiments were raised, and the Government declined Mr Mackenzie's offer, but agreed to accept his services in the matter of procuring recruits for the 74th and 75th. This did not please him, and he did not then come prominently to the front. On the 19th of May 1790, he renewed his offer, but the Government informed him that the strength of the army had been finally fixed at 77 regiments, and his services were again declined. He was still anxious to be of service to his country, and when the war broke out, in 1793, he again renewed his offer, and placed his great influence at the service of the Crown ; and we find a letter of service granted in his favour, dated the 7th of March 1793, empowering him, as Lieutenant-Colonel-Commandant, to raise a Highland battalion, which, being the first embodied during the war, was to be numbered the 78th, the original Mackenzie regiment having had its number previously reduced to the 72d. The battalion was to consist of 1 company of grenadiers, 1 of light infantry, and 8 battalion companies. The Chief at once appointed as his Major his own brother-in-law, Alexander Mackenzie of Belmaduthy, a son of Kilcoy, then a captain in the 73d Regiment, and a man who proved himself on all future occasions well fitted for the post. The following notice, headed by the Royal arms, was immediately posted throughout the Counties of Ross and Cromarty, on the mainland, and in the Island of Lews :—

"Seaforth's Highlanders to be forthwith raised for the defence of his Glorious Majesty, King George the Third, and the preservation of our happy constitution in Church and State.

"All lads of true Highland blood willing to show their loyalty and spirit, may repair to Seaforth, or the Major, Alexander Mackenzie of Belmaduthy; or the other commanding officers at headquarters, at . . . . . where they will receive high bounties and soldier-like entertainment.

"The lads of this regiment will live and die together, as they cannot be draughted into other regiments, and must be reduced in a body, in their own country.

"Now for a stroke at the Monsieurs, my boys! King George for ever! Huzza!"

The machinery once set agoing, applications poured in upon Seaforth for commissions in the corps from among his more immediate relatives, and from others who were but slightly acquainted with him.*

The martial spirit of the people soon became thoroughly roused, and recruits came in so rapidly that on the 10th of July 1793, only four months after the granting of the Letter of Service in favour of Seaforth, the regiment was marched to Fort-George, inspected and passed by Lieut.-General Sir Hector Munro, after which five companies were immediately embarked for Guernsey, and the other five companies landed in Jersey in September 1793, after which they were sent to Holland.

On the 13th of October in the same year, Mackenzie offered to raise a second battalion for the 78th, and on the 30th of the same month the King granted him permission

---

* Besides Seaforth himself, and his Major mentioned in the text, the following, of the name of Mackenzie, appear among the first list of officers :—

Major.—Alexander Mackenzie of Fairburn, General in 1809.

Captains.—John Mackenzie of Gairloch, "Fighting Jack," Major in 1794, Lieutenant Colonel the same year, and Lieutenant General in 1814; died the father of the British Army in 1860; and J. Randoll Mackenzie of Suddie, Major-General in 1804, killed at Talavera 1809.

Lieutenant.—Colin Mackenzie, Lieutenant-Colonel 91st Regiment.

Ensigns.—Charles Mackenzie, Kilcoy ; and J. Mackenzie Scott, Captain 57th Regiment ; killed at Albuera.

to raise five hundred additional men on the original letters of service. This was not, however, what he wanted, and on the 28th of December following he submitted to the Government three alternative proposals for raising a second battalion. On the 7th of February 1794, one of these was agreed to. The battalion was to consist of eight battalion and two flank companies, each to consist of 100 men, with the usual number of officers and non-commissioned officers. He was, however, disappointed by the Government ; for while he intended to have raised a second battalion for his own regiment, an order was issued, signed by Lord Amherst, that it was to be considered a separate corps, whereupon the Lieutenant-Colonel-Commandant addressed the following protest to Mr Dundas, one of the Secretaries of State :—

"St Alban Street, 8th February 1794.

"Sir,—I had sincerely hoped I should not be obliged to trouble you again ; but on my going to-day to the War Office about my letter of service (having yesterday, as I thought, finally agreed with Lord Amherst), I was, to my amazement, told that Lord Amherst had ordered that the 1000 men I am to raise were not to be a second battalion of the 78th, but a separate corps. It will, I am sure, occur to you that should I undertake such a thing, it would destroy my influence among the people of my country entirely; and instead of appearing as a loyal honest chieftain calling out his friends to support their King and country, I should be gibbeted as a jobber of the attachment my neighbours bear to me. Recollecting what passed between you and me, I barely state this circumstance ; and I am, with great respect and attachment, sir, your most obliged and obedient servant.   (Signed)   "F. H. MACKENZIE."

This had the desired effect, the order for a separate corps was rescinded, and a letter of service was granted in his favour on the 10th of February 1794, authorising him, as Lieutenant-Colonel-Commandant, to add the new battalion, of which the strength was to be one company of grenadiers, one of light infantry, and eight battalion companies to his own regiment. The regiment was soon raised ; inspected and passed at Fort-George in June of the same year by Sir Hector Munro ; and in July following the King granted permission to have it named, as a distinctive title, " The Ross-shire Buffs." The two battalions were amalgamated in June 1796. Another battalion was raised in 1804 —Letter of Service, date 17th April. These were again amalgamated in July 1817.* Though the regiment was not accompanied abroad by its Lieutenant-Colonel-Commandant, he continued most solicitous for its reputation and welfare, as we find from the various communications addressed to him regarding the regiment and the conduct of the men by Lieutenant-Colonel Alexander Mackenzie of Fairburn, appointed Lieutenant-Colonel from the first battalion,† and then in actual command ; but as the history of the 78th Highlanders is not our present object, we must meanwhile part company with it and follow the future career of Francis Humberston Mackenzie. As a reward for his eminent services to the Government he was appointed Lord-Lieutenant of the County of Ross, and, on the 26th October 1797, raised to the dignity of a peer of the United Kingdom, as Lord Seaforth and Baron Mackenzie of Kintail, the ancient dignities of his house, with limitation to heirs male of his body. His Lordship, having resigned the command of the 78th, was, in 1798, appointed Colonel of the Ross-shire Regiment of Militia. In 1800 he was appointed Governor of Barbadoes, an office which he held for six years, after which he held high office in Demerara and Berbice. While Governor of Barbadoes he was at first extremely popular, and was distinguished for his firmness and even-handed justice, and he succeeded in putting an end to slavery, and to the practice of slave-killing in the island, which at that time was of very common occurrence,

---

* For these particulars we are mainly indebted to Fullarton's Highland Clans and Regiments, and to Stewart's Sketches.

* J. Randoll Mackenzie, also from the first battalion, was appointed senior major.

and deemed by the planters a venial offence punishable
only by a small fine of £15. In consequence of this humane
proceeding he became obnoxious to many of the colonists,
and, in 1806, he finally left the place. In 1808 he was made
a Lieutenant-General. These were singular incidents in
the life of one who may be said to have been deaf and
dumb from his youth; but who, in spite of these physical
defects—sufficient to crush any ordinary man—had been
able, by the force of his natural abilities and the favour of
fortune, to overcome them sufficiently to raise himself to
such a high and important position in the world. He took
a lively interest in all questions of art and science, especially
in natural history, and displayed at once his liberality and
his love of art by his munificence to Sir Thomas Lawrence,
in the youth and struggles of that great artist and famous
painter, and by his patronage of others. On this point a
recent writer says—"The last Baron of Kintail, Francis,
Lord Seaforth, was, as Sir Walter has said, 'a nobleman of
extraordinary talents, who must have made for himself a
lasting reputation, had not his political exertions been
checked by painful natural infirmities.' Though deaf from
his sixteenth year and though labouring under a partial
impediment of speech, he held high and important ap-
pointments, and was distinguished for his intellectual acti-
vities and attainments. . . . . His case seems to con-
tradict the opinion held by Kitto and others, that in all
that relates to the culture of the mind, and the cheerful
exercise of the mental faculties, the blind have the advantage of the deaf. The loss of the ear, that 'vestibule of the
soul,' was to him compensated by gifts and endowments
rarely united in the same individual. One instance of the
Chief's liberality and love of art may be mentioned. In
1796 he advanced a sum of £1000 to Sir Thomas Lawrence
to relieve him from pecuniary difficulties. Lawrence was
then a young man of twenty-seven. His career from a boy
upwards was one of brilliant success, but he was careless
and generous as to money matters, and some speculations by
his father embarrassed and distressed the young artist. In

his trouble he applied to the Chief of Kintail. 'Will you,' he said in that theatrical style common to Lawrence, 'will you be the Antonio to a Bassanio?' He promised to pay the £1000 in four years, but the money was given on terms the most agreeable to the feelings, and complimentary to the talents of the artist. He was to repay it with his pencil, and the Chief sat to him for his portrait. Lord Seaforth also commissioned from West one of those immense sheets of canvas on which the old Academician delighted to work in his latter years. The subject of the picture was the traditionary story of the Royal hunt, in which Alexander the Third was saved from the assault of a fierce stag by Colin Fitzgerald, a wandering knight unknown to authentic history. West considered it one of his best productions, charged £800 for it, and was willing some years afterwards, with a view to the exhibition of his works, to purchase back the picture at its original cost. In one instance Lord Seaforth did not evince artistic taste. He dismantled Brahan Castle, removing its castellated features, and completely modernising its general appearance. The house, with its large modern additions, is a tall, massive pile of building, the older portion covered to the roof with ivy. It occupies a commanding site on a bank midway between the river Conon and a range of picturesque rocks. This bank extends for miles, sloping in successive terraces, all richly wooded or cultivated, and commanding a magnificent view that terminates with the Moray Firth."*

The remarkable prediction of the extinction of this highly distinguished and ancient family is already known to the reader, and its literal fulfilment is one of the most curious instances of the kind on record. There is no doubt that the "prophecy" was widely known throughout the Highlands generations before it was fulfilled. Lockhart, in his "Life of Sir Walter Scott," says that "it connected the fall of the house of Seaforth not only with the appearance of a

---

* Review of "The Seaforth Papers" in the *North British Review*, 1863, by the late Robert Carruthers, LL.D.

deaf 'Cabarfeidh,' but with the contemporaneous appearance
of various different physical misfortunes in several of the
other Highland chiefs, all of which are said to have actually
occurred within the memory of the generation that has not
yet passed away. Mr Morrit can testify thus, for that he
heard the prophecy quoted in the Highlands at a time when
Lord Seaforth had two sons alive, and in good health, and
that it certainly was not made after the event," and then he
proceeds to say that Scott and Sir Humphrey Davy were
most certainly convinced of its truth, as also many others
who had watched the latter days of Seaforth in the light of
those wonderful predictions.*

His Lordship outlived all his four sons, as predicted by
the Brahan Seer. His name became extinct, and his vast
possessions were inherited by a stranger, Mr Stewart, who
married the eldest daughter, Lady Hood. The sign by
which it would be known that the prediction was about to
be fulfilled was also foretold in the same remarkable manner, namely, that in the days of the last Seaforth there
would be four great contemporary lairds, distinguished by
physical defects described by the Seer. Sir Hector Mackenzie, Bart. of Gairloch, was buck-toothed, and is to this

* " Every Highland family has its store of traditionary and romantic beliefs.
Centuries ago a seer of the Clan Mackenzie, known as Kenneth Oag (Odbar),
predicted that when there should be a deaf Caberfae the gift land of the estate
would be sold, and the male line become extinct. The prophecy was well known
in the North, and it was not, like many similar vaticinations, made after the
event. At least three unimpeachable Sassenach writers, Sir Humphrey Davy,
Sir Walter Scott, and Mr Morritt of Rokeby, had all heard the prediction when
Lord Seaforth had two sons alive. both in good health. The tenantry were, of
course, strongly impressed with the truth of the prophecy, and when their Chief
proposed to sell part of Kintail, they offered to buy in the land for him, that it
might not pass from the family. One son was then living, and there was no immediate prospect of the succession expiring ; but, in deference to the clannish
prejudice or affection, the sale of any portion of the estate was deferred for
about two years. The blow came at last. Lord Seaforth was involved in West
India plantations, which were mismanaged, and he was forced to dispose of part
of the "gift-land." About the same time the last of his four sons, a young man
of talent and eloquence, and then representing his native county in Parliament,
died suddenly, and thus the prophecy of Kenneth Oag was fulfilled.—

        Of the name of Fitgerald remained not a male
        To hear the proud name of the Chief of Kintail."
—*The late Robert Carruthers, LL.D., in the North British Review.*

day spoken of among the Gairloch tenantry as "An Tighearna stòrach," or the buck-toothed laird. Chisholm of Chisholm was hair-lipped, Grant of Grant wsa half-witted, and Macleod of Raasay was a stammerer.[*]

To the testimony of those whose names we have already given, we shall add that of a living witness. Duncan Davidson of Tulloch, Lord-Lieutenant of the county of Ross, in a letter addressed to the writer, dated May 21, 1878, says—"Many of these prophecies I heard of *upwards of 70 years ago*, and when many of them were *not* fulfilled, such as the late Lord Seaforth surviving his sons, and Mrs Stewart Mackenzie's accident, near Brahan, by which Miss Caroline Mackenzie was killed."

One cannot help sympathising with the magnificent old Chief as he mourned over the premature death of his four fine sons, and saw the honours of his house for ever extinguished in his own person. Many instances are related of his munificent extravagance at home, while sailing round the West Coast when visiting the great principality of the Lews, and calling on his way hither and thither on the other great chieftains of the West and Western Islands. Sir Walter Scott, in his "Lament for the last of the Seaforths," adds his tribute—

> In vain the bright course of thy talents to wrong,
> Fate deadened thine ear and imprisoned thy tongue,
> For brighter o'er all her obstructions arose
> The glow of thy genius they could not oppose
> And who, in the land of the Saxon or Gael
> Could match with Mackenzie, High Chief of Kintail
>
> Thy sons rose around thee in light and in love,
> All a father could hope, all a friend could approve ;
> What 'vails it the tale of thy sorrows to tell?
> In the spring-time of youth and of promise they fell !
> Of the line of MacKenneth remains not a male,
> To bear the proud name of the Chief of Kintail.

This sketch of him cannot better be closed than in the language of one whom we had occasion already to

---

[*] For full details of this remarkable instance of family fate, see "The Prophecies of the Brahan Seer."—A. & W. Mackenzie, Inverness.

quote with approbation :—"It was said of him by an
acute observer and a leading wit of the age, the late
Honourable Henry Erskine, the Scotch Dean of Faculty,
that 'Lord Seaforth's deafness was a merciful interposition to lower him to the ordinary rate of capacity in
society,' insinuating that otherwise his perception and
intelligence would have been oppressive. And the apt-
ness of the remark was duly appreciated by all those who
had the good fortune to be able to form an estimate from
personal observation, while, as a man of the world, none was
more capable of generalizing. Yet, as a countryman, he
never affected to disregard those local predilections which
identified him with the County of Ross, as the genuine
representative of Kintail, possessing an influence which,
being freely ceded and supported, became paramount and
permanent in the County which he represented in the Commons House of Parliament, till he was called to the peerage
on the 26th October 1797, by the title of Lord Seaforth and
Baron of Kintail, with limitation to heirs male of his body,
and which he presided over as his Majesty's Lord-Lieutenant.   He was commissioned, in 1793, to reorganise the 78th
or Ross-shire Regiment of Highlanders, which, for so many
years, continued to be almost exclusively composed of his
countrymen.   Nor did his extraordinary qualifications and
varied exertions escape the wide ranging eye of the master
genius of the age, who has also contributed, by a tributary
effusion, to transmit the unqualifed veneration of our age to
many that are to follow.   He has been duly recognised by
Sir Walter Scott, nor was he passed over in the earlier
buddings of Mr Colin Mackenzie ; but while the annalist is ·
indebted to their just encomiums, he may be allowed to
respond to praise worthy of enthusiasm by a splendid fact
which at once exhibits a specimen of reckless imprudence
joined to those qualities which, by their popularity, attest
their genuineness. Lord Seaforth for a time became emulous
of the society of the most accomplished Prince of his age.
The recreation of the Court was play ; the springs of this
indulgence then were not of the most delicate texture ; his

faculties, penetrating as they were, had not the facility of detection which qualified him for cautious circumspection ; he heedlessly ventured and lost. It was then to cover his delinquencies elsewhere, he exposed to sale the estate of Lochalsh ; and it was then he was bitterly taught to feel, when his people, without an exception, addressed his Lordship this pithy remonstrance—' Reside amongst us and we shall pay your debts.' A variety of feelings and facts, unconnected with a difference, might have interposed to counteract this display of devotedness besides ingratitude, but these habits, or his Lordship's reluctance, rendered this expedient so hopeless that certain of the descendants of the original proprietors of that valuable locality were combining their respective finances to buy it in, when a sudden announcement that it was sold under value, smothered their amiable endeavours. Kintail followed, with the fairest portion of Glenshiel, and the Barony of Callan Fitzgerald ceased to exist, to the mortification, though not to the unpopularity of this still patriarchal nobleman among his faithful tenantry and the old friends of his family."*

His Lordship married, on the 22d of April 1782, Mary Proby, daughter of Baptist Proby, D.D., Dean of Lichfield, and brother of John, first Lord Carysfort, by whom he had issue, a fine family of four sons and six daughters, first, William Frederick, who died young, at Killearnan ; second, George Leveson Boucherat, died young at Urquhart ; third, William Frederick, who represented the County of Ross in Parliament, 1812, and died at Warriston, near Edinburgh, in 1814; and fourth, Francis John, a midshipman in the Royal Navy, died at Brahan, in 1813. They all died unmarried. The daughters were, Mary Frederica Elizabeth, who succeeded him ; second, Frances Catherine, died without issue ; third, Caroline, accidently killed at Brahan, unmarried ; fourth, Charlotte Elizabeth, died unmarried ; fifth, Augusta Anne, died unmarried ; and sixth, Helen Ann, married the Right Honourable Joshua Henry Mackenzie of

* Bennetsfield MS.

the Inverlael family and anciently descended from the
Barons of Kintail, a Lord of Session and Justiciary, by the
title of Lord Mackenzie, with issue, two daughters.

Lord Seaforth, having survived all his male issue, died
on the 11th of January 1815, at Warriston, near Edinburgh,
the last male representative of his race. His lady outlived
him, and died at Edinburgh on the 27th February 1829.
The estates, in virtue of an entail executed by Lord Seaforth, with all their honours, duties, and embarrassments,
devolved upon his eldest daughter, then a young widowed
lady,

XXII. MARY ELIZABETH FREDERICA MACKENZIE, LADY HOOD,

Whom Scott commemorated in the well-known lines—

> And thou, gentle dame, who must bear to thy grief,
> For thy clan and thy country the cares of a Chief,
> Whom brief rolling moons, in six changes have left
> Of thy husband, and father, and brethren bereft ;
> To thine ear of affection how sad is the hail
> That salutes thee the heir of the line of Kintail.

She was born at Tarradale, Ross-shire, on the 27th of March
1783, and married at Barbadoes on the 6th of November
1804, Sir Samuel Hood, afterwards K.B., Vice-Admiral of
the White, and, in 1806, M.P. for Westminster. Sir Samuel
died at Madras, on the 24th December 1814, without issue.
Lady Hood then returned to Great Britain, and, in 1815, took
possession of the family estates, which had devolved upon
her by the death of her father without male issue, when, as
we have seen, the titles became extinct. She married,
secondly, on the 21st of May 1817, the Right Honourable
James Alexander Stewart of Glasserton, a cadet of the
house of Galloway, who assumed the name of Mackenzie,
was returned M.P. for the County of Ross, held office under
Earl Grey, and was successively Governor of Ceylon, and
Lord High Commissioner to the Ionian Islands. He died
on the 24th of September 1843. Mrs Stewart-Mackenzie
died at Brahan Castle on the 28th of November 1862, and

was buried in the family vault in the Chanonry or Cathedral of Fortrose. Her funeral was one of the largest ever witnessed in the Highlands of Scotland, several thousands of persons being present on foot, while the vehicles numbered over 150. By the second marriage she left issue—Keith William Stewart-Mackenzie, now of Seaforth; Francis P. Proby, died without issue; George A. F. W., married a daughter of General T. Marriott, and died in 1852 without issue; Mary F., married the Honourable Philip Anstruther, with issue; Caroline S., married J. B. Petre, and died in 1867; and Louisa C., who married William, second Lord Ashburton, with issue—one daughter. Mrs Stewart-Mackenzie and her husband were succeeded by their eldest son,

XXIII. KEITH WILLIAM STEWART-MACKENZIE,

Now of Seaforth, late an officer in the 90th Regiment, and Colonel-Commandant of the Ross-shire Rifle Volunteers. He married first, Hannah, daughter of James Joseph Hope-Vere of Craigiehall, with issue—James Alexander Francis Humberston Mackenzie, younger of Seaforth, a captain, 9th Lancers; Susan Mary, married the late Colonel John Constantine Stanley, second son of Edward, Lord Stanley of Alderley, with issue, two daughters; Julia Charlotte S., married the late Arthur, 9th Marquis of Tweeddale; and Georgina II., died young.

He married secondly, Alicia Almeira Bell, with issue, one daughter.

THE CHIEFSHIP.

IT has been pointed out that the male line of Colonel Alexander Mackenzie of Assynt became extinct on the death of Francis Humberston Mackenzie, last Lord Seaforth, who died in 1815, surviving all his male issue. It will also be remembered that the male line of George, second Earl of Seaforth, who died in 1651, terminated in Kenneth, XIXth Baron of Kintail, leaving issue only Lady Caroline. It has also been shown that the lineal descent of the original line of Kintail was divested from heirs male in the person of Anna, Countess of Balcarres, daughter of Colin, first Earl of Seaforth; and the male line of Colonel Alexander Mackenzie of Assynt having terminated in the last Lord Seaforth, we must carry the reader further back to a collateral branch to pick up the legitimate succession, and, as far as possible, settle the question of the present Chief. ship of the Clan.

Various gentlemen have been and are claiming this highly honourable position, and this is not to be wondered at, when it is kept in mind that whoever establishes his right therto, establishes at the same time his right to the ancient honours of the House of Kintail. It has been already pointed out that the original title of Lord Mackenzie of Kintail did not come under the attainder which followed on the part which Earl William took in the Rising of 1715; therefore the present Chief of the Mackenzies, in virtue of that position, as heir male of the first Lord Mackenzie of Kintail, is entitled to assume that title; and thus it becomes a most important duty in a work like this, to make the question as clear as possible and finally dispose of it once and for all.

We have before us the claim and pedigree of a Captain Murdoch Mackenzie, "of London," who claimed "the titles, honours, and dignities of Earl of Seaforth and Baron Mac-

kenzie of Kintail," in virtue of the claimant's pretended
descent from the Honourable John Mackenzie of Assynt,
second son of Kenneth, third Earl of Seaforth. According
to this pedigree, the Honourable John Mackenzie had a son,
" Murdoch Mackenzie of Lochbroom, who, having shown a
disposition of enterprise like his kinsman Earl William, left
his native parish in 1729 or 1730, first for Aberdeen and
afterwards for Northumberland, where, in consequence of
the unsettled state of Scotland, he resided with his family."
Murdoch had a son, John Mackenzie, " born in Beadnall,
Parish of Bamborough, County of Northumberland, 1738,
married Miss Isabella Davidson in 1762, and died in 1780,
in his forty-second year." This John had a son, " Captain
Murdoch Mackenzie, the claimant, born at Beadnall, County
of Northumberland, 1763; married, 1781, Miss Eleanor
Brown, of the same place, and has issue. He commanded
the ship, Essex, transport, 81, of London, during the late
war. Being desirous to see his clan in the North, in
1790 he visited the late Francis Lord Seaforth, who, in the
true spirit of Scotch sincerity, hospitality, and nobility, received him with demonstrations of pleasure. After talking
over family matters, his Lordship candidly said that Captain
Murdoch ought to have been the peer in point of primo-
geniture." A short account of the family accompanies the
pedigree, which concludes thus :—" In consequence of the
death of the last peer, it has been discovered in Scotland
that the titles and family estates have devolved upon Captain Murdoch Mackenzie, of London. This gentleman is
naturally anxious to establish his rights, but being unable
to prosecute so important a claim without the aid of sufficient funds, he has been advised to solicit the aid of some
individuals whose public spirit and liberal feelings may
prompt them to assist him on the principle that such timely
assistance and support will be gratefully and liberally rewarded. Captain Mackenzie hereby offers to give his bond
for £300 (or more if required) for every £100 that may be
lent him to prosecute his claim —the same to become due
and payable within three months after he shall have re-

S

covered his title and estates." We have not learnt the result of this appeal, but Captain Murdoch Mackenzie certainly did not establish his claim either to the titles or to the estates of the last Lord Seaforth.

It is, however, placed beyond doubt by the evidence produced at the Allangrange Service in 1829, that Kenneth (not Murdoch) was the name of the eldest son of the Honourable John Mackenzie of Assynt, and there is no trace of his having had any other sons. By an original Precept issued by the Provost and Magistrates of Fortrose, dated 30th October 1716, the son of the late John Mackenzie of Assynt is described as " Kenneth Mackenzie, now of Assynt, grandchild and apparent heir to the deceased Isobell, Countess Dowager of Seaforth, his grandmother on the father's side." In the same document he is described as her "*nearest* and lawful heir." It will thus appear that Captain Murdoch Mackenzie's genealogy is incorrect at the very outset; and if further proof be wanted that the descendants of John Mackenzie of Assynt are extinct, it will be found in the fact that the succession to the representation and honours of the family of Seaforth devolved on the male issue of Colonel Alexander of Assynt and Conansbay —a younger son, and in the parole evidence given by very old people at the Allangrange Service.

The claim of Captain Murdoch Mackenzie having failed, we must go back another step in the chain to pick up the legitimate succession to the honours of Kintail, and here we are met by another claim, put forward by the late Captain William Mackenzie of Gruinard, in the following letter :—

11 Margaret Street, Cavendish Square,
London, 24th October 1829.

MY DEAR ALLANGRANGE,—Having observed in the *Courier* of the 21st inst., at a meeting at Tain, that you were proceeding with the Seaforth Claims, I take the earliest opportunity of communicating to you a circumstance which I am sure my agent, Mr Roy, would have informed you of sooner, did he know that you were proceeding in this affair; and which, I think probable, he has done ere this ; but lest it might have escaped his notice, I deem it proper to acquaint you that on Mr Roy having discovered, by authenticated documents, that I was the lineal descendant of George, Earl of Seaforth, he authorised an English counsellor to make application to the Secretary of State to that effect, who made a reference to the Court of Exchequer in Scotland to examine the evidence—Mr Roy having satisfied them with having all which he required to establish my claim. I therefore am inclined to address you in order that you may be saved the trouble and expense attending this affair. Indeed, had I known you were taking any steps in this business, be assured I would have written to you sooner.

I had not the pleasure of communicating with you since your marriage, upon which event I beg leave to congratulate you, and hope I shall soon have the pleasure of learning of your adding a member to the Clan Kenneth.—Believe me, my dear Mac, yours most sincerely,

(Signed) WM. MACKENZIE.

George F. Mackenzie of Allangrange,
by Munlochy, Ross-shire.

The Gruinard claim is founded on a Genealogical Tree in possession of the representatives of the Family, by which John, I. of Gruinard, is made out to be the son of George of Kildun, second son of George, second Earl of Seaforth. It is generally believed among the clan that the descendants of this George, who was the *second* George of Kildun, are long ago extinct; but whether this be so or not, it can be conclusively shown, by reference to dates, that John, I. of Gruinard, could not possibly have been his son. And to the conclusive evidence of dates may fairly be added the testimony of all the Mackenzie MSS. which we have perused, and which make any reference to John of Gruinard. In every single instance where he is mentioned, he is described as a *natural* son of George, second Earl of Seaforth. Before he succeeded Earl George was known as (first) George of Kildun, hence the confusion and the error in the Gruinard Genealogical Tree. The "Ancient" MS. so often referred to in this work, and the author of which was a contemporary of John, I. of Gruinard, says that Earl George "had also ane *naturall* son, called John Mackenzy, who married Loggie's daughter." The author of the Ardintoul MS., who was the grandson, as mentioned by himself, of Farquhar Macrae, Constable of Islandonain Castle in Earl Colin's time, and who died advanced in years in 1704—consequently almost, if not contemporary with John of Gruinard—describing the effects of the disastrous battle of Worcester, informs us that Earl George, who was then in Holland, was informed of the result of the battle "by John of Gruinard, *his natural son*, and Captain Hector Mackenzie,

who made their escape from the battle," and that the tidings
"unraised his melancholy, and so died in the latter end of
September 1651." The Letterfearn MS. is also contemporary, as the author of it speaks of Earl Kenneth as "*now*
Earl of Seaforth," and of Kildun in the present, while he
speaks of his father in the past tense, and says, "He (Earl
George) left *ane natural son*, who *is* called John, who *is*
married with Loggie's daughter."

It may be objected, however probable it may be
that these MSS. are correct, that they are not authentic.
We have before us, however, a certified copy of a sasine,
dated 6th of February 1658, from the Part. Reg. Sasines
of Inverness, vol. 7, fol. 316, from which we quote as follows :—" Compearit personally John M'Kenzie, *naturall*
broyr to ane noble Erle Kenneth Erle of Seaforth Lord of
Kintail, &c., as bailzie in that part," on behalf of ": the noble
Lady, Dame Isabell M'Kenzie, Countess of Seaforth, sister
german to Sir Gerge Mackenzie of Tarbet, Knight, future
ladie to the said noble Erle." There is still another document having a most important bearing on this question, recently discovered in the office of the Sheriff-Clerk of Tain.
It is a discharge by Patrick Smith of Braco, dated and
registered in the Commissar Books at Fortrose, on the 4th
December 1668, in which he describes the parties as " Kenneth, Earl of Seafort, Lord Kintail, as principal, and John
Mackenzie of Gruinyard, designit in the obligatione vnder-
wrytten his *naturall* brother as cautioner." Further, George
of Kildun married, first, Mary Skene, daughter of Skene of
Skene, in 1661, as will ·be seen by·a charter to her of her
jointure lands of Kincardine, &c. (see Part. Reg. Sas. Invss.,
vol. ix., fol. 9). He married, secondly, Margaret, daughter
of Urquhart of Craighouse. It will at once occur to the
reader how absolutely impossible it was that George of
Kildun, who only married his first wife in 1661, could have
had a son, John of Gruinard, who obtained a charter in his
favour of the lands of Little Gruinard, &c., in 1669, and
who is, in that charter, designated "of Meikle Gruinard,"
while John of Gruinard's *wife* has lands disponed to her in

1655, *i.e.*, six years before the marriage of his reputed father George of Kildun ? Further, how could John of Gruinard's second son, Kenneth, have married, as he did, the widow of Kenneth "Og," fourth Earl, who died in 1701, if John, his father, had been the son by a second marriage of "George of Kildin," who married his first wife in 1661 ? This is absolutely conclusive.

Kenneth, third Earl of Seaforth, according to the Gruinard genealogy John of Gruinard's uncle, was born at Brahan Castle in 1635. He is described as "a child" in 1651 by a contemporary writer, who says that the Kintail people declined to rise with him in that year during his father's absence on the Continent, because he was but a *child*, and his father, their master, was in life." Colin, first Earl of Seaforth, died in 1633, and the author of the Ancient MS. informs us that "Earl George, being then the Laird of Kildun, married before his brother's death, the Lord Forbes's daughter." Thus, George of Kildun could not have been born before 1636 or 1637 ; and the date of his first marriage, twenty-four years later, tends to corroborate this. How, then, could he have a married son, John of Gruinard, whose *wife* obtained lands in 1655, *i.e.*, when Kildun himself was only about 18 years of age, and when John, then designated of Gruinard, was, in 1656, old enough to be cautioner for Earl Kenneth ? Proof of the same conclusive character could be adduced to any extent, but, in the face of the authentic documents already quoted, it appears quite superfluous to do so.

John, I. of Gruinard, could not possibly have been a son of the second George Mackenzie of Kildun. He was, undoubtedly, the *natural* son of the first George, who succeeded his brother Colin as second Earl of Seaforth, and it necessarily follows that the representatives of John of Gruinard have no claim whatever to the Chiefship of the Clan, or to the ancient honours of the family of Kintail. But the claim having been made, it was impossible, in a work like this, to pass it over, though we would have much preferred that the question had never been raised.

ALLANGRANGE LINE.

Having thus disposed of the Gruinard claim, and the legitimate representation of the later Peers in the male line having become extinct, to pick up the chain of succession of the ancient House of Kintail, we must revert to Kenneth, first Lord Mackenzie. It will be remembered that Kenneth had seven sons—

1. *Colin*, his successor.

2. *John* of Lochslinn, who left an only daughter, Margaret.

3. *Kenneth*, who died unmarried.

By his second wife, Isabel Ogilvie of Powrie, he had—

4. *Alexander*, who died young.

5. *George*, who succeeded his brother Colin as second Earl of Seaforth, and whose line terminated in Lady Caroline.

6. *Thomas* of Pluscardine, whose male line is also extinct, but is represented in the female line by Arthur Robertson, now of Inshes, Inverness.

7. *Simon*, after the death of his brother designated of Lochslinn, and whose representative became and now is the heir male of the ancient family of Kintail, and Chief of the Clan Mackenzie.

SIMON MACKENZIE of Lochslinn married, first, Elizabeth, daughter of the Rev. Peter Bruce, D.D., Principal of St Leonard's College, St Andrews, son of Bruce of Fingask, by Elizabeth, daughter of Alexander Wedderburn of Blackness. By her he had five sons and one daughter. The first son was the famous

Sir GEORGE MACKENZIE of Rosehaugh, Lord Advocate. His history is well known, and it would serve no good purpose to give a meagre account of him such as could be done in the space at our disposal. He wrote various works of acknowledged literary merit, and his "Institutes" is yet considered a standard work by lawyers. He left an autobiography in MS., published in Edinburgh by his widow in 1716. The small estate of Rosehaugh, where his residence lay, was in his time profusely covered over with the shrub known as the Dog Rose, which suggested to the famous lawyer the idea of designating that property by the name of " Vallis Rosarum," hence Rosehaugh.

Sir George married, first, Elizabeth, daughter of John Dickson of Hartree, and by her had three sons—(1) *John* (2), *Simon*, and (3) *George*, all of whom died young ; and two daughters—

1. *Agnes*, who married James Stuart Mackenzie, first Earl of Bute.[*]

2. *Elizabeth*, who married, first, Sir Archibald Cockburn of Langton, with issue ; and secondly, the Honourable Sir James Mackenzie of Royston, Bart., with issue—George, who died without succession, and two daughters, married, with issue. Sir George married, secondly, Margaret, daughter of —— Halliburton of Pitcur, by whom he had two sons and two daughters, all of whom died without issue except

George, who succeeded his father as second of Rose-haugh, married, and had an only daughter, who died without issue. It will thus be seen that the male line of Sir George Mackenzie of Rosehaugh also became extinct.

SIMON MACKENZIE, second son of the Honourable Simon of Lochslinn, married Jane, daughter of Alexander Mackenzie, I. of Ballone, brother to Sir John Mackenzie of Tarbat, and uncle to George, first Earl of Cromarty. The marriage contract is dated 1663. Simon died at Lochbroom in the following year, and left an only and posthumous son,

I. SIMON MACKENZIE, first of Allangrange, an advocate at the Scottish Bar. The property of Allangrange was acquired in the following way :—Alexander Mackenzie, I. of Kilcoy, third son of Colin Cam, XI. of Kintail, had four sons, of whom the youngest, Roderick, obtained the lands of Kilmuir, in the Black Isle, became a successful lawyer, Sheriff-Depute and Member of Parliament, and was knighted by Charles II. Sir Roderick Mackenzie, then of Findon, acquired by purchase of several properties, a very considerable estate, which, at his death in 1692, and on that of his only son the following year, were divided among his daughters, as heirs-portioners. The third of these daughters, Isobel, married (August 22, 1693) Simon Mackenzie, the advocate, and brought him as her portion the Estate of ALLAN, formerly the property and residence of Seaforth, and which was thenceforth called by the name of Allangrange. By her he had issue—

.1. *Roderick*, who died before his father, unmarried,

2. *George*, who succeeded.

3. *Kenneth*.

4. *William*, a captain in the Dutch army, issue extinct.

5. *Simon*, died in the West Indies, without issue.

6. *Lilias*, died unmarried.

7. *Elizabeth*, married, in 1745, John Matheson of Fernaig.

8. *Eliza*, married Ludovic, son of Roderick Mackenzie, V. of Redcastle.

9. *Isobel*, married Murdo Cameron at Allangrange.

He married, secondly, on the 28th August 1718, Susanna Fraser, daughter of Colonel Alexander Fraser of Kinneries, known as the "Coroner"—male issue extinct. He was drowned in the river Orrin, returning from a visit to Fairburn, in February 1730, and was succeeded by his eldest surviving son,

II. GEORGE MACKENZIE, who, in May 1731, married Margaret, grand-daughter of Sir Donald Bayne of Tulloch. The male representation of the Baynes terminated in John; and his daughter, Margaret, carried the lineal descent of that old and respectable family into the house of Allangrange. The Baynes were not originally a Ross-shire family, but a branch of the Clan Mackay which settled in the vicinity of Dingwall in the sixteenth century. By Margaret Bayne George had issue, five sons—

1. *Simon*, who died young, in 1731.

2. *William*, who became a Captain in the 25th Regiment, died unmarried, before his father, in 1764.

3. *George*, died young.

4. *Alexander*, died unmarried, in 1765.

5. *John*, who succeeded his father.

6. *Margaret*, who married, as his second wife, Alexander Chisholm of Chisholm, with issue.

7. *Isobel*, who married, in 1767, Simon Mackenzie of Langwell, a Captain in the 4th Regiment, with issue.

8. *Mary*, married Kenneth Chisholm, Fasnakyle, with issue.

9. *Margaret*, married John Chisholm, Comar, with issue.

George had six other daughters, all of whom died young or unmarried. He died in 1773, and was succeeded ·by his eldest surviving son,

III. JOHN MACKENZIE, at an early age appointed Examiner of Customs in Edinburgh. He married, first, in 1781, Catherine Falconer, eldest daughter and co-heiress of James Falconer of Monkton, and grand-daughter of the Right Honourable Lord Halkerton and the Honourable Jane Falconer. By the acquisition of this lady's fortune, Allangrange was able to devote himself to agricultural pursuits, for which he had a strong predilection, and in which he was eminently successful. His wife died in 1790. By her he had issue—

1. *George Falconer*, who succeeded him.

2. *Jane Falconer*, who married John Gillanders of Highfield, with issue ; and two other daughters, both named *Margaret Bayne*, who died young.

He married, secondly, Barbara, daughter of George Gillanders, first of Highfield, relict of John Bowman, an East Indian merchant in London, without issue. He died in 1812, and was succeeded by his only son,

IV. GEORGE FALCONER MACKENZIE, who was, in 1829, served male heir to his ancestor, the Honourable Simon Mackenzie of Lochslinn, and heir male in general to Simon's father Kenneth, first Lord Mackenzie of Kintail, as also to Lord Kenneth's brother Colin, first Earl of Seaforth.*

---

* The following gentlemen composed the jury in the Allangrange Service :— Sir James Wemyss Mackenzie of Scatwell, Bart., M.P. ; Sir Francis Alexander Mackenzie of Gairloch, Bart. ; Colin Mackenzie of Kileoy, advocate ; William Mackenzie of Muirton, W.S. ; Alexander Mackenzie of Millbank ; Hugh Ross of Glastullich ; Alexander Mackenzie of Woodside ; Simon Mackenzie Ross, younger of Aldie ; Hugh James Cameron, banker, Dingwall ; Alexander Gair, banker Tain ; John Mackenzie, David Ross, Hugh Leslie, William Fraser, and Donald Stewart, the last five, writers in Tain.

He matriculated his arms accordingly in the Public Register of the Lyon Office of Scotland, and on the 9th of January 1828, married Isabella Reid Fowler, daughter of James Fowler of Raddery and Fairburn, in the County of Ross, and Grange in Jamaica, and by her had issue—

1. *John Falconer*, who succeeded him.
2. *James Fowler*, now of Allangrange.
3. *George Thomas*, married Ethel Newman in London.
4. *Sophia Catherine*, died young.
5. *Anna Watson*.

He died in 1841, and was succeeded by his eldest son,

V. JOHN FALCONER MACKENZIE, who died, unmarried, in 1849, and was succeeded by his next brother,

VI. JAMES FOWLER MACKENZIE, now of Allangrange, Chief the Mackenzies, and heir male to the dormant honours of the ancient family of Kintail and Seaforth. He is yet (1879) unmarried.

The Honourable Simon Mackenzie of Lochslinn had three other sons by the first marriage—(1) Thomas, I. of Loggie; (2) John, I. of Inchcoulter, or Balcony; and (3) Colin, Clerk to the Privy Council and Commissioner in Edinburgh. Issue of all three extinct.*

THE OLD MACKENZIES OF DUNDONNELL.

The Honourable SIMON MACKENZIE of Lochslinn, fourth son of Kenneth, first Lord Mackenzie of Kintail, married, secondly, in 1650, Agnes, daughter of William Fraser of Culbockie, relict of Alexander Mackenzie, I. of Ballone, brother of Sir John Mackenzie of Tarbat. Failing the line of Allangrange, all the male issue of the Honourable Simon Mackenzie by his first marriage will have become extinct, when the Chiefship must be looked for among the descendants of his second marriage with Agnes Fraser, as above.

---

* See **Findon's** Genealogical Tables and the Allangrange Service.

By this marriage, the Hon. Simon Mackenzie had issue—

1. *Kenneth Mòr*, I. of Glenmarksie and Dundonnell.

2. *Isobel*, married Murdoch Mackenzie, VI. of Fairburn.

3. *Elizabeth*, married the Rev. Roderick Mackenzie, laird and minister of Avoch, grandson of Sir Roderick Mackenzie, Tutor of Kintail, with issue—John, II. of Avoch, forfeited for having taken part in the Rising of 1715; several other sons, all of whom, except Roderick, predeceased their father; and four daughters—(1) Christian, married Sir Kenneth Mackenzie of Scatwell ; (2) Isobel, married Alexander Matheson of Bennetsfield; (3) Margaret, married John Macrae of Dornie; and (4) Anne, who married the Rev. Lewis Grant.

·I. KENNETH MOR MACKENZIE had the lands of Glenmarksie, and, in 1690, acquired the lands of Dundonnell from the Mackenzies of Redcastle. He afterwards acquired the lands of Meikle Scatwell, of which he had a sasine, in 1693. He married Annabella, daughter of John Mackenzie, I. of Gruinard, by whom he had issue—

1. *Kenneth*, his heir.

2. *Alexander*, of whom nothing can be traced.

3. *Colin Riabhach* of Ardinglash, who married Annabella, daughter of Simon Mackenzie, Loggie, issue extinct.

4. *Simon*, of whom nothing is known.

5. *Barbara*, who married Alexander, II. of Ballone.

6. *Sibella*, who married John Mackenzie, II. of Ardloch.

7. *Annabella*, who married James Mackenzie of Keppoch, in Lochbroom, brother of Ardloch, with issue. Kenneth Mòr was succeeded by his eldest son,

II. KENNETH MACKENZIE, II. of ·Dundonnell, who married Jean, daughter of The Chisholm of Chisholm, by whom he had

1. *Kenneth*, his heir.

2. *Alexander*, a Captain 73d Regt., died in 1783.

3. *John*, who married Barbara, daughter of Mackenzie of Ardloch, with issue, several sons, who died young, and two daughters, one of whom married Alexander Mackenzie of Riabhachan, Kishorn, with issue. He was succeeded by his eldest son,

III. KENNETH MACKENZIE, who married, in 1737, Jean, daughter of Sir Kenneth Mackenzie, first Baronet of Scatwell, by whom he had

1. *George*, his successor.
2. *Kenneth*, a W.S., died in 1790.
3. *William*, an Episcopolian Minister, with issue.
4. *Roderick*, with issue.
5. *Alexander*, a Captain, died in India without issue.
6. *Simon*, a Captain, married, and died in Nairn in 1812.
7. *Lewis*, also a Captain, who died in India.
8. *Janet*, married Colin Mackenzie, brother to George Mackenzie of Kildonan, Lochbroom. She died in 1783.
9. *Isabella*, died unmarried.

Kenneth's wife died in 1786. He died in 1789, and was succeeded by his eldest son,

IV. GEORGE MACKENZIE, who married Abigail, daughter of Thomas Mackenzie, V. of Ord, by whom he had

1. *Alexander*, who died young.
2. *Kenneth*, who succeeded his father.
3. *Thomas*, who succeeded his brother, Kenneth.
4. *Jane*, who married the Rev. Dr Ross, Lochbroom.

George was succeeded by his eldest surviving son,

V. KENNETH MACKENZIE, who, in 1817, married Isabella, daughter of Donald Roy of Treeton, without issue He left the estate to his brother-in-law, Robert Roy, W.S. who lost it after a long and costly litigation with

VI. THOMAS MACKENZIE, second surviving son of George, IV. of Dundonnell, and next brother of Kenneth. The estate was ruined by law expenses, and had to be sold. It was purchased by Murdo Munro-Mackenzie of Ardross, grandfather to the present proprietor, Murdo Mackenzie of Dundonnell. (See Mackenzies of Ardross.)

Thomas Mackenzie, VI. and last of the old Mackenzies of Dundonnell, married Anne, eldest daughter of Alexander Mackenzie, VI. of Ord, and by her had issue—

1. *George Alexander*, born at Teanassie, Beauly, 10th July 1818, and married Louisa, daughter of Captain Stewart, Ceylon Rifles, without issue.

2. *Thomas*, who went to California, and of whom no trace.

3. *John Hope*, now residing at Tarradale, Ross-shire, married, in Ceylon, Louisa, daughter of Captain Stewart, and relict of his deceased brother, George Alexander, without issue.

4. *Helen*, married the Honourable Justice Charles Stewart, in Ceylon, without issue.

5. *Isabella*, who resides in Elgin, unmarried.

THE MACKENZIES OF HILTON.

I. DUNCAN MACKENZIE, first of Hilton, second son of Alexander "Ionraic," sixth Baron of Kintail by his first marriage with Anna Macdougal of Dunolly, was designated by the title of the barony of Hilton, in Strathbran, bounded on the north by Loch Fannich, on the south by the ridge of the northern hills of Strathconan, on the east by Achnan-Allt, and on the west by Ledgowan. A part of the barony lay in Redcastle. He married a daughter of Ewen Cameron, XII. of Lochiel, and by her had one son.

II. ALLAN MACKENZIE (from whom this family, is called "Clann Allan"), who married a daughter of Alexander Dunbar of Conzie and Kilbuyack, third son of the Sheriff of Moray. She, after his death, married Kenneth, I. of Allan (now Allangrange), second son of Hector Roy, I. of Gairloch. By her Allan had two sons—

1. *Murdoch*, his heir.

2. *John*, ancestor of the Mackenzies of Loggie.

He was succeeded by his eldest son,

III. MURDOCH MACKENZIE, who married a daughter of Innes of Inverbreakie, and by her had one son,

IV. JOHN MACKENZIE, who married Margaret, daughter of Dunbar of Inchbrock, with issue—

1. *Murdoch*, his heir.

2. *Alexander*, who, in 1640, married Margaret, natural daughter of John Roy Mackenzie, IV. of Gairloch.*

3. *Colin*, who, educated at the University of Aberdeen, where he received his degree of Master of Arts, applied himself to theology, and became minister of Killearnan, where he died. He married a Miss Dundas, by whom he had several children, of whom Kenneth Mackenzie, well known as deacon of the goldsmiths in Edinburgh.

4. His eldest daughter married John Sinclair, Caithness.

5. His second daughter married John Matheson, Lochalsh, father of Farquhar Matheson, Fernaig, whose son John

---

* Marriage Contract in Gairloch Charter Chest.

Matheson, first of Attadale, became progenitor of the present family of Ardross and Lochalsh.

He was succeeded by his eldest son,

V. MURDOCH MACKENZIE, who married Mary, eldest daughter of Murdoch Murchison of Auchtertyre, minister of Kintail, and by her had—

1. *Alexander*, his heir.

2. *Roderick*, who married the eldest daughter of Alexander, third son of Murdoch Mackenzie, II. of Redcastle, by whom he had a son, Colin, who died unmarried in 1682.

3. *Colin*, married Isobel, daughter of Donald Simson, Chamberlain of Ferintosh, and by her had two sons, Alexander and Roderick, whose lineal succession will be afterwards detailed, when we come to show how the grandson of Roderick came to carry on the main line, as XI. of Hilton. He also had one natural son.

4. *Murdoch*, married Agnes Helen, daughter of Donald Taylor, a Bailie of Inverness (1665), and by her had one son, Alexander, who entered young into the service of Kenneth, Earl of Seaforth, and in the year 1709 was made one of the Chamberlains to Earl William. He married, in 1709, Katherine, daughter of the Viscount of Stormont, by whom he had several children, whose succession is unknown. His only daughter, Jean, married Hector Mackenzie, and by him had a son, Kenneth (a Jesuit in Spain, who died without issue), and several daughters.

5. *Isobel*, married Donald Macrae, minister of Kintail.

He was succeeded by his eldest son,

VI. ALEXANDER MACKENZIE, who was twice married: first, to Annabella, second daughter of John Mackenzie, I. of Ord, without issue; and secondly, to Sibella, eldest daughter of Roderick Mackenzie, I. of Applecross, relict in succession of Alexander Macleod of Raasay, and Thomas Graham of Drynie. By her he had one son,

VII. EVAN MACKENZIE, who married Elizabeth, daughter of Colin Mackenzie, IV. of Redcastle, by whom he had

1. *John*, his heir.

2. *Colin*, who succeeded John as IX. of Hilton.

3. *Florence*, who married Alexander Macrae, son of Donald Macrae, minister of Kintail.

He was succeeded by his eldest son,

VIII. JOHN MACKENZIE, who married a daughter of Thomas Mackenzie, IV. of Ord, by Mary, fourth daughter of John Mackenzie, III. of Applecross. He joined the Earl of Mar in 1715, and was killed at Sheriffmuir, where he commanded a company of the Mackenzies. Having no issue, he was succeeded by his next brother,

IX. COLIN MACKENZIE, who married Catherine, daughter of Christopher Macrae of Arrinhugair. He matriculated himself in the Lyon Herald's office, and received for his armorial bearing, AZURE, a hart's head caboss'd, and attired OR, a Highland dirk, shafted gules between the atterings for difference. Above the shield a helmet befitting his degree, with a mantle gules doubling argent and a wreath of his colours is set. For his crest, two hands holding a two-handed sword in bend proper. He died in 1756, aged 65, leaving two sons and one daughter—

1. *John*, who married Helen, daughter of Roderick Mackenzie, VII. of Fairburn. He died, without issue, before his father, in 1751.

2. *Alexander*, who succeeded his father.

3. A daughter, married to John Macdonell, XIII. of Glengarry.

He was succeeded by his eldest surviving son,

X. ALEXANDER MACKENZIE, who married Mary, daughter of George Mackenzie, II. of Gruinard. He died without legitimate issue, but left a natural son, Alexander, well known and still kindly spoken of as "Alastair Mor Mac Fhir Bhaile Chnuic," Seaforth's principal and most successful recruiting sergeant when raising the 78th Highlanders. Many a curious story is still related of Alastair's successful efforts to procure willing, and often hesitating, recruits for the regiment of his chief. He married Annabella Mackenzie, who long outlived him, and was well known and highly respected for many years as " Banntrach an t-Shearsan," in Strathbran. Alastair was a constant and conspicu-

ous figure at all the Ross-shire markets, where his popularity
and address never failed to secure a recruit for the famous
" Buffs." Many of his descendants, in the third generation,
occupy responsible positions throughout the country.

This baron was succeeded in the estates and barony by
the heir of line (next of male kin), Alexander, great-grandson of Colin, third son of Murdoch Mackenzie, V. of Hilton.

The male line of Alexander Mackenzie, the sixth baron,
having become extinct, the heir and representative was
sought for among the issue of his brothers. The next brother was Roderick, who, as already shown, left one son,
Colin, who, in 1682, died without issue. The next after
Roderick was Colin, who, by Isobel Simson, left two sons—

1. *Alexander* (Sanders), who became chamberlain to
Culloden. He married Helen, daughter of William Munro
of Ardullie, and by her had two sons and two daughters—
(1) Colin, who died unmarried, but left a natural son, Alexander, from whom are descended several respectable families
in Ferrintosh. (2) Donald, who married Jean, daughter of
Thomas Forbes of Raddery, and of the lands of Fortrose as far
as Ethie. He was buried in the Cathedral of Fortrose, on the
western gable of which is a tablet to his memory, erected
by his wife. By her he had one son, Alexander, drowned
with his father in 1759 when fording the Conon opposite
Dingwall, and then—the son being unmarried—perished
the legitimate male succession of his paternal grandfather,
Alexander. Donald had several daughters—(1) Mary, who
married Colin Mackenzie, minister of Fodderty, and first of
the family of Glack. She was with her father when he was
drowned, but she was saved ; (2) Jean, married Colin Murchison ; (3) Isobel, married David Ross ; (4) another married Mr Mackenzie of Ussie, and had two sons, Donald and
Frank ; (5) Anne, married Lewis Grant ; and (6) Helen,
married Alexander Mackenzie of Ardnagrask, afterwards at
Logie-side, from whose son, Bailie John Mackenzie of Inverness, are numerous descendants. Alexander's (Sanders)
eldest daughter Mary, married Donald Murchison, son of
John Murchison of Auchtertyre ; the second, Elizabeth,

T

married William Martin of Inchfure, whose daughter, Annie, was celebrated for her beauty, and married Norman,
XVIII.th Baron of Macleod.

2. *Roderick*, who acquired Brea in Ferrintosh, in wadset,
which remained in the family for two generations. By
marriage he acquired the ruined castle of Dingwall (the ancient residence of the Earls of Ross) and its lands, as also
the lands of Longcroft. He was called Mr Rory Mackenzie of Brea, and married Una (Winifred), daughter of John
Cameron, town-clerk of Dingwall, by whom he had three
sons—(1) John Mackenzie of Brea, called, " John the Laird,"
who resided at Tarradale, and married in 1759, Beatrix,
daughter of Alexander Mackenzie, VIII. of Davochmaluak,
by Magdalen, daughter of Hugh Rose, XIII. of Kilravock,
and by her had seven sons and four daughters—Rory, who
died unmarried ; Alexander, who succeeded as XI. of Hilton, and of whom afterwards ; Kenneth of Inverinate, who
married Anne, daughter of Thomas Mackenzie, IV. of Highfield and VI. of Applecross (by Elizabeth, daughter of
Donald Mackenzie, V. of Kilcoy), by whom he had two sons
and six daughters—Thomas, who succeeded as X. OF AP-
PLECROSS [see Genealogy of that Family] ; and Alexander,
who married Harriet, daughter of Newton of Curriehill, by
whom he had four children—Kenneth, died unmarried ;
Alexander, a lieutenant in the Royal Engineers, died unmarried ; Marion married Charles Holmes, barrister, without issue ; Harriet, unmarried. Kenneth's six daughters
were—Jane, died unmarried ; Elizabeth married her cousin,
Colonel John Mackenzie, XII. of Hilton ; Flora married
Rev. Charles Downie ; Catherine, Mary, and Johanna, died
unmarried.

The other sons and the daughters of " John the Laird "
were—Colin, " the Baron," born at Tarradale, 3d December
1759, died unmarried ; Peter, died unmarried ; Duncan,
married Jessie Mackenzie, daughter of Mackenzie of Strathgarve, without issue ; Arthur died unmarried ; Magdalen
died unmarried ; Marcella (Medley) married the Rev. Dr
Downie ; Annie died unmarried ; Mary married, in 1790,

the Rev. Donald Mackenzie, minister of Fodderty; Elizabeth died unmarried.

Roderick's other sons were—(2) Colin Mackenzie, minister of Fodderty, first of the family of Glack; and (3) Peter Mackenzie, M.D., a surgeon-general of the army, and a knight of Nova Scotia—died unmarried.

Alexander was succeeded in the lands and barony of Hilton by

XI. ALEXANDER MACKENZIE, second son of John Mackenzie of Brea, already shown to be the great-grandson of Colin, third son of Murdoch Mackenzie, V. of Hilton, and his heir of line. He was born at Tigh-a-Phris, Ferrintosh, on the 3d July 1756; educated at the University of Aberdeen, and afterwards bred a millwright, to qualify him for the supervision of family estates in the West Indies. He became a Colonel of local militia in Jamaica, and subsequently, upon the death of his maternal grandfather, and of his cousin, Lieutenant Kenneth Mackenzie, at Saratoga, he succeeded to the estate of Davochmaluag. The adjacent properties of Davochpollan and Davochcairn, having been already acquired by his father. were by him added to Davochmaluag, and to the combined properties he gave the name of Brea, after the former possession of his family in the Black Isle. He was a distinguished agriculturist, and was, with Sir George Mackenzie of Coul, and Major Forbes Mackenzie, the first to introduce Cheviot sheep to the Highlands, for their waste lands. He greatly improved the estate of Brea, in Strathpeffer, and laid it out in its present beautiful form. His land improvements, however, proved unremunerative; and his Hilton estates were heavily encumbered in consequence of the part taken by the family in the Risings of 1696, 1715, and 1745; and great losses having been incurred in connection with the West Indian properties, he got into pecuniary difficulties, and the whole of his possessions, at home and abroad, were sold either by himself or by his trustees. He married Mary James in Jamaica, and by her had four children—

1. *John*, his heir.

2. *Alexander*, who married his cousin Charlotte, daughter of the Rev. Dr Downie, and died in Australia, leaving issue, eight children—(1) Alexander, unmarried; (2) Downie, died unmarried; (3) John; (4) Kenneth, who married Miss Macdonald, a grand-daughter of Macleod of Guesto; (5) Charles, unmarried; (6) William, unmarried; (7) Mary James, married to her cousin, Kenneth Mackenzie, XIV. of Hilton; and (8) Jessie, unmarried.

3. *Kenneth*, a W.S., who married Anne Urquhart, without issue. He married, secondly, Elizabeth Jones, with issue, and died in Canada, where his widow and children reside, in Toronto.

4. *Mary*, unmarried, in Australia, very aged, in 1878.

He died at Lasswade, and was succeeded as representative of the family by his eldest son,

XII. JOHN MACKENZIE, Colonel of the 7th Regiment of Bengal Cavalry, and for many years superintendent of the Government breeding stud at Buxar. He married, in 1813, Elizabeth, daughter of his uncle, Kenneth Mackenzie of Inverinate, and died at Simla in 1856, leaving—

1. *Alexander*, his successor.

2. *Kenneth*, who became XIV. of Hilton.

3. *Mary*, married Dr James, of the 30th Regiment.

4. *Anne*, married General Arthur Hall, 5th Bengal Cavalry.

5. *Elizabeth Jane*, unmarried.

He was succeeded by his eldest son,

XIII. ALEXANDER MACKENZIE, who died in 1862, in New South Wales, unmarried, and was succeeded by his brother,

XIV. KENNETH MACKENZIE, the present representative of the ancient House of Hilton, residing at Tyrl-Tyrl, Taralga, near Sydney. He married Mary James, daughter of Alexander Mackenzie, his uncle, and by her he has—

1, *John ;* 2, *Kenneth ;* 3, *Downie ;* 4, *Flora ;* and 5, *Jessie.*

THE MACKENZIES OF GLACK.

COLIN MACKENZIE, third son of Murdoch, V. of Hilton,

had two sons. The male issue of Alexander, the eldest—
as appears in the Hilton genealogy—became extinct in
1759, when his grandson, Alexander, was drowned, but his
succession in the female line was carried on by his grand-
daughter, Mary, who married Colin Mackenzie, I. of
Glack. The second son, Roderick, was designated of Brea.
He married Una (Winifred), daughter of John Cameron of
Longcroft. His grandson, Alexander, son of John, succeeded as XI. of Hilton. The second son of Roderick
Mackenzie of Brea, born in 1707, became

I. COLIN MACKENZIE, first of Glack. He was educated
at the University of Aberdeen, and afterwards, in 1734,
settled as minister of Fodderty. He was on terms of intimacy with the celebrated Lord President Forbes of Culloden,
with whom he maintained a constant correspondence; and
this, with his clerical calling, kept him from taking part in
the Rising of 1745, though all his sympathies were with the
Jacobites. He received, in his district, the earliest news of
the landing of Prince Charles, which reached him at night,
when he at once crossed Knockfarrel to Brahan Castle,
where, finding his Lordship in bed, without awaking his
lady, he told him what had happened. Seaforth* having
only lately had his estate restored to him, was not disposed
to show ingratitude to the Government, and was easily prevailed upon to disappear from Brahan for a time. He
therefore started for the West Coast during the night
unknown to any one, accompanied by Colin Mackenzie,
just as the Prince's army was on its march eastward. Both
were in retirement near Poolewe when two ships laden with
Seaforth's retainers from the Lews sailed into the loch, who
were at once directed to return to Stornoway, Seaforth
waving towards them with the jaw-bone of a sheep, which
he was picking for his dinner.†

---

* We shall continue, as the most convenient course, to call him Seaforth,
though at this period the title had been forfeited.

† In this way, it is said, was fulfilled one of the predictions of the Brahan
Seer—"That next time the men of Lews should go forth to battle, they would
be beaten back by a weapon smaller than the jaw-bone of an ass."

Meantime, Seaforth's lady, not knowing the whereabouts or intentions of her husband, entertained the Prince
at Brahan Castle, and urged upon the aged Earl of Cromarty and his son, Lord Macleod, to call out the clan.
Subsequently, when the Earl of Cromarty and Lord Macleod were confined in the Tower of London, for taking part
in the rebellion, and when the Countess with ten children,
and bearing a twelfth, were suffering the severest hardships
and penury, Colin Mackenzie, at great risk to himself,
voluntarily collected the rents from the tenants (giving them
his own receipt, in security against their being required to
make second payment to the Government commissioners),
and carried the money to her ladyship in London.   In return
for this, he was afterwards appointed, by Lord Macleod,
chaplain to Macleod's Highlanders, raised by his lordship
—now the 71st Highland Light Infantry.   The appointment proved more honorary than lucrative, as he had to
furnish a substitute, at his· own expense, to perform the
duties pertaining to the office.   It was this Colin who first
recognised the health-giving properties of the Strathpeffer
mineral spring, and who, by erecting a covered shed over it,
first placed it in a condition to benefit the suffering.   He
inherited a considerable fortune in gold from his father,
and from his mother the ruined castle of Dingwall (the old
seat of the Earls of Ross) and its lands, as also the lands of
Longcroft.   He gave the site of the castle of Dingwall,
then valued at £300, to Henry Davidson of Tulloch, as a
contribution towards the erection of a manufactory which
he proposed to establish for the employment of the surplus
male and female labour in Dingwall and its neighbourhood,
but which was never commenced.   He sold its other lands,
and those of Longcroft, to his nephew, Alexander Mackenzie, XI. of Hilton.   Subsequently, he purchased the estate
of Glack, in Aberdeenshire, of which he was afterwards
designated.   In his ninety-fifth year, shortly before his
death in 1801, he conducted the opening services of the
Parish Church of Ferrintosh (Urquhart), towards the erection of which he largely contributed, to commemorate the

saving and washing ashore of his wife upon her horse near its site, on which occasion her father and only brother were drowned. The Rev. Colin Mackenzie married, first, Margaret (not Jean, as stated in the Spalding Club volume of the Kilravock papers), daughter of Hugh, IV. of Clava, by whom he had issue an only daughter, Margaret, who died young, 22d September 1746. He married, secondly, his second cousin, Mary, eldest daughter of Donald Mackenzie, Balnabeen, by his wife Jean, daughter of Thomas Forbes of Raddery, a bailie of Fortrose, in whose memory a tablet is erected on the Cathedral there, bearing the following inscription :—" Sub spe beatae resurectionis in Domino, hic conduntur ceneres Thomae Forbesii quondam ballivi Fortrossensis, mortui 21, Sepulti 25 Maii 1699, qui in indicium grati erga Deum animi et charitates erga homines 1200 lib. Scot. ad sustentandam evangelii prædicationem hac in urbe dicavit. Monumentum mariti unpensis extmendum curavit Helena Stuart relicta conjux hic etiam sexpeleindiam sperans." By her—who, as already shown, carried on, in the female line, the succession of Alexander (Sanders), eldest son of Colin, third son of Murdoch, V. of Hilton—he had

1. *Roderick*, his heir.

2. *Donald*, educated in theology at the University of Edinburgh, appointed minister of Fodderty and chaplain to the 71st Regiment of Highlanders—his father having resigned these offices in his favour. He was noted as a great humorist, and said to be at heart more imbued with the spirit of a soldier than with that of a minister. He was twice married ; first, to Mary, daughter of his uncle, John Mackenzie of Brea (" The Laird "), by whom he had two sons and two daughters—Colin, a Colonel of Royal Engineers, married Anne Petgrave, daughter of John Pendrill of Bath, without issue ; John, of whom afterwards as IV. of Glack ; Elizabeth, who married Lieutenant Stewart, R.N., with issue ; and Mary, died unmarried.

3. *Forbes*, a Captain in the North British (Ross-shire) Militia, afterwards Major in the East of Ross Militia, and

for thirty-seven years a Deputy-Lieutenant of the county. He was a noted agriculturist. It was he who, at Muirton of Barra, in Aberdeenshire, first cleared land of large boulders, by blasting and building them into fences. He reclaimed and laid out the greater part of Strathpeffer, where, on Fodderty, he was the first to apply lime to the land, and to grow wheat north of the Forth. He was the first to import Clydesdale horses and shorthorn cattle into the·Northern Counties; and was, as already mentioned—with Sir George Mackenzie of Coul and his cousin Hilton—the first to introduce Cheviot sheep into the Highlands. He married Catherine, daughter of Angus Nicolson, Stornoway, and grand-daughter of him who commanded and brought to Poolewe, for Prince Charles' standard; the 300 men sent back by Seaforth to the Lews, already mentioned. By her he had three sons and three daughters—(1) Nicolson, a surgeon in the army, unmarried, wrecked near Pictou, in 1853, and there drowned attempting to save the lives of others; (2) Roderick, heir of entail to Foveran, a Colonel in the Royal Artillery, married, in 1878, Caroline Sophia, daughter of J. A. Beaumont of Wimbledon Park; (3) Thomas, a Major in the 78th Highlanders; (4) Mary, married the Rev. John Kennedy, D.D., Dingwall, by whom she has two daughters—Jessie, unmarried; and Mary, married John Matheson, Madras, son of the late Rev.· Duncan Matheson, Gairloch; (5) Dorothy Blair, died unmarried; (6) Catherine Eunice, married to the late Adam Alexander Duncan of Naughton, Fife, by whom she has one daughter; and (7) Catherine Henrietta Adamina.

4. *Anne*, married Hector Mackenzie, a Bailie of Dingwall, and son of Alexander Mackenzie of Tollie, by his second wife, Catherine, daughter of Bayne of Delny, and younger half-brother of Alexander Mackenzie, I. of Portmore.

5. *Mary*, married Capt. John Mackenzie, VI. of Kincraig.

6. *Joanna*, married Dr Millar, in the Lews.

7. *Una*, died unmarried.

8. *Beatrix*, married Peter Hay, a Bailie of Dingwall. ·

9. *Isabella*, died unmarried.

10. *Jean*, married the Rev. Colin Mackenzie, Stornoway.
He was succeeded by his eldest son,

II. RODERICK MACKENZIE, who was twice married;
first to Margaret, daughter of Sir Alexander Mackenzie,
Bart., X. of Gairloch, without issue; secondly, to Christina,
daughter of John Niven, brother to Clava, with issue—

1. *Harry*, died unmarried, in 1828.

2. *John*, of whom afterwards as III. of Glack.

3. *Roderick*, of Thornton, died unmarried, in 1858.

4. *James*, a Major in the 72d Highlanders, died unmarried, in India, in 1857.

5. *Mary*, became Lady Leith of Westhall, Inveramsay
and Thornton, in her own right, and is now the widow of
the late General Sir Alexander Leith, K.C.B., of Freefield
and Glenkindie—without issue.

6. *Rachel*, died unmarried.

7. *Christina*, of Foveran, died unmarried.

8. *Jean Forbes Una*, died unmarried.
He was succeeded by his eldest surviving son,

III. JOHN MACKENZIE, who inherited Thornton from
his brother Roderick, Foveran from his sister Christina, and
who acquired Inveramsay by purchase. He died unmarried,
in 1877, and was succeeded by his cousin, a son of his uncle
Donald,

IV. JOHN MACKENZIE, fourth and now of Glack, twice
married; first to Anne, daughter of Thomas Macgill, without issue; and secondly, to Margaret Campbell, daughter of
John Pendrill, Bath, by whom he has

1. *Duncan Campbell*, Rector of Shephall, married to Louisa,
daughter of Colonel O. G. Nicolls, by whom he has three
sons and four daughters—Donald, a Lieutenant in the
Royal Marines; Alan, Lieutenant in the Highland Rifle
Militia; Malcolm, Helen, Edith, Lilian, and Amy.

2. *John Pendrill*, married to Adelaide, daughter of Col.
Henry Thornton, by whom he has two daughters—Lucy
Eleanor, and Margaret Pendrill.

3. *Roderick B.*, married Josepha P., daughter of R. Igna-
tius Robertson, without issue.

4. *Margaret Campbell Pendrill*, unmarried.

5. *Mary*, unmarried.

THE MACKENZIES OF LOGGIE.

ALLAN MACKENZIE, II. of Hilton, had, by his wife, daughter of Alexander Dunbar of Conzie, third son of the Sheriff of Moray, two sons—(1) Murdoch, who, we have seen, succeeded as III. of Hilton ; (2) John, who was served heir to, and designated of, Loggie, a barony situated in the parish of the same name, now forming the western portion of the more modern parish of Urquhart, in the Black Isle.

I. JOHN MACKENZIE, first of Loggie, was the oldest cadet of the House of Hilton, from whom descended several persons distinguished for their literary attainments and valour. He married a daughter of Mackenzie of Gairloch (supposed to be John, the second baron) by whom he had one son, who succeeded,

II. ALLAN MACKENZIE, who married a daughter of Alastair Roy Mackenzie of Achilty, by whom he had—

1. *Donald*, his heir.

2. *William* (Murdoch?), who left an only daughter married to Murdoch Mackenzie, first of Little Findon, third son of Alexander Mackenzie of Killichrist, II. of Suddie.

He was succeeded by his eldest son,

III. DONALD MACKENZIE, who was three times married; first to· Catherine, fourth daughter of Murdoch Mackenzie, II. of Redcastle, without issue; secondly, to Annabella, eldest daughter, by his second marriage, of Alexander Mackenzie, V. of Gairloch. By her he had—

1. *Colin*, educated in medicine at the University of Aberdeen, and, going abroad, studied at Leyden and Paris under the most famous professors. Having received his degree of Doctor of Medicine at the University of Rheims, he returned home. But his adoption of extravagant theological doctrines, and his immoral conduct in his youth, caused him to be disinherited by his father, whereupon he again returned to the Continent. Having stayed abroad for several years, he returned to Inverness, where he practiced medicine with

success, and had a yearly pension settled on him until his death there, at a great age, in February 1708. Although a great admirer of the fair sex, so much so that he made choice of one of them for his spiritual guide, he died unmarried. This lady was the famous Antonia Bourignon, who tried to show that Christianity was quite worn out in the world, and that she was sent by God to restore it upon the old footing, as it was established originally by Christ and his Apostles.

2. *Alexander*, his successor.

3. *John*, educated in theology at the University of Aberdeen, and for several years chaplain to General Major Mackay's Regiment. After the Revolution he was appointed minister of Kirkliston, near Edinburgh, from which he soon retired to London, and having died there unmarried, was buried in St Martin's Church, Westminster.

4. *Murdoch*, who succeeded as V. of Loggie.

5. *Margaret*, first married to Roric Mackenzie, V. of Fairburn; secondly, to Hector Mackenzie of Bishop-Kinkell. .

6. *Christian*, married John Mackenzie, I. of Gruinard.

7. *Annabella*, married Mackenzie of Loggie, Lochbroom.

He married, thirdly, Anne, daughter of the Rev. Donald Morrison, minister in the Lews, by whom he had an only daughter, who married Angus Morrison, minister of Contin. He had also a natural son, Rory, a captain in the Confederate army under King William, who died in Holland unmarried, and is said to have been a gentleman of great honour and generosity. He was succeeded by his second son,

IV. ALEXANDER MACKENZIE, who was twice married; first, in 1667, to Jean, daughter of Alexander Mackenzie of Ballone; and secondly, to Catherine, second daughter of William Mackenzie of Belmaduthy, without issue by either. He was succeeded by his brother,

V. MURDOCH MACKENZIE, educated at the University of Aberdeen, but his inclination leading him to the army, he entered the Earl of Dumbarton's Regiment, where, by his merit and valour, he soon raised himself to the rank of captain. In Monmouth's rebellion, at the battle of Sedgmoor, on the 6th of February 1685, "the valiant Colonel Murdoch Mackenzie, under the command of Lord Feversham, signally distinguished himself." He and his company attacked the enemy with such bravery and resolution, that— excepting the officers—there were only nine of his men who were not either killed or wounded; and he himself had the honour of taking the Duke of Monmouth's standard, "twisting" it out of the standard-bearer's hand, and presenting it afterwards to King James VII. at Whitehall. For this service he was promoted to a colonelcy. He died in London, and was buried at St Martin's Church, Westminster. He married an English lady, by whom he had two sons and three daughters—

1. *Murdoch*, his heir.

2. *George*, a youth of promising parts, killed in a duel.

There is no record of the names or marriages of the daughters. He was succeeded by his eldest son,

VI. MURDOCH MACKENZIE, who continued to reside in London, and whose representatives are unknown.

THE MACKENZIES OF GAIRLOCH.

This family is descended from ALEXANDER, SIXTH
BARON OF KINTAIL, by his second wife, Margaret, daugh-
ter of Macdonald of Morar called by the Highlanders "Mac
Dhughail Mhorair." By this lady he had

I. HECTOR ROY MACKENZIE, generally known as "Eachainn Ruadh," the first of the family of Mackenzie who obtained possession of Gairloch. Hector played such an
important part in the history of his time that it will be
necessary to describe somewhat in detail the various matters of moment in which he was concerned. This has been,
to some extent, already done in his capacity of Tutor or
Guardian to his nephew, John of Killin, IX. of Kintail.

It has been conclusively established [pp. 81-82] that
Kenneth a Bhlair, VII. of Kintail, died in 1491, and that
his son, Kenneth Og, killed in the Torwood by the Laird of
Buchanan in 1497, outlived him and became one of the
Barons of Kintail, though there is no account of his ever
having been served heir. It has been affirmed that Duncan,
Kenneth a Bhlair's elder brother, predeceased him, and that,
consequently Hector Roy succeeded in the usual way, he
being the eldest surviving brother of the Chief, as legal
guardian of Kenneth Og, VIII. of Kintail. We have not
been able to establish this assertion ; but Duncan's name
does not appear after his brother's death in 1491 in any of
the MS. histories of the Clan nor in any official document
that we have seen in connection with it. The writer of the
Ardintoul MS. informs us distinctly that Duncan was dead,
and that Hector, his (John's) younger uncle "meddled with
the estate." The Earl of Cromarty says that "Hector Roy,
being a man of courage and prudence, was left Tutor by his
brother to Sir Kenneth, his owin brother-vterin Duncan
being of better hands than head. This Hector heiring of
Sir Kenneth's death, and finding himself in possession of
ane estait, to which those only now haid title whose birth-
right wes debatable, viz., the children begot by Kenneth
the 3d on the Lord Lovat's daughter, with whom he did at

first so irregularly and unlawfully cohabit." This objection, however, could not have applied to Duncan, nor to his son Allan, and it is difficult to understand on what ground Hector could have attempted to obtain possession of the estates for himself, unless it be true, as established to some extent hereafter, that he was joint-heir of Kintail; for it is beyond question that Allan, Duncan's eldest son and heir, who was entitled to succeed before Hector, was then alive. There is no evidence whatever to show that Hector Roy was at any time appointed Tutor to John of Killin until an arrangement was finally made between themselves, by which Hector was to act as such, and to keep the estates in his own hands, until John came of age.

Hector was undoubtedly in possession of vast estates in his own right at this period. When the factious party of the nobility, known as the Lords of the Association, took up arms against King James III., Alexander of Kintail sent his sons, Kenneth and Hector, with a retinue of 500, to join the Royal standard; but Kenneth, hearing of the death of his aged father, on his arrival at Perth, returned home at the request of the Earl of Huntly; and the Clan were led by Hector Roy to the battle of Sauchieburn, near Stirling; but after the defeat of the King's forces, and the death there, in 1488, of the King himself, Hector, who narrowly escaped, returned to Ross-shire and took the stronghold of Redcastle then held by Rose of Kilravock for the rebels, and placed a garrison in it. He then joined the Earl of Huntly and the other clans in the North who were again rising to avenge the death of the King; but meanwhile orders came from the youthful James IV., who had been at the head of the conspirators, ordering the Northern chiefs to lay down their arms, and to submit to the existing state of things. Thereupon Hector, yielding to necessity, submitted with the rest, and he was "not only received into favour, but, to reward his past fidelity, and also to engage him for the future, the young King, who at last saw his error, and wanted to reconcile to him those who had been the friends of his father, made him a present of the Barony of Gairloch in the western circuit of Ross-shire, by knight-service after the manner of that age. He likewise gave him Brahan in the low country, now a seat of the family of Seaforth, the land of Moy, in that neighbourhood, and, after-wards, Glasletter (of Strathglass), a royal forest which was made a part of the Barony of Gairloch. Not far from the pleasant valley of Strathpeffer is the Castle Leod, part of Hector's paternal estate, afterwards a seat of the Earl of Cromarty; Achterneed, near adjacent, also Kinellan, were likewise his, and so was the Barony of Allans, now Allan-grange, a few miles southward. In the chops of the High-lands he had Ferburn the Wester, and both the Scatwells, the Greater and the Less. Westward in the height of that country he had Kenlochew, a district adjoining to Gerloch on the east, and southward on the same track *he had the half of Kintail, of which he was left joint-heir with his brother Kenneth, chief of the family.*[*]

The original charters of Gairloch are now lost, but a " Protocol" from John de Vaux, Sheriff of Inverness, whose jurisdiction extended to the Northern counties, is conclusive as to their having existed :—

To all ande syndri to quham it afferis to quhays knawledge thir present letres sall to cum Johnne the Vaux burges off Dygvayll and Shireff in this pairt sendis gretyng in Gode euerlastande to yhur vniuersite (you universally) I make it knawyne that he the commande off our souerane lordis letres and precess under his quhyt wax direet(ed) to me as shireff in that part past, and grautis me to haff gwyne to Hector McKennyeh herytahyll stayt and possessioune of all and syndri the landis off Gerloch with thair pertineus after the forme and tenor off our souerane lordis chaiter maide to the forsaide Hector tharvpone the quhylkis land with their pertinens extendis yherly to tuelff merkis off auldo extent lyande be-twix the watteris callyde Innerew and Torvedene within the Shireffdome of In-uerness ande I grant me to haff gyffyne to the forsaide Heetor Herytahyll state and possessioune of all ,and syndri the forsaide landis with thair pertynens saffande vtheris menis ryehtis as owys (use) and eustum is charge—and in our souerane lordis nayme and myn as Shireff that nay man vex inquiet nor strubyll (trouble) the said Heetor nor his ayris in the pecyahyll brukynge and joysinge (enjoyment) of the landis forsaides vnder all payne and ehargis that efter may folow in wytness oft the quhylkis I haff append to thir myn letres off sesyng my seyll at Alydyll (? Talladale) in Garloch the x day of the moneth off December the zher off Gode ane thousande four hundreth nynte and four zheris befor thir

_____

[*] MS. History of the Family of Gairloch. Another MS. says that his pos-sessions in Kintail were "bounded by the rivers Kilfilene and Croe."

witnes Schir Doull Rurysone vicar of Urcharde, Murthy beg, Mak murquho,
Johnne Thomassone, Kenneth Meynlcyssoune ; Donalde Meynleyssoune ; Doull
Rluresone, and Duncan Lachlanscunc serieando with vtheris diuerse.

The next authentic document in his favour is a Precept,
by the King to the Chamberlain of Ross, commanding the
latter to obey a former precept given to Hector of the
males, &c., of Braane and Moy, as follows :—

> Chalmerlane of Ross, we grete·you weill fforsamekle as we direct(ed) oure
> speciale letres to you obefor (of before) making mentioun that we had gevin to
> oure louit Hector Roy Makkenze the males and proffites of oure landis of Braane
> and Moy with ariage cariange and vther pertinence tharof lyand within oure lord-
> schipe of Rosse for his gude and thankfull service done and to be done to us in-
> during oure will and that it was oure will that he had broukit and joisit (enjoyed)
> the saidis landis with all proffitis tharof induring our will and sa the tenandis
> now inhabitaris tharof hrouk thare takkis and nocht removit tharfra, the whilk
> letres as we are sckirlye (surely) infornit ye disoheit in great contemptioun and
> lichtleing of our autoritie riale (royal authority). Herfor we charge you zit as
> obefor that ye suffir the said Hector to brouk and jois the saidis landis and tak vp
> and haue all males fermez proffitis ariage cariage and deu seruice of the saidis
> landis and that the tenandis and inhabitaris tharof to answer and obey to him
> and to nane vtheris quhill (till) we gif command be oure speciale letres in the
> contrar, and this on na wise ye leif vndoue as ye will incur our indiguatioun and
> displeasour.   Thir our letrez senc and vnderstaud deliuer thame agane to the
> berar to be kepit and schevin be t'ie said Hector apoun compt for your warand
> befor our Comptrollar and auditoriouis of our chekker at your nixt compt, and
> after the forme of our said vther letres past obfore gevin vnder our signet at
> Edinburgh the fift day of Marche (1508) and of Regne the tuenty zere.
>
>   (Signed)   JAMES R.

It will thus be seen that Hector Roy had extensive
possessions of his own, and the dispute between him and
his nephew, John of Killin, fully described [pp. 81-101], has
probably arisen in respect of Hector's rights to the half of
Kintail which his father had left him jointly with his eldest
brother, Kenneth a Bhlair, VII. of Kintail. He kept possession of Islandonain Castle until compelled by an order
from the Privy Council to give it up to John of Killin in
1511, and it appears from proceedings before the Privy
Council [see pp. 98-99] that, from 1501 to 1508, Hector
continued to collect the rents of Kintail without accounting
for them ; that he again accounted for them for one year,
in 1509 ; and for the two following years the second time
retained them, while he seems to have kept undisturbed

possession of the stronghold of Islandonain throughout. We can find no record of his answer to the summons to appear before the Privy Council, if he ever did put in an appearance; but in all probability he kept possession to compel his nephew to come to terms with him about his joint rights to Kintail, without any intention of ultimately keeping John of Killin out of possession. This view is strengthened by the fact that John obtained a new charter under the Great Seal granting him Kintail anew on the 25th of February 1508-9*—the same year in which Hector Roy received a grant of Brahan and Moy—probably following on an arrangement of their respective rights in those districts; also from the fact that Hector does not appear to have fallen into disfavour with the Crown for his conduct to John of Kintail; for only two years after he brought the action against Hector before the Privy Council, he receives a new charter, under the Great Seal, of Gairloch, Glasletter, and Coirre-nan-Cuilean, dated 8th of April 1513,† "in feu and heritage for ever," and he and his nephew appear ever after to have lived on the most friendly terms. Gairloch, originally the possession of the Earls of Ross, and confirmed to them by Robert Bruce in 1306 and 1329, was granted by Earl William to Paul M'Tyre, and his heirs by Mary Grahame, for a yearly payment of a penny of silver in name of blench ferne in lieu of every other service except the foreign service of the King when required. In 1372 King Robert II. confirmed the grant. In 1430 King James I. granted to Nele Nelesoun (Neil son of Neil Macleod) for his homage and service in the capture of his deceased brother, Thomas Nelesoun, a rebel, the lands of Gairloch.‡

Though Hector Roy was in possession of Crown Charters to Gairloch, he found it most difficult to obtain possession from the Macleods, and their chief Allan MacRory. This Allan married, first, a daughter of Alexander Ionraic, .VI. of Kintail, and sister of Hector Roy, by whom he had

---

* Reg. of the Great Seal, vol. xv., fol. 80.
† The original charter is in the Gairloch Charter Chest.
‡ Origines Parochiales Scotiae, vol. ii., p. 406.

U

issue two (or three) sons.   He married, secondly, a daughter
of Roderick Macleod of the Lews, by whom he had one son.
Roderick determined to murder all the male issue of the
Macleods of Raasay, and those of Gairloch by Mackenzie's
daughter, that his own grandson, by Allan's second marriage, might succeed.   With this view he invited all the
members of the two families—with whom he was connected
by his marriage with the widow of Mackay of Reay, a
daughter of Mackenzie of Kintail—to the Island of Isay,
pretending that he had matters of great consequence to
communicate to them.   All the members of both families
and their more immediate relatives and friends accepted the
invitation.   Roderick feasted them sumptously, on their
arrival, at a great banquet.   In the middle of the festivities
he informed them of his desire to have each man's advice
separately, and that he would afterwards make known to all
of them the momentous business to be considered, and
which closely concerned each of them.   He then retired
into a separate apartment, and called them one by one,
when they were each, as they entered, stabbed with dirks
through the body by a set of murderous villains whom he
had appointed for the purpose.   Not one of the family of
Raasay was left alive except a boy nine years of age, who
was being fostered from home, and who had been sent
privately, when the news of the massacre had gone abroad,
to the Laird of Calder, who kept him in safety during his
minority.   He afterwards obtained possession of Raasay,
and became known as Gillechallum Garbh MacGhille-
challum.   Macleod of Gairloch's sons, by Hector Roy's
sister, were all murdered.   Roderick placed his own grandson in an inner room, where, walking with his brutal relative,
he heard one of his brothers cry on being stabbed by the
assassins' dirk, and said, " Yon's my brother's cry."   " Hold
your peace," old Rory replied, "yonder cry is to make you
laird of Gairloch; he is the son of one of Mackenzie's
daughters."   The boy, dreading his own life might be
sacrificed, held his tongue, "but afterwards he did what in
him lay in revenging the cruel death of his brothers and

kinsmen on the murtherers."* The same writer informs us
that "this was the first step that Hector Roy Mackenzie
gote to Gairloch. . . . His brother-in-law, Allan Macleod, gave him the custody of their rights, but when he
found his nephews were murdered, he took a new gift of it
to himself, and going to Garloch with a number of Kintail
men and others, he took a heirschip with him, but such as
were alive of the Shiol 'ille Challum of Garloch, followed
him·and fought him at a place called Glasleoid, but they
being beat, Hector carried away the heirschip. After this
and several other skirmishes, they were content to allow him
the two-thirds of Gairloch, providing he would let themselves
possess the other third in peace, which he did, and they kept
possession till Hector's great-grandchild put them from it."

The Earl of Cromarty, and the other MS. historians of
the family, corroborate this. Earl George says that Hector
"incited to revenge" by the foul murder of his nephews,
made some attempts to oust the Macleods from Gairloch
during John of Killin's minority, but was not willing to
engage in a war with such a powerful chief as Macleod of
Lews, while he felt himself insecure in his other possessions,
but after arranging matters amicably with his nephew, cf
Kintail, and being now master of a fortune and possessions
suitable to his mind and quality, he resolved to avenge the
murder and to "make it productive of his own advantage."
He summoned all those who were accessory to the assass-
ination of his sister's children before the Chief Justice.
Their well-grounded fears made them absent themselves
from Court. Hector, according to another authority, produced the bloody shirts of the murdered boys ; whereupon
the murderers were declared fugitives and outlaws, and a
commission granted in his favour for their pursuit, " which
he did so resolitly manadge that in a short tyme he kiled
many, preserved some to justice, and forced the remainder
to a compositione advantagious to himselfe. . . . His
successors, who were both active and prudent men, did

* Ancient MS. History.

thereafter acquire the rest from their unthrifty neighbours."
The greatest defeat that Hector ever gave to the Macleods
" was at Bealach Glasleod, near Kintail, where most of them
were taekin or killed." At this fight Duncan Mòr na
Tuaighe, who so signally distinguished himself at Blar-na-
Pairc, was present with Hector, and on being told that four
men were at once attacking his son Dugal, he answered,
" Well, if he be my son there is no hazard for that," a
remark which turned out quite true, for the hero killed the
four Macleods, and came off himself without any serious
wounds.*

In acknowledgment of the King's favour, Hector
gathered his immediate followers in the west, joined his
nephew, John of Killin, with his vassals, and fought, in
command of the Clan, at the disastrous battle of Flodden,
from which both narrowly escaped; but most of their followers were slain. Some time after his return he successfully fought the desperate skirmish at Druim-a-chait,
described at pp. 86-90, with only 140 men against 700 of
the Munros, Dingwalls, Maccullochs, and other tribes, under
the command of William Munro of Fowlis, on which
occasion Sheriff Vass of Lochslin was killed at a bush near
Dingwall, " called to this day Preas Sandy Vass," or Alex.
Vass's bush, a name assigned to it for that very cause.†

Hector, during his life, granted to his nephew, John of
Killin, his own half of Kintail, Kinellan, Fairburn, Wester
Brahan, and other possessions situated in the Low Country,
which, as will be seen hereafter, brought his son, John Glassich, into trouble.‡

Hector Roy was betrothed to a daughter of the Laird of

---

* " Duncan in his old days was very assisting to Hector, Garloch's predecessor, against the Macleods of Gairloch, for he, with his son Dugal, who was a
strong, prudent, and courageous man, with ten or twelve other Kintailmen, were
alwise, upon the least advertisement, ready to go and assist Hector, whenever,
wherever, and in whatever he had to do, for which cause there has been a friendly
correspondence betwixt the family of Gerloch and the MacRas of Kintail, which
still continues."—*Genealogy of the MacRas.*

† Gairloch MS.

‡ Gairloch MS.

Grant, but she died before the marriage was solemnised. He, however, had a son by her called Hector Càm, he being blind of one eye, to whom he gave Achterneed and Culte-Leod, now Castle Leod, as his patrimony. Hector Càm married a daughter of Mackay of Farr, by whom he had two sons, Alexander Roy and Murdo.* Alexander married a daughter of John Mòr na Tuaighe MacGillechallum, a brother of Macleod of Raasay; by whom she had a son, Hector, who lived at Kinellan, was nicknamed the Bishop, married a daughter of Macleod of Raasay, and left a large family, one of whom was afterwards married to Murdo Mackenzie of Achilty. Hector Càm's second son, Murdo, also left issue.

Hector Roy, after the death of Grant's daughter, married Anne Macdonald, a daughter of Ronald MacRanald, gener-ally called Ronald Bàn, the Laird of Moidart. She was the widow of William Dubh Macleod of Harris, Dunvegan, and Glenelg, by whom she had a daughter, who, by Hector Roy's influence at Court, was married to Rory Mor of Acha-ghluineachan, ancestor of the Mackenzies of Fairburn and Achilty, after she had by him a natural son, Murdoch, who became progenitor of the family of Fairburn. By this marriage Hector had four sons and three daughters.

1. *John Glassich*, his heir.

2. *Kenneth* of Meikle Allan, now Allangrange, who married a daughter of Alexander Dunbar of Kilbuyack and widow of Allan Mackenzie, II. of Hilton.

3. *John Tuach*, who inherited Scatwell, and

* "These were both succeeded by the son of Alexander, a slothful man who dotingly bestowed his estates on his foster child, Sir Roderick Mackenzie of Coigeach, in detriment to his own children, though very deserving of them, Captain Hector Mackenzie, late of Dumbarton's Regiment, and also a tribe in the Eastern circuit of Ross, surnamed from one of their progenitors, Mac Eanin, *i.e.*, the descendants of John the Fair.—*Gairloch MS.* Another MS. gives the additional names of—"Richard Mackenzie, vintner in Edinburgh, grandson of Alexander Mackenzie of Calder, Midlothian ; Duncan Mackenzie, an eminent gunsmith in London ; and James Mackenzie, gunsmith in Dundee." It also adds that of the successors of the Mac Eanins in Easter Ross, were "Master Alexander Mackenzie, an Episcopal minister in Edinburgh ; and preceptor to the children of the present noble family of Cromarty, whose son is Charles Mackenzie, clerk to Mr David Munro of Meikle Allan."

4. *Dugal Roy.*

The daughters married respectively, Bayne of Tulloch, John Aberach Mackay, and James Bayne Fraser of Bunchrew, a natural son of Lord Lovat, killed at Blar-na-Leine, ancestor of the Frasers of Reelick. Hector had also a son, John Beg, who, according to some authorities, was illegitimate, and from whom descended some Mackenzies who settled in Berwick and Alloa.

Hector died in 1528. On the 8th of September of that year, a grant is recorded to Sir John Dingwall, "Provost of Trinity College, besyd Edinburgh, of the ward of the lands of Garlocht, quhilkis pertenit to umquhill Achinroy Mackenzie." He was succeeded by his eldest lawful son,

II. JOHN GLASSICH MACKENZIE, who appears from the above-quoted document to have been a minor at his father's death. His retour of service is not extant, but an instrument of sasine, dated 24th of June 1536, in his favour, is in the Gairloch charter chest, in which he is designated "John Hector-son," and in which he is said to be heir, served and retoured to his father, Hector Roy Mackenzie, of the lands of Gairloch, and the Grazings of Glasletter and Coirre-nan-Cuilean. John is said to have objected to his father's liberality during his life in granting, at the expense of his own successors, to his nephew, John of Killin, so much of his patrimonial possessions. According to the Gairloch MS. already quoted he gave him his half of Kintail, Kinellan, Fairburn, the Wester Brahan, and "other possessions in the Low Country besides." John thought these donations exorbitant, and therefore "sought to retrench them by recovering in part what with so much profusion his father had given away, and for that, a feud having ensued betwixt him and his chief, he was surprised in his house by night, according to the barbarious manner of the times, and sent prisoner to Iland Downan, and there taken away by poison in A.D. 1550. His brother Dugal, who sided with him, and John (Beg), his natural brother, were both slain in the same quarrel."[*]

* Gairloch MS. Another MS. says that John Tuach was assassinated the same night.

A bond, dated 1544, has been preserved by the Spalding Club, to which John Glassich's name, among others, is adhibited, undertaking to keep the peace, and promising obedience to Kenneth, younger of Kintail (Kenneth na Cuirc), as the Queen's Lieutenant.[*] John's obedience does not appear, however, to have been very complete. Mackenzie of Kintail having, according to another authority, received information of John's intention to recover if possible part of the property given away by his father, sent for him to Brahan, where he came, accompanied by a single attendant, John Gearr. The Chief charged him with designs against him, and John's asseverations and vindication proving unsatisfactory, he caused him to be apprehended. His attendant, John Gearr, seeing this, drew his two-handed sword and made a fierce onslaught on the Chief who sat at the head of the table and smartly bowed his head under it, or he would have been cloven asunder. John Gearr was instantly seized by Mackenzie's guards, who threatened to tear him to pieces, but the Chief, admiring his fidelity, strictly charged them not to touch him. John Gearr was questioned as to why he had struck at Mackenzie himself and took no notice of those who apprehended his master, when he boldly replied that "he saw no one else present whose life was a worthy exchange for that of his own Chief." The sword made a deep gash in the table, and the mark, which was deep enough to admit of one's hand being placed edgeways in it, remained in it until Colin, first Earl of Seaforth, caused the piece to be cut off, saying, that "he loved no such remembrance of the quarrels of his relations."

John Glassich, by all accounts, was neither too circumspect in his conduct at home and among his neighbours, nor a dutiful and loyal subject to his Sovereign. In 1547 his property was forfeited to the Crown, for refusing to join the Royal Standard, and the escheat thereof granted to the Earl of Sutherland, as will be seen by the following document :—

* Spalding Miscellany, vol. iv., p. 213.

Ane lettre maid to Johnne Erle of Suthirland his airis assignais ane or ma o
the gift of all gudis mouable and vnmouable dettis takkis stedingis cornis obliga-
tionis sowmes of money gold silver cunzeit and vncunzeit and vtheris gudis
quhatsumouir quhilkis pertenit to Johne Hectorsoune of Garloch and now per-
teining to our souerane lady he reson of eschete throu the said Johnis tresonable
remaning and hyding at hame fra the oist and army devisit to conuene at Peblis
. the x day of Julii instant for recoucring of the hous at Langbalme furth of oure
auld Inymies handis of Ingland in contrare the tennour of the lettres and pro-
clamationis maid thairupon Incurrand thairthrou the panis contenit thairuntill
or ony vther wise sal happin to perlene to us our souorane he resoun fuirsaid
wyth power etc. At Sanct androis the xxiiij day Julii The year of God Im.
Vc. xlvij (1547) yeris.*

There is no trace in the Privy Council Records of the
reversal of this forfeiture; but it does not appear to have.
affected the succession. Indeed it is not likely that it
even affected the actual possession, for it was difficult even
for the Earl of Sutherland, backed up by Royal authority,
to wield any substantial power in such an out-of-the-way
region as John Glassich's possessions in the west. We have
already stated that in 1551 the ·Queen granted to John
Mackenzie of Kintail and his apparent heir, Kenneth na
Cuirc, a remission for the violent taking of John Glassich,
Dougal, and John Tuach, his brothers, and for keeping
them in prison, thus usurping "thairthrou our Souerane
Lady·is autorite." Neither of them is spoken of in this remission as being then deceased, though tradition and the family
MS. history has it that John Glassich was poisoned or starved
to death at Islandonain Castle in 1550.† It is possible,
however, that Kintail found it convenient to conceal John's
death until the remission had been already secured. Only

* Reg. Sec. Sig., xxi., fol. 31b..

† One of the family MSS. has it that by his marriage "he got the lands of Kinkell, Kilbokie, Badinearb (?), Pitlundie, Davochcairn, Davochpollo, and Foynish,
with others in the Low Country, for which the family has been in the use to
quarter the arms of Fraser with their own. This John, becoming considerably
rich and powerful by these different acquisitions, became too odious to and
envied by John, Laird of Mackenzie, and his son Kenneth then married to
Stewart, Earl of Athole's daughter, that they set upon him, having previously
invited him to a Christmas dinner, having got no other pretence than a fit of
jealousy on account of the said Earl's daughter, bound him with ropes and carried
him a prisoner to Islandownan, where his death was occasioned by poison admin-
istered to him in a mess of milk soup by one MacCalman, a clergyman and
Depaty-Constable of the Fort."

six weeks after the date of the "respitt" we find John Glassich, referred to in the Council Records, under date of 25th July 1551, as the "omquhile (or late) Johne McCanze of Garlocht," his lands having then been given in ward to the Earl of Athol "ay and quhill (till) the lauchful entre of the rychtuis air or airis thairto being of lauchfull age."[*]

Though Hector Roy Mackenzie obtained a charter of Gairloch in 1494, the Macleods continued for a time to hold possession of a considerable portion of it. According to the traditions of the district they had all to the east and south east of the Crasg, a hill situated on the west side of the churchyard of Gairloch, between the present Free and Established Churches. At the east end of the Big Sand, on an elevated and easily defended rock, stood the last stronghold occupied by the Macleods of Gairloch—to this day known as the "Dun" or fort. The foundation is still easily traced. It must have been a place of considerable importance, its circumference being over 200 feet. Various places are still pointed out in Gairloch where desperate skirmishes were fought between the Macleods and the Mackenzies. Several of these spots, where the slain were buried, look quite green to this day. The "Fraoch Eilean," opposite Leac-na-Saighid, where a naval engagement was fought, is a veritable cemetery of Macleods, ample evidence of which is yet to be seen. Of this engagement, and of those at Glasleoid, Lochan-Neigh, Leac-na-Saighid, Kirkton, and many others, thrilling accounts are still recited by a few old men in the district; especially of the prowess of Domh'ull Odhar Mac Ian Leith, and the other Kintail heroes who were mainly instrumental in establishing the Mackenzies of Gairloch permanently and in undisputed possession of their beautiful and romantic inheritance. Hector Roy and John Glassich succeeded in driving the Macleods out of the country, but they often returned, accompanied occasionally by their relatives, the Macleods of Lews, whose Chief, until the death of Torquil Dubh Mac-

---

[*] Reg. Sec. Con., vol. xxiv., fol. 84.

leod of the Lews, the Macleods of Gairloch and Raasay acknowledged as their superior.

John Glassich married Agnes, daughter of James Fraser of Foyness, with issue—

1. *Hector*, his heir.

2. *Alexander*, and

3. *John*, who succeeded each other in succession.

He had also two natural sons before his marriage— *Alexander Roy* and *Hector Caol.**

John Glassich died in 1550, at Islandonain Castle, was buried in the Priory of Beauly, and succeeded by his eldest lawful son,

III. HECTOR MACKENZIE, in whose favour there is a sasine dated 6th May 1563,† in which he is described as "Achyne Johannis McAchyne," and bearing that the lands had been in non-entry twelve years, thus carrying back the date of his succession to the year 1551, when they were given in ward to John, fourth of the Stewart Earls of Athole.

---

* *Alexander Roy* had a son John, who lived at Coirre Mhic Dhomhnuill in Torridon, and who had a son, Mr Murdoch Mackenzie, Chaplain to Lord Reay's Regiment in the Bohemian and Swedish service, under Gustavus Adolphus. This clergyman was afterwards made Bishop of Moray and Orkney in succession. He had a son, Sir Alexander of Broomhill and Laird of Pitarrow in Kincardine, father of Colonel Alexander Mackenzie of Hampton, Virginia, who left his English estates to his nephew, Mr.Young of Castleyards, Kirkwall. He had also a daughter, Jacobina Mackenzie, who settled in Dundee. The Bishop had a brother, Alexander, who settled in Strathnaver, at that time the property of Lord Reay, of whom were descended Mr Hector Mackenzie, an Episcopal clergyman at Inverness, and father to James and Alexander, ministers in Edinburgh. The learned Dr James Mackenzie of Drumshiuch, a distinguished physician, and author of "The History of Health," and Mr William Mackenzie, schoolmaster, afterwards lost on the coast of Guinea, were also grandsons of this Bishop Mackenzie. He had another son, Mackenzie of Groundwater, who left a son, Thomas Mackenzie, a merchant in Kirkwall, whose brothers were the learned Murdoch Mackenzie, navigator to his Majesty "known by his accurate surveys of the Western Coasts of Great Britain and Ireland, and whose abilities will render him famous to posterity," and James Mackenzie, a writer, once in the service of the Earl of Morton, in the Orkney Islands, and author of a treatise on Security. Another of the Bishop's descendants was James Mackenzie, author of one of the Gairloch MS. histories, to whose services we are not a little indebted, though he attempts to make his ancestor legitimate at the expense of correct genealogy. *Hector Caol* left a numerous tribe in Gairloch, still known as Clann Eachainn Chaoil, and said to be distinguished by their long, slender legs.

† Gairloch Charter Chest.

Hector died—probably killed, like his brothers—without issue, in September 1566, and was succeeded by his next lawful brother,

ALEXANDER MACKENZIE, who has a retour, as heir to "Hector, his brother-german," in the lands of Gairloch—namely, "Garloch, Kirktoun, Syldage, Hamgildail, Malefage, Innerasfidill, Sandecorran, Cryf, Baddichro, Bein-Sanderis, Meall, Allawdall, with the pasturage of Glaslettir and Cornagullan, in the Earldom of Ross, of the old extent of £8;" but not to any of the other lands which Hector Roy is said to have left to his descendants. This retour is dated 2d December 1566.* Alexander did not long possess the estates, for he died, to all appearance—probably killed—a few weeks after his succession, without making up any titles. It is, therefore, not thought necessary to reckon him as one of the Barons of Gairloch.

It is very probable that the brothers, Hector and Alexander, met with the same fate as their father, John Glassich, John Tuach, and John Beg, and by the same authors. This is in accordance with local tradition, and an old MS. which says that Agnes Fraser fled with John Roy "to Lovat and her Fraser relatives," adds regarding the fate of his brothers—" In those days many acts of oppression were committed that could not be brought to fair tryales befor the Legislator." "She was afterwards married to Chisholm of Comar, and heird his family, here she keepd him, in as conceald a manner as possible, and, as is reported, every night under a Brewing Kettle; those who, through the barbarity of the times, destroyed the father and uncles, being in search of the son, and in possession of his all excepting his mother's dower. He was afterwards conceald by the Lairds of Moydart and of Farr, till he became a handsome man and could putt on his weapon, when he hade the resolution to waitte of Colin Camme Mackenzie, Laird of Kintail, a most worthy gentleman who established him in all his lands, excepting those parts of the family

* Ing. Retour Reg., vol. i., fol. 22, and Origines Parochiales.

estate for which Hector and his successors hade an undoubted right by writs."

He was succeeded by his brother,

IV. JOHN ROY MACKENZIE, Hector Roy's third son,
who was still a minor, though his father had been dead for
15 or 16 years, and the estate was, in 1567, given in ward
by Queen Mary, who "granted in heritage to John Baner-
man of Cardenye, the ward of the lands and rents belonging
to the deceased Hector Makkenych of Garloch, with the relief of the same when it should occur, and the marriage of
John Roy Makkenych the brother and apparent heir of
Hector."* In 1569, John Roy being then of "lauchful age,"
is served and retoured heir to his brother-german, Hector, in
his lands of Gairloch,† as specified in the service of 1566,
passing over Alexander, undoubtedly because he never made
up titles to the estate. The retour of 1569 gives the date of
Hector's death as 30th September 1566. In 1574 John Roy
has a sasine which bears that the lands were seven and
a-half years in non-entry. This takes it back to the date
of Hector's death, three months before the gift of ward to
John Bannerman. In the same year he acquired half the
lands of Ardnagrask from Lovat, partly in exchange for
the rights he had inherited in Phoineas from his mother, he
being described by Lovat in the disposition, according to
an old inventory, as "the son, by her first husband, of his
kinswoman Agnes Fraser." From this it may be reasonably assumed that John Glassich's widow had made over
her rights to her son during her life, or that she had by this
time died.

We find from the old inventory already quoted that there
was a Charter of Alienation by Hugh Fraser of Guisachan,
dated 29th May 1582, and it appears from it that John Roy
acquired Davochcairn and Davochpollo, in Strathpeffer, in
1574, from this Hugh Fraser, and that in the first-named year
he also obtained from him the lands of Kinkell-Clarsach
and Pitlundie, in terms of a Contract of Sale dated 26th of

---

* Origines Parochiales Scotiae, p. 406, and Reg. Sec. Sig., vol. xxxvi. fol. 6.
† Inq. Retour Reg., vol. i., fol. 22, and Origines Parochiales.

January 1581. The charter is confirmed by James VI. in 1583. It appears from his daughter's retour of service * that the baron's eldest son, John, died in 1601. He had been infeft by his father in Davochpollo and Pitlundie, and married Isabel, daughter of Alexander Mackenzie of Fairburn, by whom he had a daughter, also named Isabel, who married Colin Mackenzie of Strathgarve, brother to Kenneth, first Lord Mackenzie of Kintail, and first of the Mackenzies of Kinnock and Pitlundie. Colin entered into a lawsuit with Alexander of Gairloch, probably in connection with this marriage, " to cut him out of his Low Country estate."† In 1657 she mortgaged Davochpollo and Pitlundie to her cousin, Kenneth of Gairloch; and her successor, John Mackenzie of Pitlundie, completed the sale to him, which brought the property back to the Gairloch family.‡

In 1606 John Roy received a charter of resignation in favour of himself in life-rent, and of his son Alexander in fee, erecting Gairloch into a free barony; and in 1619 he obtained another charter,§ under the Great Seal, in which Kinkell is included in the Barony, and constituted its chief messuage. John Roy built the first three stories of the Tower of Kinkell, " where his arms and those of his first wife are parted her pale above the mantlepiece of the great hall."‖

The only son of Roderick Macallan of Gairloch, who

* Ing. Retours Reg., vol. viii., fol. 284b.

† Colin of Kinnock, who entered a lawsuit against Alexander Mackenzie of Gairloch, meaning to cut him out of his Low Country estates, and being powerfully supported by Mackenzie of Fairburn and Mr John Mackenzie of Tolly, minister of Dingwall, a plodding clergyman, kept him sixteen sessions at Edinburgh ; the last year of which Gairloch and his brother Kenneth seeing Lord Kintail insulted by the Earl of Glencairn, who was supported by most of those on the street, put on their armour and came directly to his assistance, and rescuing him from imminent danger brought him to their lodging. No sooner was the tumult over than they embraced very cordially, and the whole matter in debate was instantly taken away, and Gairloch got a present of 600 merks to finish the Tower of Kinkell, of which his father (John Roy) only built three stories—*Gairloch MS.*

‡ Papers in the Gairloch Charter Chest.

§ These charters are in the Gairloch Charter Chest.

‖ Gairloch MS.

survived the massacre by his uncle, Roderick Macleod of the
Lews, in the absence of young Macgillechallum Garbh of
Raasay, under the care of the Laird of Calder, possessed
himself of Raasay and took up his quarters in Castle Broch-
ail, the ancient residence of the Chiefs of the Macleods ; and
of which the ruins are still to be seen on the east side of the
island. Seeing this, Donald Macneill, who previously sent
young Macleod of Raasay to be under the protection of Calder,
brought back the rightful heir, and kept him, in private,
until an opportunity occurred by which he could obtain
possession of the castle. This he soon managed by coming
to terms with the commander of the stronghold, who preferred the native heir to his relative of the Gairloch Macleods. It was arranged, that when Macneill should arrive at
the castle with his charge, access should be given to him. The
commander kept his word, and Macgillechallum Garbh was
soon after proclaimed Laird of Raasay.

In 1610 the severe skirmish at Lochan-Neigh, in Glen
Torridon, was fought between the Mackenzies—led by Alexander, since his brother's death in 1601, the apparent heir
of Gairloch—and the Macleods, under command of John
MacAllan Mhic Rory, only surviving male representative of
Allan Macleod of Gairloch, accompanied by his uncle, John
Tolmach Macleod. John MacAllan was taken prisoner ;
many of his followers were killed, seventeen or eighteen
taken prisoner, and the few who escaped with John Tolmach were pursued out of the district. In the following
year (1611) Murdoch Mackenzie, a younger son of Gairloch,
accompanied by Alexander Bayne, apparent heir of Tulloch, and several men from Gairloch, sailed to the Isle of Skye
in a vessel loaded with wine and other commodities. It is
asserted by some that Murdoch's intention was to apprehend
John Tolmach, while others maintain that his object was to
secure the daughter of Donald Dubh MacRory, who was a
cousin of John MacAllan, at the time a prisoner in Gairloch,
and his heir of line, in marriage. The latter is the most
probable, and is the unbroken tradition in Gairloch. By
such a union, failing issue by John, who was well secured in

captivity by John Roy, the ancient rights of the Macleods would become vested in the Gairloch family, and a troublesome dispute would be settled for ever, especially if John Tolmach was secured at the same time. We may easily conceive how both objects would probably become combined ; but whatever may have been the real object of the trip to Skye, it in the end proved fatal. The ship found its way —intentionally on the part of the crew, or forced by a severe storm—to a sheltered bay off Kirkton of Raasay, where the young laird, a son of Macgillechallum Garbh, at the time resided. Here it was deemed advisable to cast anchor ; and young Raasay, hearing that Murdoch Mackenzie was on board, consulted a friend, Macgillechallum Mòr Machomhnuill Mhic Neill, who persuaded him to visit the ship as a friend, and arrange to secure young Mackenzie by stratagem, with the view to get him afterwards exchanged for their relative, John MacAllan Mhic Rory, still a prisoner in Gairloch. Acting on this advice, young Raasay, Gillechallum Mòr, and twelve of their men, started for the ship, leaving word with his bastard brother to get all the men in Raasay in readiness to go out to their assistance in small boats as soon as the alarm was given. Mackenzie received his visitors in the most hospitable and unsuspecting manner, supplying them with as much wine and other viands as they could consume, and sat down with them himself. Four of his men, however, felt a little suspicious, and fearing the worst consequences, abstained from drinking. Alexander Bayne of Tulloch and the rest of Murdoch's men partook of the good things to excess, and ultimately became so drunk that they all retired to sleep below deck. Mackenzie sat between Raasay and Macgillechallum Mòr, without any concern, when the former, seeing him alone, started up, turned suddenly round upon him, and told him that he must become his prisoner. Murdoch instantly got up in a violent passion, laid hold of Raasay by the middle and threw him down, exclaiming, " I would scorn to be your prisoner." One of Raasay's followers seeing his chief treated thus, drew his dirk and stabbed Mackenzie through the body, who, finding himself wounded, jumped back to draw his sword, and his foot coming against some obstruction, he stumbled and fell overboard. Those on shore having heard the row, came out with their small boats, and seeing Mackenzie, who was a dexterous swimmer, manfully making for Scousar on the opposite shore of Skye, pelted him with stones, and drowned him. The few of his men who kept themselves sober, seeing him thus perish, resolved to sell their lives dearly, and fighting like heroes, they killed the young Laird of Raasay, Macgillechallum Mòr, author of all the mischief, and his two sons; but young Bayne of Tulloch and the six inebriated companions who followed him under deck hearing the uproar, attempted to come up, and were all killed by the Macleods as soon as they presented themselves through the hold. But not a soul of the Raasay men ultimately escaped alive from the swords of the four heroes who kept themselves free from the influence of the viands, and who were ably supported by the crew of the vessel. The small boats now began to congregate around the ship, and the Raasay men attempted to get on board; but they were thrown back and slain, and pitched into the sea without mercy. The shot and ammunition having become exhausted, all the pots and pans, and other articles of furniture which could be made of any service were hurled at the Macleods, while our four abstainers plied their more warlike weapons with deadly effect. Having procured a lull from the attempts of the enemy, they began to pull in anchor, when a shot from one of the boats at a distance killed one of the four heroes, Hector MacKenneth, "a pretty young gentleman." The other three seeing him killed, and all of them being more or less seriously wounded, they cut their anchor cable, hoisted canvas, and sailed away before a fresh breeze, with their horrid cargo of dead bodies lying about the deck. As soon as they got out of danger, they determined to throw the bodies of Raasay and his men overboard, that they might receive the same treatment as their own master, whose body they were unable to search for. It is reported that none of the bodies were ever found, except that of Macgillechallum Mòr, which came ashore, and was afterwards buried in Raasay. They carried the bodies of Bayne of Túlloch and of his companions to Lochcarron, where they were properly buried. The three survivors were John Mac-Eachainn Chaoil, John MacKenneth Mhic Eachainn, and Kenneth MacSheumais. The first named lived for thirty years after, dying in 1641; the second died in 1662; and the third in 1663—all very old men. Among the slain was a son of Mackenzie of Badachro, a cadet of the House of Gairloch, who is said to have signally distinguished himself.* This sanguine skirmish seems to have been the last which took place between the Mackenzies of Gairloch and the Macleods, and the former appear to have held undisputed possession of the whole of Gairloch from that day to this. Their conduct has, however, for years been such that they deemed it prudent to obtain a remission from the Crown for their lawless conduct, which was duly granted, in 1614, by James VI.†

* Allangrange, Ardintoul, and Letterfearn MSS., and Sir Robert Goidou's Earldom of Sutherland. For traditional Gaelic account, taken down from the recitation of Kenneth Fraser in Gairloch, see *Celtic Magazine*, vol. iii., pp. 192-4.

† The document, slightly modernised in spelling, is as follows :--"James R. —Our Sovereign Lord understanding the manifold cruel and barbarous tyrannies and oppressions so frequent within the Highlands and Isles, of that (part of) his Highness's Kingdom of Scotland, before his Majesty's departure furth of the same, that one part of the inhabitants thereof being altogether void of the true fear of God, and not regarding that true and loyal obedience they ought to his Majesty in massing and drawing themselves together in troops and companies, and after a most savage and insolent form committing depredations, rieves, 'slouthis," and cruel slaughters against the most honest, godlie, and industrious sort of people dwelling within and bewest the said bounds, who were a ready prey to the said oppressors, so that the said honest and peaceable subjects were oft and sundry times, for defence of their own lives, their wives and children, forced to enter into actions of hostility against the said limmers and broken men who oft and diverse times invaded and pursued them with fire and sword, reft and spuilzied their whole goods, among whom his Majesty understanding that his Highness's lovites and true and obedient subjects, John Mackenzie of Gairloch, Alexander, Kenneth, Duncan and William Mackenzie, his sons, dwelling within the Highlands most 'ewest' the Isles of Skye and Lewis, who many and sundry times before his Majesty's going to England, has been most cruelly invaded and pursued with fire and sword by sundry of the said vagabonds and broken men dwelling and resorting in the Skye and Lewis and other bounds of the Highlands where they dwell, and has therethrew sustained many and great slaughters, depredations

X

John Roy purchased or rented the tithes of his lands, which appear to have led him into no end of disputes. A certain Mr Alexander Mackenzie was appointed minister at Gairloch—the first after the Reformation ; and in 1583 he had to get a decree from the Lords of the Privy Council and Session ordaining the teind revenue to be paid to him. At the Reformation Sir John Broik appears to have been

and heirschips, so that in the very action of the said invasions and hostilities pursued against them, the said persons in defence of their own lives, their wives' and children's and of their goods, has slain sundry of the said invaders and lim- mers, taken others of them, and thereafter put them to death, to the great com- fort of his Majesty's good, honest, and true subjects who were subject to the like inroads, invasions, and tyrannies of the said vagabonds and fugitives and settling of his Majesty's peace within the bounds ; and his Majesty being noways willing that the said John Mackenzie of Gairloch and his said sons' forwardness in their own defence, and withstanding of the foresaid open and violent hostilities and tyran- nies of the said broken men which has produced so much and good benefit to his Majesty's distressed subjects, shall suffer any hurt, prejudice, or inconvenience against the said John Mackenzie of Gairloch and his said sons, which his High- ness by these letters decrees and declares to have been good and acceptable service done to his Highness and the country : Therefore, his Majesty, of his especial grace, mercy, and favour, ordains ane letter to be made under his High- ness's Great Seal in due form to the said John Mackenzie of Gairloch, Alexander, Kenneth, Duncan, and William Mackenzie, his sons, remitting and forgiving them and every one of them all rancour, hatred, action, and crime whatsoever that his Majesty had, has, or anywise may lay to the charge of the said John Mackenzie or his said sons, or any of them, for the alleged taking and appre- hending, slaying or mutilating of the said vagabonds and broken men, or any of them, or for art and part thereof, or for raising of fire against them, in the taking and apprehending of them, or any of them, at any time preceding his Majesty's going to England, and of all that has passed or that may pass thereupon, and of every circumstance thereanent and suchlike. His Majesty, of his especial grace, taking knowledge and proper motive, remits and forgives the said persons, and every one them, all slaughters, mutilations, and other capital crimes whatsoever, art and part thereof committed by them, or any of them, preceding the day and date hereof (treason in our said Sovereign Lord's own most noble person only excepted), with all pains and executions that ought and should be executed against them, or any of them for the same, exonerating, absolving, and relieving the said John and his said sons, and all of them, of all action and challenge criminal and civil that may be moved thereupon to their prejudice for ever : Discharging hereby all judges, officers, magistrates, admini- strators of his Majesty's laws, from granting of any proofs, criminal or civil, in any action or causes to be moved or pursued against the said John Mackenzie or his sons foresaid for anything concerning the execution of the premisses : Dis- charging them thereof and their officers in that employed by them, and that the said letter be extended in the best form with all clauses needful and the precepts be directed orderly thereupon in form as effeirs. Given at Theobald's, the second day of April, the year of God, 1614 years,"—*Gairloch Charter Chest.*

rector of the Parish; after which it was vacant until, in 1583, King James VI, presented this Alexander Mackenzie to "the parsonage and vicarage of Garloch vacand in our Souerane Lordis handis contenuallie sen the reformatioun of the religioun within this realme by the decease of Sir John Broik."* In 1584 Mr Alexander Mackenzie let the teinds to John Roy for three lives and nineteen years more, for an annual payment of £12 Scots. In 1588 the Crown granted a similar tack for a like payment. In 1612 Mr Farquhar MacGillechriost raised an action against John Roy and his son Alexander for payment of teind. A certain Robert Boyd became cautioner for the Teind of 1610; but the action went on for several years, and was apparently won by Mr Farquhar MacGillechriost, who, in 1616, let the teind of Gairloch, for nineteen years, to Alexander Mackenzie, Fiar of Gairloch, for £80 Scots yearly. Alexander then surrendered to Colin, Lord Mackenzie of Kintail, the tithe of his lands of Letterewe, Inverewe, Drumchorc, and others, who, on his part, as patron of the Parish, bound himself not to sanction the set of the tithes to any other than the said Alexander and his heirs.†

John Roy Mackenzie married, first, Elizabeth, daughter of Angus Macdonald of Glengarry, by his wife, Mary, daughter of Kenneth Mackenzie (na Cuirc) X. of Kintail, by his wife, Elizabeth, daughter of John, Earl of Athol, and by her had issue—

1. *John*, who married, as already seen, Isabel, daughter of Alexander Mackenzie II. of Fairburn, by whom he had an only daughter, also named Isabel, who married Colin Mackenzie of Kinnock. John died before his father in 1601.

2. *Alexander*, his successor.

3. *Murdoch*, killed unmarried, at Raasay, in 1611.

4. *Kenneth*, I. of Davochcairn, who married, first, Margaret, daughter of James Cuthbert of Alterlies and Drakies, Inverness, with issue—present representation unknown; and secondly, a daughter of Hector Mackenzie, IV. of Fairburn,

---

* Reg. Sec. Sig., vol. xlix., fol. 62.
† Papers in the Gairloch Charter Chest.

also with issue—present representation unknown. He died at Davocheairn in 1643, and was buried at Beauly.

5. *Duncan* of Sand, who married a daughter of Hugh Fraser of Belladrum, by whom he had issue, two sons and three daughters. He died at Sand of Gairloch from the bite of a cat at Inverasdle, in 1635, and is buried at Gairloch. The sons were Alexander, who succeeded him at Sand, and John, who married a daughter of Mr George Munro, minister of Urquhart, and resided in Ardnagrask. Katherine, the eldest daughter, married, first, a son of Allan Mac-Ranald Macdonald, heir male of Moydart, then residing at Baile Chnuie, or Hilltown of Beauly, and secondly, William Fraser of Boblanie, with issue—seven daughters, all married, one to Mr Ross of Bindale; another of Sand's daughters married Thomas Mackenzie, brother of Alexander Mackenzie, V. of Aehilty, and the third married Duncan MaeIan vie Eachainn Chaoil.

Alexander, who succeeded his father at Sand (retour 1647), married a daughter of Murdo Mackenzie of Kernsary—situated at the northern extremity of Loch Maree—fifth son of Colin Cam, XI. of Kintail, by his wife Barbara daughter of John Grant, XII. of Grant. Murdoch married a daughter of Alexander Mackenzie, II. of Fairburn, by whom he had, in addition to the daughter who became the wife of Alexander Mackenzie of Sand, an only lawful son, John, killed in 1645 at the Battle of Auldearn, in command of the Lews Mackenzie Regiment, whereupon the lineal and sole representation of the Kernsary family reverted to the descendants of Alexander Mackenzie of Sand, through Mary, his wife. By her Sand had two sons and two daughters. He was succeeded, in 1656, by the eldest son, Hector, who also appears to have succeeded his uncle John, in Ardnagrask. He married Janet Fraser, with issue—John, who died at Ardnagrask in 1759, and left a son, Alexander, who got a new tack of Ardnagrask for forty years, commencing in May 1760;* and who married

* Gairloch Papers,

Helen Mackenzie, daughter of Donald, great-grandson of Murdo Mackenzie, V. of Hilton (by his wife, Jean Forbes of Raddery), by whom he had a large family of five sons and six daughters. The eldest son, John, a merchant in, and Bailie of, Inverness, was born at Ardna-grask in 1762. He married Prudence, daughter of Richard Ord, Merkinch, Inverness, by his wife, Elizabeth, daughter of John, third son of Alexander, VII. of Davochmaluag,* by whom he had five sons and two daughters. Three of the sons died without issue, one of whom was John, a merchant in Madras. Alexander married Maria Lascelles of Blackwood, Dumfries, with issue—John Fraser, who married Julia Linton, with issue; Alexander, who married Adelaide Brett, Madras, with issue; and four daughters, Margaret, Jane, Frances, and Maria, two of whom married, with issue.

Bailie John's second surviving son, the Rev. William Mackenzie, married Elizabeth MacLaren, by whom he had issue—John Ord, married, without issue; James, married, with issue; Richard, married Louisa Lyall, with issue; Henry, of the Oriental Bank Corporation; Gordon, of the Indian Civil Service; and Alfred, of Townsville, Queens-land; also Louisa, Isabella, Maria, and Williamina, all of whom married, the first three with issue.

The Bailie's daughters were Elizabeth, who married Montgomery Young, with issue; and Jane, who married Provost Ferguson, of Inverness, with issue—John Alexander, married, with issue; Mary, married Walter Carruthers of the *Inverness Courier*, with issue; and Agnes Prudence, married to the Rev. G. T. Carruthers, one of Her Majesty's Chaplains, in India.

6. *William* Mackenzie of Shieldag, who married a daughter of the Rev. Mr Murdo Mackenzie, minister of Kintail, with issue, seven sons and seven daughters, and a natural son, John Mòr, who married a natural daughter of Murdoch Mackenzie of Redcastle.

---

* See Davochmaluag genealogy.

7. A daughter married Fraser of Foyers.

8. *Katrine*, married Fraser of Culbokic.

9. Another *Katrine*, married Fraser of Struy.

10. *Janet*, married, first, George Cuthbert of Castlehill, Inverness (marriage contract 29th June 1611); and secondly, Neil Munro of Findon.*

11. A daughter married Alastair Mòr, brother of Chisholm of Comar.

John Roy married, secondly, Isabel, daughter of Murdoch Mackenzie, I. of Fairburn, and by her had issue—

12. *Captain Roderick* of Pitglassie, who served in the army of the Prince of Orange, died unmarried in Holland, in 1624.

13. *Hector* of Mellan, who married the widow of the Rev. John Mackenzie of Lochbroom; and secondly, a daughter of Alexander Mackenzie IV. of Achilty, by whom he had issue, five sons.

14. *John*, a clergyman, who married a natural daughter of Alexander Mackenzie, I. of Kilcoy, with issue, four sons and two daughters. He died at Rhynduin in 1666.

15. *Katrine Og*, married Fraser of Belladrum.

16. *Isabel*, married, first, Alastair Og Macdonald† of Shirness, or Cuidreach, brother-german to Sir Donald Macdonald of Sleat, and ancestor of the Macdonalds of Cuidreach and Kingsburgh, in the Isle of Skye. She married, secondly, Hugh Macdonald of Skirinish.

John Roy had also a natural son, Kenneth Buy, by a woman of the name of Fraser, who married a daughter of Alexander Mackenzie, IV. of Achilty; and two natural daughters, one of whom married Donald Bain, Seaforth's Chamberlain in the Lews, killed in the battle of Auldearn, in 1645; and the other, Margaret, married Alexander, "second lawful son" of John Mackenzie, IV. of Hilton.

---

* Marriage contract in Gairloch Charter Chest, dated 5th February 1627.

† The marriage contract is in the Gairloch Charter Chest, dated 23rd Jan. 1620. This gentleman, in the mouth of November 1625, killed a man in Uist named Alexander Mac Iau Mhic Alastair, for which he received a remission from Charles I., dated at Holyrood, the first of August 1627, and which Macdonald appears to have deposited in the Gairloch Charter Chest on his marriage with Isabel of Gairloch.

He died at Talladale in 1628, in the 80th year of his age; was buried in the churchyard of Gairloch, and succeeded by his eldest surviving son,

V. ALEXANDER MACKENZIE, who was advanced in years at his father's death. He appears to have been most active in the duties pertaining to the head of his House during the life of his father, and led his followers against the Macleods in their repeated incursions to re-possess themselves of Gairloch. "He was a valiant worthy gentleman. It was he who made an end of all the troubles his predecessors were in in the conquering of Gairloch from the Shiel Vic Gilie Challum."* Very little · is known regarding him, his career being so much mixed up with that of his father. Under the charter of 1619 he was infeft in the barony as Fiar, and he immediately succeeded on his father's decease. In 1627, while still Fiar of Gairloch, he obtained from his son-in-law, John Mackenzie of Applecross (afterwards of Lochslinn), who married his daughter Isobel, a disclamation of part of the lands of Diobaig, previously in dispute between the Lairds of Gairloch and Applecross.† In 1637 Alexander proceeded to

---

* Applecross MS.

† In the Gairloch Charter Chest there is a feu charter of endowment by John Mackenzie of Applecross, in implement of the contract of marriage with his betrothed spouse, Isobel, daughter of Alexander Mackenzie, younger of Gairloch, dated 6th of June 1622. After John of Lochslinn's death she married, secondly, Colin Mackenzie of Tarvie; and there is also a sasine in favour of Margaret, second lawful daughter of this Colin of Tarvie, by Isobel of Gairloch, and spouse of Matthew Robertson of Davochcarty, in implement of a marriage contract. A little piece of scandal seems, from an extract of the Presbytery Records of Dingwall, of date 3d of March 1666, to have arisen about this pair—Matthew Robertson and Margaret Mackenzie. "Rorie McKenzie of Dochmaluak, compearing desyred ane answer to his former supplication requiring that Matthew Robertson of Dochgarty should be ordained to make satisfaction for slandering the said Rorie with alledged miscarriage with Matthew Robertson's wife. The brethren considering that by the witness led in the said matter there was nothing but suspicion and jealousies, and said Matthew Robertson being called and inquired concerning the said particular, did openly profess that he was in no wayes jealous of the said Rorie Mackenzie and his wife, and if any word did escape him upon which others might put such a construction, he was heartily sorry for it, and was content to acknowledge so much to Rorie Mackenzie of Dochmaluak, and crave pardon for the same, which the Brethren taking into their consideration, and the Bishop referring it to them (as the Moderator reported), they have, ac-

acquire part of Logic Wester from Duncan Bayne, but the matter was not arranged until 1640, in the reign of his successor.

Alexander married, first, Margaret, daughter of Roderick Mòr Mackenzie, I. of Redcastle, by his wife, Finguala, or Florence, daughter of Munro of Fowlis, with issue—

1. *Kenneth*, his heir.

2. *Murdo*, "predecessor to Sand and Mungastle,"* who married a daughter of John Mackenzie, III. of Fairburn, with issue—a daughter, Margaret, who married Colin Mackenzie, I. of Sanachan, brother to John Mackenzie, II. of Applecross.

3. *Hector*, "portioner of Mellan," who married a daughter of Donald MacIver, and "of whom a small tribe in Gairloch."

4. *Alexander*, a cornet in Sir George Munro's Regiment; "an officer under Cromwell, whom he afterwards left, and was wounded on the King's side at the battle of Worcester, leaving a succession in Gairloch by his wife, Janet, daughter of Mackenzie of Ord." He lost an eye at Worcester, and was consequently ever after known as "Alastair Càm," or One-eyed Alexander. That he was not killed at Worcester,

---

cording to the Bishop's appointment, ordered the said Matthew Robertson to acknowledge so much before the Presbytery to the party, and to crave his pardon in anything he has given him offence. The which being done by the said Matthew Robertson, Rory Mackenzie of Dochmaluak did acquiesce in it without any furder prosecution of it."

* There is great confusion about the families of the various Sands which we have not been able to clear up. The following is from public records:—"In 1718 on the forfeiture of the Fairburn estate, *Alexander* Mackenzie of Sand appeared and deponed that *Murdoch* Mackenzie of Sand, his father, had a wadset of Mungastle and certain other lands from Fairburn. In May 1730 *Alexander* Mackenzie of Sand purchased Mungastle for 3000 merks from Dundonell, who had meantime become proprietor of it. In January 1744 *Alexander* Mackenzie of Sand, son of the preceding Alexander, was infeft in Mungastle in place of his father. In 1741 the above Alexander (the younger) being then a minor, and John Mackenzie of Lochend being his curator, got a wadset of Glenarigolach and Ridorch, and in 1745 Alexander being then of full age, apparently purchased those lands irredeemably. In March 1765 Alexander Mackenzie of Sand, with consent of Janet Mackenzie his wife, sold Mungastle, Glenarigolach, &c. One of the witnesses to this deed of disposition is Alexander Mackenzie, eldest son to Alexander Mackenzie, the granter of the deed."

as stated in one of the Gairloch MSS., is conclusively proved by the marriage contract, in the Ord charter chest, which shows that he married Janet, daughter of John Mackenzie, of Ord, in 1652, a year *after* the battle of Worcester, fought in 1651. The marriage contract is dated "Chanonrie 21 July and 6th August 1652." His descendants are still well known in Gairloch as "Sliochd Alastair Chàim," or the descendants of Alexander the One-eyed, one of them being the late John Mackenzie of the "Beauties of Gaelic Poetry," who was fifth in legitimate male descent; as also the Author of this History, who is, both on the male and female side, sixth in succession. Alexander Cam's immediate successors settled in North Erradale, Gairloch, the half of which they held down to the beginning of the present century. He died in Gairloch, and was buried with his descendants in the Eastern Chapel, in the Churchyard there.

5. *Isobel*, married John Mackenzie of Applecross (afterwards of Lochslinn), brother-german to Colin, first Earl of Seaforth, poisoned at Tain. By him she had issue, a daughter, who married Sir Norman Macleod, father of John Macleod of Muiravenside and Bernera, advocate. Isobel married, secondly, Colin Mackenzie of Tarvie, third son of Sir Roderick Mackenzie of Coigeach, Tutor of Kintail, with issue. She married, thirdly, Murdoch Mackenzie, V. of Achilty, without issue.

6. *Margaret*, married Alexander Ross of Cuilich, from whom came the family of Achnacloich.

7. Another married Robert Gray of Skibo, with issue.

Alexander of Gairloch married, secondly, Isabel, daughter of Alexander Mackenzie, progenitor of the families of Coul and Applecross, with issue—

8. *William* of Multafy and I. of Belmaduthy.

9. *Roderick*, married Agnes, daughter of Alexander Mackenzie, I. of Suddie, with issue.

10. *Angus*,* married the eldest daughter of Hector Mackenzie, IV. of Fairburn, without issue.

---

* This Angus " was a brave soldier, and commanded a considerable body of Highlanders under King Charles the Second at the Torwood. He, with Scrym-

11. *Annabella*, married Donald Mackenzie, III. of Logie with issue.

12. *Janet* (? Isabella), married Alexander Mackenzie of Pitglassie, progenitor of the Mackenzies of Ardross.

Alexander had also a natural daughter, who married George, fourth son of John Mackenzie, I. of Ord.

He died, as appears from an entry in an old inventory of his successor's retour of service, on the 4th of January 1638,* in the 61st year of his age, at Island Suthain, in Loch Maree, where traces of his house are still to be seen. He was buried with his wife " in a chapel he caused built near the Church of Gairloch" during his father's lifetime, and was succeeded by his eldest son,

VI. KENNETH MACKENZIE, a strong loyalist during the wars of Montrose and the Covenanters. He was fined by the Committee of Estates for his adherence to the King, under the Act of 3d February 1646, entitled " Commission for the moneys of Excise and Processe against delinquents." The penalty was a forced loan of 500 merks, for which the receipt, dated 15th March 1647, signed by Kennedy, Earl of Cassilis, and Sir William Cochrane, two of the Commissioners named in the Act, and by two or three others, is still extant. Seaforth was, at the time, one of the Committee of Estates, where probably his influence was exercised in favour of leniency to the Baron of Gairloch ; especially as he was himself privately imbued with strong predilictions in favour of the Royalists. Kenneth commanded a body of Highlanders at Balvenny under Thomas

geour of Dudhope and other loyalists, marched at a great rate to assist the Macleans who were cut to pieces by Cromwell's dragoons at Inverkeithing, but to their great grief were recalled by the Earl of Argyll, general of the army.—*Gairloch MS.*

* In this service we find "Kirktoun with the manor and gardens of the ssme," and, after a long list of the townships, the fishings of half the water of Ewe, and the rivers Kerry and Badachro, we have "the loch of Lochmaroy, with the islands of the same, *and the manor place and gardens in the Island of Ilinrory*, the loch of Garloch, with the fishings of the same," from which it appears that the residence on Island Rory Beg, the walls of which and of the large garden are yet distinctly traceable, was at least as early as that on Island Suthain in which Alexander died.

Mackenzie of Pluscardine, and his own brother-in-law, the Earl of Huntly ; but when the Royalist army was surprised and disarmed, he happened to be on a visit to Castle Grant and managed to escape.

In 1640 he completed the acquisition of Logic Wester, commenced by his predecessor, but not without having had recourse to the money market. He granted a bond for 1000 merks, dated 20th of October 1644, to Hector Mackenzie, *alias* MacIan MacAlastair Mhic Alastair, in-dweller in Eadill-fuill. On the 14th of January 1649, at Kirkton, he granted to the same person a bond for 500 merks ; but at this date Hector was described as "indweller in Androry," and, again, another dated at Stankhouse of Gairloch (Tigh Dige), 24th of November 1662 ; but the lender is on this occasion described as living in Diobaig. For the two first of these sums Murdo Mackenzie of Sand, his brother-german, was collateral security.

In 1657 Kenneth was collateral security to a bond granted by this brother, Murdoch Mackenzie of Sand, to Colin Mackenzie, I. of Sanachan, brother-german to John Mackenzie, II. of Applecross, for 2000 merks, borrowed on the 20th March of that year ; the one-half of which was to be paid by the delivery at the feast of Beltane, 1658, of 50 cows in milk by calves of that year, and the other half, with legal interest, at Whitsunday 1659. Colin Mackenzie, I. of Sanachan, married Murdoch's daughter, and the contract of marriage is dated the same day as the bond, and subscribed at Dingwall by the same witnesses.

From a discharge by Kenneth Mackenzie of Assynt, dated 17th November 1648, Kenneth of Gairloch appears to have been cautioner for George, Earl of Seaforth, in a bond granted by him for a loan of 5000 merks.

In 1658, by letters of Tutorie Dative from Oliver Cromwell, he was appointed Tutor to Hector Mackenzie, lawful son of Alexander Mackenzie, lawful son of Duncan Mackenzie of Sand, Gairloch. There is nothing further to show what became of the pupil, but it is highly probable that on the death of Alexander, son of Duncan of Sand, the farm

was given by Kenneth to his brother, Murdoch, and
that the 2000 merks, borrowed from Colin Mackenzie of
Sanachan, who married Murdoch's only daughter, Margaret,
may have been borrowed for the purpose of stocking the
farm. The dates of the marriage, of the bond, and of the
Tutoric Dative, so near each other, strongly support this view.

Kenneth of Gairloch married, first, Katharine, daughter
of Sir Donald Macdonald of Sleat, without issue. The
contract of marriage is dated 5th September 1635, the marriage portion being "6000 merks and her endowment 1000
libs. Scots yearly."* In 1640 he married, secondly, Ann,
daughter of Sir John Grant of Grant, by Ann Ogilvy,
daughter of the Earl of Findlater. There is a charter by
Kenneth in her favour of the lands of Logie Wester, the
miln and pertinents thereof, with the grazings of Tolly, in
implement of the marriage contract, dated 4th of December
1640, with a sasine of the same date, and another charter of
the lands and manor-place of Kinkell and Ardnagrask,
dated the 15th August 1655, with sasine thereon, dated 5th
September following. By her he had—

1. *Alexander*, his heir.

2. *Hector* of Bishop-Kinkell, who married Mackenzie
of Fairburn's widow, and with her obtained the lands of
Bishop-Kinkell.

3. *John*, who died unmarried.

4. *Mary*, who married Alexander Mackenzie, younger
of Kilcoy.

5. *Barbara*, married, first, Fraser of Kinneries, and
secondly, Alexander Mackenzie, I. of Ardloch, by both of
whom she had issue.

6. *Lilias*, married Alexander Mackenzie, I. of Ballone,†
by whom she had an only daughter, Margaret, who married,
first, Sir Roderick Mackenzie of Findon, with issue, and
secondly, George Mackenzie, II. of Gruinard.

---

* Gairloch MS.

† The marriage contracts of the three daughters are in the Gairloch Charter
Chest, and are dated respectively, 21st March 1664, 30th March 1667, and 20th
July 1670.

He married thirdly, Janet, daughter of John Cuthbert of Castlehill; marriage contract dated 17th December 1658; the marriage portion being 3000 merks, and her endowment 5 chalders victual yearly, with issue.

7. *Charles*, I. of Letterewe, who, by his father's marriage contract, got Logie Wester, purchased by Kenneth in 1640. In 1696 it was exchanged by Charles, with his eldest halfbrother, Alexander VII. of Gairloch, for Letterewe. Charles married Ann, daughter of John Mackenzie, II. of Applecross, with issue. [See Mackenzies of Letterewe.]

8. *Kenneth*, died unmarried.

9. *Colin*, I. of Mountgerald.

10. *Isabella*, married Roderick Mackenzie, brother of John Mackenzie, II. of Applecross, and

11. *Annabella*, married George Mackenzie, a younger brother of Davochmaluag.

According to the retour of service of his successor, Kenneth died in 1669,* was buried in Beauly, and succeeded by his eldest son,

VII. ALEXANDER MACKENZIE, who, by a charter of resignation, got Logie Wester included in the barony of Gairloch. It had, however, been settled on his step-mother, Janet Cuthbert, in life-rent, and after her, on her eldest son Charles, to whom, after her death, Alexander formally disponed it. They afterwards entered into an excambion by which Alexander re-acquired Logie Wester in exchange for Letterewe, which became the patrimony of the successors of Charles.

---

* There is in the Proceedings of the Society of Antiquarians of Scotland for 1871 a notice of the Priory Church of Beauly, by Captain White of the Ordnance Survey, in which we find the following about the later gravestones, which he describes as florid and staring without being rich, and presenting an unvarying uniformity of type :—"One example will describe all the rest. It is a slab in the north aisle of date 1669, with the cognisance of a stag's head on the top, and death's head, sand-glass, and cross-bones at the bottom. In the centre part is a verse from the book of Job, with *memento mori* written underneath. Round the margin is the following inscription—'Heir lyes ane honorable man called Kenneth McKenzie sumtyme Laird of Gairloch who departed the 22d of April 1669.'" This stone is the only monumental record of the Gairloch family in the Priory, which existed before the time of the present Baronet.

In 1671 Alexander acquired Mellan Charles, and the second half of the water of Ewe.*

A tradition is current in the family that when Alexander sought the hand of his future lady, Barbara, daughter of Sir John Mackenzie of Tarbat, and sister-german to the first Earl of Cromarty, and to Isobel, Countess of Seaforth, he endeavoured to make himself appear much wealthier than he really was, by returning a higher rental than he actually received, at the time of making up the Scots valued rent in 1670, in which year he married. This tradition is corroborated by a comparison of the valuation of the shire of Inverness for 1644, published by Mr Charles Fraser-Mackintosh, F.S.A.S., in "Antiquarian Notes," and the rental of 1670, on which the ecclesiastical assessments are still based. In the former year the rental of the Parish of Gairloch was £3134 13s 4d, of which £1081 6s 8d was from the lands of the Barony, equal to 34½ per cent. ; while in the latter year the valued rental of the parish is put down at £3400, of which £1549 is from the Barony lands, or 45½ per cent. It is impossible that such a rise in the rental could have taken place in the short space of twenty-six years ; and the presumption is in favour of the truthfulness of the tradition which holds that the rental was over-valued for the special purpose of making the Baron of Gairloch appear more im-

* Regarding this place there is the following refereuce in the records of the Presbytery of Dingwall, under date, 6th of August 1678 :—"That day Mr Roderick Mackenzie, minister at Gerloch by his letter to the Presbytery declared that he had summonded by his officer to this Presbytery, Hector McKenzie in Mellan in the Parish of Gerloch, as also John, Murdoch, and Duncan McKenzie, sons to the said Hector, as also, Kenneth McKenzie his grandson, for sacrificing a bull in ane heathenish manner in the Island of St Ruffus, commonly called 'Ellen Moury, in Lochew,' for the recovering of the health of Curstane McKenzie, spouse to the said Hector McKenzie, who was formerly sick and valetudinarie ; who being all cited, au not compearing, are to be all summonded again pro 2d." The case was called against them again on the third of the following September, but they never appeared, and the matter was allowed to drop. The island of St Ruffus is evidently Isle Maree ; Lochmaree, being then desiguated Lochewo, as Kenlochewe and Letterewe unmistakeably testify. The name Loch Maree must, however, have also been known then, for in a charter under the Great Seal to John Mackenzie of Gairloch and his son Alexander, dated 26th of August 1619, it is called "Loch Maroy."

portant in the eyes of his future relatives-in-law than he really was. In 1681 he had his rights and titles ratified by an Act of Parliament, printed at length in the Folio edition.

He married, first, Barbara Mackenzie of Tarbat, with issue—

1. *Kenneth*, his heir.

2. *Isobel*, who married John Macdonald of Balcony, brother to Sir Donald Macdonald.

He married, secondly, Janet, daughter of William Mackenzie, I. of Belmaduthy, on which occasion Davochcairn and Ardnagrask were settled upon her in life-rent, and on her eldest son at her death, as appears from a precept of Clare Constat, by Colin Mackenzie of Davochpollo, in favour of William, his eldest surviving son.* By her he had—

3. *Alexander*, who died unmarried.

4. *William*, who got the lands of Davochcairn, and married, in 1712, Jean, daughter of Roderick Mackenzie, V. of Redcastle, with issue, one son, Alexander, of the Stamp Office, London; and several daughters. Alexander has a *Clare Constat* as only son in 1732. He died in 1772, leaving a son, Alexander Kenneth, who emigrated to New South Wales, where many of his descendants now reside; the representative of the family, in 1878, being Alexander Kenneth Mackenzie, Boonara, Bondi, Sydney.

5. *John*, who purchased the lands of Lochend (now Inverewe), with issue—Alexander Mackenzie, afterwards of Lochend; and George, an officer in Colonel Murray Keith's Highland Regiment; also two daughters, Lilias, who married William Mackenzie, IV. of Gruinard, and Christy, married to William Maciver, Turnaig, both with issue.

6. *Ann*, who married Kenneth Mackenzie, II. of Torridon, with issue. She married, secondly, Kenneth Mackenzie, a solicitor in London.

He died in December 1694, at 42 years of age; for in his general retour of sasine, 25th February 1673, he is said to be then of lawful age. He was buried in Gairloch, and succeeded by his only son by the first marriage,

* Original in the Gairloch Charter Chest.

VIII. Sir Kenneth Mackenzie, created a Baronet of Nova Scotia, by Queen Anne, on the 2d of February 1703. He was educated at Oxford, and afterwards represented his native county in the Scottish Parliament. He strongly opposed the Union, considering it, if it should take place, "the funeral of his country."* After the succession of Queen Anne he received from her, in December 1702, a gift of the taxed ward feu-duties, non-entry and marriage dues, and other casualties, payable from the date of his father's death, which, up to 1702, appear not to have been paid. Early in the same year he seems to have been taken seriously unwell, whereupon he executed a holograph testament at Stankhouse, dated 23d May 1702, witnessed by his uncle, Colin Mackenzie of Findon, and by his brother-in-law, Simon Mackenzie of Allangrange. He appoints as trustees his "dear friends" John, Master of Tarbat, Kenneth Mackenzie of Cromarty, Kenneth Mackenzie of Scatwell, Hector Mackenzie, and Colin Mackenzie, his uncles, and George Mackenzie of Allangrange. He appointed Colin Mackenzie, then of Findon, and afterwards of Davochpollo and Mountgerald, as his Tutor and factor at a salary of 200 merks Scots. In the following May, having apparently to some extent recovered his health, he appeared in his place in Parliament. By September following he returned to Stankhouse, where he executed two bonds of provision, one for his second son George, and the other for his younger daughters.

He married, in 1696, Margaret, youngest daughter, and, as is commonly said, co-heiress of Sir Roderick Mackenzie of Findon ;† but the Barony of Findon went wholly to Lilias the eldest daughter, who married Sir Kenneth Mackenzie, 1st Baronet and IV. of Scatwell ;‡ another of the

---

* "Kenneth of Gerloch having finished his studies at Oxford and become ane agreeable gentleman under the auspices of George, Earl of Cromarty, was one of the members of Parliament for the shire of Ross, in the reign of Queen Anne, and was made a knight Baronet, but dyed before the conclusion of Union twixt Scotland and England."—*Gairloch MS.*

† Marriage contract dated 21st April 1696 in Gairloch Charter Chest.

‡ The marriage contract of Lilias is in the Ord Charter Chest, and is dated 6th of July 1682.

daughters married Simon Mackenzie of Allangrange. There was a fourth unmarried at the date of Margaret's contract of marriage; and the four took a fourth part each of Sir Roderick's movables and of certain lands not included in the Barony. At the date of his marriage Kenneth had not made up titles; but by his marriage contract he is taken bound to do so as soon as he can ; his retour of service was taken out the following year.

By his marriage he had—

1. *Alexander*, his heir.

2. *George*, who became a merchant in Glasgow.

3. *Barbara*, married in 1729, George Beattie, a merchant in Montrose.

4. *Margaret*, who died in 1704.

5. *Anne*, who married, in 1728, Murdo Mackenzie younger of Achilty.

6. *Katharine*, who died young.

Sir Kenneth also had a natural daughter, *Margaret*, who married, in 1723, Donald Macdonald, younger of Cuidreach. Sir Kenneth's widow, about a year after his decease, married Bayne of Tulloch. Notwithstanding the money Sir Kenneth received with her, he died deeply involved in debt, and left his children without proper provision. George and Barbara were at first maintained by their mother, and afterwards by Colin of Findon, who married their grandmother, relict of Sir Roderick Mackenzie of Findon, while Alexander and Anne were in a worse plight.

He died in December 1703, only 32 years of age ; was buried in Gairloch, and succeeded by his eldest son,

IX. SIR ALEXANDER MACKENZIE, the second Baronet, a child only three and a-half years of age. His prospects were by no means enviable; he and his sister Anne for a time, having had, for actual want of means, to be "settled in tenants' houses." The rental of Gairloch and Glasletter at his father's death amounted only to 5954 merks, and his other estates in the low country were settled on Sir Kenneth's widow for life ; while he was left with debts amount-

Y

ing to 66,674 merks, or eleven years' rental of the whole estates. During Sir Alexander's minority, the large sum of 51,200 merks had been paid off, in addition to 27,635 in name of interest on the original debt; and thus very little was left for the young Baronet's education. In 1708 he, his brother, and sisters were taken to the factor's house —Colin Mackenzie of Findon—where they remained for four years, and received the rudiments of their education from a young man, Simon Urquhart. In 1712 they all went to school at Chanonry, under Urquhart's charge, where Sir Alexander remained for six years, after which, · being then 18 years of age, he went to Edinburgh to complete his education. He afterwards made a tour of travel, and returning home in 1730 married his cousin, Janet of Scatwell, on which occasion a fine Gaelic poem was composed in her praise by John Mackay, the famous blind piper and poet of Gairloch, whose daughter became the mother of William Ross, a bard even more celebrated than the blind piper himself. If we believe the bard the lady possessed all the virtues of mind and body;* but in spite of all these advantages the marriage did not continue a happy one; for, in 1758, they separated on the grounds of incompatibility of temper; after which she lived alone at Kinkell.

When, in 1721, Sir Alexander came of age, he was compelled to procure means to pay the provision payable to his brother George and to his sisters, amounting altogether to 16,000 merks, while about the same amount of his late father's debts was still unpaid. In 1729 he purchased Cruive House and the Ferry of Skuddale. In 1735 he bought Bishop Kinkell; in 1742 Logie Riach; and, in 1743 Kenlochewe, which latter was considered of equal value with Glasletter in Kintail, which was sold about the same time. He also, about 1730, redeemed Davochcairn

---

* The poem, "Beannachadh Baird do Shir Alastair MacCoinnich," is preserved by the late John Mackenzie at page 96 of his "Beauties of Gaelic
Poetry." A more complete version is given by the writer from an old MS. in
his possession, found among the Gairloch papers, at pages 192 5 of the Transactions of the Gaelic Society of Inverness, vol. iii. and iv.

and Ardnagrask from the widow of his uncle William; and
Davochpollo from the widow, and son, James, of his grand-
uncle, Colin of Mountgerald. In 1752 he executed an
entail of all his estates; but leaving debts at his death,
amounting to £2679 13s 10d more than what his personal
estate could meet, Davochcairn, Davochpollo, and Ardnagrask, had eventually to be sold to pay his liabilities.*

In 1738 he pulled down the old family residence of
Stankhouse, or "Tigh Dige," at Gairloch, which stood in a
low, marshy, damp situation, surrounded by a moat, from
which it derived its name, and built the present house on
an elevated plateau, surrounded by magnificent woods and
towering hills, with a southern front elevation—altogether
one of the most beautiful and best sheltered situations in the
Highlands; and he very appropriately called it Flowerdale.
He vastly improved his property, and was in all respects a
careful and good man of business. He kept out of the Forty-
Five. John Mackenzie of Meddat applied to him for aid in
favour of Lord Macleod, son of the Earl of Cromarty, who
took so prominent a part in the Rising, and was afterwards in
tightened circumstances; but Sir Alexander replied, in a
letter dated "Gerloch, 17th May 1749," as follows :—

Sir,—I am favoured with your letter, and am extreamly sory Lord Cro-
maitie's circumstances should obliege him to sollicit the aide of small gentlemen.

*The state of religion seems to have been for a long time, and up to Alex-
ander's time, in a very unsatisfactory state in the Presbytery of Gairloch, now
that of Lochcarron. "In March 1725, we find the Presbytery of Gairloch
obliged to hold a meeting at Kilmorack, as the Presbytery, to use the language
of the record, had no access to meet in their own bounds, since they had been
rabbled at Lochalsh on the 16th September 1724, that being the day appointed
for a parochial visitation there. From a petition which Mr Sage, the first
Presbyterian minister of Lochcarron, settled there in 1726, presents to the Presbytery, in 1731, praying for an act of transportability—we see that he considered
his life in danger—that only one family attended regularly on his ministry ; and
that he dispaired of being of any service in the place." The same writer informs
us that not further back than the middle of the eighteenth century the inhabitants of Lochcarron in this Presbytery " were involved in the most dissolute bar-
barism. The records of Presbytery, which commence in 1724, are stained with
an amount of black and bloody crimes, exhibiting a picture of wildness, ferocity,
and gross indulgence consistent only with a state of savagism."—*New Statistical
Account of Lochcarron.*

I much raither he hade dyed sword in hand even where he was ingag'd then be necessitate to act such a pairt. I have the honour to be nearly related to him, and to have been his companion, but will not supply him at this time, for which I beleive I oau give you the best reason in the world, and the only one possible for me to give, and that is that I cannot.*

The reason stated may possibly be the correct one; but it is more likely that Sir Alexander had no sympathy whatever with the cause which brought his kinsman into such a pitiable position, and would not, on that account, lend him any assistance.

Several of his leases, preserved in the Gairloch charter chest, contain some very curious clauses, some of which would make those who advocate going back to the "good old days" draw their breath; but notwithstanding conditions which would now be called tyrannical and cruel the Laird and his tenants understood each other, and got on remarkably well. The tenants were bound to sell · to him all their marketable cattle "at reasonable rates," and to deliver to him at current prices all the cod and ling caught by them; and, in some cases, were bound to keep one or more boats, with a sufficient number of men as sub-tenants, for the prosecution of the cod and ling fishings. He kept his own curer, cured the fish, and sold it at 12s 6d per cwt. delivered in June at Gairloch, with credit until the following Martinmas, to a Mr Dunbar, merchant, with whom he made a contract binding himself, for several years, to deliver, at the price named, all the cod caught in Gairloch.†

---

* Fraser's Earls of Cromartie, vol. ii., p. 230.

† The following is an extract from a lease granted by Sir Alexander to the great-great-grandfather of the author, John Mor Mackenzie, grandson of Alastair Cam Mackenzie, fourth son of Alexander, V. of Gairloch, by his wife, Janet Mackenzie of Ord. The lease is for 20 years, "of the equall half of the quarter lands of Airidale a Pris, or North Airidale. . . . as presently occupied by him;" is dated the 5th of September 1760; but is not to take effect until Whitsunday 1765, five years being, at the time, to run of the old lease. John Mor binds himself to pay Sir Alexander "all and hail the sum of one hundred and thirty-one marks and a half Scots mony, two marks three shillings and fourpence money for said Crown rent, ten merks ten shillings and eightpence in lieu of Peats, or as the same shall reasonably from time to time be regulated by the proprietor, a mark of Crove mony, Twenty marks mony foresaid of Stipend, or as the same shall hapen to be setled twixt the landlord and minister. Two long carryages, Two

Sir Alexander married, in 1730, Janet, daughter of Sir Roderick Mackenzie, second Baronet and V. of Scatwell, with issue—

1. *Alexander*, his heir.

2. *Kenneth*, who died in infancy.

3. *Roderick*, a captain in the army, killed at Quebec before he attained his majority.

4. *William*, a writer, died unmarried.

5. *James*, died in infancy.

6. *Kenneth* of Millbank, factor and tutor to Sir Hector, the 4th Baronet, during the last few years of his minority. He married Anne, daughter of Alexander Mackenzie of Tolly, with issue—(1) Alexander, County Clerk of Ross-shire, perhaps the most popular, and, at the same time, the most reckless member of the Clan that ever existed. His father left him £20,000, and, for years, he had about £1000 per annum as factor for Lovat and Tulloch ; but he spent it all and a good deal besides, and died in poverty in 1861. He married, and had issue—Alexander, in New Zealand ; Kenneth, married twice in India, and died in 1877 ; and Catharine, who married Murdo Cameron, Leanaig; (2) Janet, who married the Rev. John Macdonald, Urquhart, with issue;

custom wedders, a fedd Kidd, a ston of cheese and halfe a ston weight of Butter, eight hens or as usuall eight men yearly at their own expense to shear Corn or cutt Hay, a Davach of Ploughing, and four horses for mucking." John also "obleigs himselfe to attend Road duty yearly four days with all his servants and sub tenants or pay a yearly capitation, optionall to the Landlord, dureing the lease under break of tack, and to sell all the cod and ling (that) shall be caught by him and his forsaids at the current price to our order and to dispose of all mercat catle to our Drover at reasonable rates, also under break of tack." He has also to pay "a fine or grassum" at the term of Whitsunday 1765, "all and hail the sum of two hundred and fifty marks Scots mony and the like sum at the end of every five years of this tack making in all the sum of one thousand marks Scots mony," &c., &c. The document is holograph of Sir Alexander ; and it is arranged that it shall be registered for conservation in the Books of Council and Session, so that letters of borning and all needful executions may pass thereon in proper form. The elder John Mor Mac Alastair died during the currency of the lease. He was succeeded in it by his son, John Mor Og, to whom, in 1785, a lease is granted of the whole of Erradale, jointly with his relative, George Mackenzie, at a rental of £24 and a grassum of 40 guineas. In 1790 the rent is increased to £32 and the grassum to £50 ; in 1795 to £40 of rent and £50 of grassum ; and five years later the lease is again renewed at the same rent,

(3) Catherine, who married Alexander Mackenzie, a merchant in London, and grandson of Alexander Mackenzie of
Tolly, with issue, an only daughter, Catherine, who married
Major Roderick Mackenzie, VII. of Kincraig, with issue;
(4) Jane, who, in 1808, married the Rev. Hector Bethune,
minister of Dingwall, with issue—Colonel Bethune, died
without issue; Rev. Angus Bethune, Rector of Seaham;
Alexander Mackenzie Bethune, Secretary of the Peninsular
and Oriental Navigation Company; and a daughter, Jane,
who married Francis Harper, Torgorm. Mrs Bethune died
in 1878, aged 91 years.

7 and 8. *Margaret* and *Janet*, died young.

·9. Another *Janet*, married Colin, eldest son of David,
brother of Murdo Mackenzie, VII. of Achilty. Murdo
leaving no issue, Colin ultimately succeeded to Achilty,
though he seems afterwards to have parted with it, as, in
1784, he has a tack of Kinkell, and dies there, in 1813, with
his affairs involved.

Sir Alexander had also a natural son, Charles Mackenzie, ancestor of the later Mackenzies of Sand, and two
natural daughters, one of whom, Annabella, by a daughter
of Maolmuire, or Miles MacRae, of the family of Inverinate,
married John Bàn Mackenzie, by whom she had a daughter,
Marsali or Marjory, who married John Mòr Og Mackenzie
(Ian Mòr Aireach), son of John Mòr Mackenzie, grandson
of Alexander Càm Mackenzie, fourth son of Alexander,
V. of Gairloch, in whose favour Sir Alexander granted the
lease of North Erradale, already quoted.

He died in 1766, in the 66th year of his age, was buried
with his ancestors in Gairloch,* and succeeded by his eldest
son,

X. SIR ALEXANDER MACKENZIE, third Baronet, called
"An Tighearna Ruadh," or Red-haired Laird. He built
Conon House between 1758 and 1760, during his father's
lifetime. His mother, who continued to reside at Kinkell,

---

* The old chapel and the burying place of the Lairds of Gairloch appear to
have been roofed at this date; for in the Tutorial accounts of 1704 there is au
item of 30 merks for "harling, pinning, and thatching Garloch's burial place."

where she lived separated from her husband, on his decease claimed the new mansion built by her son eight years previously, on the ground that it was situated on her jointure lands; but Sir Alexander resisted her pretensions, and ultimately the matter was arranged by the award of John Forbes of New, Government factor on the forfeited estates of Lovat, who then resided at Beaufort, and to whom the question in dispute was submitted as arbitrator. He compromised it by requiring Sir Alexander to expend £300 in making Kinkell Castle more comfortable, by taking off the top storey, re-roofing it, and rebuilding an addition at the side, reflooring, plastering, and papering all the rooms.

Sir Alexander, in addition to the debts of the entailed estates, contracted others on his own account, and finding himself, in consequence, much hampered, he tried, but failed, to break the entail, though a flaw has been discovered in it since, to which Sir Kenneth, the present Baronet, called the attention of the Court; whereupon the entail was declared invalid. He then entered into an agreement to sell the Strathpeffer lands and those of Ardnagrask, in contemplation of which Henry Davidson of Tulloch bought the greater portion of the debts of the entailed estates, with the view of securing the consent of the Court to the sale of Davochcairn and Davochpollo to himself; but on the 15th of April 1770, before the transaction could be completed, Sir Alexander suddenly died from the effects of a fall from his horse. His affairs were seriously involved, but having been placed in the hands of an Edinburgh accountant, his creditors afterwards received nineteen shillings in the pound.

He married, first, 29th Nov. 1755, Margaret, eldest daughter of Roderick Mackenzie, VII. of Redcastle, by whom he had issue, one son,

    1, *Hector*, who succeeded him.

She died 1st December 1759.

He married, secondly, in 1760, Jean, daughter of John Gorry of Balblair, and Commissary of Ross, with issue—

    2. *John*, who raised a company, almost entirely in Gairloch, for the 78th Regiment of Ross-shire Highlanders

when first embodied; and of which he obtained the captaincy.
He rose rapidly in rank. On May 3, 1794, he obtained his
majority; in the following year he is Lieutenant-Colonel
of the Regiment; Major-General in the army in 1813; and
full General in 1837. He served with distinction and without cessation from 1779 to 1814. So marked was his daring
and personal valour that he was popularly known as "Fighting Jack" among his companions in arms. He was at the
Walcheren expedition; at the Cape; in India; in Sicily;
Malta; and the Peninsula; and though constantly exhibiting numberless instances of great personal daring, he was
wounded only once, when on a certain occasion he was struck
with a spent ball on the knee, which made walking somewhat troublesome to him in after life. At Tarragona he
was so mortified with Sir John Murray's conduct, that he
almost forgot that he himself was only second in command,
and charged Sir John with incapacity and cowardice, for
which the latter was tried by Court Martial—General Mackenzie being one of the principal witnesses against him. ·
Full of vigour of mind and body, he took a lively interest
in everything in which he took a part, from fishing and
shooting to farming, gardening, politics, and fighting. He
never forgot his native Gaelic, which he spoke with fluency
and read with ease. Though a severe disciplinarian, his
men adored him. He often said that it gave him greater
pleasure to see a dog from Gairloch than a gentleman from
anywhere else. When the 78th returned from the Indian
Mutiny the officers and men were feted at a grand banquet
by the town of Inverness, and as the regiment marched
through Academy Street, where the General resided, they
halted opposite his residence (now the Lancashire Insurance
Office); and though so very frail that he had to be carried in a
chair, he was taken out and his chair placed on the wide
steps at the door, where the regiment saluted and warmly
cheered their old and distinguished veteran commander,
who had so often led their predecessors to victory; and then
the oldest officer in, and "father" of, the British army.
He was much affected, and wept with joy at again meeting

his beloved 78th—the only tears he was known to have shed since the days of his childhood. He married Lilias, youngest daughter of Alexander Chisholm of Chisholm, with issue—(1) Alastair, who first served in the army, but afterwards settled down, and became a magistrate, in the Bahamas, where he married an American lady, Wade Ellen, daughter of George Huyler, Consul General of the United States, and French Consul in the same place, with issue— a son, the Rev. George William Russel Mackenzie, an Episcopalian minister; and (2) a daughter, Lilias Mary Chisholm, unmarried. Alastair afterwards left the Bahamas, and went to Melbourne as Treasurer for the Government of Victoria, where he died, about twenty-five years ago. The General died on the 14th of June 1860, aged 96 years, and was buried in the Gairloch aisle at Beauly.

3. *Kenneth*, born 14th February 1765, a Captain in the army, served in India, and was at the siege of Seringapatam. He soon after retired and settled down as a gentleman farmer in Kerrisdale, Gairloch. He married Florence, daughter of Farquhar Macrae of Inverinate, with issue— three sons and four daughters; (1) Alexander, a Captain in the 58th Regiment, who married a daughter of William Beibly, M.D., Edinburgh, with issue; (2) Hector, a merchant in Java, where he died unmarried; (3) Farquhar, a settler in Victoria, where he married and left issue—Hector, John, Violet, Mary, and Flora; (4) Jean, married William H. Garrett, of the Indian Civil Service, with issue—two sons, Edward and William, and four daughters, Eleanor (now Mrs Gourlay, The Gows, Dundee); Flora, Emily, and Elizabeth; (5) Mary, married, first, Dr Macleod, Dingwall, without issue; and secondly, Murdo Mackenzie, a Calcutta merchant, also without issue; (6) Christian Henderson, married John Mackenzie, writer, Tain, a son of George Mackenzie, III. of Pitlundie, with issue—two sons, both dead, one of whom left a son, Charles; (7) Jessie, married Dr Kenneth Mackinnon, of the Corry family, H.E.I.C.S., Calcutta.

4. *Jean*, died young.

5. *Margaret*, married Roderick Mackenzie, II. of Glack, Aberdeenshire, with issue ; and

6. *Janet*, who married Captain John Mackenzie, Woodlands, son of George Mackenzie, II. of Gruinard, without issue.

He had also a natural daughter, Janet, who married John Macpherson, by whom she had Hector Macpherson, merchant, Gairloch ; Alexander Macpherson, blacksmith, and several others.

The second Lady Mackenzie of Gairloch, Jean Gorry, died in 1766, probably at the birth of her last daughter, Janet, born on the 14th October in that year, and Sir Alexander himself died on the 15th of April 1770. He was buried at Gairloch, and was succeeded by his eldest son,

XI. SIR HECTOR, fourth Baronet, better known among his Gairloch tenantry as "An Tighearna Storach," or the Buck-toothed Laird. A minor, only twelve years of age when he succeeded, his affairs were managed by trustees appointed by his father. These were John Gorry; Provost Mackenzie of Dingwall, and Alexander Mackenzie, W.S., respectively, son and grandson of Charles Mackenzie, I. of Letterewe ; and Alexander Mackenzie, of the Stamp Office, London, son of William Mackenzie of Davochcairn. These gentlemen did not get on so harmoniously as could be wished. The first three opposed the last, supported by Sir Hector, and by his grandfather and uncle of Redcastle. In March 1772, in a petition in which Sir Hector craved the Court for authority to name his own factor, he is described as "being now arrived at the age of fourteen years." The differences between the trustees finally landed them in Court, on the question, Whether the agreement of the late Sir Alexander to sell the Ardnagrask and Strathpeffer lands should be carried out ? and, in opposition to the majority of the trustees, the Court decided that these lands should not be sold until Sir Hector arrived at an age to judge for himself. Securing this decision in his favour, Sir Hector, thinking that Mr Gorry was acting too much in the interest of his own grandchildren—Sir Alexander's children

by the second marriage—appointed a factor of his own—
Kenneth Mackenzie, his half uncle, the first "Millbank."

In 1789 he obtained authority from the Court to sell
the lands which his father had previously arranged to dispose
of to enable him to pay the debts of the entailed estates.
He sold the lands of Davochcairn and Davochpollo to
Henry Davidson of Tulloch, and Ardnagrask to Captain
Rose, Beauly, who afterwards sold it to Mackenzie of Ord.

He was, in 1815, appointed Lord-Lieutenant of his
native County. He lived generally at home among his
devoted tenantry; and only visited London once during his
life. He regularly dispensed justice among 'his Gairloch
retainers without any expense to the county, and to their
entire satisfaction. He was adored by his people, to whom
he acted as father and friend, and his memory still continues
green among the older inhabitants, who never speak of him
but in the warmest terms for his kindness, his urbanity
and frankness, and for the kind and free manner in which
he always mixed with and spoke to his tenants. He
was at the same time believed, by all who knew him,
to be the most sagacious and most intelligent man in
the county. He employed no factor after he became
of age, but dealt directly and entirely with his people,
ultimately knowing every one on the estate personally; so
that he knew how to treat each case of hardship and consequent inability to pay that came before him; and to distinguish feigned from real poverty. When he became frail
and old he employed a clerk to assist him in the management, but he wisely continued landlord and factor
himself to his dying day. When Sir Francis, his eldest
son, grew up, instead of adopting the usual folly of sending elder sons to the army that they might afterwards
succeed to the property entirely ignorant of everything connected with it, he gave him, instead of a yearly allowance,
several of the farms, with a rental of about £500 a year,
over which he acted as landlord or tenant, until his father's
death, telling him "if you can make more of them, all
the better for you." Sir Francis thus grew up, interested

in, and thoroughly acquainted with all property and county business, and with his future tenants, very much both to his own advantage and that of those who afterwards depended upon him.

Sir Hector also patronised the local Gaelic bards, and appointed one of them, Alexander Campbell, better known as "Alastair Buidhe Mac Iamhair," his ground-officer, and allowed him to hold his land in Strath all his life rent free.* He gave a great impetus to the Gairloch cod fishing, which he continued to encourage as long as he lived.

Sir Hector married, in August 1778, Cochrane, daughter of James Chalmers of Fingland, without issue; and the marriage was dissolved on the 22d of April 1796. In the same year, the marriage contract bearing date "9th May 1796," within a month of his separation from his first lady, he married, secondly, Christian Henderson, daughter of William Henderson, Inverness, a lady who became very popular with the Gairloch people, and still affectionately remembered in the West as "A Bhantighearna Ruadh."† By her he had issue—

1. *Francis Alexander*, his heir.

2. *William*, a merchant in Java, and afterwards in Aus-

---

* Dr John Mackenzie of Eileanach, Sir Hector's only surviving son, makes the following reference, under date of August 30, 1878, to the old bard :—" I see honest Alastair Buidhe, with his broad bonnet and blue great-coat (summer and winter) clearly before me now, sitting in the dining room at Flowerdale, quite ' raised ' like, while reciting Ossian's poems, such as 'The Brown Boar of Diarmad,' and others (though he had never heard of Macpherson's collection) to very interested visitors, though as unacquainted with Gaelic as Alastair was with English. This must have been as early as 1812 or so, when I used to come into the room after dinner about nine years old." The bard was the author's great grandfather on the mother's side, and was, on his mother's side, descended from the Mackenzies of Shieldag.

† Dr John, her only surviving son, writes of her and her father thus :—" His second wife was only child of William Henderson, from Aberdeenshire (cousin of Mr Coutts, the London banker, with whom, in consequence of the relationship, my elder brothers, Francis and William, were on intimate terms in Stratton Street, Piccadilly, where Lady Burdett Coutts now lives), who set up a Bleach-field at the Bught, Inverness, by a daughter of Fraser of Bught. . . . . Henderson followed his daughter to Conon, as tenant of Riverford, where, till very old, he lived, and then moved to Conon House, till he died about 1816, loved by all, aged 97. I think he is buried in the Chapel Yard, Inverness."

tralia. He died, unmarried, in 1860, at St Omer, in France.

3. *Hector*, married Miss Fraser, eldest daughter of General Sir Hugh Fraser of Braelangwell; was Captain in H.E.I.C.S., and died in India, without surviving issue.

4. *John*, now of Eileanach. He studied for the medical profession, and took his degree of M.D. He was one of the trustees of Sir Kenneth, the present Baronet, during his minority, and afterwards, for several years, Provost of Inverness. He married, 28th September 1826, Mary Jane, only daughter of the Rev. Dr Inglis of Logan Bank and Old Greyfriars, Edinburgh, Dean of the Chapel Royal, and sister to the present Lord Justice-General Inglis, President of the Court of Session, with issue—(1) Colonel Hector, born August 24, 1828, went to India in his twentieth year, was at Chilianwallah and Goojerat, and, afterwards, until he retired in 1877, in the Civil Service chiefly as Judicial Commissioner for Central India at Nagpore. He married, May 9, 1855, Eliza Anne Theophila, eldest daughter of General Jamieson, of the H.E.I.C.S., without issue; (2) John Inglis, died in 1843, in his sixth year; (3) Harry Maxwell, born 16th May 1839, a Captain in the Royal Artillery. He married on the 7th September 1872, Georgina Caroline, eldest daughter of the late Captain Ponsonby, Deputy Quarter-Master-General in Scinde, and has issue, four children—three sons and one daughter; (4) Mary, married Duncan Davidson, now of Tulloch, by whom she had Eoin Duncan Reginald, a settler in Queensland; Hector Francis, in New Zealand; Alastair Norman, in Queensland; Lucy Eleonora, married, in 1873, Allan R. Mackenzie, yr. of Glenmuick and Kintail, with issue —one daughter; Mary Macpherson; and Victoria Geraldine; (5) Christina Isabella, married, November 23, 1853, Charles Addington Hanbury of Strathgarve, Ross-shire, and Belmont, Herts, with issue, four sons and four daughters—Harold Charles, of the Carabineers; John Mackenzie Basil; David Theophilus, Mary Florence, Kithe Agatha, who married, April 1877, Horace William Kemble of Oakmere, Herts; Isabel, and Maria Francis Lisette; (6) Kithe Caroline mar-

ried, April 12, 1865, Francis Mackenzie Ogilvie, third son
of Thomas Ogilvie of Corriemony, with issue, seven children ;
(7) Lisette, married June 28, 1878, Frederick Louis Kinderman, son of — Kinderman, founder of the house of Keith
and Co., London and Liverpool; (8) Georgina Elizabeth,
married, January 26, 1860, Duncan Henry Caithness Reah
Davidson, younger of Tulloch, with issue—Duncan ; John
Francis Barnard ; Mary ; Elizabeth Diana ; Adelaide Lucy ;
Georgianna Veronnica ; and Christina Isabella.

5. *Roderick*, a Captain in the army, afterwards sold out,
and became a settler in Australia, where he died. He married Meta Day, an Irish lady, sister of the present Bishop
of Cashel, without issue.

Sir Hector also had three natural children, by Jean
Urquhart, which was the cause of his separation from his
first wife. He made provision for them all. The first,
Catherine, married John Clark, leather-merchant, Inverness,
and left issue. Another daughter married Mr Murrison,
contractor for the Bridge of Conon, who afterwards settled
down, after the death of the last Mackenzie of Achilty, on
the farm of Kinkell, by whom she had issue, of whom the
Stewarts, late Windmill, Inverness.   A son, Kenneth,
originally in the British Linen Bank, Inverness, afterwards
died in India in the army.

His widow survived him about twelve years, first living
with her eldest son, and, after his marriage, at Ballifeary,
now called Dunachton, on the banks of the Ness. Though
he came into possession of the property under such very
unfavourable conditions; though his annual rental was under
£3000 a year; and though he kept open house throughout
the year at Conon and Gairloch, he was able to leave, or
pay during his life, to each of his younger sons, the handsome sum of £5000. When pressed, as he often was, to go
to Parliament, he invariably asked, " Who will then look
after my people ?"

He died 26th of April 1826; was buried in the Priory
of Beauly, and succeeded by his eldest son,

XII. SIR FRANCIS ALEXANDER, fifth Baronet, who,

benefiting by his father's example, and his kindly treatment
of his tenants, grew up interested in all county matters.
He was passionately fond of all manly sports, shooting,
fishing, and hunting. He resided during the summer in
Gairloch, and for the rest of the year kept open house at
Conon. During the famine of 1836-7 he sent cargoes of
meal and seed potatoes to the Gairloch tenantry, which,
with some heavy bill transactions he entered into to aid an
old friend, William Grant of Redcastle, at the time carrying on the Haugh Brewery, Inverness, involved him in
temporary financial difficulties. This induced him, in 1841,
to get his brother, Dr John Mackenzie of Eileanach, to take
charge of his affairs, when he went himself with his lady
for a few years to reside in Brittany, where his youngest
son, Osgood Hanbury Mackenzie, now of Inverewe, was
born. To get clear of the liability incurred with Mr Grant,
Dr John had ultimately to pay down £7000.

In 1838 he published a work on agriculture, " Hints for
the use of Highland Tenants and Cottagers, by a Proprietor," 273 pages, with English and Gaelic on opposite
pages, which shows his intimate knowledge with and the advanced views he held on the subject, as well as the great
interest he took in the welfare of his tenantry—for whose
special benefit the book was written. It deals, first, with
the proper kind of food and how to cook it ; with diseases
and medicine, clothing, houses, furniture, boats, fishing implements, agricultural implements, cattle, horses, pigs, and
their diseases ; gardens, seeds, fruits, vegetables, education,
morals, &c., &c., while illustrations and plans are given of
suitable cottages, barns, outhouses, and farm implements.

He married, first, in the 31st year of his age, 10th
August 1829, Kythe Caroline, eldest daughter of Smith-
Wright of Rempstone Hall, Nottinghamshire, with issue—

1. *Kenneth Smith*, his heir, the present Baronet, born in
1832.

2. *Francis Harford*, Kerrisdale, born 1833, unmarried.

He married, secondly, 25th October 1836, Mary, daughter of Osgood Hanbury of Holfield Grange, Essex, the pre-

sent Dowager Lady Mackenzie of Gairloch, with issue—

3. *Osgood Hanbury*, born 13th May 1842, and, in 1862, bought Kernsary from his brother, Sir Kenneth, and Inverewe and Turnaig, in 1863, from Sir William Mackenzie of Coul. On 26th June 1877, he married Minna Amy, daughter of Sir Thomas Edwards-Moss, Baronet of Otterspool, Lancashire, with issue, a daughter, Mary Thyra.

Sir Francis died, 2d June 1843, from inflammation of the arm, produced by bleeding—then a common practice for almost all manner of complaints—by his personal friend, Robert Liston, the celebrated surgeon. He was succeeded by his eldest son,

XIII. SIR KENNETH S. MACKENZIE, sixth and present Baronet, universally admitted to be one of the best landlords in the Highlands. Following the example of his father and grandfather, he deals directly with his people, without any factor or go-between, except an estate manager at Gairloch—and takes a personal interest, like his ancestors, in every man on his property. He takes an active part in all County matters; is Convener of the Commissioners of Supply, and Deputy-Lieutenant and Magistrate for the County of Ross. In 1854 he was appointed Attaché to Her Majesty's Legation at Washington, which, however, he never joined. In 1855 he received a commission as Captain in the Highland Rifle (Ross-shire) Militia, was afterwards promoted to be Major, and ultimately retired. He still commands a company of Rifle Volunteers raised on his Gairloch property. In 1860 he married Eila Frederica, daughter of Walter Frederic Campbell of Islay, with issue—

1. *Kenneth John*, his heir, born in 1861.
2. *Francis Granville*, born in 1865; and
3. *Muriel Katharine*.

THE MACKENZIES OF BELMADUTHY.

I. WILLIAM MACKENZIE, first of Belmaduthy, was the eldest son of Alexander Mackenzie, V. of Gairloch, by his second marriage with Isabel, daughter of Alexander Mackenzie, progenitor of the families of Applecross and Coul.

William married Mary, daughter of James Cuthbert of Altcrlies and Easter Draikies, Inverness, with issue—

1. *Alexander*, his heir.

2. *Isabel*, married to John Munro of Tayres.

3. *Catherine*, married Alex. Mackenzie, IV. of Loggie.

4. *Janet*, married Alexander Mackenzie, VII. of Gairloch.

5. *Jean*, married Hugh Baillie of Kynmylies, Sheriff-Clerk of the County of Ross.

6. *Mary*, married Murdo Mackenzie of Sand.

William and his wife both died in one week, in 1658, and were buried in Fortrose. He was succeeded by his only son,

II. ALEXANDER MACKENZIE, who married Catharine, daughter of Sir Kenneth Mackenzie, I. of Coul, with issue—

1. *William*, his heir.

2. *Kenneth*, I. of Pitlundie.

3. *George*, I. of Culbo, who married Mary, daughter of Alexander Forrester of Cullenauld, with issue—(1) Isabel, who married Fraser of Achnagairn, with issue ; (2) Anne, married Dr John Mackenzie ; and (3) Catharine, who married John Mackenzie, III. of Gruinard, with issue. Leaving no male issue, his nephew, William, II. of Pitlundie, succeeded to Culbo.

4. *Anna*, married Alexander Mackenzie, M.D., eldest son of Bernard Mackenzie of Sandylands.

Alexander was succeeded by his eldest son,

III. WILLIAM MACKENZIE, who married, first, Margaret, daughter of Alexander Rose of Clava, with issue—

1. *John*, his heir.

2. *George*, M.D., surgeon of the Queen's Dragoons.

3. *Hugh*, a merchant in Fortrose.

4. *Alexander*, commander of a ship in the Guinea trade. The latter three died unmarried.

5. *Catharine*, married Wm. Tolmie, merchant, Fortrose.

6. *Elizabeth*, married John Matheson of Bennetsfield.

7. *Jean*, married Simon Mackenzie, I. of Scotsburn.

8. *Isobel*, married William Mackenzie, a Lieut.-Colonel in Montgomery's Highlanders.

z

He married, secondly, Elizabeth, daughter of Sir Kenneth Mackenzie, IV. of Scatwell, Bart., by whom he had—

1. *Kenneth*, a doctor of medicine at Reading.

2. *Roderick*, I. of Flowerburn.

3. *Lilias*, who married Roderick Macleod of Cadboll.

He was succeeded by his eldest son,

IV. JOHN MACKENZIE, who married Rebecca, daughter of John Mackenzie, I. of Delvine, with issue—

1. *William*, his heir.

2. *John*, died young.

3. *Kenneth*, a merchant at Patna, married a Miss Mackenzie in the East Indies.

4. *Margaret*, who died unmarried.

5. *Rebecca*, married John Aird, a London merchant.

He was succeeded by his eldest son.

V. WILLIAM MACKENZIE, Advocate, who married Maria, daughter of John Lancaster, Cambridge, with issue—

1. *John*, his heir.

2. *William*, who married a daughter of Mr Hay, Huntingdon, without issue.

3. *George*, married a Miss Lynch, without issue.

4. *Cecilia*.   5. *Maria*.   6. *Rebecca*.   All unmarried.

He was succeeded by his eldest son,

VI. JOHN MACKENZIE, who married Margaret, daughter of Mr Hay, Huntingdon, with issue—

1. *John Kenneth*.   2. *Anne Maria*.   3. *Catherine*.

Present representation unknown.

THE MACKENZIES OF PITLUNDIE AND CULBO.

I. KENNETH MACKENZIE, first of Pitlundie, was the second son of Alexander Mackenzie, II. of Belmaduthy, by his wife, Catharine, daughter of Sir Kenneth Mackenzie, I. of Coul. He married Anne, daughter of Hector Mackenzie of Bishop Kinkell, brother of Alexander, VII. of Gairloch, with issue—

1. *William*, his heir.

2. *Margaret*, who, in 1727, married John Matheson, I. of

Attadale, of whom the family of Alexander Matheson of Ardross and Lochalsh.

He was succeeded by his only son,

II. WILLIAM MACKENZIE of Pitlundie and Culbo, getting the latter as heir to his uncle, George, I. of Culbo. He married a daughter of George Mackenzie of Inchcoulter, with issue—

1. *George*, his heir.

2. *William*.

3. A daughter, who married Alexander Mackenzie of Cleanwaters.

4. *Anne*, who married Roderick Mackenzie of Achavannie, with issue.

He was succeeded by his eldest son,

III. GEORGE MACKENZIE, Sheriff-Substitute of the Counties of Ross and Cromarty. He married Anne, daughter of Alexander Mackenzie, last and VIII. of Davochmaluag, with issue—

1. *William*, his heir.

2. *Alexander*, who died unmarried.

3. *Kenneth*, Captain, H.E.I.C.S., killed at Java, in 1811.

4. *Duncan Henry*, major, Madras H. Artillery, who married Mary Mackinnon of Corry; died in 1834; and left issue —George William, who died unmarried, and Lieut.-Colonel Lachlan Mackinnon of the Madras Army, unmarried.

5. *George* of Drynie, a writer in Dingwall, who married Catherine, daughter of John Macrae, Sheriff of Dingwall, by whom he had issue—John, a surgeon in the Madras Army, died unmarried in 1872; George William, English Chaplain at Frankfort, who married a Miss Fanny Taylor; Charles, died unmarried; Duncan; Anne, married Thomas Ballantine, with issue—a daughter; Elizabeth Proby, married Rev. W. Hutchins, Vicar of Louth, Lincoln, with issue; Isabella, married Rev. William Baden Powell, Vicar of Newick, Sussex; and Margaret, unmarried. George died in 1865.

6. *John*, a writer in Tain, married Christian, daughter of Capt. Kenneth Mackenzie of Kerrisdale, with issue—George,

who died young; and Kenneth, who died unmarried. John died in 1852.

7. *Elizabeth*, who married James Macdonell, W.S., of the family of Glengarry, without issue.

8. Another, married Thomas Simpson, son of the minister of Avoch, with issue.

9. *Anne*, died unmarried.

He died in 1802 (his wife dying in 1832), and was succeeded by his eldest son,

IV. WILLIAM MACKENZIE, M.D., of the H.E.I.C.S. He married Margaret, daughter of Thomas Allan, with issue—

1. *George Kenneth*, died young.

2. *William Ord*, M.D., Deputy-Inspector-General of Army Hospitals, who became his heir.

3. *Thomas Allan*, Major, 3d Light Cavalry, Bombay, who married Clara, daughter of J. Birdwood, judge, Bombay Civil Service, with issue, William and Allan Stanley, the last of whom died young.

4. *Duncan Proby*, married .Cecilia, daughter of John Dudgeon, Edinburgh, with issue.

5. *George Richard*, married Elizabeth, daughter of Thos. Scott, W.S., Edinburgh.

6. *Robert Cleghorn*, married Ellen Maria, daughter o Colonel Flexman, Tasmania, with issue—two daughters. He died in 1866.

7. *Agnes*, married Charles Garstin, Bengal C. Service, with issue—two sons and three daughters.

8. *Margaret Anne*, died unmarried,

He sold the estate of Pitlundie in 1805 to Mr Graham of Drynie; died in 1866, and was succeeded in Culbo by his eldest surviving son,

V. WILLIAM ORD MACKENZIE, now of Culbo, M.D., Deputy-Inspector-General of Army Hospitals. He married Mary Susan, daughter of the late Henry Holmes, London with issue—

1. *Montague Allan-Ord ;*

2. *William Henry Allan-Ord ;*

3. *Stuart Allan-Ord ;*

4. *Edith Allan-Holmes ;*

5. *Gertrude Helen Allan-Holmes ;*

6. *Margaret Douglas Allan-Holmes ;* and

7. *Mary Susan Allan-Holmes,* who died young.

THE MACKENZIES OF FLOWERBURN.

I. RODERICK MACKENZIE, first of Flowerburn, was second son of William, III. of Belmaduthy, by his second wife, Elizabeth, daughter of Sir Kenneth Mackenzie, IV. of Scatwell, Bart. He married Grace, daughter of Alexander Mackenzie of Inchcoulter, with issue—

II. An only daughter, who married a Mr Kilgour. She succeeded to the estate, and may be called second of Flowerburn. By Mr Kilgour she had issue—

1. *Roderick Kilgour,* her heir.

2. *Elizabeth Townsend.*

She was succeeded by her only son,

III. RODERICK KILGOUR-MACKENZIE, who married Anne, second daughter of John Grant of Glenmorriston, with issue—

1. *Roderick,* his heir. He assumed the name of Mackenzie; died in 1812 ; and was succeeded by his only son,

IV. RODERICK MACKENZIE, who married Harriet, daughter of Colonel Grogan of Scafield, County Dublin, with issue—

1. *Roderick Grogan,* his heir.

2. *Elma,* married Major John M'D. Smith, Madras Staff Corps, with issue.

3. *Georgina Adelaide,* married Major Roderick Mackenzie, now of Kincraig.

He was succeeded by his only son,

V. RODERICK GROGAN MACKENZIE, now of Flowerburn, who married Eva, daughter of Sir Evan Mackenzie of Kilcoy, Baronet, with issue.

THE MACKENZIES OF LETTEREWE.

KENNETH MACKENZIE, VI. of Gairloch, married, as his third wife, in 1658, Janet, daughter of John Cuthbert of Castlehill, Inverness, and by her had issue—

I. CHARLES MACKENZIE of Mellen Charles, and I. of
Letterewe, who, by his father's marriage contract, got Logie-
Wester, which he afterwards exchanged with his half-brother,
Alexander, VII. of Gairloch, in 1696, for the lands of Letter-
ewe. He married Anne, daughter of John Mackenzie, II.
of Applecross (sasine 1687), by whom he had issue—

    1. *Murdoch*, his heir.

    2. *Mr Hector*, minister of Fodderty, previously librarian
in the University of Aberdeen, who married a Miss Baillie,
by whom he had one daughter, who married Mackenzie of
Park.

    3. *Alexander* of Tolly, Provost of Dingwall, progenitor
of the Mackenzies of Portmore, Muirton, &c.

    4. A daughter, who married her cousin, Roderick Mac-
kenzie, II. of Sanachan, second son of Roderick Mackenzie,
I. of Applecross.

    5. *Annabella*, married to Mr Maciver, Gress, Lews.

He was succeeded by his eldest son,

II. MURDOCH MACKENZIE, who married Catharine,
daughter of Simon Mackenzie, I. of Torridon, relict of
John Mackenzie of Dalmartine killed at Sheriffmuir, by
whom he had—

    1. *John*, his heir.

    2. *Janet*, who married the Rev. James Robertson, the
famous "Ministear Laidir" of Lochbroom, with issue.

Murdoch Mackenzie was at Sheriffmuir, and also at
Glenshiel in 1719; and, when an old man, he was anxious
to be out again in 1745, but his wife managed to prevent
him. There is a tradition in the family that she poured hot
water on his feet and scalded them to keep him out of the
Forty-five. He was succeeded by his eldest son,

III. JOHN MACKENZIE, who married his cousin, Katharine, daughter of Alexander Mackenzie of Tolly, Provost
of Dingwall, and by her had—

    1. *Murdoch*, his heir.

    2. *Alexander*, who succeeded his brother Murdoch as V.
of Letterewe.

    3. *John*, Sheriff-Substitute of the Lews district of Ross-

shire, who married, first, Johanna, daughter of Alexander Mackenzie, Badachro, by whom he had surviving issue (1), John Mackenzie, Auchinstewart, Wishaw, who married in Australia, Miss Anna Baird, with issue—a son, John Alexander, an Engineer in the service of the Peninsular and Oriental Company's service.

"The Sheriff" married, secondly, Christina, daughter of the Rev. Hugh Munro, minister of Uig, in the Lews [representative of the Munros of Eriboll, Sutherlandshire], with issue—(2), John Munro Mackenzie of Mornish, Mull, who married Eliza, daughter of Patrick Chalmers, Wishaw, by whom he has two sons—John Hugh, married Jeanie, daughter of Thomas Chalmers, Longcroft, Linlithgow; Patrick; and three daughters—Harriet, Christina, and Helena. (3) Hugh Munro Mackenzie, Distington, Cumberland, who married Alexa, daughter of Captain Martin Macleod of Drynoch, Ontario, with issue—two sons and three daughters, Martin Edward, Hugh Munro, Christina, Jeanie, and Kate. (4) Katharine, who married her cousin, Capt. James Robertson Walker, R.N., of Gilgaran, Cumberland, without issue.

4. *Annabella*, who married her cousin, James Robertson, collector of customs at Stornoway, son of the "Ministear Laidir" of Lochbroom, by whom she had, among others, Katharine, who married Lewis Maciver, Gress, Stornoway. By this marriage Katherine Robertson had, among others, Evander Maciver, factor for the Duke of Sutherland at Scourie, who married Mary, daughter of Donald Macdonald of Skeabost, Skye, with issue—Duncan, a settler in Queensland; Lewis, at Scourie; Murdo Robertson, and John Macdonald, merchants in Cape of Good Hope; and a daughter, Mary, who married Francis Shand Robertson, Richmond, Surrey, with issue.

5. *Catherine*, who married her cousin, Charles Robertson, another son of the "Ministear Laidir," residing in London.

6. *Anne*, who married John Macintyre, tacksman of Letterewe, with issue.

John was succeeded by his eldest son,

IV. MURDO MACKENZIE, a Captain in the 78th Highlanders, who died in India without issue. He was succeeded
by his next brother,

V. ALEXANDER MACKENZIE, who married Catherine,
daughter of James Macdonald of Skeabost, with issue—

1. *John*, his heir.

2. *James*, midshipman, H.E.I.C.S., died without issue.

3. *Murdo*, a doctor, H.E.I.C.S., died without issue.

4. *Hector*, in the Customs at Cape of Good Hope, who
succeeded his brother John as VII. of Letterewe.

5. *Donald Alexander*, who emigrated in early life to the
United States, where he became a merchant, and married,
with issue—Charles, a lawyer in good practice, the present
representative, of the family of Letterewe ; and Alexander,
a Captain of Engineers in the United States army, married
in 1872, with issue—a son, Donald.

Donald Alexander died in 1872, leaving a widow, who
still survives, at Dubuque, Iowa.

6. *Jessie*, married Donald Macdonald, Lochinver, who
died at Cape of Good Hope in 1855, leaving issue—(1)
Donald, an Engineer, at the Cape, married, with issue—two
sons and a daughter ; (2) Alexander J., married, in London,
Caroline Heugh, with issue—two daughters ; (3) Murdo,
married, in London, Laura Foley, niece of the famous sculp-
tor of that name, by whom he has four sons and a daughter ; (4) Katherine, who married W. S. Kirkwood, Edinburgh, with issue—four sons and two daughters ; now
residing with her mother in London.

7. *Katherine*, died unmarried.

8. *Emily*, living in London, unmarried.

He was succeeded by his eldest son,

VI. JOHN MACKENZIE, a W.S. in Edinburgh, who died
there unmarried, and was succeeded by his eldest surviving brother,

VII. HECTOR MACKENZIE, who, in 1835, sold the
estate to Meyrick Bankes of Winstanley Hall, Lancashire.
He died, unmarried, in 1860, at Algoa Bay, Cape of Good
Hope, when he was succeeded as representative of the
family by his next brother,

VIII. DONALD ALEXANDER MACKENZIE, a merchant at Dubuque, United States of America, where he died in 1872, and was succeeded as representative of the family by his eldest son,

IX. CHARLES MACKENZIE, a lawyer in the United States. The representative of the family in this country is John Mackenzie, Achenstewart, Wishaw.

THE MACKENZIES OF PORTMORE.

ALEXANDER MACKENZIE OF TOLLY was third son of Charles Mackenzie, I. of Letterewe, by Anne, daughter of John Mackenzie, II. of Applecross. He married, in 1740, Annabella, daughter of Sir Donald Bayne of Tulloch ; and her descendants, as representatives of that ancient family, bear its cognisance in the centre of their shield, a wolf's head ppr. He became Bailie, and afterwards Provost of Dingwall, and exercised a considerable political influence, having greatly aided Lord Macleod in his candidature for the County of Ross, as will be seen from the Cromarty papers. During a riot which occurred in Dingwall conse- · quent on an election, Mrs Mackenzie, whilst looking out of a window of her own house, was accidentally shot. By her Provost Mackenzie had issue—

1. *Alexander*, I. of Portmore.

2. *Katharine*, married her first cousin, John Mackenzie, III. of Letterewe, with issue.

3. *Charlotte*, married the Rev. John Downie, minister of Gairloch and Urray, with issue.

He married, secondly, Katharine, daughter of Bayne of Delny, with issue—

· 1. *Ronald*, a Captain in the army, died without issue.

2. *Hector*, a Bailie of Dingwall, married Anne, daughter of the Rev. Colin Mackenzie, minister of Fodderty, with issue—(1) Alexander, merchant in London, married his cousin, Catherine, daughter of Kenneth Mackenzie of Millbank, with issue, two daughters—Catherine, married Major Roderick Mackenzie of Kincraig, and Anne, who married the Rev. John Macdonald, of Calcutta ; (2) Colin, Lieuten-

ant in the Royal Navy, died without issue; (3) Henry, died
without issue; (4) Hectorina, who died in 1850. Bailie
Mackenzie married, secondly, a daughter of Mr Mackenzie,
Ussie, with issue—(5) Jane, married John Mackenzie; (6)
Annabella, married William Kemp of Comrie; (7) Anne,
married Kenneth Mackenzie of Millbank.

I. ALEXANDER MACKENZIE, his eldest son and heir,
who afterwards became first of Portmore, settled in the
South, and became a W.S.; but all his life he kept up a close
connection with his native county, having intimate business
relations with all the principal landowners, among whom he
was familiarly known by the soubriquet of "Sandy the
Signet." He purchased the estate of Seaton, in East
Lothian, but afterwards sold it to Lord Wemyss, after
which he purchased the estate of Portmore, in Peebleshire.
He married Anne, eldest daughter of Colin Mackenzie, VI.
of Kilcoy, by his wife Martha, eldest daughter of Charles
Fraser of Inverallochy, whose mother was Lady Erskine,
daughter of the Earl of Buchan. Thus the families of Kilcoy and Portmore deduce descent from the Royal Houses
of Stewart and Plantaganet, as also from the Dukes of Bur-
gundy.

He died in 1805, and was buried in the Greyfriars,
Edinburgh, latterly the burying-place of the family, leaving
issue :—

1. *Alexander*, who died in infancy.

2. *Alexander*, Lieutenant-Colonel 21st Dragoons, died
in the West Indies in 1796, aged 27.

3. *Colin*, who succeeded to Portmore.

4. *John*, died young.

5. *George Udny*, died young.

6. *Charles*, died young.

7. *William*, I. of Muirton (Ross-shire), W.S. Edinburgh.
He married, first, Mary, daughter of James Mansfield of
Midmar, with issue—(1) Alexander, II. of Muirton, and now
of Meikle Scatwell, a W.S. He married his cousin, Marion,
daughter of John Mansfield of Midmar, with issue—William
Garioch, died without issue in Gibraltar, 1876; John Mans-

field, W.S., Edinburgh; Alexander James, in Natal; Douglas
Hay, who succeeded to the estate of Meikle Seatwell by will
of his aunt, Mrs Douglas, and, dying without issue in 1873,
bequeathed it to his father; George Vansittart, a merchant
in Leith; James Dalrymple, in New Zealand. Alexander,
II. of Muirton, sold the estate to Colonel Ainslie; (2) James
Mansfield, died without issue; (3) William, M.A., in Holy
orders, married Isabella Trotter, Natal, with issue; (4)
Marion, married Captain Fred. H. De Lisle, R.N., Guernsey, without issue.

William, I. of Muirton married, secondly, Alice, daughter of Andrew Wauchope of Niddry Marischal, without
issue. He died in 1856, and was succeeded in the lands of
Muirton by his eldest son, Alexander, as above.

8. *Sutherland*, Manager of the Scottish Union Insurance
Company, died without issue.

9. *John*, banker in Inverness, married Mary Charlotte, ·
only daughter of Robert Pierson of Riga, and died in 1854,
leaving issue—(1) Alexander, a Major-General in the Army,
who, in 1860, died without issue. (2) John Robert, a Major-
General, and late Colonel of the 105th Regiment, married
Amelia Wilson, daughter of James Wilson, banker, Inver-
ness, with issue. (3) Colin, a Major in the Madras Staff
Corps, married Victoria, eldest daughter of Dr Charles
Mackinnon, of the Corry family, with issue. (4) Charlotte,
married, first, John A. Fraser, Lieutenant, 93d Highlanders,
with issue — John A. Mackenzie, Lieutenant, R.N.;
William Forbes Mackenzie; Charlotte A.; and Mary
E. (5) Mary Anne, married, first, George Grogan of Sutton,
Dublin, with issue—Edward George, Lieutenant, 42d
Highlanders, who married Meta, daughter of Admiral Sir
William King Hall, K.C.B., with issue; Mary Esme,
married Lieutenant and Adjutant Andrew Scott Stevenson,
42d Highlanders, with issue. Mary Anne married, secondly,
Colonel St George Stepney, C.B., Coldstream Guards,
without issue. (6) Elizabeth, married Captain George
Harkness, Madras, N.I., with issue. (7) Katharine, married
Captain Charles Harkness, and died in 1857, without issue,

Martha; Annabella; Jean; Elizabeth; and *Catharine,* all died unmarried.

He was succeeded by his third and eldest surviving son,

II. COLIN MACKENZIE, a W.S. in Edinburgh, and afterwards one of the Principal Clerks of Session, and Deputy Keeper of the Signet. He was one of the oldest friends of Sir Walter Scott, who alludes to him in his poems. He married Elizabeth, daughter of Sir William Forbes, Bart., of Pitsligo, and died in 1830, leaving issue—

1. *Alexander,* who died young.

2. *Alexander* (a second), who died young.

3. *William Forbes,* who succeeded to Portmore.

4. *Colin,* H.E.I.C.S., died without issue.

5. *James Hay,* W.S., married Isabella, daughter of Jas. Wedderburn, Solicitor-General for Scotland, with issue —(1) Colin, W.S.; (2) James Wedderburn, who died young; (3) George Wedderburn, in Ceylon; (4) Isabella Elizabeth, married Major-General Kirkland, with issue; (5) Alice, died young; (6) Louisa Helen; (7) Anne Christina, married Edward Bannerman, with issue; (8) Jean Charlotte. James Hay died in 1865.

6. *John,* late treasurer of the Bank of Scotland, married Christina Garioch, daughter of John Mansfield of Midmar, with issue—(1) Colin, Captain in the Highland Rifle Militia, and late Captain, 78th Highlanders, F.R.G.S., F.S.A. Scot. He married Jeannette Sophie, eldest daughter of Baron Gerhard Knut A. Falkenberg of Trystop, His Swedish and Norwegian Majesty's Consul-General in British North America, with issue—Ian Duncan, Ulric Knut, Colin Mansfield, and Christina Frederica Augusta. (2) Christina Garioch, who died young.

7. *Sutherland,* Lieutenant, Royal Navy; lost on board H.M.S. "Victor," in the Gulf of Mexico, 1844, without issue.

8. *George,* Lieutenant, H.E.I.C.S., died in India, in 1844, without issue.

9. *Charles Frederick,* a Fellow of Caius and Gonville College, Cambridge, second wrangler of his year. He entered Holy Orders, and was appointed Archdeacon of

Natal, in which colony he laboured successfully for some years among the Zulus. Coming home, he was selected as the leader of the Universities' Mission to Central Africa, and was consecrated at Capetown, the first Missionary Bishop of the English Church. He afterwards proceeded to the Zambezi River, where, acting in concert with Dr Livingstone, he succeeded in liberating a large number of slaves from the hands of the drivers who conducted them to the coast; and some of these liberated slaves formed the nucleus of the Bishop's first settlement at Magomero. While descending the River Ruo to meet Dr Livingstone, Bishop Mackenzie's canoe was overturned and his quinine lost. A short residence on a swampy island brought on a fever, to which he succumbed in January 1862. His life has been written by his friend, Dr Goodwin, the present Bishop of Carlisle.

10. *Elizabeth*, married George Dundas, a Judge of the Scottish Bench, by the title of Lord Manor, with issue—(1) James, V.C., Captain in the Royal (late Bengal) Engineers. He obtained the Victoria Cross for conspicuous gallantry during the expedition to Bhotan. (2) Colin Mackenzie, Commander. Royal Navy; (3) George, died without issue; (4) William, a W.S.; (5) David; (6) Elizabeth Christian; (7) Mary Frances; (8) Helen Anne; (9) Katharine.

11. *Anne* accompanied her brother to Natal, where she remained with him during the whole period of his ministry there. She afterwards followed him to Central Africa, but hearing of his death whilst ascending the Zambezi River, she returned to England, where she started and edited a small monthly missionary periodical, called "The Net." By this, and through her own unaided efforts, she was the means of inaugurating the Memorial Mission to Zululand (in memory of her brother), of which the Bishop of Zululand is the head. She was the author of a life of Henrietta Robertson, wife of the Rev. Mr Robertson, late chaplain to the garrison of Fort-Etchowe.

12. *Katharine*, died unmarried.

13. *Jane*, died unmarried.

14. *Louisa*, married William Wilson, C.S., without issue.

15. *Alice*, married the Venerable C. S. Grubb, late Archdeacon of Natal, with issue—Louisa and Constance.

Colin died in 1830, and was succeeded by his eldest surviving son,

III. WILLIAM FORBES MACKENZIE, for many years M.P. for the County of Peebles. He was a Lord of the Treasury under Lord Derby's Government, and is chiefly known in Scotch Parliamentary circles as the author of the famous "Forbes Mackenzie Act." He married Helen Anne, daughter of Sir James Montgomery of Stanhope, Baronet, with issue—

1. *Colin*, his heir.

2. *Elizabeth Helen*, who died young.

He died in 1862, and was succeeded by his only son,

IV. COLIN MACKENZIE, late H.E.I.C.S. He is Convener of the County of Peebles; and married Katharine Alice, daughter of Samuel Wauchope, C.B., with issue—four daughters.

THE MACKENZIES OF MOUNTGERALD.

I. COLIN MACKENZIE, first of Mountgerald, was the second surviving son of Kenneth Mackenzie, VI. of Gairloch, by his second wife, Janet, daughter of John Cuthbert of Castlehill. He married, first, Dame Margaret, successively relict of Sir Roderick Mackenzie of Findon and George Mackenzie, II. of Gruinard, daughter of Alexander Mackenzie, I. of Ballone, without issue. He married, secondly, Katharine, daughter of James Fraser of Achnagairn, with issue—

1. *James*, his successor.

2. *Alexander*, who died without issue.

3. *Kenneth*, died without issue.

4. *Colin*, who succeeded his brother James.

5. *Isabella*, who married Sir Lewis Mackenzie, third Baronet and VI. of Scatwell, with issue.

6. *Anne*, who married Alexander Mackenzie, II. of Lochend, with issue.

Colin was a Lieutenant in the Scotch Fusilier Guards,

and fought at the battle of Stenkirk, after which he retired from the army, purchased the estate of Mountgerald, and built Woodlands House. He died in 1727, and was succeeded by his eldest son,

II. JAMES MACKENZIE of Mountgerald. He died without issue, and was succeeded by his eldest surviving brother,

III. COLIN MACKENZIE, a Major in the army. He married Elizabeth, daughter of Sir Roderick Mackenzie, V. of Scatwell, with issue—

IV. COLIN MACKENZIE, a Major in the army. He married Emilia, daughter of Colonel James Fraser of Belladrum, with issue—

1. *Colin*, his heir.

2. *Alexander*, who succeeded his brother Colin.

3. *Simon Fraser*, Colonel, who succeeded Alexander.

4. *Hannah*, died unmarried.

5. *Mary*, died unmarried.

6. *Eliza*, married David Dick of Glenshiel.

7. *Isabella*, married Archibald Dick, with issue.

8. *Sarah*, died unmarried.

9. *Jemima*, died unmarried.

He was succeeded by his eldest son,

V. COLIN MACKENZIE, died without issue, and was succeeded by his next brother,

VI. ALEXANDER MACKENZIE, who also died without issue, and was succeeded by his next brother,

VII. SIMON FRASER-MACKENZIE, a Lieutenant-Colonel in the Madras Cavalry. He married, first, a daughter of Colonel Pendergast, with issue, one daughter, Mary; and, secondly, Margaret, a daughter of General Stewart, without issue.

In 1855 he sold the estate of Mountgerald to Lewis M. Mackenzie of Findon, brother and predecessor of Major J. D. Mackenzie, now of Findon and Mountgerald.

THE MACKENZIES OF LOCHEND.

I. JOHN MACKENZIE of Lochend, third son of Alexander, VII. of Gairloch by his second wife, Janet, daughter of William Mackenzie, I. of Belmaduthy, married Annabella, daughter of George Mackenzie, II. of Gruinard, by whom he had issue—

1. *Alexander*, his heir.

2. *George*, a Colonel in the H.E.I.C.S., and of Murray Keith's Highland Regiment, who married Christina, daughter of Captain Munro, Braemore, with issue—(1) Captain John, who married a Miss Fraser, and left two children, George and Poyntz; (2) Poyntz, died at Guadaloup; (3) Major Alexander, married Eliza, daughter of Captain Sutherland, by whom he had a daughter, Mary, married a Mr Gordon, in Dowville, Lower Canada. He married, secondly, Miss Fanny Brown, by whom he had five sons, Alexander, Poyntz, Innes, Wemyss, and Norman, and two daughters—Hannah and Annabella. Colonel George's daughters (1) Eliza, married Colonel Alexander Mackenzie of Gruinard, with issue; (2) Lilias, married Captain Macgregor, 18th Regiment, without issue, (3) Georgina, married a Mr Euracht; (4) Christina, married Angus Macleod, Banff, with issue; and (5) Annabella, married Captain John Munro, with issue.

3. *Lilias*, who married William Mackenzie, IV. of Gruinard, with issue.

4. *Christina*, married William Maciver, Turnaig, with issue.

John Mackenzie of Lochend was Tutor to his nephew, Sir Alexander Mackenzie, second Baronet of Gairloch, in 1728. He was succeeded by his eldest son,

II. ALEXANDER MACKENZIE, who married, first, a daughter of Colin Mackenzie, I. of Mountgerald, with issue—

1. *Lewis*, who died unmarried.

2. *John*, who succeeded to Lochend.

3. *Alexander*.

4. *James*.

5. *Annabella*, who married John Maciver, with issue.

6. *Lilias*, who married Iver Maciver, Gress, Lews, with issue.

Alexander married secondly, Annabella, daughter of Sutherland of Little Tarboll, with issue—

7. *Lewis*.

8. *Elizabeth*, who married a Mr Mackenzie with issue.
He was succeeded by his eldest surviving son,

III. JOHN MACKENZIE, who married, first, a daughter
of Mr Morrison, in the Lews, with issue—

1. *Anne*, who married a Mr Gardiner.

He married, secondly, a daughter of Mr Morrison, in
the Island of Tannera, with issue—

2. *Annabella*, who married Lieutenant Morrison, R.N.,
with issue.

3. *Sybella*, married Captain Rynie, R.N., with issue.

4. A daughter married Mr Mackenzie, of the Sand
family, residing in Ullapool, without issue.

He married, thirdly, a daughter of Collector Reid,
Stornoway, with issue—

5. *John*, his heir.

6. *Daniel*, died unmarried.

7. *James*, M.D., who married a daughter of Captain
Reid of Eilean Riach, without issue.

8. *Margaret*, died unmarried.

He was succeeded by his eldest son,

IV. JOHN MACKENZIE of Lochend, who married Miss
Mackenzie Morrison, Argyll.

THE MACKENZIES OF DAVOCHMALUAG.

I. ALEXANDER MACKENZIE, the first of this family, was second son of Kenneth Mackenzie, VII. of Kintail (Kenneth a Bhlair), by his second wife, Agnes, daughter of Hugh, VIth Lord Lovat. He married Margaret, daughter of Sir William Munro of Fowlis, with issue—

1. *Roderick*, who succeeded him.
2. *Hector*, married, with issue.
3. A daughter, married Fraser of Belladrum; and
4. A daughter, married William Ross of Invercharron.

He was succeeded by his eldest son,

II. RODERICK MACKENZIE, who married Anne, daughter of Donald Macdonald of Sleat, with issue—

1. *Kenneth*, his heir.
2. *John Dubh.*
3. *Mary*, who had a natural son, Alexander, progenitor of the family of Applecross and Coul, by Colin Cam, XI. of Kintail. She afterwards married, first, John Mor Grant, with issue; and, secondly, Cameron of Glen-Nevis.

Four other daughters married, respectively, Mackenzie of Kildun; Murdoch Mackenzie, III. of Achilty; Iver MacIver, Lochbroom, and Donald MacChoinnich Mhic Mhurchaidh.

He was succeeded by his eldest son,

III. KENNETH MACKENZIE, who married a daughter of Ross of Balnagown, with issue, three sons—

1. *Alexander*, his heir.
2. *John*, minister of Lochbroom, married his cousin, a daughter of Hector, son of Alexander, I. of Davochmaluag, with issue—William and Kenneth.
3. *Kenneth.*

He had also a natural son, Murdo, Chamberlain of the Lews, married to a daughter of George Munro of Kaitwall, with issue—several sons.

He was succeeded by his eldest son,

IV. ALEXANDER MACKENZIE, who married Margaret, daughter of Hector Munro of Fowlis, with issue—

1. *Roderick*, his heir.

2. *Colin*, who married Mary, daughter of the Rev. Mr Mackenzie, minister of Sleat, with issue.

3. The eldest daughter, married Robert Gray.

4. Another married Alexander MacRa of Inverinate; and

5. A third married Murdo Matheson, Balmacarra.

He was served heir on the 30th December 1618, and was succeeded by his eldest son,

V. RODERICK MACKENZIE, who married Janet, daughter of Fraser of Belladrum, with issue—

1. *Kenneth*, his heir.

2. *John*, a Captain in Colonel Hill's Regiment.

3. *George*, who married Annabella, daughter of Kenneth Mackenzie, VI. of Gairloch, with issue.

4. *Roderick*, married a daughter of Mackenzie of Fairburn, with issue.

5. *Hector*, merchant in Edinburgh, unmarried.

6. *Margaret*, married Alexander Mackenzie, II. of Tarvie, with issue.

7. A daughter married Bain of Knockbain.

8. Another married the Rev. John Mackenzie, Lochbroom.

He was a strong loyalist. His estates were confiscated and a garrison placed in his house by Oliver Cromwell, and he suffered great hardships during the Commonwealth. His friends took the officer who commanded the garrison in Davochmaluag house by surprise, and, in exchange for the officer's release, Mackenzie secured his peace. A sasine to him is dated 1640. He was succeeded by his eldest son,

VI. KENNETH MACKENZIE, who married, first, Mary, daughter of Sir Kenneth Mackenzie, first Baronet of Coul, with issue—

1. *Alexander*, his heir.

2. *Roderick*, who married a daughter of Kenneth Mackenzie of Dundonnell, with issue.

3. *Kenneth*, who married a daughter of the Rev. John Mackenzie, minister of Fodderty and Archdeacon of Ross, with issue.

4. A daughter, married, in 1689, Alexander Forrester of Cullenauld.

5. A daughter, married Roderick, a brother of Sir Alexander Mackenzie, II. of Coul; and

6. A third married Donald Mackenzie, brother of Mackenzie of Fairburn'; all three with issue.

He married, secondly, the widow of Mackenzie of Gairloch, without issue.

He was succeeded by his eldest son,

VII. ALEXANDER MACKENZIE, who married, first, Janet, daughter of Sir Alexander Mackenzie, II. of Coul, with issue—an only daughter, Janet, who married Æneas Macleod of Camuscurry, with issue; marriage contract 28th April 1715; tocher 3000 merks. She married, secondly, John Mackenzie, chirurgeon, Fortrose. He married, secondly, Elizabeth, daughter of Alexander Rose of Clava (marriage contract 1695), with issue—

1. *Alexander*, his heir.

2. *Kenneth*, who married a Miss Gordon, and died in Jamaica, leaving issue—two sons.

3. *John*, who married his cousin, Mary, daughter of his uncle Roderick, who emigrated to, and resided in, Carolina, and by her had a son, Captain John, who married abroad, and had issue—one daughter, Elizabeth, who died at Brighton in 1856, without issue. *John* had also one daughter, Elizabeth, who married, first, Richard Ord, Inverness, and by him had three sons and two daughters. Of the sons, William, M.D., H.E.I.C.S., died without issue; John, a merchant in London, married, and had issue; Richard, died young. The eldest daughter, Mary, married Donald Fraser, solicitor, Inverness, and by him had two sons and two daughters, John of Bunchrew (died 1876), who married Hester Lomax, with issue—four sons and five daughters; Richard, who died without issue; Eliza, who married George Arbuthnot of Elderslie, Surrey; and Catharine, who married Lieutenant-Colonel Patrick Vans-Agnew, C.B., of Barnbarroch, Wigtonshire, both with issue. The second daughter, Prudence, married Bailie John Mackenzie, of Inverness, son of

Ardnagrask, with issue [for which see the Mackenzies of Sand and Ardnagrask in the Gairloch genealogy]. Elizabeth married, secondly, as his second wife, Farquhar Maera of Inverinate, without issue.

4. *Roderick*, who died unmarried.

5. *Mary*, married William Mackenzie of Achilty and Kinellan, a brother of Sir Alexander Mackenzie, V. of Coul.

6. *Margaret*, married Captain Joseph Avery, who afterwards went to Carolina, and left issue.

7. *Frances*, married John Maclcod of Bay, with issue—one daughter.

8. *Christian*, married William Tolmie, first a merchant at Fortrose, and afterwards at Dunvegan, Isle of Skye, with issue—two sons and two daughters.

He was appointed Sheriff-Substitute of Ross in 1698; and was succeeded by his eldest son,

VIII. ALEXANDER MACKENZIE, the last Baron of Davochmaluag, Sheriff-Substitute of Ross, who married, first, Magdalene, daughter of Hugh Rose, XV. of Kilravock (marriage contract 1723), with issue—an only son

1. *Kenneth*, who died before his father of consumption, at Cowes, in the Isle of Wight, in 1753, while serving an apprenticeship with George Mackenzie, merchant there.

2. *Jean*, who married, first, William Mackenzie, son of Donald Mackenzie, V. of Kilcoy, without issue; and secondly, Alexander Mackenzie of Fairburn, with issue—an only son, Kenneth, Lieutenant in the 21st Regiment, serving under General Burgoyne in America, where he was killed, unmarried, at Saratoga, in September 1777.

3. *Beatrice*, married John Mackenzie of Brae, with issue.

4. *Mary*, married Farquhar MacRa of Inverinate, with issue.

5. *Magdalane*, married the Rev. Alexander Mackay, minister of Barvas, in the Lews, without issue.

He married, secondly, Anne, daughter of Roderick Mackenzie, IV. of Applecross, and widow of Alexander Mackenzie of Lentran, with issue—a daughter, Anne, who married George Mackenzie, III. of Pitlundie, Sheriff-Substitute of Ross, with issue.

Alexander was Captain of an Independent Company in 1746. He died without male issue in 1776, and was succeeded by his grandson,

IX. KENNETH, a son of his eldest daughter, Jean, a Lieutenant in the army, and killed, as already stated, without issue, at Saratoga in 1777; and having survived his cousin, Roderick Mackenzie, eldest son of John Mackenzie of Brae, the lineal representation of the family devolved upon Alexander, XI. of Hilton, second son of John Mackenzie of Brae; who, being bred a millwright, went abroad, and carried on that business in partnership with others, in Jamaica. He was still alive there in 1780, married, with issue.

THE MACKENZIES OF ACHILTY.

The progenitor of this family was the third son of Kenneth Mackenzie, VII. of Kintail, by Agnes of Lovat. He was originally designated of Acha-ghluincachan, but afterwards known as

I. RORY MOR MACKENZIE, first of Achilty. He was a very powerful man, and many instances of his prowess are still related among his countrymen; the most noted of which is his defeat of the famous Italian before King James V. [described pp. 76-80]. He married, first, a daughter of Farquhar MacEachainn Maclean, and by her had—

1. *Alastair Roy*, his heir.

2. *Alastair Dubh*, died without issue.

3. *John Roy*, married, with issue.

He married, secondly, a lady of the name of Grant, widow of Ross of Balnagowan, with issue. By a daughter of William Dubh Macleod he had four natural sons, of whom Murdoch, legitimatised by King James V. in 1539, became progenitor of the family of Fairburn. The other three—Alexander, John, and Roderick—were legitimatised by the same King in 1541. Rory Mor died 17th March 1533, was buried at Beauly, and succeeded by his eldest son,

II. ALASTAIR ROY MACKENZIE, who married a daughter of Chisholm of Strathglass, with issue—

1. *Murdoch*, who succeeded.

2. *Rory*, married, with issue—a daughter, who married Duncan Fraser of Munlochy, and Donald, married, with issue.

3. *John*, married the Good-man of Tullochgorm's daughter, with issue—a son, Alexander, who lived at Struy.

He died at Lochbroom in 1578, was buried there, and succeeded by his eldest son,

III. MURDOCH MACKENZIE, who married a daughter of Roderick Mackenzie, II. of Davochmaluag, with issue—

1. *Alexander*, his heir.

2. *Murdoch*, I. of Ardross and Pitglassie, progenitor of the present Mackenzies of Dundonnell.

3. *Kenneth*, of whom nothing is known.

4. *Rory*, who married, first, a daughter of Alastair Mac-
Allan, by whom he had Murdo Mackenzie, afterwards
Bishop of Ranfoe in Ireland. He married, secondly, a
daughter of Hector Mackenzie, son of Murdoch Mackenzie,
I. of Fairburn, by whom he had—

5. *Alexander.*

6. *Hector*, and four daughters who married respectively
Allan Mackenzie of Loggie; Dougal Mac Ian Oig; Rory
Clark; and Lachlan Mac Mhurchaidh Mhic Eachainn, of
Gairloch.

8. *Isobel*, who married Alexander Mackenzie of Inchcoulter, with issue.

He died 14th March 1609, was buried in Lochbroom,
and was succeeded by his eldest son,

IV. ALEXANDER MACKENZIE, who married a daughter
of David Chambers, with issue—

1. *Murdoch*, his heir.

2. *John*, who married a daughter of Kenneth Mackenzie,
I. of the Old family of Davochcairn.

3. *Thomas*, married a daughter of Duncan Mackenzie,
I. of Sand ; and several daughters, who married respectively
James Macleod, Assynt; Ranald MacGillespick ; Angus
Mac Dhughail Mhic Dhughail; Hector Mackenzie, Mel-
lan (Gairloch); Kenneth Buidhe Mackenzie, natural son of
. John Roy, IV. of Gairloch ; and Duncan Mackenzie, Mhic
Ian.

He died at Kildin, was buried at Dingwall, and was
succeeded by his eldest son,

V. MURDOCH MACKENZIE, who married, first, a daugh-
ter of Hector Mackenzie, son of Alexander Roy, son of
Hector Càm, natural son of Hector Roy Mackenzie, I. of
Gairloch, without issue. He married, secondly, a daughter of
Hector Mackenzie, IV. of Fairburn, relict of Kenneth Mac-
kenzie, I. of Davochcairn, with issue—

1. *Alexander*, his heir.

2. *Isobel*, who, in 1701, married Kenneth, son of John
MacIver Turnaig.

He married, secondly, Isabel, daughter of Alexander

Mackenzie, V. of Gairloch, relict successively, of John Mackenzie of Lochslinn, and Colin Mackenzie, I. of Tarvie.
He was succeeded by his only son,

VI. ALEXANDER MACKENZIE, Chamberlain of the
Lews and Assynt in 1735. He married Christian Mackenzie, with issue—

1. *Murdoch*, his heir.

2. *David*, married, with issue.

He was succeeded by his eldest son,

VII. MURDOCH MACKENZIE, who, in 1728, during his
father's lifetime, married Anne, third daughter of Sir Kenneth
Mackenzie, first Baronet and VIII. of Gairloch, without
issue. He was succeeded by his nephew, a son of his brother David,

VIII. COLIN MACKENZIE, an officer in the 78th Regiment, who married Janet, third daughter of Sir Alexander
Mackenzie, second Baronet and IX. of Gairloch. He seems
to have been the last who possessed the property, as in
1784 he has a tack of Kinkell, where he died in 1813, with
his affairs much involved. He had a son John who died
without issue. The property passed into the hands of
the Mackenzies of Applecross.

THE MACKENZIES OF ARDROSS, NOW OF DUNDONNELL.

The immediate progenitor of this family was Murdoch
second son of Murdoch Mackenzie, III. of Achilty.
He purchased the lands of Pitglassie and Kildin; and
married Catharine, daughter of John Mackenzie of Tolly,
with issue—

1. *Kenneth*, who, in 1699, married Agnes Fraser, and
died before his father, without issue.

2. *Alexander*, who succeeded his father.

3. *John*, of Rapach, who married Anne, daughter of
Colin Mackenzie, III. of Kincraig, without issue.

4. *William*, Episcopal minister of Rosskeen, married a
daughter of Fraser of Belladrum. He was admitted minister of Rosskeen before the 9th of August 1665, and died

14th March 1714 (Dr H. Scot's Festi). He had a son described in 1709 as "John, his eldest son." He also had a son called "Black Colin," who had the farm of Achintoul in Rosskeen, and married, with issue—(1) Alexander, who married Lilias Mackenzie, daughter of Colin Mackenzie, II. of Kincraig, and by her had a daughter who married, first, Alexander Ellison, and secondly, Alexander Aird, ancestor of the Rev. Gustavus Aird, Free Church minister of Creich. (2) George, married a daughter of Gordon of 'Embo, with issue—Colin; John; and three daughters, Mary, Nelly, and Margaret, who died at Invergordon 30 to 35 years ago, and "were as primitive in their appearance and dress as if they had come out of Noah's ark."

William also had three daughters, who married respectively the Rev. Allan Clark, minister of Glenelg; the Rev. Duncan MacCulloch, minister of Urquhart, and Andrew Fraser, Chamberlain of Ferrintosh.

Alexander of Ardross died in 1655, was buried at Dingwall, and succeeded by his second and eldest surviving son,

I. ALEXANDER MACKENZIE, who married Janet (? Isabella) daughter of Alexander Mackenzie, V. of Gairloch, with issue—

1. *Murdoch*, his heir.

2. *Kenneth*, in Ulladale, who had a son, Alexander; retour as heir general in 1715.

3. *Hector*, apprenticed to learn chirurgery in 1682.

4. *William*, married, in 1681, Christian, daughter of Colin Mackenzie, II. of Kincraig.

5. *Alexander*.

6. *Roderick*.

7. *Isobella*, married, in 1678, as his second wife, Alexander Mackenzie of Inchcoulter, brother-german to Sir George Mackenzie of Rosehaugh.

He bought the lands of Ardross during his father's lifetime, in 1644, formerly the property of Ross of Tolly, and sold the lands of Pitglassie and Kildin. He was served heir in 1662 ; died in 1674, and was succeeded by his eldest son,

II. MURDOCH MACKENZIE, who married a daughter of Grant of Elchies, in Strathspey, with issue—

1. *John*, his heir.

2. Another son, who died in 1761.

3. *Murdoch*, Tacksman of Clynes in 1745.

4. *Rory*. 5. *Anne*. 6. *Margaret*, who married, in 1709, Gregor, heir of Robert Grant of Gartenmor.

He was buried at Ardross, and was succeeded by his eldest son,

III. JOHN MACKENZIE, who married Helen, daughter of T. Erskine of Pittoderie, celebrated for her great beauty, by whom he had issue—

1. *Roderick*, his heir.

2. *Murdoch*, who succeeded as V. of Ardross.

3. *Margaret*, married James Muir of Stonywood, with issue.

4. *Rachel*, or Barbara, who married George Paton of Grandholm, with issue.

5. *Jean*, and several others—in all a family of fifteen sons and daughters.

He was buried at Ardross, and succeeded by his eldest son,

IV. RODERICK MACKENZIE, who died without issue, and was succeeded by his eldest brother,

V. MURDOCH MACKENZIE, who, in 1743, married Bathia, daughter of John Paton of Grandholm. In his time was concluded in the House of Lords before Lord Mansfield, a law-suit which existed for four generations with the Rosses of Achnacloich or Tolly, concerning the validity of the sale of the property to Alexander, second of the family, a process which ruined the Rosses and involved Ardross deeply in debt. He died, and was buried at Ardross, leaving issue, an only daughter, who succeeded to the property,

VI. MARGARET MACKENZIE, who, in 1763, married Captain James Munro of Teaninich, with issue—

1. *Hugh Munro*, Captain in the 78th Regt., who succeeded to the estate of Teaninich, and, in 1794, died unmarried.

2. *Murdoch*, who resumed the name of Mackenzie, and

succeeded his mother in the lands of Ardross and Dundonnell.

3. *Colonel Hector*, who died unmarried in 1827.

4. *Major-General John Munro*, H.E.I.C.S., who married 'Charlotte, daughter of Dr Blacker, with issue—(1) James St John, late Major 60th Rifles, who died in 1818, was married, and left issue—Maxwell, Lieutenant 48th Regt., and others; (2) John; (3) Stuart Caradoc; (4) Maxwell William; and (5) Charlotte, who, in 1834, married the Hon. George A. Spencer, with issue.

5. *Catherine*, married Thomas Warrand of Warrandfield, Inverness, with issue—Robert, a Major in the 6th Inniskilling Dragoons; and three sons and a daughter, all of whom died young.

6. *Bathia*; and 7. *Alexina*, both of whom died young.

Margaret was buried at Ardross, and was succeeded by her second son,

VII. MURDO MUNRO-MACKENZIE, retoured in 1795. He sold Ardross to the Duke of Sutherland, and, in 1835, purchased the estate of Dundonnell from Thomas Mackenzie, VI. of the Old family of Dundonnell. By the death of his elder brother, Hugh, without issue, Murdo became the head of the family of Munro of Teaninich. He went to India, but before he was able to embark in any pursuit, he was, in consequence of the death of his mother, called home to take possession of the estate, which was very much involved, his clear annual income therefrom being at first only about £60. He continued to be harassed for upwards of thirty years by constant litigation at an enormous cost. He purchased the River Shin with borrowed money, speculated in salmon fishings and lands, sold the whole, in 1832, to a company who soon after sold it to the Duke of Sutherland, who, in his turn, sold part of it to Alexander Matheson of Ardross, M.P. He took this step intending to go to Canada, but was prevented from doing so by altered circumstances, and the state of his eyes, which were failing him. In 1834 he purchased the estate of Dundonnell, and, in 1838, the detached portions of the Cromarty estates, including the forest of Fannich. He married Christina, daughter of Robert Ross, tacksman of Strathcullanach, on the Balna-gowan estates. By her he had issue—

1. *Hugh*, who, in 1813, died young.
2. *John*, who died in 1815.
3. *Hugh*, who succeeded him.
4. *Kenneth*, who succeeded his brother Hugh.
5. *Robert*, a Lieutenant-Colonel H.E.I.C.S., in Brisbane, Queensland, married, with issue.
6. *James*, died unmarried.
7. *Murdo*, died unmarried.
8. *Mary*, married Major-General Francis Archibald Reid, C.B., with issue.
9. *Helen*, married Simon Mackenzie-Ross of Aldie, whom she survives, without issue.

He died at Dundonnell, was buried there, and was suc-ceeded by his eldest surviving son,

VIII. HUGH MUNRO-MACKENZIE, who spent his whole time in beautifying, improving, and increasing his estates, upon which he regularly resided. He died unmarried, in 1869, leaving his fee-simple estates of Mungasdale, Gruinard, and Strath-na-Scalg, to an illegitimate daughter, who after-wards married Mr Catton.

He was buried at Dundonnell, and was succeeded by his brother,

IX. KENNETH MUNRO-MACKENZIE, who, trained to the medical profession, qualified in Edinburgh, and after-wards practised successively in Dublin, London, France, and Italy, and eventually emigrated to New South Wales, whence, after 34 years in different capacities, and after establishing his family in good positions there, he returned, in 1870, to his native county to take possession of his late brother's property. This, however, he only succeeded in doing after years of expensive litigation carried on against him by his brother's natural daughter, Mrs Catton, who attempted to overthrow the family settlements and obtain possession of the whole estates for herself; but instead of doing so she ruined her own property, which had to be sold to pay the lawyers.

He married, in 1838, Julia Smith, relict of Captain
Edmund Harrison Cliffe, of Sydney, New South Wales,
with issue—

1. *Murdo*, his heir, who accompanied his father home
from Australia, and now of Dundonnell.

2. *Hugh* of Bundanon, Shoulhaven, N.S.W., who married,
in 1876, Bella Mary, eldest daughter of T. T. Biddulph of
Earie, Shoulhaven, with issue—Bella, May, and Hugh.

3. *Helen*, married, in 1870, John Robinson of Shoulhaven, N.S.W., with issue.

4. *Mary*, married, in 1860, James Thomson of Burrier,
Shoulhaven, N.S.W., with issue—five sons and three daughters.

5. *Julia Anna*, married, in 1867, the Rev. Robert Speir
Willis, M.A., of the Church of England, Incumbent of
Manly Beach, Sydney, N.S.W., with issue—one son and
one daughter.

Kenneth died in 1878, was buried at Dundonnell, and
was succeeded by his eldest son,

X. MURDO MUNRO-MACKENZIE, now of Dundonnell.

THE MACKENZIES OF FAIRBURN.

This family is also descended from Roderick Mòr Mackenzie of Achilty, by a daughter of William Dubh Macleod of the Lews, by whom he had a natural son,

I. MURDOCH MACKENZIE, first of Fairburn, legitimatised
by letters of legitimation granted by James V., dated 1st
July 1539. Later on, March 16, 1541, there are letters of
legitimation, " Alexandro Mackenzie Seniori, Joanni juniori,
et Roderico, bastardis filiis naturalibus, quondam Roderici
Maekenze." Murdo, for some time, lived at Court, was a
Gentleman of the Bedchamber to James V., and obtained a
charter for his lands, dated 1st April 1542, afterwards confirmed by Queen Mary in 1548. He married, first, Margaret, daughter of Urquhart, Sheriff of Cromarty, with
issue—

1. *Alexander*, his heir.

2. *John*, I. of Tolly, minister of Dingwall, who married

Margaret, daughter of Ballindalloch, with issue—Murdoch, II. of Tolly (and others), who married Catherine, daughter of James Innes of Inverbreakie, with issue. '

3. *Annabella*, who married, first, Thomas Mackenzie of Lochluichart and Ord, with issue ; and secondly, Alexander Mackenzie, progenitor of Coul, also with issue.

4. A daughter' married Ross of Priesthill.

Murdoch married, secondly, a daughter of Rory Mac-Farquhar, with issue—

5. *Roderick* of Knockbaxter.*

6. *John*, I. of Corry.

7. *Hector*, Chamberlain of Lochcarron.†

8. *Isabel*, married John Roy Mackenzie, IV. of Gairloch.

9. A daughter married Donald Glass Macdonald ; and

10. *Mary*, married Wyland Chisholm, Kinkell.

He died in 1590, and was succeeded by his eldest son,

II. ALEXANDER MACKENZIE, who married a daughter of Walter Innes of Inverbreakie, with issue—

1. *John*, his heir.

2. *Hector*, who succeeded his brother John.

3. *Isobel*, who married John Mackenzie, eldest son of John Roy, IV. of Gairloch, who died in 1601, before his father, without male issue. She married, secondly, Bayne of Tulloch.

4. A daughter married Murdo Mackenzie of Kernsary, with issue.

Alexander was succeeded by his eldest son,

III. JOHN MACKENZIE, who married Janet, daughter of Torquil Macleod of Coigeach. He had no male issue.

Four daughters married respectively—the eldest Murdo Mackenzie of Sand ; Agnes, first, Murdo MacCulloch of Park, and secondly, Roderick Mackenzie, II. of Corry ; Isobel, John Mackenzie of Pitlundie ; and Annabella, Roderick Mackenzie, Ardlair ; the last three being heirs

---

* One of the sons of Roderick of Knockbaxter was Rory, minister of Gairloch in 1678, and ancestor of the second family of Kernsary.

† For the descendants of the issue of the second marriage, see Findon's Tables, sheet V.

portioners. There is a sasine of Monar to John of Fairburn in 1620. He died in, 1645, and was succeeded by his
next brother,

IV. HECTOR MACKENZIE, who married, first, Agnes,
daughter of Valentine Chisholm of Comar, with issue—

1. *Roderick*, his heir, who succeeded ; and five daughters,
who married respectively, Roderick, son of Bayne of Tulloch,
and, secondly, Angus, third son of Alexander Mackenzie,
V. of Gairloch, by Isobel Mackenzie of Coul ; another married Kenneth Mackenzie, I. of Davochcairn, and, secondly,
Murdoch Mackenzie, V. of Achilty; the third married the
Rev. Alexander Mackenzie, minister of Lochcarron; the
fourth, Roderick, second son of Colin Mackenzie, I. of Kincraig ; and the fifth, Mr Alexander, third son of Mr John
Mackenzie of Tolly, by his second marriage with a daughter of Thomas Fraser of Struy.

Hector was succeeded by his only son,

V. RODERICK MACKENZIE, who first married a daughter
of Patrick Grant of Glenmoriston, without surviving issue.
He married, secondly, in 1663, Margaret, daughter of Donald
Mackenzie, III. of Loggie, with issue—

1. *Murdoch*, his heir.

2. *John* of Bishop-Kinkell.

3. *Colin*.   4. *Donald*.

He was succeeded by his eldest son,

VI. MURDOCH MACKENZIE, who, in 1673, married Isobel,
daughter of the Hon. Simon Mackenzie of Lochslinn, with
issue—

1. *Roderick*, his heir; 2. *Kenneth;* 3. *George;* and 4.
James.

He was succeeded by his eldest son,

VII. RODERICK MACKENZIE, who, in 1712, married
Winniewood, daughter of William Mackintosh, younger of
Borlum, with issue—

1. *Alexander*, his heir.

2. *Kenneth*, married Ann MacRa, with issue.

3. *Colin*.

He was succeeded by his eldest son,

VIII. ALEXANDER MACKENZIE of Fairburn, to whom the estates, forfeited in 1715, were restored in 1731. He was succeeded by his eldest son,

IX. RODERICK MACKENZIE, who, in 1768, married Catharine, daughter of William Baillie of Rosehall, with issue—

1. *Alexander*, his heir.

2. *William*, died without issue.

3. *Mary*, married James Massey, without issue. Mary married secondly, Colonel Robert Murray Macgrigor, with issue.

4. *Barbara*, who married, first, Kenneth Murchison of Tarradale, with issue—the late Sir Roderick Impey Murchison, President of the Royal Geographical Society, who married a daughter of General Hugonin, without issue; and the Hon. Kenneth Murchison.

5. *Janetta Catharine*, married, first, Robert Sutherland; secondly, Lieutenant Hull.

6. *Barbara*, who married Richard Hort, Royal Horse Guards Blue.

He was succeded by his eldest son,

X. ALEXANDER MACKENZIE, created a Baronet, Major-General in the army. He was the last of the Mackenzies of Fairburn, died unmarried in 185-, and is buried in the St Clement's aisle of the old Church of Dingwall.

THE MACKENZIES OF KILLICHRIST AND SUDDIE.

KENNETH A BHLAIR, VII. of Kintail, had a fourth
son by his second marriage with Agnes of Lovat, of whom
descended the families of Suddie, Inverlael, Little Findon,
Ord, Langwell, Highfield, and other minor branches. The
three-first named being extinct in the male line, it is needless
to enter further into detail than is necessary to show their
intermarriages with other Mackenzie families. The progenitor of these families was known as

I. KENNETH MACKENZIE of Killichrist, or Gilchrist.
He was Priest of Avoch, Chaunter of Ross, and perpetual
Curate and Vicar of Coirbents, or Conventh. He resigned
this vicarage into the hands of Pope Paulus, in favour of the
Priory of Beauly. We find a presentation by James, Bishop
of Moray, to Mr Kenneth Mackenzie, of the vicarage of
Conventh, dated June 27, 1518.* He has a charter of the
lands of Suddie from James V. in 1526. He would
not refrain from marriage, notwithstanding the orders of
the Roman Church promulgated some time previously, and
the Bishop attempted to depose him with the result described at p. 80. He married Helen Loval, daughter of
Robert Loval of Balumbie, Forfarshire ; his brother, John
of Killin, IX. of Kintail, and the lady's father, being parties
to the contract of marriage, dated 1539, by which it was
agreed that in case of his decease before her she was to
have an annuity of 600 merks Scots and other perquisites.

By this marriage Kenneth of Killichrist had—

1. *Alexander*, his heir.

2. *Thomas* of Kinlochluichart, and afterwards I. of Ord.

3. *John* Caol, or Slender, married, with issue.

4. *Roderick*, who married, and had two sons—Alexander
and John, and a daughter, who married, first, a Mr Macdonald ; and secondly, the Rev. Kenneth Mackenzie of the
Torridon family, minister of Sleat, in Skye.

---

* Antiquarian Notes, p. 160.

He was succeeded by his eldest son,

II. ALEXANDER MACKENZIE of Killichrist, who had a charter from James VI., dated 1571, of the lands of Suddie, granted to his father in 1526 by James V. He married Agnes, daughter of Roderick Mackenzie, third son of Allan, II. of Hilton, and progenitor of Loggie,* with issue—

1. *Kenneth*, his heir.

2. *John*, Archdean of Ross, I. of Inverlael, who had a son, Kenneth, II. of Inverlael, without male issue; and the Rev. Mr Thomas, who became III. of Inverlael, and had a son, John, who succeeded, and another, Thomas, a W.S., who died unmarried. John, the Archdean and I. of Inver-lael, had also a third son, Alexander, a W.S., who died un-married; and, a fourth, the Rev. James Mackenzie, minister of Nigg, from whom the late Right Honourable John Holt Mackenzie, without issue, and the late Joshua Henry Mackenzie of Belmont, Lord of Justiciary, who married Helen Ann, youngest daughter of Francis Humberston-Mackenzie, last Lord Seaforth, with issue—two daughters, Frances Mary and Penuel Augusta.

3. *Murdoch*, I. of Little Findon, who had a son, John, II. of Little Findon ; and

4. *Kenneth.*

5. *Alexander*, a natural son, who became a Colonel in the army; was Governor of Tangiers; and, by a German lady, had two sons, who served in the French army, and two daughters, one of whom, Penelope, married Allan Mac-donell, Chief of Clan Ranald, killed at Sheriffmuir in 1715.

Alexander was succeeded by his eldest son,

III. KENNETH MACKENZIE, who first married the widow of James Gray of Skibo, with issue—a daughter, who mar-ried John Dunbar of Avoch, and secondly, Lachlan Mack-intosh of Cullochy. He married, secondly, in 1605, Cath-arine, daughter of Roderick Mor Mackenzie, I. of Redcastle, with issue—

1. *Alexander*, his heir.

* Findon is incorrect here.

2. *Margaret*, who married Fraser, Tutor of Foyers.

He was succeeded by his only son, who became FIRST of the

MACKENZIES OF SUDDIE.

I. ALEXANDER MACKENZIE, first of this family, married Mary, daughter of Mr Bruce of Airth, with issue—

1. *Kenneth*, his heir.

2. *Colin*, who married Janet, daughter of John Mackenzie of Ardcharnich and Langwell, with issue—Alexander, an officer in the Horse Guards; Thomas, killed, in the Scots Guards, in Spain; John, a Lieutenant-Colonel in Collier's Regiment in Flanders; and Colin, in Lauder's Regiment, killed in Flanders; present representation unknown.

3. *Elizabeth*, married George Leslie, Sheriff-Clerk of Inverness, with issue.

4. *Agnes*, married Roderick, son of Alexander Mackenzie, V. of Gairloch, with issue; and

5. *Magdalen*, married Alexander Graham of Drynie.

He has a sasine of Suddie in 1650, and another in 1672. He was succeeded by his eldest son,

II. CAPTAIN KENNETH MACKENZIE, who served in Dumbarton's Regiment in France in 1666, and afterwards as a Royalist in Scotland. He married Isobel, daughter of John Paterson, Bishop of Ross, with issue—

1. *Kenneth*, his heir.

2. *George*, killed with Lord Mungo Murray at Darien.

3. *Margaret*, married William Macleod of Bernera.

4. *Elizabeth*, married, as his first wife, Colonel Alexander Mackenzie of Conansbay, son of Kenneth Mor, third Earl of Seaforth, without issue; and

5. *Alice*, married, first, in 1698, John Macdonald of Balcony, only son of Sir James Macdonald of Sleat; and secondly, John Maclean, a medical doctor in Inverness.

He was killed in Lochaber in 1688, and was succeeded by his eldest son,

III. KENNETH MACKENZIE, who, in 1706, married Katharine, daughter of John Shaw of Sornbeg, Ayrshire, with issue—

1. *William*, his heir.
2. *John*, a Lieutenant-Colonel in the army.
3. *Mary*, married Norman Macleod of Macleod.
4. Another daughter.

There is a sasine in his favour dated 1695. He was succeeded by his eldest son,

IV. WILLIAM MACKENZIE, last of Suddie, who married Margaret, daughter of Sir Alexander Mackenzie, Bart., V. of Coul, with issue—

1. *Alexander*, who died before his father, without issue.
2. *Major-General John Randoll Mackenzie*, killed at Talavera in 1809, without issue.
3. *Janet;* and
4. *Katharine*, who both died without issue.
5. *Henrietta Wharton*, who became her father's heir, in 1810, and married, for her second husband, Sir James Wemyss, fourth Baronet of Scatwell, M.P., and Lord-Lieutenant for the County of Ross, to whom she brought the Suddie estates, and had issue—Sir James John Randoll Mackenzie, present Baronet of Scatwell, who, about 1850, sold or alienated the estates.

THE MACKENZIES OF ORD.

KENNETH, first of Killichrist, fourth son of Kenneth a Bhlair, VII. of Kintail, had, as we have seen, a second son, Thomas of Kinlochluichart, who, in 1598, obtained from Kenneth, XIIth Baron, and, afterwards, first Lord Mackenzie of Kintail, a tack of the lands of Ord. Thomas married, first, Isobel, daughter of Roderick MacAllan Macleod of Gairloch, with issue—

1. *Murdoch* Mackenzie of Scatwell, without issue; who, in 1619, talzied the estate of Scatwell to his foster-brother, Kenneth Mackenzie, I. of Scatwell, son of Sir Roderick Mackenzie of Coigeach, Tutor of Kintail; and
2. *Kenneth*, who became progenitor of the Mackenzies of Langwell; and of the family of Mackenzie-Ross of Aldie, who adopted the addition of Ross on succeeding to the property of Ross of Aldie.

Thomas of Kinlochluichart married, secondly, Annabella, daughter of Murdoch Mackenzie, I. of Fairburn, and had issue—

3. *John*, who afterwards became proprietor of Ord.

4. *Thomas*, who died before 1628, and had two sons, John of Wester Kessock, who married Margaret Maclean, and another son, who died without issue in 1642.

5. *Murdoch*, servitor to the Tutor of Kintail, died in 1628, unmarried. This Murdoch, by his last will, dated 13th January 1628, left his brother-german, John Mackenzie of Ord, executor and legatee, and bequeathed 400 merks Scots, and fifteen bolls victual or the value thereof to the children of his late brother Thomas.. He also left three hundred and twenty-one merks Scots to Thomas Graham, his sister's son, and the annual rent of one thousand merks to Isobel Cuthbert, wife of his said brother and executor, and discharged his sisters of all the monies they borrowed of him. Thomas Mackenzie died before 1619. His eldest son,

I. JOHN MACKENZIE, became the first of the family of Ord who possessed the property, and was designed thereof, though it was held in tack by his father. He was commonly called Ian Dubh a Ghiuthais, or Black John of the Fir. He obtained a charter, dated 23d July 1607, from Kenneth, XIIth Baron and first Lord Mackenzie of Kintail, of the lands and mill of Ord, and the half of Corrievoulzie and Strathvaich, and on the 15th of September 1637, George, second Earl of Seaforth, gave him a regular free charter.

He married Isobel, daughter of Alexander Cuthbert of Drakies, by his wife, Christian Dunbar, who long survived him, and by her had issue—

1. *John*, his heir.

2. *Thomas*, progenitor of the Mackenzies of Highfield.

3. *James*, who married a daughter of Mr Farquhar Clark. He is a cautioner, along with his brother, Kenneth of Ord, to Thomas Mackenzie of Inverlael, from which he is discharged on the 18th of May 1659, and, witness to the registration of the marriage contract of his brother John, at Inverness, 20th February 1666.

4. *George*, who married, first, a natural daughter of Alexander Mackenzie, V. of Gairloch, and secondly, Janet, daughter of Mr Linen, minister of Fairnly—issue one son, Alexander, who went in the expedition to Darien, and afterwards settled and married in Jamaica, where his posterity still exist.

5. A daughter married Mackenzie of Tarradale.

6. *Annabella*, married, in 1650, Alexander Mackenzie, VI. of Hilton.

7. *Janet*, married, in 1652, Alexander Càm Mackenzie, fourth son of John Roy, IV. of Gairloch, with issue—Alexander MacAlastair Chàim, the writer's ancestor.

Two daughters married respectively, a son of the Rev. John Clark, minister of Lochalsh, and Murdo Mackenzie Mhic Mhurchaidh.

He witnessed the burning of the Church of Cilliechriost by the Macdonalds of Glengarry in 1602 ; died before the 1st of December 1644, and was succeeded by his eldest son,

II. CAPTAIN JOHN MACKENZIE of Ord, who fought under Montrose against the Covenanters, and was in consequence summoned to appear before the Presbytery of Dingwall on the 5th of March 1650, as a Malignant, but he having been "a long time in the Isles, and but lately come to the country, he confessed his accession to the Rebellion of that Bloody and Excommunicated Traitor, James Graham, and to the late Insurrection in the North (1649), and to have been at the head of a company in the same at Balvenny, professing his grief for the same, and desiring to be received to the Covenant and Public Satisfaction." He was referred to the Commission of the General Assembly, to be held in May ensuing. On the 19th of November following he again compeared before the same Presbytery, supplicating to be received to "Public Repentance" for his accession to the several rebellions, when he was ordained "to make his repentance to James Graham's unnatural rebellion, the unlawful engagements, and the late insurrection in the North, in the kirk of Dingwall, in his own habits, the next Sabbath, and to be received, and to subscribe the

Declaration." On the 13th October 1653, he was appointed
to keep the Earl of Seaforth's Forest of Fannich, for which
he was to receive a certain number of bolls victual yearly.
On the 22d of April 1655 he was tried by Court Martial in
Edinburgh, for plundering the lands of Fowlis on the 9th
November preceding, was found guilty, and sentenced to
repair the damage to the extent proved by Fowlis, out of
his lands of Ord, and to be committed to prison until the
General's pleasure should be known thereon.

He married Magdalene, daughter of William Fraser of
Culbokie ; marriage contract dated 21st July 1633 ; tocher
2500 merks Scots. By her he had issue—

1. *Thomas*, his successor.

2. *Kenneth*, whom we find as a witness to a bond, dated
27th April 1724, by Thomas Mackenzie of Ord, and his
eldest son Alexander, to John Mackenzie of Highfield. He
married, in 1702, Elizabeth, daughter of Assynt, with issue
—one son, Kenneth.

3. *Annabella*, married, 28th April 1698, to Charles Maclean in Brae.

4. *Helen*, married, 25th April 1700, James Murray,
tenant in Culloden.*

He died before 19th February 1686, and was succeeded
by his eldest son,

III. THOMAS MACKENZIE. He redeemed the wadset
of Corrievoulzie on the 6th and 8th of March 1697, duly and
lawfully premonishing and warning John Mackenzie, in-
dweller in Wester Kessock, and Margaret Maclean, his
spouse, to repair to the Tolbooth of Fortrose, commonly
called the Charter House, on the 15th of May next, and
there any time betwixt the sun rising and the down passing·
of the same, to receive from Thomas Mackenzie of Ord, or
any other in his name, the sum of fifty thousand merks
Scots, whole and together in ane sum, all copper and lay-
money excepted, and upon receipt thereof to deliver up the

---

* Ord MS. Findon says the daughters were Janet, married to Donald Macdonald, in South Uist (contract 1711), probably a second marriage ; and Florence,
married Kenneth Mackenzie, Kenlochewe.

Wadset of Corrievoulzie, &c., to him. On the 23rd of August 1716 he entered into an obligation with Kenneth Bayne of Tulloch and John Mackenzie of Highfield, by which, upon their satisfying Colin Graham of Drynie for a debt contracted between him and Ord, the latter is to make an ample disposition to them and their heirs, of all his lands lying within the Sheriffdom of Ross, with reservation always, during all the days of his life, of the sum of one hundred and twenty merks Scots, five bolls of bear, five bolls of malt, five bolls of oatmeal, five bolls of bear meal yearly, out of the rents of said lands ; and it was specially provided that as soon as the sum of four thousand merks Scots was paid by Kenneth Bayne and John Mackenzie, that they should be obliged to give the said Thomas Mackenzie one chaldron of victual, or one hundred merks Scots yearly, over and above the reservation above-mentioned.

He married Mary, daughter of John Mackenzie, II. of Applecross, by whom he had—

1. *Alexander*, his heir.

2. *Magdalene*, who married William Mackenzie, uncle to Sir John Mackenzie of Coul (marriage contract 18th July 1716). He had also a natural son, Kenneth, a private, in 1725, in Colonel Tyrell's Regiment.

He was succeeded by his only son,

IV. ALEXANDER MACKENZIE, who married Jean daughter of John Mackenzie, II. of Highfield, before the 29th of June 1725, with issue—

1. *Thomas*, his heir.

He died before 10th October 1748, and was succeeded by his only son,

V. THOMAS MACKENZIE, who, educated at Fortrose, married Ann, youngest daughter of Sir Kenneth Mackenzie, first Baronet and IV. of Scatwell (contract dated 15th June 1750). She had a jointure, in case of her surviving him, of five chaldrons of victual rent, and three hundred merks Scots yearly, namely, three chaldrons of victual out of the lands of Broomhill, Ballavulàich, and Milltown of Ord, two chalders of the first and readiest of the rents of the Mill of

Ord, and the sum of three hundred merks out of the lands of Corrievoulzie, Strathvaich, Stronchondrum, and Bruthach-nam-Bò. By her he had issue—

1. *Alexander*, his heir.

2. *Elizabeth*, married Alexander, only son of George Gillanders of Highfield, Chamberlain to Kenneth, last Earl of Seaforth, with issue (contract dated 17th April 1777).

3. *Abigail*, married George Mackenzie, IV. of Dundonnell, with issue.

He died in 1803, and was succeeded by his only son,

VI. ALEXANDER MACKENZIE, who, during his father's life-time, was, by deed of settlement of Katharine Bethune, and Alexander Macdonald, her husband, dated 3d December 1785, appointed sole executor to Macdonald's only child Kenneth, whom failing, the said Alexander Mackenzie, younger of Ord, to be sole heir, "and this as a token of gratitude to the worthy family of Ord." He married Helen, daughter of Neil Maeinnes, Collector of Taxes, Aberdeen, with issue—

1. *John*, who died before his father, unmarried.

2. *Thomas*, his successor.   .

3. *Alexander*, a Captain in the 25th Regiment, Native. Infantry, H.E.I.C.S., who married Hannah Fraser, niece of Fraser of Belladrum, with issue—(1) Alexander, H.E.I.C.S., who married a daughter of Colonel Birch, with issue—four sons and four daughters; (2) Charles-Archdale, and three daughters, Helen, Emilia, and Anna. He died in India 15th June 1837.

4. *Anne*, married her cousin-german, Thomas Mackenzie, VI. and last of the Old Mackenzies of Dundonnell.   ·

5. *Margaret*, married a Mr Maclean, Granada, with issue—an only daughter, Helen.

6 & 7. *Eliza* and *Helen*, died unmarried.

He was succeeded by his eldest surviving son,

VII. THOMAS MACKENZIE, now of Ord, Vice-Lieutenant of the County of Ross, born in December 1797. He married, on the 27th of April 1825, Anna Watson, daughter of James Fowler of Raddery, and Grange in Jamaica, by whom he has an only son,

1. *Alexander Watson*, born 31st August 1827, Captain, 91st Regiment. He married, 10th June 1857, Angel-Babington, daughter of the Rev. Benjamin Peile, with issue— two sons and two daughters—(1) Thomas Arthur, born 17th September 1859, Sub-Lieutenant 42d Highlanders; (2) Alexander Francis, born 18th April 1861 ; (3) Beatrice Anna; (4) Anna Watson.

·THE MACKENZIES OF HIGHFIELD.

I. THOMAS MACKENZIE, first of this family, was the second son of John Mackenzie, I. of Ord, by Isobel, daughter of Alexander Cuthbert of Drakies. He married Agnes, daughter of Murdoch Matheson of Balmacarra, with issue—

1. *John*, his heir.

2. *Lachlan*, married, with issue.

He was succeeded by his eldest son,

II. JOHN MACKENZIE, who married Margaret, daughter of James Maclean, a Bailie of Inverness, with issue—

1. *Thomas*, who died before his father, without issue.

2. *James*, his successor.

3. *Colin*, of Meikle-Scatwell, who married Catharine, daughter of Alexander Mackenzie of Lentran, without issue.

4. *William*, of Strathgarve, who married Janet, daughter of Alexander Mackenzie of Lentran, and by her had John, II. of Strathgarve, and Alexander, who died without issue. John had William, III. of Strathgarve, and three daughters. This William has a sasine in 1747. He left a son, John, issue unknown; and another son, William, died in India without issue.

5. *Elizabeth*, married Donald Mackenzie, V. of Kilcoy.

6. *Jean*, married Alexander Mackenzie, IV. of Ord.

7. *Catharine*, married, 1747, Robert Ross of Achnacloich. He has a sasine in 1730, and was succeeded by his second and eldest surviving son,

III. JAMES MACKENZIE, who married, Mary, daughter of Roderick Mackenzie, IV. of Applecross, with issue—

1. *Thomas*, his heir.

2. *William ;* 3. *Alexander ;* and 4. *John*, died young.

5. *Alexander* of Breda, Aberdeenshire, who married
Maria Rebecca, daughter of Colonel William Humberston
Mackenzie of Conansbay, and sister of the last Lord Seaforth, with issue—(1) William, a Lieutenant in the 78th
Regiment, died at Breda in Holland of a wound he had received the previous day at the taking of Merxew, 1814;
(2) Thomas, a midshipman, R.N., drowned at sea; (3)
Frederick, R.N., murdered at Calcutta, 1820; (4) Francis,
R.N., drowned at sea in 1828; (5) Colin, all without issue;
and (6) Alexander, Captain, 25th Regiment, and Adjutant
of the Ross-shire Militia, who took a great interest in the
history of his Clan, and collected a large amount of information and valuable MSS.   He married Lilias Dunbar,
daughter of James Fowler of Raddery, with issue—(1)
James Evan Fowler, died unmarried; (2) Alexander,
now at Fortrose; and three daughters, who died unmarried.   He died in 1872.   Alexander of Breda also had
four daughters, two of whom, Louisa and Gertrude Elizabeth,
died unmarried; Margaret, married the Rev. Charles Grant,
minister of the Episcopal Church of Scotland, with issue—
nine children.   She died in 1871.   The other, Mary Gibbs,
married on the 25th March 1827, George Skues, Lieutenant,
Royal Marines, Aberdeen.   By this marriage she had issue
—(1) William Mackenzie, M.D., Surgeon-Major in the
Army, who married Margaret, daughter of Christopher
Hyre, Newfoundland, with issue—three sons and five
daughters, George Edward Mackenzie; Frederick William
Mackenzie; Charles Ayre Mackenzie; Mary Isabella Mac- ·
kenzie; Margaret Caroline Mackenzie; Gertrude Eliza
Mackenzie; Minnie Mackenzie, and Elsie Mackenzie; (2)
Edward Walker, Staff-Surgeon in the Army, died at Cal-
cutta, unmarried, in 1862; (3) Frederick Mackenzie, a Sur-
geon-Major in the Army, married Maria Theresa Malcolm,
by whom he has issue—two sons, Frederic Mackenzie and
Edward George, and two daughters, Mary Theresa and
Margaret Sarah; (4) Richard Alexander, residing in
America; (5) John Richards; (6) Georgina Mary, and two
daughters, who died in infancy.

6. *Margaret*, married Alexander Mackenzie of Muirton of Kilcoy, with issue.

7. *Elizabeth*, married Donald Matheson of Attadale.

8. *Anne*, married James Rose of Cuilich, with issue; and six other daughters who died unmarried.

He was succeeded by his eldest son,

IV. THOMAS MACKENZIE, who afterwards succeeded his uncle, John Mackenzie, as VI. of Applecross.

He received the estate of Applecross from his maternal uncle, John, V. of Applecross, and, in 1781, he sold the estate of Highfield to George Gillanders, commissioner for Seaforth, and purchased Lochcarron from Sir Alexander Mackenzie of Delvine for £10,000. He married Elizabeth, daughter of Donald Mackenzie, V. of Kilcoy, with issue— John, VII. of Applecross, and several others. (For the succession see Applecross genealogy.)

THE MACKENZIES OF REDCASTLE AND KINCRAIG.

I. RODERICK MOR MACKENZIE, progenitor of the families of Redcastle and Kincraig, was the third son of Kenneth Mackenzie, X. of Kintail, by his wife, Elizabeth Stewart, daughter of John, second Earl of Athol. Roderick was a distinguished warrior, and took a prominent part in the frequent encounters between the Mackenzies and the Macdonalds of Glengarry, and often commanded the Clan on these occasions. In 1608 he received a charter under the Great Seal of the lands of Redcastle. He married Florence, daughter of Robert Munro, XVth Baron of Fowlis, with issue—

1. *Murdoch*, his heir.
2. *Colin*, I. of Kincraig.
3. *Isabel*, married Hugh Mackay of Bighouse, with issue.
4. Another married Alexander Macleod of Tallisker.
5. *Margaret*, married, as his first wife, Alexander Mackenzie, V. of Gairloch, with issue.
6. *Helen*, married Thomas Dunbar of Grange.
7. *Catharine*, married, first, in 1605, Kenneth Mackenzie, III. of Killichrist, with issue; and secondly, Thomas Chisholm of Kinneries.
8. *Agnes*, married John Dunbar of Bennetsfield; and
9. Another married one of the Baynes of Tulloch.

Roderick Mòr was succeeded by his eldest son,

II. MURDOCH MACKENZIE, who married Margaret, daughter of William Rose, XI. Baron of Kilravock, with issue—

1. *Kenneth*, who died young.
2. *Roderick*, who became his heir.
3. *Alexander*, who married Miss Paterson, with issue.
4. *Mr John*, schoolmaster at Chanonry, who died in 1640, unmarried.
5. *William*, M.D., died in Spain, without issue.
6. *Margaret*, married Alexander Chisholm of Comar.
7. *Finguala*, married Roderick Mackenzie, I. of Applecross.

8. *Catherine*, married Donald Mackenzie, III. of Loggie. Others married respectively, Alexander Fraser of Reelig ; Rev. William Mackenzie, minister of Tarbat ; Alexander MacRa, Chamberlain of Kintail ; Fraser, son of Fraser of Foyers, and secondly, Hugh, brother of Fraser of Culduthel.

Murdoch has a sasine as heir to his father in 1615. He was succeeded by his second and eldest surviving son,

III. RODERICK MACKENZIE, who married Isobel, daughter of Alexander Mackenzie, I. of Kilcoy, with issue—

1. *Colin*, his heir.

2. *Alexander*, an advocate, died unmarried.

3. *Charles*, and

4. *Anne*, who married John Mackenzie, II. of Scatwell, with issue—an only daughter, Lilias, who married, in 1679, Colin Mackenzie, III. of Kincraig.

He has a sasine in 1629 and one in 1638. He was fined the sum of £2000 for taking part in the wars of Montrose against the Covenanters, and was for some time imprisoned in Edinburgh with Thomas Mackenzie of Pluscardine. During his absence on this occasion General Carr besieged his castle, the only place which still held out in the interest of the King ; killed the commander, who exposed himself on the ramparts, and set fire to the castle, and razed the walls to the ground. He was liberated from prison on the intercession of his maternal uncle on payment of 7000 merks Scots. In 1690 he excambed with Kenneth Mackenzie, I. of Dundonnell, formerly of Glenmurkle, the lands of Acha-ta-Donill, Blachlach, &c., belonging to Redcastle, for the davoch of Meikle Scatwell, of old occupied and possessed by Allan and Alexander Mackenzie. He was succeeded by his eldest son,

IV. COLIN MACKENZIE, a very prudent man, who amassed a large fortune, and, in 1676, made an entail of the Barony of Redcastle, which he, however, neglected to have registered, a fact only discovered long after his death. He married, first, the eldest daughter of Sir Kenneth Mackenzie, Baronet, I. of Coul, with issue—

1. *Roderick*, his heir.

2. *Colin* of Rossend, married, with issue—Colin, W.S., and Charles, a goldsmith. He took part in the Rising of 1715, and suffered in consequence.

3. *John*, of whom no trace.

4. *Jean*, who is described as the eldest daughter on her tombstone in Tain, married, in 1679, John Urquhart of Newhall.

5. *Margaret*, married, in 1680, Alexander Fraser, younger of Belladrum.

6. *Elizabeth*, married, in 1685, Evan Mackenzie, VII. of Hilton, with issue.

7. *Anna*, married, in 1687, Lachlan Mackintosh of Daviot, with issue.

He married, secondly, Marjory, daughter of John Robertson of Inshes, widow of Angus Mackintosh of Daviot, without issue. He was killed at Killearnan in 1704, and was succeeded by his eldest son,

V. RODERICK MACKENZIE, called by the Highlanders "Ruairi Dearg," or Red Rory, who married Margaret, daughter of James, XVIth Baron of Grant, by Lady Mary (or Margaret) Stewart, only daughter of James, fourth Earl of Moray, by Lady Anne Gordon, daughter of George, VIth Earl of Huntly. There is a sasine to her, "as sister to Ludovic Grant *nunc de* Freuchy," dated 1680. By this lady he had—

1. *Roderick*, his heir.

2. *Ludovic*, who married Eliza, daughter of Simon Mackenzie, I. of Allangrange.

3. *James*, M.D., in London.

4. *Alexander*, who married, in 1721, Margaret, daughter of Charles Mackenzie of Cullen.

5. *Isobel*, married, in 1718, Æneas Macbean of Kinchyle.

6. *Jean*, married, in 1712, William Mackenzie of Davochcairn.

7. *Anne*, who died unmarried.

He married, secondly, Katharina, daughter of Charles Mackenzie of Cullen.

He wrote a MS. history of his own family, died in 1725, and was succeeded by his eldest son,

VI. RODERICK MACKENZIE, by the Highlanders called
" Ruairi Mor," who married, first, in 1707, Margaret, daugh-
ter of Sir James Calder of Muirtown, widow of Alexander
Dunbar of Westfield. with issue—

   1. *Roderick*, his heir.
   2. *Captain Colin*, married Mary, daughter (or grand-
daughter) of Sir John Cochrane of Ochiltree, second son
of the first Earl of Dundonald, with issue — Kenneth
Francis, H.M. Consul in the West Indies, and two daughters—Rose, who married John Wilson, and Margaret, who
married Gilbert Robertson of Kindeace. Kenneth Francis
married Anne Townshend. She died in 1847. He died in
1831, aged 83, and left issue—(1) Charles ; (2) James Joseph,
who married Marian, daughter of Edward Impey, B.C.S.,
and died without issue in·1872 ; (3) Kenneth, died, without
issue; (4) Colin, Lieutenant-General, 48th Regiment, Madras .
Army, who, was, in 1844, Assistant Political Agent at
Peshawur, and, afterwards, a hostage with the Afghans
in 1842. He married, first, 26th May 1832, Adeline Marian,
daughter of James Pattle of the Bengal Civil Service, with
issue—Adeline Anne, who married Major-General Henry
Hoseason, Madras Army, with issue—eight children ; Mary
Julia, married Major Herbert Clogstorm, with issue—four
children ; Rose Prinsep married, first, Lieutenant David
Arnot ; and secondly, Captain Francis Pictet, Madras Army,
with issue—six children ; (5) Anne ; (6) Isabella Jessy,
married, 17th October 1839, James Baines of Ludlow, with
issue ; (7) Mary Cochrane, married, 17th March 1835, James
King King of Staunton, Herts, with issue ; (8) Elizabeth
Margaret, married, 15th August 1832, Lieutenant-General
Thomas D. Carpenter, Madras Army, with issue; (9) Amelia
Frances, married, in 1838, the Rev. Thomas King of Staun-
ton Park, Herts, with issue ; and (10) Townshend, died with-
out issue. Lieutenant-General Colin married, secondly,
Helen Catherine, daughter of Admiral James Erskine
Douglas.

   Charles Mackenzie, eldest son of Kenneth Francis, as
above, married Rebecca Molyneux. He died in New York

C 2

in 1865, and left issue—Charles Francis, who married Lucie de Mornet, with issue—Charles. ᛚ. ꜱ. /ᴌ

3. *Thomas.* 4. *John.* 5. *William.*

Nine other sons and two daughters, of whose issue nothing is known.

By her first husband, Alexander Dunbar of Westfield, this lady had seven sons and one daughter—the latter married to Sir William Dunbar of Hempriggs, with issue—thus having altogether a family of twenty-one sons and three daughters. Roderick Mòr died, 29th of March ·1751, at Redcastle, and was succeeded by his eldest son,

VII. RODERICK MACKENZIE, known among his countrymen as Ruairi Bàn, who married, in 1730, Hannah Anna Murdoch of Cambodden, Galloway, with issue—

'1. *Kenneth*, his heir.

John v. 403 2. *Captain Colin*, who became VI. of Kincraig, by the *.9 405* will of the then proprietor, he having had no son to leave it to.

3. and 4. *Alexander* and *Roderick*, died in infancy.

. 5. *Margaret*, married, in 1755, Sir Alexander Mackenzie, third Baronet and X. of Gairloch, with issue. She died 1st September 1759.

6. *Mary*, born 1732, and died, unmarried, at Lettoch, Redcastle, in 1828, aged 96.

7. *Elizabeth*, born 1746, married August 1782, Major-General Colin Mackenzie, with issue—Alexander Wedderburn, who died, unmarried, 4th January 1838, at Park House, Dingwall; and Hannah Margaret Cochrane, who died, unmarried, 2d February 1858, at Golder's Green, Hendon.

8. *Christina*, born 1749; and

9. *Jean*, born 1752, married Robert Anderson, Glasgow, and died, in 1819, without issue.

His wife died at Redcastle on the 21st of April 1755, in the 39th year of her age. He died at Inverness, 10th May 1785, and was succeeded by his eldest son,

VIII. CAPTAIN KENNETH MACKENZIE, born February 21, 1748, and married at Edinburgh, 17th August 1767,

Jean, daughter of James Thomson, Accountant-General of Excise in Scotland, with issue—

1. *Roderick*, his heir.

2. *Hector*, who married at Edinburgh, 29th March 1800, Diana Davidson, daughter of Dr Davidson, of the H.E.I.C.S., Leeds, with issue—Robert Davidson Mackenzie, Adjutant, 1st Bombay Light Cavalry, who died of cholera, 22d December 1822, at Sholapore, India, without issue. His mother died at Garlieston, aged 76, 7th August 1852.

3. *Boyd*, who married William MacCall of Newton-Stewart, without issue ; and

4. *Hannah*, the last surviving child of Kenneth of Red-castle, married William MacCa of Barnshalloch, and died at Creebridge, Newton-Stewart, 8th August 1849, aged 83.

Kenneth was tried for the murder of one Kenneth Mac-kenzie, *alias* Jefferson ; was found guilty and sentenced to be hanged. He was, however, afterwards pardoned ; divorced his wife ; went abroad ; entered the Russian service ; and was killed in 1789 near Constantinople, where he was Assistant Consul, in a duel with a man, Smith, captain of a merchant ship, to whom he had entrusted all his pro-perty when he got into trouble about Jefferson. He figures in Kay's famous Edinburgh portraits as one of the Bucks of the City.

He was succeeded by his eldest son,

IX. RODERICK MACKENZIE. He never took possession of the estate, but, being much encumbered, sold it, in June 1790, to James Grant of Corriemony, for £25,450, whose nephew, Patrick Grant, in 1828, sold it to Sir William Fettes of Comely Bank, Bart., for £135,000. Sir William's trustees re-sold it to Colonel Hugh D. Baillie, whose descendants now possess it.

Roderick, the last direct male representative of the House of Redcastle, died, in 1798, at Jamaica, unmarried, when the representation of the family devolved upon his uncle, Captain John Mackenzie, VI. of Kincraig.

THE MACKENZIES OF KINCRAIG.

I. COLIN MACKENZIE, second son of Roderick Mor Mackenzie, I. of Redcastle, was the first of this family. He married Catherine, daughter of the Rev. John Mackenzie of Tolly, minister of Dingwall (sasine to her 15th September 1617) with issue—

1. *Colin*, his heir.

2. *Roderick*, who married, first, Isabel, daughter of Hector Mackenzie, IV. of Fairburn, and secondly, Elizabeth, daughter of John Bayne of Tulloch; sasine to him in 1652, and one to her in 1656.

3. *Margaret*, who, in 1638, married, first, Gilbert Robertson, II. of Kindeace, and secondly, John, son of Hugh Ross of Balnacloich.

4. *Florence*, married, in 1643, David Cuthbert, Inverness.

5. *Agnes*, married, first, in 1672, Alexander Bayne of Knockbain, and secondly, the Rev. John MacRa, minister of Dingwall, author of the Ardintoul MS. History of the Mackenzies, and of a MS. Genealogy of the MacRas.

6. A daughter married John Clunes, son of a Bailie of Cromarty.

Colin married, secondly, a daughter of Innes of Inverbreakie, relict of Murdo Mackenzie of Tolly, with issue— James, who married Catherine Innes.

He died in 1649, and was succeeded by his eldest son,

II. COLIN MACKENZIE, who married Agnes, daughter of Duncan Bayne of Delny, with issue—

1. *Colin*, his heir.

2. *Duncan*, a Lieutenant-Colonel, Scots Guards, married, and, in 1724, died without issue.

3. *Lilias*, married Mr William Mackenzie, minister of Roskeen.

4. *Katharine*, married, as his second wife, in 1680, William Grant of Ardoch.

5. *Florence*.

6. *Christian*, married, in 1681, William Mackenzie, brother to Murdoch Mackenzie, II. of Ardross.

7. *Agnes*.

He married, secondly, Christian Munro, relict of William Ross, Knoekgartie (contract of marriage 16th March 1680). He was succeeded by his eldest son,

III. COLIN MACKENIZE, who, in 1679, married Lilias, daughter of John Mackenzie, II. of Scatwell, with issue—

1. *Colin*, his heir.

2. *John*, who succeeded as V. of Kincraig.

3. *Anne*, who married John Mackenzie of Rapoch, brother to Alexander Mackenzie, I. of Ardross.

4. *Barbara*, who married James Mackenzie.

He was succeeded by his eldest son,

IV. COLIN MACKENZIE, who married (he being her third husband) Margaret, daughter of Sir Roderick Mackenzie of Findon, without issue.

He was succeeded by his next brother,

V. JOHN MACKENZIE, a Captain in Lochiel's Regiment. He married Christina (Findon says Katharine), daughter of James Menzies of Comrie, without issue.   She died at Kincraig 21st December 1775.   Captain John was dangerously wounded at Malplaquet in 1709.   His last commission was in the 42d Highlanders.   In December 1760 he made a disposition of the lands of Kincraig to Roderick Mackenzie, VII. of Redcastle, in trust for the second son of the latter, John, then only nine years old.

He died a few days after, and was succeeded by his remote cousin,

VI. CAPTAIN JOHN MACKENZIE, second surviving son of Roderick Bàn, VII. of Redcastle, born at the latter place in 1751.   His descendants, since the death of Roderick, IX. of Redcastle without issue in 1798, carry on also the representation of the main line of that family.   He married Mary, daughter of the Rev. Colin Mackenzie, minister of Fodderty, with issue—

1. *Roderick*, his heir.

2. *Colin*, Lieutenant in the 71st Regiment, killed at Vittoria, 21st June 1813, without issue.

3. *John*, died without issue, 20th August 1822, off St Helena, returning home from Java.

4. *Kenneth Francis,* Colonel 64th Bengal Native Infantry, married, 6th January 1832, Margaret, daughter of the Rev. Thomas Taylor, D.D., of Tibbermore, with issue—Captain Roderick Boyd, died at Cheltenham, 5th October 1867, unmarried; Lieutenant Wedderburn; Hannah; Thomas Harry, died young; Mary Christina, married, 17th December 1849, Colonel Brown-Constable, with issue — twelve children; Margaret Jane, married, 10th October 1850, Major-General H. F. Waddington, of Monmouthshire, with issue—six children, two of whom married, with issue; Isabella Fraser, died young; and Annie Colina, married, 31st October 1866, Thomas H. Knolles, with issue—five children. Colonel Kenneth Francis died at sea in 1856.

5. *Hector,* Major H.E.I.C.S., unmarried.

6. *Hugh,* Colonel, late 2d Bengal Europeans, married, first, Anne, daughter of Thomas Duncan, advocate, Aberdeen, by whom he had — Captain Harry Leith, R.A., married twice, with issue; John Hugh, M.D.; Thomas Duncan, Bombay Civil Service, married, 25th April 1871, with issue; Mary Janet, married, 31st July 1866, Surgeon-Major Kilgour, with issue; and Sarah Anne, still unmarried. Colonel Hugh married, secondly, Edith S. Hastings, Oxfordshire, also with issue.

7. *Charles Fitzgerald,* H.E.I.C.S., married the Hon. Mrs Fergusson, daughter of Lord Kirkcudbright, and died without issue, 5th September 1850.

Colin of Kincraig also had

8. *Maxwell,* a natural son, Lieutenant-Colonel of the 71st Regiment, killed at Bayonne in 1813, and to whom, and his brother Colin, there is a monument, by Chantry, erected in the Church of Rosskeen.

9. *Mary,* married, January 28, 1813, Major-General Sir D. Macleod.

10. *Johanna Ch. Menzies,* died unmarried in 1794.

11. *Margaret,* married Donald Macintyre, Calcutta, with issue—Major-General John Macintyre, Madras Artillery, who, in 1857, married Marianne, daughter of Alexander N. Shaw, Bombay Civil Service; Colonel Donald Mac-

intyre, V.C.; Colina Maxwell, married, in 1844, Dr William Brydon, "the last man," or sole survivor of 13,000 in the disastrous retreat from Cabul to Jellalabad in 1842, and who died in 1873, with issue—eight children ; Mary Isabella, married, in 1849, General James Travers, V.C.; and Charlotte Anne.

12. *Jane Pettey*, died young.

13. *Isabella*, married, first, Captain Allan Cameron, with issue ; and secondly, General Sir Hugh Fraser, K.C.B., of Braelangwell, with issue. She died in 1852.

14. *Elizabeth Jane*, died unmarried in 1832. ·

Captain John of Kincraig served in Lord Macleod's Regiment, the 73d, now 71st Highlanders, and was wounded at Gibralter in 1780. His wife died at Park House, Dingwall, 4th January 1838. He died at Kincraig, 29th April 1822, aged 72 years, and was succeeded by his eldest son,

VII. RODERICK MACKENZIE, Major H.E.I.C.S., who married, in 1836, Katharine, daughter of Alexander Mackenzie, son of Bailie Hector Mackenzie of Dingwall, descended from the families of Letterewe and Gairloch, with issue—

1. *Roderick*, his heir, now of Kincraig.

2. *Katharine*, died unmarried in 1870.

3. *Eliza Jane*, married George Martineau.

4. *Mary Ann.*

5. *Alice*, who married Alexander Edmonds.

Major Roderick died at Kincraig on the 6th April 1853, and was succeeded by his only son,

VIII. CAPTAIN RODERICK MACKENZIE, now of Kincraig, who, on the 5th of February 1867, married Georgina Adelaide, daughter of Roderick Mackenzie, late of Flowerburn.

THE MACKENZIES OF CROMARTY.

This branch of the great Mackenzie family, next to the principal House of Kintail and Seaforth, played the most important part in the history of the country. The Mackenzies of Cromarty are descended from Sir Roderick Mackenzie of Coigeach, Tutor of Kintail, who in his day took such a conspicuous part in the affairs of Clan Kenneth. His career is noticed to a large extent in the history of the family of Seaforth; is otherwise pretty generally known, and need not here be enlarged upon. He was the second son of Colin Càm Mackenzie, XIth Baron of Kintail, by Barbara, daughter of John Grant of Grant, XIIth Baron. He was a brave and resolute man, shown by the manner in which he seized M'Neil of Barra by stratagem, and brought that arch pirate, of whom Queen Elizabeth had complained, to the Court of King James, at Holyrood. When brought into his Majesty's presence, the pirate, who, much to the surprise of all, was a tall, well-favoured man of reverened aspect, with a long grey beard, proved more than a match for the King. When asked what could induce him to commit so many piracies and robberies on the Queen of England's subjects, he replied he thought he was doing the King good services by troubling "a woman who had murdered his mother." On which, James cried out, "The Devil take the carle! Rorie, take him with you again, and dispose of him and his fortune as you please." On another occasion, when Sir Roric was passing through Athole on his way to Edinburgh, in the interest of his ward, he was stopped by the men of Athole for passing through their country without the leave of their lord. The Tutor of Kintail dismounted and sought-out a stone, on which he began to sharpen his claymore. The Athole men, from a safe distance, asked him what he was doing there. "I am going to make a road," was the ready answer. "You shall make no road here." "Oh, I don't seek to do so; but I shall make it between your lord's head and his shoulders if I am hindered from pursuing my lawful business." At this the

Athole men retired, and, on reaching their lord, told him what had happened. "It was either the Deil or the Tutor of Kintail," he said, "let him have a free path by here for ever." That he was stern in his Tutorship is proved by the following proverb still current in Ross-shire:—"There are but two things worse than the Tutor of Kintail—frost in spring and mist in the dog days." He married Margaret, daughter and co-heiress of Torquil Macleod, known among the Highlanders as "Torquil Cononach," of the Lews, Coigeach, and Assynt. By this marriage he obtained Torquil's mainland possessions, which were previously, however, in 1605, granted by Torquil to Kenneth Mackenzie, X. of Kintail, Sir Roderick's eldest brother. He bought Milton and Tarbatness from the Munros. He had issue—

1. *John*, his heir, afterwards Sir John Mackenzie of Tarbat.

2. *Kenneth*, I. of the family of Scatwell.

3. *Colin*, I. of Tarvie.

4. *Alexander*, I. of Ballone.

5. *James*; and 6. *Charles*, died unmarried.

7. *Margaret*, who married Sir James Macdonald of Sleat, with issue.

He had also a natural son, the Rev. John, Archdean of Ross, died in 1666 in the Parish of Tarbat, who, by his wife, Christian, daughter of John Wemyss of Lathocker, had the Rev. Roderick Mackenzie, first of Avoch, in 1671 Sub-Chaunter of Ross, and several other children.

Sir Roderick was knighted in 1609 for the part he took, with his brother Kenneth, first Lord Mackenzie of Kintail, in pacifying the Lews and civilising the inhabitants.

He died in 1628, and was succeeded by his eldest son,

SIR JOHN MACKENZIE of Tarbat, created a Baronet of Nova Scotia, 21st May, in the same year, and married Margaret, daughter of Sir George Erskine of Innerteil, a Lord of Session, with issue—

1. *George*, his heir.

2. *John*, died young.

3. *Sir Roderick*, M.P. for Cromarty in 1700, and for

Fortrose in 1703, and afterwards Lord Prestonhall, who married, first, Margaret, daughter of Dr Burnet, Archbishop of St Andrews, with issue—Alexander Mackenzie of Fraserdale, who, in 1702, married Amelia, eldest daughter of Hugh, Xth Lord Lovat, with issue—several sons and daughters, and whose representation was proved extinct in 1826, when Alexander Mackenzie, Lieut.-Colonel H.E.I.C.S., assumed the dormant Baronetcy, as heir male collateral of Sir Kenneth, brother of John, second Earl of Cromarty, and was at the same time served heir male to George, first Earl of Cromarty. Lord Prestonhall married, secondly, Margaret, daughter of Haliburton of Pitcur, and relict of Sir George Mackenzie of Rosehaugh, without issue.   There is a sasine to this Roderick (Lord Prestonhall) as third son, dated June 1654.

4. *Alexander*, I. of Ardloch, whose representatives are now the real heirs male to the Cromarty titles.

5. *Kenneth*, married, and had one son, Kenneth, who died without issue.

6. *James*, M.D., died unmarried.

7. *Margaret*, married, first, Roderick Macleod of Macleod, without issue ; and secondly, Sir James Campbell of Lawers, Perthshire.

·8. *Anne*, married Hugh, IXth Lord Lovat, with issue.

9. *Isabel*, married Kenneth, third Earl of Seaforth.

10. *Barbara*, married Alexander Mackenzie, VII. of Gairloch, with issue.

11. *Catherine*, who married Sir Colin Campbell of Aberuchil, with issue.

Sir John Mackenzie of Tarbat died in 1654, and was succeeded by his eldest son,

I. SIR GEORGE MACKENZIE, who made a distinguished figure in the history of his country during the reigns of Charles II., James II. (VII. of Scotland), and William III. In 1661, at the early age of 31, he was made a Lord of Session.   He subsequently held the offices of Lord-Justice-General and Clerk-Register of Scotland.   When Maitland got into favour Sir George shared the fall of his patron, Lord Middleton, but on the death of the Duke of Lauder-

dale, he again got into favour, and to the close of the reign
of King James he held the principal sway and power in Scottish affairs. He was accessory, if not not the principal, in
putting Spence and Carstairs to the torture of the boot and
thumb-screws after the rebellion of Argyll. In 1685 King
James created him Viscount Tarbat, Lord Macleod and
Castlehaven. During the reign of William III. his influence
became much diminished, but he afterwards got into favour,
and, on the accession of Queen Anne, he again got into
Royal favour, and was by her, in 1703, raised to the dignity
of Earl of Cromarty, and made Secretary of State for Scotland. He subsequently resigned this office for his old post
of Justice-General; and recompensed Her Majesty's favours
by strongly advocating, with voice and pen, the Union of
the two Kingdoms, of which he was the first proposer. In
1710, after 60 years of active public service, he retired into
private life.

The Earl undoubtedly possessed ability of a very high
order, though as a politician he was very unsettled in his
principles. "As a judge," Smibert says, that he "was ad-
dicted to the old practice of considering the litigants rather
than their causes;" and Carstairs says, that "he habitually
falsified the minutes of Parliament, and recorded in its name
decisions and orders never really made"—a heavy charge
to bring against any statesman, and a most difficult thing
to do. In the course of his long and checkered career he
had been a member of so many Ministries, and, in fact,
changed sides so many times that it was not to be expected
that he should escape misrepresentation. "Some do com-
pare him to an eel," wrote Lockhart of Carnwath, "and
certainly the character suited him exactly. . . . He
had sworn all the most contradictory oaths, and complied
with all the opposite Governments since the year 1648, and
was humble servant to them all till he got what he aimed
at, though often he did not know what that was." Almost
every statesman in that age was as changeable as he, but he
possessed a wonderful capacity for business which distinguished few of his rivals. He is admitted on all hands to

have been, in private life, a gentleman of the most refined habits. He wrote well on various subjects, his chief productions being Essays on the Union of the two Kingdoms of England and Scotland ; on the Gowrie Conspiracy; and a " Plain Explication " of the Prophecies of Daniel and St John. He also wrote the MS. history of his own Clan, so often quoted and referred to in this work.

He married, first, Anne, daughter of Sir George Sinclair of Mey, with issue—

1. *Roderick*, who died young.

2. *John*, who became his heir.

3. *Kenneth*, who, in 1704, obtained a baronetcy, with his grandfather's patent of creation, as Sir Kenneth Mackenzie, Baronet of Grandvale and Cromarty.* He died in 1729, having been married to Anne Campbell, with issue—Sir George, the second Baronet, also M.P., who married Elizabeth, daughter of Captain John Reid, Greenwich, without issue ; and, in 1741, his affairs having become embarrassed, he sold Cromarty to Sir William Urquhart of Meldrum. He died in 1748, and was buried at Dingwall; his lady survived him 59 years, and died at Inverness in 1807, aged 84; Colin; James; Campbell; and Gerard, all died young, or unmarried ; Kenneth, who, in 1748, succeeded his brother Sir George, as third Baronet, and died unmarried in 1763 ; Catherine, who married Dr Adam Murray, of Stirling ; and several other daughters.

4. *James*, on the 8th February 1704, created a Baronet by Queen Anne, as Sir James Mackenzie of Royston, and,

---

* Sir Kenneth and his younger brother, Sir James Mackenzie of Royston, were created baronets in the same year, the patent of the latter being dated 8th of February 1704. Sir Kenneth's patent (which is to his heirs male for ever), was dated 29th of April 1704, and contained the original precedency of the patent of his grandfather, Sir John, who was created a baronet of Nova Scotia in 1628. Sir Kenneth was a member of Parliament for the County of Cromartie in the reigns of King William and Queen Anne. He warmly supported the treaty of Union, was one of the members nominated by the Parliament of Scotland, on 13th February 1707, to sit in the United Parliament of Great Britain, and was chosen member for the County of Cromartie at the general election in 1710. A new writ for that county was ordered on 22d January 1729, in consequence of his decease, and his eldest son, Sir George, was elected in his place.—*William Fraser's Earls of Cromartie.*

in 1710, he became a Lord of Session, by the title of Lord Royston. The Baronetcy was limited to heirs male, and Lord Royston having died in 1744 without surviving male issue, the Baronetcy became dormant.* By his marriage with Elizabeth, daughter of Sir George Mackenzie of Rosehaugh, Lord Royston had issue—George, married, and died before his father, without issue ; Anne, married Sir William Dick of Prestonfield ; and Elizabeth, married Sir John Steuart of Grandtully, with issue.

5. *Margaret*, married Sir D. Bruce, of Clackmannan.

6. *Elizabeth*, married Sir George Brown of Coalstown.

7. *Jean*, married Sir Thomas Stewart of Balcaskie.

8. *Anne*, married the Honourable John Sinclair, son of Lord Murkle.

Earl George married, secondly, Margaret, Countess of Wemyss, without issue. He died in 1714, was buried at Dingwall, and was succeeded by his eldest son,

II. JOHN, second Earl of Cromarty. He does not appear to have taken any prominent part in public affairs, and kept out of the Rising of 1715. Notwithstanding the division made of the family estates to make provision for the two baronetcies, he continued to possess extensive properties in the Counties of Ross, Inverness, Elgin, and Fife. He married, first, Lady Elizabeth Gordon, daughter of the first Earl of Aboyne, without issue. He divorced this lady,

---

* In the year 1730 Lord Royston, with the concurrence of George Mackenzie, his son, obtained an Act of Parliament, authorising him, with the consent of Charles Erskine of Tinwall, Lord Advocate, the Honourable William Maule of Panmure, and others, or any two of them, to sell the barony of Royston for the purpose of discharging the debts affecting it. The Act declared that Lord Royston should not, by selling the barony of Royston, be considered as contravening the entail of the barony. The Act further provided that the trustees should lay out the surplus of the price in the purchase of other lands in fee-simple, which should be settled on Lord Royston, and the other surviving heirs of entail, according to their different rights and interests, and in the same order and course of succession secured to them respectively by the estate of the barony of Royston. The barony was purchased by John, second Duke of Argyll, wdo made it one of his residences, and called it Caroline Park. . . . Lord Royston possessed for some time the superiority of Little Farnese, which had been given to him for a freehold qualification in the shire of Cromartie. Some years before his death he purchased the lands of Avoch from Mackenzie of Delvin, and to this property he gave the name of Farnese.—*William Fraser's Earls of Cromartie.*

and married, secondly, the Honourable Mary Murray, daughter of the third Lord Elibank, with issue—

1. *Lord George*, his heir.

2. *Captain Roderick*, married twice, with issue—one daughter; and Captain Kenneth of Cromarty, who succeeded, in 1789, to the estates, and died without male issue in 1796.

3. *William*, died at sea, without issue.

4. *Patrick*, married, without male issue.

5. *Gideon*, died without male issue.

6. *Mary ;* 7. *Anna ;* 8. *Helen*, died young or unmarried.

He married, thirdly, Anna, daughter of Hugh, Xth Lord Lovat, with issue—

9. *James.* 10. *Hugh.* 11. *Norman*, without surviving issue.

12. *Emilia*, who, in 1740, married Archibald Lamont of Lamont, with issue.

He died in 1731, and was succeeded by his eldest son,

III. GEORGE, third Earl of Cromarty, so well known in history in connection with the Rising of 1745, that it is unnecessary here to give more than a very brief notice of him. It would indeed be impossible, in the space at our disposal, to give a detailed account of his unfortunate career; and this is all the less necessary from the magnificent monument to this family, recently compiled by Mr William Fraser for His Grace the Duke of Sutherland, and printed for private circulation—" The Earls of Cromartie."

He joined Prince Charles and fought at the battle of Falkirk at the head of a body of 400 or 500 of his Clan, and was afterwards, 15th April, the day before the battle of Culloden, taken prisoner with his eldest son, Lord Macleod, and all his officers in Dunrobin Castle by two companies of Sutherlands and Mackays, he having previously detached himself from the main body of the Highland army with the view of seizing the Castle of Dunrobin, and repressing the adherents of the Government in the far North. He was sent to London and imprisoned in the Tower. His vacillating conduct and uncertain correspondence with the

famous Lord President Forbes are well-known, he having
actually written to him as late as October 1745, saying that
he was then "stirring actively in the cause of the Government." He was tried, found guilty of high treason, and
sentenced to death; but was afterwards pardoned through
the bold entreaties of his wife. In support of his own application for mercy, she waited personally on the Lords of
the Cabinet, and presented a separate petition, pleading for
mercy, to each of them, and on the Sunday after sentence
of death was passed upon him, she went to Kensington
Palace, dressed in deep mourning, accompanied by Lady
Stair, to make a personal appeal to His Majesty for the
Royal clemency. She was far advanced in pregnancy, and
though a woman of strong mind, who had hitherto exhibited
great fortitude in her distressing position, on this occasion
she completely broke down, and gave way to grief. Taking
her stand in the entrance of the chapel, through which the
King had to pass, she waited his arrival, and when he approached where she was, she fell on her knees, seized him
by the coat-tails, presented her petition, and fainted away
at his feet. He immediately seized her and raised her up,
took the petition, and handed it to the Duke of Grafton,
one of his attendants. He then requested Lady Stair to
conduct her to one of the apartments; and the Dukes of
Hamilton and Montrose, the Earl of Stair, and other
courtiers, having supported her petition by a personal application to the King, His Majesty, on the 9th of August,
granted a pardon, and allowed his Lordship to be at once
set at liberty.* He lived for several years in seclusion and

---

* Making all allowance for the strong and mingled influences which bore on
the Gael at this epoch—loyalty, hope, fear, and interest, being all more or less
called into action—we cannot pardon such cases of deceit as those of Lovat and
Cromarty. Well might the latter dread the issue when carried captive to London. He saw the necessity—to preserve one hope of life—of making a complete
submission and confession of guilt. He pleaded that he had ever been well disposed towards the existing Government, but had been misled by false counsel
and pretences. He might more truly have said, perhaps, that erroneous hopes
of personal and family aggrandisement had formed his main actuating motive in
joining the rebellion, though we must always make allowance for the natural
fears of injury from those who had actually first risen as insurgents. "Join us

poverty, mainly supported by the contributions of his old tenants and retainers on the forfeited estates. ·

Earl George, married Isabella, daughter of Sir William Gordon of Invergordon, with issue—

1. *John, Lord Macleod*, his heir.

2. *William*, died young.

3. *George*, a Colonel in the 71st Regiment, who died unmarried in 1788.

4. *Isabella*, married George, VIth Lord Elibank, with issue. In 1796 she succeeded her cousin, Captain Kenneth, in the estates.

5. *Mary*, married, first, Captain Clark, London; secondly, Thomas Drayton, South Carolina; and thirdly, John Ainslie, Charlestown.

6. *Anne*, married, first, the Honourable Edmond Atkin, of South Carolina; and secondly, Dr John Murray of Charlestown.

7. *Caroline*, married, first, a Mr Drake of London, and secondly, Walter Hunter of Polmood and Crailieg.

8. *Jean.*

9. *Amelia*, died young.

10. *Margaret*, married in 1769, John Glassford of Douglastown, Dumbarton, with issue; and

11. *Augusta*, married Sir William Murray of Achtertyre, with issue.

He died in 1766, and was, in 1784, succeeded in the estates by his eldest son,

IV. LORD MACLEOD, Major-General in the army, by whose noble conduct the shattered fortunes of the family

---

or you will be treated as foes." Such was the common cry at the time. Though the high-minded conduct of such a man as old Balmerino in the same emergency, when he stood before the peers of England, erect, and even proud of his cause, excited sympathy of a higher nature, yet the miserable position of the Earl of Cromarty—whose wife was then about to increase an already large family, and whose youthful heir, Lord Macleod, had been also drawn into the insurrection, though confessedly a mere instrument in the hands of others—affects one with feelings of sincere compassion. We must not honour but we must pity. It is said that the Countess led her ten children to the feet of the King as petitioners for the lives of their father and brother. The appeal was irresistible.—*Smibert's Highlanders.*

were, to some extent, relieved. Disdaining to live on the charity of his friends and a burden to his father, he went to Sweden as a soldier of fortune; worked his way in the · Swedish army, and, in 1775, returned to his native country, after twenty-seven years of distinguished foreign service, full of fame and honours, with the rank of Lieut.-General. In 1754 the Lovat estates were restored to General Fraser by George III.; and this emboldened Lord Macleod on his return to petition his Majesty for the restoration of his ancestral possessions ; but his application was not complied with. When Lord Macleod joined his father against the established Government he was only eighteen years of age, and on account of his extreme youth he obtained an unconditional pardon, dated 22d June 1748. In 1777 he was presented at Court, when Grorge III. received him very graciously ; and in return for the gracious treatment of his Sovereign in first pardoning him, and now so generously receiving him, he offered to raise a Highland Regiment, which offer was accepted, and in a very short time, though he was without property or any political connections, a fine body of 840 men was raised by him among his Highland countrymen. To this number 236 Lowlanders and 34 English and Irish, were added by some of his friends, making in all a full regiment of 1100 men, embodied at Elgin, and inspected there by General Skene in April 1778. Immediately after, Letters of Service were issued to · raise a second battalion of the same size as the first. This was soon done, no less than 1800 of the men being from the old possessions of his Lordship's ancestors—a splendid set of men with excellent constitutions, and of most exemplary conduct. He was himself appointed Colonel of the first battalion, and his brother, the Hon. Lieut.-Colonel Mackenzie, commanded the second battalion. The Regiment was called Macleod's Highlanders, and numbered the 73d, now the 71st Highlanders. In 1779 Lord Macleod accompanied his Highlanders to India, and fought at their head in the Carnatic against Hyder Ali, under Major-General Sir Hector Munro, where the regiment greatly distinguished itself, though it was nearly cut to pieces at the battle of Conjeveram. In 1782 his Lordship was promoted to the rank of Major-General, and in the following year returned home. As an acknowledgment for his distinguished services, an Act of Parliament was passed, on the 18th of August 1784, by which the forfeited estates of the Earldom of Cromarty were restored to him, on payment of the sum of £19,000 to relieve the property of existing burdens.

He married, in 1786, Isabella, daughter of James, XVIth Lord Forbes, without issue. The mansion was almost entirely demolished after the " Forty-five;" but it was by him rebuilt and enlarged ; and the policies put into good order and properly attended to. He died in 1789, and was succeeded in the estates by his cousin-german,

V. CAPTAIN KENNETH MACKENZIE of Cromarty, who, in 1796, died without male issue. He was the last direct male heir, and on his death the representation of the family, carrying with it the dormant honours of Cromarty and Tarbat, went into the family of Ardloch. He was succeeded in the property by Lord Macleod's eldest sister,

VI. LADY ELIBANK. She died in 1801 without male issue, and was succeeded by her eldest daughter,

VII. THE HONOURABLE MARIA MURRAY, who, in 1790, married Edward Hay of Newhall, brother to George, VIIth Marquis of Tweeddale. Her only sister, the Hon. Isabella Murray, died unmarried in 1849. By her marriage with Mr Hay, Lady Murray had—

1. *John Hay*, who assumed the name of Mackenzie in addition to his own, and succeeded to the estates.

2. *Dorothea*, married Sir D. Hunter Blair, with issue.

3. *Isabella*, married John Buckle, with issue.

4. *Georgina Ann*, who married James, Vth Earl of Glasgow, with issue.

She was succeeded by her only son,

VIII. JOHN HAY-MACKENZIE, who, in 1828, married Anne, daughter of Sir Gibson-Graig, Baronet, with issue.

1. *Anne*.

He died at Cliefden in 1849, and was succeeded by his only child,

IX. ANNE HAY-MACKENZIE of Cromarty, who, on the 27th of June 1849, married His Grace the third and present Duke of Sutherland. In 1861, during the premiership of Lord Palmerston, Her Grace, by a new creation, was made Countess of Cromarty, Viscountess Tarbat of Tarbat, Baroness Macleod of Castle Leod, and Baroness Castlehaven of Castlehaven, with remainder to her second son, Viscount Tarbat. Thus, after the death of the present Duchess of Sutherland, should the old title ever be restored, there would be two Earls, with all the titles exactly similar, excepting that the rightful Earl would also inherit the Nova Scotia Baronetcy; as also that of 1704.

As it is possible these honours may yet be claimed, it may be interesting to note in a more concise manner the facts concerning them. The original patent of a Nova Scotia Baronetcy to Sir John Mackenzie of Tarbat, by Charles I., dated 21st May 1628, was to him "*suosque hæredes masculos quoscunque de tempore in tempus in posterum per perpetuo*," and the re-grant of 29th April 1704, to his grandson, Kenneth, second son of George, first Earl of Cromarty, being confessedly to *restore* the Baronetcy—now absorbed in the Earldom—intact, "as the samen was given to the umquhile Sir John Mackenzie of Tarbat," was to Kenneth and his heirs male "*in perpetuum*," and was therefore granted with the same succession presumedly to heirs male whomsoever.

Sir Kenneth Mackenzie of Grandvale and Cromarty, first Baronet of this re-grant, dying without issue in 1729, the dignity was enjoyed by his eldest son, Sir George, second Baronet, who died without issue in 1748, and by his youngest son, Sir Kenneth, third Baronet, who died, also without issue, at Tain, in 1763. At his death it is clear that the succession would then, under the patent of 1704, devolve upon his heir male, who at this time was no other than George, the attainted third Earl of Cromarty, who had survived all male descendants of the patentee, but whose honours, having been attainted in 1746, had been restored by the pardon under the Great Seal granted to him, 20th

October 1749. Thus was this Baronetcy absorbed a second time in the Earldom of Cromarty, nor does it appear that it was ever assumed by George, third Earl (who died in Poland Street, London, September 29, 1766), or by his son, Lord Macleod, who obtained a pardon dated 26th January 1748, and who, dying without issue, 2d April 1789, ended the direct line both of the Earldom and the Baronetcy.

The succession then opened to his cousin, Captain Mackenzie of Cromarty, who obtained the estates; but he also died without issue in 1796, without having assumed either title.

Taking the term "*hæredibus masculis*," according to the opinion of Mr John Riddell, the advocate and author, "in the sense of our law, as an equivalent to heirs male whatsoever," the representation of the Tarbat Baronetcy would then revert to the brothers of George, first Earl of Cromarty, the next of whom was Roderick, Lord Prestonhall. But here again the fatality to heirs male, which has dogged the steps of the Cromarty titles in so extraordinary a manner, ended the succession in the children of his son, Alexander of Fraserdale. Mr Riddell, in his opinion upon the revival of 1826, says, "I certainly saw proof of the male extinction of the Prestonhall branch several years ago." That is, in one of the Lovat actions of Fraserdale, or Macleod of Macleod; and, after that family, the succession of the descendants of Alexander of Ardloch, fourth son of Sir John Mackenzie of Tarbat, was proved, in the Service at Tain, 30th October 1826, in the person of Lieutenant-Colonel Alexander Mackenzie, eldest son of Colonel Robert Mackenzie of Milnmount, who assumed the dormant Baronetcies of Tarbat and Royston, and who, dying without issue, 28th April 1841, was succeeded by his only brother, Sir James Sutherland Mackenzie, who also died unmarried, 24th November 1858. Since then these Baronetcies have remained dormant, no effort to assume them having been made by the next heir male, although it has been quite in his power to do so.

It is obvious from what has already been shown, that the representation of the Earldom of Cromarty, granted to George, Viscount Tarbat, 18th September 1703, the succession of which is "*hæredibus masculis et talliæ*," devolves upon the same head as the above-named Baronetcies. It is not, however, clear whether the pardon obtained by George, third Earl, is sufficient to remove the attainder, or whether an Act of Parliament would not be further necessary, although the attainted male-blood is at an end. Since this question was debated, the restoration of the Airlie and other forfeited peerages have, in a great measure, cleared the ground, and in the new creation of 1861 the older title and honours could be in no way affected or disturbed.

THE MACKENZIES OF ARDLOCH.

The first of this family on which now devolves the representation of the original Earldom of Cromarty and the baronetcies of Tarbat and Royston in the male line was

I. ALEXANDER MACKENZIE, fourth son of Sir John Mackenzie of Tarbat, created a Baronet of Nova Scotia in 1628, by his wife, Margaret, daughter of Sir George Erskine of Innerteil, a Lord of Session and Justiciary. Alexander, to whom there is a sasine as "fourth son," dated June 1654, married Barbara, daughter of Kenneth Mackenzie, VI. of Gairloch, by his second wife, Ann, daughter of Sir John Grant, Baron of Grant, and relict of Fraser of Kinneries. By her Ardloch had issue—

1. *Roderick*, died young.

2. *John*, his successor.

3. *James* of Keppoch, who married Isabella, daughter of Kenneth Mackenzie I. of Dundonnell, with issue—(1) Alexander, married Henrietta Mackenzie of Fisherfield (sasine 1773); (2) Simon of Keppoch, who had Alexander of Kildonan; (3) George of Kildonan, married Ann, daughter of Roderick Mackenzie of Kernsary, with issue—James. He died in 1809, aged 109 years; (4) Colin, of Jamaica, married Janet, daughter of Kenneth Mackenzie III. of Dundonnell, without issue; (5) Mary, married Donald, grandson of John

Mackenzie, I. of Gruinard, with issue; (6) Isabella, who married Allan Mackenzie, of the family of Hilton. James sold Keppoch in 1730.

5. *Barbara*, who married Roderick, son of George Mackenzie, II. of Gruinard, with issue.

6. *Ann*, married William, son of George Mackenzie, II. of Gruinard, with issue.

7. *Margaret*, died unmarried; and three others who married respectively, Sinclair of Dunbeath; Gordon of Auchintoul, a cadet of the Gordons of Embo; and Colin Mackenzie of Kildun.

He died in 1736,* and was succeeded by his eldest surviving son,

II. JOHN MACKENZIE, who married Sybella, daughter of Kenneth Mackenzie I. of Dundonnell, with issue—

1. *Alexander*, his heir.

2. *Kenneth*.

3. *John*.

4. *Annabella*, and other daughters; issue unknown.

He was succeeded by his eldest son,

III. ALEXANDER MACKENZIE, who married Margaret, daughter of Robert Sutherland of Langwell, in Caithness, twelfth in descent from William de Sutherland, fifth Earl of Sutherland, and his lady, the Princess Margaret Bruce, sister and heir of David II., King of Scotland, with issue—

1. *James*, a Major in the army, who married a daughter of Mackenzie of Fairburn, and had one son, who died before his father.

2. *Robert* of Milnmount, Colonel H.E.I.C.S., who married, first, a daughter of Mackenzie of Bayfield, without issue male; and secondly, Katharine, daughter of Colonel Sutherland of Uppat, Sutherlandshire, by whom he had Sir Alexander Mackenzie, Baronet of Tarbat and Royston, a Lieutenant-Colonel H.E.I.C.S., who, on the 30th October 1826, assumed the dormant baronetcies of Tarbat and Royston, as heir male collateral of Sir Kenneth Mackenzie,

---

* Findon says 1726, but he was alive in 1733, as appears from an Inverness sasine.

brother to John, second Earl of Cromarty; and in the same
year he was served nearest and lawful heir male, at Tain, to
George, first Earl of Cromarty. He died, unmarried, in
1841, and was succeeded in the baronetcies by his next
brother, Sir James Sutherland Mackenzie, who, in 1858,
died without issue. A sister, Elizabeth, married Lieutenant
Sutherland, Royal Navy, with issue; and another, Margaret,
married the Rev. James H. Hughes, a chaplain in H.E.I.C.
Service, Bombay, with issue. On the death of Sir James
the baronetcies and other dignities of the Cromarty family
reverted to his cousin, John Mackenzie, Lochinver, son of
Kenneth Mackenzie, Ledbeg, Assynt, who has, however,
never assumed the titles.

   3. *George*, was minister in Caithness, and died unmarried
in 1825.

   4. *Kenneth* of Ledbeg, married, first, a daughter of
Mackenzie of Elphin, with issue—(1) John of Lochinver,
who now is heir male to the Tarbat and Cromarty honours.
He was twice married, without issue; (2) Robert; (3) James;
(4) Charles; (5) Royston, all of whom died without surviving issue; (6) Jane; (7) Georgina; (8) Jessie, married the
Rev. John Kennedy, minister of Redcastle, who died in
1841, and left issue, one of whom is the Rev. John Kennedy,
D.D., now of Dingwall.

   5th, 6th, and 7th sons of Alexander, III. of Ardloch,
died unmarried.

   8. *Murdoch*, married Janet, a daughter of Kenneth Mackenzie of Dundonnell, without issue.

   9. *Alexander*, married a daughter of Mackenzie, Stron-
chrubie, and had a son, James, who died in Assynt, unmarried, and two daughters, one of whom, Margaret, married
Kenneth Macleod, and Anne, who died unmarried.

   Failing the male succession of this family, which, however, it will be found extremely difficult, if not quite impossible, to trace, should the representatives of Kenneth
Mackenzie of Ledbeg become extinct in the male line, the
dormant honours of Tarbat and Cromarty will revert to the
family of Scatwell.

THE MACKENZIES OF SCATWELL.

Sir Roderick Mackenzie of Coigeach, Tutor of Kintail, by Margaret, eldest daughter and co-heiress of Torquil Macleod of the Lews, had a second son, the progenitor of this family,

I. KENNETH MACKENZIE, first of Scatwell. He married, in 1634, Margaret, eldest daughter and co-heiress of Robert Munro, the Black Baron, XXth of Fowlis, and with her received the handsome " tocher " of 15,000 merks, and had issue—

1. *John*, his heir.

2. *Jean*, who married a son of Munro of Lumlair.

3. *Anne*, who married MacCulloch of Park, with issue.

4. *Catherine*, married Kenneth Mackenzie, I. of Langwell..

He married, secondly, Janet, daughter of Walter Ross of Invercharron, and relict of Thomas Ross of Priesthill, life rentrix of Priesthill, Ulladale, &c., with issue—

5. *Roderick*, who died young.

6. *Alexander*, who succeeded his half-brother, John, as III. of Scatwell.

7. *George*, died young.

8. *Kenneth*, who succeeded his brother, Alexander, as IV. of Scatwell, and was afterwares created a Baronet of Nova Scotia in 1703.

9. *Isabella*, married John Macleod of Corrtullich, Tutor of Macleod of Macleod.

10. *Christian*, who married, first, John Gray of Arboll, and secondly, George Gordon of Ospidale, without issue.

He had a sasine of Little Scatwell in 1619, and a charter of Allangrange, from George, Earl of Seaforth, in 1636. He died at Lochluichart, 3d March 1662, of which place he has a sasine in 1634, and was buried in St Clement's Chapel, Dingwall, on which occasion, according to the Wardlaw MS., " My Lord Lovat paraded there with near 100 horse and 500 foot," to do honour to " a gallant and a great spirit."

He was succeded by his only son by the first marriage,

II. JOHN MACKENZIE, who has a sasine in 1667, and

married Anne, daughter of Roderick Mackenzie, III. of Redcastle, with issue—an only child, Lilias, who married Colin Mackenzie, III. of Kincraig, with issue ; sasine to her in 1679. He died 13th May 1677, and was succeeded by his half-brother,

III. ALEXANDER MACKENZIE, who married Janet Ross of Ulladale, who died in March 1699. He died without issue, 18th March 1680, and was succeeded by his brother,

IV. SIR KENNETH MACKENZIE, created·a Baronet of Nova Scotia by Queen Anne, 22d Feb. 1703, six weeks after the elevation of his cousin-german, George, Lord Tarbat, to the Earldom of Cromarty. Dr George Mackenzie informs us that " he was a member of the Union Parliament, and joined those patriots of the country who stood by the ancient and inalienable privileges of the nation." In 1688 he acquired by purchase from his relative, Sir George Mackenzie of Rosehaugh, and Mary Haliburton, his wife, the lands of Pittonachty. About the same time he married Lilias, eldest daughter of Sir Roderick Mackenzie of Findon, third son of Alexander Mackenzie, I. of Kilcoy, who, on the death of her father and mother, and that of her only brother the year following, was, 12th October 1693, served heir of Taillzie and provision to her father in the lands of Findon, and she brought this property to her husband. In 1696 the fortunes of the family of Scatwell having thus been much improved, a dwelling-house was erected by Kenneth and his wife at Findon, into which they removed from Lochluichart ; and the family continued to reside in it until the erection of the new mansion at Pittonachty by Sir Roderick Mackenzie, the second baronet, in 1795. The old residence at Findon, now used as a farm house, still bears the following inscription on the lintel of the main door :—

" Omnia terrena per vices sunt aliena,
 Nunc mea, nunc hujus,
 Post mortem nescio cujus,
         Nulli certa domus."
" K. MK. 16. 96 L. MK."

By Lilias of Findon, who died 21st October 1703, Sir Kenneth had issue—

1. *George*, who, in 1705, died unmarried.

2. *Roderick*, who succeeded as second baronet.

3. *Alexander*, who died young.

4. *Simon*, I. of Scotsburn.*

5. *Margaret*, who married, first, Æneas Macleod of Cadboll, with issue; and secondly, Roderick Mackenzie, IV. of Applecross, with issue.

6. *Isabel*, who married, first, Kenneth Bayne of Tulloch, without issue; and secondly, Roderick Chisholm of Chisholm, with issue.

7. *Elizabeth*, married William Mackenzie, III. of Belmaduthy, with issue.

8. *Margaret*, who married James Cuthbert, merchant, Inverness.

He married, secondly, in 1707, Christian, eldest daughter of the Rev. Roderick Mackenzie, minister and Laird of Avoch, grandson, by a natural son, of Sir Roderick Mackenzie of Coigeach, without issue. He married, thirdly, Abigail, daughter of John Urquhart of Newhall, with issue—

9. *Kenneth*, H.E.I.C.S.

10. *Jean*, who married Kenneth Mackenzie, III. of Dundonnell, with issue. She died in 1786.

11. *Ann*, who, in 1750, married Thomas Mackenzie, V. of Ord, with issue.

In 1728, two years before his death, he mortified a sum of 900 merks for the education and benefit of the poor in the parish of Avoch. He died in 1730, and was suceeded by his eldest surviving son,

V. SIR RODERICK MACKENZIE, second baronet, who, in 1710, married Janet, daughter of Ludovic, XVIIth Baron of Grant (now represented by the Earl of Seafield), by whom he had—

1. *Lewis*, his heir.

2. *Captain Alexander*, married, first, his cousin, Lilias,

---

* For his descendants see Findon's Mackenzie Genealogies, sheet 10.

daughter of Simon Mackenzie, I. of Scotsburn, with issue ; and secondly, Janet, daughter of John Mackenzie, III. of Torridon, with issue ; but the male representation by both marriages is now extinct.*

3. *Janet*, who married Sir Alexander Mackenzie, second Baronet and IX. of Gairloch, with issue.

4. *Elizabeth*, married Colin Mackenzie II. of Mount-gerald, with issue.

5. *Margaret*, who married James Cuthbert of Milncraig.

Sir Roderick succeeded in 1730, and died in 1750, being succeeded by his eldest son,

VI. SIR LEWIS MACKENZIE, third baronet, who married, in 1739, Isabella, eldest daughter of Colin Mackenzie, II. of Mountgerald, with issue—

1. *Roderick*, his heir.

2. *Colin*, born in 1746, on the day of the battle of Cul-loden, a merchant in London, with Mark Sprot, the then eminent financier, and who married Janet, daughter of J. Sprot, Edinburgh. He has a sasine of Little Findon in life-rent, dated September 2, 1771. By this lady he had issue—(1) Colin, died, unmarried, in 1841 ; (2) Mark, died, unmarried, in 1856; (3) Lewis, Major in the Royal Scots Greys, who married Nancy, daughter and heiress of Samuel Forrester Bancroft, with issue—*(a)* Lewis Mark Mackenzie, I. of Findon and Mountgerald, who died, unmarried, in 1856. He obtained the estate of Findon by deed of arrange-ment from his cousin, Sir James John Randoll Mackenzie, VIth Baronet of Scatwell, in 1849, and purchased Mount-gerald from Colonel Simon Mackenzie in 1855. He was succeeded, as II. of Findon, &c., by his next brother *(b)* Augustus Colin, who also died, unmarried, in 1865 ; when the only surviving brother *(c)* Major James D. Mackenzie, who served both in the 79th and 14th Regiments, author of the " Mackenzie Genealogies " recently published, suc-ceeded to the property, as III. of Findon and Mountgerald, and married, in 1858, Julia Stanley, daughter of Dr Samuel

---

* See Finlon's Mackenzie Genealogies, sheet 10.

Clutsam, T.C.D., with issue; *(d)* Ernest Bancroft, died, unmarried, in 1861 ; *(e)* Colin, died young; *(f)* Nancy Copley, married Thomas Antony Lister of Gargrave, with issue— Nancy M. Augusta; *(g)* and Julia Louisa, married Baron Iver H. Rosen-krantz, Chamberlain to the King of Denmark and Minister at the Court of Italy, with issue.

3. *Lewis*, died in the West Indies, unmarried.

4. *George*, Colonel in the 72d Regiment, who married Joan, daughter of John Campbell of Wellwood, Ayrshire, with issue—(1) Lewis, Captain in the 72d Regiment, who married Jane, daughter of William Logan, with issue—one daughter, Margaret; (2) John Campbell, Lieutenant 5th Regiment, married, in 1810, Marie Barbier Deshayeux, at St Jean de Luz, with issue—George Salvador, Lieutenant, H.E.I.C.S., drowned in 1844 in the Ganges ; Admiral John Fraser Campbell, who married, in 1850, Annabella, daughter of the Rev. Dr Stirling, minister of Craigie, with issue; Francois, Major H.E.I.C.S., married, in 1854, Julia, daughter of John Mercer, of Maidstone, with issue ; Lilias, died unmarried ; and Louisa Georgina, married, in 1843, as his second wife, Dr Stair M'Quhae, with issue ; (3) George, died young; (4) another George, died unmarried; (5) Isabel, died young ; (6) Catherine, died unmarried ; (7) James, who married William Forrester Bow, M.D., with issue—three sons.

5. *Lilias*, who died, unmarried, in 1777.

Sir Lewis was served heir to his father in 1752. His marriage contract is dated 1739. His wife died in 1786 at Findon. He died in 1756, and was succeeded by his eldest son,

VII. SIR RODERICK MACKENZIE, fourth baronet, who, in 1764, married Katharine, daughter of Sir James Colquhoun of Luss, by Lady Helen Sutherland, daughter of William, Lord Strathnaver, with issue—

1. *Lewis*, Colonel of the Ross and Cromarty Rangers, who, in 1794, married Grace, daughter of Thomas Lockhart of Newhall, and died before his father, in 1810, without issue.

2. *James Wemyss*, who succeeded his father.

3. *Helen*, who, in 1790, died unmarried.

4. *Katharine Morrison*, who, in 1819, died unmarried.

In 1795 he built, on the estate of Pittonachty, the present mansion, to which, with the property, he gave the name of the adjoining estate of Roschaugh, and removed his family to it from the old house at Findon. He also built the present Church of Urquhart, or Ferrintosh, the old one having become untenable from the accumulation of interments within it. He died in 1811, and was succeeded by his eldest surviving son,

VIII. Sir James Wemyss Mackenzie, fifth baronet, M.P., and Lord-Lieutenant for the County of Ross. He resided for a time in Jamaica, and was a paymaster in the army.· He married, in 1810, Henrietta Wharton, daughter and heiress of William Mackenzie, IV. of Suddie, by Margaret, daughter of Sir Alexander Mackenzie, V. of Coul. She was previously married to Captain Robert Pott of Galallan, without issue; and on the death of her brother, Major-General John Randoll Mackenzie, of the 78th Highlanders, at Talavera, in 1809, she brought to Sir James Wemyss Mackenzie of Scatwell the estate of Suddie. By her he had an only child—

Sir James John Randoll, the present baronet.

He died in 1843, and was succeeded by his only son,

IX. Sir James John Randoll Mackenzie, VIth and present baronet, who, born in 1814, married, in 1838, Lady Anne Wentworth-Fitzwilliam, daughter of Charles William Wentworth V. Earl Fitzwilliam, K.G. She died in 1879 without issue.

In 1849 he obtained a dis-entail of the Scatwell estates, and soon after alienated or sold them. The estate of Findon went, under a deed of arrangement, to his cousin, the late Lewis Mark Mackenzie, grandson of Colin, second son of Sir Lewis Mackenzie, VI., and third baronet of Scatwell, and is now in possession of his brother, Major James Dixon Mackenzie of Findon and Mountgerald, heir presumptive to the Scatwell baronetcy, and, failing the representation of the Mackenzies of Ardloch, heir male to the Tarbat and Royston Baronetcies, and to the original Earldom of Cromarty. The estate of Scatwell was sold to Mr Murray of Polmaise; Lochluichart to Lord Ashburton; Roschaugh, in 1864, was sold to James Fletcher, now of Roschaugh, while that of Suddie was in the hands of the trustees under Sir James John Randoll Mackenzie's marriage settlement.

THE MACKENZIES OF BALLONE.

I. ALEXANDER MACKENZIE, the first of this family, was fourth son of Sir Roderick Mackenzie, Tutor of Kintail, by his wife, Margaret, daughter and co-heiress of Torquil Macleod of the Lews. He has a sasine of the lands of Achaghluineachan, Lochbroom, in 1635, where Ballone (now Inverbroom) is situated. He married Agnes, daughter of Hugh Fraser of Culbokie, relict of Kenneth Mackenzie of Inverlael, with issue—

1. *Alexander*, his heir.

2. *Jane*, who married Simon, brother of Sir George Mackenzie of Roschaugh, with issue.

He married, secondly, Lilias, daughter of Kenneth Mackenzie, VI. of Gairloch, with issue—an only daughter.

3. *Margaret*, who married, first, Sir Roderick Mackenzie of Findon, with issue; and secondly, George Mackenzie, II. of Gruinard.

He also had a natural son, Colin, who was Chamberlain to Lord Tarbat, and had a sasine of Kildonan in 1684.

He was succeeded by his only son,

II. ALEXANDER MACKENZIE, who married Barbara, daughter of Kenneth Mackenzie, I. of Dundonnell, and niece to Sir George Mackenzie of Roschaugh, with issue—

1. *Alexander*, his heir.

2. *Colin*, who married Mary, daughter of Mackenzie of Achilty.

3. *Kenneth*, who married, first, Barbara, daughter of Colin Mackenzie, without surviving issue; and secondly, Barbara, daughter of Roderick Mackenzie, son of George Mackenzie, II. of Gruinard, with issue.

4. *Anne*, who married Roderick Mackenzie of the family of Achilty, with issue—four daughters.

He died in 1726, and was succeeded by his eldest son,

III. ALEXANDER MACKENZIE, who married Catharine, grand-daughter of George Mackenzie, II. of Gruinard (sasine in 1742), with issue—

1. *Alexander*, drowned at sea.

2. *John*, who succeeded.

3. *Mary*, married Roderick Mackenzie of Kernsary.

4. *Catherine*, married Colin Knight, in the Lews.

5. *Margaret*, married, first (sasine 1697), James MacRa of Conchra, Lochalsh, only son of Rev. John MacRa, minister of Dingwall, with issue; and secondly, Colin Chisholm of Knockfin, with issue.

6. *Isobel*, married Alexander Stronach, minister of Lochbroom, with issue.

7. *Barbara*, died unmarried.

8. *Alexandrina*, married Alexander Macrae, Strathmore, with issue.

He was succeeded by his eldest surviving son,

IV. CAPTAIN JOHN MACKENZIE, who married, first in 1770, Margaret, daughter of Roderick, son of George Mackenzie, II. of Gruinard, with issue—

1. *John*, his heir, a shipowner in the Lews.

2. *Hector*, who married Mary Tolmie, Dunvegan, Skye, with issue—an only son, John T. Mackenzie, shipowner, Dunvegan.

3. *Barbara*, married Captain Campbell, with issue.

4. *Catherine*, married William Mackenzie (of the Hilton family), Ullapool, with issue—one son, John, and two daughters.

Captain John married, secondly, Ann, daughter of Mackenzie of Acha-na-h'airde, with issue—

5. *George*, who went to America, and married a Miss Fraser at St Ann's, there.

6. *Alexander*, who also went to America, first established himself in business with his cousin, Roderick Mackenzie, in St Francois, a small town on the St Lawrence.

He afterwards bought a farm in the township of Wickham, and married a Miss Sarah Duncan of Grantham, by whom he had six children—(1) James Mackenzie, Lapeer, Michigan, U.S.A., who married, first, in July 1867, Georgina Hunter of Gardiner, Maine, issue—one son, Harvard Hunter, who died young. He married, secondly, in 1875, his first wife having died in 1868, Miss Amanda Hart, by whom he has a son, Harrison Hart, and a daughter, Emily Sarah; (2) Roderick Munro; (3) Andrew Duncan; (4) Norman; (5) Alexander Stronach; and (6) Henry, all of whom are still alive.

7. A daughter, who married William Mackenzie, Dornie.

8. *Margaret*, married a Mr MacRa, in Strathglass.

9. *Georgina*, married a Mr Maclennan, in Coigeach.

10. A daughter, married Wm. Macdonald, in America.

He sold the estate of Ballone to Henry Davidson of Tulloch, and emigrated to America, where most of his descendants now reside. He was succeeded, as representative of the family, by his eldest son,

V. JOHN MACKENZIE, shipowner in the Lews, who married Barbara Maciver, Gress, in that Island, with issue —an only son,

1. *John*, his heir, who married, with issue, all of whom died young, except one daughter who still survives. He also had three daughters, the eldest of whom died unmarried; the second married Mr Macleod, Valtos, Lews; and the third married Mr Morrison, rope manufacturer, Stornoway, whom she survives, with issue—two sons and a daughter.

He was drowned at sea on his way from America, when he was succeeded, as representative of the family, by his only son,

VI. JOHN MACKENZIE, who married, and died without male issue, when he was succeeded, as representative of the family, by his cousin, the only son of his uncle Hector,

VII. JOHN T. MACKENZIE, shipowner, Dunvegan, who married Miss H. Ferguson, Selkirk, with issue—Murdo Tolmie, medical student in Edinburgh University, and other children.

THE MACKENZIES OF KILCOY.

I. ALEXANDER MACKENZIE, first of this family, was third son of Colin Càm Mackenzie, XIth of Kintail, by his wife, Barbara, daughter of John, XIIth Baron of Grant. He married, in 1611, Jean, daughter of Sir Thomas Fraser of Strichen, and has a charter of Kilcoy in 1618. By this lady he had—

1. *Colin*, his heir.

2. *Thomas*, who has a sasine in 1678.

3. *Alexander*, I. of Muirtown of Kilcoy, who married Marie Cuthbert of Drakies. He had a sasine of "the lands of Muiren" in 1657, and a charter to "Alexander in the Muir" in 1666. By Marie of Drakies he had issue—(1) Colin, his heir; (2) the Rev. John, minister in Badenoch; another son, and one daughter. He was succeeded as II. of Muirtown by his eldest son, Colin Mackenzie, W.S., who married Margaret, daughter of Sir James Grant of Moyness, with issue—(1) Kenneth, his heir; (2) Simon, who died abroad; and three daughters. Kenneth, his eldest son, succeeded as III. of Muirtown, and, in 1724, married Mary, second daughter of Charles Mackenzie of Cullen, with issue —(1) Alexander, his heir; (2) Colin, M.D., who died unmarried; and (3) James, who also died unmarried. Alexander, the eldest son, succeeded as IV. of Muirtown, and married Margaret, daughter of James Mackenzie, III. of Highfield, with issue, four daughters, who married respectively, Hugh Rose of Cuilich; Black of Calder; Alexander Cumming; and the youngest, Margaret, Bailie James Shaw of Inverness, who died 21st January 1801. By this marriage Barbara had issue—(1) Alexander Mackenzie Shaw, who succeeded to the property after his father's death, who must have bought up the shares of his wife's three sisters, as he undoubtedly left the whole to his eldest son, a minor, only seventeen years of age, when his father died. It was, however, left in the hands of a Mr Fraser, who managed to squander the funds which should have been invested for the second son, William, a Colonel, H.E.I.C.S. (married with

E 2

issue), and ten daughters, who survived their father; and to make up the deficiency, not only Muirtown, but Waternish, in Skye, and Woodside, near Fortrose, also the property of Bailie Shaw at his death, had to be sold. Muirtown was bought by a Mr Reid, who afterwards re-sold it to William Mackenzie of Portmore, W.S. Alexander Mackenzie Shaw married, in 1804, Mary Laing, with issue—(1) Gilbert Shaw, born in 1806, late a judge in Jamaica, and now residing at Tongland, Kirkcudbright; (2) Gilbert, died young; (3) Henry Bridgewater; (4) Alexander; (5) John; (6) Mary, died unmarried; (7) Hectorina, married Mr Sprott; and (8) Eleanor, who married Mr Scabank.

4. *Sir Roderick* Mackenzie of Findon, with issue.

5. *Isobel*, married Roderick Mackenzie, III. of Redcastle. with issue.

6. A daughter, married Ross of Pitcalnie, Tutor of Balnagowan.

7. A daughter, who married, first, Duncan Bayne of Tulloch; and secondly, in 1651, George Munro, younger of Lumlair.

8. A daughter, who married Maclean of Borera.

He had also three natural daughters, who married respectively, Hector Mackenzie of Fairburn; Neil Bayne, in Uist; and Mr John, son of John Roy Mackenzie, IV. of Gairloch.

He married, secondly, Barbara Dunbar, with issue—one daughter; and was succeeded by his eldest son,

II. COLIN MACKENZIE, who married, in 1640, Lilias, sister of Sir Alexander Sutherland, Lord Duffus (sasine 1649), with issue—

1. *Alexander*, his heir.

2. *Roderick* of Dalvennan, advocate, who married Margaret, sister of John Cathcart of Castletown, without issue male. He has a sasine of the lands of Allangrange in 1672.

3. *Charles* of Cullen, who, in 1682, married Florence, daughter of John Mackenzie, II. of Applecross, with issue, a son, who died young; Abigail, who married Alexander Mackenzie of Lentran; Mary, who married Kenneth Mac-

kenzie, III. of Muirtown, with issue; Katharina, married Roderick Mackenzie, IV. of Redcastle; Florence, married Duncan MacRa of Inverinate, with issue; and Margaret, who married Alexander Mackenzie, brother of Redcastle.

4. *Thomas*, I. of Cleanwaters, who, in 1680, married Margaret, daughter of Matthew Robertson of Davochcarty, with issue—Colin, who married Florence, daughter of Simon Mackenzie, I. of Torridon, with issue—a son, Alexander, who married a daughter of William Mackenzie, II. of Pitlundie, by whom he had one son who died young.

5. *John*, who, in 1683, married Isobel Mackenzie, with issue—two sons, one of whom, Charles, married and had a son, Alexander, who succeeded to the property of Cleanwaters.

Colin was succeeded, in 1682, by his eldest son,

III. ALEXANDER MACKENZIE, who, in 1665, married Mary, daughter of Kenneth Mackenzie, VI. of Gairloch, by whom he had an only son—

1. *Roderick*, his heir.

In 1658 he bought the lands of Allan (now Allangrange) from Seaforth's trustees, and, in 1682, he sold it to his uncle, Sir Roderick Mackenzie of Findon, whose daughter, Isobel, carried it to Simon Mackenzie, progenitor of Allangrange.

He died in 1687, and was succeeded by his only son,

IV. RODERICK MACKENZIE, who married, in 1689, Annabella, daughter of Sir Donald Bayne of Tulloch, with issue—

1. *Donald*, his heir.

2. *John*, who died without issue.

3. *Lilias*, who married Donald Dingwall, Provost of Dingwall.

He was succeeded by his eldest son,

V. DONALD MACKENZIE, who, in 1716, married Elizabeth, daughter of John Mackenzie, II. of Highfield, with issue—

1. *Roderick*, who died young.

2. *Colin*, his successor.

3. *James*, who died young.

4. *William*, who married Jean, daughter of Alexander Mackenzie, VIII. of Davochmaluag, without issue.

5. *Alexander*, who died in Holland, without issue.

6. *Kenneth*, Tutor of Kilcoy, who married Janet, daughter and heiress of Sir Robert Douglas of Glenbervie, Baronet, author of the "Peerage" and "Baronage," with issue.

7. *Elizabeth*, who married Thomas Mackenzie, IV. of Highfield and VI. of Applecross, with issue.

He was succeeded by his eldest surviving son,

VI. COLIN MACKENZIE, who, in 1747, married Martha, eldest daughter of Charles Fraser of Inverallochy. Through this lady the family of Kilcoy claim to be heirs to the old Earldom of Buchan, conferred, in 1469, upon James Stewart, half-brother of James II., by the second marriage of his mother, Queen Jane, to Sir James Stewart, the Black Knight of Lorn. In 1617 a Crown charter of *Novadamus* is granted to the then Countess Mary of Buchan, who married James Erskine, with the precedence of the former charter to herself and her husband in life-rent, and the heirs male of their marriage, whom failing to *his* nearest heirs male whatsoever. In 1625 the Earl and Countess had another charter of the Earldom with the same limitation. In 1633 the charter of 1625, and a decree of 1628, giving the Earldom of Buchan precedence over those of Eglintoun, Montrose, Cassilis, Caithness, and Glencairn, were ratified by Act of Parliament. These charters make the Kilcoy claim quite hopeless, not because they are not the rightful heirs, but because the Earldom was given in 1617 by a charter to the heirs male of James Erskine, though he had no more right to it than he had to the throne itself, beyond having married the Countess Mary of Buchan, now represented by the Mackenzies of Kilcoy. Nothing can annul a charter but another Crown charter, and as a matter of fact and justice, the Cardross Erskines have no more right to represent and sit as the Earls of Buchan of 1469 than they have to be Kings of Great Britain. By this lady Kilcoy had issue—

1 *Donald*, who died young.

2. *Charles*, his heir.

3. *Colin*, a Lieutenant in the 71st Regiment, killed in the American War, without issue.

4. *Alexander*, who, on succeeding to his mother's pro- perty of Inverallochy, assumed the additional name of Fraser, and became the well-known Lieutenant-General Alexander Mackenzie-Fraser of Inverallochy and Castle Fraser, Colonel of the 78th Regiment, and M.P. for the County of Ross. He married Helen, sister of Francis Humberston Mackenzie, last Lord Seaforth, with issue—(1) Colonel Charles Mackenzie-Fraser, his heir, and after his father's death at Walcheren in 1809, II. of Castle Fraser and Inverallochy. He married Jane, daughter of Sir John Hay of Hayston, with issue—*(a)* Alexander, who died in 1843; *(b)* John Wingfield, died in 1846; *(c)* Charles Murray, died in 1846; *(d)* Francis Mackenzie, died in 1849; *(e)* Kenneth, died young in 1836. All these died without issue. *(f)* Colonel Frederick Mackenzie-Fraser, III., and now of Castle Fraser, married Lady M. Blanche, daughter of the Earl of Perth. She died in 1874, without issue. *(g)* Catherine, who died, unmarried, in 1856; *(h)* Mary Elizabeth, died, unmarried, in 1847; *(i)* Eleanor Jane, married the Right Rev. George Tomlinson, D.D., Bishop of Gibraltar, with issue (she died in 1858); *(j)* Grace Harriet; and *(k)* Augusta Charlotte, who married Robert Drummond, with issue. Colonel Charles, II. of Castle Fraser, died in 1863. (2) Lieutenant-Colonel Frederick Alexander Mackenzie-Fraser, his brother, married, first, Emma Sophia, daughter of Hume Macleod of Harris, with issue—Frederick Charles, married, with issue, and died in 1877; Colin; and Isabel, who died unmarried. He married, secondly, Georgina Augusta, daughter of the Honourable Sir Charles Bagot. Lieutenant-General Alexander had also two daughters, (3) Marianne and (4) Helen, both of whom died unmarried.

5. *Anne*, who married Alexander Mackenzie, W.S., I. of Portmore, with issue.

6. *Elizabeth*, died young.

7. *Jean*, married Alexander Elphinstone of Glack, with issue.

8. *Elizabeth;* 9. *Martha;* 10. *Margaret;* 11. *Janet*, all of whom died young or unmarried.

Colin of Kilcoy died in 1758, and was succeeded by his eldest surviving son,

VII. CHARLES MACKENZIE, who married, in 1781, Jane G., third daughter of Patrick Grant of Glenmoriston, with issue—

1. *Colin*, his heir.

He died in 1813, and was succeeded by his only son,

VIII. SIR . COLIN MACKENZIE, who, in 1836, was created a Baronet, with remainder to his second son. He married Isabella, daughter of Ewen Cameron of Glen Nevis, with issue—

1. *Charles*, superseded.

2. *Evan*, his heir.

3. *Colin*, died, unmarried, in 1868.

4. *Jane*, married James Wardlaw, Major, H.E.I.C.S., with issue.

He died in 1845, and was succeeded by his second son,

IX. SIR EVAN MACKENZIE, Baronet, now of Kilcoy, who, in 1844, married Sarah Anne Philomena, daughter of J. Parks, Sydney, with issue—

1. *Colin Mackenzie*, younger of Kilcoy, Captain 79th Cameron Highlanders.

2. *Edith Millicent*.

3. *Eva*, who married Major Roderick Mackenzie of Flowerburn, with issue.

4. *Sarah Anne Philomena*.

MACKENZIE-DOUGLAS OF GLENBERVIE.

I. GENERAL SIR KENNETH MACKENZIE-DOUGLAS, Baronet of Glenbervie, first of this family, was the eldest son of Kenneth Mackenzie, Tutor of Kilcoy, sixth son of Donald Mackenzie, V. of Kilcoy, by his wife, Janet, daughter and heiress of Sir Robert Douglas of Glenbervie, Baronet. He assumed the additional name of Douglas on succeeding to his mother's property of Glenbervie; and was, in 1831, created a Baronet. He married Rachel, only child and heiress of Robert Andrews of Hythe, Kent, with issue—

1. *Robert Andrews*, his heir.

2. *Kenneth*, Lieutenant 58th Regiment, died in Ceylon, without issue.

3. *Alexander Douglas*, who married, and died in 1848, leaving issue.

4. *Edward*, died, in 1835, without issue.

5. *Lyndoch*, Lieutenant 97th Regiment, married Laura, daughter of Major-General Sir Archibald Campbell, Baronet, with issue—three daughters, Helen, Laura, and Jessie.

6. *Donald*, married Emily Jane, daughter of Hugh Kennedy of Cultra, County Down, with issue—Donald Sholto Mackenzie; Kenneth Nigel Mackenzie; and Emily Mackenzie.

7. *Rachel*, married Captain Snodgrass, 96th Regiment. He was succeeded by his eldest son,

II. SIR ROBERT ANDREWS MACKENZIE-DOUGLAS, Baronet, who married Martha, daughter of Joshua Rouse, Blenheim House, Hants, with issue—

1. *Robert Andrews*, his heir.

2. *Kenneth*.

3. *Elizabeth*, who married Sir Francis George Augustus Fuller-Elliot-Drake, baronet, with issue.

He died in 1843, and was succeeded by his eldest son,

III. SIR ROBERT ANDREWS MACKENZIE-DOUGLAS, third and present Baronet of Glenbervie, Captain 57th Regiment.

. . .

THE MACKENZIES OF APPLECROSS.

The immediate progenitor of the family of Applecross was Alexander Mackenzie of Coul, so often referred to in the main part of this work, and who so greatly distinguished himself in the wars with Glengarry and Macleod of the Lews. He was a natural son of Colin Càm, XI. of Kintail, by Mary, eldest daughter of Roderick Mackenzie, II. of Davochmaluag, by his wife, Ann, daughter of Donald Macdonald of Sleat, ancestor of Lord Macdonald of the Isles. Alexander became a great favourite with his brother Kenneth, afterwards created first Lord Mackenzie of Kintail, as also with Sir Roderick Mackenzie of Coigeach, and his distinguished brothers of Kilcoy and Kernsary. He has a sasine of half the lands of Applecross and others, as a "natural son of Colin Mackenzie of Kintail," dated 10th of March 1582. He has another, in 1607, from Roderick Dingwall of the lands of Kildun, and one in 1619 of the lands of Pittonachty, or Roschaugh, and Castleton. It is said that Alexander when quite an infant was sent home to his father, Colin of Kintail, to Brahan Castle, who consulted his lady, Barbara, daughter of Grant of Grant, as to what he should do with the little stranger. She was naturally incensed at her husband's infidelity and the proposed addition to her family circle, and indignantly replied —"Cuir 'sa Chuil e," that is "put him in the ash-hole or corner." The Baron perceived ,the imprudence of further offending his lady; but being naturally of a humane disposition, and anxious to act honourably to his innocent offspring, he went out with the boy, and on his return informed his lady that he had acted upon her suggestion, and left him in the *Coul.* He secretly sent Alexander to the place then, and to this day, called "A Chuil," or Coul, to be nursed and brought up by a respectable woman who then resided there, and thus carried out the letter, if not the spirit, of his lady's request; and at the same time performed his duty towards his afterwards distinguished son.

His grandson, John, the second Laird of Applecross,

who, in 1669, wrote a genealogy of his clan down to 1661, gives the following account of the progenitor of his family: —" He was happy in his youth by the comeliness of his person, and agility of body, to be looked upon by Kenneth, Lord Kintail, his brother, and all his followers, being then engaged in their hottest feuds with the Clan Ranald and Macleods of Lewis, as the fittest man to command what force his brother was to make use of on these occasions, wherein he failed not their expectations, managing that command (which he enjoyd until the Tutor of Kintail put a period to all these troubles by the transaction with Glengarry, and utter extirpation of the Macleods of Lewis) with so much courage and expedition, that albeit during the whole tract of these broils there passed not any action of moment wherein he was not signally concerned, yet in all of them his constant success brought no less honour to him-self than advantage and reputation to his party. This, with his singular industry and upright dealing in affairs, got him so much of the love of his brethren, especially Lord Kenneth, who on his death-bed honoured him with the gift of his own sword in testimony of his esteem and affection for him, and so much of the respect of his friends and neighbours, and the good opinion of the country people, that, without difficulty or the least grudge of any person whatsoever, he in a short time purchased a considerable estate, which he still augmented by the same means during the rest of his life." He purchased Applecross, and other lands which exceeded in extent the lands of Coul bestowed on him by his father.

He married, first, Annabella, daughter of Murdoch Mac-kenzie, I. of Fairburn, by his first wife, Margaret Urquhart, daughter of the Laird and Sheriff of Cromarty. She was relict of Thomas Mackenzie, I. of Ord. By her Alexander had issue—

1. *Roderick*, infefted by his father in the estate and Barony of Applecross.

2. *Isabel*, who married, as his second wife, Alexander, V. of Gairloch, with issue.

3. *Marjory*, who married the Rev. William MacCulloch of Park, minister of Fodderty.

He married, secondly, Christian, daughter of Hector Munro of Assynt, with issue—

4. *Kenneth*, at first of Assynt and afterwards of Coul.

5. *Alexander*, who died unmarried in 1639.

6. *Hector* of Assynt, who married a daughter of Hugh Fraser of Belladrum, with issue. Sasine to him in 1650.

7. A daughter, married Alexander Chisholm of Comar.

8. Another, married Sir Alexander Innes of Coxtoune.

He has a charter from James VI., dated 28th July 1617, in favour of "Alexandro Mackenzie de Coul, et Christianæ Munro ejus spousæ, terrarum ecclesiasticarum de Uladil, &c.," in Inverness-shire, and has a second charter to him and his second wife of the lands of Pittonachty, Wester Haldock, Pitfla, &c., in the same county, dated 28th June 1621; while there is another, dated 12th July 1634, to "Alexandero Mackenzie de Coul, et Kennetho ejus filio, terrarum de Urquhart, &c." He was a most prudent man, and besides the large patrimony bestowed on all his children, left a large sum of money for pious uses and for the children of gentlemen among his own relations. He died at an advanced age at Pittonachty in March 1650, was buried in a tomb he caused to be built for himself at Chanonry, and was succeeded in the lands of Applecross by his eldest son,

I. RODERICK MACKENZIE, whom we shall call the first of Applecross—his father having been both of Applecross and Coul. He married Finguala, or Florence, daughter of Murdoch Mackenzie, II. of Redcastle, with issue—

1. *John "Mollach,"* his heir.

2. *Colin*, I. of Sanachan, who married a daughter of Murdo Mackenzie of Sand, Gairloch, with issue [see 'Findon's Tables].

3. *Sibella*, who first married Alexander Macleod, V. of Raasay, with issue; secondly, Thomas Graham of Drynie, and thirdly, Alexander Mackenzie, VI. of Hilton.

4. A daughter, married Lachlan Mackinnon, eldest son

of Mackinnon of Scalpay, Tutor of Mackinnon of Strath-ardale, with issue.

5. A daughter, married the eldest son and heir of William Mackenzie, Shieldag, Gairloch.

He received the estate of Applecross as his patrimony during the life of his father, whom he predeceased on the 6th of July 1646, and was buried in his father's tomb at Chanonry. He was succeeded by his eldest son,

II. JOHN MACKENZIE, called "Ian Mollach," or Hairy John, who married a daughter of Hugh Fraser of Belladrum, with issue, four sons and five daughters—

1. *Alexander*, his heir.

2. *Roderick*, who married Isabella, daughter of Kenneth Mackenzie, VI. of Gairloch, with issue. The descendants of this Roderick now represent the Old Mackenzies of Applecross, in the male line, John Mackenzie, V. of Apple-cross, having died without issue, when the estates went, as will be seen, into the possession of his sister Mary's eldest son, James Mackenzie, IV. of Highfield. Several of Roderick's descendants are still alive, male and female—one of the latter being Mrs Farquhar Macrae, Strome Ferry Hotel (north side), who has a fine family—a son and several daughters.

3. *Kenneth*, I. of Aldeny, who married a daughter of John Matheson of Bennetsfield, with issue.

4. *John*, called "Ian Og," one of the four famous Johns killed in 1715, under his brother Alexander, who was Lieutenant-Colonel of Seaforth's 1st Regiment, at Sheriff-muir.. He married a daughter of the Rev. John MacRa, the last Episcopalian minister of Dingwall, with issue; for which, and the issue of Kenneth of Aldeny, see Findon's Tables.

5. A daughter, married Sir Donald Bayne of Tulloch, with issue.

6. *Catharine*, married Simon Mackenzie, I. of Torri-don, with issue.

7. *Ann*, married, in 1684, Charles Mackenzie, I. of Letterewe, with issue.

8. *Mary*, married Thomas Mackenzie, III. of Ord, with issue; and

9. *Florence*, married, in 1682, Charles Mackenzie of Cullen, third son of Colin Mackenzie, II. of Kilcoy.

John had a sasine in 1663. He purchased the Baronies of Tarradale and Rhindoun. In his grandfather's life-time he obtained a charter under the great seal in favour of "Johanni Mackenzie de Applecross, terrarum de Lochslyne, Newton de Lochslyne, &c."

He was succeeded by his eldest son,

III. ALEXANDER MACKENZIE, who married, first, Anne, daughter of Alexander Fraser, Tutor of Lovat, by his wife Sibella (Elizabeth), daughter of Kenneth, first Lord Mackenzie of Kintail, with issue—

1. *Roderick*, his heir.

2. *Kenneth*, a merchant in Inverness, married a daughter of —— Rose, Merkinch.

3. *Colin*, a doctor in Edinburgh, who married Miss Dunbar of Linkwood.

4. *Sibella*, married, in 1697, the Honourable John Mackenzie of Assynt, second son of Kenneth Mor, third Earl of Seaforth, with issue—Kenneth, who married Frances, his cousin, daughter of Colonel Alexander, without issue.

5. *Anne*, married, first, in 1707, Alexander Mackenzie, II. of Kinchulladrum, with issue—Anne, his only child in life, in 1766; secondly, John MacRa of Dornie; and, thirdly, Colin Mackenzie (Gruinard family),a goldsmith in Inverness.

6. A daughter, married the Rev. Archibald Macqueen, minister of Snizort, Skye.

7. Another married William Mackenzie of Shieldag.

8. *Mary*, married Malcolm Macleod, VII. of Raasay.

He married, secondly, Margaret, daughter of Mackenzie, of Fairburn, with issue—one son, Simon, in the Foot Guards. He married, thirdly, in 1713, Christian, daughter of Fraser of Belladrum, issue—one daughter, who married her cousin, Roderick Mackenzie of Achavannie, son of John Og, killed at Sheriffmuir.

He joined the Earl of Mar in 1715, and was Lieutenant-

Colonel of Seaforth's 1st Regiment, for which he was attainted of high treason, and the estates forfeited to the Crown.

He was succeeded by his eldest son,

IV. RODERICK MACKENZIE, who has a sasine of Kinchulladrum, of which place he was designed, in 1721 ; and who, in 1724, re-purchased the estate of Applecross from the· Court of Enquiry for £3550.

He married, first, Anne, only daughter of Alexander Macdonnell, XI. of Glengarry, by his first wife, Ann, daughter of Hugh Lord Lovat, and by her had issue—

1. *John*, his heir.

2. *Alexander*, a Captain in Marjoribanks' Regiment, in the Dutch service, who died unmarried.

3. *Kenneth*, a watchmaker in London, died unmarried.

4. *Mary*, who married James Mackenzie, III. of Highfield, whose eldest son and heir, Thomas, IV. of Highfield, inherited Applecross from his uncle John, and carried on, in the female line, the representation of the family.

5. *Anne*, who married, first, Alexander Mackenzie, I. of Lentran ; and, secondly, as his second wife, Alexander Mackenzie, VIII. of Davochmaluag, with issue.

6. Another daughter married the Rev. John Maclean, minister of Kintail.

He married, secondly, Margaret, daughter of Sir Kenneth Mackenzie, first Baronet and IV. of Scatwell, and widow of Æneas Macleod of Cadboll, with issue—an only daughter, Lilias (or Eliza), who married Alexander Chisholm of Chisholm, with issue.

He was succeeded by his eldest son,

V. JOHN MACKENZIE, who married Anne, only daughter of Sir Colin Mackenzie, fourth Baronet of Coul, without issue.

He left the estate of Applecross away from his brother Kenneth,* to the son of his sister Mary, Thomas Mackenzie,

---

* This John, the last of this family,'deprived his brother, Kenneth, of the property, and passed it in favour of Thomas Mackenzie of Highfield, his sister's son. In order to set aside the legal succession, and in order to prevent his

IV. of Highfield, by whom he was succeeded as

VI. THOMAS MACKENZIE, sixth of Applecross and IV. of Highfield. He married Elizabeth, only daughter of Donald Mackenzie, V. of Kilcoy, by whom he had issue—

1. *John*, his heir; an advocate in Edinburgh.

2. *James*, died unmarried, in India.

· 3. *Colin*, died unmarried, in India.

4. *Donald*, a Captain in the 100th Regiment of Foot, married Anna, daughter of James Macleod, IX. of Raasay, with issue—two sons and six daughters, John; Thomas; and Elizabeth, died unmarried; Flora Loudon, married General Sir Alexander Lindsay, H.E.I.C.S.; Jane, married James Macdonald, Balranald, North Uist; Anne married Christopher Webb Smith, B.C.S.; Isabella Mary, married Dr Lauchlan Maclean; and Maria, married John Mackenzie, the famous piper, known as the "Piobaire Bàn," with issue. She still survives in Liverpool.

5. *Thomas*, died unmarried.

6. *Jean*, died unmarried.

7. *Anne*, married Kenneth Mackenzie of Inverinate, brother of Alexander Mackenzie, XI. of Hilton.

Other three daughters, Catherine, Mary, and Elizabeth, died unmarried. In 1781 Thomas sold the estate of Highfield to George Gillanders, commissioner for Seaforth; and about the same time bought Lochcarron from Sir Alexander Mackenzie of Delvine, for £10,000 sterling. It was previously bought from Seaforth by Sir Alexander for one-half that sum.

He was succeeded by his eldest son,

VII. JOHN MACKENZIE of Applecross and Lochcarron,

brother, Kenneth, from marrying, he allowed him only £80 yearly for his subsistence during his lifetime, which small allowance made it inadequate for him to rear and support a family, so that in all probability this has been the cause of making the family extinct. After this Kenneth the succession should have reverted back to Roderick Mackenzie, a descendant of Roderick, second son of John, II. of Applecross, who went to Nova Scotia in 1802, or failing the family of this Rory, next to his brother's family, Malcolm, who died a few years ago in Kishorn, and failing heirs of that family to the other descendants of John of Applecross, viz.:—Kenneth of Auldinie, and John, killed at Sheriffmuir in 1715. —*MS. of the Family, written in 1828.*

who married, in 1787, Elizabeth, daughter of Alexander Elphinstone of Glack, Aberdeenshire, with issue—

1. *Thomas*, his heir.

2. *Eliza*, who afterwards succeeded to Applecross. Three sons, John; Alexander; and Frederick, died young.

This laird made a new disposition of the estates, by which, in consequence of a quarrel, he cut out his only surviving brother, Captain Donald and his daughters—his two sons having previously died unmarried—from the succession. The property, under this new settlement, first, went to his son and heir, Thomas, and his issue; secondly, failing these to his daughter Elizabeth; and thirdly, failing her and her issue, to Thomas, the eldest son of his sister Anne, who, as already seen, married Kenneth Mackenzie of Inverinate, W.S.; and, failing him and his issue, to the other children of the same sister.

He was succeeded by his eldest and only surviving son,

VIII. THOMAS MACKENZIE, for many years, and to the day of his death, in 1827, Member of Parliament for the County of Ross. He died, unmarried, and was, in terms of the above-named settlement, succeeded by his sister,

IX. ELIZABETH MACKENZIE. She was in delicate health when her brother died, and continued so to her death, two years later, in 1829. She was never served heir, and, dying unmarried, she was, in terms of the settlement made by her brother, succeeded by her cousin-german,

X. THOMAS MACKENZIE of Inverinate, W.S., Edinburgh, who afterwards represented the County of Ross in Parliament from 1837 to 1847. He married Margaret, daughter of George Mackenzie of Avoch, with issue—five sons and three daughters—

1. *Kenneth John*, his heir.

2. *George Alexander*, a merchant in Liverpool, who married Elizabeth, daughter of John Cay of Charlton, with issue—one daughter, Mabel Georgina. He died in 1874.

3. *Thomas*, W.S., Edinburgh, the present representative of the family.

4. *Francis James*, died, unmarried, in 1875.

5. *Duncan Davidson*, died, unmarried, in 1863.

6. *Margaret.* 7. *Anne Jane;* and

8. *Geddes Elizabeth*, married John Cay, W.S., Edinburgh.

He sold the estate 'of Applecross, in 1857, to the Duke of Leeds, and Inverinate to Alexander Matheson, now of Ardross and Lochalsh.

He was succeeded, as representative of the family, by his eldest son,

XI. KENNETH JOHN MACKENZIE, who died, unmarried, in 1868, when he was succeeded by his next brother,

XII. GEORGE ALEXANDER, who, as shown above, died in 1874, leaving issue—an only daughter. He was succeeded by his next elder brother,

XIII. THOMAS MACKENZIE, a Writer to the Signet, Edinburgh, the present representative of the Mackenzies of Highfield and Applecross.

THE MACKENZIES OF COUL.

The distinguished Alexander Mackenzie of Coul and Applecross, natural son of Colin Càm, XIth Baron of Kintail, by Mary of Davochmaluag, had, among others, whose names are given under APPLECROSS,

I. SIR KENNETH MACKENZIE, at first designated of Assynt, but, in 1649, he has a sasine of the lands of Coul. He was a "man of parts," and in great favour with Charles II., who created him a Baronet by royal patent to him and to the heirs male of his body, dated 16th October 1673. He was also appointed Sheriff-Principal of the Counties of Ross and Inverness, these being then one county, and under the jurisdiction of one Sheriff.

He married, first, the eldest daughter of Alexander Chisholm of Comar, with issue—

1. *Alexander*, his heir.

2. *Simon*, I. of Torridon and Lentran.

3. *John*, I. of Delvine.

4. *Roderick*, married a daughter of Alexander Mackenzie, VII. of Davochmaluag.

5. The eldest daughter married Colin Mackenzie, IV. of Redcastle, with issue.

6. *Agnes*, married Sir John Munro of Fowlis, with issue.

7. *Jane*, married Alexander Baillie, IX. of Dunain.

8. *Christian*, married John Dunbar, younger of Bennetsfield.

9. *Lilias*, married John Munro of Inverawe, with issue.

10. *Mary*, married Kenneth Mackenzie, VI. of Davochmaluag, with issue.

11. Another daughter married Gordon of Cluny.

He married, secondly, a daughter of Thomas Mackenzie of Inverlael, with issue—two sons, who died young ; and four daughters —

12. *Catharine*, married Alexander Mackenzie, II. of Belmaduthy, with issue.

13. A daughter married Ross of Aldie.

14. A daughter, married Maciver of Turnaig ; and

15. Another, married Maciver Turnaig's brother.

The estate of Turnaig continued the property of the Coul family, until sold to Osgood H. Mackenzie of Inverewe, in 1863. He was succeeded by his eldest son,

II. SIR ALEXANDER MACKENZIE, second Baronet, who married, first, Jean, daughter of Sir Robert Gordon of Gordonstown, Tutor of Sutherland, with issue—

1. *John*, his heir.

2. *Colin*, who succeeded as IV. of Coul.

3. A daughter, who married Mackintosh of Cullachy.

4. *Janet*, married, in 1695, Alexander Mackenzie, VII. of Davochmaluag, with issue.

He married, secondly, Janet Johnstone of Warriston, by whom he had three sons—William, Simon, and James ; and a daughter, Margaret, who married Andrew Brown of Dolphinton, with issue.

He obtained a charter under the Great Seal, in 1681, by which his lands of Coul and others were, upon his own resignation, erected into one free barony in favour of himself and heirs male, holding of the Crown. He afterwards, in 1702, made a deed of entail by which all his estate was settled upon heirs male of his own body. He died shortly after, and was succeeded by his eldest son,

F 2

III. SIR JOHN MACKENZIE, third Baronet, who married, first, Margaret, daughter of Hugh Rose of Kilravock, with issue—an only daughter, who married Bayne of Delny.

He married, secondly, in 1703, Helen, daughter of Patrick, Lord Elibank, with issue—two daughters, one of whom married Sir George Hope of Kirkliston, Baronet; the other died unmarried.

He joined the Earl of Mar in 1715, was attainted for high treason; but dying without issue male the titles and estates were assumed by his next brother,

IV. SIR COLIN MACKENZIE, fourth Baronet, who was made Clerk to the Pipe in the Exchequer, which office he held during his life. He married Henrietta, daughter of Sir Patrick Houston of Houston, with issue—

1. *Alexander*, his heir.

2. *William* of Achilty and Kinnahaird, who married Mary, daughter of Alexander, VII. of Davochmaluag, with issue, now extinct in the male line. John, the last male representative of the family, in 1850, left for Melbourne in the ship *Owen Glendower*, which was never since heard of.

3. *Anne*, married John Mackenzie, V. of Applecross, without issue.

He died in 1740, in the 67th year of his age, and was succeeded by his eldest son,

V. SIR ALEXANDER MACKENZIE, fifth Baronet. He obtained a charter, under the Great Seal, to himself and his heirs male, as heir to his grandfather, of the whole estate of Coul, dated 1742. He married Janet, daughter of Sir James Macdonald of Sleat, Baronet, with issue—

1. *Alexander*, his heir.

2. *James*, died unmarried.

3. *Henrietta*, married Thomas Wharton, without issue.

4. *Margaret*, married William Mackenzie, IV. and last of Suddie, with issue.

5. *Stewart*, married William Dallas of Cantray, with issue.

6. *Christina*. 7. *Janet*.

He died in 1792, and was succeeded by his eldest son,

VI. MAJOR-GENERAL SIR ALEXANDER MACKENZIE,

sixth Baronet, an officer in the H.E.I.C.S. He married Catharine, daughter of Robert Ramsay, with issue—one son. He died in 1795, and was succeeded by his only son,

VII. SIR GEORGE S. MACKENZIE, seventh Baronet, married, first, Mary, daughter of Donald Macleod of Guineas, with issue—

1. *Alexander*, his heir.

- 2. *William*, who succeeded as IX. of Coul.

3. *George*, died, unmarried, in 1839.

4. *Robert-Ramsay*, succeeded as X. of Coul.

5. *John*, late minister of Ratho, born 1813, married, in 1839, a daughter of the famous Thomas Chalmers, D.D., without issue. He died in London in 1878.

6. *Donald Macleod*, an Admiral in the Royal Navy, born in 1815, married, in 1865, Dorothea, daughter of Admiral Sir Michael Seymour, G.C.B., without issue.

7. *James*, a minister, married Philadelphia, daughter of Sir Percival Hart Dyke of Lullingstone, Kent, Baronet. He died, without issue, in 1857.

8. *Margaret*; 9. *Catherine*; 10. *Mary*, died unmarried.

He married, secondly, Catherine, daughter of Sir Henry Jardine, with issue—

11. *Henry Augustin Ornano*, who, born in 1839, married Mary Ann, daughter of Louis Bone, with issue—two sons and a daughter.

He died in 1848, and was succeeded by his eldest son,

VIII. SIR ALEXANDER MACKENZIE, eighth Baronet, an officer in the Bengal army, H.E.I.C.S. He died unmarried, in 1856, and was succeeded by his next brother,

IX. SIR WILLIAM MACKENZIE, ninth Baronet, who married Agnes, daughter of R. D. Smyth of Ardmore, Derry, and died without issue in 1868, when he was succeeded by his next surviving brother,

X. SIR ROBERT RAMSAY-MACKENZIE, tenth Baronet, who, born in 1811, married, in 1846, Louisa Alexandrina, daughter of Richard Jones, a member of the Legislative Assembly of Sydney, Australia, with issue—

1. *Arthur G. Ramsay*, his heir.

.2 *Mary Louisa*, married Alexander Archer.

3. *Katharine E.* 4. *Louisa S.;* and 5. *Frances P.*
He was educated at the High School of Edinburgh,
and, in 1867, appointed Premier of the Executive Council,
and Colonial Treasurer of Queensland, having previously
held the offices of Colonial Secretary and Colonial Treasurer.
He died in 1873, and was succeeded by his only son,

XI. SIR ARTHUR G. RAMSAY-MACKENZIE, eleventh
and present Baronet, born in 1865, a minor.

THE MACKENZIES OF TORRIDON.

I. SIMON MACKENZIE, first of Torridon and Lentran,
was second son of Sir Kenneth Mackenzie, first Baronet
of Coul, by his first wife, a daughter of Alexander Chisholm
of Comar. He has a sasine of the half of Arcan on disposition in 1697. He married Catharine, daughter of John
" Mollach " Mackenzie, II. of Applecross. She has a sasine
in 1672 and another in 1694. By her he had issue—

1. *Kenneth*, his heir.

2. *Alexander*, I. of Lentran, Tarradale, and Rhindoun,
who married, first, Anne, daughter of Roderick Mackenzie,
IV. of Applecross (sasine, 1745), with issue—(1) Alexander,
who died young; (2) Roderick of Tarradale, a captain in
Marjoribank's Regiments, killed in America, without issue;
(3) John Mackenzie of Arcan, secretary to the Highland
Society of London, well known as " John Mackenzie of the
Temple," so intimately connected with the editing and publication of Macpherson's Gaelic Ossian. He succeeded to the
property, which he afterwards sold or alienated—Rhindoun to
The Chisholm; Tarradale to Dr Murchison, his nephew; and
Arcan to his sister Elizabeth, relict of John Mackenzie of
Sanachan. He died unmarried—the last male representa-
tive of the family of Lentran. The daughters were—(1)
Anne, married Donald Macrae, Camusluinie, Kintail, with
issue; (2) another married Alexander Murchison of Auchter-
tyre, with issue; (3) Janet, married William Mackenzie of
Strathgarve, with issue; (4) Catharine, married Colin
Green, Scatwell, without issue; (5) Isabella, married Colonel

Mackay of Bighouse, Sutherlandshire, without issue ; and (6) Elizabeth, who married Captain John Mackenzie of Sanachan and Tullich, Lochcarron, who in right of his wife succeeded to Arcan. She died without issue.

3. A daughter, married Archibald Macdonald of Barisdale, with issue.

4. *Anne*, married, in 1694, Farquhar MacRa of Inverinate, with issue.

5. *Catharine*, married Roderick Mackenzie of Auldeny.

6. *Florence*, married Colin Mackenzie, II. of Cleanwaters.

Simon was succeeded by his eldest son,

II. KENNETH MACKENZIE, who, in 1703, married Ann, daughter of Alexander Mackenzie, VII. of Gairloch, with issue—

1. *John*, his heir.

2. *Mary*, who married Colin Mackenzie, Bailie of Dingwall, with issue—(1) Kenneth, who married Margaret Macdonald in Skye, with issue—Alexander, who died young in Jamaica ; John, a lieutenant in the 78th Regiment, died in India, without issue ; and Donald, died young. He had also several daughters—Janet, married John Chisholm, Dingwall, where she died, without issue, in 1870, aged 95 ; Mary, and Margaret Anne, both died unmarried, the latter in 1856; Alexanderina, married Captain Munro of the 42d Highlanders. (2) John, a merchant in Bishopgate Street, London, who married a daughter of his partner, Alexander Mackenzie of the Coul family, with issue—Colin Alexander, known as "the Ambassador"; Kenneth, who died young ; John, a colonel in H.E.I.C.S.; Alexander, of Christ Church, Oxford, who died unmarried ; and Caroline, who married Dr William Wald, without issue. (3) Alexander, died young. (4) Mary, who married Murdoch Mackenzie, Bailie of Dingwall, without issue. (5) Anne, who married Andrew Robertson, Provost of Dingwall and Sheriff-Substitute of Ross, grandson of Colin Robertson of Kindeace, with issue—Anne, who married, as his second wife, Sir John Gladstone, Baronet of Fasque, with issue—the famous statesman, William Ewart Gladstone of Hawarden, M.P.,

Prime Minister of Great Britain from 1868 to 1874. (6) Fanny, who married John Mackenzie of Kinellan, with issue—Colin, who died young; Alexander, who married Mary Macdonald; Margaret, who married Farquhar Matheson; and Mary, Christy, and Janet, all of whom died unmarried. (7) Betsy, married a Mr Simpson; and (8) Elizabeth.

He entertained Prince Charles Edward in 1745, and was shortly afterwards succeeded by his eldest son, ·

III. JOHN MACKENZIE, who married Isobel, daughter of Kenneth Mackenzie, II. of Dundonnell (sasine in 1741), with issue—

1. *Kenneth*, his heir.

2. *John*, who succeeded as V. of Torridon.

3. *Janet*, who married, as his second wife, Captain Alexander, second son of Sir Roderick Mackenzie, second Baronet and V. of Scatwell, with issue. She died in 1808.

He fought with Prince Charles at the battle of Culloden, and is said to have been "one of the prettiest men in Scotland." The following extract is from a letter, dated 10th September 1878, from his grandson, the late Bishop Mackenzie of Nottingham, in reply to a request from the writer that he would kindly communicate anything he knew about his more immediate ancestors :—" He led into action the few Mackenzies who fought in that battle. He was a nephew of Macdonald of Keppoch (one of the seven men of Moidart), and was personally requested by Lady Seaforth to take up arms for the Prince, and he attached himself, with the personal following who attended him, to his uncle's standard. The Macdonalds, in strong resentment for having been placed on the left instead of the right of Charles Edward, refused to charge when ordered by their commander. Keppoch, uttering the touching exclamation, 'My God! that I should live to be deserted by my own children!' then charged, accompanied by my grandfather and his small following. He soon fell pierced by balls; and then, while my grandfather wept over him, exhorted him to leave the field as the brief action was already over, and the dragoons were already scattering over the field in pursuit. Some of the Macdonalds placed. themselves under their Chief's favourite nephew, as he is called in Scott's account of the battle. Tradition says that some of them were disposed to run when they saw parties of the dragoons approaching them, but that Torridon spoke briefly, ' Keep together men. If we stand shoulder to shoulder these men will be far more frightened at us than we can be of them. But remember, if you scatter, they have four legs to each of your two, and you will stand singly but small chance against them.' They took his advice, and he led them in fair order off the field.

" It is further reported that he was proscribed after the battle, and that his life was saved by Sir Alexander Macdonald of Sleat, ancestor of the present Lord Macdonald, who was one of the Royal Commissioners. Sir Alexander urged that Torridon was a young and inexperienced man, and not likely to be dangerous to the Government, on account of the distance and comparative smallness of his wild Highland estate; however, it is said that he added— ' Torridon is a great favourite with the ladies, and if you *hang Torridon* it is certain that half the ladies of the country will *hang themselves.*' This reasoning is said to have prevailed ; and it is certain that the estate descended to my eldest brother in right of inheritance, without having been confiscated."

He was succeeded by his eldest son,

IV. KENNETH MACKENZIE, who married Miss Cockerell, daughter of a solicitor, in London. He sold the estate to his brother John. By his wife he had issue—

1. *Kenneth Cockerell,* who married, and had—(1) Kenneth Cockerell, who died without issue; (2) John Scott, of the Manchester and Liverpool Railway Company, married, and died in 1859, leaving an only son, who died since without issue.

2. *Isabella,* died without issue.

He was succeeded by his next brother,

V. JOHN MACKENZIE, who purchased the estate from him ; and whose descendants have now become the heirs male of his predecessors, Kenneth's descendants having, as we have seen, become extinct. He married Anne Isabella, daughter of Isaac Van Dam, in the West Indies, with issue—

1. *John*, his heir.

2. *Anthony Van Dam*, died, unmarried, in 1824.

3. *Charles*, Rector of St Benet, London, and Prebendary of St Paul's Cathedral, who now represents the family.

4. *Henry*, a clergyman of the Church of England, consecrated Bishop Suffragan of Nottingham in 1870. He resigned his Episcopal duties in 1877, but retained the title of Bishop, and the offices of Archdean of Nottingham, and Canon and Sub-Dean of the Cathedral of Lincoln. He died in 1878. He married, first, Elizabeth, daughter of Robert Ridley, of Demerara, with issue—an only daughter, Edith, who married the Rev. H. Fellowes. He married, secondly, Antoinette, daughter of Sir James Henry Turing of Foveran, Baronet, with issue—a large family, of whom 11 survive.

John Mackenzie, V. of Torridon, died in 1820, and was succeeded by his eldest son,

VI. JOHN MACKENZIE, who married Katharine Yallop, and died without issue in 1852. He sold the estate to James Alexander Stewart-Mackenzie of Seaforth, and was, at his death succeeded, as representative of the family, by his eldest surviving brother,

VII. THE REV. CHARLES MACKENZIE, Rector of St Benet, London, and Prebendary of St Paul's Cathedral, who married Henrietta, daughter of Henry Simonds of Reading, Berkshire, with issue—

1. *Henry Douglas*, married Miss Suttar, Bathurst, N.S.W., with issue—one son, Dudley B. Douglas, and two daughters. He has also four daughters, all unmarried.

THE MACKENZIES OF DELVINE.

I. JOHN MACKENZIE, first of this family, was third son of Sir Kenneth Mackenzie, first Baronet of Coul, by his first wife, Miss Chisholm of Comar. He married, first, a daughter of the Laird of Lentran, with issue—one son, George, who married, and died before his father without issue in 1722. He married, secondly, a daughter of

Sir Robert Gordon of Gordonston, with issue—William, who married and died in England, before his father, without issue. He married, thirdly, Margaret, daughter of Hay of Alderston, with issue—

1. *Alexander*, who became heir on the death of his half-brother.

2. *Kenneth*, Professor of Law in the University of Edinburgh, who married Grizel Hume, daughter of Brown, I. of Dolphinton. By this marriage Kenneth, who died in 1756, had two sons and two daughters. The second son, Andrew, was a W.S., and married a daughter of Campbell of Achlyne. The daughters died unmarried. The eldest son, John, succeeded his father-in-law, and became JOHN MACKENZIE, II. OF DOLPHINTON. He married Alice, daughter of Robert Ord, Lord Chief-Justice of the Exchequer, in 1773. By her he had six sons and three daughters. Four of the sons, Robert, Kenneth, John, and George, died unmarried, as did also two of the daughters, Mary and Anne. Grace married William Baillie, with issue. Kenneth, the sixth son, was a Major in the 4th Regiment, and married a Miss Solomon in America, by whom he had four sons and three daughters. The eldest surviving son of John succeeded him as RICHARD MACKENZIE, III. OF DOLPHINTON, who died in 1850. He married Jane, daughter of Captain Hamilton, 73d Regiment, by whom he had issue—JOHN ORD MACKENZIE, IV. and now of Dolphinton, W.S., who married Margaret, daughter of Sir Thomas Kirkpatrick of Closeburn, with issue. Richard also had three other sons, Kenneth, Richard James, and George.

3. *Thomas*, who died young.

4. *John*, Chief Clerk of Session, married Miss Renton of Lamerton, without issue. D. 14ᵗ June 1778.

5. *Donald*, surgeon in the Army, died, 1741, unmarried.

6. *Anne*, married Alexander Robertson of Faskally, with issue. She died in 1772.

7. *Helen*, married Crawford Balfour of Bingry.

8. *Rebecca*, married John Mackenzie, IV. of Belmaduthy.

Five other daughters, *Janet, Catharine, Mary, Christina*, and *Jane*, died unmarried.

John Mackenzie, I. of Delvine, died in 1731, and was succeeded by his second and eldest surviving son,

II. ALEXANDER MACKENZIE, who married, with issue —an only daughter,

III. MARGARET MACKENZIE, who married George Muir of Cassencairie, with issue—an only son. She died in 1767, and was succeeded by her son,

IV. SIR ALEXANDER MUIR-MACKENZIE, created first Baronet of Delvine in 1805. He married Jane, daughter of Sir Robert Murray of Hillhead and Clermont, Baronet, with issue—one son, and eight daughters, seven of whom died unmarried. The eldest, Susan, married Robert Smythe of Methven in 1817. He died in 1835, and was succeeded by his only son,

V. SIR JOHN WILLIAM PITT MUIR-MACKENZIE, second Baronet, who married Sophia Matilda, daughter of James Raymond Johnstone of Alva and Hangingshaw, with issue—

1. *Alexander*, his heir.

2. *Robert Smythe*, born 1842, captain, Royal Horse Artillery; married Anne, daughter of Captain C. Gordon, with issue.

3. *Cecil C.*, lieutenant, Royal Engineers, died unmarried.

4. *Kenneth Augustus*, born 1845, and married.

5. *Montague Johnstone*, born 1847.

6. *John William Pitt*, born 1854, and married.

7. *Georgiana Mary*, married.

8. *Lucy Jane Eleanora*, married in 1859, Bentley Murray of Monkland.

9. *Sussannah Anne Eliza.*

He died in 1855, and was succeeded by his eldest son,

VI. SIR ALEXANDER MUIR-MACKENZIE, third and present Baronet of Delvine, born in 1840. He served as a captain in the 78th Highlanders; and married Frances, daughter of Sir Thomas Moncrieffe, Baronet.

THE MACKENZIES OF GRUINARD.

I. JOHN MACKENZIE, first of this family, was a natural son of George, second Earl of Seaforth, who, with Captain Hector Mackenzie, conveyed the news of the defeat of the Royalists, in 1651, by Oliver Cromwell at the Battle of Worcester, to his father in Holland, where he was at the time in exile. John of Gruinard must have been born long before the Earl's marriage, for in 1651 his Lordship's heir and eldest legitimate son "was but a child" about fifteen years of age, while John of Gruinard was old enough to have fought that year at the Battle of Worcester, and convey the intelligence to his father which broke his heart, and which hastened his death in the same year.[*]

He married before 1655, for in that year there is a sasine to Christina, daughter of Donald Mackenzie, son of Allan Mackenzie, II. of Logic, in which she is designated as his wife. By this marriage he had issue—

1. *George,* his heir, who, in a sasine, dated 10th August 1685, is called by his mother "George Mackenzie, my eldest lawful son."

2. *Kenneth,* who married Frances Herbert, daughter of William, Marquis of Powis, and widow of Kenneth, fourth Earl of Seaforth, without issue, and who at her death, twenty years after the marriage, left all her plate, a small property in England, and several thousand pounds sterling to her husband; and, eventually, John, IV. of Gruinard, his grand nephew, succeeded to everything but the money, which was disputed and thrown into Chancery, where it has ever since remained.

3. *John,* a doctor in Inverness; also five other sons, and eight daughters, all married, several of them with issue [see Findon's Tables, Sheet XII.]

He has a charter of Little Gruinard and other lands in 1669, in which he is described as then "of Meikle Gruinard." He was succeeded by his eldest son.

---

[*] For a full discussion of his illegitimacy, see article on the Chiefship, page 271.

II. GEORGE MACKENZIE, who married, first, Margaret, daughter of Alexander Mackenzie, I. of Ballone, fourth son of Sir Roderick Mackenzie of Coigeach, Tutor of Kintail. She was relict of Sir Roderick Mackenzie of Findon, who died in 1692. By her he had issue—

1. *George*, his heir.

2. *Kenneth*, who married a daughter of Kenneth Mackenzie, III. of Suddie, with issue.

3. *Colin*, a goldsmith in Inverness, married, first, Anne Mackenzie, daughter of Alexander Mackenzie, III. of Applecross, widow of Alexander Mackenzie of Kinchulladrum; with issue—two daughters.

4. *Simon*, married Mary, daughter of John Mackenzie, II. of Ardloch, with issue.

5. *Donald*, married Janet, daughter of Sir Alexander Mackenzie, third Baronet and X. of Gairloch, without issue.

6. *Roderick*, married Barbara, daughter of Alexander Mackenzie, I. of Ardloch, with issue—four daughters.

7. *William*.   8. *Kenneth*.

9. *William*, a lieutenant, Royal Navy, married Ann, daughter of Alexander Mackenzie, I. of Ardloch, with issue —an only daughter, Mary Howard, who married Dr Grant, Inverness, by whom she had four sons and seven daughters.

10. *George*.

11. *Captain John* of Castle Leod, who married Geddes, daughter of his uncle, Simon Mackenzie. He bought the estate of Avoch with money left by Admiral George Geddes Mackenzie, his wife's brother. By this marriage he had George of Avoch, a merchant in London (and several other sons and daughters), who married Margaret, daughter of the Rev. William Mackenzie, minister of Glenmuick, by whom he had two daughters—(1) Geddes, who, in 1812, married Sir Alexander Mackenzie, the celebrated North American explorer, and discoverer of the Mackenzie River, by whom she had issue—Alexander George of Avoch; George Alexander; and Geddes Margaret, all three unmarried; (2) Margaret, who married Thomas Mackenzie, X. of Applecross, with issue.

There were three other sons and nine daughters, making in all twenty-three of this marriage.

George of Gruinard married secondly Elizabeth, a natural daughter of President Forbes of Culloden. There is a sasine of Meikle Gruinard in 1729 "to Elizabeth Forbes, his spouse." By her he had four sons and six daughters, making the extraordinary total of thirty-three children, nineteen of whom, at least, are known to have married, and most of them into the best families in the north.*

He has a sasine in 1696, and the marriage contract with Margaret Mackenzie, his first wife, is dated the same year.

He was succeeded by his eldest son,

III. JOHN MACKENZIE, who first married, in 1713, Catharine, daughter of George Mackenzie, I. of Culbo, third son of Alexander Mackenzie, II. of Belmaduthy, had issue—

1. *William*, his heir.

2. *John.*

3. *Annabella*, who married the Rev. Murdo Morrison of Stornoway. with issue.

4. *Lilias*, married the Rev. James Macaulay, Gairloch.

5. *Isabella*, married Alexander Mackenzie, Little Gruinard, with issue.

He married, secondly, a daughter of Mackenzie of Sand. He was succeeded by his eldest son,

IV. WILLIAM MACKENZIE, who married Lilias, daughter of John Mackenzie, I. of Lochend (now Inverewe), son of Alexander Mackenzie, VII. of Gairloch, with issue—

1. *Simon*, a captain in the 78th Regiment, who died before his father on his way home from India, unmarried.

2. *George*, killed by a fall in Jamaica, before his father's death, unmarried.

3. *John*, who became his father's heir.

---

* The celebrated wit, the late Honourable Sir George Rose of London, Master in Chancery, was a grandson of Margaret, daughter of George, II. of Gruinard, by his second marriage, with a natural daughter of President Forbes. Margaret had a daughter, Elizabeth, by George Fern, who married James Rose of London, father of Sir George.

4. *Alexander*, a Colonel in the army, and "a most distinguished soldier." He served with the 36th Regiment throughout the Peninsular War, and in the course of his service was dangerously wounded in the neck, lost an eye, and had two horses killed under him. He was well known as a most gallant and distinguished officer, and in every sense a thorough Highlander. He married Eliza, daughter of Colonel George Mackenzie, son of John Mackenzie, I. of Lochend, by whom he had one son, George, a captain in the 36th (his father's) Regiment, killed leading an escalading party at the assault of Burgos — unmarried; and one daughter, Alexanderina, who married Alexander Grove, M.D., R.N., at Greenwich Hospital, with issue—three daughters. Colonel Alexander married, secondly, Eliza, daughter of Captain James Græme, R.N., by whom he had issue—(1) George, who died unmarried in 1842; (2) Major-General Alexander Mackay Mackenzie, who became the representative of Gruinard, and died in 1879; (3) William, died young; (4) Eliza; (5) Lilias, married Sir John W. Fisher, M.D., without issue; and (6) Janet, married W. F. B. Staples, barrister, with issue.

5. *Catherine*, married the Rev. Donald Mackintosh, Gairloch, with issue—five daughters, one of whom, Annabella, married Murdo Macrae, with issue—one of whom, Mr Macrae of Kirksheaf, Tain.

6. *Margaret*, died unmarried.

William, IV. of Gruinard, raised a company of Highlanders in 1778 for Lord Seaforth's Regiment. Simon, his eldest son, went to India in command of it, and, as we have seen, he died on his return voyage, from the accidental bite of a favourite Arab horse he had with him ; when lock-jaw supervened which caused his death. This proved disastrous to the fortunes of the Gruinard family and their position in the County of Ross, as from the high character which Simon bore it may be safely inferred that the family property in his hands would have remained intact, and, probably, would have continued in their possession to this day.

William was succeeded by his third and eldest surviving son,

V. JOHN MACKENZIE, of the 73d Regiment, who married Margaret, daughter of Gun Munro of Braemore, Caithness, by whom he had issue—

1. *William*, his heir.

2. *Christina*, who married John Campbell, Poolewe, with issue—several sons and daughters.

Captain John, in 1795, sold the property—which in his time comprised Meikle Gruinard, Udrigle, and Sand, " with the pendicle thereof called Little Gruinard "—to the late Henry Davidson of Tulloch, who re-sold it to Meyrick Bankes of Letterewe, the present proprietor. He was succeeded, as representative of the family, by his only son,

VI. WILLIAM MACKENZIE, a Captain in the 72d Regiment, and said to have been the handsomest man in his day in the Highlands of Scotland. It was seen that in 1829 he claimed the Chiefship of the Clan against Allangrange, but we have conclusively shown elsewhere [p. 271] that he had no right whatever to that honour. He married Margaret, daughter of Wilson of Wilsonton, with issue—

1. *John*, who died young; and three daughters, two of whom, both named Mary, died young; the third, Margaret Innes, married Lachlan Maclachlan, Killinochannich, Argyllshire, without issue.

Captain William having left no male issue, he was succeeded, as representative of the family, by his first cousin.

VII. MAJOR-GENERAL ALEXANDER MACKAY MACKENZIE, the eldest surviving son of the distinguished Colonel Alexander Mackenzie, fourth son of William Mackenzie, IV. and brother to Captain John, V. of Gruinard. (For a full account of the services of this gallant Highland officer, see a memoir of him by the present writer in the *Celtic Magazine* for July, vol. iv., pp. 302-327.)

He married Marion, daughter of the Rev. William Colville of Newton, Cambridgeshire, and died in London in 1879, leaving issue—

1. *John*. 2. *Stuart*. 3. *Lilias*. 4. *Sybil*.

9 7 8 3 7 4 3 3 7 6 8 6 1